...ys
Woodward

with all good
wishes

Iris Danbury
1974.

Lucie Durrant went to the Canary Islands on a working holiday looking for new ideas for the jewellery that she designed. Her call on the attractive Joel Barron was of a purely business nature, but later, as she came to know him better, she began to wonder if that was all he meant to her . . .

# THE SILVER STALLION

*by*

IRIS DANBURY

MILLS & BOON LIMITED
17–19 FOLEY STREET
LONDON W1A 1DR

*All the characters in this book have no existence outside the imagination of the Author, and have no relation whatsoever to anyone bearing the same name or names. They are not even distantly inspired by any individual known or unknown to the Author, and all the incidents are pure invention.*

*First published 1973*
*This edition 1974*



*ISBN 0 263 71565 5*

Made and Printed in Great Britain by
Cox & Wyman Ltd., London, Reading
and Fakenham

# CHAPTER ONE

When she started out this morning on the journey from Las Palmas, Lucie had been full of confidence. Now, as the taxi turned off the main road and bumped down a narrow track towards the coast and the house where Joel Barron lived, each minute increased her apprehension.

Would he think she had been sent to pry? He would certainly reach that conclusion if he knew of the other reasons for her visit. On the face of it, she was merely making a routine call, a courtesy visit on behalf of Mr. Thornton, the wholesale jeweller in London.

'Just see if you can hurry him up with the new designs,' he had instructed her. 'Ask when they'll be ready. No, better not. Joel hates working to a timetable, but I'd still like a rough idea. I've a number of customers waiting.'

She could imagine that Joel Barron, the famous creative silversmith, preferred his own methods and schedule, but she saw Mr. Thornton's point.

Personally, she was excited at the thought of meeting a man who was at the peak of his career and whose name was a guarantee of good design and excellent workmanship. In a much more modest way she worked on antique and modern costume pieces in silver, sometimes set with stones, and Mr. Thornton had been helpful in purchasing and finding outlets for her designs.

The taxi stopped and the driver indicated a pair of iron gates with the name 'Villa Toledo' painted on a white board. This was the address Mr. Thornton had given her.

She paid the driver, watched him disappear down the track, then she gingerly pushed open one half of the stiff gates. A paved path led to a pink-washed villa. The front door stood open and Lucie rang a bell, but no one came. The house and garden seemed wrapped in an afternoon siesta silence, although it was barely eleven o'clock.

Then a woman appeared from the far side of the house.

'You want something?' she asked in Spanish.

'Yes – that is, I came to see Señor Baron. Is he in?'

The woman looked blank. 'Señor Barron? No.'

'But this is his address,' Lucie said, 'Joel Barron. He's a silversmith – er – he works in *argentino*—'

The woman's face cleared. 'Ah, *si*! He does not live here now.' She gave Lucie a prolonged stare. 'You are English? You want to find him?'

'Yes. On business.'

'You are his wife? His sister?'

Lucie smiled. 'Oh, no. Only a business friend.' That was hardly true, for she had not yet met him.

There was another pause while the woman regarded Lucie. 'Then I give you his address. Come with me.'

She led the way into the house and into a small sitting-room. From a writing desk she extracted a crumpled piece of paper, smoothed it out and handed it to Lucie to copy.

'Villa Sirena, Molino de la Torre, Ventura.' Lucie wrote down the address in her notebook. 'Thank you very much. Is it far to Ventura?'

The woman looked puzzled, then she laughed. 'You fly – or take steamer.'

'Oh! Then it's one of the other islands.' Lucie was alarmed at this information.

'You do not know Canary Islands a long time?' asked the other.

'No. I arrived in Las Palmas only two days ago.'

'Then you must visit all our beautiful islands.'

Lucie rose to leave. 'Thank you, *señora*. You have been kind. I must think out new plans to visit Señor Barron.'

'You return to Las Palmas now? You have the car?'

With a sense of shock at her own carelessness, Lucie realized her foolishness in allowing the taxi to leave instead of waiting for her. He had actually offered to wait, but she had said that she had no idea how long she would be detained on her call.

'No, no car. Is a taxi possible?'

The woman pursed her lips. 'No taxi here. But wait – perhaps Pablo take you in his car. Wait and I telephone.'

'Thank you.'

'You will take a glass of wine?'

Lucie accepted the wine gratefully. She needed a measure of refreshment to cope with this new situation. But first she must get back to Las Palmas.

She could hear the woman telephoning in the hall and hoped she had made it clear what she wanted, for she had no more than a smattering of Spanish and the other woman's English was difficult to follow.

The woman returned to the room. 'Pablo here in half an hour,' she announced. 'Now you give me your name? Then if Señor Barron is—' she frowned and clenched her fists—'is *colerico*—'

'Angry?' suggested Lucie.

'*Si, si* – angry. Then I tell him you are English friend.'

'Lucie Durrant. I'll write it down and my address at present in Las Palmas.' She wondered why Señor Barron should have cause to be angry, but perhaps the woman who was now living here knew him better and had experienced his temper.

In about half an hour a man came along the path shouting that he was ready and the woman accompanied Lucie down to the gates where a small covered van waited.

So this was the car! How ridiculous she had been to dismiss the taxi, but regrets were no use now. She clambered in next to Pablo and soon became aware of powerful smells of vegetables arising from the boxes and crates in the back.

Pablo asked no questions but drove stolidly until he came to the outskirts of Las Palmas. He stopped at the Triana bridge. 'Is O.K. here?' he queried.

'Yes, thank you. Perfectly O.K.' She handed him the equivalent of the taxi fare she had paid and he examined the peseta notes.

'Too much!' he muttered.

'No, keep it. Good luck.'

He shrugged, pocketed the notes with a smile, no doubt believing that all the English were not only millionaires but mad as well.

It was easy enough here near the busy market place to

take a taxi for the short distance to her hotel, and after lunch she reviewed the new position with regard to Joel Barron.

Evidently he had not given his new address to Mr. Thornton in London. Lucie mulled over the possibility of merely writing or telephoning to Mr. Barron to find out the information Mr. Thornton wanted. But there was the other matter, and that demanded a personal visit.

'If you're going to the Canary Islands, Lucie,' Mr. Thornton had said when she told him of her plans, 'my wife would very much like you to call on Joel and see if his brother's children are being well looked after.'

'His brother's children?'

'Yes. There's a girl about nine, I think, and a boy of five or so. Their mother died last year and their father, that's Joel's brother, is in Singapore. So he asked Joel to take them to the Canaries. I can't imagine why, unless it was out of spite. He said he didn't want his kids brought up by two aged maiden aunts.'

'But what am I to do?' queried Lucie. 'I can't exactly interfere.'

'No, of course not. But you could get a general impression as to whether they're running wild. Are they being educated? What sort of home has Joel and is it fit for children to live in it? That sort of thing. Mrs. Thornton will be most grateful.'

Lucie was thoughtful, wondering why Mrs. Thornton couldn't take a short holiday in the Canaries and see for herself. Also, what was the connection between her and the children?

Reluctantly she agreed to carry out Mr. Thornton's instructions. 'But you mustn't blame me if I fail to find out all you want to know.'

So now she was faced with this daunting prospect of visiting Joel Barron and inspecting the domestic atmosphere in which his niece and nephew were growing up.

She studied timetables at the hotel reception desk and found there was a daily flight to Ventura.

'But apparently it wouldn't be possible for me to return the same day?' she asked the clerk.

'No, but the following morning you could come back.'

'So I need a room for one night.'

The clerk undertook to make a reservation for the flight and also a room in a small inexpensive hotel he recommended.

'One day in Ventura is not enough, *señorita,*' he said with a smile. 'You must go again later and travel about the island.'

'Yes, I hope to do that,' she agreed. 'But first this is a business visit.'

The short flight next morning set her down at the airport near the main town and she took a taxi to what she hoped was the right address of Mr. Barron. This time she was more cautious and asked the taxi-driver to wait, for the Villa Sirena appeared to be an isolated building near the shore.

Lucie pushed her way among a tangled mass of oleanders and hibiscus bushes; long sprays of bougainvillea tapped her face and she was glad when the path was less overgrown and she came in sight of the villa.

A young girl was beating a small rug and seemed surprised at Lucie's approach.

'Señor Barron?' began Lucie. 'Could I see him?'

'He is working,' answered the girl in Spanish. 'You know him?'

'Not really,' Lucie replied in English. Then, searching carefully for the correct Spanish words, she added, 'Miss Durrant, from England. Business matter.'

The girl gave Lucie a prolonged stare from glowing dark eyes. Then she led the way into the house and beckoned to Lucie to follow.

'Wait, please,' the girl commanded, leaving Lucie in a large untidy living-room. Lucie stared about her – several armchairs, a circular table piled with assorted magazines in English, Spanish, French and German. But her eye was drawn to a display cupboard with glass doors and many pieces of silverware. She rose to examine them, knowing they were examples of the superb craftsmanship for which Joel Barron's name was a guarantee.

There were presentation pieces like salvers or cups, but also exquisite teapots and coffee jugs, cruets and cutlery. She longed to feel the pieces in her hands, caress the embossed or engraved outside surface, touch the satin-smooth interiors.

The minutes elapsed and there was no sign of Mr. Barron or the young Spanish girl. Lucie strained her ears for any evidence of what she had come to seek, children's voices, but there was nothing but silence.

Then she heard a masculine voice outside, speaking angrily in Spanish, and a moment later a tall young man with a bronzed face and hostile blue eyes erupted into the room.

'Yes? Miss – er—'

'Durrant. Lucie Durrant,' she supplied.

'Well, at the moment I'm very busy, so if you could say what you want – but I must warn you that I don't take casual orders from tourists.'

'No, Mr. Barron, it's not that. I've come from Mr. Thornton in London.'

He frowned. 'Oh!' he grunted. 'And what does he want?'

'You have some designs in hand for him, and if you could let him know about them – soon?'

He swung away from her, then turned back suddenly. 'Sit down, Miss – Derwent—'

'Durrant,' she corrected.

'Durrant, then, and tell me why Thornton has sent you all this way to ask a simple question when he could have written a letter.'

Lucie chose a straight-back chair by the table. 'He says he's written several times and you haven't replied. Perhaps he had only your old address, the one near Las Palmas.'

Mr. Barron laughed. 'Yes, of course. That move of mine has foxed a lot of people. The woman who lives there promised to send on my letters, but she rarely does, and I can't say it matters much to me.'

'I called there yesterday and she gave me this address, so I came this morning on the plane.'

He pulled a chair out and sat astride it. 'Then you're staying in Las Palmas? On holiday?'

'Partly. But I also hope to do business in the Canaries. I make jewellery pieces, mostly costume designs, and sometimes Mr. Thornton buys from me. So when he knew I was coming here to try to sell some of my samples, he asked me to call on you.'

'I see. Have you marvellous powers of persuasion to coax a reply out of me?'

She shook her head and smiled. 'None at all.'

He flashed her a keen look of appraisal. 'Modestly spoken! Then I'll give you a straight answer. Is the work ready or not? I'm afraid the answer is not. I've been too busy.'

'Mr. Thornton understands that, of course,' she said hastily. 'All he asks is some idea of a date – if possible?'

He rose and came closer to her, glaring down at her and towering over her in a manner that sent shivers of apprehension down her spine. Not an easy man to do business with at all, she thought. Not easy to cope with in any context.

'I can't work to a timetable.' He flung away from her, hands in the pockets of his jeans. 'Thornton is only one of my customers. He must take his turn.' He wheeled round again. 'Still, perhaps I've made him wait a long time. Look, Miss Derwent – Durrant, then – tell him that I'll start work on them within the next week or so. Fair enough?'

'Mr. Thornton will still want to know when you're likely to finish the work,' she pointed out.

He stared at her with an expression somewhere between hostility and admiration. 'You're a tenacious young woman, aren't you?' Then he laughed. 'All right. I'll start as soon as I can, but I'll give him a more or less definite date for completing when I'm about half-way through. You never know what snags are going to crop up. There, does that answer satisfy you?'

'Thank you, yes. I'll write to Mr. Thornton.'

'How long are you staying in the Canaries?'

'That depends on how long my available money lasts out and whether I can sell my work. I'm trying Las Palmas first, then I thought I might spend some time in Tenerife.'

He glanced ostentatiously at his watch and she took the hint. She remembered the taxi waiting. Mr. Barron was dismissing her, yes she had accomplished only half her errand. Somehow she must broach the subject of the children.

She rose to go. 'Thank you for seeing me, Mr. Barron. I know you're very busy, so—'

He accompanied her to the door, but she saw that this was not the same one by which she had entered the villa.

'Where did you leave your car?' he asked.

'I came by taxi from the airport. The man is waiting.'

'The airport? But you can't take the plane back today.'

'No. I'm staying at a hotel in the town tonight.'

'I see. Then you'd better get back there or the taxi will be costing you a fortune.' He grinned. 'Charge it up to old Thornton.'

Lucie took a deep breath. 'Mr. Barron, I hope you won't be annoyed, but there was another matter, another reason why I came here.'

'Yes?' His tone was no gentle prompting, but an aggressive monosyllable that quenched her courage.

She could not look him in the face as she murmured, 'The children. Mr. Thornton wanted to be sure that—'

'Ah, now we're coming to it. The truth is you were sent here to do a bit of spying. The silver goods were only an excuse. Well, what about the children?'

'Only that since you are their guardian, he wants to be assured that—'

'That I still have them here? That I haven't thrown them into the sea or sold them into slavery? I realize now, Miss Durrant, why you were sitting there with your ears pricked up. You were waiting for the sounds of children's joyous laughter and toddlers' prattle.'

She half smiled. 'Perhaps I was. I – I guessed they were out for the day somewhere.'

'You're right. But I think we'd better go into some explanations. Will you stay to lunch? I'll send the taxi away.'

'I haven't paid him,' she objected. 'And how shall I get back to the town?'

'We'll sort that out later.' He had already walked down a wider path than the one she had negotiated and she was left standing there, unhappily aware that she had not been as tactful as the situation demanded. Now she was an unwelcome guest whom he had been forced to invite.

In a couple of minutes he was back. 'I know it's no business of mine,' Lucie began apologetically, but he waved away her self-reproach.

'Later. First I must tell Bernarda to prepare lunch for us. Excuse me.'

From where she stood she could hear voices, so apparently a kitchen was near by and Bernarda perhaps the girl she had already met.

When he rejoined her he indicated a wooden bench outside one of the windows. 'Lunch will be a few minutes, Bernarda says. She keeps house for us – if you can call her slapdash methods housekeeping. Still, we manage.'

Lucie smiled and remained silent. Now that she was relieved of the pressure of being forced to leave Mr. Barron's villa without seeing the children she could relax a little and allow him to discuss the matter in his own way.

Evidently he did not choose to mention it, but instead asked Lucie about her own work.

'I'm only really a beginner,' she admitted. 'Oh, I've done my course at art school, but I realize how much I've still to learn.'

'Do you sell well?'

She smiled and shook her head. 'Not yet. I've had a few orders from an exhibition which Mr. Thornton arranged and several London shops and department stores take pieces on sale or return.'

'So how do you live? With your parents, I suppose?'

'No. My father died when I was small and my mother married again three years ago. She lives in Scotland – my stepfather is a farmer, but he made it fairly plain that unless I was willing to work on the farm, I wasn't exactly welcome. So I share a flat in London with three other girls.'

'And now you're chancing your luck in the Canaries.'

'Well, I have to live somewhere, so I thought a winter and spring in sunshine might be a good idea. I have a small amount of money left me by my grandmother and now that I'm twenty-one, it's available. So you could say I'm gambling with it.'

'So you're twenty-one? You don't look it.' He turned towards her, scrutinizing her pale oval face with high cheekbones, the straight nose and generous mouth, then at her dark grey eyes and brown hair with lively, warm glints as the sun caught it. Under his gaze, she felt the colour flood into her cheeks and neck and quickly turned her head away.

He was younger than she had imagined. She had assumed that so successful an artist would be somewhere in his forties, but Mr. Barron was no more than thirty, if that. Her downward gaze rested on his hands, tanned and muscular, hands that would beat metal into shape and master it, yet fashion it lovingly with delicacy and skill.

Bernarda appeared now to say that lunch was ready, and Lucie accompanied Mr. Barron into a room with wide french windows overlooking a tidier part of the garden. A long Spanish mahogany table was set at one end with two places and Bernarda served a first course of *hors d'oeuvres*, comprising several ingredients unknown to Lucie, small fish and spiced vegetables with piquant sauce.

Lucie glanced around the room and noticed that much of the wall space was covered with pictures; landscapes, portraits, still life, one or two abstracts.

'You also paint?' she queried, sensing that these were originals.

'Not me. My friend Hallam. He lives here and has a studio. In fact, it was his idea that shifted me from Las Palmas. He had this house and offered me a share of it. He pointed out the isolation and that we could both work in peace. In Las Palmas people kept descending on me and demanding teapots just like their Aunt Matilda used to have. Sometimes a whole coachload of tourists would stop close by and the courier would hopefully call and try to persuade me to show them around. I gave in the first few times, but after that – no dice.'

He paused while Bernarda served a meat dish with a hot, spicy sauce.

'I hope you won't find this too peppery,' he said as he poured some wine into her glass.

Lucie tasted the food gingerly. 'No, it's fine. Unusual flavour.'

'Hallam and I find this place very good for working. We don't interfere with each other and the arrangement provides us with companionship.'

'And the children? Are they comfortable here?'

He grinned at her. 'I thought you wouldn't let the subject rest for long! Jessica and Daniel love the place. The garden runs down to the sea. They amuse themselves on the shore or in the rock pools.'

'Yes, of course, it would be ideal.' She hesitated, then plunged on. 'But their education?'

Mr. Barron laughed. 'Depends what you mean by "education", doesn't it? They're learning some of the best things in life. There'll be plenty of time for the textbooks and algebra later on.'

She nodded and smiled, uncertain what next she could say. This was exactly what the Thorntons had feared – that the children were undisciplined, left to their own resources and likely to be backward when eventually their education really began.

'No need to worry,' Mr. Barron continued. 'Jessica is very much the nursemaid-teacher-boss where Daniel's concerned.'

'How old are they?'

'I'm not sure. I suppose Jessica's about seven and Daniel – well, he'd be four, I suppose.'

'Jessica's nine and Daniel five,' she told him. 'So Mr. Thornton told me.'

'Well, *Mrs.* Thornton would certainly know their ages. I don't know what sort of tale you've heard about my snatching the kids away from much more respectable relatives, but the truth is that Howard, their father, thought the infants would be stifled. These old aunts – oh, they're perfect darlings according to everyone who knows them – they brought up Christine, the children's mother, and she was cosseted and cocooned so much that when at last she broke free and started to earn her own living, she was like a bewildered child in a whirlpool of inexperience. When she met Howard, my brother, home on one of his leaves, she saw him as a rescuer. The marriage turned out quite well, but no thanks to the aunts, who hated Howard and saw him as a wolf who had snatched away their precious lamb.'

Mr. Barron was silent for a minute or so. Lucie thought she could see his brother's point of view. Yet why was Mrs. Thornton involved?

'Is Mrs. Thornton a relative of Christine?' she asked.

'She claims to be,' snapped Joel Barron. 'Some sort of second cousin by marriage. Actually, I think the two aunts persuaded her to be on their side when Christine died, so that they could have the children with them.'

'Will their father be away long?'

'Another year at least. Then if he has to go away again, he'll choose good boarding schools.'

'Poor mites,' murmured Lucie. 'Out of the frying-pan into the fire.' She caught herself up sharply, not having meant to say those last words aloud.

Mr. Barron glared at her, his conversational manner vanished. 'One minute you're complaining about their lack of education, the next you're lamenting that they have to go to school.'

'Oh, no,' she assured him hastily. 'Not on my own account at all. I'm only a kind of messenger.'

The meal was finished and Joel Barron rang a bell for Bernarda to clear.

'Come this way,' he invited Lucie, 'and I'll show you the garden.'

This part was much tidier for a small ornamental pool was surrounded by a flagged stone terrace backed by bushes, hydrangeas, fuchsias and spiky cacti with bright red flowers. At one corner stood a flowering bush covered with yellow blossoms and nearby a jacaranda tree not yet in bloom, for this was only October.

'I realize I came towards your house from the wrong direction,' Lucie explained. 'The path was very narrow and overgrown.'

He turned to look at her. 'Sometimes that happens to all of us. We force our way through the jungle, as it were, when all the time, if we only knew, there's a perfectly good broad way to wherever we want to reach.'

She was surprised by the tone of his voice and wondered if he were merely thinking aloud or expecting her to grasp the hidden meaning of his words.

At the end of the garden a low stone wall separated it from the shore where dark rocks dotted the sandy beach.

Ahead was the turquoise sea stretching towards the coast of Africa. Could children ask for a better playground? she reflected.

'I – er – don't want to intrude too much on your time, Mr. Barron,' she said, 'but perhaps I ought to be getting back to the town.'

'Yes, of course. Satisfied that you got what you came for?'

'Well, yes, I think so. I'll be able to tell Mr. Thornton about the work and—'

'And that the children are little models of deportment, well-behaved, with clean faces, immaculate clothes?'

'I can tell him that he need not worry about their welfare.'

'What makes you trust me?'

She forced herself to look up into his face, to see the glint of amused mockery in his blue eyes. 'I'm quite sure you would take good care of your brother's children,' she said quietly.

He smiled. 'I think you'd better see them. Don't you?'

She hesitated. 'When?'

'Tomorrow, if you like. They've gone out with Hallam today. He's off painting somewhere and he's taken Jessica and Daniel with him.'

It was on the tip of her tongue to say that perhaps she could wait today for their return. But then she realized that might be unfair to the children rather than to Mr. Barron, for at the end of a day's outing they might be tired and not at their best.

'Yes,' she said at last. 'If I may come again tomorrow?'

'Sure. I'll drive you back to Corvario. I take it you're staying in the town?'

She felt slightly guilty because she was taking up his time, but remembered that it was Mr. Barron who had sent away the taxi and invited her to stay for lunch.

The drive back to the main town seemed to take less than half the time she had spent in the taxi on the outward journey. At the entrance to her hotel she thanked him.

'What time tomorrow?' he queried. 'Ten o'clock?'

'Yes, that would be all right.'

'Hallam or I will call for you. No need for a taxi.'

He slammed the car door and had driven away before she could make any further reply.

As she crossed the small reception hall, she realized that she would have to cancel tomorrow morning's return flight to Las Palmas and also she would need an extra night at the hotel.

After she arranged these matters with the clerk, she strolled out into the street, turned a corner and found herself in a wide thoroughfare where most of the buildings were only one storey. A church stood on the corner surrounded by a wall interrupted at intervals by flights of wide steps. Five minutes' more walking brought her to a narrow street and a busy market-place where most of the stalls were being cleared of merchandise, for it was now five o'clock.

After dinner in the hotel she began a letter to Mr. Thornton, relating the outcome of her interview with Mr. Barron, but she said nothing yet about the children. That part would have to wait until tomorrow's visit.

At ten o'clock next morning she was waiting outside the hotel and in about five minutes a car drew up. A fair-haired man stepped out and came towards her. 'Miss Durrant? I'm Hallam Dayne. Joel asked me to call.'

'Thank you. I'm quite ready.'

As he drove out of the town and along the coast road he said, 'I believe we upset your arrangements yesterday. I took the youngsters out for the day, so you missed them.'

Evidently Mr. Barron had explained the situation to Hallam Dayne. Lucie murmured non-committally that it didn't matter. In her own mind she regretted that the 'inspection', as Joel Barron termed it, had been magnified into a more important affair. She had wanted to make it casual, see the children and form her own conclusions to tell Mr. Thornton.

At the Villa Sirena Mr. Barron was in the garden with the two children perched on a bench, their legs swinging.

'These are the heavenly pair,' Mr. Barron introduced them to Lucie. 'Jessica, this is Miss Durrant.'

The little girl hopped down from the bench and held out her hand to Lucie in a most grown-up manner. 'How do you do? Have you come to be our governess?'

The question took Lucie by surprise. 'Oh, no, nothing like that.'

'This is my brother Daniel. Stand up, Daniel, and look polite,' urged his sister.

Lucie made suitable acknowledgment of the small boy's shyly mumbled words.

'I'll leave you, Miss Durrant,' said Mr. Barron, 'to get acquainted with the infants. If they tell you wild tales about their wicked uncle, don't believe them.'

Mr. Barron walked away down the garden, but Hallam Dayne stayed. 'Would you like a drink of something? Coffee? Wine?'

'Coffee, please,' Lucie answered.

'And orangeade for me and milk for Daniel,' ordered Jessica.

'Yes, madam. At once, madam.' With a grin at Lucie, Hallam went indoors.

If Lucie had been shy of starting a conversation with the children, Jessica showed no such hesitation.

'You are English? That's good. Not American?'

'No, English,' replied Lucie.

'What do you do in England?'

'I work at jewellery – pendants, bracelets, rings.'

Jessica frowned. 'Oh. That's why you've come. To work for Uncle Joel.'

'Oh, no.' Lucie was appalled at this suggestion. 'No, I've come to the Canary Islands to sell my jewellery and then perhaps get orders for more.'

Hallam Dayne had now returned with the tray of drinks, and Lucie was glad of the interruption.

'Do you think you'll be successful? In selling here?' he asked.

'I have to find that out. Mr. Thornton in London seemed to think it a good idea to try.'

He sat down and picked up his coffee cup. 'I was only thinking that the competition is pretty stiff. A lot of stuff, jewellery, trinkets and so on, comes in from Spain and Italy.'

She thought his tone of voice and choice of words

sounded contemptuous. 'I wasn't thinking of trying to compete with the Spanish styles. I have my own designs, some English, some Egyptian, or Persian.'

He nodded. 'Of course. Then I wish you luck.'

But now Jessica and Daniel were impatient to be on the move. They had finished their drinks and tugged at Lucie's hands.

'We must show you the garden,' invited Jessica.

Lucie smiled and allowed herself to be drawn down the path towards the pool and its terrace and did not disclose that she had been here yesterday with their Uncle Joel.

After lunch when the children had been settled for their siesta and Hallam had gone to his studio, Joel asked Lucie her verdict after the inspection.

'Oh, I think Jessica and Daniel are charming,' she answered with enthusiasm. 'Obviously well looked after. Certainly healthy.'

'But not really being educated?' His eyebrows were raised and his mouth curved in a smile.

'You know best about that. I wasn't supposed to test their reading ability or ask them to add up a column of figures.'

'No? I thought that was part of your brief.'

'Perhaps it was at first, but now I've seen them, I agree with you that it would be good for them to enjoy themselves in your care. For a while, at any rate.'

'So the report will be reasonably favourable, I take it.'

'Certainly. I'll write to Mr. Thornton as soon as I return to Las Palmas.'

Mr. Barron sighed mockingly. 'That sets my mind at rest, Miss Durrant.'

She laughed, but made no reply.

'Where are these bits of jewellery of yours?' he asked.

'I haven't them here. They're in the manager's safe at the hotel in Las Palmas.'

'Oh, I see. The thought occurred to me that if you had some samples with you, I might introduce you to one or two people here in Ventura. It would have saved you fumbling around.'

'That's very kind of you, Mr. Barron. I have one

sample, of course – the pendant I'm wearing.'

'I'd noticed that.' He leaned forward and examined the silver plaque with a design of thistles and lilies hung on a long chain. 'Did you make this as well as design it?' he asked.

'Oh, yes.' His bent head was close below her gaze and she was sharply aware of the thick strands of his dark hair and a faint echo of the brilliantine he used. She ought to have taken off the pendant and handed it to him, instead of being separated from him by only a chain's length.

'I thought you would be working.' A woman's voice cut the silence and Joel Barron jerked his head away from Lucie, releasing the plaque as though it had suddenly seared him.

Lucie glanced up and saw a young woman of medium height with beautiful rounded Spanish features and colouring. She wore a pale cyclamen dress cut in that superbly simple style that Lucie could rarely afford.

'And as you see, I'm not.' Mr. Barron had risen and now introduced Lucie. 'Señorita del Rey – Miss Durrant from England.'

'From England? Then you are on holiday?'

'Partly,' agreed Lucie. 'Partly on business.'

The Spanish girl sat in the chair that Mr. Barron had vacated. 'Oh, business! That is very dull. Does the business keep you here for a long time?'

'Oh, no. I'm staying in Las Palmas. I came here today to – to see Mr. Barron.'

'Miss Durrant came to visit the children,' put in Joel Barron.

'Oh? To take them home?' There was a restrained eagerness about Miss del Rey's query that was immediately apparent to Lucie.

Joel laughed. 'Nothing like that. Merely to see them on behalf of a relative in England.'

The Spanish girl glanced up and gave Joel an entrancing smile. 'But if there are – no, it does not matter.'

Lucie rose. 'I think perhaps I ought to go soon, if you will excuse me.'

'But no, you must not go yet!' protested Miss del Rey with conventional insincerity.

'Well, you'll want to see the children again before you go, I take it? Miss Durrant?' queried Joel.

'Not if they have to be disturbed from their siesta.'

'Wait a little longer, and either I or Hallam will drive you back to Corvario.'

'But I have my car here,' suggested Miss del Rey. 'I could drive Miss Durrant back to – wherever it is. Oh, let us be less formal. Have you a first name, Miss Durrant? I am Rosanna del Rey.'

'With half a dozen extra surnames in between,' added Joel Barron.

'That is only Spanish style.'

'My name is Lucie.' She had always felt that her name lacked vigour, that it was pallid and faded compared with more vivid names such as Theodora or Vanessa or Katrina. Now here was this girl so aptly named Rosanna, spirited and self-assured, glowing as a rose itself.

Joel Barron settled the question of transport. 'No, Rosanna, Lucie – Miss Durrant – isn't ready to leave yet. The children will be disappointed not to see you again.'

Lucie sat down again. Joel suggested coffee and went indoors to order it.

The two girls were silent for some moments. Lucie was about to remark on Rosanna's excellent English when the Spanish girl leaned slightly forward and peered at Lucie's silver plaque pendant.

'Yes, I see now,' she laughed quietly. 'At first when I came into the garden I thought some tragedy had hurt Joel and you were comforting him. But I see now that he was looking at your pretty pendant.'

Lucie nodded. Obviously Joel Barron's attitude might have appeared slightly ambiguous, but need Miss del Rey have referred to it?

'You have not visited the Canaries before?'

'No. This is my first visit,' replied Lucie.

'And your stay – how long?'

'That depends.' She was aware of the other girl's probing and since it was true that her own plans were vague, she saw no reason why she should try to give definite answers. 'Perhaps a month – two months. I have to go to Tenerife and some of the other islands as well.'

Rosanna nodded, but it was clear that she longed to

know more about the business affairs that involved Lucie in these journeys.

Fortunately Joel Barron returned, accompanied by Bernarda with a tray of coffee and small cakes. In a few moments Hallam Dayne appeared and greeted Rosanna.

'Rosanna is our nearest neighbour,' explained Hallam. 'She lives in a villa perched on the edge of the cliff and has the advantage over us. She can see our place easily, but we have to go up on to our roof to see hers.'

'Is it a flat roof?' asked Lucie.

'Yes. I've thought sometimes of making a garden up there, but I've never got around to it.'

'You could make a swimming pool,' suggested Rosanna.

'And have the whole villa flooded if it leaked? No fear. Anyway, why bother with swimming pools when the sea is so close!'

Presently, children's voices inside the house indicated that Jessica and Daniel had no further use for siesta time and they came running out to the grown-ups in the garden.

When Jessica saw Rosanna del Rey, the child murmured *'Buenos dias,'* dropped a slight curtsey, then turned her attention towards Lucie.

'When are you coming again?' she asked. 'Tomorrow?'

'Oh, no.' Lucie flushed a little. 'I have to go back to Las Palmas.'

'Then next week?'

Lucie shook her head and smiled.

'Don't pester Miss Durrant,' broke in Joel Barron sharply. 'She has her own plans.'

Hallam offered to drive her back to Corvario, but Joel Barron accompanied her to the car.

'I shall be in Las Palmas myself next week. If you'll give me the address where you're staying, I might be able to see your jewellery samples.'

'Thank you, Mr. Barron. That would be very kind.'

'I'll telephone which day I'm coming.' He paused, then gave her a keen glance. 'But if I criticize or tell you that you've little chance of selling your stuff here, how will you take it?'

'Sensibly, I hope,' she returned. 'I might be glad to be told that I'm wasting my time on such a venture.'

He nodded approval, but said nothing more as Hallam approached and entered the car.

On the way back to Corvario Hallam seemed less talkative than on this morning's journey, and Lucie deemed that it was not her place to disturb his thoughts.

He drove past her hotel apparently absentmindedly.

'Oh, sorry,' he apologized when she pointed out the error. 'I'm afraid I was thinking of something else.'

He turned into a side alley and backed. Outside her hotel he asked, 'Shall we be seeing you again, Miss Durrant?'

'Probably not. Perhaps I may come to Ventura later on if I think I can make any sales.'

'If you do, be sure to let us know and we can have lunch or dinner. Good luck.'

She watched him drive away, uncertain as to whether his good luck wishes were sincere or he was glad to see the back of her.

She decided to use the remaining time before dinner in exploring the streets of Corvario, look at the shops and try to assess what chances there might be of selling her articles. One or two shops displayed excellent pieces, but without marked prices; in the souvenir shops there were plenty of examples of mass-produced bangles and necklaces at prices to tempt the tourist, prices with which she could not possibly compete.

Later during the evening she finished her long letter to Mr. Thornton, telling him that Jessica and Daniel were evidently very happy in their Canary Islands home and there was nothing for him or Mrs. Thornton to worry about.

'And their education?' She could almost hear Mr. Thornton asking that question.

She chewed over the query and finally added that Mr. Barron intended to look after that side of the children's welfare. Her words were ambiguous. Intended? When? When they had grown into what Mrs. Thornton would have called 'ignorant little savages'.

Lucie shrugged. She had dutifully carried out her part

of the bargain and the Thorntons must take whatever steps they thought necessary.

Next morning she flew back to Las Palmas and started on her real business, visiting shops and wholesalers with specimens of her work.

After four or five days, she was delighted with the results. She had taken more than a dozen orders and several buyers had shown interest in her more unusual pieces, the individual pendants and brooches.

She was almost bubbling with excitement when Mr. Barron telephoned that he would be at her hotel tomorrow.

'Any luck?' he asked.

'More than I'd hoped for,' she answered.

When he arrived next morning and she accompanied him to a quiet corner table in the hotel foyer, she had schooled herself into a calmer, more modest frame of mind. She watched his face as she unwrapped and displayed from the black velvet wrappings the separate samples. His expression was probably more important than his words. She could not see his eyes, but she saw the momentary lift of his eyebrows as he examined a pair of textured silver cufflinks.

'Where did you get the idea for these? Flake chocolate?'

She laughed. 'Yes. At first I was thinking in terms of wrinkled tree bark – but that's how they turned out. Flake chocolate in silver.'

He nodded to himself. 'M'm. Do you finish all the work yourself or just make the designs and turn them over to someone else?'

'All my own handiwork. There's no satisfaction unless you do the whole thing all through. I'm aware,' she added hastily, remembering that this was the great artist Joel Barron, 'that my workmanship is by no means perfect, but I'm learning all the time.'

He continued to examine the samples one by one, sometimes pointing out where she could improve either design or finish. Then he handed them all back to her and she wrapped them in the velvet coverings and replaced them in the cardboard boxes which she used.

He stood up. 'I think we both deserve lunch now.' He

waited while she handed in the cardboard boxes to the reception clerk and was given the manager's receipt. 'I see that you take some precaution instead of leaving the lot lying around in your room,' he said with a smile.

'It's not that they're all terribly valuable, although the raw material can be quite costly. But without samples I'd be lost and have nothing to show.'

He took her to a restaurant in the Pueblo Canario, the famous Canary Village in a park behind the Santa Catalina hotel.

'Have you explored this part of Las Palmas?' he asked.

'Not yet. I've spent all my time calling on possible business people.'

'But you know that there are special shows of Canary dancing and singing twice a week?'

'Oh, yes, and I've decided to come on Sunday. 'I've heard that the costumes are wonderful.'

After the meal Joel Barron suggested they should sit outside at a table in the paved square. 'We can have coffee there,' he told the waiter.

'Miss Durrant,' he began when they were seated in one of the Moorish alcoves of the square. 'I've been thinking about your visit.'

He paused so long that she felt compelled to prompt with a quiet 'Yes?'

'I was wondering – that is – well, tell me this – how long are you likely to stay in the Canaries?'

'As long as I can. I told you – until my money runs out.'

'And what commitments have you at home in England?'

She hesitated. 'None,' she said at last, bleakly. There was no one to care very much whether she stayed in the Canaries for ever. The girls in the flat had already replaced her. Only perhaps her mother might in due course make inquiries if Lucie did not write regularly.

'Then I have a proposition to make. Since your visit Jessica and Daniel have never stopped talking about you. Every day they ask when you're coming again. You've unsettled them.'

'I'm sorry about that,' she murmured.

'Bernarda, too. Of course, she's young and eager to taste city life. She wants to work in Las Palmas, or at least somewhere gayer than our isolated little hideout at Molino de la Torre. Now the children keep telling her that they like you better than they do her, so she's upped and left us.'

Lucie's eyes widened with concern. 'Oh, no!'

'Well, I expect we can replace her with another girl or an older woman to look after us, but that might not solve my problem.' He raised his head and faced Lucie squarely across the table. 'I'm asking you, Miss Durrant, if you'll come and stay indefinitely with us.'

The question jolted Lucie into speechlessness. She was aware of Joel Barron's steely blue eyes and that he was waiting for an answer.

Then she shook her head. 'I don't think I could do that,' she said quietly, not looking at him, but away across the paved square with its gay-coloured umbrellas over the tables. 'I'm not exactly undomesticated, but I wouldn't be much good. And what would happen to my work?'

Now he smiled at her as she turned towards him. 'It's not the housekeeper part that is a difficulty. We'll get someone to do the chores and cooking. I'm asking you to come for the sake of the children. I've realized that they need rather more care than I can personally give them or expect from a girl like Bernarda. As for your work, you'd be welcome to use my workshop whenever you liked.'

Lucie was again silent. Then she said, 'Then it's really a governess you want for the children?'

He sighed. 'Not exactly that either. Nor even a nurse-maid. I respect your independence more than that. You would be our guest. The financial part would probably take care of itself.'

'The *au pair* girl,' muttered Lucie.

'All right, look at it like that if you want to. But would you even consider the proposition? Come for a month or two and see how you like it. Then if you find you can't cope or you don't like the situation, we'll call it a day and you're free to go back to England or tour the rest of the islands, just as you wish.'

'But, Mr. Barron, I want to tour the islands now,' she objected. 'It's what I came for.'

'There'll be nothing to stop you going off for a few days at a time on your business trips. The real difference is that you'd be able to work at our place, make new pieces to replace those you sell and probably have more chances of selling all through the season.'

'What does Mr. Dayne say? I understand the villa belongs to him.'

'Hallam would be delighted. It was partly his idea.'

'How long could I have to think it over?' she queried.

'I don't expect you to make a snap decision. Shall we say – a week from now? That would give you time to go over to Tenerife with your samples and make a few calls. I'll give you a list of likely buyers, if that will help.'

Lucie looked down into her lap. 'I don't really know what to say. It's such an unexpected offer – something I'd never thought about.'

'Then give it all your consideration during the next day or so. If you decide to come, we'll make all the arrangements. The Villa is quite a pleasant house, but of course quiet. No life except what we make for ourselves. A tiny fishing harbour about half a mile away with a few houses. That's all.'

'But a lovely climate, unspoilt coast and a peaceful atmosphere,' she put in.

He smiled at her. 'I left that stuff for the guide books and travel brochures.'

When they strolled out of the square of the Canary Village, glanced at the shops selling pottery and trinkets, books, and dolls dressed in local costumes, Joel Barron seemed to have dismissed the subject, for he spoke of other matters, sightseeing in Gran Canaria and Tenerife, the many festivals that took place in various parts of the islands.

Perhaps she understood that in a subtle fashion he was trying to extol the advantages of staying.

When he left her at her hotel he said he was staying the night with friends in Las Palmas. 'I'm flying back tomorrow evening. Weigh up the position and let me know what you decide. I'll be careful not to promise the children anything definite.'

For the rest of the day Lucie's thoughts spun round her

head in a turmoil. What had she to lose if she accepted this offer that had descended out of the blue? To be privileged to share, even in a small way, the workshop of Joel Barron was a chance not to be thrown away lightly. The children were darlings, of course, and there was the slightest hint of blackmail there. Then what of Hallam Dayne? She had received the impression that he was coolly contemptuous of her jewellery knick-knacks and completely uninterested in her as a person.

Lucie made no decision. For the next four days she tried to shut her mind to the problem and deal exclusively with her business affairs. She flew to Tenerife and roamed about Santa Cruz, visiting some of the addresses Mr. Barron had given her. She returned to Las Palmas and concentrated on writing out her orders clearly in her notebook.

All the time one part of her mind was debating the question of taking the plunge and staying in Ventura at the Villa Sirena for at least several months. The faces of Jessica and Daniel floated before her. Joel Barron would always see that they had physical care while they were in his charge. But was that enough? In his own way he might love them as a devoted uncle, but surely they needed at this point in their lives a woman, even a young woman, who would enter into their childish games, laugh with them, soothe their hurts when they fell down, and make them feel cherished.

Lucie realized that the decision had already been made days ago.

## CHAPTER TWO

On the short plane journey to Ventura Lucie had time to reflect on the wisdom or otherwise of the step she was taking. Until now during the last few days she had been too busy to give herself time to think. Several rush visits to shops, buying a dress or two, a pair of slacks and a jacket, for she guessed that Las Palmas would have more variety than those in Ventura, arranging to leave the hotel and book her plane passage, writing letters to Mr. Thornton to give him her new address – all these things had occupied her to the exclusion of any contemplation of the situation she might find herself in at the Villa Sirena.

Whatever risks she was taking or regrets that might arise, it was too late now, for the plane would soon touch down and Mr. Barron would be there to meet her as he had promised. His reply to her letter accepting his offer had been by telegram and therefore terse. 'Come Thursday stop Will meet you at airport.' No signature. No 'kind regards' or anything like that. Perhaps he was already regretting what might be an impulsive offer.

The sight of him waiting at the airport as she passed through the customs was enough to send her spirits soaring. He took charge of her luggage, stowed it in his car and gave her a smile of welcome that both startled and disquieted her. It was not so much his smile which he might have bestowed on any of his guests, but her own reaction. The relationship between her and Mr. Barron had changed naturally, since she was now to be a guest in his household and before this she had been no more than an acquaintance more or less in the course of his business.

'Good journey?' he asked now as he drove off.

'Yes, very pleasant.'

He pointed out one or two interesting places and she watched the sandy-coloured landscape punctuated with palm trees, occasional flat-roofed white houses and clusters of prickly pear near the roadside.

While she answered him a deeper layer of her mind was warning her that she must not allow herself to believe that Joel Barron had any other purpose in inviting her to his house than the true one, that of caring for the children. She must certainly not interpret a warm or cordial smile, a few friendly words, as evidence that he found her attractive.

At the Villa Sirena Jessica and Daniel were at the gate to welcome her.

'I told Daniel you'd come back and live with us,' said Jessica confidently.

'And here I am,' responded Lucie, as she hugged the children in turn without restraint.

They rushed up the stairs ahead of her to show her to her room, and Joel Barron followed with her suitcases.

'I hope you'll like the room,' he said.

'Oh, I do. It's charming.'

There were two windows, one with a sea view and a small balcony, the other looking out across the hills. The walls, painted a cool water green, contrasted well with the dark warm browns of the Spanish mahogany furniture. A huge wardrobe stood in one corner awaiting Lucie's not very extensive collection of clothes. Rugs in soft colours carpeted the smooth grey marble floor.

'Shall I help you unpack?' queried Jessica eagerly.

'I'm told that lunch will be ready in about half an hour,' Joel was saying from the doorway, 'so come down as soon as you're ready – and don't let the youngsters pester you.'

Lucie smiled.

'Pester!' murmured Jessica with the utmost contempt. 'Uncle Joel, we never pester anyone!' But Uncle Joel had disappeared down the corridor.

'There's a bathroom next door to you,' pointed out Jessica helpfully. 'Our room is on the other side.'

'You and Daniel?'

'Yes. Daniel is a bit afraid of being in a room by himself,' explained Jessica. 'But next year he'll be six, so he won't be frightened then of sleeping by himself.'

'I'm not afraid now!' protested Daniel stoutly.

Jessica gave him a glance that combined the expression of a fond, protective sister with a disbelief of Daniel's courage, in the dark.

Then she turned her attention to helping Lucie unpack, trotting about with coat-hangers, setting shoes on the shoe-rack, talking all the time about Uncle Joel or Uncle Hallam, the girl Bernarda who had left.

'Bernarda was nice, but she wouldn't let us go into the kitchen when she was cooking.'

'Perhaps she didn't want you to be hurt with burns or scalding water,' pointed out Lucie.

'Oh, no, it wasn't that,' declared Jessica. 'She said that she didn't want us getting under her feet all the time, but my view is—' she paused with dramatic significance – 'that she didn't want us to see what she put in the food.'

Lucie laughed. 'Well, all cooks have their pet recipes and don't want others to spy on them.'

'The food here took some getting used to,' sighed Jessica. 'In England we had all sorts of nice things like chocolate pudding and trifles and jellies, and sometimes damson pies.'

'And what do you get here instead of those?'

'Bananas.' Jessica wrinkled her nose in disgust.

'We have melon sometimes,' put in Daniel. 'I like melon.'

'Perhaps when I've been here a bit longer we'll be able to make you a banana and melon trifle,' promised Lucie. 'How would that be?'

'Sounds nice,' agreed Jessica. 'Look, here's your bathroom.' She turned the key in the lock and unbolted the door of the adjoining bathroom.

Lucie had not expected to find such expensive-looking plumbing in an isolated house on a small Canary island, but the turquoise tiled walls to match the panelled bath, the gleaming towel rails with soft white and turquoise towels and a chestnut brown bath mat added up to a delightful sense of luxury.

She noted the door on the opposite side leading to the children's bedroom.

'What a good arrangement to have this bathroom between our rooms,' she said.

Jessica was at the wash-basin rinsing her hands, then exhorting Daniel to do likewise before lunch.

The two children escorted Lucie downstairs to the

dining room where Mr. Barron was waiting, a trifle impatiently, it seemed.

'I hope you haven't let the kids talk you to death,' he said.

Lucie smiled. 'No, indeed. They've both been most helpful showing me around.'

A middle-aged woman served the meal and Lucie assumed this was the new housekeeper. Hallam Dayne did not appear and when Jessica remarked on Uncle Hallam's absence, Joel Barron belatedly explained that when he was working he often skipped lunch or had a light meal and a bottle of wine taken up to his studio.

'But he isn't working today,' pointed out Jessica. 'He went down to the harbour.'

Joel gave the child a sharp glance. 'How do you know he hasn't come back?'

'Well, it was only just before you and Lucie came,' continued Jessica relentlessly. 'He said he wasn't going to be one of the reception committee – whatever that means.'

'You shouldn't tattle, Jessica,' reproved her uncle.

Lucie hastily asked a question about the nearby harbour in an effort to divert the conversation, for Jessica had gone scarlet at receiving the curt rebuke.

'It's not quite half a mile along the coast,' Joel answered. 'A tiny fishing harbour with a huddle of houses. Hardly big enough to call a village. But useful to us for food supplies sometimes. One of the men usually brings us fish and in his spare time does the garden for us.'

'That's Alberto,' put in the irrepressible Jessica, who had recovered her poise. 'He's nice, but he speaks funny Spanish.'

Joel laughed. 'He has a fearful dialect. I can't always understand what he says, but he keeps an eye on our boat for us.'

'Oh? You have a boat? What sort?' Lucie asked the question merely to keep the ball rolling, for apart from rowing a dinghy on the Serpentine, she was ignorant of boats in general.

'A small cabin cruiser,' replied Joel. 'But we're thinking of getting a yacht soon. Hallam and I share the one we have now.'

'When we behave ourselves properly,' said Jessica demurely, 'Uncle Joel or Uncle Hallam take us out in the boat.'

'I see,' Lucie smiled. 'It's a special treat.'

'Well, we're always being threatened,' returned the child. 'It's "Don't do this and don't do that – or you won't get a boat ride." So we have to be very good.'

'Good heavens!' exclaimed Joel. 'The boot's on the other foot. Hardly a day goes by that we're not pestered to take them skylarking round the bay.' He shook his finger at Jessica. 'Be careful, madam, or you'll be left at home next time.'

Jessica smiled disarmingly, but said no more. Already at so early an age she had learned when not to claim the feminine privilege of the last word.

Lucie spent the afternoon alone in her room. The children were shepherded to their room to lie on the beds, whether they slept or not. Joel retired to his workshop and no doubt Señora Matana, the housekeeper, needed her siesta after a morning's cooking and other work in the house.

So far Lucie had been delighted with her welcome into Mr. Barron's household, apart from that one stray reference to Hallam Dayne's absence at lunch. If Jessica failed to understand, Lucie knew perfectly well what was meant by the phrase 'reception committee' in connection with herself.

She decided that where Mr. Dayne was concerned she must walk very warily indeed, for he was the owner of the villa, even though Joel Barron no doubt paid his share.

At dinner, however, her anxiety vanished, at least for the time being, for Mr. Dayne gave her the most friendly greeting, apologizing for his absence earlier in the day.

'I went out in the boat,' he explained. 'She's not been running well lately, so I made a short trial trip.'

She intercepted the surprised look on Joel Barron's face and guessed that he knew nothing of the boat's malfunctioning.

'We must take Miss Durrant out some time,' he said quietly. 'Unless, of course, you hate boats or are a bad sailor.'

'I like boats, but I haven't sailed in rough seas, so I don't know what sort of sailor I am,' she replied.

'It's rare that we get much rough weather around here,' Joel Barron assured her. 'The occasional storm, a gale perhaps, but on the whole a calm sea.'

'And a prosperous voyage, I trust?' Hallam finished the quotation with a smile at Lucie. 'One thing we can do, I think, is discard this formality of "Miss Durrant" and "Mr. Barron" and so on. I hope I may call you Lucie?'

'Yes, of course.' In her mind already she had been calling the two men by their Christian names, so it was easier now to avoid a careless familiarity that might offend either of them.

The next morning the two children escorted her down to the tiny village of Molino de la Torre and she saw the little harbour, hardly more than a curving piece of wall, where two fishing-boats swung lazily at their moorings.

'There's our boat!' pointed out Daniel. 'Come and see it.' He dragged her by the hand along the uneven harbour wall and she looked down on the cabin cruiser, smartly painted, the deck protected by a canvas cover.

'A fine boat,' she commented. 'What's her name?'

'*La Sirena*,' answered Jessica. 'I think it means "mermaid", but it's called that because it belongs to our house, the Villa Sirena.'

Daniel was leaning perilously over the edge of the quay. Lucie caught her breath sharply. 'Daniel! Be careful!' She took a step or two towards him and grasped his hand. 'You mustn't fall in the water.'

'He's tumbled in several times,' commented Jessica. 'Someone always fishes him out.'

'But can you swim?' she asked the small boy.

'Nearly!' he replied indignantly. 'Well, almost nearly,' he amended.

Jessica grimaced, but not unkindly. 'I try to hold him up, but he sinks. Too fat!'

'Then we shall all have to take turns to teach you to swim well, Daniel,' suggested Lucie.

'Can you swim and dive and water-ski?' queried Jessica.

'Oh, heavens, not all of them. I swim – moderately, but I can't dive very well and I've never been water-skiing.'

'You should see Uncle Hallam on skis,' put in Daniel. 'He's very clever. He can hold on with only one hand and he goes ever so fast.'

Accompanied by the two children Lucie explored the rest of the tiny village, the huddle of houses close to the harbour, the inn with a couple of tables outside.

'That's where Alberto lives,' Jessica pointed out a small white cottage where orange-coloured fishing nets hung on the walls to dry.

Several days went by with Lucie feeling as though she were one of the island's winter holidaymakers. She had come in October to make full use of the winter tourist season. Now in early November she wondered how she could fulfil the orders she had taken for jewellery so that they did not miss the Christmas trade.

'My intention was, of course, to take as many orders as possible,' she explained to Joel, 'and then fly home to make the articles and return here to deliver them. After that, I would possibly get more orders.'

He smiled at her. 'Commuting! Well, I told you that you were free to use my workshop whenever you wanted to work there.'

'Yes, I know, but I don't want to intrude when you're working and, apart from that, I haven't my tools here, nor the material.'

'M'm.' Joel was thoughtful for a few moments. 'I could supply the tools and probably the material. What you're really saying is that you want to work on your own without my breathing down your neck.'

She flushed a little. 'I'm still not much more than a novice and I make mistakes. I could easily work in my own bedroom. Then I wouldn't be in your way.'

He gave her a keen glance that caused the flush in her cheeks to deepen and she was aware of her pulses beating faster.

'Just as you like,' he said abruptly, and walked away down the garden.

Lucie felt angry with herself. Joel had intended to help her and she had clumsily rejected his assistance while still needing his co-operation in the matter of tools and material.

She went slowly upstairs to her own bedroom and surveyed it with a view to working space. There was plenty of room and all she needed was a small sturdy table. While the practical part of her mind dealt with methods of working, a deeper layer was warning her of danger. She was drawn to Joel and respected him as a professional artist; she was attracted to him as a man because he had shown her kindness and generosity, but she knew she must not allow herself to drift into a warmer relationship.

Quite apart from any possible reciprocal response on his side, she was not ready for any deep emotion. A recent disastrous experience had left her drained of any desire for a new attachment. Not even Mr. Thornton had known that Lucie had more than one reason for escaping from an English winter to the Canary Islands. Selling jewellery was only part of the complex situation, for she was trying to put behind her those harsh memories, the sense of treachery that she had confided to no one. One of her flatmates had guessed some of the reasons for Lucie's departure, but Lucie smiled without revealing any details.

'Uncle Joel is taking us out in the boat,' Jessica informed Lucie next day.

'Oh, good. In the morning or afternoon?'

'Afternoon – when we've had our siesta. You know he couldn't take us in the mornings. He works in his old shed.' Jessica's blue eyes widened with mock fear. 'Ooh! It's more than we dare do – go and worry him in the shed.'

'Shed? It's his workshop where he makes the most beautiful silver tea services and trays and so on.'

'Yes, I know. He bangs about with hammers.' Jessica giggled. 'Sometimes Daniel and I stand outside and every time Uncle Joel give a clang, we say "Ding dong ding dong" – but we don't let him hear us or he'd be cross.'

Lucie laughed. 'Quite right. If he heard you, he might dong the silver in the wrong place and then it would be spoilt. What time is he expecting you to be ready this afternoon?'

About four o'clock, I expect. You must be ready also.'

'Why? Am I invited?'

'Of course. He said I wasn't to forget to tell Lucie. So I've told you. He never calls you Miss Durrant now, does he?'

'Well, no. But neither do you and Daniel.'

'Oh, "Miss Durrant" all the time would make you sound like an old dragon of a schoolteacher.'

The mention of 'schoolteacher' reminded Lucie that nothing was being done to help the children's education. She had originally declared that she did not wish to be considered as a governess, but now that she was here with Jessica and Daniel, she had come to the conclusion that an hour's instruction in simple subjects every day might not be a bad thing. Yet she could not take this step without Joel's knowledge or consent and she must tackle the subject very diplomatically.

Hallam appeared for lunch, but not Joel. 'He's working,' he explained for Lucie's benefit, then cast a glance at Jessica and Daniel. 'Apparently the two brats have insisted on being taken for a boat ride, so poor Uncle Joel has to do without his lunch.'

Jessica looked up from her plate and stared at Hallam with indignant candour in her blue eyes. 'Señora Matana took his lunch down to the shed. I saw it – three plates all covered and a bottle of wine.'

Hallam laughed. 'There can't be anything going on in this house that Jessica doesn't see or hear about. She has the makings of a perfect spy.'

'Spy?' echoed Daniel. 'Who's a spy? I like to hear about spies.'

Lucie gently urged the children to concentrate on their food and discuss spies another time.

Later in the afternoon she settled herself in a long chair in the garden and read one of Joel's books which she had borrowed from his collection. Some distance away she could hear the occasional clang of metal from the workshop and smiled, remembering Jessica's 'Ding dong'. Eventually she must have dozed for a while, the book unheeded, for she opened her eyes to find Hallam regarding her.

'Sorry if I disturbed you,' he apologized.

'I wasn't asleep,' she maintained in spite of his disbelieving expression.

'Are you really interested in silver work?'

His question startled her. She sat up and swung her legs off the long chair on to the ground. 'Of course! What makes you think I'm not?'

He smiled lazily, but she was not looking at his mouth. His grey eyes were hard as stones. 'Oh, girls often take up some profession or craft because they're interested in the end-product. They're not really concerned with the work that has to be done before they reach their goal.'

'You think I took up making jewellery because I'm more interested in pretty ornaments for women to wear?' she asked mildly.

He lit a cigarette. 'Well, it's possible that you chose jewellery because you thought you had a talent that way, and it was a less crowded profession than some others, but you might just as easily have gone in for the stage or dress-designing or journalism.'

Lucie shook her head. 'I don't understand what you mean. I *wanted* to design silver pieces and other kinds of ornaments. I use stone sometimes and I enjoy the work of rubbing it down and shaping and polishing it. It isn't only the end-product that counts with me.'

'Then you're a little different perhaps from the average run of career girls.'

She had the feeling that he was baiting her, but for what purpose?

'Surely in your own work as a painter, you're not only interested in the finished picture. You must enjoy the process of applying paint and seeing your ideas take shape under your brushes.'

'Of course. But I'm twenty-six and since I was sixteen I've never done anything else except draw and paint. It really is my work – the same as Joel is a professional.'

Now Lucie smiled at the taunt. 'And you think I'm a mere dilettante, whiling away my time until—' Then she stopped abruptly in confusion.

He laughed quietly. 'Until you marry, you were going to say.'

'Marriage is a long way from my thoughts or my present plans,' she said coolly.

'I wonder!' he murmured softly. 'But you mustn't be offended. Joel and I are in the habit of speaking our thoughts plainly and I hope you'll do the same while you're here with us.'

'Perhaps I've learned to guard my tongue – most times,' she added hastily, remembering that unfortunate blunder of only a moment ago.

'And you're not offended with me?' His casual tone implied that he was indifferent as to whether she were offended or otherwise.

'Of course not,' she assured him.

'Then would you like to come up to my studio? I don't promise to show you all my work or any efforts not yet completed.'

She glanced at her watch. Ten minutes to four. 'Well – er – now?' she queried.

'Yes. Why not?'

'Perhaps I could come another time. I'm supposed to be going with the children in the boat – with Joel.'

His expression changed at once to a mixture of surprise and derision. 'Oh? I didn't realize – then of course you must go. Joel doesn't give out his invitations lightly to all comers. I hope I haven't delayed you. Go and enjoy yourself.'

He walked towards the villa, leaving her standing there bewildered, unsure how much she had offended him. She regretted very much refusing his invitation to visit his studio, for she had already been warned by Joel, Señora Matana and Jessica that Hallam's studio was definitely out of bounds to everyone except by personal invitation.

He, too, apparently did not issue his favours lightly, and now she understood his meaning when he referred to that same characteristic in Joel.

All the same, Lucie had the uneasy feeling that Hallam had either known or at least guessed that she would be accompanying the children on the boat trip. He had then timed his offer to face her with the choice of visiting the studio or going with Joel. Perhaps he had merely wanted to delay her so that Joel would be annoyed at being kept waiting.

But now there was no more time for reflection. She hurried up to her room, hoping not to meet Hallam on the way, and changed her dress for a pair of yellow linen slacks and a white jumper.

Jessica and Daniel were already outside the porch impatiently waiting to start.

'You look nice,' commented Jessica admiringly to Lucie.

'Not only nice, but very suitably dressed,' came Joel's remark as he joined the trio. 'Come on, all of you. This way for the *Skylark*!'

They walked a short distance along the dunes avoiding the tufts of succulents and prickly pears. Away to the right was the road dotted with a few palms and beyond that, one of the mountain peaks making up the long chain that ran like a backbone through the length of the island. Lucie had already on previous walks noticed the curious shape of the peak, for its slopes were dented by long hollows as though giant hands had playfully scored it when it was hot and malleable.

'Is it that shape because it's volcanic?' she asked Joel now as he walked beside her, with the children racing and skipping ahead.

'Volcanic to start with and probably changed its shape several times with various upheavals, but those marks are caused by erosion. Wind and water have a powerful influence on the landscape.'

Now they took the rough path that led down to the shore and then cut across the narrow neck of land that sheltered the harbour and village of Molino de la Torre.

In a few minutes after Joel had checked supplies of oil and petrol, Lucie and the two children were aboard and heading out to the glittering turquoise sea.

Lucie's brown hair blew across her face and she tied a scarf over her head. Outside the harbour the boat rocked for a few moments as it caught the crosswind. Jessica and Daniel laughed and shouted with glee, but Lucie wondered if she had been wise to eat the small assorted shellfish, followed by *canelloni* at lunch. But as Joel changed course *La Sirena* settled into a steady motion, seeming to skim the rippling waves and Lucie was less apprehensive that she would disgrace herself in front of Joel and two hardy little sailors.

'We could go to Corvario, if you like,' Joel offered.

'Oh, yes, yes, please!' cried Jessica.

'You, madam, will wait to be asked,' admonished Joel. 'What about you, Lucie?'

'Yes, I'd like to if it's convenient for you. Not too far?'

'Oh, no. I sometimes take the boat there instead of going by car.'

He made a wide U-turn to head for the opposite direction and now he pointed out to Lucie the various places of interest.

'There's our villa!' called Jessica as they passed. Then a few moments later Joel indicated a villa perched high up on the cliff.

'That's where Rosanna lives.'

Lucie gazed at the white villa clinging so precariously to the rocks that it seemed in danger of falling into the sea.

Since Lucie's arrival at the Villa Sirena, Rosanna had not called or, at least, if she had, then Lucie had not been there at the time, and now she wondered if the Spanish girl were a frequent visitor or spent her time elsewhere in perhaps livelier surroundings.

But now Joel was nearing the port of Corvario, reduced his speed and slid into a vacant mooring in the harbour.

'I suppose you two want ice-creams,' he said to the children when he helped them ashore.

'Yes, please,' they said in unison.

He led the way to a café facing the quay and ordered for Jessica and Daniel, with coffee for Lucie and himself.

'Since I'm here,' he said after a while, 'I might as well make a call at a shop in the town. They have material on order for me. Could you keep Jessica and Daniel with you?'

'Certainly,' Lucie replied. 'I'll be glad to look around this part of the town. I haven't seen the harbour until now.'

'I shan't be more than about half an hour,' he told her, 'so don't stray too far away. I'll meet you down by the boat.'

She watched him stride off across the square, a tall, broad-shouldered man in dark brown trousers and beige jacket, a man with the air of one who knew exactly where he was going and stepped out decisively.

How heartening it would be, she thought, if he were approaching instead of receding and he came towards one with that firm step! But she reined her imagination. She knew so little about Joel, whether he was married or had been married at some time, and it was hardly her concern to find out.

Jessica and Daniel were familiar with the harbour and eager to point out places and people.

'That old man over there sleeps all day long,' observed Jessica, indicating a fisherman lying on the quay with a pile of rolled-up nets for his pillow.

'Probably he's out all night fishing and then he's tired next day,' said Lucie.

'Oh, no, he doesn't fish. He cleans the streets in the middle of the night with a hose.'

'Then he still has reason to be tired in the daytime. Anyway, how do you know what he does at night?'

'He told me,' answered Jessica.

'In one of his waking moments, apparently?'

'If you don't believe me. I'll go and ask him,' declared Jessica. 'His name is Juan.'

'No, no, please don't disturb him. Of course I believe you,' added Lucie hastily.

Daniel was intrigued with a man who was selling small wooden animals that danced on an elastic string. He fingered a gay little horse and Lucie asked the seller the price. She handed over a few pesetas and was well rewarded by Daniel's gratitude.

'You mustn't ask for things, Daniel,' scolded his sister. Then she turned to Lucie with that adult air that sat so precociously on a girl of nine. 'You mustn't give in, Lucie, or you'll never have any money where Dan's concerned. Anyway, I expect you paid too much for it. Uncle Joel says you should never give people more than half of what they ask.'

'I don't think I'm very good at bargaining,' admitted Lucie. 'Perhaps I shall learn.'

By the time the children had shown her all the absorbing features of the quays, the tiny alleys, the two rival inns and the various boats including a smart white-painted yacht anchored out in the harbour, Lucie guessed it would be time to return to the boat.

'Heavens! Uncle Joel will be waiting for us. It's nearly an hour since he left.'

They hurried down to the mooring only to find that Joel had not yet returned, but he came along in a few minutes.

'Sorry to keep you waiting,' he apologized. 'But I was detained at the shop longer than I expected and then I met—'

'We've only just come,' confessed Daniel. 'We haven't been waiting.'

Jessica shot him a warning glance, but Lucie said, 'That's right.'

'Good.' He stepped into the boat first so that he could help the children aboard and then Lucie. He had cast off and swung out into the wide sea before he said, 'I met Rosanna. You remember her – Miss del Rey.'

Lucie nodded.

'She's invited us to go to dinner at her villa tomorrow night.'

By 'us' Lucie interpreted that he meant himself and Hallam and she thought no more of the arrangement until the following afternoon when Joel said to her, 'Will the children be all right, do you think? We shan't be home late.'

Lucie stared at him, puzzled. 'But I shall be here as usual.'

'No. I thought you understood that you were included in Rosanna's invitation.'

'No, I didn't.'

'Well, you'd better come with us or she'll be offended. Be ready about eight.'

'I don't like leaving Jessica and Daniel in the house by themselves.'

'Then ask Señora Matana to stay until we come home. Tell her she can have a few extra pesetas.'

Señora Matana lived in the village of Molino and came every day to the Villa to cook and clean. Usually she went home after the evening meal was finished. At such short notice Lucie doubted whether the woman would be willing to stay late.

A middle-aged woman of comfortable plumpness, she

was preparing dinner when Lucie entered the kitchen. In laboured Spanish with a few English words here and there, she explained the position.

'Until what time?' asked the woman.

Lucie shook her head. 'I'm not sure. Not too late. Perhaps eleven or midnight.' She was aware that this was probably not quite true, for she had learned that Spanish evening meals started late and any entertainment that followed was likely to be protracted until well after midnight.

Señora Matana nodded assent.

'Either Señor Barron or Señor Dayne will take you home in the car,' Lucie added, hoping that this would turn out to be true.

'*Si, si, señorita.* Perhaps you can take a message to my home? Then they will know.'

'Of course. Tell me the address.'

'Calle Verde, eight. The little girl will tell you where to find it.'

When Lucie sought out Jessica for guidance, the girl said, 'You won't find it until you know the village better. The house is in a small street. Shall I come with you?'

'Might be a good idea,' agreed Lucie.

'We'd better take Daniel. He'll only get into some scrape or other if I'm not there to keep him out of mischief.'

As the trio walked the short way along the dunes, then the beach, Lucie wondered if Jessica's protective attitude towards her brother was tending to stifle the boy. The girl had almost taken on the rôle of the two elderly aunts from whom Joel had detached both the children. Jessica and Daniel really needed companions of their own respective ages.

On this occasion Lucie was glad of Jessica's guidance, for she would never have discovered the house by herself and would merely have wasted time hunting up and down the streets. Calle Verde was no more than a narrow passage ascending a steep flight of steps between two houses.

'It's like a hole in the wall, isn't it?' remarked Jessica.

Half-way up, another passage turned right and number eight was tucked into a corner. A girl about five or six years old answered the door and Lucie began her message, but Jessica asked in Spanish, 'Where is your mother? Tell her to come.'

In a few moments a young woman came to the door.

'Señora Matana—' began Lucie, but this alarmed the woman, who immediately jumped to the conclusion that some accident or illness had happened to her mother. After some minutes of explanation between Lucie's tenuous grasp of Spanish, Jessica's helpful interpolations and the young woman's anxious questions, the situation became clear that Señora Matana would not be home until at least '*medianoche*' and that the daughter was to cook the evening meal for the family.

Lucie gave a great sigh when she and the two children had walked some distance away.

'I see I shall have to learn Spanish fast if I'm to cope with problems like this. How have you managed to pick up so much?' she asked Jessica.

'I talk to Alberto when he does the gardening and sometimes Uncle Joel speaks in Spanish for me to learn. He says it's always a good thing if you can grow up by-lingy – is that the right word?'

'Bi-lingual,' supplied Lucie. 'It means you speak two languages like a native, and that's a great asset. You must teach me, Jessica. All I know is a few isolated words, and they won't get me far.'

When they were back in the Villa Sirena again, Jessica was curious about Lucie's evening out.

'Rosanna – oh, Señorita del Rey, we're not supposed to call her Rosanna – she must like you, Lucie.'

Lucie shook her head. 'I've met her only once, so she doesn't know me at all to like or dislike me.'

'She doesn't like us, Daniel and me. She says we're a handicap. What does that mean?'

'A drawback. A disadvantage.'

'Yes, that's what she means. She says Uncle Joel ought not to have taken us away from England.'

'I suppose Uncle Joel knows best about that,' was Lucie's diplomatic comment. 'Now I must get myself ready.' She was reluctant to encourage Jessica's gossip about the two men or Rosanna.

'Will you show me your dress before you go?' queried Jessica.

'Of course. I'll come in and show myself off.'

Lucie's wardrobe for special evening occasions was sparse. She had come to the Canaries to occupy herself mostly in the daytime and had not envisaged decking up for the evening. She possessed only a single outfit, a long skirt printed in a flowing pattern of subtle shades of purples and mauves, with a wide, matching belt, and a tailored shirt with full sleeves and button cuffs in plain lavender. She had bought the outfit in London mainly because it was an easy-care fabric and the print by a famous designer.

Her dark hair was shoulder-length and curled at the ends. She took extra trouble with her make-up, using only light eye-shadow, a pale rose lipstick. Finally she dabbed on some perfume she had bought inexpensively in Las Palmas.

'Ooh, you smell nice,' was Daniel's comment when she paraded for the children's benefit.

'Pretty dress,' Jessica eyed Lucie up and down. 'When can I wear a long skirt like that?'

Lucie kissed the child. 'Oh, a few more years yet. You don't want to grow up before your time.'

When she joined the two men standing by the car, she was glad she had put on her best rig-out, for they wore black ties and white dinner jackets, so evidently dining at Rosanna's was an occasion.

She saw Joel's eyes light up with approval and her heart gave a queer little jerk.

Hallam gave her a cool stare of appraisal, then said, 'You'd better sit in the back. I'd hate to get that skirt tangled up in my gears.' He settled in the driving seat. Joel held open the rear door for Lucie, began to follow her, but changed his mind, apparently, for he slammed the door shut and chose the passenger seat next to Hallam.

In the mirror she caught a fleeting glimpse of Hallam's smile, as he glanced at Joel. Then his features straightened into his usual expression and he started the car.

Hallam drove a short distance along the road, then took a right turn at the fork and now climbed a twisting road that was little more than a track.

'We don't always come by car,' explained Joel, turning

towards Lucie. 'There's a path up from the shore to Rosanna's, but it's rather rough and certainly not one to attempt in the dark either up or down.'

As soon as Rosanna received her guests in the spacious hall of the villa, Lucie realized that she had not really been invited. The Spanish girl's dark eyes momentarily betrayed the fact, although she recovered quickly and gave Lucie almost an effusive welcome, only slightly overdone.

Lucie's spirits sank to zero. Had Joel merely misunderstood, or had he deliberately included her for some obscure reason of his own?

Rosanna's mother, Señora del Rey, was an older replica of her daughter. Dark-haired without a trace of silver, plumper, her face only slightly more mature, she had the same bright-eyed sparkle that Rosanna used to such great effect.

During the pre-dinner sherries Lucie was invited to sit beside Señora del Rey, who spoke very reasonable English, if not as fluent as her daughter's.

'You are here – how long?' she now asked.

'Just over two weeks.'

'No, I mean – how long for the future? When you are leaving?'

Lucie realized that the older woman did not know of the changes that Joel had made.

'I am here indefinitely – that is, a long time. All the winter. Perhaps I shall go home in the summer.'

Señora del Rey nodded comprehension if not approval.

'You have not a home in England? Your mother? Father?'

Briefly Lucie explained her home circumstances and also that she had come to Ventura to work as well as keep an eye on two children.

'Ah, Joel has the assistant?'

'Oh, no, I am not capable of his beautiful work. I make little pieces of jewellery.'

The Señora's eyes danced. 'Oh, then you must earn much money. Jewellery is valuable.'

Lucie shook her head. 'Not yet. I have a great deal to learn and my kind of pieces are quite inexpensive to buy.'

Rosanna indicated that it was time to move into the dining room, where five places had been set at a round table. Lucie was seated between Señora del Rey and Hallam, while Rosanna sat between the two men and strategically divided her attention between them.

Occasionally Hallam addressed a remark or two to Lucie, but he was usually much more interested in Rosanna's conversation. Now that she had met the Spanish girl again, Lucie speculated on whether either of the two men were in love with Rosanna. Or both?

Señora del Rey claimed her attention, asking questions about Joel's household, sometimes referring to Joel himself for enlightenment in Spanish.

The long meal seemed endless to Lucie, who still smarted with the impression that she was an uninvited guest. Yet at the end of the evening she thought there might be another view.

They had all moved to the large drawing-room with its wide, curved windows opening on to the sea. After a while Rosanna drifted out with Joel to accompany her on the narrow terrace where a stone wall offered protection from falling on to the rocks below.

Hallam and Señora del Rey were superficially playing a card game, but obviously teasing each other, mostly in Spanish. For some time Lucie sat a few yards away, uneasy and dejected because she was so much a stranger here. Presently Hallam turned towards her, snapping on his charm like a torchlight. 'Why, Lucie, you mustn't look so doleful, although we've neglected you quite shamefully. Come over here and talk to us.'

He had risen to guide her to a chair and his arm slid around the back of her waist. At that moment Joel entered from the windows with Rosanna, and Lucie's face flamed as she met his gaze. Hallam's free-and-easy gestures might mean nothing to anyone, but she certainly did not want Joel to imagine that she was not above flirting with Hallam.

It was at this point that she perceived the purpose of the evening. She had been brought here for inspection. The del Reys wanted to find out more about her and whether she were a suitable person to be in the same house as Hallam and Joel as well as fit to associate with the two children.

She reflected now that she might have misinterpreted Rosanna's initial expression of surprise; perhaps there had been a different reason quite unknown to Lucie, since, of course, the two girls had lacked opportunity so far of getting to know each other.

It was long after midnight when the two men and Lucie left the del Reys and she hoped that Señora Matana would not be too resentful at the late hour.

Joel was driving and Hallam sat in the back of the car with Lucie. When they arrived at the Villa Sirena, Hallam alighted first. 'I'll tell the Señora that we're back,' he said over his shoulder as he walked towards the front door. 'And you can drive her back to Molino.'

The Spanish woman had to be roused from a deep sleep in an armchair in the kitchen and Hallam accompanied her to the car.

*'Gracias, señora,'* murmured Lucie. *'Muchas gracias.'*

When Hallam returned Lucie was at the foot of the stairs.

'Good night, Hallam,' she said. He came closely behind her and wound his arm about her waist. She stiffened, then tried to mount the stairs faster. On the landing she pulled herself away.

'I must see if the children are all right,' she said quietly.

He grasped her shoulder and planted a light kiss on her temple. 'You looked very sweet tonight, Lucie.'

'Thank you,' she muttered, and moved quickly away, opening the door of the children's bedroom and shutting it behind her.

Jessica stirred at the sound of the door. 'It's all right,' whispered Lucie, switching on the light. But the girl turned over and was immediately asleep again.

Lucie paused. If she went through the intervening bathroom between this room and her own, she need not go out again on to the landing. Hallam might still be there and she did not want to meet him again now.

Fortunately the door between the bathroom and her own room had not been bolted or locked again.

She sat on her bed and stared into space. Hallam's attitude mystified her. Until now he had been almost openly contemptuous of her ideas about work, regarding her as a girl filling in the time until an eligible husband came along. Yet tonight on two occasions he had intentionally conveyed to her a light awareness of her as a woman. Why? Because for the first time he had seen her dressed up for a social occasion? She glanced now at her long skirt and frivolous blouse top.

She jumped up jerkily from the bed and started to undress. Possibly she was making far too much of a masculine arm touching her and a good-night peck on her face. She remembered that Hallam was an artist and no doubt much affected by the visual aspect of women and their clothes. Of his charm there could be no doubt, and possibly he behaved to many girls in a casually affectionate manner.

A few minutes later she heard the sound of the car being put away. Joel had returned. As she brushed her hair and met her reflection in the mirror, she was forced to admit that she would have preferred that butterfly caress to have been given by Joel and not Hallam.

## CHAPTER THREE

SINCE she had come to live at the Villa Sirena, Lucie found the evenings the least enjoyable part of the day.

After dinner when the children were in bed, the two men usually spent the rest of the evening in the sitting-room where windows opened on to the terrace, but Lucie felt herself to be an encumbrance, the unwelcome third party. She doubted whether Joel and Hallam could talk as freely in her presence as they had in the past. Occasionally one or other went out to the village or to Corvario, possibly to see their friends, but that situation was no improvement, for she felt ill at ease alone with either of the men, although for different reasons.

On the other side of the house was a large drawing-room, more feminine in character, but apparently not much used. She hesitated to isolate herself there and often took the easy way out by retiring early to her own bedroom to read for a while.

Now, on the evening following the visit to the del Reys, she was aware of greater disquiet. Whenever she caught Hallam's glance, mocking, challenging, she looked away quickly, knowing that he probably relished her confusion.

Immersed in her own thoughts, she was brought sharply to reality by Joel's voice. 'Lucie! Are you listening?'

She blinked at the exasperation in his tone. 'I'm sorry, Joel. I'm afraid I was far away.'

'Obviously in a world of wonderful dreams,' murmured Hallam.

'Lucie—' began Joel, then stopped.

'Yes?'

'I'm afraid that we – that is, Hallam and I – have offended the local conventions of propriety. Señora del Rey and Rosanna have pointed out to us the iniquity of allowing a young woman – and one of our own country-women at that – to remain under our roof.'

Lucie's face showed immediate alarm. 'You mean you

want me to go – to leave?'

'Oh, nothing like that,' replied Joel hastily. 'It's a matter of—'

'What he means,' broke in Hallam, 'is that in Spanish eyes you shouldn't be sleeping here without another woman in the house to protect you from two impressionable and warm-hearted men.'

'Oh,' said Lucie flatly. 'I hadn't thought of that.'

'Our unusual household is apparently the talk of the village, if gossip is to be believed,' continued Hallam.

'But did Bernarda stay here overnight?' She had just remembered the young girl who had left suddenly.

'She did,' Joel answered. 'No one seemed to object to that, least of all Bernarda herself, although one might have imagined the opposite view.'

Hallam laughed. 'Evidently the villagers decided that Bernarda was in no danger if left to our mercy. She was not exactly a raving beauty.'

The inference was not lost on Lucie, although she was not disposed to accept at more than superficial level any compliments that Hallam might offer her.

'Then what do you want me to do?' she now asked. She judged it a time for plain speaking.

As neither of the two men answered immediately, she continued, 'I could probably find a room in the village and go there every night. But what about the children? They'd be left alone if you were both out during the evenings.'

Joel nodded. 'Oh, we haven't thought of anything nearly so drastic as turning you out to shack up somewhere in the village. No, Hallam has a plan which we think might work well.'

She looked inquiringly at the artist, inwardly already dubious about his motives.

'I have a cousin,' Hallam began. 'She's comfortably middle-aged and widowed. She lives in a boarding-house on the outskirts of Nottingham. It was already in my mind to invite Georgina here for a longish holiday over Christmas. In fact, I'd mentioned it to her when I was last in London and saw her. She'd probably be delighted to come here a bit sooner and stay longer. It might only be a temporary measure, but you could see, Lucie, how you get on together.'

Lucie could visualize immediate advantages. If the cousin were companionable, it would alter this uneasy triangle that Lucie regretted she had created with the two men. There would be an extra person in the house, an additional contact for the two children and an older woman who could be consulted in the case of illness.

'Georgina is quite domesticated,' continued Hallam. 'She ran her own home until her husband died a few years ago. She'd be able to take the children off your hands for a large part of the day. Then you'd be able to do your jewellery work.'

As she glanced towards Joel she caught his look, half apologetic, half encouraging, combined with some other quality too elusive to identify.

'So far you haven't done any work since you've arrived,' he pointed out.

'I must start soon to catch up with my orders,' she replied.

'Well?' queried Hallam. 'How does the suggestion strike you, Lucie?'

'I think it's an excellent idea. When do you think she will come?'

Hallam considered. 'If I telegraph as soon as possible, I expect she could arrive within about a week, perhaps a shade more. She might have arrangements to make at her boarding-house, passport if she hasn't one, and so on. At any rate, I'll try to persuade her to come at the earliest moment.'

Lucie smiled. 'I'm looking forward to seeing her, and I'm sure we shall get on well together.' It was a courageous prophecy, but this was Hallam's house and he had control over who should live there, so she knew she must be determined from the start to like his cousin.

He rose now and came towards her. 'In the meantime, you'll have to entrust your reputation to a silversmith who has obviously fled to these islands to escape his creditors, and an artist – well, we all know what *they*'re like, with their riotous living and crazy escapades.' He bent down to pinch her cheek lightly between his thumb and finger, then straightened up. 'I'm going down to the village,' he said to Joel.

Lucie saw that Joel was staring at Hallam, his brows furrowed, a severe downward twist to his mouth. Her heart momentarily leapt with a spurt of excitement. Could it be that Joel was becoming just a little jealous of Hallam's easy philandering? Now he merely nodded towards Hallam and suggested to Lucie, 'You said you wanted to see some of the rest of my collection of silver, I'll show you now.'

Now it was Hallam's turn to regard his friend with some surprise. Lucie did not dare to construe Joel's offer as a challenging counterstroke to Hallam's easy-going affectionate attitude, but Hallam might take it that way.

In any case Lucie was delighted to receive such a mark of favour from Joel when he unlocked one of the cupboards and took out some of the pieces that were such eloquent examples of his skill and craftsmanship. There were sets of cutlery and rose-bowls; coffee jugs and candlesticks, ornate salvers and a bundle of half a dozen salt spoons.

She fingered the goblets and presentation cups and admired the satin-smooth interiors, the chased designs outside.

'Of course, you realize that not all this lot is my own unaided work. This, for instance, is a copy of a Roman bowl from the Regency period, and here's a decanter, probably Victorian.'

Lucie let out a gasp of delight at this latter article, a piece of graceful design, but embellished with a network of silver-gilt ornamented with ivory and lapis-lazuli.

'I've never seen anything so beautiful,' she murmured, handing it back to Joel in case her hands trembled and she dropped it.

'These little vases had quite a vogue a few years back.' He handed her a slender vase about nine inches high. 'People gave them for wedding presents and that sort of thing, but the fashion has died out now. People buy chromium plate instead.'

'These have a slightly Lalique style about them,' she commented.

His friendly smile warmed her. 'Only someone like you who understands silver would spot that.'

'But these pieces are not so terrifying as much of Lalique's work. When you look at the illustrations you think it's all quite lovely. Then a second look tells you that the beautiful curve is a serpent or an animal with devouring jaws.'

Joel stood back, hands in his pockets, and laughed.

'How well you've studied him! Perhaps the period in which he lived influenced him a great deal. At the end of the nineteenth century values were changing, and he certainly made a break with the rather fusty traditions, the ornate, the superimposed decoration that sometimes hid the shape of the article.'

Lucie was enjoying herself for the first time in this intimate company with Joel. They had a common ground for discussion and her self-consciousness had vanished. She realized that without Hallam's mocking presence, she and Joel could find a harmony that might be merely fleeting, but was gratifying while it lasted.

She was therefore all the more vexed with herself when her careless words tore the delicate fabric apart.

He had finished showing her his collection and then took out a book of drawings and designs which he had made at one time or another, either as commissioned articles or for sale through commercial channels.

As they sat together at the table and he turned the pages, she became aware of his nearness. When his hand brushed hers as he pointed out a design, a thrill shot through her and unconsciously she drew an inch or two farther away from him.

Then when he had shut the book and put it away in a drawer, she heard herself saying those clumsy words that altered everything.

'Thank you, Joe, for showing me such a lovely collection. Perhaps one day I might have a few odds and ends to show you when I've more experience of working in silver. Now I'd better go up to my room – or if Hallam finds us alone here without a chaperone, he'll—' She broke off in confusion, her face becoming scarlet.

Joel had turned round swiftly and stood against the tall cupboard. He glared at her and his blue eyes had that same hostile look that she remembered on the first day she had met him.

'Hallam? I see. His opinions count with you. Yes, you'd better go, Lucie. Good night.'

He held the door open for her and she walked out, her head held high, as she mumbled 'Good night, Joel,' but her spirits had sunk to the very abyss of desolation.

In her room she flung herself into an armchair, feeling more ashamed and self-humiliated than she could remember for a long time. How could she have repaid Joel's kindness, his professional understanding, with a crude, flippant remark that a schoolgirl would have hesitated to say!

Now he would think that left alone with him she was anxious to play the coquette. Then another aspect presented itself. Her reference to Hallam might make Joel believe that she had fallen in love with the artist. That would be disastrous – yet, on reflection, no more disastrous than to betray to Joel himself that he was the man to whom she was more attracted.

Where did Rosanna come into this? It seemed clear to Lucie that both Joel and Hallam cared greatly for the opinion of the del Reys. Lucie had been taken for inspection last night and now it was imperative that another woman should enter Hallam's household.

In a way, she saw that she ought to be flattered. She and Rosanna had met briefly on that first visit to the Villa Sirena and now that Lucie appeared to be a semi-permanent member here, Señora del Rey had demanded a more conventional arrangement. Lucie thought that the del Reys were not so much concerned with her as with the avoidance of any breath of scandal that might attach to either of the two men. That surely must mean that somewhere was a hint of a future alliance. Joel? Hallam?

She sighed, deciding that it must be Joel who loved Rosanna and had therefore willingly consented to Lucie's inspection. In the depths of her misery, Lucie could not even feel flattered that she might be regarded as a menace to Joel or Hallam.

By next morning she felt calmer and knew that she must take up the routine of life at the villa. After she had spent an hour or so with Jessica and Daniel on the beach she decided that she must pluck up courage to start work on her jewellery orders.

She gathered her order sheets and design sketches and timidly knocked on the door of Joel's workshop, a shed a few yards away from the back of the villa.

'You said that perhaps I might work in here sometimes,' she said hesitantly.

'Yes, yes, of course. Come in and shut the door. I don't want these papers blown about.' He was standing at a desk and apparently engaged on designs.

'It's time you got down to some work,' he continued in the same harsh tone. His meaning was clear – he had not invited her to Ventura to be solely the children's companion. He had believed he was helping her in her profession at the same time.

'Yes, I've been lazy,' she admitted immediately. 'Now I'll make up for lost time.'

They discussed the material and tools she might need and as he bent his head close to hers, she was again assailed by an almost suffocating awareness of his masculine nearness. His face was within an inch of her own and no doubt Hallam would have seized the opportunity to plant a meaningless kiss on her cheek. But Joel was different, and in any case his affections were engaged elsewhere.

Yet while he added up quantities of sheet silver and alloys, wire of varying thicknesses, she realized that she had never before experienced this drowning sensation, not even with that other man in her life who had maintained that he loved her and then cruelly cheated her of all her expected happiness.

But now she must not think of either the past or the future. She must live firmly in the present and confine herself to a professional outlook and capacity.

'I've nearly finished those designs for your Mr. Thornton in London,' he said, after a while.

'Oh, good. He'll be pleased to receive them.'

For the rest of the morning until lunch time she worked on a bracelet of linked oblong plaques each ornamented with a sign of the zodiac. Absorbed in her task, she did not notice when Joel went out of the workshop, leaving an uncompleted candlestick on the bench. There was also an unfinished horse, a magnificent creature about nine inches long, with a proud head and flying tail.

Had he gone out because her presence irritated him or was a second occupant merely in the way?

At lunch he did not appear, and Hallam explained that Joel had gone into Corvario.

'What have you been making?' asked Jessica.

'A bracelet,' Lucie answered.

'Can I see it?'

'Not until it's finished.'

'Will you make me a bracelet?'

Lucie smiled gently. 'Yes, if you want one, but not yet. I have a lot of orders to make first. Then I'll make something very special for you.'

Jessica's face lit with pleasure.

'What will you make for me?' Daniel wanted to know.

'Boys don't wear jewellery,' Jessica put in before Lucie could reply.

'They do. Men wear things.' Daniel stoutly maintained. 'Uncle Hallam does. He wears a cross on a chain.'

Hallam burst into laughter. 'Two impossible brats! How can one hope to keep anything secret from them?' He turned towards Daniel with a mock frown. 'One man shouldn't give away another. How would you like it if I told Lucie all your secrets?'

'I haven't any secrets.'

Hallam shook a finger at the small boy. 'Wait a little, my lad, and you'll have plenty that you don't want the girls to know.'

'The trouble with Daniel,' said Jessica in her charmingly pompous manner, 'is that when he sees things, he can't keep quiet. Now I—'

'Oh, you're the very essence of discretion,' interrupted Hallam. 'Look at that time when you – oh, never mind. I'll spare you this time.' He turned towards Lucie. 'Take care, Lucie, or these urchins will worm every mystery out of you and then gaily spread it to whoever will listen.'

Jessica pouted, 'I'm not a tell-tale.'

'Darling, you are, but you don't know it, and everyone takes it for your childish innocence.'

It was noticeable, thought Lucie, that the two children apparently liked Hallam equally with Joel and that they were always at ease with him, perhaps even more than their uncle, for they had been forced to recognize him as their guardian, while Hallam was an extra pseudo-uncle, available sometimes for games and play and without responsibilities towards them.

During the afternoon when Hallam was apparently in his studio and the children in their room, Lucie looked around for a small table that she might use for working in her bedroom.

She tiptoed into the kitchen where Señora Matana lay sprawled in an armchair and was noisily enjoying her siesta. There was no spare table here, for the daily housekeeper needed them all. Obviously, she could not take one from Joel's workshop, even if available, but she remembered that Alberto, the fisherman-gardener, used a small shed for his tools and flower-pots.

The door was locked and she turned away, intending to ask Alberto next time she saw him. But then the rusty old hinge of the door caught her eye. With a little manipulation, she found it possible to detach the hinge from the crumbling woodwork and squeeze herself through the opening.

In the dimness she stumbled over some flower-pots, but eventually saw two tables, one placed upside down on the other. The top one was a garden table of white-painted iron and was occasionally used on the terrace, but the other, an oblong, wooden one, had apparently not been used for a long time. She doubted if she could extricate it through the door opening and she had already tried to unlock the door. Perhaps the best thing would be to ask Alberto if she could have it for her own use.

She pushed herself through the opening and replaced the pieces of hinge as best she could. Her cream trousers and red and white striped shirt had become soiled while she was grubbing about in the shed and she walked towards the house to change.

Joel was alighting from his car and eyed her with some surprise.

'Fallen down on a flower-bed?' he inquired with a smile.

'Not exactly. I'm afraid I've been trespassing. I broke into the garden shed. I was looking for—' she broke off in embarrassment.

'Alberto would be glad of your help, if that's what you intend. Part of our place is a jungle.'

Desperation forced her to say the truth baldly. 'I was looking for an old table. I thought I could use it – in my room.'

'I'm sure we could find you an extra piece of furniture if you want it.'

Now her face was reddening. 'I don't want to spoil a good table. I want it to work on.'

She was looking down at the ground and only when she became aware of his silence did she face him. His expression was one of indifference.

'I – I – thought it might be an idea,' she stumbled along. 'I don't suppose you want anyone else working in your work-place. It's probably irritating when you—'

'Who said I found it irritating?' he demanded, his eyes alight with anger. 'If I choose to let you use part of the space, then you should accept it and not jump to some false conclusion.'

She was on the verge of smiling and opened her mouth to tell him that she would be delighted to work alongside him, but he was too quick for her.

'Still, if you want to work alone – and it's obvious that I'm the one who irritates – then have it your own way.' His tone was harsh and hurtful.

'I didn't mean—'

'I'll ask Alberto to find a suitable table for you,' he snapped, 'although it may take a day or so to clean it up. You'll have to be patient about that.'

'Yes. Thank you. I don't mind cleaning it up myself, if Alberto can spare the one I saw in his shed.'

'He'll do the cleaning for you.' He had turned away abruptly, but now swung back towards her. 'How did you get in? Wasn't Alberto there?'

She felt the colour rise again in her cheeks. 'I broke in. The door was locked and I struggled through the hinged side. It's rather broken.'

'Then we must have the door repaired. We can't have you spoiling your clothes like that.'

'I'll go in and change,' she said hastily, and hurried towards the front door of the Villa. At the foot of the stairs she turned briefly and saw him standing by the car, but she could not be sure whether he were laughing. Probably at something else – or even at her stupidity in forcing locked doors instead of asking for what she wanted.

Upstairs in her room, she scolded herself yet again for her clumsiness of manner with Joel. In trying to relieve him of her presence when working, she had merely given him the impression that it was she who could not concentrate.

As she pulled on a pair of green linen slacks, wriggled into a clean cream shirt, and brushed her hair, she reflected that perhaps it would be for the best if she worked separately. Then she would not hear this constant hammering of her heart whenever she and Joel were alone together.

She glanced into the children's room and saw they were both in their swimming suits.

'Come with us,' invited Jessica. 'Uncle Hallam is taking us to the beach.'

'Oh, that's nice.'

'Are you wearing your swimsuit?' Jessica asked.

'Well, no. I didn't know you were going. But I'll go back and put it on. I shan't be more than a few minutes.'

When she rejoined the children they were already downstairs in the hall and Hallam stood waiting for her. He was wearing a gaily striped towelling bath-robe, so evidently he also intended to swim.

It was an idyllic place to live, she thought, as she sat for a while on a slab of rock above the waterline. A few yards down the garden, over the wall by means of rough steps and you were down on a sandy beach with the glittering sapphire blue water stretching out to the horizon.

At this point, Hallam said, the beach shelved very gently down and it was safe for the children, but away beyond the clutter of rocks, the slope was steeper.

'I don't advise you to bathe there, unless you happen to be a very strong swimmer,' he advised Lucie.

'I'm only a very moderate one,' she admitted.

'Both the children know that it's out of bounds. Still, one has to keep an eye on them.'

When she entered the water and swam around for a short time, she saw Daniel teetering on the edge where the waves frothed around his feet.

She splashed towards him. 'Come on, Daniel, I'll hold you up.' She lifted the boy off his feet and set him down on the surface on his back. 'Now move your legs and work with your arms. I shan't let you go.'

It was Daniel's usual tendency to sink in the middle like a pair of nutcrackers, but Lucie had experienced the same fault herself until she had confidence in the buoyancy of the sea.

Now she held the boy with one hand, in the small of his back, then gently withdrew that support. He swam placidly several strokes until he realized Lucie was no longer holding him. He promptly sagged and swallowed water, but she rescued him.

'See? You can swim by yourself now. Next time you'll have to do twelve strokes without help from me.'

Daniel blinked the water out of his eyes. 'I fall down to the bottom of the sea,' he complained.

'You won't next time,' she assured him. 'Out now. Enough for one day.'

She called to Jessica who was swimming parallel with the shore as she had been instructed. 'You can go in again later,' she promised.

To her surprise, Hallam had disappeared. Then she heard him call, 'Lucie!' She looked up and saw him halfway up the rock path. 'I'm going up to Rosanna's. I'll be back later.'

A jagged rock hid him from view as he apparently climbed higher. Jessica came splashing out of the water and towelled herself.

'Is that the way to Miss del Rey's villa, then?' Lucie asked the girl.

'Yes. It's very rough – big stones to climb. We mustn't go there, Uncle Joel told us. It's dangerous!'

Lucie could well appreciate the danger. Along the part that she could see there was no wall or railing to prevent anyone falling on to the rocks below. No doubt higher up near the villa there was more protection.

Jessica spread herself on a towel and Lucie followed suit. She thought lazily that it was a blissful way to spend an afternoon; tomorrow she would begin work in earnest, set herself a schedule and not allow herself to be beguiled into idleness on the shore.

She glanced up and looked towards the spot where a few moments ago Daniel had been busy collecting stones to fill his bucket. The child had disappeared.

'Daniel!' she called. Then she saw him clambering up the forbidden rocks. She ran towards him, yet at the foot she paused, anxious not to frighten him into panic and perhaps a fall.

'Daniel!' she coaxed softly. 'Come down here now. You've done your exploring.'

But the boy gave her a confident smile. 'I'm all right, I know the way. Uncle Hallam goes up here.'

'I know, darling, but it's too steep for you.' She mounted towards him, the sharp rocks hurting her feet. Out of sheer devilment, Daniel climbed higher until he came to a flat piece of rock.

'You come up here, Lucie,' he demanded. 'Then I'll come down.'

When she reached the place where he stood, she saw that it was almost like a rough platform. Beyond it the path wound up to the del Reys' villa, but that, too, was rough and without much protection.

'Now we'll sit down here for a minute while I get my breath,' she said quietly. 'Then we'll go down together. But you ought not to have climbed up. Don't do it again, please, Daniel. You frighten me.'

He giggled at her, but sat as she requested.

Somewhere above, probably in the gardens of the villa, there were voices, then laughter, followed by Hallam's voice. 'Need you be concerned about a plain little thing like her?'

The girl, evidently Rosanna, laughed again. 'But she's not plain. She's very attractive. When she came here, I was . . .' the words faded away.

'I don't find her attractive,' returned Hallam. 'She's not a patch on you. Believe me . . . anyway, I'm asking my cousin. Then everything will be . . .'

Lucie rose abruptly from the flat rocks. 'Come on, Daniel, we must go.'

Perversely, he wanted to stay longer, but she insisted,

almost dragging him by the hand down the steep path between the rocks.

For the moment she could not allow her concentration to veer from getting Daniel and herself safely down to shore level, but when they both reached safety on the sandy beach, Lucie gave her mind to what she had just heard.

Of course listeners never hear any good of themselves, but she had not eavesdropped by intent. She could well understand that in the eyes of an artist such as Hallam, she would appear just that – 'a plain little thing'. Yet he had not been above trying to flirt with a plain little thing. Or was that the reason? Perhaps he thought it safe to pay an occasional attention to someone not wildly attractive. Plain girls were grateful for a kiss and a smile where the raving beauties took it for granted as the small change paid as homage to their good looks.

'I think it's time we went home,' she said to the two children. She gathered the towels, Daniel's bucket with his cherished collection of stones, pulled on her own slacks and shirt over her bikini.

Jessica was scolding Daniel at length. 'It was very naughty of you – you might have been killed! Poor Lucie had to go to look for you. Why must you be such a bad boy?'

Daniel gave her his disarming grin and went racing towards the wall of the villa.

In spite of the gravity of the situation in which the boy had been so carelessly disobedient, Lucie could not help smiling to herself. Even at so young an age he was already learning the technique of avoiding feminine strictures by running away.

When the children were bathed and then settled in the kitchen for their evening meal, Lucie had more time for reflection. Now it occurred to her as she changed for the evening that perhaps Hallam had intended her to hear his comments. It was quite possible that he had known she was near; he could easily have heard her voice calling to Daniel and the boy's answers.

He obviously wanted to make it clear to her that he was not in any way smitten by her charms. Probably he had gone up to Rosanna's villa to tell her of the new arrangement to be made for his cousin to join his household. Naturally he needed to reassure Rosanna and her mother that the due proprieties were being observed, but evidently she needed to be convinced too, that Lucie was unlikely to offer any rivalry to herself.

At this idea, Lucie laughed at her reflection in the mirror. 'Not a patch on you . . .' Hallam's words echoed. She could never hope to achieve Rosanna's magnetic attraction.

Then Lucie's laugh faded. Was it Hallam who was in love with the Spanish girl and was forced to convince her that there was no cause for jealousy?

And Joel? Gradually Lucie felt a great wave of hope rise within her. If Joel were free, if he did not love Rosanna, then what dizzy prospects the future might hold! Lucie's heart skipped about like a mad thing, but she sobered herself down before she went into the dining-room for dinner.

Only one place was laid. Apparently neither of the two men were expected in and Señora Matana was a little impatient to serve the meal to Lucie as fast as possible.

'If you like, I'll clear away and wash up,' Lucie offered.

The elderly Spanish woman beamed her thanks. Yes, it would be good if she could leave early tonight. Her son was coming to see her.

In the kitchen washing the dishes, Lucie reflected on the day's events. One way and another it had been quite a day, first working alongside Joel, then almost flinging his good offers in his face; the incident on the beach and the snatch of conversation between Hallam and Rosanna. Finally her flights of fancy emphatically quelled by the non-appearance of either of the men. Yet that was probably all to the good, she mused. It would have been difficult tonight to have faced Joel and Hallam across the dinner-table and altogether impossible to have spent the rest of the evening trying not to say the wrong thing or give an unguarded glance.

The situation might be easier when Hallam's cousin arrived from England.

# CHAPTER FOUR

As soon as Lucie made an appearance after breakfast the following morning, Joel called to her that Alberto was here and might find her a suitable worktable.

'Oh, thank you.' She had better put a good face on the matter now, having caused some trouble by breaking into the garden shed, and Joel was evidently quite determined that she should have her table and not intrude again into his workshop.

She accompanied Joel to the shed. Alberto, an elderly man slightly bent, with a mahogany tanned face and black hair and beard slightly sprinkled with grey, greeted Lucie with a *'Buenos dias'*. Joel explained rapidly in Spanish what was wanted and the man nodded.

The shed door was already open and she walked in towards the table she had decided was suitable. Alberto set it down outside on the paved path and Joel examined the legs critically.

'Rather wobbly here, but probably it will stand firm on an ordinary floor,' he said to Lucie. 'Will it do?'

'Splendidly,' she agreed with enthusiasm. Again, she was aware of the half-amused glance he gave her.

'Right, then Alberto will clean it up for you.' He spoke in Spanish to the gardener. Then he examined the broken hinge which Lucie had manipulated yesterday to enable her to enter the shed.

'That needs mending or new hinges,' he pointed out to Alberto. 'With a door like that anyone could break in and steal your prize plants.' He exchanged glances with Lucie, but she thought it safer to smile and say nothing.

Hallam came into the garden to join the others. When the purpose of the table had been explained to him, he said pointedly to Lucie, 'Oh, I thought you were intending to work with Joel. What do you do to each other? Gossip? Or is Joel afraid you'll steal his designs?'

Lucie controlled her temper, although she was furiously angry with Hallam for making his insinuations in the presence of Joel. Alone, she might have retorted that she and Joel had more respect for each other's work than to idle or to cheat.

Now Joel merely laughed. 'Don't take any notice of Hallam, Lucie. He enjoys teasing.' He walked away to his workshop, leaving Lucie and Hallam together. After a moment's hesitation, she turned to go towards the villa.

'Lucie!' he called. 'Don't go yet!' She turned, but did not retrace her steps towards him. He came slowly to her. 'Why did you disappear from the beach yesterday? When I came down from Rosanna's, you'd all cleared off.'

She stared at him. 'It was time the children went in. I didn't see any point in staying or waiting for you.' She was not going to give him the satisfaction of knowing whether his remarks about her had been overheard, so she made no reference to Daniel's escapade.

'You take your duties with the children pretty seriously, don't you?'

She was surprised by this sudden change of topic. 'I came here to see that they were properly looked after, but I'm not a nursemaid, nor even a governess.'

'Do you have to send reports home to whoever it is who is anxious about them?'

'Certainly not. I wrote to Mr. Thornton after my first visit here. If I mention Jessica and Daniel in my letters, my comments are not reports.' She paused, then faced Hallam. 'Are you hinting that I'm spying on Joel because he's the children's guardian?'

Hallam laughed. 'Nothing of the sort! What an idea! Well, in the future, when my cousin Georgina arrives, you'll be able to get on with your own work much better. She'll take quite a lot of responsibility off your hands.'

For a moment she was silent, then she spoke her thought bluntly. 'That sounds very much as though you're hoping I'll take the hint and leave here after your cousin has settled in.'

'Really, Lucie, you do jump to the most extraordinary conclusions. The last thing I want is your departure. The children adore you and so—'

She challenged him to finish that sentence.

'And so will Georgina when she comes,' he finished smoothly. He had known, of course, that she was trying to trap him into saying 'and so do I'. But he was too practised, too adept in recognizing the ways in which women's minds worked, to be caught in that snare.

He gave her the kind of smile that might have melted her rancour if she had been the least fraction in love with him. 'Come, Lucie, and let me show you my studio. You can't make excuses today. Joel has gone into the monastery of his workshop and your table won't be ready yet, so you can't work.'

She allowed herself to be conducted to his sanctum adjacent to his bedroom and waited while he unlocked the door. The room was large with windows on both the north and east aspects of the villa. Since all the rooms were provided with venetian blinds and shutters to the windows, it was easy enough to block out the early morning sun from the east. The two easels each held an unfinished work covered by a cloth, and Lucie, aware that most artists dislike exhibiting their paintings in progress, asked no questions about the subjects.

Canvases were stacked on the floor around the walls; a few were framed and hung and Lucie saw at once several portraits of Rosanna del Rey. Here was the lovely Spanish girl demurely smiling, in a flame-coloured shirt, in traditional costume of the island, in a pensive mood and holding a single poinsettia flower in her hand; half a dozen other poses.

There were landscapes not only of Ventura scenes, but some of Venice and Rome, Morocco and Spain.

'I'd done quite a deal of work before I settled down here,' he told her. 'But naturally I can't stay in one place too long. I bought this villa because it was cheap and suited me for a while, but eventually I shall set out again – Greece, Turkey, Persia – an enormous number of places that one wants to paint.'

She wandered around the studio, examining the pictures, admiring the strength of his contrasts, or the delicate tonal values. In her opinion, Hallam was an excellent artist. There were several nudes and she supposed these were earlier works. She could not imagine Rosanna posing in the nude.

'In a way I envy you and Joel,' Hallam said after a pause.

'Why?'

'Because you two can really work anywhere – in a dusty old shed when it's raining, in a basement or attic. Town or country, it doesn't matter as long as you have light enough to see what you're doing. With painting it's different. Except for portraits and possibly abstracts, we have to go out and catch our scene.'

'Don't some people take photographs or colour slides and work from those in the studio?'

'Some do.' His smile was sarcastic. 'But not artists. That method becomes almost like mass-produced stuff. When you have time, Lucie, I'd like to paint you. Keep still for a moment.'

As she obeyed and he studied the angles and contours of her face, she wondered uneasily what this suggestion would entail. He picked up a sketching block and began to rough in a portrait with thick charcoal strokes.

'H'm, I could make something of you, I think.'

'Not for a few days,' she suggested. 'I ought to get some of my orders finished.'

'Of course. In any case I have to go to England to arrange with Georgina and help her to settle her affairs for the time being. So I'll wait until I come back.'

'Then you've heard from her? She's willing to come?'

'I'm positive she's willing, but I haven't heard definitely yet. Tomorrow most likely there'll be a cable in reply to mine.'

When she finally left the studio and joined Jessica and Daniel in the garden, Lucie was glad of a respite from Hallam's rather overpowering persuasion. In his presence she frequently found herself yielding to his opinions, his suggestions, not always because she wanted to but because he was usually offering a challenge, daring her to disagree or refuse.

Joel was not like that. If he lacked Hallam's mercurial characteristics, that was an advantage, for then you knew that Joel was dependable, that once he had undertaken a task he would eventually fulfil it. True, Mr. Thornton, the London jeweller, had cause to complain of delay in the matter of work, but Joel could not be hurried in those matters.

When she returned to her room after lunch, the worktable was in position by a window, the top covered with a piece of thick green baize cut to fit and on it a collection of small tools, hammer, chisel, pincers, wire-cutters, together with her unfinished pieces of work and an amount of sheet silver and lengths of fine wire for chain links.

She smiled sadly at the sight, uncertain whether Joel was unduly anxious to eject her from his own workshop or whether he was trying to do her a favour by setting her up with a working place of her own. She hoped it was the latter reason, but suspected that the former applied.

In an effort to forget the vagaries of the two men whose household she had so impulsively and unwittingly joined, she concentrated on the jewellery, cutting and shaping and polishing the pieces. She finished three of the zodiac sign bracelets, packed them into a box and put them inside the enormous wardrobe which seemed to mock her sparse amount of clothing. When she visited Las Palmas to deliver some of her orders, she would take the opportunity to buy a couple of outfits.

At dinner Hallam announced that his cousin Georgina had cabled. She would be delighted to stay indefinitely, but must have a week to arrange matters in England.

'What's her name?' Lucie asked. 'I mean her married name. I can't keep referring to her as Cousin Georgina.'

Hallam laughed. 'She'll be Georgina from the moment she steps inside the door. Actually her name is Mrs. Frensham.'

Joel had arranged that when Hallam flew to England he would take with him the new designs for Mr. Thornton and deliver them by hand to the jeweller.

'So if you've any commissions for me, Lucie, I'll be delighted to carry them out,' Hallam offered a couple of days later.

Lucie considered for a few moments. 'There is something I'd like. At the flat where I used to live, I left a small case of tools. At the time I decided to spend the winter in the Canaries, I intended to go back later. My plans depended on whether I could obtain any orders here. So if you could possibly pick them up? I'll give you the address.'

'I'll be delighted,' Hallam returned with such cordiality that she warmed towards him, regretting her doubts as to his sincerity.

'If you think of anything else before I go, let me know and if I can possibly oblige you, I will,' he continued.

It was later on that same day when Lucie was sitting in the garden by the pool for a breath of fresh air that Hallam came sauntering along and dropped into a chair beside her.

'How goes the work?' he asked.

'Very well. I've finished a number of bracelets, some brooches and pendants. Now I have to start on earrings.'

'H'm. It's a case of he works fastest who works alone. I tried once sharing a studio in London with a fellow-artist, but it didn't turn out well. We both got on each other's nerves. I chatter while I work, he liked absolute silence.'

Lucie laughed. 'There's not much silence with silver workers. We're either hammering or banging, making little irritating clonks and dongs, except of course when I'm knitting chains.'

'Knitting?'

'I call it that – looping one link through the next.'

Hallam lit a cigar. 'I was wondering, Lucie, if you could spare time tomorrow to sit for me.'

'Tomorrow?' she echoed, trying to gain a few seconds' time to consider. A sharp prickle of apprehension ran through her, warning her of possible danger ahead.

'Yes, tomorrow. You could surely spare me a morning, however busy you are. Anyway, you have the advantage that you can work by artificial light, whereas I can't.'

She recalled his offers earlier in the day when he had promised help in London. She could hardly refuse now to sit for her portrait. She told herself she should be honoured.

'Yes, of course. What time, and what do you want me to wear?'

Hallam smiled with the corners of his mouth turned down. 'Good question. I wasn't suggesting—' he broke off and laughed. 'You've a yellow silk shirt. I don't mind what else – skirt, trousers, anything. I'm only doing head and shoulders.'

She nodded. 'And the time?'

'Let's say half past nine.'

'I'll be there,' she promised. He rose abruptly and walked towards the villa. She wondered how many sittings he would require and hoped that he would not occupy too much of her time, for she wanted to send some more samples of her work back to Mr. Thornton for his comments.

After dinner Lucie sat for a while in the sitting-room with the two men who smoked and chatted. She took no part in the conversation and was occupied in mending a dress for Jessica.

'Lucie, I'm going to Corvario tomorrow morning,' Joel said suddenly. 'Want to come? Jessica and Daniel can stay here with the cook and we could have lunch in the town.'

Lucie caught her breath sharply. Across the room she was conscious of Hallam. His eyes were slightly narrowed and a half smile curved his mouth. Oh, if Joel had asked her earlier, she thought, before she had made that promise to sit for Hallam.

'I – I'm sorry, Joel, but I'm – Hallam asked me to sit for him tomorrow morning,' she stammered.

Joel's pleasant expression was replaced by one of controlled resignation. To Lucie, watching him with apologetic eyes, it seemed that he had pulled down a shutter over his features, obscuring with indifference whatever he might feel.

'Oh, all right,' he said coolly. 'Forget it.'

'Sorry, Joel.' Hallam's voice held only superficial sincerity in Lucie's opinion. 'I thought while I was waiting for a day or two before I go to England, I'd fill in the time with a portrait. I don't want to work on anything outdoors because the light changes. But of course, I can easily do something else if you want to take Lucie.'

In a few words Lucie realized that he had successfully relegated her to the status of a fill-in task between more important commissions and at the same time made it impossible for Joel to insist on taking her away from a prearranged sitting.

This was a reversal of the incident when Hallam had

invited her to visit his studio, probably knowing that she was going out in the boat with Joel. Lucie was furious. Hallam had probably known on this occasion something of Joel's plans, but he had shoved his oar in first and tied her to an unbreakable arrangement.

She longed to say outright that she would prefer to go with Joel, but that would be too blatant and merely succeed in embarrassing Joel, while Hallam would smile at defeat and later congratulate her on her magnetic attraction that pulled two men at the same time in opposite ways. Perhaps she should have been flattered by such simultaneous offers, but she did not believe that either man regarded her as a prize worth struggling for.

When she arrived next morning in the studio she was deliberately ten minutes late.

'Sorry I'm late,' she apologized rather too airily, and his oblique glance swiftly told her that he knew the reason. He was still busy with preparations, setting out colours on a palette, selecting sticks of charcoal.

'I thought perhaps you'd ratted on me and gone with Joel,' he said, not looking at her.

'I don't believe you thought anything of the kind,' she said evenly.

'I hope you don't regret missing the chance of an outing with him.'

'No doubt I shall survive,' she returned.

He took time over posing her, moving her shoulders, her head. 'Let your hands lie loosely in your lap. You're tensing them up and it affects your shoulders.'

She obeyed. Then his hand tilted up her chin and she saw that his eyes glittered with amusement. She schooled herself for the careless kiss he might give her, in passing, as it were, but if he was aware of her thought, he was happy to disoblige her.

He began work with a fierce concentration that surprised her, making bold charcoal strokes on the canvas and apparently only occasionally glancing at the face of his sitter.

'I talk volubly while I'm painting, but take no notice and don't answer me,' he warned her.

'I won't.'

'There! You've twisted your mouth.'

She said 'Sorry' mentally and kept her gaze fixed on the spot he had indicated.

After a time he said crossly, 'You must think more pleasant thoughts, Lucie. You're frowning and blinking all the time. I shall begin to wish you'd gone off with Joel unless you can add a little to my gaiety.'

She tried to resume her relaxed expression, but after a while he put down his palette and brush. 'We'll stop for a few minutes and you can rest. Walk about and loosen your muscles.'

He went out of the studio and returned in a few minutes with a tray of coffee. She was gazing out of the north window at the hills. At this time of day they appeared camel colour with lighter streaks of sand; on the lower slopes were terraced fields with an occasional white house dotted here and there or a solitary palm tree standing sentinel over a plantation.

She turned to take the cup of coffee from Hallam. 'Do you find this a satisfying landscape to paint?' she asked.

He wrinkled his lips before replying. 'In a way, yes, but only for a time. As I told you, I don't usually want to stay in one place too long. A year or two, perhaps, then I want new colours, new effects of light, different people to paint.'

She smiled, adding to herself that he also required different girls to kiss, to pass the time pleasantly in their company.

The next hour progressed more smoothly. Hallam gave her short resting periods and although he chatted to himself all the time, he seemed more satisfied with her posing.

'Right!' he said at last. 'That's enough for today.'

Lucie rose and stretched her arms above her head and he stopped in the act of wiping a brush to regard her.

'You must pose like that for me some time,' he said with a grin.

'I doubt if I could hold it for long.' After a moment she asked, 'Will you want me tomorrow?'

His grey eyes held amusement and his eyebrows rose in a query. 'I should have to consider exactly what you mean.'

She was instantly annoyed at her careless lack of caution. 'Then do you require me to sit for you again tomorrow?'

He bent to attend to his brushes. 'Ah, now I understand. No, Lucie, my darling, you're free to do what you please. I can't do any more for a day or so until some of the paint is drier.'

Joel did not come in to lunch, but Lucie knew that he had not been expected. She was, however, surprised when Hallam said to her shortly before dinner, 'I'm going out for the evening, Lucie. I'm taking Rosanna to dinner at a little place along the coast. You'll be all right?'

'Oh, yes, of course. Señora Matana will be here for a little while yet.'

'Joel may not come home until pretty late. Once he gets into Corvario he meets some of his cronies and they sit in a café for hours.'

She heard Hallam's car drive away a few minutes later and pondered on the fact that he had now made it clear that if he had occupied a little time with Lucie earlier in the day, now it was Rosanna's turn.

The thought also presented itself that Joel could not be in the company of Rosanna tonight, since Hallam was her escort, and even this tenuous reflection gave her a warm happiness.

'Come and read to us when we're in bed,' pleaded Jessica, when she heard that Hallam had gone out for the evening.

'All right,' agreed Lucie. 'But only for twenty minutes, then I must have my dinner. I can't keep Señora Matana waiting. She wants to get home.'

'You could bring your dinner here and eat it,' was Jessica's cunning suggestion.

Lucie gave in, volunteered to do the washing-up and sent Señora Matana off home early with a good parcel of food.

She had been reading stories for more than half an hour and Daniel was already asleep when there was a light tap on the door.

'Lucie? It's Joel here.'

She opened the door quickly.

'I saw the light on here,' he explained, 'so I guessed you were here.' He came across to Jessica sitting up in bed and frowned at her. 'Time you were asleep, young woman. Let Lucie have a few minutes' peace in the evenings.'

Jessica snuggled down in bed, closed her eyes and held up the most innocent face. 'You may kiss me good night, Uncle Joel. I'm practically asleep already.'

He obeyed and added an affectionate little tug at the girl's nose.

When Lucie bent to kiss her, Jessica sprang up, flinging her arms around Lucie's neck. 'Darling Lucie, must you go?'

'Yes, pet, I must. Good night.'

Lucie extricated herself quickly and joined Joel on the landing.

'Have you had a meal?' she asked. 'Can I get you anything?'

'No, I'm not hungry. Come downstairs and we'll have a drink of something.'

On the opposite side of the hall from the sitting room was a small room sparsely furnished and often used by the children as a play-room. Across the corner a verandah lounge had been built jutting out into the wide terrace. A marble-topped table and several easy chairs indicated that it was intended to be used at times when the evenings might be too chilly to sit outside, but when a current of air was needed through open windows.

It was here that Joel directed Lucie to sit with him when he brought a bottle and glasses and poured drinks. He flung himself into a chair and his long legs sprawled out in front of him. 'Had a good day?' he asked. 'How did the sitting for Hallam go?'

Lucie gave a small chuckle. 'I'm not sure. You'd better ask Hallam about that. I doubt if I was a really good poser.'

He glanced across at her. 'Too honest? Your face shows your thoughts too often and most of the time the sitter must make her mind a blank.'

She was grateful for the dim lights on the verandah, only a couple of amber lamps in the form of shells, for otherwise Joel might have seen her alarmed expression. She sipped her wine first before replying in a controlled voice, 'I must try then not to be so transparent in future if I have a give-away face.' She was concerned in case he had already interpreted stray thoughts that had flitted across her features in unguarded moments.

He spoke about the children. 'When Georgina, this cousin of Hallam's, arrives, you'll have more free time for your own work.'

'I was thinking that – with your permission, of course I might help their education along in an elementary way. I could teach Daniel to read and Jessica could learn to do sums. We might even advance to geography in due course.'

Joel studied her and even in the dim amber light his gaze was enough to undermine her determination to regard him in no more than a friendly way.

'We pledged ourselves not to turn you into a governess, Lucie,' he said after a long pause. 'You've already become more or less a nursemaid to those two imps.'

'Only because I've wanted to. No one has compelled me.'

'Except Jessica and Daniel themselves,' he pointed out, and as he moved to refill the glasses, she saw the grin on his face. 'Those two are probably the most powerful people in this house. You must be careful, my dear Lucie, that you don't become their slave.'

'I'm sure there's no fear of that,' she said mildly, but she was warmed by the way in which he had called her 'my dear Lucie'. Spoken like that, it meant practically nothing – a manner of speech.

When he was silent for a while, she queried gently, 'And you? Did you have a good day?'

'No,' he grunted, 'a frustrating one. My car broke down a few miles from Corvario on the way there and I had to get a lift into the town. Nothing that I'd ordered from my suppliers was ready – oh, the steamers were late or there'd been a mix-up in the sizes of the sheets – the wrong thickness, all that sort of thing. Then the people I wanted to see – of course I missed them because I'd arrived later than I expected.' He sighed. 'Oh, well, one has to accept all that in exchange for living here, I suppose.'

'It's a lovely place to live in,' she murmured.

'M'm. Sometimes I think it's too lovely. The climate – eternal spring – makes one lazy. It's true that not so many tourists come here the way they flock to Las Palmas and Tenerife. All the same, the atmosphere is conducive to a holiday mood, and that's bad for work.'

'I've felt that, too. I've dawdled and dallied over my own stuff.'

'In London, I had a grim little workshop in a yard with a couple of men to do the rough jobs. Then I felt that life was passing me by and all that the future held was a bigger and better workshop and a small army of employees, so I'd be turning out factory stuff eventually. I came first to Tenerife and then Las Palmas for a holiday and it struck me that I could work here. People like Thornton and others told me I was mad, idiotic. I was throwing up a most successful career to become a one-man arty-crafty concern and would probably end up by becoming a beachcomber.'

'That hasn't happened yet,' she pointed out. 'You work very hard.'

'Oh, I turn out a fair amount of stuff one way and another. Perhaps I don't know what I want. I'm not keen on spending so much time on repeat orders, yet I'm equally against becoming a factory.'

'Couldn't you employ someone else to do the repeat orders?' she asked. 'Someone in England? If they have your designs to copy, they ought not to go wrong.'

He snorted. 'That wouldn't do at all unless I were there to supervise the work at every stage. As to getting someone here who could really be trusted to work competently, that's probably quite impossible. Ventura isn't exactly overloaded with qualified silversmiths.'

'No, I see the difficulty.' Lucie began to wonder if he were testing her, throwing out a feeler to see if she were interested in becoming his assistant. A wave of joy rose within her, but died away almost instantly. She would be useless in his kind of work; she had been trained in quite a different branch. Yet, of course, she knew the rudiments of the art even though she lacked the skill born of practice. But she would not be led into such a serious error as offering her assistance; that offer must come from Joel and he must make it direct.

They talked of other matters – books and music, places in England, cities and villages. He told her of one holiday in Spain where he had visited a house in the province of Castile.

'At one time this had been a small castle, but half of it was in ruins and the family lived in a few rooms. The extraordinary part was that although the curtains hung in tattered ribbons and the upholstery was threadbare, the owners, an old man and his two sisters, dined off gold plate. Apparently their means were so restricted that they ate frugally – actually I was quite ashamed of my appetite, and curbed it when I saw their portions.'

'I don't think I've ever seen a gold dinner service,' said Lucie.

'This was the real thing. I tried very tactfully to tell them that they were sitting on a fortune if only they could bring themselves to sell their treasures,' Joel shrugged. 'But no good. They said they owed it to their descendants to keep the gold plates, the pictures on the panelled walls. They didn't seem to realize that they could have enjoyed much more comfort in their own lifetimes.'

'And were there sons and daughters to inherit?'

Joel laughed. 'None of these three was married or had children. The estate would go to some distant nephew and when the time comes, I'll bet he'll sell the lot for whatever it will fetch, for obviously there's no money left there.'

'How was it you were able to visit this family?' she asked.

'I'd been touring through a large part of Spain, visiting museums and collections of silver wherever they could be seen and I was told of this family who lived in poverty in the midst of valuables. Somehow they had lost their land and all they had left was the ruined castle and its contents. Gold dishes and candlesticks, bowls and ornaments of all kinds stood around, all solid gold. I asked if they weren't afraid of being robbed or burgled. They laughed and told me that their servants would protect them. That was probably the most pathetic part of the situation, for all they now possessed was one old devoted couple, a man of nearly eighty, I should think, and his wife who cooked and cleaned.'

'They were living in the past – when they were wealthy and well looked after,' commented Lucie.

'Yes. Time had gone ahead of them. I regretted there

was nothing much I could do to help them. I contacted one of the Spanish museums and suggested that a suitable offer could be made, but I don't think anything came of it.'

He told her of other places and countries he had visited and she was surprised when, glancing at her watch, she noticed the time was long past midnight.

He saw that glance. 'Yes, Lucie, it's late. We'd better make a move.' He paused, then added, 'You're a good listener. I've spent most of the evening rambling away and you've let me go on without interruption or wanting to put in your oar. M'm, I feel better than I did when I came home.'

She glowed at receiving this unexpected compliment.

He rose and switched off the lights on the covered verandah. 'Stay there a minute and I'll put on these other lights.' Lucie walked a step or two across the darkened room and tripped against a chair leg. She felt his hand across her shoulder to steady her and a tremor shot through her.

As the lights came on she asked, 'What am I to do about the children's lessons?' She made a determined effort to bring herself under control by asking a casual question.

They were out in the hall now. 'The lessons? Oh, yes, do as you like – but don't let it take up too much time.'

'Any idea where Hallam went tonight?' he queried. 'I doubt if he's come home yet.'

'He said he was dining at a little place along the coast – I don't know the name.'

Joel smiled a trifle crookedly. 'Not alone, I'll warrant.'

Lucie hesitated. She had no desire to play the rôle of gossipmonger in the household.

Joel smiled again. 'With Rosanna, I expect.'

She nodded confirmation and as the hall lights caught his face she saw again that curious 'shut' look that descended across his features.

As she went upstairs to her room she reproached herself for having obviously caused him pain by confirming what he had already guessed. Yet what else could she have said when Joel asked a direct question? She wished she could have understood the situation better between the two men and Rosanna. Were they rivals? Was it Hallam who was trying to drive a wedge between Joel and Rosanna, taking her out to dinner when Joel's back was turned? Or it could be that Hallam was more favoured by Rosanna and Joel unhappy because of defeat.

As she turned her head this way and that on her pillow, Lucie could find no satisfactory answer to these useless questions. Certainly they were useless, for they did not concern her. She was here in Ventura for only a limited time and after her departure she would probably never know what happened. There might at some time in the future be a brief notice of the engagement or wedding of Rosanna to 'the noted English silversmith, Joel Barron', or perhaps, 'the promising artist, Hallam Dayne'.

But the thought that sustained Lucie just before she fell asleep was that tonight Joel had at least been content, if not wildly happy, in her company; that for an hour or so he had talked out his worries and that she, on her part, had basked in the warmth of his friendship. More than that she could neither claim nor expect, but it was not enough. She longed for Joel's love, a reciprocal ardour to match her own in its intensity and durability. She knew that he would not give his love unthinkingly, bestowing an idle caress here or there. With Joel an affection would go deeply.

Now she recognized that Vincent, that other man in her life, had never kindled in her the same emotion that she felt for Joel. At the time when her world had crashed, she imagined it would be the end of love for her, but now she knew that while it had not been counterfeit, her attachment had been only a vague shadow. If eventually she was forced to root out of her heart this affection for Joel, it would take much longer to heal the wound and forget.

## CHAPTER FIVE

THE day before Hallam was due to leave for England to fetch his cousin Georgina back with him, Lucie gave him the box of jewellery pieces intended for Mr. Thornton.

'He doesn't have to make up his mind whether he wants to buy them,' she told Hallam. 'He can write later.'

'And I won't forget to go to your old address and pick up the case of tools,' he promised.

Joel glanced across sharply. 'What tools did you want? I could probably supply anything. Why didn't you ask?'

Lucie's face flamed scarlet, for she was aware of Hallam's nonchalant manner as he walked a step or two across the terrace.

'I thought it would be better to have my own in case I broke or damaged yours, and as Hallam is going to London—'

Joel shrugged. 'Independent, as usual,' he muttered.

'It's no trouble,' Hallam assured him earnestly. 'I'm only too willing to do Lucie a small service if I can.'

So Hallam was now casting himself in the rôle of a friend most eager to help a girl, in sharp contrast with Joel's ungracious attitude.

Lucie opened her mouth to make some retort, but thought better of it and remained silent. Hallam had not asked her for another sitting for the portrait and she was now more firmly convinced that arranging the sitting on that particular morning had been only a device to thwart Joel's idea of taking her to Corvario. Further, having started a portrait of her, he had an excellent excuse for requesting her to continue the sittings at some later date.

Later in the day when Joel was elsewhere, Hallam said to Lucie, 'And I take it I'm to give a good report about the children?'

'Report?' she echoed, although she knew quite well what he meant.

'To the Thorntons. You want me to praise Joel, don't you? Tell them that he's a wonderful guardian and that no one need worry.'

'Of course,' she answered coolly. 'But they knew that in the first place.'

'Then why did they send you to investigate?'

'That's not quite correct,' she retorted. 'All that Mrs. Thornton was concerned about was the children's education.'

'And I can assure her that now you're taking charge of that side, she need have no qualms.'

She tried to make light of his sarcastic tone, for she would not give him the satisfaction of knowing that he had needled her. 'Don't make it sound as though I'm a governess. I'm just helping with reading and a few sums.'

His eyes danced as he swung an arm around her waist and kissed her cheek. 'Sweet Lucie,' he murmured. 'I can always tell when you get angry with me. I've never seen before grey eyes that gave off green sparks.' He released her and she mustered a smile.

'It's just as well I don't take you too seriously.'

'And Joel? Do you take him seriously?' He wagged a finger at her. 'Let me warn you. You may think he's rock-steady and all that, but he's fire itself when it comes to romance.'

'Indeed!' Lucie faced him with a pertness that was usually foreign to her.

'Indeed, yes. But of course the fire soon goes out. Oh, he can be a charmer when he likes, but don't be misled.'

'Thanks for the warning,' she said airily as she walked away. 'I'll remember what the gipsy said.'

In some ways Lucie was relieved to be without Hallam's presence in the house. He intended to be away about a week, he said, according to whether Georgina was ready or not. His absence might stretch to a fortnight, for he hoped to make arrangements for a one-man show of his paintings next year and he also intended to amuse himself in London at theatres and the opera, as well as call on some of his friends.

'I shan't have time to think of your rebuffs,' he had told Lucie as he bade her good-bye, giving her a slightly lingering farewell kiss. 'I shall be gadding about. I might even look up some of my former girl-friends, although I expect they're all safely married by now with a pram in the front porch.'

'What did you expect?' queried Joel derisively. 'That they'd be waiting for you to return like Peer Gynt when they were silver-haired women?'

Lucie had developed a flexible routine since Joel had given her permission to give the children a few lessons. Each morning she accompanied the pair to the beach where the swimming session was followed by reading. The difficulty of suitable books in English had been solved temporarily by Joel who had bought several books for children in Spanish and then translated the lessons for Lucie to copy out.

'We'll get Hallam to bring back a selection,' he had promised. 'In the meantime, Jessica and Daniel can learn Spanish at the same time.'

Lucie had laughed at this estimate of their respective abilities. 'It might be a good thing if they grew up really bi-lingual, but one can't force them.'

So now she diligently spelt out difficult words for Daniel, then listened to Jessica, who was naturally much more advanced, and was absorbed in pony adventure books or tales of travel.

Sometimes half-way through the morning Joel came out from his workshop, and joined them, often bringing with him a jug of fruit drink.

For Lucie it had become a very pleasant way of spending the mornings. In the afternoons she worked in her room, piecing together silver chains, twisting and hammering metal for brooches, setting small gemstones into ornaments. Then came a period of relaxation with Jessica and Daniel before their light evening meal. It was the evenings that Lucie enjoyed most of all. Not that Joel was always home for dinner, but when he was there, the meal prepared by Señora Matana was eaten to the accompaniment of Joel's conversation. Afterwards, he might plead that he had correspondence or technical reading to attend to, but occasionally he sat with her in what she now called the Twilight Verandah, the oblong bay that cut across one corner of the villa.

In one sense, the pattern of days was heavenly, almost like being a married couple, she told herself, a married pair with the children upstairs in bed and the quiet part of the day to be enjoyed. In another sense, she was uncertain as to how long she could maintain this purely friendly attitude towards him. She was constantly on her guard lest a chance word or careless gesture might break the fragile camouflage that she had established between herself and this man to whom she had so prodigally given her heart and who was totally unaware of such a gift.

Then suddenly the pattern was demolished. One morning Joel came down early to join Lucie and the children on the sandy beach. He was wearing black swimming trunks and when he had taken a short swim by himself farther out than Lucie deemed it advisable for the children, he came thrusting through the gentle, lazy waves and romped with Jessica and Daniel, tossing the small boy in the air and catching him only inches before the child hit the sea.

'Now let's see how well you can swim,' he challenged Daniel. 'I'll race you!'

'Oh, shame!' exclaimed Lucie. 'He isn't up to championship standard yet. Come on, Daniel, show Uncle Joel how you float and swim on your back.'

But the excitement and general jollity was too much for Daniel, who started gamely enough, but collapsed as much through giggling as through self-consciousness.

'He always folds up in the middle,' commented Jessica. 'Look at me, Uncle Joel. I can swim a long way.' She promptly flung herself on the water and battled across the sea in the direction of Africa.

'Not too far out, pet!' called Lucie in alarm. 'Turn round and come back!' But Jessica apparently did not hear.

Lucie plunged in to follow the girl, but Joel with strong overarm strokes forged ahead to overtake Jessica. Lucie slackened speed when she saw the child cling to her uncle as Joel brought her safely inshore.

'You went out too far!' Lucie gently scolded her. 'You must always swim parallel with the shore – the same way as the land. Do you understand?'

Jessica was now all smiles, her composure recovered,

but Lucie realized that there had been a few terrifying moments when the child knew she was far out of depth and ready to panic.

'But I can swim ever so well, can't I?' she appealed to Joel.

'Too well, perhaps,' he answered. 'You're not old enough to go out a couple of miles. I might not be there next time, so always do what Lucie tells you.'

'Now where's Daniel?' exclaimed Lucie apprehensively.

But there was Daniel placidly floating on top of the water, effortlessly, his face turned to the turquoise sky, his hands, gently paddling at his sides like little pink water weeds.

'Bless me!' shouted Joel. 'The boy can float!'

'Sh!' warned Lucie. Too late, for Daniel turned his head at this interruption and fell about in the shallow water.

'Come on, out! Both of you!' commanded Lucie.

Joel called, 'Yes, ma'am. Indeed, ma'am.'

'Oh, I didn't mean you as well,' she said apologetically, but he grasped her hand, seized one of Jessica's and they all splashed ashore, to be confronted by the unexpected sight of Rosanna.

'I could hear you all having such a merry party that I simply had to come down and join you,' she greeted them.

Rosanna, wearing a black and orange bikini with an orange and green towelling wrap hung loosely on her shoulders, was so exquisitely evenly tanned that Lucie guessed that the Spanish girl spent much of her time sunbathing.

'Daniel can swim,' Jessica said proudly, with a slight touch of sarcastic defiance in her tone.

Rosanna's dark eyes flashed a keen glance at the girl. 'But of course. English children always learn to swim, even though the sea is icy in your country.'

'But it's warm here,' continued Jessica. 'Don't you like to swim?'

'Hush, dear,' urged Lucie mildly. 'You shouldn't ask too many questions.'

Rosanna laughed. 'Joel and Hallam – and others – have

tried to teach me to swim, but I do not feel at home in the sea. I like only to be lazy in our pool.'

Lucie understood that slightly boastful tone that Jessica had used about Daniel's prowess. That child was going to be a menace to other women when she grew up.

Rosanna turned towards Joel. 'Has Hallam gone to England?'

'Yes. He left nearly a week ago. Didn't you know?'

She raised her luminous eyes mockingly. 'Does anyone ever tell me anything?'

'Sorry, I thought you knew.' Joel was shaking sand out of his espadrilles before putting them on.

'I was away for a day or two on my brother's yacht,' explained Rosanna.

Joel turned towards Lucie. 'Remember that elegant yacht we saw in Corvario when I took you there by boat?'

She nodded. 'Yes, a beautiful ship.'

'That belongs to Rosanna's family. Occasionally we're commanded to lunch or dinner on board and then we smarten ourselves up and hope to arrive bandbox-fresh.' He looked at Rosanna. 'Next time we'll bring Lucie, if we may – give her a chance of inspecting a luxury-class vessel.'

Rosanna gave Lucie a cool smile. 'Yes, of course. We might arrange it when Hallam returns and brings the new housekeeper with him.'

How cleverly Rosanna managed to demote the women-folk in Hallam's and Joel's household, thought Lucie. Georgina was the new 'housekeeper' and Lucie had no doubt that she herself was already dubbed 'the children's governess'.

Rosanna pulled her wrap around her shoulders and rose to her feet. 'I must go now, Joel. You are welcome for lunch if you choose.'

'I'm not very respectably dressed,' he objected, looking down at his faded maroon shorts and fawn shirt. 'But at least I'll come with you up that dangerous path. It's very risky. Why don't you do something to make it safer?'

Rosanna gave him a dazzling smile. 'Then perhaps we should have no need of our charming escorts.'

'You'll take the children back when you're ready, Lucie?'

Joel's query was unnecessary. Rosanna's possessive manner as she grasped Joel's arm to help her over the rocks made Lucie wince with sheer jealousy. Not even from herself now could she disguise the fact that she was so hopelessly in love with Joel that every small, unthinking courtesy he showed to another girl was a rapier wound to the heart.

On subsequent mornings Rosanna found it convenient to join Lucie and the children on the beach, apparently indifferent as to whether Joel were there or not. She would spread herself comfortably on her towels and sunbathe, closing her eyes as a signal that she did not wish to be disturbed.

Lucie saw no reason why she should try to prevent Jessica and Daniel from enjoying themselves in noisy play. Rosanna had her own garden and swimming pool if she chose to use it, and in any case this part of the beach was immediately outside the Villa Sirena, so Lucie considered that the inmates had a prior right.

All the same one morning when Jessica and Daniel were having a mild fight and some sand was accidentally spattered over Rosanna's unsuspecting face, Lucie was contrite.

'I'm terribly sorry,' she apologized. 'Jessica, you must tell Miss del Rey how sorry you are. You, too, Daniel. You were both to blame.'

Jessica gave Rosannna an uncharitable glance. 'I'm very sorry if I disturbed you,' she said in a chilly, grown-up voice.

Daniel stood there, giggling, but managed to splutter 'Sorry!' before he ran off to play in a safer place.

Rosanna sat up, wiping her face with tissues, examining her features in a small mirror – no doubt, Lucie thought a trifle maliciously, in case some permanent damage had been done.

'Those two are really rather a wild pair,' Rosanna observed when Jessica had gone out of earshot. 'They really should be sent to good schools in England.'

'They'll both go in due time,' Lucie assured the other.

'I can't think why Joel has landed himself with his brother's family. Surely there were other relatives in England?'

Lucie shook her head. 'I don't know about that.' She was not willing to offer information. Rosanna must know the children's circumstances at least as well as Lucie.

'No doubt matters will improve when this new housekeeper arrives,' continued Rosanna.

'She's not coming here in quite the capacity of a housekeeper, I think. Mrs. Frensham is Hallam's cousin. It may be that after a while she might take over some of the household duties. At present, the villa and the cooking and everything else are rather a lot for Señora Matana.'

Rosanna turned an animated face towards Lucie. 'Then you must look forward to that, I'm sure. The children would be taken off your hands and you'd have all the time you want to do your jewellery work, so that you'd be free, even to go back to England or wherever you want to stay.'

Lucie was both amused and irritated by Rosanna's complacent reorganization of the Villa Sirena household and its occupants' duties.

'We shall have to wait and see how Mrs. Frensham fits in and what part of the household she wants to manage.'

'Naturally. Is she old? Or young?'

Lucie smiled. Rosanna was already trying to test out the opposition. 'Not exactly either. Middle-aged, I'm told.'

'You don't resent her coming here?'

'Why should I?' Lucie faced Rosanna. 'I understood that it was at your suggestion – or your mother's and yours – that it was thought advisable to have an older woman in the villa while I'm staying here. After all, there are two young men to be protected.'

Rosanna's eyebrows lifted. 'Oh, but no. It was for your protection.'

Lucie's gentle sarcasm had been lost on the Spanish girl.

'It doesn't imply a very good opinion of Joel and Hallam if it looked as though I were at their mercy.'

Rosanna shrugged. 'For my part, it would not matter, but you understand my mother was worried.'

'For you? Or Joel? Or me?' cut in Lucie quickly.

Rosanna stared. Then she turned her face away. 'For

you most of all – but it is also a delicate situation. You see' – now she turned towards Lucie with a confidential air – 'Joel is so very fond of me. He loves me very much, so naturally my mother feels it is important that he – that everyone – should be discreet.'

'How long did the young girl Bernarda live at the villa?' queried Lucie.

'Bernarda?' Rosanna shrugged. 'Oh, was that her name? I don't know. There have been several girls there to cook and clean since Hallam came.'

Lucie bit back the words that almost came tumbling out. '*Since Hallam came.*' So that was it! It apparently did not matter so much if a succession of girls came and went while only Hallam had lived there, but now Joel would be tarred with the same brush of suspicion.

Did this anxiety on the part of the del Reys, mother and daughter, really mean that Rosanna was in love with Joel?

'Yes, of course, I see that you had my best interests at heart,' Lucie said. 'Spanish girls in the house are not quite the same as an English one. Naturally, you would also be anxious on behalf of Joel. You are going to marry him?'

She shot the question at Rosanna, hoping to surprise the girl into a moment's confusion or hesitation, but Rosanna's face did not move a muscle until her lips parted in a smile.

'You are interested in that possibility, of course.' The words were a statement, not a question. 'Many decisions have to be made before a betrothal takes place. Perhaps in England you make hasty arrangements, but here it is different. I have three brothers, all married – my father died five years ago – and since I inherited part of his estate, my brothers would not wish me to marry without their consent.'

Lucie remained silent, thinking that the situation was a little hard on Joel – or indeed any other suitor for Rosanna – if the prospective husband had to please all three brothers simultaneously.

'There is also the fact that Joel is not Spanish,' continued Rosanna, 'although that is not an obstacle. Nowadays many Spanish girls marry foreigners.' She smiled in the most friendly way at Lucie. 'So you see although there are difficulties, we both know that in the end everything will come right.'

Lucie was left to ponder on whether 'we both know' meant herself and Rosanna or referred to the girl and Joel.

Rosanna considered it a good moment to gather her towels and cushions, suntan oil and lotions, and leave the beach. As she knelt collecting her odds and ends, she gave a sudden exclamation. 'Oh, *dolor*!'

To Lucie's dismay a stream of suntan oil had spurted across the pages of a library book from which, earlier, she had been reading to the children.

'Oh, I do apologize,' Rosanna was wiping the pages and actually making matters worse. 'The stopper must have come out of the bottle.'

Lucie picked up the book before Rosanna could do any more damage. 'It's unfortunate,' she said, giving the other an accusing glance, but Rosanna had turned her head away.

'Is it badly damaged?' she now asked.

'I don't know. I'll attend to it indoors.' Fairly or unfairly, Lucie was convinced that the spill was no accident. The book had been well out of reach of Rosanna's various cosmetics. Perhaps this was a petty revenge for the children having spattered her with sand. Or was it a warning to Lucie not to ask awkward questions or seek to find out to much about Joel and his affections?

'You must let me pay for the book,' Rosanna was saying.

'It came from the library in Las Palmas. Joel brought it when he went over there last week.'

'Oh, I see.' Rosanna sounded quiet. 'Then if they make a fuss, Joel can pay for it. You must not be the loser, Lucie.'

After Rosanna had gone up the path to her villa, unaided by masculine company this time and apparently well able to tackle the formidable, dangerous climb, Lucie found those last words echoing in her brain. 'You must not be the loser, Lucie.'

But if matters turned out the way Rosanna hinted, then Lucie would certainly be the loser.

As soon as Jessica saw the damaged book, she said immediately, 'She did that on purpose!'

'Hush, dear. You mustn't make accusations. It was an accident,' maintained Lucie stoutly. She saw disbelief in Jessica's dark blue eyes and added hastily, 'I can clean it up, I think.'

She spent more than an hour during the afternoon trying to eradicate the stains, ironing the pages through blotting paper, dabbing with various grease-removers, finally applying fuller's earth and hoping for the worst marks to vanish. How on earth would she explain this to Joel? she wondered. She could hardly lay the blame on Rosanna. She decided that next time she took books to the beach, she would take more care of them and tuck them away somewhere out of harm's way.

Later in the afternoon, her mind beset by problems, she worked badly on two silver plaques, cutting the metal wrongly and having to change her mind as to their eventual shape. Her spirits drooped and were not lifted when Joel did not appear for dinner.

Señora Matana informed her that he had gone to the village earlier and would not be back until later in the evening. As usual, Lucie offered to clear away the meal and wash up so that Señora Matana could leave sooner for her own home. She was in the kitchen finishing the dishes when Joel came in.

'Hallo! Making yourself useful?' he greeted her.

She turned with a tureen in her hands. 'It seems a pity to keep Señora Matana here so late when there's only one person to serve, so I offered.'

'Dear Lucie!' he murmured. 'I don't know what we'd all do without you.'

To her own amazement her composure cracked, the tureen slipped from her hands to crash in fragments on the tiled floor. Then, horrified, she burst into tears.

'Don't cry, Lucie dear,' he whispered. 'It's only a very ordinary piece of china, easily replaced.'

'I know,' she sobbed. 'Silly of me.' She could not tell him that she was not lamenting the loss of a dish, but that her tears were caused by that caressing tone of his voice, the way he had said 'Dear Lucie'.

He was picking up some of the pieces and she controlled herself and dried her eyes.

'That's better,' he said when he straightened up. Then he put his hands gently on her shoulders. 'No good crying over one shattered bit of crockery!' He bent his face towards hers and kissed her gently on the lips. Then he seemed to thrust her away from him and walked a couple of steps across the kitchen, his hands in his trouser pockets.

She stood by the sink almost transfixed and scarcely heard him when he said, 'How about a boat trip tomorrow? We could take all day off and go to one of the good beaches down the coast. You've seen practically nothing of the island since you came.'

She blinked away the remaining tears and smiled. 'That would be lovely. Isn't it marvellous that you can plan trips in this climate and be almost sure that the weather will be good? In England you have to wait and see if it rains.' She was gabbling away to hide the sudden joy she felt at the prospect of spending a whole day in his company. Tomorrow Rosanna would come down to the beach in vain. Unless—? The thought that he had already invited Rosanna hit her like a blow on the head.

'The children will love the idea,' she said.

Jessica and Daniel were always ready to be thrilled by a boat ride and were up early next morning after Lucie tiptoed into their room and woke them with the news. Jessica, ever the little mother, pattered about giving orders to her brother, deciding what he should wear. 'We must take jackets with us in case the wind is cold.'

'Did Uncle Joel say anything about the food?' she asked Lucie.

'No. What should he have said?'

'Sometimes we take food with us and cook it on the boat,' she answered gleefully. 'Oh, it tastes very nice.'

Lucie nodded. 'I'll ask as soon as I see him,' she promised.

She ate her own breakfast and went downstairs to tell Señora Matana of the day's arrangements. On the kitchen table were packages, evidently food.

'Are we taking these parcels with us?' she asked.

Señora Matana answered, '*Si, si, señorita*. But there is more – wait.'

The assorted packages already seemed enough for a dozen passengers, but Joel carried the large hamper down to the little harbour and stowed it aboard the boat. Then he stepped ashore again.

'Stay here, all of you. I have to find Alberto.'

Lucie kept an eye on Jessica and Daniel to see that they did not fall overboard and spoil the trip at the outset. She was conscious of a bubbling joyousness at the prospect of the day's outing and doubly glad that apparently Rosanna was not included.

After twenty minutes or so, Joel returned with a large fish wrapped in a piece of straw matting. 'How well can you cook, Lucie?' he asked.

'That depends on what's to be cooked,' she answered cautiously, eyeing the fish with some dismay.

'Not to worry,' he assured her. 'I'm a dab hand at outdoor cooking.'

'When you did some cooking on the beach one day, you burnt all the fish,' pointed out Jessica.

Joel adopted a mock-sorrowful expression. 'Really, Jessica, you're an *enfant terrible*! Can't I be allowed to do a little boasting so as to impress Lucie?'

She gave her uncle a wicked grin. 'I know what you said I am. It's French for "that terrible child".'

'I shall call you names in German or Greek. That'll fox you,' he threatened, as he cast off from the mooring.

He steered a safe distance from the shore, but not so far out that Lucie could not enjoy the changing contours and colours of the coastline. This morning the mountains that ran the length of the island like a backbone were misty mauve and pale sandy shades, dissolving into the sharp greens of maize crops on the lower slopes and the darker hues of banana plantations.

'That little town,' pointed out Joel, as they passed a cluster of white houses with a tiny harbour, 'is Ventura's Blackpool.'

Lucie laughed up at him. 'Blackpool?' Where is the long promenade and the famous tower?'

He laughed, too. 'It's name is Pozo Negro, so that means Black Pool.'

Jessica and Daniel were occupied with their fishing lines and Lucie sat by the taffrail enjoying the wind that ruffled her hair, the sense of being near to Joel, and the snatches of nonsensical conversation in which he indulged from time to time. This was a new Joel, a light-hearted, more carefree Joel than the silversmith intent on his work, impatient of interruptions or delays.

A lighthouse in the distance caused him to veer farther from the shore. 'Plenty of hidden rocks and reefs inshore,' he told her.

Daniel shouted, 'I've caught one!' but when he pulled up his line there was only a long drift of seaweed hanging on the end.

'Oh, bad luck!' sympathized Joel. 'Try again. Look, wait a minute and I'll bait the hook for you.'

The boy obeyed and delightedly cast his line again, this time with a morsel of fish on the end as bait.

'I don't believe there are any fish in this sea,' complained Jessica. 'Here, Daniel, you can take my line as well. I'm tired of fishing.'

'Tut, tut!' mocked her uncle. 'You mustn't give up like that, Jessica. Where is your persistence, your endurance, your tenacity of purpose?'

'Too many long words for me, Uncle Joel. I know what you mean – why don't I stick at it?'

He sighed. 'What chance have I against such a matter-of-fact, down-to-earth little horror?'

'Lucie never calls me a little horror.'

'She's too polite.'

The boat was turning in a wide circle as they approached an enormous sand beach stretching, it seemed, for miles in a vast curve. A few houses, a couple of modern hotels with gardens and palm trees, that was all.

'We can run the boat on to the beach. There's no harbour here – yet. One day the tourist development will change it all, for better or worse, I don't know which.'

He jumped over the side into a foot of water, dragged the boat a little farther, then lifted the two children on to the sand, and lastly Lucie. As his hands clasped her waist she felt a heady tremor run through her, but quelled it instantly as he set her feet on the ground.

When *La Sirena* was properly secured, he clambered aboard again for the hamper, which Lucie took from him while he brought the large fish and a number of other odds and ends. They walked a short distance along the sandy beach until Joel selected a spot where tough clumps of bushes made a shield from the slight breeze.

'There isn't a soul about,' remarked Lucie. Far away she could see two or three specks moving about near one of the hotels.

'No. I like this place for that reason,' replied Joel. He was busily unpacking the hamper to find drinks for the children, but shut it again when he had handed them beakers of orangeade.

'Now see if my boy-scout technique will serve me,' he muttered, as he began to gather sticks for a fire. Jessica and Daniel ran about helping, until Joel said there were enough. Lucie had taken off her sandals which had become slightly wet when she landed, and now rolled up her blue linen trousers to the knees. Oh, this was fun, she told herself. After her father died, her mother had not been able to afford many holidays. A few days at Brighton, perhaps, or a week or so in the summer with a cousin who lived on the outskirts of St. Albans, that had been the most that could be managed. Since she had left school, of course, Lucie had spent holidays in Cornwall or the Lakes, but she had never before been involved in this kind of small family party.

While the fire gathered its strength, Joel was busy cutting the fish into thick cutlets. He had found a flat stone and wielded a large knife with unerring skill. He produced a toasting fork which he handed to Lucie.

'Stick it firmly on the end and hold it – like that,' he instructed.

Jessica and Daniel were ready to do their share. 'I'll get the plates ready,' offered Jessica, while Daniel obligingly acted as bellows and blew on the fire for Lucie's benefit.

'You'll never taste fish better than this,' observed Joel, licking his fingers after he had demolished one cutlet and now proceeded to cook a second.

'Lovely,' pronounced Lucie. 'What fish is it?'

He shook his head. 'I've forgotten the name. They have all kinds of different fish here in these waters, some we don't know at all in England. But what does the name matter? Have some more.'

She laughed and shook her head. 'I can't eat any more. All right, half a piece, then.'

He opened a second bottle of red wine and refilled her glass. She thought she had never enjoyed an open-air meal so much in the whole of her life. After the fish there were small cakes and cheese to follow with bananas and oranges.

'We have quite an amount of food left for another meal,' said Joel when even the children admitted they could eat no more. 'We shall need that later, but the fish was better cooked while it was so fresh.'

'Did Alberto catch it last night?'

Joel grinned. 'So he said, but I'm never quite sure that he hasn't bought it from another man and is then selling it to me at a profit.'

'Doesn't he always go out fishing himself?'

'No, only when it suits him. The same as he does our garden – when it suits him. I must get him to cut down some of that jungle at the back of the villa.'

She remained silent remembering those words of his when she had first come to the Villa Sirena. 'We force our way through the jungle when all the time, if we only knew, there's a perfectly good broad way to wherever we want to reach.'

Was there ever going to be a good broad way for her or must she always struggle through the jungle of doubt and indecision, the charmed moments followed by the depressions of misunderstanding?

Jessica and Daniel had almost to be pegged down to the sand before they would be persuaded to take a short siesta after lunch.

'It's the same as being at home,' grumbled Jessica.

'One hour, then you can rush around all you want to,' promised Joel. 'But one hour lying down. That's an order.'

'I'll lie down when you and Lucie do,' she offered.

Lucie obediently stretched herself out, face to the sun, and only too willing to surrender herself to this blissful day and all its happenings.

Joel said, 'I must finish my cigar first.'

Jessica settled herself comfortably, caught Lucie's eye and actually winked.

Lucie closed her eyes and gave herself up to that dreamlike state, neither waking nor sleeping, when pictures float before the eyes, scenes come and go vaguely, yet one is aware of one's surroundings, the faint rustle of the waves on the shore, the cry of a bird, distant voices. Yet she must have actually slept, for when she opened her eyes, the children were playing with Joel a few yards away. Presently he flung himself down beside her, as she sat up and brushed the sand from her hair.

'Too energetic for me, those two,' he murmured. 'I must be ageing fast.'

'You? And not yet thirty?' she hazarded. She guessed he was still in his twenties, but could not be sure.

'Two more years before that milestone, but they make me feel an old man.' He gave a hearty yawn and for a few minutes appeared to be asleep. Then he sat up, leaned forward and hugged his knees. He fumbled in his shirt pocket for matches and a cigar.

Occasionally she kept a watchful eye on the two children in case they strayed too far, but sitting slightly behind Joel, she was able to fix her glance on him, noting the line of his jaw, the straight nose, the untidy mass of his dark hair tumbling over his brow.

Suddenly he turned towards her so swiftly that she realized she had been caught staring. She smiled uncertainly, knowing that colour was slowly rising into her cheeks.

'D'you think you'll fit in all right with Georgina?' he asked. 'What I mean is, you don't think you're being – supplanted – elbowed out, as it were?'

'Oh, no, nothing like that. Not from what I've heard from Hallam.'

Now she was sorry that even the mention of Hallam had been made to cast the slight shadow on this halcyon day.

'M'm, Hallam,' Joel muttered. 'D'you find him difficult? He's not an easy fellow to understand.'

'Oh, no,' she said more quickly than she had intended. 'Apart from not being a very good sitter, I think – I mean I've found him a very pleasant companion.'

Joel was silent for a minute or so and Lucie regretted making a rather enthusiastic defence of Hallam. Yet she could scarcely tell Joel that she distrusted his friend and the man with whom he shared a house.

'He's a charmer right enough,' murmured Joel more to himself perhaps than to her. He suddenly swerved his head towards her. 'You're not falling for him, are you?'

Under the intent gaze of his dark blue eyes she had to keep a grip on herself and not let him see the blunt truth. She laughed lightly. 'No, of course not! It would never do! As you say, he's a charmer, probably very attractive to girls, but I'm not likely to fall for him – or indeed anyone.'

She knew she was talking too quickly and too much as that last lie came tumbling out.

'Yet you must have known some men before now,' he pursued. 'What did you say you were? Twenty-one? I can't believe that romance has utterly passed you by.'

She stared ahead at the sea and the sharp line of the horizon. 'I – I had one shattering experience,' she said at last. Perhaps it would help to eradicate the final pangs of that unhappy affair if she could tell Joel. He would understand then that she was not a girl at a loose end looking for the chance of a light-hearted romance with any handy young man, but one who would hesitate to commit herself to a new love unless it were sincerely and deeply felt.

'Tell me,' he prompted. But at that moment Jessica and Daniel came running up and flung themselves down beside Lucie.

'I'm thirsty,' announced Daniel, and as Lucie poured drinks into beakers, she could not decide whether to be glad or sorry that she had not yet disclosed the account of that past heartbreak.

During the rest of the day there were only fleeting moments when she and Joel were alone and she decided that the mood in which Joel would have listened to her revelations had gone.

There was food to be eaten and Joel suggested that Lucie might like to have tea at the hotel not far off.

'Just a pot of tea, I mean,' he explained. 'We've enough food here, even for these ravenous young wolves.'

'No, I'd rather not go to the civilized places today,' she replied. 'I like this kind of happy-go-lucky day. Anything formal would spoil it.'

Some time later they clambered aboard *La Sirena* and headed northwards along the coast. In the evening light the mountains assumed a sharp cut-out appearance as though they were two-dimensional and part of a stage set. When Joel neared the little harbour of Molino de la Torre, their home base, he said, 'I believe I could run the boat up the beach outside our villa. I've often done it before and it would save us carting all this gear, the hamper and so on, from the village.'

He sped past the harbour entrance, then slowed down to turn. He made a good landing, but just as he was stepping ashore a voice called out from the rocks above.

Lucie saw Rosanna half-way up the path. So now it was known all about the day's sailing and who had made up the party.

'Had a good day?' called out Rosanna.

'Yes, a very good one,' replied Joel, turning his attention to beaching the boat safely and hauling out the children.

This time Lucie managed to land on the soft sand without Joel's aid, for she did not want to receive such attentions from Joel under the critical eye of Rosanna. It was only a short distance from the sea's edge to the garden of Joel's villa and the children were already up and over the rough steps carved in the wall. As Joel and Lucie walked slowly along the paved path towards the villa, he said, 'And was it a good day, Lucie?'

'Oh, yes, Joel, a very good day. I've enjoyed every minute of it.' She was aware of the enthusiasm in her voice, but there was no reason to disguise that. Why should she be half-hearted about admitting the pleasure he had given her?

Yet it was noticeable that as soon as he had finished dinner he excused himself. 'I must catch up on some of my drawings,' he said, and she knew better than to follow him to the sitting-room where he would be working at his desk.

It was some time later when she passed him in the hall and he was telephoning. From the snatch of phrases she caught, she gathered that he was explaining the day's outing to Rosanna. Lucie wondered if he would have found that necessary if Rosanna had not already seen the boat and its passengers returning.

## CHAPTER SIX

WHEN Hallam's cousin Georgina arrived and settled in, Lucie laughed to herself, struck by the ridiculous irony of the situation whereby a great fuss had been made about the proprieties of Lucie living alone with two young men. Surely it was an even graver offence to have left her in the villa with only one man while the other went to England for over a fortnight? The del Reys, mother and daughter, seemed to have odd ideas, especially when it was apparently Joel about whom they were so concerned.

As Hallam had prophesied, Mrs. Frensham was 'Georgina' from the start, even shortened to 'Georgie' by the children. In her middle fifties, she was on the plump side, with the kind of hair that had once been bright red but was now fading into a fairish grey. Her china blue eyes twinkled with fun and good humour and she was quickly enslaved by Jessica and Daniel.

'Oh, it was such a delight when I received Hallam's first invitation to spend Christmas here, but when his cable asked me to come sooner and stay longer, I didn't think such good fortune could fall in my lap.'

Lucie had personally checked all the details of Georgina's room across the landing from Lucie's own. It faced north but was decorated in warm tangerine shades with antique cream furniture.

Georgina was charmed with the room and told Lucie so on several occasions. 'My own home was comfortable and as attractive as I could make it, but when my husband died – three years ago – it was too large and too expensive for me to keep going. So I sold it along with most of the furniture and my solicitor advised me to invest the money in an annuity.'

'But the boarding house where you live – are you comfortable there?' asked Lucie.

Georgina grimaced. 'Comfortable, yes. But it becomes a little dreary after a while. The same routine – even the same meals on a kind of monthly rota.' She laughed. 'When you know that dinner on the first Wednesday in the month will be lamb chop and peas followed by treacle tart, you want to opt out and go off somewhere and have lobster salad or else a ridiculous picnic meal of bread and cheese and pickles.'

'You won't get meals here of a boring sameness. In fact, sometimes I haven't the faintest idea of what I'm eating, but Señora Matana is a good cook, and I enjoy foreign food anyway.'

When Georgina had been at the Villa Sirena about a week she suggested to Lucie that Christmas preparations had better be made. 'It's already the first week in December.'

'I know. Christmas will be here before I've half finished my orders. I must certainly go over to Las Palmas during the next few days. But we must try to give the children some sort of English Christmas if we can.'

'Las Palmas!' murmured Georgina softly. 'What a magical name that is! You read about it in cruise brochures, see pictures of the hotels, the beaches, the promenades. It must be a wonderful city. Perhaps it might be possible for me to go there for a few days later on?'

'Oh, I'm sure that could be managed,' Lucie assured her.

Later in the day a possible plan occurred to her. First she cautiously sounded out Joel.

'Both the children need some new clothes,' she began. 'I thought I might combine a shopping trip for them with my own business calls. Georgina is longing to see Las Palmas, so I suppose it would be all right if we four spent a few days there and left you and Hallam on your own? Señora Matana will look after you both and see that you don't starve.'

Joel at the time was perched on the edge of the stone wall that ran along the terrace outside the villa. He took so long to reply that Lucie began to be apprehensive that she had made a most unwelcome suggestion. He was regarding her with a faint smile on his lips and an expression on his face that she could not quite fathom.

'And how do you suppose Hallam and I managed before you descended on us with your ministrations?'

'Very well, I expect, in a bachelor kind of way,' she returned with a laugh. 'At least we'll be taking the children off your hands.'

'That will leave us entirely carefree,' he mocked. 'Yes, of course, go whenever it suits you. If you tell me the date when you've settled it, I'll probably be able to make arrangements for you all – the flight, hotel and all that.'

'Thank you, Joel.'

'That reminds me that the Thorntons are evidently spending a holiday in Tenerife just after Christmas. Most certainly Mrs. Thornton will want to pay us a flying visit, so it might be as well to get Jessica and Daniel nicely kitted out. Otherwise I shall be criticized for meanness and allowing the children to go about in rags.'

Lucie smiled delightedly. 'We'll put on a good show when they come – unless of course they turn up unexpectedly, and catch us all grubbing about on the beach.'

Georgina was overjoyed at the prospect of a visit to Las Palmas. 'Nothing so exciting has happened to me in the last three years. I'm so grateful to Hallam for letting me come.'

She spent time inspecting the children's clothes, mending those still in reasonable condition, discarding others outgrown or worn out. She began to learn a few Spanish words from Señora Matana and even more from Jessica, who was beginning to fancy herself as a linguist. While Lucie worked hard on her current orders so that she would have plenty to take to Las Palmas and elsewhere, Georgina took over the rather makeshift lessons in reading and arithmetic.

Then two days before the date fixed for departure, Hallam suggested that Lucie might give him another sitting for the portrait.

'I'm rather busy just now,' she demurred. 'Could it wait until after I come back?'

'I shall lose interest in it then altogether,' he answered testily. 'You girls are all alike – flattered to death in the first place, and then it's a bore.'

'Oh, no, Hallam, not a bore. Only that we're going to Gran Canaria the day after tomorrow and – oh, all right,' she said hastily, noticing the black look on his face and the sullen droop of his mouth. 'When? Today or tomorrow?'

Lucie was always sharply aware that she was living in

Hallam's house and she must try not to offend him to the point where trouble might arise between him and Joel.

Hallam instantly regained his more attractive expression. 'That's the girl! What about this afternoon?'

She agreed. No doubt she could make up for the loss of time by working during the evening after dinner or early tomorrow morning.

The yellow silk shirt which she had worn for the previous sitting was now slightly crumpled, for she had put it on yesterday. If she had known about Hallam's sudden need for her attendance, she would have reserved it. With the aid of a small travelling iron, she smoothed the collar and shoulders.

When she went to his studio after lunch, she found him sprawling full-length on the couch. He picked up a wine bottle by his side and offered her a drink.

'There's a glass on the shelf there,' he pointed out.

'No, thanks. I had enough wine with lunch.'

He seemed in no hurry to start posing her and she waited, becoming more irritated as the minutes went by.

'Where do you want me to sit?' she asked at last.

'Over there, as usual.' He gestured with the wine bottle. Then he suddenly rose, stretched his arms above his head, flexing his muscles. Lucie paid little attention. She was already aware of Hallam's slim, lithe figure, more elegant perhaps than Joel's burly breadth; the two men were about the same height, so she had to look up to both of them an equal distance from her own level.

For a time he worked with great concentration, talking sometimes to himself but not to Lucie. Eventually he gave her a chance to rest and relax.

'I suppose I'm not yet allowed to see your progress,' she said as she moved her shoulders to and fro.

'No, indeed. Not for some time.'

'Because artists never want to show the work until it's finished or because the sitter might be irrevocably shocked?' she queried.

'Both, probably. The painter doesn't want to lose his sitter too soon, however unflattering the portrait may eventually turn out to be.'

After ten minutes or so he picked up his palette and

brushes again. He gave her several keen glances. 'D'you think we might have a slightly more plunging neckline?'

Lucie glanced down at the open-necked shirt she was wearing. As she hesitated to undo the next button, Hallam's voice rasped, 'Oh, don't be so tiresomely squeamish. You'd do it fast enough for Joel if he asked you.'

'Joel *wouldn't* ask me,' she flared at him, wrenching the button. 'Does that suit you?'

'Darling Lucie, don't get so het up over silly trifles,' he said, smiling. 'You've upset all the collar now.' He put down his palette and came over to her, rearranging the shirt opening. She felt his hands lightly brush her breasts and although the colour rose in her cheeks, her heart beat no faster or more erratically because of his touch. She was seething with anger and humiliation and thought wrathfully that if Hallam had any sensitivity at all, he would abandon this particular sitting, for some of her emotions must surely be reflected in her face.

More than half an hour went by and now Hallam, too, was silent, not even chattering to himself. Then he said suddenly, 'So you've persuaded Joel to take you by boat to Las Palmas.'

'By boat?' she queried sharply. 'No, I thought we were going by plane.'

'Then it must be good news for you. He thinks you and Georgina shouldn't be left loose in Las Palmas.'

'He didn't tell us this,' Lucie said slowly, but now she could not prevent the angry tension in her face relaxing.

He swung towards her, palette in hand. 'What a marvellous change of expression! Two seconds ago you were sullen and your eyes were glazed. One snippet of news has made all the difference. Keep it like that, Lucie.'

For a horrified moment she suspected that Hallam had merely told her of Joel's decision in order to remove the dull look from her features.

'Is it really true?' she asked. 'Or is it just a ruse to cheer me up?'

The words were fatally chosen, for he immediately pounced on the implication. 'Then Joel's company on the trip is a cheering thought for you?'

She did not answer, fearing to give him further admissions which he might twist to his own advantage.

'More cheering than if I were coming with you?' he queried.

'It will be an advantage to have Joel with us when we are buying clothes for the children,' she answered as coolly as she could.

He made a derisive grunt. 'Is that all the use you could find for him? A handy cheque book? No, dear Lucie, you can't fool me like that. I'm sorry for you.'

At first she refused to rise to the bait of demanding why he need be sorry for her.

After a long pause, he said, 'They're a well-matched pair. They're both ruthless and demanding, but they'll manage. Rosanna will adore being the wife of a rather unusual artist in silver. Joel will proudly display her. After all, he won't always continue to live here, stuck on one of the smaller Canary Islands. Rosanna longs to travel – she wants to see Paris, New York, Buenos Aires. Joel will be able to provide just those opportunities.'

Every word Hallam uttered struck a wounding blow to all Lucie's secret aspirations. She supposed that she had known all along that Joel was not for her, but the dream had been sweet. Yet need Hallam have so brutally torn aside the filmy veil of hope?

She remained silent, trying to pretend that Hallam was merely talking to himself and that she was not expected to answer, but this proved defeatist, for he pursued the same topic, drilling on the same spot as though he were determined to pierce her nerve.

'I don't think you realized what you were up against when you came here,' he said now, not addressing her, but intent on his painting. 'You're sweet and tremendously attractive, but you're too soft – well, too soft for a man like Joel. I doubt if he's ever realized that you were setting out to hook him.'

Now she knew that he was hoping she would bounce up from her stool, eyes flashing, furious at his insults, but she refused to give him that satisfaction. Instead, she smiled, forgetting her pose and turned her head towards him.

'You must think I'm a very green girl,' she said smoothly. 'I came here for a definite purpose and only a limited time, and that purpose was not to ensnare either you or Joel.'

'Why then did you stay once you had seen that the two children were not exactly neglected?'

'Because Joel asked me.'

'And you were really green enough to think he's already fallen for you?'

'Nothing like that!' she snapped. 'I had other reasons for wanting to be out of England for a time.'

'Oh? Interesting.'

For a few moments she did not speak. Why should she tell Hallam? Her past was no business of his.

'I can guess,' he murmured. 'An unhappy love affair.'

'It wouldn't perhaps occur to you that I was running away from the police!' she said with biting sarcasm.

'Not in your case, darling Lucie.'

'No, of course not. I'm too soft. I'd stay there and take what punishment was coming to me.'

'And the man?' prompted Hallam. 'Why didn't you fight for him?'

Now she stared at him. 'Fight? Because he was married.'

The words were almost torn from her and she regretted the disclosure.

'Oh, bad luck, darling!' he exclaimed as he put down his brushes and came towards her. 'I'm sorry, I didn't really mean to hurt you by raking up those old memories. Does it still smart?'

He stood close to her and dropped one hand on her shoulder.

'I've cried all the tears long ago. I can think about it without bitterness. I've only told you now because I want to make you understand that I haven't come to your house to find a husband. I'm not ready to love again.'

'Tell me about it,' he urged, and his tone was so sympathetic that she was almost fooled.

'There's very little to tell,' she said coldly. 'It's happened before now to other girls. I didn't believe it could happen to me. The hardest part was that he wasn't even separated from his wife. He was living quite happily with her. He was just one of those men who find it easy to commute between London and Edinburgh – a share in a flat with two other men and a home in Scotland. His work as a salesman kept him travelling and sometimes I didn't see him for a week or two – while he was touring the North. Equally, of course, there were times when his wife didn't see him for a few days – while he was busy in London.'

Lucie laughed, a brittle little sound. 'Oh, don't worry about me, Hallam. I'm well able to resist even the most irresistible man now. I've learned the hard way.'

Hallam shook his head. 'You mustn't let this affair spoil your life.'

'I've no intention of that!' she retorted. 'But perhaps I've made you see that you're quite safe from me or my wiles, and the same applies to Joel.'

She rose abruptly. 'Evidently you've finished the sitting for the time being, so if you don't mind, I'd like to go. I've crowds of things to do before we go to Las Palmas.'

She went to her room and stood staring out of the window for a time, yet seeing nothing of the camel-brown hills, the distant clumps of palm trees or the occasional white house dotting the lower slopes. She had the feeling that she had been unwise to give her confidences to Hallam, even though he had practically goaded her into telling him. She could never be sure of his trustworthiness or discretion. At some later date he might easily twist the substance of what she had told him, reveal it by hints or innuendoes and represent her in an unfavourable light.

However, the damage was done, and it was ironic that a short time ago she had been on the verge of relating to Joel the unhappy episode with Vincent, and circumstances had prevented her. Now it was Hallam to whom she had told her secret history.

She sighed at her own want of reticence and turned her thoughts to the coming trip to Las Palmas. The bright spot on that horizon was that Joel was accompanying her and Georgina with the children.

Joel took the opportunity before dinner to explain to Lucie that he had changed his plans and would take the party in *La Sirena*. 'It's not for the sake of saving money on the plane trip, but it's really more convenient for all of us, instead of trundling back and forth between airports.'

'I like that better,' announced Jessica. 'Anyone can travel by plane, but we have our boat. Can we stay and sleep on the boat?'

Joel laughed. 'I think not. There isn't room for all of us.'

'But we did that once before,' she persisted. 'You took us, Daniel and me, and we slept in the bunks.'

'All right for children, but not very comfortable for ladies,' he told her.

A journey in the cabin cruiser was a new experience for Georgina and for the first hour or two she took refuge in the saloon.

'How long does it take to get to Las Palmas?' she asked Lucie.

'About five hours by steamer, I think, but Joel will do the journey in about half that time.' Lucie added that more comforting thought at the sight of Georgina's slightly green face.

'I'm a poor sailor, I fear,' muttered Georgina, but to her own surprise she went on deck when Daniel shouted to her that land was in sight.

'As though it hasn't been in sight for most of the time,' commented Joel with a laugh. 'The children would have you believe, Georgina, that we've been casting about on the wide Atlantic since dawn.'

'Well, I feel better if I can see that land is not too far away,' she answered.

He had booked a hotel a little distance from the harbour and opposite a small park. In the taxi he said, 'I think you'll like the situation – near the shopping streets of Triana and the old part of the town and some of the more interesting sights.'

Lucie was pleased with his choice, for she knew this part of Las Palmas better than the more fashionable and newer districts of Las Canteras.

Georgina exclaimed with delight when she found a bouquet of carnations, a bottle of wine and a large dish of fruit in her room. She picked up the card. 'With the Manager's compliments.'

'Oh, what a splendid idea to welcome you like this!'

After lunch the two children were eager to explore the little park opposite, which was no more than a square of grass and trees with a children's playground.

'Siesta first and playtime afterwards,' commanded Lucie. 'Then we'll all go out.'

'Uncle Joel doesn't like shopping,' complained Jessica. 'He calls it "traipsing about" and it makes him tired.'

'Uncle Joel won't be traipsing about with us. He has more important things to do.'

'I don't like shopping much,' put in Daniel. 'It's boring.'

'Any more moans out of you two and I shall ask Uncle Joel to throw you both in the sea,' threatened Lucie. 'No one is shopping today, but Georgina and I thought we might look at some of the shops and find out where we can buy the nicest clothes for you.'

'All right, come along, Daniel.' Jessica's resigned tone was comic. 'Anyway, I haven't had any new clothes for a long time,' she added wistfully.

'All the more reason why we should shop carefully now and buy you some new outfits that you'll like.'

When the children were finally settled in their room for probably no more than an hour, Lucie and Georgina discovered that the hotel possessed a roof garden and a swimming pool. The two women stretched themselves in long cane chairs and Lucie studied the street map of the town that extended for nearly six miles along the shore and across the narrow isthmus joining the peninsula with its grid-iron pattern of streets.

She made notes of the various places she had to visit to deliver her jewellery orders, so that she could avoid needless journeys.

'I could probably do a couple later this afternoon,' she suggested to Georgina. 'I have several addresses in Triana and close by.'

'I'll take charge of Jessica and Daniel if you want to go to places on your own,' offered Georgina.

'Good. I'll meet you in the Plaza near the Cathedral. Look, here it is on the map. What time? About half past five or six o'clock? That would give you time to stroll along the streets and look in the shops.'

Lucie selected the pendants, bracelets and rings, checked the addresses of the shops and stores and set out. Before she left Ventura, she had made out all her invoices, for Joel had advised her to deliver the goods only against settlement by cash or cheque. 'Don't be fobbed off with someone who says that they will get the manager to attend to the account later. You have to pay out for the material in the first place and you must expect to be paid on the nail.'

But today she had no difficulties. All the traders, whether Spanish or among the many Indian, Syrian, Turkish or Moroccan races, appeared to be delighted with her wares. For every order she had made extra pieces to offer and after she had finished today's tour, she returned to the Plaza to meet Georgina and the children. She was in a most contented mood.

During the past few weeks she had been experimenting with various ornaments, mostly pendants, in the shape of animals or fish. She had always been attracted to the fascinating little sea-horses in aquaria and when she made the first one with a bony little body, a fine curly tail and tiny garnets or peridots for the eye, Joel had complimented her on her skill.

'I shall only make a few on spec,' she told him. 'I don't know whether they'll sell.'

'They ought to catch on like wildfire. Oh, I shall have to consider my insecure position. I see that now I've a most formidable rival in silverware.'

His praise and his mock fears were music in her ears. Now she could tell him tonight that she had not only sold all her samples but the buyers were asking for more.

'I'm so happy,' she told Georgina when they met. 'I'm bloated with money and one man gave me a bottle of banana wine as a bonus. What shall we do, Georgina? Drink ourselves silly?'

'Is it nice wine?' asked Jessica, eager to try anything once.

'Lovely flavour,' replied Lucie, heady with her own success. 'But not to be sampled in public places. We'll take it home and you shall try it.'

Joel congratulated her at dinner. 'You'll be turning yourself into a factory soon. But watch out that you don't get into the mass-produced racket. When you go on your rounds the other days, hold back in some cases, make the buyers eager for your exclusive designs. That way you should probably jack up the prices quite a bit.'

Lucie laughed. It was all very well for Joel Barron, famous artist in silver, to urge her to withhold articles in the hope of higher prices. She needed to be successful on a much humbler level.

The days in Las Palmas fled by on wings, it seemed. Lucie tried to compress all her business calls into the first three days, including a flight to Tenerife, so that she might be entirely free then to accompany Georgina and the two children on sightseeing pleasures. Joel had various matters to attend to during most of the daytime, but in the evening when the three adults met for dinner, after Jessica and Daniel were safely in bed, it became an animated exchange of news and points of interest.

After dinner Joel usually took Lucie and Georgina out somewhere to a café or bar. One evening they all went to an expensive night-club high up at the back of the town, a smart, beautifully-designed piece of architecture, with a superb floor-show. On another occasion they visited the luxury hotel in the Doramas Park and drank wine in the elegant courtyard, surrounded by well-dressed men and women.

But the place Lucie liked best was the Santa Catalina Park near the docks and in the heart of the city. Here, under a canopy of trees with interlaced branches, an endless cosmopolitan crowd sat at umbrella-shaded tables or strolled about the tiled paths between beds of shrubs and palms, meeting their friends or meditating over a single drink.

The square, not in any way vast, throbbed with life as diverse in its attractions as the multi-nationals who milled about at all hours. Japanese jostled with Italian sailors, Hindu women in floating saris moved gracefully between Scandinavian tourists. A row of cafés on one side of the square provided refreshments, and Lucie often wondered if the waiters ever had any time off duty for going home to sleep.

'Open night and day,' she said to Joel. 'Don't the cafés ever shut?'

'Not if they can help it, while there are still customers,' he said with a grin. 'I think they do actually close somewhere about two or three in the morning and open again at dawn.'

There were kiosks selling magazines or fancy goods and souvenirs; sometimes women with baskets of flowers for sale roamed between the tables.

On Sunday at midday the party went to the Pueblo Canario, the Canary village built as a typical example of the island architecture. This, Lucie remembered, was the place where Joel had taken her to lunch on that first visit to Las Palmas and made his surprising offer that she should go to Ventura and more or less take the children under her care.

She had not guessed then at that meeting that only a comparatively short time later would find her so deeply in love with this man that she would have flung away every vestige of material success, of economic security, or physical comfort, for the slender chance of sharing his life, working beside him and caring for him wherever he chose to live.

Joel had prudently reserved a table from which they would all have an uninterrupted view of the dancers. Lucie had already seen one of these displays of folklore dance and song in the most colourful costumes, and Joel must have witnessed the scene many times, but to Georgina, it was enthralling.

'I'm having the time of my life,' she said eagerly, as the dances began.

Jessica and Daniel remembered being taken some time ago. 'But it was in the evening,' pointed out Jessica, 'and Daniel fell asleep.'

'I didn't!' he objected. 'I only shut my eyes.'

'Well, you'll probably see some new dances and hear other songs, even if you've been before,' cut in Joel.

'Oh, they look so pretty,' murmured Georgina, as she watched the girls in their wide skirts, usually with an overskirt of a different colour bordered or lace-edged and often looped up at the back almost like a bustle. Most of them wore a white silky jacket which flared just below the waist, and their hats were small and perched on their heads with a coloured scarf hanging down at the back.

The men wore wide-sleeved shirts with a kind of sleeveless cardigan in bright colours over white breeches or tunics.

Georgina was busily sketching some of the costumes in some blank pages of her diary. 'You could buy some nice postcards in colour,' Joel informed her.

'Good. I shall want to remember all these. I do wish I'd brought my camera.'

'I can give you some colour slides,' offered Joel.

The songs were accompanied by guitars and tambourines, castanets and whistles, but some of the girls also played a typical Canary instrument which Joel said was called a *timplé*.

'It looks and sounds almost like a ukelele,' observed Lucie.

'I'd like to have one of those,' suggested Daniel.

'You couldn't play it,' declared Jessica scornfully. 'You'd have to learn music.'

'Then I'll learn music. I can sing a tune.'

When at last the dancing and singing were finished, Daniel led the grown-ups towards one of the shops in the Canary Village.

'Look, this is a shop where they sell those *timplés*,' he pointed out to anyone who would listen.

Lucie looked at Jessica with a woman-to-woman look. 'Shall we buy him one?'

Jessica nodded and smiled. 'If it will keep him quiet. Although that's the last thing that will happen.'

In the shop it was Joel who kept trying out these small five-stringed instruments only about a foot long, picking them up and listening to his own rough versions of The Campbells are Coming and Little Brown Jug.

'Perhaps we should buy Uncle Joel a *timplé* as well,' said Lucie loudly enough for him to hear.

He looked up, his eyes alight with fun and merriment and his glance caused her to stammer out what she wanted to the assistant. She had not been prepared and she veiled her own eyes lest she should give herself away.

'And, Jessica, what would you like?' she asked the girl. 'Something you fancy?'

'That's nice.' She pointed to a small doll in a delightful

Gran Canaria costume. 'But I'm getting rather old for dolls.'

Lucie and Georgina exchanged glances, but Lucie said tactfully, 'They're not really dolls, dear. They're souvenirs, specially for the Canary dancers.'

During the next day or so Joel often found time to accompany Lucie, Georgina and the two children on their sightseeing excursions. Jessica and Daniel were particularly interested in the Zoo, situated high up in the Doramas Park, and went several times to see favourite animals. In the House of Columbus, a beautiful old house with a collection of documents, pictures, globes and model ships of the explorer's time, a couple of exotic parrots lived in the courtyard. The birds delighted the children, especially when shrieks and abusive noises were directed at the visitors.

Again, Lucie experienced that excited yet deeply contented feeling of a family party doing the sights. It had not been difficult to love Jessica and Daniel, and now with Georgina almost as a friendly aunt, Lucie could not help imagining Joel in the rôle of husband and father.

'We have an invitation tonight to some friends of mine,' he told the two women before dinner one evening, when only two or three days of the holiday were left. 'They live in a magnificent house in the old Vegueta district, one that still has real Canary balconies and so far has escaped being pulled down.'

Lucie wore one of her newly purchased outfits, a filmy blouse of patterned nylon with long balloon sleeves, and a full-length skirt of supple cyclamen silk. Without trying to doll up she must certainly not let Joel down in front of his friends.

When the three stepped out of the taxi, Lucie could see even in the soft moonlight the splendid façade of the house with carved wooden balconies to some of the first floor windows. On one side a more elaborate balcony turned the corner and displayed a sculptured figure holding a shield with the arms, no doubt, of the family who lived here.

Entrance through a solid, iron-studded door led into one of the loveliest courtyards Lucie had ever seen. Hidden floodlighting illuminated masses of hibiscus and poinsettias grouped round a small fountain in the middle; almond trees stood at the corners and in turn supported trails of bougainvillea and creepers with pale yellow flowers.

'What a marvellous place!' was Georgina's comment. 'You'd have no idea that such a place was hidden away behind the street.'

Then Joel conducted the two women through one of the Moorish arches ahead into a very large room. It was only dimly lit with small lamps in the corners and Lucie had only a vague impression at first of some half a dozen people.

Joel was making introductions, then stopped before a girl in a high-backed Spanish armchair. 'Rosanna, of course, you know.'

Rosanna! Lucie jerked herself into awareness. It now dawned on her in dismay that she was being introduced to several of the del Rey family. She had not taken in that Manuel, Camaro, Leandro and others were the men's Christian names, and Joel had not thought it necessary to add their surnames. Several other women smiled and greeted Lucie and Georgina, but Lucie was glad when at last she was able to sit down. Someone handed her a glass of wine and she made an effort to control her trembling fingers as she took it.

So Joel had spent some of his time in Las Palmas only because Rosanna was here, Lucie derided herself for a vain fool, believing that he had not found her company distasteful or unbearable. Oh, when would she learn not to judge Joel's actions in relation to herself, but to Rosanna?

The rest of the evening was a long-drawn-out desolation to Lucie. Several of the guests chatted to her and to Georgina, while it was only natural that Joel should remain at the far end of the room close to Rosanna.

Lucie gathered that this beautiful house was the home of Rosanna's eldest brother. Two of the other men were also her brothers, accompanied by their wives. There was talk of the yacht party tomorrow and Lucie found that she had accepted the invitation to lunch on board.

On the way home in the taxi she felt she could not take part in the chatter that Georgina maintained about the house, the patio, the exquisite furniture or the lively people they had met tonight. She felt bruised in spirit because Joel had unwittingly enticed her to a high pinnacle and then hurled her into an abyss of despondency. Now it seemed she was committed to meeting Rosanna and others of her family tomorrow on the yacht. Joel ought to have warned her, she thought angrily, yet later, her calmer self demanded why he should go to that trouble when he probably had not the least inkling of the dismay and disquiet that she would suffer.

She slept badly and next morning Georgina eyed her at breakfast with a questioning air. Lucie impulsively thought of pleading illness in order to avoid the lunch party, but decided that she must face the situation as calmly as possible.

Daniel was delighted when told of the invitation, but Jessica adopted her resigned expression. 'Oh, yes, it's a beautiful yacht, but it's not like an ordinary boat. You must try not to scratch the paint and remember to put the cushions back in the proper place. It's "*Si*, Señorita del Rey," and "*No*, Señorita del Rey" all the time.' She gave Lucie a crafty little grin. 'I'll bet she didn't really want to have us on board if we could have been left somewhere else. She doesn't like us. But Uncle Joel wouldn't want us to be left out.'

Jessica's matter-of-fact appraisal of Rosanna and her staunch belief in her uncle acted as a tonic to Lucie's weary spirits. 'We'll all wear our nicest and most suitable clothes,' she said briskly, 'and show Miss del Rey that we're quite accustomed to luncheons aboard luxury yachts any day of the week.'

Georgina threw Lucie an encouraging smile and the latter wondered how much Georgina guessed of the one-sided love that was so great a torment.

Yet aboard the del Reys' yacht, *Mirabelle*, Lucie enjoyed herself more than she would have thought possible. From the time that Joel conducted the party into the motor launch that took them out to the yacht until nearly midnight when it returned with them to the quayside, Lucie found a new gaiety to mask her dejection.

She wore new white trousers and a sleeveless sun-top of strawberry pink with a white woolly jacket as protection against the wind, and felt as smart as Rosanna or the other women.

The decks of *Mirabelle* were spacious by any standards and under a striped awning there were long tables set out with bottles and glasses in addition to small dishes of shrimps and shellfish, strips of red peppers, small pieces of cucumber or gherkin, tiny pieces of vegetables in a piquant sauce – there was no end to the variety of these small appetizers.

'One is always tempted to make an entire lunch off these nice little titbits,' Lucie remarked to Georgina, as she watched Daniel embark on his third helping. 'Enough just now, please, Daniel,' she implored. 'Or you won't be able to eat the real lunch later on.'

In the main Rosanna almost ignored Lucie, apart from one or two polite remarks, but the Spanish girl cornered Georgina after a while. From a short distance off Lucie watched the trio, Rosanna sitting gracefully in a white-painted folding chair, Georgina next to her and sitting at their feet, Joel on a pile of cushions. His back was towards Lucie, so she could not see his expression, but from the upward tilt of his head she guessed he was interested in what Rosanna was saying.

The luncheon was long and elaborate, served in a beautiful saloon where the walls were decorated with murals of old Spanish galleons. More than a dozen people sat at an oval table headed by the wife of the eldest del Rey brother. Several other young men and girls whom Lucie had not previously met were fellow-guests, but although the girls were quite attractive, none of them could compare with Rosanna's luminous beauty.

After lunch the party scattered around the yacht to find places where they could sprawl at ease and doze, or rock themselves in hammocks specially erected by the deck-hands. Jessica and Daniel needed no persuasion to take their siesta in hammocks. Small groups of twos and threes spent the time chatting or reading, but Señora Anna-Maria, the wife of the middle brother, invited Lucie on a tour around the yacht.

Apart from the dining saloon there were several other lounges, as well as a playroom for children. The cabins – Lucie thought that perhaps they should be called staterooms – were most expensively furnished and in the most lovely colour schemes – sapphire blue and pale green, another in magenta and cream. The bathrooms were dreams of luxury with marble floors and walls and subtle lighting that gave the impression one was already on the ocean bed.

'Do you spend much of your time on the yacht?' Lucie asked her guide.

Anna-Maria smiled. 'Not very much. It belongs to Manuel, you understand. He is the oldest of the brothers. My husband, Camaro, is the second and we live in Tenerife. But sometimes we come to stay in the house at Las Palmas or on the yacht. That is often when there is family business to be discussed. There are several estates which belong to the three men and Rosanna also has to be told for the sake of her dowry.'

Yes, Rosanna's dowry. Lucie had seen last night as well as this morning the easy manner in which Joel was accepted by Rosanna's brothers. She remembered that conversation some time ago when Rosanna had said that her brothers would have to consent to her marriage. Obviously there would be no difficulties where Joel was concerned.

Aloud she said, 'I think I've seen this yacht in the harbour at Corvario, haven't I?'

Anna-Maria nodded. 'Sometimes we have to visit the mother, Señora del Rey on the island Ventura.'

'Yes, the house where I'm living – I'm staying,' she hastily corrected, 'is at Molino de la Torre, close to Rosanna's.'

Lucie had expected that the yacht visit would end late afternoon or early evening, but Joel showed no signs of wanting to leave. Evidently he was not afraid of outstaying his welcome, she thought, and was then ashamed of the contemptuous spirit in which that idea had been framed. Naturally he was reluctant to tear himself away from Rosanna's company.

At about five o'clock, a steward served coffee and cakes and then a couple of the men played deck quoits with the children. After a while Joel appeared at Lucie's elbow. 'How about quoits? We'll make up a foursome.'

'I've never played,' she confessed, unwilling to make a

fool of herself in front of Rosanna and the others.

'Simple enough. Even Daniel is quite a dab at it.'

Rosanna elected not to play, murmuring that it was all too strenuous for her, and Lucie and Joel were opposed by a young Spanish girl and a man called Pedro. After a few initial fumbles, Lucie soon acquired the hang of the game and with Joel as her partner won easily.

'Enjoying today?' he asked her when they sat down to rest in a couple of chairs by the rail.

'Certainly. It's not every day that one can hobnob with the rich,' she answered jauntily, 'and sample the taste of luxury.' She glanced across at him and saw that his eyes which only a moment ago had held laughter and friendliness were now veiled as he gazed at the deck and his mouth had taken a firm but downward curve. What had she said that annoyed him? To cover her momentary anxiety she rushed on, 'Shall we be expected to go ashore soon?'

'Why? Don't you want to stay?' His voice was so abrupt that she almost flinched.

'Of course, but I thought—'

'They expect us to stay to dinner.'

She glanced ruefully down at her white slacks and pink sun-top. A formal dinner aboard a luxury yacht in such casual clothes?

'You needn't worry about clothes,' he reassured her. 'No one dresses up for meals here.'

But Rosanna had decided to wear a low-cut evening dress of dark ruby brocade from which her sun-tanned neck and shoulders rose in luscious curves. Her almost black hair was piled high and decorated with a jewelled comb. A ruby and topaz necklace of very ornate design flashed and sparkled as she moved and there was also a wide gold mesh bracelet studded with rubies and brilliants. Among the company of guests in casual daytime clothes, Rosanna appeared like an exotic hothouse flower tossed in the midst of a bunch of buttercups and daisies. The two girls who did not belong to the del Rey family gave Rosanna envious glances bordering on the hostile, but no one commented.

Then towards the end of the meal Rosanna spoke to Lucie who sat almost opposite. 'That little pendant you are wearing – what does it represent?'

Lucie fingered the ornament on a slender silver chain. 'It's a sea-horse.' Then she added with a touch of defiance, 'I make them – by the dozen.'

'How clever of you! Is it silver?'

Lucie understood now the reason for this dressing-up on Rosanna's part. The apparent ostentation was for Joel's benefit, to point the contrast between the girl with a wealthy background and a distinguished family, and the insignificant little working girl who made trumpery gift-shop ornaments.

'Not solid silver, of course,' replied Lucie evenly. 'An alloy.'

'You wouldn't understand how Lucie and I work,' cut in Joel unexpectedly. 'We're not living in the days of your Spanish ancestors when they could pick up all the gold and silver for the asking. We manipulate alloys of different metals into what we think are artistic shapes, and the value lies in our work, not in the intrinsic value of the metal.'

Rosanna's smile curved her lips but did not reach her dark brown eyes. 'Of course. No doubt you help Lucie to make her – animals.'

'You're ignorant, my dear Rosanna,' retorted Joel. Lucie realized that everyone else had stopped talking to listen to this dialogue. 'Sea-horses are fish, not animals, and the idea is entirely Lucie's own.' He grinned at Rosanna. 'Soon, you'll be discarding that fine necklace of precious stones to wear one of Lucie's sea-horses on a piece of ribbon. They're selling all over the islands like hot cakes and every girl will need one while the craze lasts.'

Lucie was warmed and elated by the spirited defence that Joel was making on her behalf. When towards midnight the motor-launch ferried them from the yacht to the quay, she was further exhilarated by his remarks as they waited for a taxi.

'I wonder who she was trying to impress,' he muttered. 'I've never known her to doll up like that on the yacht. No one ever does, no more than a clean shirt or a white jacket and the girls in a cotton dress, perhaps.'

'Perhaps the jewellery was meant to impress Lucie,'

Georgina remarked. 'It would serve her right if her expensive knick-knacks fell overboard or were stolen,' she added indignantly.

Joel and Lucie laughed at that, but the taxi came along at that moment, sparing Lucie the necessity of replying.

She lay awake in the darkness for some time, reflecting on the day's events, chagrin at finding Rosanna the obvious object of the invitation to the yacht, then Joel's ranging himself on Lucie's side and the final criticism of Rosanna's ostentatious behaviour at dinner. Perhaps it was only wishful thinking, but could it be that Joel was not so enamoured of Rosanna as Lucie had imagined? Even if that were true, it did not mean that he was ready to fall into Lucie's arms or anyone else's for that matter. Still, it was comforting to know that your rival possessed imperfections. It seemed that Rosanna had not yet succeeded in her conquest of Joel, in spite of what Hallam had maintained, that the match was a foregone conclusion.

# CHAPTER SEVEN

On the whole, Lucie considered that the trip to Las Palmas had been enjoyable and worth while. It seemed that all the members of the party had been able to combine business with pleasure. Lucie had delivered her orders successfully and received many more commissions; with Georgina she had shopped for clothes for the children and, in addition, several packages of school books, maps and puzzles to help in the makeshift lessons that now constituted their education.

Georgina was delighted with Las Palmas and the fact that she had been able to buy lengths of beautiful materials, Thailand silk, brocades, nylon, for making up into dresses at a later date.

'If only I could get hold of a sewing machine,' she said to Lucie, 'I could make all kinds of outfits for the children as well as myself. I've always made quite a lot of my own clothes.'

Even Joel had found opportunities for seeing business acquaintances and for purchasing material and equipment for his work.

If, Lucie reflected, there had been several small areas where her depression had been distressing, then this was something to be endured – as a rainy day in a fortnight's sunshine holiday.

In some ways she was glad to be home – that was how she regarded the Villa Sirena on the little island. Georgina was a tremendous help in so many ways, taking charge of Jessica and Daniel when Lucie needed to work hard at her jewellery, delighting them with the jellies and trifles they loved so much and which Señora Matana, good cook though she was, really had little time to attend to. In return, Georgina learned to concoct some of the Spanish and Canary specialities and often lightened Señora Matana's work.

'She is good, that one,' the housekeeper remarked to Lucie when Georgina had taken the children off to the beach for combined arithmetic lessons and a swimming session.

'I'm very glad she has come here,' replied Lucie sincerely.

The older woman hovered by Lucie's side, as though she wanted to say something else, and Lucie looked up expectantly.

'Was there something—' she asked.

The housekeeper's brown face looked sombrely apologetic. 'The Señora from England – does she stay a long time?'

'Oh, I hope so.'

There was obviously a matter that still troubled Señora Matana.

'Is it – she will stay and I must go?' At last the words were out and Lucie jumped up hastily.

'No, no, nothing like that,' she tried to reassure the woman. 'No question. We need you. It's only that Georgina likes to help you so that you don't have so much work to do.'

There were tears glistening in Señora Matana's dark eyes. *'Gracias, señorita, gracias.* I have to work, for my husband is often ill. He has the bad back – from fishing.'

'You mean he was injured when he was out fishing?'

The woman nodded. 'Six months ago. He fell on the boat. He cannot walk very well.'

Lucie remembered the tiny house in Molino where she had taken a message. 'Your daughter looks after him?' she queried.

'*Si*. But she has two children also and no husband. He is dead.'

'Oh, that is sad.'

'He was drowned and the other man with him when the boat was lost in the storm.'

Lucie sighed, seeing this pathetic family struggling to eke out an existence on the money that Señora Matana earned in Hallam's house. Now she saw the need to reassure the woman even more emphatically that Georgina would certainly not be taking her place.

'We shall always want you, dear Señora Matana,' she said, grasping the woman's sinewy, sun-tanned arm. 'We couldn't do without you. Don't be afraid.'

The conversation had been carried on in a mixture of Spanish and English, for Lucie had by now grasped a few more phrases and the housekeeper had picked up a smattering of English, but Lucie tried to make it clear that the woman's position was safe from dismissal.

Yet after Señora Matana had gone back to the kitchen Lucie remained thoughtful. The house was Hallam's and he of course had the responsibility of employing what staff he chose. If Georgina stayed permanently, or at least until the children were sent back to England for schooling, was he likely to dispense with the Spanish woman's services?

Lucie could not believe this would happen, for in the first place, there was a lot of work to keep a house of the size of the Villa Sirena clean and tidy as well as do all the cooking. Secondly, Hallam was not mean in money matters and no doubt Joel shared the expenses of the upkeep of the household.

The talk with Señora Matana had set Lucie's thoughts in the direction of Hallam. Since the Las Palmas visit he had seemed to be his usual exuberant self, yet she felt there was an air of suppressed triumph about the way he looked at her when she caught his glance.

So far he had not asked her to sit again for him, but she had washed and pressed the yellow silk shirt and put it away in her wardrobe. She would never wear it again if she could help it, except for the purpose of the portrait – if he ever finished it.

Then, as though by some form of telepathy, Hallam asked her if she would pose next day. 'I expect to finish it then.'

When she went to his studio, she cleared her mind of all previous pinpricks and sat with what she hoped was the placid expression he demanded.

Yet he was dissatisfied. 'You've gone wooden,' he exclaimed disgustedly.

'Sorry. What do you want me to do?'

'Think about something that excites you,' he snapped.

'I'll try,' she offered. Then a devil's thought came into her head. What would it be like to be wrapped in Joel's arms, feel his kisses on her face, hear his murmured words of love?

'That's better,' Hallam said after a long pause, during which he had worked furiously, flinging down brushes, mixing colours on his palette, and daubing energetically at the portrait she could not see. 'Thinking about Joel has made a vast improvement.'

'Who said I was thinking about Joel?' she demanded.

'Hold it – your tongue, I mean. I don't need to be told. A jealous man always knows if the girl is dreamy about his rival.'

Now Lucie laughed and altered the set of her shoulders. 'Jealous? What cause would you have to be jealous of anyone where I'm concerned?'

He did not answer for a moment, turning to frown at her, dabbing at the canvas, and turning again towards her.

'Because I don't like to see you break your heart over Joel.'

'I'm cured of all that,' she lied.

'Oh? I'm glad to hear it. In that case, I might even discover that perhaps you have a very tiny regard for me.'

'You flatter yourself, Hallam,' she said lightly, trying to keep this conversation from going in the wrong direction. 'Must I fall in love with one or the other of you just because I live in the same house?'

'Well, no. Still, it's always possible that when a girl turns her back on one man, she finds another facing her – just as attractive.'

Now Lucie remained silent for a minute or two. What was Hallam up to? What was he trying to tell her?

'I think I started off with you, Lucie, my darling, on the wrong foot.'

'How do you mean?'

'When I first came to live here, Rosanna practically fell over herself to show me how welcome I was. We spent a lot of time together, sailing between the islands, sometimes over to Las Palmas wining and dining and dancing and all that. I painted several portraits of her – some of them are still here – and one way and another I was really enjoying myself. Then I met Joel in Las Palmas – we'd known each other in England some years ago – and, like a fool, I invited him to come and live here.'

'Why was it foolish?' she asked when he paused so long.

'Because, stupid, Rosanna transferred her attentions to him straightaway and I was out on a limb.'

'I see. But you told me how well matched they were,' she reminded him.

'So they may be, but it doesn't soothe me to think so. When Joel mentioned that he wanted to bring you here to keep an eye on the children, I was all in favour of the idea. I thought, Right, my lad. You fix your sights on Lucie and I'll get Rosanna back.'

She smiled. 'So I was to be just a pawn in the game?'

'Not exactly. Anyway, it didn't work out like that. Joel didn't seem to be madly taken with you, so I decided that if you weren't exciting enough for him, you might be worth my giving you a second look.'

'Thank you for the compliment,' she snapped. How arrogant could Hallam be?

'Oh, don't take offence. I didn't mean that in a slighting way. I'd started off by treating you coolly, but after a while I began to like your damned independent ways, your spurts of fiery temper, even your looks – which are nothing to shout about – all right, don't come at me with a dagger in your hand! – but you know yourself that you're no ravishing beauty. Yet I've come to like your serious little face and watch the expressions flit across it.'

'Material for the artist,' she said quietly.

For a few moments he did not speak. Then she asked, 'Do you really love Rosanna?'

'M'm, not sure now. I was mad about her for a while, but now I don't really care.' He put down his brushes and came across to her, his arms outstretched. 'Lucie, sweet, we could have fun together.' His arms closed around her, but she held herself rigid, yet not struggling to free herself. He kissed her lips with passionate intensity that aroused no response on her part. He sat on the long stool beside her and crushed her in an iron embrace that held no tenderness. When for an instant he loosened his grip, she pushed him away.

'No, Hallam.' She stood up quietly, with all the dignity

she could muster. 'It's not me you want to kiss and hug, it's just a girl who happens to be handy.'

'Darling, don't say that!' He sat on the stool, a foolish grin on his face. 'I'm fond of you.'

'Fond!' she echoed with a little laugh. 'You don't love me. You wouldn't even pretend that. You wouldn't want to marry me—'

'Oh, marriage – that's something different altogether.'

'I don't suppose you'd fall into that trap.'

'Not for a long time to come,' he admitted. 'But you told me you weren't looking for a husband.'

'I'm not.'

'Liar! Not even Joel?'

Lucie reddened slightly. 'I'm willing to take my time. I shall never make demands on Joel.'

'Then in the meantime, be nice to me,' he coaxed.

She faced him and smiled. 'If I said I was willing to fill in the time with you, you'd be insulted.'

He rose and walked to his easel. 'In some ways, you're quite a girl. Iron-hard – and I thought you were soft. Oh, well, it was a good try.'

He began to clean his brushes and she tried to peep at the canvas on the easel, but he was too quick for her and threw the cover over the painting before she could glimpse more than a corner of the picture.

'Don't cheat,' he said. 'You'll see it when it's really finished.'

When she left the studio, she went across the landing to her own room and met Georgina coming out of the room where Daniel now slept. Georgina had persuaded the small boy to sleep alone in the room next to hers. 'Jessica ought to have her own room to herself now, and Daniel is no longer a baby,' she had said to Lucie.

Daniel had surprisingly agreed without a murmur when he knew that Georgina would be within call in the next room. 'Of course I'm not a baby,' he said stoutly. 'I'm not afraid of the dark.'

At that moment Jessica had been about to burst into contradictions, but Lucie had silenced her with a finger on her lips, and subsequently pointed out to the girl how much better not to have Daniel under her feet in her own room.

'Perhaps Uncle Hallam will have it redecorated for you some time,' Lucie promised. 'I'll ask him.'

So now Lucie almost scuttled along the wide corridor, aware that her hair was untidy, her face probably flushed.

'You seemed to be talking a lot in there,' Georgina said lightly. 'I thought painters always wanted their sitters to be silent.'

'Hallam likes to talk – usually to himself. Sometimes I answer.' Lucie took refuge quickly behind her bedroom door. Had Georgina heard any particular sentences or only a couple of voices? Not that she would eavesdrop deliberately.

Apparently there were to be no more sittings for that particular portrait, and Lucie was thankful. She wanted a long interval between this afternoon's violent encounter and her next meeting with Hallam in the privacy of his studio or, indeed, anywhere else.

She and Georgina were occupied with Christmas preparations, some of which they wanted to keep secret from the children.

'They don't want us to know what they're doing,' Jessica told her brother one morning loudly enough for both Lucie and Georgina to hear. 'Sometimes people put Christmas presents in the wardrobes or under the beds, so that we won't find them until Christmas Day.'

Lucie laughed silently with Georgina. 'Thanks for the warning,' she whispered. 'We won't hide anything in the wardrobes or under the bed.'

The best place she could think of was Joel's workshop. 'The children know they mustn't come poking around here,' she said to him one day, 'so perhaps I can hide this parcel under the bench.'

'Good idea. What is it?' He was working on the silver horse, fashioning its flying mane.

'As though I should tell you!' she declared with mock indignation. 'How do I know that you're to be trusted?'

He shot her a glance that amazed her by its hostility. Then his attention was again on his work. 'No, you don't know if I can be trusted,' he said heavily.

She could think of nothing to say, nothing that sounded anything but lame or trite. She left the workshop hastily, but stood outside for a few moments, asking herself why Joel could be so kind and then so harsh and hostile by turns. He had misinterpreted her rather feeble joke about being trusted, but surely he need not take her words at face value.

She could only assume that he had been annoyed at her interruption when he was working on the silver stallion. Possibly it was intended as a gift for Rosanna and he was trying to keep it secret.

At dinner that evening there was nothing in his attitude to explain his surliness, but Hallam gave Lucie several glances that tried to indicate an intimate, secret bond between him and herself. On each occasion she looked swiftly away, only to encounter Joel's intercepting gaze.

When, a week before Christmas, Hallam announced his intention of spending the holiday and part of the New Year in England, Lucie was profoundly grateful. An impossible wish, of course, but she would have been glad if he had said his stay would extend six months or more.

'I have a couple of exhibitions to attend to,' he told Lucie and Georgina, 'and, quite frankly, I don't think I can stand the atmosphere here of Christmas parties and children's games and all that. You understand?'

'Of course,' replied Georgina sharply. 'Something more sophisticated would please you better.'

Hallam grinned at his cousin. 'You said that in a vinegary tone that I didn't know you could use.'

'Life is full of surprises,' she retorted. 'It surprises me that you've stayed here so long working in an unsophisticated place like Ventura.'

'Ah, but I find I can't *work* among a fun-loving crowd. I need simple surroundings and—'

'And simple people like Lucie and me,' she finished cheerfully for him.

'Lucie isn't nearly as simple as she might want some folk to believe,' he retorted. 'Are you, darling?' He turned towards her.

'How would I know?' she asked. 'It depends what you mean by simple. I don't think I'm a very complicated person.'

'Oh, you have your little intricacies,' Hallam declared. 'Like small convolutions that lead one into a maze of bewildering complexities.'

'You're getting too deep for simple folk like us,' cut in Georgina, laughing. 'Off with you and leave us to our Blind Man's Buff and Christmas pudding with silver thimbles and other such harmless delights.'

When he had gone, saying that he was going to the village of Molino, Georgina and Lucie sat for a while in silence. Then Georgina said, 'I'm not prying, Lucie dear, but has Hallam been making a nuisance of himself?'

Lucie smiled. 'Not exactly. Sometimes he's rather overpowering, but it's just his nature. He doesn't mean any real harm. A few kisses and embraces don't count with him.'

Georgina sighed. 'I'm afraid he's always had the playboy attitude to life. I doubt if he'll ever marry and settle down.'

'Few artists want to do just that.'

'Oh, he's often said that marriage is just a cage to artists of all kinds. The very thought of being compelled to support a wife and family is inhibiting in itself – those were his words one day when I tackled him about some brokenhearted girl.'

Lucie laughed softly. 'He's already made that quite plain to me.'

Georgina glanced at her companion. 'It's really Joel, isn't it? You don't have to answer.'

Lucie turned towards the older woman. 'I suppose I don't have to answer because it's all too obvious?

'I wouldn't say that. Women understand each other and see the little signs that men don't notice.' After a panse Georgina added, 'Perhaps that Spanish girl isn't as clever as she thinks she is.'

'What makes you say that?'

'Joel isn't soft enough to be taken in by a beautiful girl belonging to a wealthy family. He'll need someone different from that. Could be someone like you.'

Lucie's eyes lit up as she met Georgina's gaze. 'Too much to hope for, I think.'

'Never give up hope, my dear. It costs nothing and sometimes brings an unexpected reward.'

Joel had been instructed to obtain from somewhere a small pine or fir tree that might serve for the children's enjoyment as a Christmas tree.

'Where on earth shall I be able to get that?' he demanded. 'No one here has ever heard of such an old Anglo-Saxon custom.'

'That day we were out in the boat along the coast,' Lucie told him, 'I saw a plantation on the mountain slopes.'

'Well, if you're so sure about it, you'd better come with me on this raiding party. We can only hope that the idea doesn't catch on too easily in the Canaries or everybody will be stripping the plantations and then the forestry patrols will be after our blood.'

'All we want is a small one – about that high.' She raised her hand to a little more than her own height.

It was a day that Lucie cherished in her memory, one that cancelled out some of those smarts and pangs that Joel and Rosanna between them had managed to inflict on her.

Since the project was not to be revealed yet to the children, Joel and Lucie had to slip out of the villa early in the morning. He drove inland across the island and up the ridge of mountains, which was not the route that Lucie had first indicated, but she was so delighted to have this one day out alone with Joel that she said nothing. She rejoiced, too, that Hallam had already left for England, so she would not have to face his inquiring gaze tonight or receive his jeering remarks.

'You've never been to Betancuria,' he said, as the road twisted down into a valley. 'It was once Ventura's capital. Now it's a quiet little town rather off the tourist map.'

'Every island needs to keep some of its towns off the tourist map, if it can,' she replied.

'Ventura has wonderful beaches, many of them golden sand instead of the black lava stuff that some of the islands have to make do with, so it's only a question of time before the invading army will come with its outsize cars, skyscraper hotels, streets of shops and the rest.'

'But is it wrong that more people should have the opportunity to travel abroad and see places like this?'

He grunted. 'Most of them rarely see anything except the beach, the hotel swimming pool, the cocktail bar. They never explore. Oh, they might take a coach trip around the island, but they don't really see anything. They don't feel the atmosphere of the place.'

'I think I'm beginning to do that,' she said, 'but I've had the privilege of being able to stay much longer than the usual fortnight or three weeks.'

He nodded as he steered along the twisting road. 'True, but then you're not the stereotyped tourist.'

She remained silent for a few minutes, relishing the countryside they were passing through, the lonely palm trees standing like single sentinels over an isolated house, the windmills rising out of the brown plains. Sometimes they passed a dromedary yoked to its eternal round of a well, or a woman in a long loose black robe guiding a laden donkey.

'Sometimes the scenery here makes me think of Biblical pictures,' she commented.

'It's probably changed little since those times.'

Joel was entering Betancuria now, a town of flat-roofed white houses, with a square-towered church and small gardens dotted with dwarf palm trees. When they alighted in the town square, he pointed out the former governor's house and several other stylish houses with outside staircases running up to first floor balconies.

At a café they drank Canary wine, and ate little saucers of small fish morsels.

'I suppose they serve these little fish affairs to increase one's thirst,' Lucie observed.

'Undoubtedly,' he agreed. 'Good for trade.'

They strolled around some of the other streets, then resumed the journey. On a sloping hillside there were a few isolated fir-trees that apparently did not belong to a regular plantation. Joel had brought with him a spade and fork from Alberto's store and now he began to loosen the dry earth around the roots of the one Lucie had chosen for its symmetry. It was not a difficult task and she wrapped the wet cloth she had brought with her around the base and roots,

'These hands!' muttered Joel mournfully. 'Never again will they be fit to tinker with my teapots and entré dishes and trophies, not to say my filigree work.'

'Filigree? I didn't know you did anything so niggly.'

'Huh, I suppose you think you're the only one who can

make the dainty bits! I'm just the smith who bangs about with a ten-pound hammer.'

Lucie laughed. 'No. Even a ten-pound hammer has to be thumped in the right place.'

'Then don't think you've a monopoly of the small stuff.'

'Oh, I see. I've a rival now for jewellery. That's since I was successful with my sea-horses. Tell me, what are you making to compete with me? Seagulls? Butterflies?'

'I'm entitled to my secrets just the same as anyone else. If I won't tell Jessica, then I'm certainly not likely to reveal my cherished plans to you.'

'Have you finished the silver horse?' She could not stop the rash question escaping.

'That Arab steed intrigues you, doesn't it?' He was smiling and she was relieved. 'Suppose I say it's no business of yours?'

Lucie had never enjoyed such a day with this delicious lighthearted fooling, this absence of restraint. She forgot her own inhibitions, her fears of revealing too much of her own aspirations, and consequently behaved naturally like any other girl out for a day with a congenial man friend.

He took her to lunch at a wayside inn among the mountains where a meal was served that would not have disgraced a smart hotel – aubergines with a piquant sauce, a Canary speciality called *caldo de pescados*, made with a local fish and very tasty. There was goats' milk cheese and a delicious sweet made of almond nougat and toasted cornmeal.

'You've eaten many kinds of *turron* – this almond sweet,' explained Joel. 'This is a special island kind with the cornmeal, *gofio*.'

When they drove away from the inn, with the inn-keeper and his wife waving until the car was out of sight, Joel headed towards the coast.

'I do like the island people here,' murmured Lucie contentedly, leaning back in her seat. 'We were probably the only customers coming for a meal then and they put on that wonderful spread.'

'M'm. They're most hospitable and kind in the simplest way, which means they give you their best.'

'At home in England, we'd have been lucky to get bread and cheese, or perhaps tinned soup if we'd come to such an out-of-the-way place.'

Joel did not answer and she sensed that he needed to concentrate on driving down a winding, very rocky path to the sea edge where a beach several miles long stretched into the distance. It was quite deserted.

They alighted from the car and scrambled down to the shore. Some flat rocks made convenient perches and Joel began to smoke one of his favourite long thin cigars.

'Have you made any – sort of – long-term plans?' he asked suddenly.

Lucie had almost dozed off in the warm sunshine with the soporific rhythm of the waves lulling her ears. She blinked herself awake. 'Long-term? – well, no, not exactly.' She traced her initials in the sand at her feet. 'I haven't thought much about the future. I've been too busy with the orders and making new samples. Sooner or later, I suppose I shall have to think about it. I've enough money at the moment, but the good sales might not last. There's always something else to come along as a novelty.'

'But you could cope with market changes, I suppose?'

'I hope so, although I might have reservations about doing really trumpery stuff.'

He turned his head to smile at her. 'Well said. No lowering of good standards, eh?'

The way he looked at her made her heart jump sideways and all she could do was smile and avert her glance lest she threw herself bodily into his arms.

'What I had in mind – only vaguely, of course – was some kind of loose partnership.'

'Partnership?' She jerked her head quickly in his direction.

'Yes. It's struck me that we could probably work quite well together – even for a time, perhaps. A year or two ago I thought of starting a line in jewellery, but nobody happened along, as it were, so I didn't bother about it. But I've been considering the various aspects lately and if the idea appeals at all to you, we could possibly discuss the details. Not now. Think it over.'

Lucie sat up straight and drew in a deep breath. What was Joel offering her? The most exciting future – commercially – the chance to be linked with Joel Barron, the famous silver designer, to have her work accepted at top levels that she had never dreamed of.

'It sounds a marvellous idea,' she said softly, not daring to look at him. 'Would it mean staying here permanently?'

'H'm. Permanently is a long time. I doubt if I could promise that – even in this delectable island and sunny climate. Sooner or later changes will come – Hallam may even decide to take wing and settle for a while in another country. Painters are forced to search for their scenes. You and I are more fortunate. We have to mull over our ideas in our heads, but we can usually do that anywhere.'

'I don't mind where I work,' she said, suppressing a phrase that she longed to add – 'as long as it's where you are.'

'As I've told you, you can always use my workshop when you want to. There might be other advantages too, for me, that is – you could act as my representative, go to London and other places, arrange my displays and exhibitions. I can't always spare the time. Perhaps I don't want to spend it in planes and taxis and business lunches.' He broke off and laughed. 'That sounds as though I don't mind sending you to do such chores, but I don't mean it that way.'

'Do you think I'm capable of acting as your representative? It's an enormous responsibility.'

'I shouldn't mention the project if I didn't think you were responsible enough. Thornton is a good chap, but he has many irons in the fire. I need someone who knows something about the silver trade and who will act exclusively for me. Also, you'd be able to have your own work exhibited along with mine and that would bring you better results, probably, than merely getting Thornton to handle your stuff.'

Lucie in imagination saw the prospect widening out before her, a dazzling vista of success. 'Oh, Joel, I'm very excited about it.' Her radiant face was within a few inches of his own and suddenly he bent forward, held her chin and kissed her full on the lips.

'Right! It's a bargain – and sealed properly with a kiss.' He rose abruptly and pulled her to her feet. 'Time we moved on.'

In the car Lucie relaxed into a rosy dream. A business partnership was sometimes the first stage in a more enduring collaboration. She saw herself as Joel's accredited representative flying about the world and spreading his fame, working alongside him, sharing his confidence, even his anxieties. And perhaps – in due time, he might even realize that she was more to him than a commercial asset.

Suddenly the thought of Rosanna intruded upon her consciousness. If Joel really loved the Spanish girl and wanted to marry her, what then? Lucie could certainly not visualize Rosanna's toleration of a young partner. Then, as though a door were slowly opening and a crack of light showed, Lucie remembered the yacht party at which all the brothers had been present. Had they inspected Joel, as it were, and found him not quite suitable as a husband for their only sister?

Yet there would be little satisfaction if Joel's heart were broken by his rejection and Lucie caught him on the rebound.

By the time Lucie reached the Villa Sirena her mind was perplexed by these conflicting possibilities, but on the whole it had been a red-letter day and one to cherish, whatever the future might bring.

# CHAPTER EIGHT

DURING the last few days before Christmas, Lucie worked hard on gifts she was making for Georgina and Jessica and spent long hours alone in her room. Her absences were scarcely noticed, for Georgina, too, retired to her room and occupied herself with the sewing machine she had bought secondhand in Corvario.

Jessica and Daniel were left more or less to their own devices, but they were both well aware of the secretive goings-on in the household.

'Everyone skips away after lunch,' observed Jessica to her uncle. 'All doing secret things. Are you making hush-hush presents for Christmas?'

'Naturally. Why should I be left out?'

She gave him a mischievous grin, wound her two arms around one of his, and asked, 'You won't let me come in your workshop and have a teeny look?'

'Not likely. You wouldn't know what I was making anyway or for whom it was intended.'

'I could guess,' she declared.

'Then start guessing when you receive your own parcels on Christmas Day,' he retorted. 'Now let me go and get on with my work.' He unwound her twining arms and sent her off with a light spanking on her behind.

Many of the cooking preparations had been attended to by Georgina with Lucie's help, so that Señora Matana could spend Christmas Eve and Christmas Day with her family. Earlier, the Spanish woman had been astounded when Georgina made a traditional English Christmas pudding, luscious and black.

'When we serve it,' Georgina explained, 'we pour brandy over it and set it alight. Flambé.'

Georgina took care to include a small pudding for the Matana family, to be included with a basket of food for their Christmas.

'Do you think we should offend the family if we gave them presents?' Lucie asked Joel.

'No. I think they'd be most grateful, but not anything

obviously expensive, for they have a fierce pride, like all Spanish people.'

So on the day before Christmas Eve, Lucie, accompanied by Jessica and Daniel, took parcels to the house in Molino where the Matanas lived. A good black dress for the Señora, with two smart nylon overalls; a pretty floral cotton dress for the married daughter, toys for the two children and a supply of tobacco and cigars for the injured Señor Matana.

The family thanked Lucie with many flowery expressions in Spanish which she understood to be flattering, but which neither she nor Jessica could quite translate. The daughter also thanked the Villa Sirena for the extra food provided, a chicken, a large basket of vegetables and fruit, accompanied by sundry little packets and tins, as well as the Christmas pudding, together with a sizeable fish from Alberto.

'We have forgotten to give Alberto something nice,' Jessica reminded Lucie on the way home.

'No. Uncle Joel has a good present for him, a brand-new fishing net for his trade and a large supply of his favourite tobacco for his pleasure.'

Lucie and Georgina managed to take a short rest during the afternoon and stretched out on long chairs on the terrace.

'Isn't it odd to bask in the sun like this!' observed Georgina. 'At home, even if the day were fine, we'd be staying indoors near the fire.'

'Perhaps the Spanish are right and we're all wrong in planning meals with heavy puddings and substantial poultry dishes with all the trimmings,' returned Lucie. She turned towards Jessica, who was supervising Daniel's painting of a fine, lurid sunset coupled with bright green vegetation apparently sailing on the ocean.

'What sort of Christmases have you had in other years?' she asked.

'Some good, others – not good.' Jessica became thoughtful. 'When Mummy was here it was nice. We had lots of presents and a Christmas tree all sparkling. Then parties, and sometimes we – went to other people's houses.'

'I remember parties,' broke in Daniel. 'I won a violin –

I think it was a violin—'

'It was a banjo,' corrected Jessica.

'All right, a banjo. And another boy snatched it from me and banged it about until he broke it.' Daniel laughed with great enjoyment. 'I punched him on the nose and then he cried, so I was glad.'

Lucie and Georgina were very amused.

'Oh, everyone thinks Daniel is a softie,' explained Jessica, 'but he can stand up for himself.'

'Tell us about the other Christmas holidays,' encouraged Lucie.

'One time we were at our aunts'. I think they're great-aunts really They're very, very old.'

'They're nearly a hundred,' supplied Daniel.

'Perhaps not so much. But ninety, I expect,' continued Jessica.

Lucie and Georgina exchanged glances, knowing that in all probability the two old aunts were probably in their sixties, but seemed immensely ancient to two children.

'They were very kind to us and gave us lots to eat, but we weren't allowed to play games or make a noise. We had to hang up pillow-slips instead of stockings for our presents and—' Here Jessica broke off, suddenly rolling with laughter. 'It was very funny. After we'd gone to bed and pretended to be asleep, they came into our room and one aunt fell over a chair or something. It made ever such a noise and Daniel called out "Who goes there?" and I stuffed my head under the bedclothes because I was laughing. When they'd gone, we crept out of bed and put on the light and found out what all the presents were.'

'You put them back again, I hope, until next morning?' queried Georgina.

'Oh, yes. In the morning we thanked the aunts and told them we were very pleased with what Santa Claus had brought us. We didn't believe in Father Christmas coming down the chimney, of course, but we knew that they wanted us to say that.'

'Well, this year you'll get your presents off – well, in another way.' Lucie narrowly prevented herself from blurting out the fact of the Christmas tree already decorated with baubles and silver tinsel and now carefully hidden in Joel's workshop.

On Christmas morning Joel set up the tree in the little room with what Lucie called the 'twilight verandah', where there was plenty of space for certain parcels too large or heavy for the tree. While he and Georgina added the finishing touches, he locked the door, but Jessica and Daniel soon escaped from Lucie and tried to peer through the verandah windows.

'I shall blindfold you both,' Lucie warned them when she discovered where they were and shepherded them back to the kitchen so that she could keep a more vigilant eye on them. She was attending to the final details of the Christmas Day lunch and now insisted that the two children should stay with her until Joel called them.

'We're very anxious to see our presents,' Jessica complained.

Daniel hooted with glee. 'You tell me that we mustn't talk about presents, and now you're doing it!'

Jessica gave her brother a haughty glance. 'Christmas is different.'

Then Joel called out and the two children scampered off with Lucie following.

'First of all, we must dance round the tree,' suggested Georgina. 'That brings us all good luck for next year.'

Joel gave her a questioning glance. 'One of your old Midland customs?'

Georgina merely laughed and seized his hand. Lucie on the other side of Joel was too diffident to take his other hand, but the children had already joined with her and Georgina and begun a joyous merry-go-round, so Joel grasped Lucie's wrist, then twined his fingers in hers. Jessica was singing 'Here we go round the Christmas Tree', but after one verse and two circuits of the tree, stopped.

'That ought to be enough luck for a whole year,' she decided, screwing her head to glance up at the top branches of the tree. 'I can see my name up there on one of those parcels.'

The break-up of the circle had left Lucie's hand still firmly grasped within Joel's warm clasp and he seemed in no hurry to release it. Georgina was already busy with scissors snipping off the packages and handing them to the children. Only when she said, 'Here's one for you, Lucie,' did Lucie gently withdraw her hand, and as she did so, Joel gave her a smile that made her heart leap with fiery intensity and turned her knees to feathers.

The next half-hour created squeals of pleasure and a chaos of wrappings, murmured thanks between the adults and wild hugs from the children.

Daniel had been forced to follow a long red ribbon before he found the large cardboard box containing a small bicycle. He was all for mounting it straight away, but had to be content with ringing the bell and deafening everyone until he had seen all his other presents.

Lucie had made a necklace for Georgina of small agates connected by a fine silver chain. 'Look, Joel, isn't this a most exquisite piece of work?' the older woman commented.

Lucie waited for his verdict, although she realized that he would not go so far as to cloud Georgina's pleasure in the trinket by condemning the workmanship.

He took it into his hands and examined the necklace, the stone settings, the clasp. Then he looked at Lucie and although she expected to see his eyes expressing a different opinion from what he might say, she believed his praise to be sincere.

'Yes, it's a nice piece,' he said to Georgina. Then to Lucie, 'You must have spent a good deal of time on this, but it was worth it.'

She was warmed by his compliment and vowed that he would never catch her making a shoddy article.

Jessica was unwrapping a large box containing a complete Canary Island costume which Georgina had secretly made. This was specially for Ventura island, first a white lawn blouse with lace insertions and over it a sleeveless bodice of black velvet. Then the skirt in stripes of blue, pink and black, and over it an apron of white lawn to match the blouse. But the special features were the enormous straw hat with a tiny conical crown, a long cord looping from the edge of the brim, with black pompoms on the crown, and then immense draped, shawl-like oversleeves, caught at the wrist.

'Oh, I'm very happy!' breathed Jessica before flinging her arms around Georgina's neck in a stifling hug.

'I didn't make quite all of it,' Georgina admitted. 'There wasn't time, but I bought genuine Canary drapings for the sleeves, and of course the hat has to be bought from a shop in Ventura where the man makes them specially.'

'And shoes, too,' murmured Jessica, finding yet more accessories among the wrappings.

She was already wearing Lucie's gift, a bracelet of small linked plaques embossed with representations of small animals, fish and birds. From Joel she had received a wristwatch, sensibly waterproof in case she forgot to take it off while swimming.

But it was Joel's gifts to Lucie and Georgina that evoked their ecstatic sighs of excited gratitude. He had made Fabergé-style Easter eggs in silver for them. Lucie's was embossed with flowers in delicate coloured enamels, and when she pressed the spring, the top opened and a tiny bird inside trilled into song.

Georgina's was different and displayed a ring of dancers in Canary costume, such as they had seen at the Pueblo Canaria, the Canary village, in Las Palmas. When the top was opened, two little instruments played a tune by themselves.

'Oh, it's so beautiful!' exclaimed Georgina, turning her egg this way and that to catch the light. 'And to get all that mechanism inside for the tunes!'

Joel was laughing. 'I know that this is Christmas and not Easter, but I thought you could call them Christmas eggs.'

'I see now,' said Lucie quietly, 'that you're my most formidable rival, for these were never done with a ten-pound hammer.'

Hallam had left his presents before he went to England, boxes of chocolates for the children and expensive perfume for Lucie and Georgina. Welcome gifts at any time, thought Lucie, but without the individual touch that all the rest of the household had contrived.

She and Georgina had consulted each other over what to give Joel. 'I shall fall back on the traditional box of cigars. I've found out what kind he likes best.'

'I don't quite know what to give him,' Lucie had said hesitantly, not wanting to embarrass him in any way with an unwanted gift.

'You make articles for men as well as women,' suggested Georgina. 'Cufflinks – that sort of thing.'

Lucie guessed that Joel probably possessed all the cufflinks he needed, yet she made him a set of onyx and coral set in silver. He had provided her with lumps of onyx from the volcano in Tenerife. 'One day when you go up Mount Teide yourself, you can pick out your own pieces from the roadside. In the meantime, perhaps you can make use of these.'

She had indeed made use of them, for, cut and polished, the pieces had been converted into pendants, rings, parts of necklaces or bracelets and now cufflinks.

Now Lucie handed Joel the small box, but did not wait for his reaction or to receive his thanks. It was Jessica who said in the evening just before dinner, 'Look, Lucie. Uncle Joel's wearing your cufflinks. Aren't they pretty?'

Lucie's face reddened as Joel shot his cuffs to show her. 'I like them,' he said, and his approval caused her heart to lift. 'Thank you, Lucie.' He cupped her face in his hands and gave her a warm, swift kiss in full view of Jessica's observant gaze.

'That's the first time I've ever seen you kiss Lucie,' she remarked.

'Perhaps it won't be the last,' he retorted, as he released Lucie.

Lucie reflected cosily that this was the third kiss from Joel, not the first. They were so few that she could count them. Yet she did not dare to dream that his kisses meant anything more than a passing salutation; they demanded nothing and promised nothing.

The children had been allowed to stay up for dinner, although the traditional Christmas dinner had been eaten at lunchtime. There were games and larks until Jessica and Daniel were more than ready for bed. Some time later, Georgina and Lucie sat with Joel in the 'twilight verandah' room for a final drink and chat and after a while Lucie noticed that Georgina had disappeared.

Joel continued talking for a while, partly about the exhibition that was to be arranged in London early in the New Year.

'When Thornton comes after Christmas, I'll discuss details with him and let you know what's going to happen. There's one thing that will please him – or perhaps we should say will please Mrs. Thornton – and that's the welfare of the two children. You've made a wonderful difference to those two.'

She smiled. 'I've done very little. All they needed was somebody reasonably young to enter into their games and play, but old enough to restrain them if they walked into danger.'

'You've made them happy, Lucie, and that can't be dismissed lightly.'

'Perhaps they've contributed a little to my happiness, too,' she said quietly. At this late hour and in the soft dim lighting of the verandah she was moved towards self-revelation and actually began, 'When I first came here, I was trying to run away from reality and—'

Then there was a commotion of voices and laughter from somewhere in the hall and the next moment Rosanna stepped into the room.

'Oh, Joel! I simply could not resist coming here tonight, although I know it's frightfully late, and telling you – oh, Lucie, you're here, too.' Rosanna broke off as though she had only just noticed the other girl as one might catch sight of an intrusive fly, but the meaning was obvious.

Lucie had already risen. 'I was just going.' She collected the wineglasses and paused only long enough to ask, 'Shall I fetch you something? Wine? Or—?'

'No, thank you.' Rosanna turned immediately to Joel and Lucie heard the Spanish girl saying, 'Oh, such a marvellous present! Only *you* would think of something so exquisite as an Easter egg. When I unwrapped it, I—'

As Lucie reached the hall and shut the door of the room, a wave of purring satisfaction rose within her. So Joel had not given Rosanna the silver stallion after all. Perhaps it had not been finished in time. Or maybe he preferred to treat all his immediate circle of women acquaintances in the same way, Christmas eggs for all. Yet that did not diminish Lucie's pleasure in her own gift, for it was one she would treasure all her life, no matter if at some time in the future she would be forced to leave Ventura and Joel behind and seek a new direction for her life.

But how soon would it be before Rosanna discovered that she was not the unique possessor of one of Joel's Christmas eggs?

After Christmas was over, Georgina and Lucie helped with the preparations for the visit of Mr. and Mrs. Thornton, who were staying in Tenerife at present. One of the spare bedrooms was made already and Georgina declared on the day before they were due, 'I shall put a bouquet of flowers, a basket of fruit, mineral water and wine in their room. That in itself says "Welcome", doesn't it?'

'I agree. Wouldn't it be fun if English hotels did the same?' returned Lucie.

Georgina laughed delightedly. 'The wine part might be a toss-up between a bottle of whisky or a flagon of cider.'

'Or even elderberry wine!' added Lucie.

They were both in high spirits, and it occurred to Lucie some time later that there was a more lighthearted atmosphere in the house when Hallam was away. She brushed the thought aside as unworthy. After all, he was their host and the owner of the Villa Sirena.

Joel met the Thorntons at the airport and brought them to the villa. Jessica and Daniel had been warned to be on their best behaviour as they were to be inspected.

'Inspected? Why?' demanded Jessica.

Lucie explained that the visitors were friends of her father. 'They want to see that you're being well looked after while your father is away in Singapore.'

'Inspectors are in the police,' observed Daniel. 'Are they policemen?'

Lucie giggled. 'Not exactly. Just coming to look you over.'

'What would happen if they don't like us or don't believe that we like living here?' pursued Jessica.

Lucie was thoughtful for a moment. Then, her eyes twinkling, she said, 'I expect you'd be sent back to the aunts.'

'Oh, no, not that!' exclaimed Jessica, evidently regarding that possibility as a fate worse than death. The teasing blackmailing threat from Lucie worked miracles, for although Jessica and Daniel were by no means naughty or tiresome children, they were often boisterous and they enjoyed grubbing about on the beach and wearing old clothes much more than sitting sedately in the company of grown-ups.

Mrs. Thornton, a tall, heavily-built woman, was at first inclined to be both critical and sceptical. 'They certainly appear to be healthy,' she conceded. 'But as to their mental welfare—' she shook her head sadly.

'Their education is not being neglected,' Lucie assured her, and Georgina added weight to this assertion by producing exercise books showing the children's progress.

'M'm,' murmured Mrs. Thornton. 'Although I really think a good school would be much better, for Jessica, at any rate.'

'Daniel is still a little bit young to send away to school,' objected Georgina. 'And he's now learning to be more independent of his sister. A sudden break between the pair might not be good for either.'

Mrs. Thornton smiled frostily. 'Possibly, but then, Mrs. Frensham, you've had no children and don't quite understand the position. I've brought up a family of three.'

Georgina eyed Mrs. Thornton calmly. 'I'm afraid you're wrong to imagine that I've no experience of children. My daughter died when she was three. My son was killed in an accident. He was fifteen. A climbing accident in the school holidays.'

Mrs. Thornton momentarily lost her poise. 'I'm sorry, I didn't know.' It was evident, however, that she was suitably impressed.

Lucie was inwardly indignant. Poor Georgina! As though her losses had not been tragic enough, here was this self-satisfied woman blundering along in ignorance, without even bothering to make discreet inquiries.

During the remainder of the visit, Mrs. Thornton attempted a more gracious attitude. She admired the children's Christmas gifts, including those sent by their father from Singapore, a beautiful leather writing case for Jessica and a cunning set of Chinese boxes for Daniel.

'But you must also see the bracelet that Lucie made for me.' Jessica thrust the cherished article almost under Mrs. Thornton's nose. 'And later I'll put on my Canary costume that Georgie made for me and I'll show you one of the dances.'

Towards the end of the visit, Joel announced that everyone was invited to a party at Rosanna's villa. 'There's to be a barbecue on the beach, so that should be good fun.'

Lucie was not keen on the idea, but since the children were also invited, she had no excuse for staying at home.

It turned out to be a large party, with guests thronging in and out of many rooms and on to the several terraces at different levels. Lucie had not previously explored all the gardens at the del Reys' villa and now saw that the terraces had been cleverly contrived with half-round bays to shelter them from the wind and stone steps twisting in spiral form to the next level. She reflected that while it might be elegant for parties, it was hard work for the maids and menservants who had to clamber up and down with trays of drinks and food.

A number of benches and chairs had been placed down on the beach in the spot where the barbecue was to be held, and when it was dark Rosanna instructed everyone to come down.

Lucie took special care to guide the two children on the way down where the terraces ended and the rough rocky path to the beach began, but everyone managed to arrive in one piece. Lanterns had been placed in a circle around the barbecue itself and the scene was a vivid one to remember. Against the black mass of the cliffs the flickering shadows and dancing lights on people's faces, seen for an instant, then lost in the darkness; the red glow of the barbecue grill, the savoury smells of cooking; the laughter and wild shouts as someone burnt his fingers on a too hot portion of meat. It was all part of the texture of Lucie's long stay in the islands.

Suddenly Lucie found Joel at her elbow. 'I've done my stint at stoking the barbecue. Let someone else take over. Have you something to eat?'

She laughed. 'Too much! I'm putting on weight alarmingly in this climate. Soon I shall be looking at a bulge where my waistline used to be.'

'You're slim enough yet. No need to worry.'

She reflected that if her companion had been Hallam

instead of Joel, the former would immediately have flung his arm around her waist to verify that she still had one. Joel was not the easy-going flirtatious kind and she was glad of that. After a short while he said, 'We must run Jessica and Daniel to earth before they disappear. Come along.' He put an arm companionably about her shoulders to assist her over the rockier parts of the beach and she felt a warm glow penetrating her being. In the past she had been clumsy both in word and deed, but could it be possible that Joel preferred to advance very slowly towards love, changing from a subtle companionship to a more intense desire? With all her heart she hoped so and determined not to spoil this pleasant harmony by demanding more than he was prepared to give.

'When we find the children,' he said now close to her ear, 'we'll slip away and take them home. They'll be tired enough.'

Jessica and Daniel were sitting happily with the Thorntons and Georgina.

'Shall we take the infants off your hands?' asked Joel. 'Then you can join in whatever fun is going. Lucie and I will take them home.'

At first both Jessica and Daniel protested that they were still wide awake, but a warning glance from Lucie begged them not to make a scene in front of the Thorntons. They were both so tired, anyway, that they were glad to yield.

It took only a short time to see the children into bed.

'Are you and Uncle Joel going back to the barbecue?' asked Jessica.

Lucie had not thought about returning. 'Well, no. We shouldn't leave you in the house alone. I shall stay downstairs.'

'That's right,' murmured the child sleepily. 'Stay with Uncle Joel. He likes you. He likes you a lot.'

Lucie dared not reply to that appraisal. 'Good night, dear.' She kissed Jessica and went quickly from the room.

She guessed that Joel had probably returned to the beach and was surprised when he called, 'Out here, Lucie! Come and sit with me.'

He was on the long terrace that ran along the east and

south sides of the villa. Tables and chairs were left out there permanently and now she dropped into a chair beside him. From this point there was a view of the sea between a gap in the bushes and tonight it was silvered by the moon. The eucalyptus trees and palms sighed and rustled, occasionally a sleepy bird protested at some disturbance and in the distance laughter and shouts came from the beach below Rosanna's villa.

Lucie sat silent, unwilling to break the spell of this magic evening. Then Joel spoke. 'I've been discussing matters with Thornton and he's put various propositions into my mind.'

'Yes?' Obviously he expected her to listen or he would not have opened the subject.

'According to him, I'm wasting my substance by just tinkering about with a few designs, working entirely to please myself, when there's a fortune ready to be picked up.'

'The factory idea again?'

'Not quite. He thinks I could set up in a quiet village somewhere, with a kind of studio shop to sell some of my output, and a work-place not too far away with perhaps three or four reasonably qualified assistants. Thornton says he's inundated with orders for my work. What he's trying to stress is that I could have the best of both worlds, cater for the industrial design part, the cutlery, the tea services and coffee pots, cruets and so on and still display my more individual pieces in the shop.'

'And will you like living in an English village after a year or so in the Canaries?'

He paused before replying. 'That's what I'm not sure about. Thornton says I'm in danger of becoming a beachcomber type. Someone else with more business sense will come along and sweep the market and I'll be left with a dwindling clientèle that will eventually dry up altogether. Then I'll be pointed out as a once-prosperous silversmith before he neglected his affairs and went to pot.'

Lucie laughed. 'He paints a very gloomy picture of your future.'

'M'm, yes. He's very concerned about my future, but he doesn't quite understand all my problems. I'm concerned with my future, too, but whatever course you take, you usually involve other people in your future. Few of us could assert that we can live in a kind of one-man space capsule entirely isolated from the rest of humanity. Whatever we do is bound to affect others.'

'Of course. We can't live in a vacuum.' She was only punctuating his speeches, for her mind was intrigued by the general drift of his reasoning. Was he now abandoning the idea of the partnership he had tentatively offered her?

'How does the idea strike you?' he asked.

'Of your returning to England?' The thought was desolation itself if it meant the break-up of the tenuous relationship now existing between her and Joel. 'Well, I'm not qualified to give an opinion.'

'But I want your opinion. In England I should still want you to work with me as an associate. The fact is I'm reluctant to leave this island.'

In the space of a few seconds Lucie's spirits soared, then plummeted to the depths as he added that last sentence. This could mean only that he found it difficult to part from Rosanna.

'In your place I'd probably feel the same,' she said as calmly as she could. 'In fact, I'm really smitten myself with Ventura – and then perhaps taking the chance to explore the other islands now and again.'

'You don't feel you're drifting along in a backwater?'

'No. I could work here just as well as I could anywhere else.'

'I see.' His voice was quiet and she could not see his face in the shadow. 'Then you'd be against a return to England?'

'Oh, I didn't say that,' she said hastily. 'It's a question you have to decide.' She longed to add, 'Wherever you go, I'm willing to go with you', but she dared not let such revealing words escape from her lips.

He pushed back his chair with a harsh, grating sound and stood up. 'Time we turned in.'

'But the others? Georgina and Mr. and Mrs. Thornton? Should we wait up for them?'

'Not necessary. They can come in when they like. The doors won't be locked.'

She rose and walked towards the open french windows

of the sitting-room. As she stepped through, Joel said, 'Perhaps it isn't only the islands that hold one here by their fascination. Sometimes it can be a person who won't let go.'

She turned towards him. 'That's true.'

'You feel that, too?'

'Yes. In a way.' She understood now the strong hold that Rosanna exerted over him, but it was equally true that Lucie was chained by her own longing to the place where Joel happened to be.

There were sounds of voices and laughter as Georgina and the others came through the garden from the beach. Lucie went out again to meet them, listened to their remarks and comments about how much they had enjoyed the barbecue.

'I'm asleep on my feet,' said Mrs. Thornton. 'But it was a marvellous party.'

'Lucie!' Georgina drew the other slightly aside. 'You should have seen Rosanna's face when she was boasting about her Christmas egg from Joel and I told her that both you and I had received similar ones, but not of course identical. She thought she was the only one—' Georgina broke off to laugh at the memory.

'Then she knows that all three of us—' began Lucie.

'All three of us!' echoed Georgina. 'She imagined she was the only one to receive such a gift.'

Lucie turned quickly to see if Joel had heard Georgina's announcement, but he had gone, probably with the two Thorntons.

Much later in the night Lucie was still awake, trying to equate Joel's idea of returning to work in England with his admitted reluctance to leave Ventura – and Rosanna. Yet he had declared that he wanted Lucie to work with him – as his associate. Did he mean that he intended to marry Rosanna, take her to England and there set up a new business with Lucie as a working partner? If this were the case, then Joel was decidedly a man who wanted not only the best of both worlds but was determined to have his cake and eat it.

Lucie's pride rebelled at the idea of being an appendage to a famous silversmith if those were the terms that she was offered. She could stay here if she chose, find somewhere else to live and work as she pleased.

But the children? Tonight Joel had not mentioned them or any future plans for them. Was he assuming that Lucie and Georgina would remain here at Ventura to look after Jessica and Daniel when he and Rosanna were married and went elsewhere? It had always been clear to Lucie that Rosanna regarded the two children as a couple of drawbacks. Even Jessica knew that. Certainly Rosanna would never tolerate starting her married life – with any partner – by being hampered with two children not her own.

Lucie wrenched her thoughts away from Joel and his problems and composed herself for sleep, but the niggling idea recurred. She regretted that Georgina had disclosed the truth about the three Christmas eggs. Rosanna would not be amused at all.

# CHAPTER NINE

ALTHOUGH Joel disclosed nothing further of the plans he had in mind, there were several occasions when Lucie longed to ask him to clarify them in so far as she herself was concerned. He was extra busy and spent most of his time in his workshop preparing material for his forthcoming exhibition in London.

Once when she had timidly entered the workshop in search of a particular tool she required for her own work, he had been in one of his most unwelcoming moods.

'Anything you want?' he asked brusquely.

'Only a pair of small pliers.'

The silver stallion was on one end of the bench, apparently finished – a glorious piece with its lean, slender body, mane and tail flying, three legs extended in flight with only one hind hoof to anchor it to the stand.

'Is it finished?' She indicated the beautiful creature.

'Yes, finished.' He picked up a black polishing cloth and flung it over the horse. Then he snatched up a pair of pliers and thrust the tool into her hands. 'I'm busy, Lucie, so if you wouldn't mind—'

She scuttled out of the workshop as fast as possible, puzzled as to his unfriendly attitude. It seemed to her that all the delicate fabric of a warm friendliness built up so gradually during these last few weeks had been ripped to fragments. Was it something she had done? Some careless words that had offended him? She searched her memory for some clue, but could find none. Or was it her reference to the silver horse?

Hallam came back from England full of energy and enthusiasm. He had arranged his spring exhibitions, enjoyed himself at no end of parties and junketings and seemed eager for work.

'I must paint Jessica in her Canary costume,' he promised, thereby delighting the child.

Either Lucie or Georgina usually helped Jessica into her costume for each of the sittings, and one morning when Lucie was engaged in this task of adjusting the various items of the elaborate dress, Lucie's foot caught in a piece of curtain often used for draped backgrounds. Several canvases stacked along the wall fell down in a heap and Lucie bent to pick them up. One or two landscapes, an abstract and a couple of nudes. Then she realized with a shock that one of the nudes was evidently Bernarda, the girl who had kept house for the two men before Lucie came.

She pushed the canvas between two others so that Jessica would not see it, for she would be sure to recognize Bernarda. For the rest of the day Lucie worried over the situation. Had Bernarda posed for Hallam in the nude or only for a head and shoulders portrait as Lucie had sat for hers? In art circles there were always rumours and gossip that it was easy enough to paint a portrait and then attach it to a different figure. If Bernarda had discovered what had happened was this perhaps one of the reasons why she had left so suddenly? Or had she been scared away by Hallam's insistence on her posing without her clothes?

When she had an opportunity Lucie asked Señora Matana if she had known Bernarda.

'*Si, si, señorita.*' The older woman glanced up from her task of preparing vegetables. Then she shook her head. 'Not good girl.'

'No?'

'No. She like men. Gone to Las Palmas now.' Señora Matana smiled. 'Plenty of men there.'

So perhaps Bernarda had been more than willing to fall in with Hallam's wishes.

The next time Lucie accompanied Jessica to the studio, she took the chance of seeing if there were any more dubious evidence of composite portraits. Most of all, she wanted to see her own, but each time she had asked Hallam to show it to her, he had fobbed her off with the excuse that he had some finishing touches to put to it. 'You shall see it when it really is complete.'

With that she had to be content, for she could hardly ransack his studio with Hallam looking on and finding amusement in her discomfiture.

Joel had decided a date on which he would fly to England, taking his display collection with him. The silver stallion had been packed along with the set of chessmen in silver and onyx, the Regency coffee jugs, the newly-designed sets of cutlery. Some of the heavier items like salvers and entrée dishes, cups and trophies had already been dispatched.

Yet still, only a couple of days before his departure, Joel had not spoken again to Lucie of his ideas about partnership or working with him either in England or here in Ventura. She was at a loss to understand his attitude and could decide only to be patient and let the initiative come from him. Once or twice she thought of tackling him boldly, but the right opportunities never seemed to present themselves.

Then Rosanna called in the late afternoon. 'I hear Joel is going to England,' she said to Lucie. 'I must see him before he goes. Is he in the place where he works?'

'I think so.' Lucie accompanied the other girl to the door of the workshop, but left immediately Joel opened the door and Rosanna stepped inside. No doubt they could both make their tender farewells in private, thought Lucie bitterly.

Just before dinner Georgina said casually, 'Hallam and Joel won't be with us. Hallam said he'd be out for the evening and Joel is finishing off something special, but he wants to see you down on the boat after dinner.'

'Who? Joel?'

'Yes. He has something to discuss with you.'

Lucie maintained enough calm to eat her meal, but her spirits were exhilarated. At this last minute almost he was going to take her into his confidence. She easily forgave him all those frustrating delays and uncertainties. To-night her future would be resolved.

When she caught Georgina's glance she smiled and looked away. Not even to Georgina could she disclose her hopes or fears.

'Is it the idea to go out on the boat for a midnight cruise?' teased Georgina, smiling.

'Perhaps. It's moonlight, ideal for night sailing,' Lucie returned happily.

As the table was cleared, Georgina said, 'I'm not sure that I like the idea of your walking along to the harbour in the dark.'

'Nonsense!' exclaimed Lucie. 'Señora Matana does that jaunt every night of her life.'

'All right, then you can both go together. I'll wash up and do all the rest.'

Lucie had to curb her impatience while the older woman pottered about the kitchen tidying up, but at last the two set off along the road by the shore. At the harbour, Lucie said, 'I can see where the boat is. There are lights on board.'

She crossed the short gangplank and jumped lightly to the deck. The saloon door was closed, but she slid it open and went inside. Joel was bending down and had his back towards her. Then he turned and straightened and she saw with a feeling near to horror that it was Hallam, not Joel.

In a couple of strides he had put himself between her and the saloon door. 'Lucie darling! What brings you down here at this time of night?'

'A mistake,' she stammered. 'I thought – it was Joel – I came—'

'Of course you came when Joel called to you,' he said silkily.

'Why are you here?' she demanded.

He laughed. 'Perhaps I've been hoodwinked, too. I was expecting to meet Rosanna here.'

'On the boat? That's a lie! She'd never come here at night.'

'No? You don't know Rosanna. In any case, I think she might possibly have intended to come here to bid me a touching farewell.'

'Why? You're not going away.'

Hallam laughed. 'No, but I've heard rumours that she intends to marry a wealthy and noble Spaniard. Both Joel and I are in the rejected basket. Throw-outs, that's what we are.'

Lucie relaxed for a moment. Up till now she had been poised for a headlong flight, but if what Hallam now said was true, Lucie imagined she could account for Joel's surliness lately.

'So you see, my darling Lucie, there's a chance for you now – with Joel, I mean. You could quite easily catch him on the rebound, as they say.'

'I've no wish to *catch* him like that,' she flung at him. She turned towards the sliding door of the saloon. 'I'll leave you to wait for Rosanna – if she comes.'

'Not so fast!' He pulled her from the door and into his arms in one swift movement. 'As you say, perhaps Rosanna won't come, and in that case I'm perfectly willing to dally a little time with you.'

'No! Not with me!' She was fighting to keep cool and not lose her head. 'In any case, you'd better go now – and I said now! – or Joel will be coming along any minute.'

'Perhaps he won't turn up any more than Rosanna has,' taunted Hallam. 'It could be that he doesn't even know you're here waiting for him, waiting for his goodnight kiss.'

She managed to get one hand free and dealt him a stinging blow on the cheek.

'Vixen!' he shouted, putting up his hand to his reddened cheek.

In that instant of his relaxation, Lucie darted to the door, but the catch was firmly in the slot and it was too stiff for her to pull quickly.

Hallam seized her again and held her imprisoned. 'So it's violence now. I didn't really believe you could be so spiteful. I see I shall have to chastise you.'

'Hallam! Let me go! If you don't I shall shout and someone in the harbour will hear me.'

'Shout away! No one will take the slightest notice. If anyone hears, they'll believe it's just the rowdy English having a party.'

She closed her eyes in sheer misery. If Joel were really coming, he would be here any moment. How could she possibly allow him to find her in this compromising situation with Hallam? If the message had been false and Joel knew nothing of it, then somehow she must escape from the boat and Hallam's clutches. If only she could get out of the saloon!

'It's always been Joel, hasn't it?' Hallam was saying. 'Ever since you came, you set your sights on him.'

'Why should that have mattered to you?' she demanded.

'Why? Because in the first place you destroyed the harmony between me and Joel. You came between us.'

'I didn't! Any harmony that ever existed you destroyed yourself.'

'And secondly, I'm mad about you, Lucie. Just as mad as I once was about Rosanna. All the time I was in England I kept seeing your serious little face – no other girl meant anything to me.'

'Spare me your pretty speeches!' She almost hissed the words at him as she tried to wriggle free. 'You've made them too often to all those other girls. I'm not impressed.'

'Then perhaps this will impress you.' His lips were on hers, crushing her mouth, as he pushed her down on one of the upholstered bunks on the side of the cabin. She was nearly suffocated in his grasp, and even when the sound of the sliding door being wrenched open impinged on her ears, she was still powerless to move.

Hallam drew away from her and now she saw Joel standing there, his face taut, his eyes dark and hostile.

'So she was expecting you after all!' said Hallam. 'Sorry, chum, I got here first.'

Lucie raised herself from the bunk and struggled to her feet, only too aware of her dishevelled state.

'Joel!' she began. 'Please – please listen—'

The contempt in his gaze shrivelled her. 'Sorry I intruded. I didn't realize the situation, but don't let me stop your – pleasure.'

That last word was like a whiplash to Lucie. She tried to rush towards Joel, but Hallam's arm caught her and held her.

'The fact is I'm only a poor substitute,' Hallam said. 'Lucie's heart really belongs to another man – only unfortunately he's married already.'

Momentarily she forgot Joel, for she was appalled at this crude disclosure.

'Hallam! How – could you! You might have spared—'

The sliding door was closing with a harsh, grating sound and Joel had gone.

Hallam smiled. 'Well, that's settled. Now we can have a bit of peace – unless, of course, Rosanna takes it into her head to interrupt us.'

But for Lucie there was no time to lose. With a strength far beyond her own capacity, she wrenched open the door and was out on the deck. As she tore across the gangplank she nearly overbalanced and fell, but regained her balance and stepped ashore. Her one thought was to find Joel, but which way had he gone? She looked about the small square facing the harbour, but there was only one table outside the café and neither of the two men sitting there was Joel. He had probably gone back to the Villa Sirena, and now she began to run along the narrow road by the shore.

'Joel!' she called out into the night. 'Joel!' There was no moon now, for black clouds darkened the sky. Sobbing and gasping for breath, she ran along the rough path. Twice she fell over boulders, picked herself up and ran on again.

At last she saw the lights of the villa and hurried these last few steps, praying that Joel would be there and would listen to her explanations.

She slowed her pace through the garden, trying to see if anyone were on the terrace, for she knew that she presented a horrifying spectacle. There was no one there.

Lucie cautiously approached the main door which was open, and crept quietly up the stairs. She had almost reached the safety of her own room when Georgina came out of Jessica's room.

'Lucie! What's happened?'

Lucie fled into her bedroom with Georgina following. 'I can't tell you!' Lucie flung herself on the bed and sobbed heartbreakingly.

Georgina sat beside her. 'Tell me, dear. Was it Joel?'

Lucie shook her head and sobbed afresh.

'But your dress! The sleeve is all torn and all the front is dusty and soiled. Let me help you. Spill it out, please!' Georgina's voice was so sympathetic that Lucie's tears flooded down her cheeks.

'In a moment,' she mumbled, and Georgina wisely let the girl cry.

Lucie sighed deeply and sat up, noticing for the first time the torn sleeve where Hallam had wrenched it apart.

'Hallam was there – not Joel,' she said flatly. 'Who

gave you that message, Georgina?'

'Hallam himself.'

'It was a frightful trick,' said Lucie in a low, flat voice. 'It might not have been so bad if he hadn't also told Joel to come to the boat and find us there.'

'But, Lucie dear, *I* passed it on to Joel.' Georgina closed her eyes in anguish. 'Oh, what have I done?'

Lucie looked up in surprise. 'What do you mean?'

'Joel came in after dinner and asked if I could fix him a snack. As you know, Señora Matana went along with you earlier, so I made Joel a cold meal and took it out to him on the terrace. When he finished eating, he showed no signs of going and I reminded him that you'd gone down to the boat.'

Lucie bowed her head in dismay. 'What then?'

'Naturally, I thought he'd forgotten. He seemed surprised. I told him that Hallam had given me his message that Joel wanted to see you down on the boat.'

'Of all the treachery!' Lucie whispered. 'Using you, Georgina, to set a trap for me. It's the lowest thing I've ever heard. No, I'm sorry. He's your cousin.'

Georgina had risen, her face flushed and her eyes blazing. 'Don't excuse him because we're related. When I see him, I shall tell him what I think of him.' After a while she sat by Lucie, holding the girl in her arms. 'What happened? Did Hallam make love to you?'

'He was brutal, and timed his embraces so well that he'd be sure that Joel would come in. If I could have run away first, I'd have done so.'

'Oh, if only I hadn't told Joel!' whispered Georgina. 'I would never have done anything to harm you two. I was hoping that you'd come together. Joel would make a good husband and you're the kind of wife he needs.'

'Don't blame yourself, Georgie dear.' It was Lucie's turn to try to comfort the other woman. 'How could you know? You gave Hallam's message to me in good faith and also to Joel. You couldn't know that Hallam would be there on the boat.'

Lucie stood up, surveyed her torn dress and took it off. 'Joel looked at me with such contempt. I shall never forget his face and his eyes.'

'Perhaps it's just as well that he's going to England the

day after tomorrow. We all need a breathing space to cool down, but not before I've had my say to Hallam.'

'Has Joel come home?' Lucie asked. 'Is he in the house?'

'I haven't seen or heard him,' replied Georgina. 'Now, let me bring you a drink and you can go straight to bed and try to forget some of tonight's upset. Nothing ever seems quite so bad in the morning.'

Lucie hoped that might be true. Surely she had touched the depths of degradation, and one could not linger there for ever.

Yet when she awoke next morning and the memory of the night before flooded over her, she was not prepared to receive an even more shattering blow.

Georgina brought Lucie's breakfast of coffee and rolls. 'I thought I'd save Señora Matana the trouble,' she explained in answer to Lucie's querying glance.

'There's also a letter for you,' she continued quietly. 'Joel left very early this morning for Las Palmas.'

'I see. He's gone a day earlier than he intended,' said Lucie in a flat voice. In her mind she added *He couldn't bear to be in the same house with me. Not even for one more day.*

Georgina went unobtrusively from the room and Lucie turned the enevelope over and over. It was addressed with the one word 'Lucie'. With trembling fingers she opened it and pulled out the two sheets.

'Dear Lucie [it began],

This is not an easy letter to write. I think I've known for quite a while that it was Hallam who meant so much to you, although I hoped perhaps for your sake more than mine that you would recognize that his affections are not always intended to be durable.

I'm sorry you couldn't have been more honest with me. I tried more than once to discover your real feelings when I spoke of my tentative plans for returning to England. When we talked – that night after the barbecue – I thought I'd made it plain that you were the girl who was making me reluctant to leave the islands and while you apparently wanted to stay here, I couldn't bring myself to try to persuade you to return to England with me.

But when you told me so clearly that Hallam was the anchor that tied you here, I knew then that the sooner I went back alone, the better.

Why didn't you tell me the truth? Enticing me down to the boat last night to watch a blatant exhibition of your intentions was quite unnecessary.

I had the impression that you and I would make good partners – in every sense – for I wanted to marry you, but naturally you have a right to choose your own way of life. Let me then wish you luck and happiness, whether your future lies with Hallam or not.

I see now that idling along in the Fortunate Isles was probably a mistake for me. One becomes attached to the wrong people.

I shall have to come back later for a day or so to pack up the rest of my goods, but after that you can completely forget me. I shall never trouble you again.

JOEL.'

Lucie stood by the window, the letter crumpled in her hands. Dry-eyed, she stared out but saw nothing of the turquoise sea, the headland in the distance or the rooftops of the houses in the village. She was hearing Joel's voice again when he had talked of his ideas for the future and then '... sometimes it can be a person who won't let go.' and again ... 'want you to work with me as an associate.'

Gradually a fierce rage welled up in her. Why couldn't he have been more honest, too? He had accused her of a lack of plain speaking. Yet he had expected her to guess the answers to his riddles. She stamped about the room, storming inwardly with fury. Wasn't that just like a man! Afraid of committing himself, he had cloaked his words with vague half-meanings.

As she dressed now she became calmer. The full realization of the happiness that might have been hers and had now vanished out of reach began to seep into her mind. To have been Joel's wife as well as his modest jewellery assistant – oh, that would have been very heaven. The cruellest part was that the door to paradise had been briefly opened for an instant, then slammed shut again in her face.

Yet she did not wholly blame Hallam for the disaster. She scourged herself for the naïve, ingenuous fool who had played into Hallam's hands. It had been mean to use Georgina as a messenger, but Lucie ought to have been more on her guard where Hallam was concerned; she could have checked with Joel and last night's spectacle would never have happened. Yet would Joel still have gone to England without making her aware of his real intentions?

She smoothed out the crumpled sheets of his letter. There was no mention of love. He wanted a partner and he was prepared to marry the girl who had the right qualifications in the business sense.

Lucie took out the Christmas egg he had given her. How many other girls at various times had received these lovely replicas with his monogram, the letters J.B. entwined in a scripted scroll? Farewell gifts? She realized how little she knew of his background. Mrs. Thornton had hinted that Joel had broken a few hearts in his time and that there was little to choose between him and his brother Howard, the children's father.

'I don't doubt he's amusing himself out in Singapore or wherever he's gone now with a pretty little Chinese girl or whatever colour takes his fancy,' she had said to Lucie.

But Mrs. Thornton was completely prejudiced against the Barron brothers, so Lucie forced herself to dismiss such observations.

Now she wrapped up the Christmas egg and put it away in a drawer. When eventually she returned to England she would keep it and look at it sometimes to remind her of a period in her life when a trusting eagerness had led only to broken hopes.

'Hallam says that it was Rosanna who gave him that message,' Georgina said to Lucie later in the day. 'She came out of Joel's workshop and met Hallam in the garden – so he says.'

Lucie looked sharply at Georgina. Was that the hint of a doubt in Georgina's opinion? After all, she knew Hallam over a longer period than anyone else here in

Ventura.

'I see,' Lucie said now. 'Then why did he go down to the boat if he knew that Joel would be meeting me there?'

Georgina frowned. 'I asked him that question. He said he misunderstood and thought that Rosanna would be there to see him.'

'That's what he told me – that he was expecting Rosanna. But I didn't believe it then and I'm sure it's not the truth now.' She sighed. 'But, anyway, let's forget the whole thing. There's no sense in having an inquest now. Joel's gone and I shall go, too, as soon as I can.'

Georgina's face became distressed. 'But the children? Jessica and Daniel will be heartbroken.'

'Children soon forget their heartbreaks. With grown-ups it takes a little longer.' Lucie whirled around towards the other woman. 'Surely, Georgie, you must see that I can't stay here in this house a moment longer than necessary!'

'No, I don't see that at all!' snapped Georgina in a more authoritative voice than Lucie had ever heard from her. 'Joel engaged you to be a companion to those two. He gave you the opportunity to do your own work and helped you in every way to make successful sales. Now because of an unfortunate scene you want to run away like a whipped dog.'

'Perhaps I feel like a whipped dog,' retorted Lucie.

'Stay here until you've finished both your tasks. In any case, you have orders to fulfil and deliver to all those shops in Las Palmas and elsewhere.'

'I could soon catch up with those and finish the work,' declared Lucie. 'As to the children, you're here now. They love you and they'll be quite happy with you.'

'That's something you must settle with Joel when he comes back from England.'

'I couldn't face him!' cried Lucie in anguish. 'How could I look at him after the way he looked at me – on the boat – struggling to free myself from Hallam's arms?'

Georgina took both of Lucie's hands. 'Lucie dear, you must learn to face catastrophe. You have to stare at it and never admit defeat. How do you think I coped when I lost both my children – and then my husband?'

'Yes, you know what it is to suffer,' murmured Lucie humbly.

'Joel isn't so completely lost to you as if he had died. There's always the chance that he'll come back.'

Lucie managed the ghost of a smile. 'He'll come back here to this villa, but not to me in the way you mean.'

'You can't be sure of that. If he really loves you – and I think he does – then his love is a poor thing if it can be destroyed by a moment's trickery that landed you in the arms of the wrong man.'

Lucie was silent for a few moments. 'Thank you, Georgie. You're always a help, and I'm probably abominably selfish thinking only of myself. Jessica and Daniel do count quite a lot with me. But I shall have to leave later on.'

## CHAPTER TEN

JESSICA's portrait in her Canary costume was nearly finished and Hallam said he needed only one more sitting. Lucie had avoided him as much as possible in the days immediately following that visit to the boat. Hallam himself was rather subdued and rarely came in for meals.

On the morning when Jessica was to pose for her last sitting, Lucie tried to find her own portrait, but there was little time to rummage, for Hallam came into the studio.

'Looking for something?' he inquired amiably.

'No. All right, yes – my portrait.'

'Be patient. You shall see it in due time. Now you can safely leave me alone with Jessica.'

In her over-sensitive state at present, even that small gibe was not lost on Lucie, but she refused to reply.

Jessica was giggling. 'I've seen my picture,' she boasted. 'Uncle Hallam hasn't done my feet. They're just blobs.'

'And how did you manage to see that?' he queried.

'I peeped under the cloth when you weren't looking.'

He made a playful swipe at her. 'If you're not careful, I shall give you only blobs for legs and blobs for arms—'

'And blobs for face. No, then it wouldn't be a portrait.' Jessica laughed with gleeful relish.

'Now, quiet, please. Stand still and don't giggle,' he admonished.

As Lucie left the studio and went downstairs she reflected on some of Hallam's better qualities. The two children adored him, he played games with them, helping Daniel with the construction outfit which the boy had been given among his Christmas presents. Lucie had watched the pair one day building a graceful single-span bridge, Hallam making suggestions and Daniel placing the girders in position. She had never heard Hallam speak crossly to either Jessica or Daniel. Was it only grown-up girls like Lucie herself who brought out the worst in him?

A day or so later he announced that a private viewing

would take place in his studio at five o'clock sharp.

'This is a great occasion,' he told Jessica especially. 'So mind you bring your best manners with you.'

Lucie was slightly reluctant to accompany the others as they trooped upstairs to the studio at five o'clock, but she desperately wanted to know the truth about her own portrait.

Hallam had placed a row of chairs across the studio for his visitors, including Señora Matana and Alberto, who had been called in from his gardening tasks.

Hallam had fixed a skeleton screen with struts at the back and a ledge in front to hold the lower edge of each canvas.

'Now, Number One in the catalogue,' he began in his best showman manner. He put up a portrait of Jessica, head and shoulders, slightly untidily dressed but catching all the childish merriment of her expression.

'Where's the catty-dog?' Daniel wanted to know.

Hallam frowned at the laughter from the others and picked up a long mahl-stick. 'Any more giggling out of you lot and I shall shut up shop. And I'm the catalogue, Daniel.'

'Catty-dog. Catty-dog,' murmured the boy under his breath. But the next picture silenced him, for it was of himself. A rather solemn-faced fair little boy peered from the canvas.

Then came Señora Matana wearing her best black dress, followed by Georgina.

'I didn't know you'd sat for Hallam,' remarked Lucie.

'It was probably a case of any handy face being useful,' answered Georgina with a smile.

Now it was Hallam's turn to guffaw. 'Ha! That puts someone I know in her place!'

Lucie flushed slightly, but let the taunt pass. There were portraits of first Joel, then Alberto, and when she gazed at Joel's semi-profile showing his strong jawline, she was glad not to see his eyes.

The picture of Jessica in her Canary costume was next to be displayed and both Georgina and Lucie exclaimed with admiration.

'Oh, it's lovely!' was Georgina's verdict. Hallam had

posed the girl in her striking costume in an attitude as though she were about to start dancing. Under the enormous Mexican-type straw hat, Jessica's delicate features and dark hair were diminished but enhanced by a lively expression.

'Well, that's the lot!' declared Hallam, looking at Lucie as though daring her to challenge him. 'Oh, no, I forgot – one more.'

Lucie stared at the portrait of herself with incredulity. Could that vision be her ordinary little self? Hallam had told her on several occasions that she was anything but beautiful, yet here was this ravishing girl masquerading in paint.

'Well?' Hallam queried. 'No comment?'

'It flatters me very much,' she said in a low tone.

'Oh, no, indeed,' cut in Georgina. 'It's a very true likeness. It's *you*.'

'When are you going to paint me again, Uncle Hallam?' Jessica broke the awkward little silence which had fallen.

'Don't be greedy! Do you think I've nothing better to do than waste my colours and canvases on a pert little miss like you?' Hallam ruffled Jessica's hair. 'Off you go.'

It happened that Lucie was last to leave the studio, and Hallam queried, 'Satisfied?'

'It's a splendid portrait,' she answered smoothly.

'You thought I'd painted a nude body on your head, didn't you?'

She hesitated, then said boldly, 'I'm glad you didn't.'

'I'm sorry about – the other night.'

'Let's both forget it,' she said, and fled across the wide landing to the shelter of her own room, where she continued her work on silver charms to hang on bracelets.

A few days later Jessica brought an English newspaper to Lucie in the garden. 'There's something about Uncle Joel here,' she announced.

Lucie took the paper, but the words blurred before her eyes.

'What does it say?' Jessica's impatient tone recalled her. 'I could read most of it, but there's a bit there—'

'I'll read it to you. It says that Uncle Joel has won the

Prix Cellini for his silver horse. You remember he showed it to you one day. Also – "Mr. Joel Barron took other awards for a set of chessmen, as well as a new design in coffee service. He has received several offers to purchase his silver exhibits and says he will consider them, except for the Silver Stallion, which is not for sale. He may decide later to present it to one of the museums, but in the meantime all his collection will go on tour to various galleries." There's a bit more,' added Lucie, 'about the notable people who were present at the dinner where Joel was given his Prix Cellini.'

Jessica frowned. 'What's a preacher-leen – whatever it was you said?'

Lucie laughed. 'Not a preacher. Look. Prix – that means prize, as you know – and Cellini. Benvenuto Cellini was the great Italian artist who lived in medieval times. He worked in gold and silver and was also a sculptor. So this prize named after him is the highest award that a silversmith – like Uncle Joel – can win.'

'Oh, that's nice. Does he get money for his prize?'

Lucie shook her head. 'No, dear, only the honour and a medallion of Cellini's head.'

When Jessica had taken the newspaper away to show it to Georgina. Lucie remained thoughtful. How would the results of this exhibition now affect Joel's plans? Yet those plans were surely of little interest to her, since she would never be able to share in them.

Lucie was working in her bedroom at pendants and necklaces when Georgina came in. 'I hope I'm not interrupting, but what would you think of an idea I have to go off on the spree to Las Palmas and perhaps Tenerife – you and I and the two children? We could do the same as on our previous trip, stay at hotels a few days here and there. You could take your orders and deliver them to various places. We might also hire a car, self-drive, then we could go about just where we like.'

Lucie looked up at the other woman. 'I think it's an excellent notion. We could all do with a change of scene.' She knew that Georgina's suggestion sprang from a generous, sympathetic heart. For the present the Villa Sirena held too many associations with Joel for Lucie. Every time she went into his workshop she was aware of his presence there. Here she had watched him using the heat-gun to keep a piece of silver warm and malleable; his engraving designs were thumb-tacked on the wall; on this bench had stood the beautiful silver stallion of which she had been allowed only occasional glimpses during its making.

Although his behaviour was at present faultless, Hallam's presence in the house was at times disquieting. He owned the villa and she recognized that it was she who must eventually remove herself if she was to find peace.

So she welcomed Georgina's idea and worked feverishly during the next few days at her jewellery orders while Georgina telephoned or went to Corvario making arrangements for flights to Las Palmas and hotel accommodation.

Jessica and Daniel were excited at this unexpected treat.

'Poor Uncle Hallam!' murmured Jessica. 'He's going to be left here all alone.'

'He'll have Señora Matana to look after him,' pointed out Georgina.

'M'm.' The girl wrinkled her nose. 'But he'll miss us.'

'It might be just what the doctor ordered,' put in Hallam, who had just come up to join the others. 'A couple of weeks without you two noise-boxes around might work wonders for my shattered nerves.'

After a pause Jessica said mischievously, 'You'll have to win a prize when you go to England again. Uncle Joel won a prize for his silver things.'

Hallam laughed. 'I can't compete with Joel, my pretty Jessica. He's the man who'll always win the prizes, and not only for his silver things, as you clumsily put it. I'm the chap who believes he's up in the top ten and suddenly the prize is snatched away by someone else.'

He glanced at Lucie as he said the last words, but she turned her face away. She was not to be drawn into conversations that might possibly lead on to dangerous ground.

The holiday that Georgina had planned in the other islands was an unqualified success and Lucie yielded to complete enjoyment. This time there was no visit to the home of the del Reys in Las Palmas or an evening on the yacht with Rosanna doing her best to give Lucie an inferiority complex. Georgina was a competent driver and always planned journeys well within the scope of the two children, so that they did not get bored or restless.

All over the interior of the island of Gran Canaria the almond trees were in bloom, clothing the valley slopes with a dazzling veil of pinkish-white so that the contours between the mountains appeared to be covered in mist.

On different days Georgina studied her maps and routes and chose various ways of exploring all the island; along the east coast route through the tomato lands down to the new resort of Maspalomas, or another day through the central mountains of Tejeda where the twisting roads wound about the slopes of old volcano craters; or along the north coast through interesting little towns set in orchards of plum and cherry and apricots.

In Las Palmas the streets and small gardens were ablaze with the mauve glory of the jacaranda trees and the sharp stabbing red of the African tulip trees, and everywhere tamarisks were in bloom along with red poinsettias, the national flower of Canary.

The party spent lazy days on the beaches in between the sightseeing tours and Daniel had at last really learned to swim, both breast-stroke as well as back-stroke. Most of all he loved just floating, which Jessica scornfully called 'Sheer laziness!'

Tenerife was an island of delight to Georgina, as well as Lucie, for the latter had not had much chance to explore until now.

As soon as she had delivered her various orders, she and Georgina took the children down to the massive harbours of Santa Cruz to watch two large liners berthed there, along with dozens of other ships.

Then there were the Dragon trees to see, one in La Laguna and the other in Icod.

'Over a thousand years old,' Georgina told the two children, at Icod, as they stared at the gnarled, twisted trunks and cactus-like leaves.

'I wouldn't like to try to climb that one!' declared Daniel.

'No, you'd soon be lost in those branches,' agreed

Georgina.

When the party went up the snow-tipped volcano Teide in the centre of the island, Lucie remembered that it was possible to collect pieces of onyx from the mountainsides and even from the road edge, and at convenient stopping points she and Georgina gathered some well coloured lumps showing the exquisite blues and purples typical of rough onyx. Only for a few moments did Lucie allow her mind to dwell on the cufflinks she had given Joel or his remark earlier that when she visited Teide she could collect her own samples.

In Santa Cruz one day they all lunched at the luxury Hotel Mencey which had once been the Governor's residence and still retained the aura of dignified splendour in its panelled interiors, spacious grounds and its little secret courtyard garden where unseen fountains splashed and birds quarrelled noisily in the creepers.

Home again, Lucie felt all the better for the diversion, but was unprepared to find that Hallam had left the day before for England.

'Did you know?' she asked Georgina.

'More or less. Not exactly the day, but I knew his intention. He had his exhibitions to attend to – and – er – perhaps he wasn't all that anxious to be here when Joel returns.'

'And when is Joel returning?' asked Lucie smoothly.

'I don't think he's decided that yet. It might be several weeks ahead.'

Lucie did not reply, but she was now determined to leave as soon as she could and certainly before Joel came back.

'It seems funny without Uncle Joel *and* Uncle Hallam,' remarked Jessica one afternoon. 'No men in the house, only women – except Daniel, of course, and he's not a man.'

'What am I? A donkey, then?' was Daniel's sharp query.

'Jessica means that you're still a boy,' soothed Lucie. 'You have to wait a few years before you're a man.'

Daniel stumped away indignantly, leaving Lucie and Jessica in the garden.

'Not that I mind women,' continued Jessica

reflectively. 'Unless they're very old – like the aunts. Mummy was nice – she was very pretty – a bit like you.' Jessica cast a swift glance at Lucie's face. 'Only she was fair – her hair shone like gold and smelt lovely. And her eyes were blue. Daniel's like her, but I think I'm more like Daddy. He has dark hair.'

Lucie remained silent, realizing that the child was really speaking her thoughts aloud. It was the first time that Lucie had ever heard Jessica mention her mother, and she perceived how vulnerable the child was under the thin veneer of precocious mannerisms.

'You remember your mother very well,' murmured Lucie encouragingly.

'Oh, yes. She was always laughing, especially when Daddy was home. Daniel doesn't remember her so well because he was younger, but she used to play with us and tell us stories – just the same as you do, Lucie.'

Lucie smiled and gave Jessica an affectionate hug.

'It would be a good idea if you and Uncle Joel got married. Then you'd be a real auntie to us and we could live with you for ever and ever.'

Lucie's face flamed, but she laughed lightly. 'I don't think that's very likely.'

'Why not? You don't prefer Uncle Hallam, do you?'

'No, of course not. But I don't expect I shall be marrying either of them.'

'M'm, pity. Uncle Joel's more your type. Besides, Uncle Hallam might take you off somewhere else to live and then we'd lose you. I wouldn't like it if you went away and never came back.' With sudden sweetness Jessica planted a kiss on Lucie's face, then went running down the garden.

It would be a wrench to part from two such attractive children, Lucie mused, but the break would have to come.

'We're invited to lunch tomorrow with Rosanna del Rey,' Georgina mentioned to Lucie at dinner.

'Including Jessica and Daniel?'

'Oh, yes. I told her on the telephone that we couldn't leave them here, and she seemed eager for us to take them.'

Lucie speculated on Rosanna's reason for this sudden

invitation, but even next day when they were all seated in the handsome dining-room of the del Reys' villa, she could find no specific motive.

After the meal they sat on one of the terraces, a large, paved space adjacent to the swimming pool. After a while Georgina left Lucie and Rosanna together. 'I'd better see that the children don't get into mischief,' she said, as she went down a flight of stone steps that led to the next terrace down.

Rosanna immediately pulled her chair closer to Lucie's as though about to talk confidentially. 'I saw the accounts in the newspapers about Joel's success,' she began. 'We are most proud of him.'

Lucie murmured that she, too, was very glad.

'And Hallam has also gone to England?'

'He has exhibitions to attend to.'

'Naturally. You must miss both men very much.'

'I'm very busy with my work,' replied Lucie.

'Ah, but you've just come back from holidays, so you now have to work hard?'

Lucie agreed.

Rosanna leaned back in her long cane chair. 'It was very pleasant to have those two men running about for me, most anxious to give me pleasure,' she said lazily. 'Hallam often told me he was in love with me, but I didn't believe it. Joel never told me – but secretly I think he was a little bit in love with me but wouldn't tell me.' Rosanna laughed, then shook her head. 'Of course, I could not have married either of them.'

Lucie glanced across quickly at the other girl. 'No?'

'Never. There are too many difficulties. Hallam is an artist, but—' Rosanna shrugged, 'he does not count. But Joel – if I really wanted to marry him, then my brothers would be glad to establish him in a place where he had other people to do all that work on his silver. He should not be hammering and – scribbling or whatever it is – there must be workmen to do that for him.'

Lucie drew a deep breath. 'But Joel is an *artist* in silver, not a mere banger of metal. He needs to do everything individually, not hand it over to others – like a factory.'

'Perhaps. But the del Reys do not usually work with their hands.'

'No, of course not,' Lucie said quietly. Rosanna's remarks had lifted her spirits considerably, but she would still go home before Joel returned. 'There is one thing I would like to ask you. Before Joel went to England, did you give Hallam a message that he wanted to meet me at the harbour?'

Rosanna frowned. 'Message? No. I did not see Hallam that day, I think. I do not remember any message.'

Lucie smiled. 'Thank you. It wasn't important.' For once she believed that Rosanna was speaking the truth. Hallam had used her, as he used everyone, as cover for his own intrigues.

'I'm going back to—' Lucie began, when a scream sounded from below, followed by a shout and then a confused murmur of voices. Lucie rose immediately. One of the children . . . those dangerous steps from the terrace to the rocks below . . .

She ran down the first flight and met Jessica, white-faced, racing up towards her.

'Georgie! She's fallen down!'

Lucie hurried down the remaining twisting flights of steps to the spot where Georgina sat hunched up, nursing one of her ankles.

'Nothing to worry about,' muttered Georgina. 'Just my ankle. Probably sprained.'

'What happened?' asked Lucie.

'Daniel and I were at the bottom,' explained Jessica, 'and Georgie was by herself.'

'I only caught my heel in a rut somewhere – and just fell,' added Georgina.

By this time Rosanna had summoned several of the staff, and three maids and a manservant were ready to assist Georgina, but the latter could not put any weight on the damaged ankle and the man picked her up and carried her up the steps.

'I've already telephoned for a doctor,' Rosanna said, and Lucie gave her a quick smile of gratitude for prompt action.

In one of the sitting-rooms at the villa, Georgina was made comfortable on a settee, and given some reviving brandy.

'It wasn't because one of the children perhaps was too

venturesome?' queried Lucie.

'Oh, no, nothing like that. They mustn't be blamed. They both went down quite properly and safely. I think I took my attention off my feet for a moment to look at the scenery.'

'We must have a fencing made for the steps,' declared Rosanna's mother, Señora del Rey. 'They are dangerous.'

Lucie had long thought that some sort of protection was overdue.

The doctor from Corvario came promptly, examined Georgina's ankle and diagnosed a bad sprain with the possibility of a slight fracture.

'You must not walk on it for at least a week,' he said sternly. 'I will come again tomorrow.'

Lucie explained that Georgina did not live in the del Reys' villa, but at the Villa Sirena.

The middle-aged doctor's dark eyes lit with interest. 'Oh, that is where the celebrity lives – Señor Barron who makes the silver. Yes, then I shall come there tomorrow.'

After he had left, Rosanna instructed her chauffeur to drive Georgina and the others home to Sirena. 'He will take Señora Frensham upstairs to her room, for now you are without men in the villa.'

Lucie thanked her warmly. 'Yes, it is a little awkward with both Hallam and Joel away.'

'I am so sorry that this has happened.' Rosanna's face was genuinely troubled. 'If you need more help, you must tell me and I will do what I can.'

Lucie noted this more considerate side of Rosanna's nature and began to feel that perhaps she had allowed prejudice to influence her previous judgment of the girl.

Georgina was made comfortable in bed in her own room at the Villa Sirena. Jessica and Daniel eventually tiptoed into the room.

'May we stay?' asked Jessica softly. 'We'll be quiet.'

'Of course. I'm not ill,' replied Georgina.

All the same Lucie considered that Georgina needed sleep to recover from the shock. When she went downstairs to tell Señora Matana to prepare a very light evening meal, she reflected again how unfortunate it was that neither Joel nor Hallam were at home.

Until the doctor's visit next day she had not thought of her own half-formed plans, but when he said that Georgina would probably need at least ten days' rest in bed, Lucie was worried. The accident meant that Lucie could not in any circumstances leave until Georgina was completely well.

'He's an old fusspot,' was Georgina's comment. 'Miles behind the times. Nowadays you have to walk about even after serious operations. I shall be all right on two sticks as soon as I get downstairs.'

'I don't think you ought, but if you insist—' Lucie gave in.

'Besides, I can rest my foot just as well on a sofa in the drawing-room and Jessica and Daniel can get on with their lessons there.' She made a grimace at Jessica who was sitting on the foot of the bed. 'Don't think, the pair of you, that you're skipping lessons. You've had your holiday.'

Jessica laughed. 'Yes, Georgie teacher. We might have known.'

So Lucie, with the aid of Señora Matana, managed to transfer Georgina each day to the spacious drawing-room on the south side of the villa, where the windows opened on to the terrace. Since Georgina had come to the villa, the two women had often made use of this well-furnished room with its easy chairs, several settees and small tables. 'When the men want to be by themselves,' she had said to Lucie, 'they can stay in their untidy sitting-room. We'll be more comfortable in here.' Oddly enough, Joel or Hallam often joined the others after dinner.

One afternoon, when Georgina declared that her ankle was now almost as good as new, Lucie was sitting at a small table assembling a necklace of cornelians and small pearls linked by silver chain. Jessica was reading and Daniel was occupied with his metal construction outfit building a lorry.

Somewhere out in the hall came the sound of voices and Lucie's head shot up, listening, but the children's keener ears had detected the owner of one of the voices and they both rushed out of the room.

'Uncle Joel! Uncle Joel!'

Lucie dropped her pliers, jumped to her feet and looked round wildly for means of escape, but there was no time, for the next instant Joel was in the room, with Jessica and Daniel hanging on to his arms.

'He's home!' exclaimed Jessica unnecessarily.

'What's all this I hear about accidents?' he demanded of Georgina.

Lucie was glad of the babel of voices and explanations that ensued, for she gained a moment's respite in which to regain some sort of composure. Joel's greeting was friendly enough on the surface, but she thought she detected a coolness in his attitude, a withdrawal of geniality. On her part, she could scarcely adopt anything else but an air of subdued politeness.

Yet it was a relief in some ways to have him in the house even if only for the sake of emergencies like Georgina's accident.

There were congratulations all round on Joel's success in London. His chessmen had been sold to an American collector and Mr. Thornton was taking orders for coffee services, dishes, chalices – anything that would bear the entwined J.B. monogram that was Joel's mark.

'On your way to a fortune,' murmured Georgina.

'On my way to becoming a factory,' he replied with a tinge of sadness.

Lucie noticed that he did not ask how she had fared with her own work, but Georgina supplied that information.

'We went for a spree in Las Palmas and Tenerife,' she told Joel, 'and Lucie had wonderful success with everything she made.'

His reaction seemed to Lucie extremely lukewarm and as soon as she could escape she took refuge in her room on the pretext of finishing the necklace there.

Later in the evening it was impossible to avoid him, for first he asked for the key to Hallam's studio. Then he said, 'You'd better come with me, Lucie.'

Reluctant and mystified, she waited while he unlocked the door. He picked up a large, flat parcel lying on the model's throne. 'It's for you,' he told her.

'For me?'

'Undo it. That's what parcels are for.'

He gave her that smile that always melted her resolution and set her heart hammering, but now she controlled herself.

The parcel contained the portrait Hallam had painted of her.

'I thought he was taking all the portraits to London to his exhibition,' she said.

'Evidently not that one. He wanted you to have it.'

He came closer and peered over her shoulder and his nearness made her want to fling herself into his arms. But that would be a disaster.

'It's a good one,' he observed.

She stood looking at her own face, but saw nothing of the colours or shadows in paint. She was wondering why Hallam had made this gesture.

'Lucie, I want you to understand that I'm staying here only a few days, just long enough to settle up everything.' He had walked away to the other side of the studio. 'I've already arranged some matters with Hallam – about sharing the house and so on. I intend to return to England – unless something quite unforeseen prevents me.'

'Yes. And the children?'

'I don't want to take them back just yet. I'm not sure where I'm going to live. That depends on someone else. So if you and Georgina are agreeable, I'd like to leave them here for a while. In the autumn my brother will be home and then we shall discuss the children's future, their schools and so on.'

Lucie straightened and put down the portrait on a bench. 'Please don't count on me, Joel. I'm leaving for England as soon as I can – that is, as soon as Georgina is fit to walk about without trouble. In fact, but for her accident, I should have gone over a week ago.'

He did not turn towards her. 'I see. May I ask if you've made definite plans?'

'I shall ask Mr. Thornton for advice.' She deliberately made her voice cold and curt, for only in that way could she control the tears that threatened to shame her.

'Do the children know – that you're going soon?'

'No, I haven't told them. I'd rather not – until I must.'

She picked up the portrait and its wrappings and Joel said hastily, 'Hallam said you must be careful of that. The picture hasn't been varnished yet, so the paint must be allowed to dry.'

'All right. Thank you.'

Lucie went out of the studio into her own room. Her emotions were frozen. Did she only imagine that vestige of tenderness in Joel's voice? Who was the someone else who influenced his choice of a place to live? Surely he must know that Rosanna had no intention of marrying him. Or was that why he needed to return to England to forget her?

Gradually during the next few days it leaked out that Joel had brought presents back from England for the various members of the household. Jigsaw puzzles for Daniel, a jewel box for Jessica, an elegant handbag for Georgina. Tantalizingly, they were doled out one at a time, starting with Daniel. For Lucie there appeared to be nothing, and she told herself fiercely that she wanted nothing from Joel. She had the Christmas egg and now the portrait from Hallam, so each man had given her a sample of his work. It should be enough. Yet she was hurt, raging against the cruel gap that had set her and Joel so far apart.

She felt disinclined for work and spent much of her time on the beach with the two children. Soon she would be leaving this lovely climate, so she might as well make the most of it now. True to his word, Joel intruded very little on the rest of the household. He was either in his workshop, ostensibly packing up his tools and equipment, or he was driving to Corvario. Occasionally he went out in the boat, *La Sirena*. Perhaps, he, too, was equally reluctant to leave the island.

'So Joel is leaving us the day after tomorrow,' Georgina remarked during an afternoon when she and Lucie were on the beach a little distance from the villa.

'Oh? Is he?'

Georgina sighed heavily. 'You're very foolish to be so stubborn, Lucie dear.'

'Stubborn? I? Nothing to be stubborn about. I've my own life to live and I shall go back to England as soon as I can.'

'A stupid misunderstanding, that's all,' snapped Georgina crossly.

'Rather more than that,' corrected Lucie.

'Daniel! Daniel!' Jessica's shouts came from farther along the beach. Then she came running up to the two women. 'Isn't he a tiresome little boy! He seems to have disappeared.'

Lucie was on her feet in an instant. 'Where was he when you last saw him?' she asked Jessica.

'On the edge of the water. He was floating and then splashing about—'

'Jessica dear, run home quickly and see if you can find Uncle Joel.' The child was off before Lucie finished her sentence.

'I'd better go in and swim to see if I can find him,' said Lucie to Georgina.

'He's probably playing about behind some rocks. Don't take any risks, Lucie!'

The sea was smooth with only tiny ripples, yet Lucie could not see a glimpse of a small head bobbing about anywhere. She swam back to the beach where Georgina waited. 'No sign of him?'

Georgina shook her head. 'He can't have gone far.'

Joel appeared with Jessica at his heels. 'I'll take the boat. You, Georgina, had better look for him around here. Jessica can help you, but don't tire yourself.'

'I'll come with you in the boat,' offered Lucie.

Joel half turned and hesitated. If he refuses my help, thought Lucie, then I shall know there's no chance ever again of coming to an understanding with him.

'But you're wet. You can't—'

'I've a thick towelling wrap here.'

'All right, put it on and let's go.'

He outdistanced her along the shore and by the time she reached the harbour, he was already switching on the engine and about to cast off the mooring ropes.

Lucie jumped aboard and he shot out of the little harbour. She wrapped the towelling around her, but when they were out of the sheltered harbour, the sun and wind would dry her much faster.

A small boat danced on the water some distance away and Joel steered towards it. 'Seen anything of a small boy swimming?'

The two men shook their heads and Joel veered away sharply.

'The current would take him this way,' Joel muttered, 'unless, of course, he panicked.'

Lucie's lips were trembling too much to answer, but she remembered Daniel's delight when he had learned how to float without doubling up in the middle and sinking. What if he had discovered that he was too far from the shore? She prayed that he was somewhere safe on land and not in the sea at all, no matter what mischief he might have been up to, hiding away somewhere.

Joel circled in a wide curve, then turned the boat towards Molino harbour again. A fishing boat was just entering and a man on board waved his arms, but it was too far off for Joel's voice to carry.

At the quay a knot of half a dozen men gathered near one of the boats. Then someone called to Joel in Spanish. Joel yelled back. 'He's safe,' he muttered to Lucie. 'Someone's found him.'

He leapt ashore without tying up his own boat and Lucie tried to follow him, but as she fumbled for the mooring rope, she suddenly blacked out in a whirling dizziness, and the next thing she knew she was being hauled out of the boat on to the quay.

Then she was in a car, holding Daniel wrapped in blankets, and soon they were back at the villa. Lucie dashed up to her room to dress, for she was still wearing her swimming suit and towelling wrap.

A very subdued Daniel had been put to bed with hot water bottles in case he caught a chill and Lucie heard explanations from Joel and Georgina.

'A fishing-boat coming in to the harbour happened to spot him,' said Joel. 'The men said that Daniel wasn't at all alarmed, floating on his back and occasionally swimming a stroke or two.'

'He hadn't realized he was so far out of his depth or he'd have panicked,' added Georgina.

'The men fished him out of the water, wrapped him up in blankets and had just landed when we came back to the harbour.' Joel turned towards Lucie. 'But what happened to you? When I came back to the boat with Daniel, you were just about to fall overboard.'

'I – I felt faint – with anxiety, I suppose, and then the relief. It was my fault – about Daniel. I should have looked after him better.'

'Don't blame yourself,' said Georgina. 'I must take my share, too, even though Daniel knows he mustn't just float away without looking where he's going.'

At that, Joel laughed. 'Difficult when you're floating.'

But something in Lucie cracked and the tears began to rain down her face. Blindly she turned to get away and seek refuge in the privacy of her room, but Joel was too quick for her. He waited, holding her in his arms, dabbing at her tear-stained cheeks, until she was calmer. Then he kissed her, not those little casual kisses he had given her from time to time, but with the intensity of a man caressing his beloved.

'Why have you held me at arm's length for so long?' he whispered.

Lucie raised her face, then glanced around the room. Georgina had discreetly disappeared. 'I thought you were the one that didn't want to touch me with a barge-pole.'

He held her close against him, kissing her neck and her ears. 'Damn it! I fell in love with you almost as soon as you came here, but you were so independent, and I respected that. You put up a great wall between us.'

'But Rosanna? I thought you – might have been a bit in love with her.'

'Rosanna? Who put that idea into your head? Hallam, I suppose.' Joel laughed. 'Rosanna del Rey will never marry a chap who works with his hands and occasionally makes them dirty.'

So he knew that, too! Rosanna had probably made that clear to him.

'It was Hallam who worried me,' Joel was murmuring against her hair. 'I couldn't be sure if you loved him—'

'Never. I went to the boat because—'

'I know all about that,' he interrupted her. 'And my letter to you was a cowardly thing to do. If I'd stayed to listen to your explanations, I'd have known the truth, but I was so mad with Hallam—'

Lucie put up a hand to twine around his neck. 'Let's

both forget it, shall we?' It was then that she knew what heavenly bliss it was to be embraced by Joel and feel the sweet comfort of his arms about her. After a while she said, 'But I wasn't very certain of your intentions. I thought you wanted me only as a business partner – and that wasn't enough for me.'

'Darling! Together we can do wonderful things, but you must have your entire freedom to do the work you want to do – jewellery or anything else. Come with me to the workshop. I've something to show you.'

Out there, he whipped the cloth from the silver stallion and there it was in its dazzling splendour. 'I brought it back from London, although it was supposed to go on tour with the rest. It's for you.'

'For me?'

'I made it for you.'

So this was why he had not brought her a present from England! Her ecstasy soared to a point of rapture beyond any emotion she had ever experienced. To own the beautiful silver Arab that had won the Cellini award, to know that Joel had made it specially for her – oh, it was overwhelming!

He gave the horse into her hands and she caressed the lovely curved, muscular body, touched the flying mane, the delicate upraised legs. 'It's more than I deserve,' she whispered.

'No, it's not enough. I'll make beautiful things for you, Lucie dearest.'

At dinner Lucie was bubbling with delight. Georgina's face held a serene satisfaction. Jessica had been allowed to stay up to dinner tonight, since the afternoon had been so disrupted by Daniel's escapade. The silver horse took pride of place in the centre of the table and Lucie could scarcely take her eyes off it.

'It's a lovely horse,' said Jessica admiringly.

'And it belongs to Lucie,' chimed in Joel, 'but I was determined not to part with it until she said she'd marry me.'

Lucie put down her knife and fork with deliberation and pointed to the horse. 'Then you ought to have it back. You still haven't asked me to marry you.'

'What a way to make a man propose! Right in the

middle of his fish medley.'

There was wine-drinking and toasting and laughter. Then at the end of the meal, Jessica came round the table to Lucie.

'I'm ever so glad you're going to be a real auntie. You will if you marry Uncle Joel, won't you?'

Lucie put her arms around the girl. 'Yes. And will you and Daniel call me Auntie then?'

Jessica made a little grimace. 'Of course not! You'll always be just Lucie.' Then she scowled and adopted that severe expression that the others knew so well. 'But you and Uncle Joel took an awfully long time to make up your minds. Daniel and I thought it would happen long ago.'

The others laughed and Lucie said humbly, 'Sorry if we were slow.' She kissed Jessica with warm affection.

Much later Joel and Lucie sat in the 'twilight verandah' and discussed their plans for the future.

'I saw a nice house in Dorset when I was in England. Old, but modernized, plenty of space, and a good barn for working in. Near a village were I could have a studio sort of shop, as old Thornton suggested. But you'd have to see it first.'

'Why did you look at houses, Joel?' she asked.

'I knew I had to get away from here if you sent me packing, but then again, I couldn't take the house – or any house – unless I could see you walking about in the rooms.'

She snuggled up to him and it was paradise itself to feel that at last the cold wall between them had disappeared.

'Hallam wants to sell this place,' Joel continued. 'He's footloose – and likes to be fancy-free – so I thought I might also buy some little place here in the Canaries on one of the islands. Then we could use it for long holidays, perhaps escape some of the winter in England.'

'And the children would love it! What about Georgina if Hallam sells this villa?'

'I've spoken to her about that. She'd like to stay here and look after a little holiday place for us. Naturally, she'll want to visit us in England sometimes. You won't mind that?'

'I love Georgina and I'll look forward to her visits. And the children. Our house – wherever it is – must always be home to them.'

'I'm glad you feel that way.' Joel bent to kiss the tip of her nose. 'They'll be off to school in the autumn and you'll meet Howard, my brother. Oh, yes, of course, I must let him know I'm getting married.'

Lucie sniffed. 'It might be as well. I hate these clandestine affairs.' She laughed as he tweaked her hair.

They went out to the terrace and gazed at the shining strip of moonlit sea. Lucie shivered slightly at the memory of Dan's adventure this afternoon, when that same sea might have spelt disaster. But now Joel was close beside her, his arm about her and the future was a brilliant pathway stretching out to the horizon.

'Georgina helped,' he said suddenly. 'She said that when two people are apparently on opposite sides of an iceberg, the best thing to do is for one of the pair to go round the edges and join the other. Sound sense.'

'Dear Georgina,' murmured Lucie. 'But for her, we'd still be on opposite sides of the iceberg.'

'But never again?' he queried.

'Never again,' she said decisively. 'Love melts icebergs with its warmth.'

As she turned she saw that a shaft of moonlight slanted through the open door of the verandah and in its beam the silver horse on the marble table seemed poised, ready for flight. But Lucie would never let him go.

'Thank you, Joel,' she whispered. 'I'm very lucky to have you both – you – and the silver stallion.'

# Mills & Boon's Paperbacks

## APRIL

UNWANTED BRIDE by Anne Hampson

The last time Caryn had seen her husband Sharn was at their wedding – a marriage of convenience so that both could claim an inheritance. But now she needed help and journeyed to Sharn's Outback home. Surely he wouldn't refuse to assist her? Yet Sharn had told no one about his wife and didn't seem at all willing to take on the responsibilities of a husband!

FAIRWINDS by Rebecca Stratton

Tara was engaged to Clifford Hautain. She was sure she loved him. But why did she find his brother Philip so intriguing? It wasn't as if Philip was interested in her – he obviously preferred the charms of the sophisticated Elwyn, who made it clear to Tara that he was her property. Yet . . .

THE RED PLAINS OF JOUNIMA by Dorothy Cork

Two weeks after she arrived in Australia from England Pippa found herself in the middle of the Outback on the sheep station at Jounima doing battle with Skye Bannerman. 'Skye's an ogre,' someone had told Pippa, and after her initial encounter with him she was inclined to agree. But perhaps he had another more attractive personality to show to the sophisticated Angela Glas?

DARK ANGEL by Elizabeth Ashton

Francesca Temple came to Italy to stay with her parents and to introduce them to her fiancé Desmond. But fate decreed that her visit was to end in her marriage to another man – the disturbing Angelo Vittorini. Could Francesca ever understand the enigmatic man who was her husband? Could she ever love him?

STORMY ENCOUNTER by Roumelia Lane

Janet was naturally worried when she heard that someone was trying to cheat her mother out of her rights and she went to Ibiza to sort things out. Just who did that odious Bruce Walbrook think he was? He might be an authority in the legal world, but she would show him that his words certainly cut no ice with her!

20p net each

# Mills & Boon's Paperbacks

## APRIL (contd.)

GALLANT'S FANCY by Flora Kidd

Miranda was prepared to help her boss in his latest take-over bid. But when it came to sweet-talking the arrogant Roger Gallant she realized that she had taken on more than she could manage!

THE BENEDICT MAN by Mary Wibberley

Lovely surroundings and a kind and considerate employer – Beth was delighted at the prospect of her new job in Derbyshire. But when she arrived at Benedict House she discovered that it was not the sympathetic Mrs Thornburn who required her services as a secretary, but her arrogant and completely unreasonable nephew. Could Beth put up with his insufferable attitude to her?

SILVER FRUIT UPON SILVER TREES by Anne Mather

It would be easy, Eve told Sophie. All she had to do was to go to Trinidad and pretend to be the granddaughter of the wealthy Brandt St. Vincente for four weeks and the money she needed would be hers. But when Sophie met the disturbing Edge St. Vincente, who thought she was his niece, and fell in love with him, she realized that perhaps it wasn't going to be that simple after all . . .

THE FEAST OF SARA by Anne Weale

Set in the strange and lonely Camargue region of France, this story tells of a young Eng'ish girl who showed herself equal to the harsh demands of life on a French farm – and to the proud spirit of a Frenchman whom she had disliked at first sight.

DESERT NURSE by Jane Arbor

After the break-up of her romance with Greg Ryder, Nurse Martha Shore took a post in a tiny hospital on a remote oil site east of Aden. She had successfully jumped out of the frying pan. Was her new job, in the burning desert heat, not ominously like the proverbial fire?

20p net each

*Née à Gevin*[...] *nt, depuis une vingtai*[...] *aliste qui ont fait l'ob*[...]
*Elle a publ*[...] lle Marie-Hélène Char[...] s Gisants, L'Amour capital, *Grand Prix du roman de la société des gens de lettres 1980,* La Passion selon Martial Montaurian, Suzanne Valadon ou La recherche de la vérité *(Bourse Goncourt de la Biographie, 1984),* Le Bunker.

Quand, au détour d'une relecture des *Hauts de Hurlevent* et d'un voyage dans le Yorkshire, une romancière telle que Jeanne Champion rencontre la figure étonnante d'une Emily Brontë, le choc est inévitable.
Au-delà de tous les commentaires suscités par la vie et l'œuvre d'Emily Brontë, c'est à un véritable voyage outre-tombe que nous convie Jeanne Champion. A travers un dialogue saisissant avec son modèle, elle a su recréer pour notre plus grand plaisir de lecture l'atmosphère de ce lieu magique où vécurent les Brontë : le sinistre presbytère de Haworth, les « Moors » austères que le vent et la pluie glacée ne cessaient de battre... Elle fait revivre, par la magie du style, par la justesse des dialogues, les mœurs et les pensées de ces personnages hors du commun que furent Charlotte et Anne (les deux sœurs), Branwell (le frère) et Emily elle-même.
Après la mort de la mère et de deux autres sœurs, l'existence de ce quatuor maudit se noua d'autant plus fortement autour de la figure étrange du père, un pasteur anglican hypocondriaque et misanthrope. Pour lutter contre la solitude, l'enfermement, les enfants se créèrent, grâce à la littérature, un univers imaginaire seul capable de tromper la mort. Cette mort qui, pourtant, aura le dernier mot : en 1848, et en l'espace de quelques mois, succomberont Branwell, Emily et Anne. Emily n'avait que trente ans...

## DU MÊME AUTEUR :

*Le cri*, roman, Julliard.
*Les miroirs jumeaux*, roman, Julliard.
*X*, roman, Christian Bourgois.
*Vautour-en-privilège*, roman, Calmann-Lévy.
*Ma fille Marie-Hélène Charles Quint*, roman, Calmann-Lévy.
*Dans les jardins d'Esther*, roman, Calmann-Lévy.
*Les gisants*, roman, Calmann-Lévy.
*Les frères Montaurian*, roman, Grasset.
*La passion selon Martial Montaurian*, roman, Grasset.
*L'amour capital*, roman, Calmann-Lévy.
*Suzanne Valadon*, Presses de la Renaissance.
*Le bunker*, roman, Calmann-Lévy.

## *Dans Le Livre de Poche :*

LA PASSION SELON MARTIAL MONTAURIAN.
SUZANNE VALADON OU LA RECHERCHE DE LA VÉRITÉ.

JEANNE CHAMPION

# *La Hurlevent*

PRESSES DE LA RENAISSANCE

*A Francis Feillet*

Quatre ouvrages m'ont tout particulièrement aidée à pénétrer dans l'univers des Brontë: *Emily Brontë; Expériences spirituelles et création poétique*, de Jacques Blondel, édité par les Presses Universitaires de France en 1956; *Le Monde infernal de Branwell Brontë*, de Daphné Du Maurier, traduit par Jane Fillion et édité par Albin Michel en 1962; *Emily Brontë: Wuthering Heights*, traduit par Pierre Leyris — choix établi et présenté par Raymond Bellour —; et enfin *Charlotte Brontë/Patrick Branwell Brontë*, récits de jeunesse choisis et présentés par le même auteur (deux livres publiés par J.-J. Pauvert en 1972). J'ajoute que les poèmes d'Emily Brontë cités dans ce livre ont été traduits par Françoise d'Eaubonne, Mireille Best et Pierre Leyris.
Que ces auteurs trouvent ici l'expression de ma gratitude.

Dans cette biographie romanesque, je mets en scène et je fais parler Emily Brontë et sa famille. Tantôt je leur prête ma voix, tantôt je les cite, elles et d'autres auteurs; dans ce dernier cas, les textes sont en italique.

Nous remercions les éditions Payot de nous avoir permis d'utiliser pour le présent ouvrage un titre rappelant pour partie celui du célèbre roman d'Emily Brontë dans la traduction française de Frédéric Delebecque: *Les Hauts de Hurle-Vent*.

*« Autour de moi des tombes grises*
*Étendent leurs ombres au loin.*
*Là, sous le gazon que je foule,*
*Silencieux, seuls, gisent les morts —*
*Là, sous le gazon, sous la glaise,*
*Voués au froid, voués au noir.*
*Malgré moi m'échappent des larmes*
*Thésaurisées par la mémoire*
*Aux dépens des années enfuies.*
*Ah ! Temps, Mort et Tourment mortel,*
*Si vous blessez, c'est pour toujours.*
*Qu'il me souvienne seulement*
*D'une moitié de la souffrance*
*Que j'ai vue, apprise, soufferte,*
*Et le Ciel même ne saurait,*
*Si pur et bienheureux soit-il,*
*Donner quiétude à mon âme.* »

Emily Jane Brontë,
17 juillet 1841.
(Traduction Pierre Leyris


* Les références complètes des textes cités sont regroupées à la fin du volume (voir p. 479).

# PROLOGUE

## 13 décembre 1985

Me fera-t-on jamais grâce d'avoir été ce que je fus, probablement par inadvertance, du moins sans préméditation, et me laissera-t-on un jour de bienheureuse indifférence rejoindre cette paix à laquelle je n'ai cessé d'aspirer de mon vivant? M'abandonnera-t-on enfin à l'oubli, au vent? Serai-je jamais libre de regagner les terres où reposent ceux que l'anonymat sauva de la voracité de l'Histoire? Lasse d'avoir rebondi dans la mémoire collective depuis bientôt un siècle et demi, mon ombre attend la délivrance. Hélas, ma prière n'a pas d'effet sur le monde qui me torture et dont, madame, vous faites partie. J'en ai pour preuve votre venue dans mon pays, ce Yorkshire éloigné des capitales. La naïveté m'avait pourtant invitée à croire que j'avais réussi à semer en cours de route mes admirateurs: écrivains à l'écoute de leurs passions, universitaires en quête d'un sujet de thèse, exégètes, curieux de tous acabits. Ce n'était qu'une illusion. Pourtant, combien d'essais, d'études n'a-t-on pas publiés sur moi, sur mon œuvre? Parce que ces ouvrages ne sont pas parvenus à cerner un mystère qui se refuse au monde, voici qu'un nouveau livre s'annonce, lequel, j'en suis convaincue, ne le cernera pas mieux. Il ressemblera plus ou moins aux précédents, portera un titre qui me déplaira sûrement. Je ne pourrai ni m'en défendre, ni l'interdire.

Ainsi, après tant d'autres mieux armés, vous osez vous mesurer à moi. Mais alors que la plupart se présentent à la porte du presbytère devenu pour le plaisir de la foule estivale le *Brontë Parsonage Museum*, vous m'apparaissez à gauche de l'église située en contrebas. Comme une voleuse, vous vous glissez dans l'ancien cimetière de Haworth. Votre hésitation face au spectacle des tombes gangrenées par la moisissure verdâtre du temps, votre recul face à toutes ces pierres tombales sous lesquelles s'additionnent les années de jeunesse fauchée par la tuberculose, le mouvement rapide de votre tête rejetée en arrière pour chercher le réconfort du ciel et mesurer la hauteur impressionnante des arbres qui surplombent le clocher, votre étonnement enfin devant ce passé enfoui mais néanmoins présent, foulé trois mois l'an par la multitude des vacanciers, tous ces gestes du corps traversé par l'émotion me rassurent. Alors que l'instant d'avant je désirais vous fuir, voilà que je me dirige vers vous, l'intruse. Je comprends soudain, au mouvement nerveux que vous venez de faire, que l'hésitation qui vous a maintenue quelques secondes plus tôt immobile à l'entrée du cimetière ne venait pas de la timidité ni du malaise que l'on peut éprouver à commettre une indiscrétion, mais tout simplement de la maladresse. Sans doute craignez-vous de glisser sur les dalles du chemin dangereux en hiver, lorsque le gel les enduit d'une pellicule de verglas ? Au-dessus de vous qui tentez d'embrasser d'un regard de navigateur l'église, le cimetière, et plus haut, derrière le muret de vieilles pierres, le jardin du presbytère, un groupe d'arbres aux branches noircies et à l'ampleur théâtrale forme comme une menace. La grandeur tragique du paysage, sa désolation vous frappent. « Étonnant ! » dites-vous. En ce lieu où rien n'a changé, où rien *ne doit* changer — seuls les arbres qui ajoutent à la dramaturgie du décor ont été plantés après notre disparition —, la réalité est saisissante. « C'est encore plus sinistre que je ne l'imaginais ! » A quoi donc, madame, se destinaient votre curiosité et votre appétit ? Ne saviez-vous pas que nous avions traversé la vie parmi les cadavres que, semaine après semaine, la communauté de Haworth venait enterrer à nos pieds ? Ne saviez-vous pas que, de nos fenêtres, nous ne pouvions voir que des tombes ? Ce paysage auquel vous aviez songé comme à un dessin que le regard contourne pour mieux le ressaisir à travers une nouvelle lecture, ce paysage s'offre à vous avec une précision presque clinique. Il ne manque au tableau ni un brin d'herbe, ni une pierre, ni une plaque de mousse, pas même une aile de corbeau.

En cet instant où tout vous semble possible, s'ouvre la première page d'un livre, celui que dans votre irresponsabilité et votre impulsivité vous avez décidé d'écrire afin de me rendre à la vie, moi qui n'aspire qu'à l'oubli. Vous m'imaginez respirant à votre rythme, voyant par vos yeux, m'interrogeant dans votre langue. Votre visage marqué par la fatigue du voyage s'éclaire brusquement ; venez-vous d'entr'apercevoir une première page ? Cette satisfaction de la pensée ravie d'avoir trouvé un bon sujet ne dure pas. Votre expression s'altère, puis se ferme. Le doute vient de surgir entre deux tombes ; votre projet est-il bien sain, et peut-on bâtir une œuvre dans un cimetière ? La mort, la mienne du moins, ne s'est-elle pas trop confessée ? A-t-on encore une oreille à lui tendre ? Il ne suffit point de trouver un titre pour assurer une œuvre, ni de hurler avec le vent pour donner froid. Le regard que vous jetez à l'église dit tout de votre inquiétude. Vous vous demandez s'il est bien sage de poursuivre votre enquête ; plutôt que de partir à la recherche de fantômes, ne feriez-vous pas mieux de visiter ce pays réputé pour son austère beauté ? Les essais savants qui m'ont été consacrés vous reviennent en mémoire. Quoi, malgré l'amoncellement de tous ces travaux, le public continuerait à me méconnaître, moi et ma famille ?

« Ne faites pas un pas de plus, madame, allez-vous-en ! »

Mais voilà que l'intuition vient de vous faire savoir que vous n'êtes plus seule. Quelqu'un vous guette que vous ne voyez pas. Quelqu'un vous souffle un ordre, et celui-là vous chagrine. Vous tremblez ; est-ce le froid et l'humidité de l'air ou la crainte d'avoir à entreprendre un travail au-dessus de vos forces ? Votre main ramène le manteau sur votre poitrine. Durant un court moment, la tentation d'abandonner votre entreprise pour rejoindre des lieux mieux connus de vous vous saisit. Ai-je gagné la partie ? Non. Le désir d'en savoir davantage vous pousse en avant. Vous remontez le cimetière, atteignez bientôt le muret qui sépare l'enceinte des morts de la lande. Les deux coudes appuyés sur les pierres, vous vous laissez aller au rêve. C'est à votre tour de contempler ce que nous n'avons cessé de voir de notre vivant ; le ciel immense, les pâturages, et plus loin, au sommet de la colline, les Moors où vous attend Cathy, l'enfant morte qui vous hante depuis l'enfance...

« *J'enfonçai le poing à travers la vitre et allongeai le bras en dehors pour saisir la branche importune ; mais au lieu de la trouver, mes doigts se refermèrent sur les doigts d'une petite main froide comme la glace ! L'intense horreur du cauchemar m'envahit : j'essayai de retirer mon bras, mais la main s'y accrochait et une voix d'une mélancolie infinie sanglotait : "Laissez-moi entrer ! Laissez-moi entrer ! — Qui êtes-vous ?" demandai-je tout en continuant de lutter pour me dégager. "Catherine Linton", répondit la voix en tremblant...* »

15 janvier 1986

Ce matin, après une nuit tourmentée — depuis mon retour de Haworth où je suis allée rendre visite à une morte, l'angoisse perturbe mon sommeil —, alors que j'ouvrais péniblement les yeux, j'ai aperçu, posé sur une chaise, le livre de Georges Bataille, *La Littérature et le Mal*. Au lieu de reprendre la lecture de ce beau texte, d'y puiser la force qui me manque, j'ai eu l'imprudence de jeter un coup d'œil à la pile de livres qui se dresse sur mon bureau. Ces travaux — pareils à des bagages encombrants, ils accompagnent inévitablement les grandes œuvres — m'ont renvoyée à mon projet. Devant cette accumulation de savoir, de recherches, d'appréciations parfois contradictoires, je me suis interrogée sur les raisons qui avaient poussé tant d'écrivains sur les traces d'une jeune fille à la vie de recluse morte de phtisie à trente ans. Si cette réflexion ne m'a pas apporté les éclaircissements que j'en attendais, elle a dénoncé en moi la lassitude, et portant plus loin ses effets, a démasqué mon impuissance à mettre en chantier, après tant d'œuvres brillantes, un travail prévu de longue date.

Depuis cette soirée — elle remonte à plusieurs années — où l'idée m'est venue de rendre vie à une grande figure de la littérature anglaise par le biais d'une biographie qui n'en serait pas une, d'un roman qui n'en serait pas un, où l'héroïne arrachée à sa gloire posthume raconterait sa vie passée... depuis cette soirée où l'idée m'est venue de rendre hommage à une grande morte dont je ne sais plus si elle est la Cathy des *Hauts de Hurle-Vent* ou Emily Brontë, fille d'un pasteur établi dans un village isolé du nord de l'Angleterre, je cherche la clef qui me permettra de pénétrer dans le presbytère de Haworth. Dressé sur une terre où règne la tristesse des saisons nordiques qui renvoient aux tempêtes, à la pétrification des hivers interminables, au crépuscule long de trois mois, il m'interdit sa porte.

> « *"Me voilà revenue à la maison : je m'étais perdue dans la lande !" La voix parlait encore, quand je distinguai une figure d'enfant qui regardait à travers la fenêtre. La terreur me rendit cruel. Voyant qu'il était inutile d'essayer de me dégager de son étreinte, j'attirai son poignet sur la vitre brisée et le frottai dessus jusqu'à ce que le sang coulât et inondât les draps du lit. La voix gémissait toujours : "Laissez-moi entrer !" et l'étreinte obstinée ne se relâchait pas, me rendant presque fou de terreur...* »

Oui, depuis des mois, et je me garde de les compter, pas une journée n'a traversé ma vie sans y laisser la trace sanglante de cette main retrouvée dans un livre dont j'avais gardé en mémoire la terrible histoire d'amour et de mort. Mais aussi, pourquoi suis-je allée rendre visite à une morte qui, à ce qu'on raconte, refusa le monde ? Pourquoi me suis-je attardée dans un cimetière au-dessus duquel croassent des corbeaux comme dans un mauvais film d'épouvante? Qu'importe. Le mal est fait. Je suis devenue, comment dire, un peu de ce Yorkshire du siècle dernier au fin fond duquel se déchirent des êtres à qui, malgré notre effroi, nous voudrions ressembler, tant leur passion nous dévore comme elle les a dévorés eux-mêmes. Sans y prendre garde, je suis devenue, non pas le reflet d'un personnage dont j'idolâtrerais le souvenir, mais l'objet d'un récit dans lequel vivent et meurent des créatures imaginaires; d'un récit à l'ombre duquel glissent des existences lointaines, des êtres aux dimensions proprement mythiques, des morts aussi farouches que des vivants, des morts plus présents dans leur incroyable réincarnation que les passants que je croise dans la rue. Et ce sentiment d'absence qui m'étreint comme à la veille d'un deuil, cette impression d'éloignement pour soi-même en même temps que d'éloignement pour les autres, ce pressentiment de l'incommunicable, de la toute-puissance d'un secret qu'il va me falloir découvrir pour le livrer ou pour le taire, je le tiens d'un fantôme dont les voiles flottent entre les pages d'un roman.

> «*Les doigts se desserrèrent, je retirai vivement les miens hors du trou, j'entassai en hâte les livres en pyramide pour me défendre, et je me bouchai les oreilles pour ne plus entendre la lamentable prière. (...) Mais, dès que je recommençai d'écouter, j'entendis le douloureux gémissement qui continuait! "Allez-vous-en! criai-je, je ne vous laisserai jamais entrer, dussiez-vous supplier pendant vingt ans. — Il y a vingt ans, gémit la voix, il y a vingt ans que je suis errante."*»

20 mars 1986

Depuis votre visite, mon ombre vaincue par votre insistance vous fait escorte malgré elle. Attirée par ce miroir que vous lui tendez, elle se laisse séduire par le simulacre d'une résurrection. Croit-elle en votre pouvoir? Sans doute, puisqu'elle s'entraîne à nier son enveloppe de mort! Emportée par le vent dont elle avait désappris la puissance, elle s'avance sur le chemin qui mène à la mémoire. Mais alors que vous devriez vous réjouir de sa hâte à se rendre à un rendez-vous qu'elle a refusé jusqu'ici, l'abondance des souvenirs qu'elle convoque sur son passage vous effraie. Comment défendre votre fragile inspiration contre les violences d'une réalité qui vous bouscule? Je sais, vous avez peur. Il y a de quoi. J'ai trop longtemps vécu dans un cimetière pour ne pas connaître le danger d'une telle promiscuité. C'est pourtant le décor dont il va falloir vous satisfaire, car c'est ici que j'ai vécu, et j'aurais mauvaise grâce à m'en plaindre; Haworth a été le seul lieu au monde où j'ai jamais souhaité demeurer. Nul endroit n'a su, comme ce village venté et perdu, solliciter ma présence. C'est dans ce presbytère gardé par des tombes que j'ai grandi; c'est entre ces sépultures que j'ai pris racine et me suis fortifiée, sous ce ciel que j'ai découvert Dieu et lui ai rendu hommage à ma façon.

A l'instant de vous inviter à me suivre sur un chemin difficile, je voudrais vous dire ceci: peu me chaut en vérité que vous fassiez de mon histoire et de celle de ma famille un bon ou un mauvais livre. D'ailleurs, réussi ou pas, ce genre d'ouvrage, je vous en avertis, de par son esprit ne plaira pas dans mon pays; les Anglo-Saxons sont gens précis; ils veulent savoir dans quel domaine on a pris le parti de les déranger : roman ou biographie ? Ce qui m'importe, c'est que vous m'abordiez avec droiture et clarté. Les éloges rendus à mon œuvre et à ma personne m'embarrassent plus qu'ils ne me flattent. Je n'y vois, la plupart du temps, qu'un bel exercice de style ou la performance d'un érudit qui croit tout connaître des remuements de mon âme. Vous-même n'êtes pas à l'abri de ce genre d'erreurs ; l'ambition de votre projet vous y expose encore plus que les autres. Mais vous ne m'écoutez pas !

Rivée à votre obsession, vous ressemblez aux spectres après lesquels vous courez. Votre pâleur me renvoie à ces visages défaits que l'on rencontre aux carrefours des cauchemars, là où les errances se croisent sans jamais se reconnaître. Accablée par ce mal d'écrire qui exige votre temps sans rien vous offrir en échange, vous allez et venez à la lisière d'un territoire où se joua notre destinée. Que le silence vous soit intolérable, cela je peux le comprendre. C'est parce que je n'ai pas pu l'assumer que ma main a écrit ce que ma bouche a tu ; c'est parce que la solitude a été trop contraignante que je l'ai peuplée d'êtres imaginaires ; c'est parce que le vent a hurlé trop fort en moi que je l'ai enfermé entre les murs d'une ferme — elle existe — à laquelle j'ai donné son nom : *Les Hauts de Hurle-Vent*, qu'il faut avoir vue au moins une fois pour en comprendre l'incroyable, l'insurpassable solitude ; c'est parce que la nature m'a confié trop de secrets, que je les ai cachés là-haut, au sommet de la colline, là où continue à régner sur des ruines un personnage de roman.

« *I am* Heathcliff ! »

Certains livres naissent de la fureur, d'autres du doute, d'autres de la foi ; *Les Hauts de Hurle-Vent*, lui, vint au monde un jour de tempête. Mais n'est-ce pas l'un de vos poètes, René Crevel, qui nous surnomma, mes sœurs et moi, *les Filles du Vent*?

«*Le Vent, lui, n'a pas de père,*
*Car au commencement était le Vent,*
*Le Vent et non le Verbe...*»

«Filles du vent...» Des six enfants Brontë, je crois que je suis la seule à l'avoir été vraiment; la seule aussi à lui avoir manifesté ma reconnaissance. Brûlée jusqu'aux veines par une histoire qui m'a été dictée par lui, j'en ai fait l'aveu bien haut: «Je *suis* Heathcliff!» l'étranger, le solitaire, le gitan. S'est-on jamais demandé pourquoi cette phrase avait fait le tour de la terre? Balayée par des rafales, elle s'est essaimée comme de la graine.

«*Aux seuls hauts du Yorkshire, le vent s'est*
*[fait chair,*
*le vent a hurlé,*
*le vent a battu...*»

Tandis que je vous parle, le jour court sur sa fin. Dans moins d'une heure, la gardienne du musée repoussera la porte sur le dernier visiteur. Elle éteindra les lumières les unes après les autres. Les ténèbres s'organiseront à l'intérieur du presbytère. Elles m'inviteront à rejoindre les lieux de ma vie passée. A peine rendue dans la petite chambre du premier étage, j'entendrai au loin l'écho de votre pas. Ce rappel de votre importune présence me poussera vers la fenêtre. Vous m'apparaîtrez comme en ce jour de décembre. Je vous verrai vous faufiler entre les tombes encore plus impressionnantes, à cette heure, que dans la pleine lumière.

Vous atteindrez le jardin, le traverserez en quelques pas, lèverez la tête en direction de la fenêtre derrière laquelle je me tiendrai : « Laissez-moi entrer ! » me demanderez-vous dans une langue étrangère. « Laissez-moi entrer ! »

« Allez-vous-en, madame ! Allez-vous-en ! Nous ne voulons pas de vous dans cette maison ! »

1er avril 1986

« *Entre toutes les femmes, Emily Brontë semble avoir été l'objet d'une malédiction privilégiée. Sa courte vie ne fut malheureuse que modérément. Mais, sa pureté morale intacte, elle eut de l'abîme du Mal une expérience profonde. Encore que peu d'êtres aient été plus rigoureux, plus courageux, plus droits, elle alla jusqu'au bout de la connaissance du Mal.* »

Où se situe ce «Mal» dont parle Georges Bataille lorsqu'il évoque l'œuvre d'Emily Brontë ? Sur quelle pente enténébrée de l'âme, au bord de quelle persécution, à la frontière de quel embrasement ? Est-il là où je crois l'apercevoir, dans l'ombre d'un Heathcliff meurtrier par amour de celle qui l'a trahi, de celle dont il nourrit l'agonie avec le poison de sa passion dévorante, ou dans la douceur insidieuse de Catherine résolue à quitter ce monde où l'on ne peut qu'être divisé ? Ce « Mal » ne tourmenterait-il pas également une mourante suspendue au cou de celui qu'elle va quitter pour mieux le persécuter pendant vingt ans, jusqu'à l'amener, lui qui ne plie devant rien ni personne, au bord de la fosse où l'attendra l'absolu d'un amour sans Dieu ni rédemption ?

Sur quoi Bataille s'est-il fondé pour prétendre qu'Emily «*ne fut malheureuse que modérément*» ? Sur la légende qui nous la décrit à la manière d'une Cendrillon soumise au rituel quotidien, silencieuse et dévouée, et comme inscrite dans une vie domestique contre laquelle elle ne se révolta jamais ? Comment croire à ce «modérément» lorsqu'on lit les poèmes qui sont parvenus jusqu'à nous, «*membres épars d'une geste romanesque inachevée*», comme les nomme si bien leur traducteur, Pierre Leyris ? Dans ces strophes, la douleur entrevue est si intense que l'on ne peut pas ne pas ressentir le dénuement, la solitude, le désespoir de celle qui les écrivit. Qui a visité Haworth au creux de l'hiver, qui s'est hasardé dans le cimetière à l'heure du crépuscule, sait que là-haut, au-delà de la vieille église, les heures portent le deuil. L'effroi d'avoir grandi en ce lieu où tout parle de l'absence, de la perte, de l'irrémédiable, ne peut être «modéré» ; il est total. «*Pour moi ni sympathie, ni soupirs, ni regret/ Que mon âme soit en partance...*»

> *Puisque le cœur est mort dès sa première enfance, Que le corps s'en aille impleuré.*

Certes, la souffrance d'Emily Brontë a été grande... et pourtant. Hier au soir, alors que j'étais plongée dans la lecture du livre de Jacques Blondel, mon œil s'est arrêté sur une phrase ; signée de la romancière, elle disait à peu près ceci : «*Je veux être telle que Dieu m'a créée.*» Ainsi me parvenait, à peine affaiblie par le temps, une pensée aussi forte qu'apaisante. Le courage, la sagesse de cette jeune fille maltraitée par le destin, sa certitude d'avoir été envers et contre toute infortune « désirée » par Dieu, m'ont redonné confiance. J'ai voulu lire dans cette profession de foi spontanée, touchante, fière aussi, une invite à pénétrer dans des lieux qui m'avaient été interdits jusque-là.

## I WISH TO BE AS GOD MADE ME

Au cœur d'une soirée, le vœu d'Emily Brontë parvenait jusqu'à moi. Atteinte dans ce qu'il y a en moi de plus sincère, mais aussi de plus menacé : l'espérance et la foi, j'ai soudainement eu la certitude de pouvoir ajouter à l'épitaphe de cette morte, lui rendre un peu de sa grandeur. Poussée vers cette jeune fille qui, par-delà le temps et la mort, me donnait une leçon de courage, j'ai entendu dans cette promesse l'appel que j'attendais depuis des mois.

Fermant les yeux, j'ai revu dans ses moindres détails ce paysage inscrit à jamais dans ma mémoire ; ce ciel aussi. Au sommet d'une colline à la pente rude à gravir, j'ai longé de nouveau la ruelle qui relie l'église à la demeure du révérend Patrick Brontë, une bâtisse que l'on a souvent dite austère, alors qu'elle n'est que simplicité et harmonie, avec sa porte à colonnades de style géorgien et ses fenêtres à petits carreaux, cinq à l'étage et quatre au rez-de-chaussée, fenêtres hautes et plutôt étroites conçues pour barrer la route au vent et au froid ; bâtisse autrefois située à l'écart du village, la dernière avant les pâturages auxquels elle tourne le dos, et devant elle le jardinet où l'on a planté un énorme bouquet d'arbres. Arrivée là, j'ai monté les marches du perron. Je m'apprêtais à frapper lorsque la porte s'est ouverte d'elle-même. Dans le vestibule désert où s'étaient croisés autrefois les membres d'une famille dont je devinais l'entente, la lumière tombait d'une ampoule laissée allumée par la gardienne. Un escalier de pierre aux marches usées en leur milieu tournait autour d'une rampe de bois. Entre les murs clairs et nus montait le silence oppressant des maisons habitées par la mort. Je suis passée devant la porte du bureau du pasteur, puis devant celle de la salle à manger, une pièce carrée qui servit également de salon et de salle de réunion pour les enfants, puis après être passée sous la voûte — elle divise le vestibule en deux parties — devant celle de la cuisine où s'activa longtemps Tabitha, la servante. Parvenue à hauteur de l'ancienne resserre à tourbe, je me suis engagée dans l'escalier, et je suis montée jusqu'au palier situé à mi-hauteur, entre le rez-de-chaussée et le premier étage, là où se trouve installée, dans un renfoncement dessiné à sa taille, la grosse horloge.

« Que venez-vous chercher ici, madame ? »

Dressé à côté de la balustrade, un homme me regardait fixement. La bouche fermée, il m'interrogeait, mais ailleurs, dans un monde qui n'était pas celui du songe, ni celui du sommeil, ni celui du cauchemar. À ses lunettes cerclées, à sa chevelure blanche, à ses traits creusés dans une chair usée par la vieillesse, je l'ai reconnu immédiatement. Alors que je croyais être venue au rendez-vous d'Emily , c'était à celui de Patrick Brontë, son père que je m'étais rendue. Ce n'était pas la jeune fille aux cheveux crantés et aux yeux clairs qui m'accueillait en haut de l'escalier, mais un vieillard autoritaire, le veuf de Maria Branwell qui, en mourant, avait abandonné à cette maison dans laquelle elle venait à peine de s'installer six enfants en bas âge et un mari désespéré.

# PREMIÈRE PARTIE

*« Monsieur, dit M. Helstone, rassemblant toute sa dignité, la grande science de l'homme est de se connaître lui-même, ainsi que le but vers lequel il dirige ses pas. »*

Charlotte Brontë, *Shirley*.
(Traduction Guy Faroux.)

*« Patrick Branty naquit le 17 mars 1777, jour de la Saint-Patrick, dans la chaumière d'Emdale située dans la paroisse de Drumballyrooney-cum-Drumgooland, en Ulster. Il était l'aîné de dix enfants, issus d'une famille pauvre, et dès son plus jeune âge, il dut lutter contre la misère et contre l'ingratitude du sol irlandais... »*

Jacques BLONDEL.

NE dit-on pas dans le monde qu'exister c'est « se faire un nom » ? Si cela est vrai, mon père, le révérend Patrick Brontë, connaissait la règle, et de l'existence il aurait dû recevoir la quintessence, car de son nom il fit toute une affaire.

Fils d'un vague Hugh Brunty ou Prunty, ou Branty, Irlandais de condition misérable qui cessa bien vite de compter ses enfants, Patrick, l'aîné, pourvu d'une solide intelligence et d'une originalité de caractère que son état de pasteur lui conseilla de taire, à part ce nom choisi par lui après maintes tergiversations, perdit tout. D'abord, à la date du 15 septembre 1821, Maria Branwell, son épouse à peine relevée de ses dernières couches ; puis, au mois de mai 1825, sa fille aînée, Maria, une fillette de douze ans dont nous ressentîmes cruellement la perte tant elle avait su semer d'amour autour d'elle ; puis, dans la même foulée sa deuxième fille, Elizabeth, emportée quinze jours plus tard par la tuberculose qui nous tua tous. Après une trêve de vingt-trois ans — dans cette destinée tragique elle prit figure de miracle —, Patrick Branwell, son fils, enfant trop aimé d'une tribu qui compta cinq filles, mourut le 24 septembre 1848 à l'âge de trente et un ans. Moi-même, d'un an moins âgée, je le suivis en décembre de la même année, précédant ma sœur Anne, laquelle nous rejoignit en mai 1849, huit mois après la mort de notre frère et cinq mois après la mienne. Charlotte fut la dernière à quitter le funèbre convoi ; elle se maria puis s'éteignit à l'âge de trente-neuf ans, à quelques mois d'un accouchement.

Notre père se retrouva donc seul avec son nom qui descendit avec lui dans la tombe. Il ne demanda aide à personne, même pas à son gendre. Arthur Bell Nicholls, auquel il voua mépris, au mieux indifférence. Seule la foi lui demeura fidèle jusqu'au bout. De cette tragédie, il reste aujourd'hui un nom que les biographes de notre famille se sont acharnés à défigurer :

Prunty, Branty, Brunty...

Mais voici son histoire.

Apprenti forgeron et aide-tisserand, notre père fut arraché à la médiocrité de sa condition par un pasteur, le révérend Harshaw, homme de cœur et de compassion. Ému par ce va-nu-pieds qui connaissait de la misère toutes les vicissitudes, et des petits métiers la précarité, Harshaw consentit à instruire à la lumière avare des chandelles le fils aîné de Hugh Brunty, ou Branty, ou Prunty, ou Bruntee, ou O'Prunty, et qu'importe !

Patrick avait à peine seize ans lorsqu'il devint instituteur, fort apprécié de ses élèves auxquels il inculqua ce qui l'occupait tout entier : le goût de l'étude et la passion du savoir : « L'analphabète ne sera jamais un homme épanoui, mais un esclave! Il lui manquera toujours l'essentiel, c'est-à-dire la connaissance! Sans elle notre esprit ne peut grandir!» Encouragé, cette fois, par le révérend Thomas Tighe, recteur de l'école paroissiale de Drumballyrooney, notre père abandonna un poste qui lui garantissait un avenir pour devenir étudiant boursier à Cambridge où il se rendit les poches vides. Certain jour, alors qu'il déambulait dans les jardins de St. John's College, il décida de refaçonner le nom qu'un obscur Irlandais lui avait donné. Assoiffé de reconnaissance et de gloire militaire, impressionné par Lord Nelson qui venait de recevoir de l'Angleterre agenouillée aux pieds de ses glorieux exploits le duché de Bronté, Patrick Brunty, plein de gratitude envers la Providence qui l'avait amené jusqu'aux hautes études, lâcha son nom comme on lâche une vieille valise. Il prit à un duché le nom qui le conduirait à la postérité.

Bronté! Pourquoi pas Brontë?

Ainsi passa-t-il de l'Irlande exsangue à l'orgueilleuse Angleterre par l'intermédiaire de deux voyelles dont il ne soupçonna jamais la charge d'ambition. Lui qui avait tellement lutté pour acquérir un peu de cette culture dont s'enorgueillissaient les classes privilégiées, imagina-t-il un instant que ce ne serait pas lui mais ses filles qui illustreraient le nom sous lequel il fut ordonné pasteur de l'Église anglicane en 1807? Je ne le crois pas. «La maternité est chez la femme ce qu'est la créativité chez l'homme! De même l'homme ne peut porter les enfants, de même la femme ne peut accoucher d'une œuvre d'art, qu'elle soit picturale, littéraire ou musicale!» Seul Branwell, son fils unique, eut droit à son attention et ses espoirs. Cette réserve faite, je m'empresse de dire ici combien mon père fut déloyalement traité par certains biographes. Mais si je veux pouvoir le défendre, il me faut d'abord dénoncer ses faiblesses ; loin de m'en offusquer, je ne vois en elles que les effets d'une société bâtie par des hommes soucieux de conserver leurs prérogatives.

« Dites-moi, chères filles, ne souhaitez-vous pas quelque jour fonder un foyer ? »

A l'image de ses contemporains, et bien qu'il demeurât toujours concaincu des bienfaits du savoir et de sa nécessité, ce « Savoir » auquel il sacrifia les nuits de son adolescence, partie de sa jeunesse, et les yeux de sa fin de vie, Patrick Brontë n'alla pas jusqu'à penser que la littérature pouvait être un passe-temps pour les femmes, à fortiori une activité honorable. En dehors des travaux ménagers, de la cuisine et de la couture, à quoi donc les filles étaient-elles bonnes à cette époque où il ne fallait point attirer l'attention sur des jupes trop savantes ? A s'établir dans la résignation du célibat ou, avec un peu de chance, à prendre place discrète auprès d'un mari choisi de préférence par un père plus soucieux de respectabilité que de bonheur. J'ajoute qu'il ne serait venu à l'esprit de personne de faire du bonheur un but. Le mari trouvé, à quoi servait-il sinon à féconder la jeune épousée, éventuellement à lui permettre d'accéder au monde, sa sensibilité, son intelligence bornée car soumise aux émotions, l'en ayant écartée depuis des temps immémoriaux ?

« Pourquoi ne me répondez-vous pas ? Ma question vous blesse ?
— Non, papa... enfin, oui et non.
— Ne voulez-vous pas avoir des enfants ?

— Certainement pas !
— Diable ! Et pourquoi ?
— Parce que nous ne sommes pas prêtes à répondre aux exigences d'un mari et qu'il nous plaît de vivre en votre compagnie ! »

Grâce à l'amour qu'elle porta à notre père, Maria Branwell échappa au triste destin que je viens de décrire, ce qui ne l'empêcha pas de succomber à la charge d'un rôle trop éprouvant pour elle : ne mit-elle pas au monde six enfants en sept ans ? Procréer, c'était alors collaborer avec Dieu, c'était apporter du sang neuf au monde. Le mien n'avait guère plus de trois ans lorsqu'elle mourut d'un cancer. Intercepté par la mort, ce message maternel ne parvint pas jusqu'à nous, en tout cas pas jusqu'à moi. Ma collaboration avec Dieu et le monde se ferait d'une autre manière. Plus tard, quand au terme de l'adolescence je tentai de rejoindre son souvenir afin de lui confier mes émois de jeune fille prête à s'ouvrir à l'amour qu'elle avait connu, je me trouvai confrontée à une réalité insupportable : l'intimité entre un homme et une femme ne pouvait aboutir qu'à la procréation, et par là, à l'épuisement et à la mort ! Cette révélation me livra au dégoût. Je me jurai d'échapper au destin qui avait fauché ma mère.

« Vous n'aimez donc pas les enfants ? Que va-t-on faire de ces curieuses filles ? »

Peut-être est-ce ici, et ici seulement, qu'il faut voir les raisons pour lesquelles, à l'inverse de notre frère qui eut pour eux tendresse et intérêt, nous, les sœurs Brontë, nous n'aimâmes jamais les enfants.

Mais j'en reviens à notre père. Lui qui avait

désiré ressembler à la belle image que l'on se faisait d'un époux, d'un père et d'un pasteur, qu'était-il devenu au lendemain des obsèques de sa femme? « Monsieur le pasteur, voulez-vous une aide? Ma fille pourrait faire votre courrier, le temps que vous repreniez pied ! »

« Vous êtes très aimable, madame, mais la douleur est pour moi une compagnie si exigeante que je ne puis en accueillir une autre, du moins pour l'instant.
— Nous craignons tous pour votre santé !
— Pour l'instant je n'ai besoin que d'oubli. Le souvenir de ces derniers mois me torture. »

Qui parmi les paroissiens se souvenait encore de cette terrible époque où le médecin, convoqué chaque jour à la cure, avait dû avouer son impuissance à guérir un mal trop sournois pour être curable? « Mais enfin, docteur, c'est impossible de la laisser souffrir ainsi ! À chaque maladie répond un traitement ! » Qui se souvenait encore de quelle façon Patrick Brontë avait protesté contre une épreuve devant laquelle il avait fini par s'agenouiller : « Oh, ma chère femme, je donnerais tout pour partager votre mal ! » Privé peu à peu d'un amour dont il n'avait guère eu le loisir de mesurer la grandeur et l'abnégation, il lui avait fallu aider notre mère à partir. Mais alors qu'elle avait toujours montré une réelle piété et une grande force de caractère, devant l'imminence de la mort la pauvre femme avait confessé des faiblesses d'enfant : « Patrick, êtes-vous sûr que Dieu existe? Êtes-vous certain que tout ceci a un sens? » Violentée par l'injustice du sort qui exigeait d'elle qu'elle abandonnât à l'incompétence d'un homme six orphelins dont l'aînée n'avait pas encore huit ans, Maria Branwell avait été sur le point de demander des comptes à Dieu : « Il ne peut vouloir une chose pareille ! » La solide foi de notre père avait su l'écarter à temps d'une révolte qui l'eût condamnée devant l'Éternel. Elle avait fini par s'en remettre à Dieu, était morte l'âme en paix.

« On va avoir le droit d'entrer dans sa chambre.
— Il faudra se tenir correctement et ne pas faire de bruit, surtout toi, Branwell, qui es si insupportable en ce moment ! »

Qui se souvenait de la matinée au cours de laquelle notre père nous avait convoqués dans la chambre mortuaire afin de dire adieu à notre mère ? Alignés le long du lit recouvert d'un immense drap blanc, nous avions déposé une fleur sur le corps et les deux mains serrées sur un crucifix. Seule, Anne, âgée de quelques mois, avait échappé à la vision d'horreur qu'est pour son enfant le cadavre d'une mère. Au moment de baiser la joue glacée de la gisante, Branwell s'était écarté en hurlant de terreur. Papa l'avait rattrapé par la manche : « Mon petit... mon petit... pourquoi cries-tu ainsi ? Prends donc exemple sur tes sœurs ! Regarde comme elles ont du courage ! » Au lieu de se calmer, notre frère s'était débattu, se refusant à un baiser : « Au secours ! » avait-il fini par crier. Devant tant d'effroi, notre père s'était décidé à lâcher prise. Laissant à ses sœurs muettes la dignité, Branwell s'était enfui. « Maria, Elizabeth, allez vite consoler votre petit frère ! » avait ordonné papa en retournant près du lit. Une heure plus tard, il avait retrouvé sa langue et ses esprits :

« Non, j'ai pas eu peur !
— Alors pourquoi as-tu crié de la sorte ?

— Parce que je voulais pas lui dire adieu ! Et d'abord, pourquoi papa y répond pas quand on lui demande où est maman ? »

Qui se souvenait de l'enterrement de la femme du pasteur ? Son mari. Ses enfants. Quelques paroissiens. Deux ou trois amis. Le fossoyeur qui l'avait portée en terre. De petite taille et naturellement frêle, le corps de Maria Branwell, amaigri par la longue et douloureuse maladie, avait été placé dans un cercueil d'enfant.

« Papa... Branwell voudrait savoir où est maman ?
— Au ciel, près de Dieu.
— Quand la reverrons-nous ?
— Bientôt.
— A l'heure de notre mort ?
— Oui, Maria, à l'heure de notre mort. C'est elle qui nous accueillera là-haut ! »

Tandis qu'à l'église on faisait l'éloge de la défunte, vantant sa ferveur religieuse, sa modestie, son élégance d'esprit, son extrême sensibilité, tandis qu'on évoquait avec lyrisme ses charités multiples, Patrick Brontë s'était-il rappelé le jour où, huit ans auparavant, il avait rencontré à Apperley Bridge, près de Bradford, la nièce de John Fennel, le directeur de l'institution où il avait été professeur ? Tandis que les orphelins reniflaient dans son dos de veuf, s'était-il laissé gagner par le souvenir ? Avait-il revu comme au premier jour de leur rencontre la charmante et douce Maria Branwell, une célibataire de trente ans, fille d'un marchand de Penzance en Cornouailles qui, les jours de fête, comptait onze enfants autour de la table, tous élevés dans la rigueur de la foi méthodiste ? Avait-il profité du sermon qu'un autre faisait à sa place pour se remémorer les lettres que la jeune femme lui avait envoyées à l'époque de leurs brèves fiançailles, lettres émouvantes, presque impudiques tant elles étaient sincères ? Et que n'eût-elle pas écrit alors, Maria Branwell, que n'eût-elle pas avoué sous le coup de cette passion dont elle avait fini par se plaindre, disant à son fiancé que l'amour terrestre l'écartait des soins qu'elle devait à Dieu ?

« Papa...
— Tais-toi, Branwell !
— J'ai oublié mon mouchoir... »

Et plus tard, tandis que notre père s'attardait aux abords d'une tombe fleurie, nous, les orphelins, avions guetté le dos de cet être, le seul sur lequel nous pouvions compter maintenant que notre mère n'était plus.

« Pourquoi il rentre pas !
— Parce qu'il est triste de laisser maman à la terre et au froid !
— Tu crois qu'on sent quelque chose quand on est là-dessous ? »

Lorsque je songe à cette terrible scène, lorsque je revois ce groupe d'enfants serrés contre une fenêtre d'où ils surveillent un père qui leur échappe déjà, je sens un immense, un monstrueux chagrin d'enfant. Ce n'est pas le mien. C'est celui de ma sœur aînée, Maria, une petiote de huit ans, menue et frêle, la seule à comprendre vraiment, en cette heure de complète déréliction, le sens du mot abandon.

Mais j'arrête là l'évocation : la souffrance de la famille Prunty, Brunty, Branty, O'Bruntee ne saurait se raconter ; elle ne regarde qu'elle.

*« La nature n'avait jamais compté faire de M. Helstone un bon mari. (...) Il pensait, aussi longtemps que sa femme gardait le silence, que rien ne la tourmentait et qu'elle n'avait besoin de rien. Au bout d'un an ou deux, elle n'était pour lui d'une grande importance sous aucun rapport; toutefois, lorsqu'un jour, brusquement, ainsi qu'il le pensa, car il l'avait à peine vue dépérir, elle prit congé de lui et de ce monde et qu'il ne trouva plus qu'une belle forme d'argile, froide et blanche, dans la couche nuptiale, il sentit la perte qu'il venait de faire, plus peut-être qu'il n'y parut... »*

Charlotte Brontë, *Shirley*.
(Traduction Guy Faroux.)

*«Sentez votre misère; soyez dans le deuil et les larmes: que votre rire se change en deuil, et votre joie en tristesse.*
*«Humiliez-vous devant le Seigneur, et Il vous élèvera!»*

Épître de JACQUES.

D'OÙ vient que je ne puisse quitter ce presbytère où me retient l'image d'un homme dressé en haut d'un escalier? Il s'enquiert avec insistance des raisons de ma visite; ai-je l'intention de m'attarder encore longtemps chez lui? Hélas, je le crains.

Va-t-on me chasser? Charlotte pourrait être ce «on», Charlotte dont je commence à sentir la présence, forte, intelligente, éveillée, ou bien Maria, cette petite fille frêle et courageuse qui tente de défendre contre ma curiosité les cinq orphelins dont elle a la charge? Ils sont tous là, bouleversés par le spectacle qui s'offre et s'offrira encore longtemps à eux, dans le cimetière où leur père continue à rendre une visite trop longue à la tombe de Maria Branwell, leur mère dont ils n'ont connu durant ces derniers mois de son agonie que les plaintes à peine étouffées, les échos de la souffrance, les protestations inutiles derrière une porte constamment fermée: «Tu crois que maman elle a mal? — Oui, très mal!»

«Qu'est-ce qu'ils font à l'intérieur?

— Ils se parlent.
— Qu'est-ce qu'ils font à l'intérieur?
— Ils attendent.
— Ils attendent quoi?
— Que Dieu vienne chercher la malade!»

Combien de fois seront-ils passés devant cette porte qu'il leur est interdit d'approcher? «Charlotte, viens vite! Branwell est en train d'écouter ce que dit maman! — Branwell! — Chut! vous allez me dénoncer! — Dépêche-toi de descendre ou je le dis à papa! — Dis ce que tu voudras! — Branwell! — Oui, papa! — Qu'étais-tu en train de faire? — J'essayais d'entendre ce que vous disiez à maman... — Et qu'est-ce que je lui disais? — Que vous prendriez toujours soin d'elle! — C'est tout ce que tu as entendu? — Que vous l'aimiez assez pour partager sa douleur; qu'elle n'était pas seule; que vous seriez toujours près d'elle! — Ne pleure pas, mon garçon! — Je pleure pas, j'ai les yeux qui coulent! — Tu sais que c'est interdit d'écouter aux portes? — Je recommencerai plus, papa. — Allez, va rejoindre tes sœurs!»

Combien de fois auront-ils traversé le palier du premier étage sur la pointe des pieds pour ne pas se faire remarquer? «Qui est là? — C'est Maria, maman! — Entre, ma petite fille, viens me dire bonjour! — Vous souffrez? — Oui, malheureusement, c'est pourquoi je ne puis m'occuper de vous en ce moment! Est-ce que je peux compter sur toi pour prendre soin de ton frère et de tes sœurs? — Je vous le promets!»

Combien de fois auront-ils aperçu dans l'entrebâillement d'une porte vite refermée le dos de Patrick Brontë penché sur l'être de douleur qu'il aurait voulu ramener à la vie, ou le profil navré du docteur incapable d'apporter un soulagement, ou la silhouette d'une amie de la famille effrayée par la progression du mal ? Combien de fois auront-ils entendu les chuchotements de la prière bousculée par l'angoisse de la mourante ? « Patrick, qu'allez-vous faire après mon départ ? Saurez-vous élever ces enfants ? Les aimerez-vous assez ? Les comprendrez-vous comme vous m'avez comprise ? »

★

Qui m'a autorisée à m'aventurer sur les traces d'une famille, jusqu'à ce palier où me parle un fantôme ?

> ... Pourquoi l'histoire porte-t-elle sur moi un regard aussi accusateur ? Que connaît-on de ma vie, de mes souffrances intimes pour m'avoir portraituré de si vilaine manière ? Tous les cadeaux que l'anonymat aurait pu me faire, la gloire de mes filles me les a retirés. Que Charlotte ait pris certains traits de mon caractère pour en vêtir un personnage de roman, c'est possible, et je ne chercherai pas à le nier — on puise l'eau à son puits — mais cela ne signifie pas que je fus Helstone, le héros de *Shirley* ! Mes enfants m'ont-ils approché d'assez près pour me connaître vraiment ? Leur ai-je jamais laissé la possibilité d'aller au-delà de la politesse et des apparences ? En cette époque de solitude morale où la bienséance interdisait les élans les plus authentiques, où l'on ne confessait rien de soi, et surtout pas ses tentations, et surtout pas son désarroi, qui connaissait qui ? Pouvais-je leur confier qu'à peine rendu au veuvage je m'étais inquiété de trouver une compagne qui leur tiendrait lieu de mère ? Pouvais-je leur raconter sans m'humilier com-

ment, avec quelle cruauté, trois célibataires, dont Mary Burder que j'avais courtisée avant de rencontrer Maria, m'avaient éconduit ?

Est-ce à moi que cette ombre s'adresse ?

Il est vrai qu'au lendemain de l'enterrement de ma chère épouse, la perspective de me retrouver seul en face de six enfants en bas âge me devint insoutenable. Je perdis la tête. Alors que j'aurais dû attendre l'apaisement que Dieu ne manqua pas de m'envoyer par la suite, je me révoltai contre mon sort. De cette révolte d'homme désarmé, mes enfants ne surent rien ou peu. Seule, l'aînée, Maria, devina ma détresse. Elizabeth Branwell, ma belle-sœur, accepta de venir vivre avec nous. Elle m'apporta un peu de paix, prit à cœur l'éducation des filles tandis que j'assumais celle de mon fils. Parce qu'il partagea longtemps ma chambre, Branwell — nous lui donnâmes le nom de sa mère pour prénom afin d'assurer la vivacité du souvenir de la morte — sut combien je souffris au cours de ces nuits où m'assaillait le souvenir : les gestes de tendresse de ma défunte femme, son sourire, ses mots chaleureux, son regard toujours affectueux, ses mains tendues vers un enfant. Seul mon fils sut combien moi, pasteur de l'Église anglicane et prédicateur réputé pour la conviction de ses sentiments, je doutai de Dieu et plus encore de sa justice...

Sur le palier du premier étage, il est là, vieillard au port militaire et à l'étonnante chevelure blanche. Il proteste, tente de se justifier. Il est vrai, certains et surtout certaines qui ont eu vent de son caractère difficile l'ont peint avec une violence extrême, lui glissant entre les mains, non pas le crucifix et le goupillon, mais un pistolet qu'il aurait porté du matin au soir, le déchargeant par une des fenêtres du presbytère pour s'assurer de son bon fonctionnement. Et l'image est si forte de cet homme d'Église réveillant chaque matin six orphelins et l'assemblée des morts étendus au pied de sa maison avec la sèche détonation d'une arme à feu pointée en direction du royaume d'outre-tombe, qu'elle nous aide à comprendre pourquoi les biographes ont eu tant de mal à l'écarter par la suite, lorsqu'il leur a fallu saisir le personnage au plus près de sa vérité.

Ainsi a-t-on prêté la violence et une sorte de rage non maîtrisée à un homme consciencieux et ardent qui s'est trouvé soudainement confronté à la population brutale et incommode d'un pays aux mœurs barbares où ne s'exprimaient bien que l'hostilité, l'alcoolisme et la misère ; celle des filatures. En ce début du XIXe siècle, elles étaient des mouroirs pour enfants. Condamnée au bagne et à la mort précoce, la jeunesse du Yorkshire raconte encore aujourd'hui son histoire sur les pierres tombales des cimetières de la région de Bradford, de Leeds et de Halifax ; rares étaient ceux qui atteignaient vingt ans.

★

A qui ne connaît pas cette superbe contrée située à la limite du West Riding du Yorkshire, la visite est vivement conseillée car elle réserve surprises et émotions.

Aussitôt dépassée la petite ville de Haworth située à flanc de coteau, juste au-dessus de la vallée de la Worth, apparaissent les Moors dans toute leur magnificence et leur sauvagerie. L'expression « à perte de vue » trouve ici son sens. Sur ces *hauts où le vent fait rage*, ce ne sont que cieux balayés et souvent menaçants, étendues désertiques, landes gorgées d'eau, arbres tordus ou foudroyés, murets de pierres. Comme le ciel auquel il emprunte sa vastitude, le paysage file aux quatre coins cardinaux. Il fait alliance avec une tristesse qui n'est pas triste à la manière ordinaire; il s'agit d'autre chose... mais comment l'exprimer? Sur les Moors, même le vocabulaire est la proie du vent!

A l'intérieur des rares fermes isolées et comme accroupies sous un toit d'ardoise, protégées des visites importunes par la distance, on se méfie toujours du visage inconnu: «Qu'apporte cet étranger? Une nouvelle du monde?» Même si les beuveries, les combats de coqs et de rats, les rixes sanglantes ont disparu avec la grande misère, la méfiance poursuit son patient travail; elle garde le paysan du curieux comme le chien bien dressé son maître.

J'allais oublier! Dans ce pays hanté par les fantômes, le brouillard joue un rôle écrasant. Du bleu pâle à l'indigo délavé, en passant par toutes les gammes de gris jusqu'au blanc de la craie écrasée, il offre ses nuances au regard qui s'effraie de son approche. Collé au pare-brise de la voiture, pour le coup aussi aveuglée que son conducteur qui n'ose pas descendre, il s'insinue dans les veines, parle au cerveau: le sentiment de solitude laisse place à celui de l'emmurement. Sur ces *hauts où le vent fait rage*, ce n'est pas le corps qui frissonne, c'est la mémoire.

«Papa, qu'est-ce que c'est qu'un esprit?
— C'est un être sans corps.
— Papa, qu'est-ce que c'est qu'un revenant?
— C'est un esprit qui revient sur ses pas.
— Papa, qu'est-ce que c'est qu'un fantôme?

— C'est une apparence.
— Papa, qu'est-ce que la vie ? Une apparence ?
— Non, Branwell, c'est un don de Dieu ! »

Aussi ne s'étonnera-t-on pas d'apprendre à travers les livres, ou les on-dit, ou même au fil d'une conversation, que les nuits de grand vent, de tempête, d'orage, les âmes errantes viennent frapper à la vitre des demeures isolées pour demander asile.

« *"Me voilà revenue à la maison : je m'étais perdue dans la lande !" La voix parlait encore, quand je distinguai vaguement une figure d'enfant qui regardait à travers la fenêtre...* »

Au pays des Brontë, rien n'a changé. Le village monte toujours la colline de chaque côté d'une rue abrupte, jusqu'à la vieille église où sonne le glas. A peine distingue-t-on les maisons neuves des plus anciennes.

« Où étais-tu encore partie, Emily ?
— J'étais là-haut, papa ! »

Lieu de repliement, de rêves interminables, d'évocations romantiques et mystérieuses dans lesquelles passe et repasse le profil du pasteur enveloppé d'une épaisse houppelande noire, ou la silhouette d'un cheval monté par un hobereau à moitié ivre... Lieu de tourmente aussi, de paix acquise à prix fort, où l'on peut arpenter des milles et des milles sans voir âme qui vive, à peine l'aile d'un oiseau ou la fourrure d'un lièvre effrayé. Entre Keighley et Haworth, les Moors attendent la visite d'une morte.

« Je n'aime pas te savoir seule ! Ne crains-tu pas les rôdeurs ?
— Non... la lande me protège.
— Écoutez-moi cette petite aventurière ! La lande ne te veut ni bien ni mal, elle se contente d'être lande ! »

Avant de quitter ce pays où j'ai enfin compris ce que signifiait le verbe «errer», je voudrais dire combien me sont apparues voyantes les couleurs du tourisme qui déverse à la belle saison un flot de visiteurs en mal de souvenirs brontéens : linge de maison, vaisselle marquée au nom de la famille, papiers à lettres, boîtes sur lesquelles est reproduit un tableau représentant les trois sœurs portraiturées par leur frère.

Quel effroi saisirait les filles du pasteur s'il leur était donné de revenir sur les lieux de leur vie passée !

*« Les longues boucles de ses cheveux noirs tombaient*
*Sur une joue d'une beauté cadavérique.*
*Il semblait jeune — usé toutefois comme ceux*
*Qui dépensent leur temps de jeunesse avant l'heure.* »

Emily Jane Brontë,
juillet 1839.
(Traduction Pierre Leyris

*« Ils durent montrer leurs peintures à Ellen. Elle examina le tableau de Branwell qui représentait les trois sœurs et qu'on avait encadré et suspendu au-dessus de l'escalier. Au moment où il fut exécuté, Emily avait à peu près quinze ans. Comme Charlotte et Anne, elle semble plus âgée que dans le tableau "au fusil", mais c'est la même bouche charnue, le même front large, les mêmes beaux yeux bien placés. Charlotte se tient d'un côté d'une colonne, Emily et Anne de l'autre. Leurs cheveux sont coupés assez courts. Au lieu de leurs collerettes, elles ont mis de grands cols à la puritaine. »*

Virginia MOORE.

LA présence de ce portrait auquel vous faites allusion et qui, je vous l'accorde, circule à tort et à travers, m'interroge plus que sa commercialisation ne vous choque. Par quel miracle ce document n'a-t-il pas été détruit avec d'autres qui étaient plus précieux que lui ?

A l'époque où il a été peint par notre frère tout à son bonheur d'artiste en devenir, qui aurait pu imaginer le destin glorieux de ce tableau de facture modeste, pour ne pas dire maladroite, où nous, les filles Brontë — de cinq les trois survivantes —, sommes représentées ? Peut-être notre père qui voyait en son fils poindre le génie ? « Çà, mon garçon, je suis tout bonnement stupéfait de découvrir en toi des talents aussi divers ! » Ou Tabitha, notre servante, émerveillée par la vague ressemblance :

« Et dire qu'a fait ça, not'e Brannii, avec

d'mauvais pinceaux, et un rien d'c'te peinture achetée à Bradford, où c'est qu'y est encore allé pour faire Dieu sait qu'é bêtise comme à son habitude d'chenapan qu'en f'ra jamais qu'à sa tête qu'a plus irlandaise qu'celle d'not'e révérend ! »

Le monde n'aura connu de nous — seule Charlotte a eu droit à plus de justice grâce au crayon de George Richmond qui a fait d'elle une jolie esquisse — que la reproduction multipliée à l'infini d'un portrait de famille peint par un débutant. Au risque de paraître contrariante, je conseillerai la prudence au spectateur trop confiant. Ce regard fixe, je peux l'en assurer, n'a jamais appartenu à Anne qui se trouve représentée en bas et à gauche du tableau. Ma jeune sœur avait des yeux superbes, d'une couleur violette que je n'ai retrouvée chez personne, une carnation pâle, des cheveux bouclés d'une manière ravissante, une expression si délicate que seul un grand talent aurait pu la rendre. Cette bouche à peine séparée du nez épais rappelle sans lui ressembler vraiment celle de Charlotte représentée à droite du tableau. Notre aînée avait hérité des traits de notre mère ; ni jolie, ni vraiment ingrate, elle se plaignit toute sa vie de cette ascendance maternelle qui, prétendait-elle, l'avait désavantagée par rapport à nous qui avions emprunté nos traits à l'Irlande des Brunty. J'ajouterai, en désignant mon portrait au centre, que si ce visage alourdi par des tempes trop larges, des joues trop pleines, ne fut pas le mien, il ne me fut pas non plus complètement étranger. Et s'il me fallait faire aujourd'hui mon autoportrait, je préférerais la description d'Ellen Nussey, l'amie de Charlotte, au pinceau de Branwell, en signalant toutefois que mes yeux n'étaient pas aussi beaux qu'elle le dit.

*« Emily Brontë à cette époque avait acquis une silhouette gracieuse, souple. Elle était la personne la plus grande de la famille, à l'exception de son père. Ses cheveux, qui étaient naturellement aussi beaux que ceux de Charlotte, étaient aussi peu gracieusement frisottés et serrés, et elle aussi avait un teint blafard. Elle avait de très beaux yeux — pleins de bonté, de vie, limpides ; mais elle vous regardait rarement ; elle était trop réservée. Leur couleur pouvait sembler gris foncé, parfois bleu sombre, cela variait. »*

Je ferai les mêmes réserves sur un autre tableau qui me représente de profil. Lorsque je le vois reproduit, j'en suis presque fâchée, car je ne me souviens pas d'avoir jamais eu un visage aussi flou, un nez aussi important, un menton aussi faible. Je n'eus guère, il est vrai, l'opportunité de me regarder ; les miroirs captaient trop de vanité pour trouver place chez un pasteur. A peine nous aperçûmes-nous dans l'eau noire d'une vitre donnant sur la nuit ou celle plus claire d'une bassine. Par manque d'appétence pour nous-mêmes, nous ne prîmes jamais plaisir à nous contempler. C'est à travers nos romans qu'on saisira le mieux nos traits, la mobilité de notre caractère, nos expressions.

Mais je m'avise que l'on pourrait voir dans ces propos une réserve à l'égard de Branwell, le portraitiste de la famille. Si réserve il y a, elle ne concerne pas le tableau lui-même mais l'artiste, son caractère, sa violence.

« Personne ne peut m'en empêcher !
— Non, en effet, c'est ton œuvre ! Mais pourquoi faire une chose pareille ? »

Je ne puis songer sans amertume à la scène

pénible qui eut lieu en cet après-midi de colère, alors que l'œuvre, sur le point d'être terminée, n'attendait plus que sa signature. Après nous avoir fait poser à tour de rôle et s'être peint lui-même au centre du tableau, Branwell, pendant que la peinture était encore fraîche, a effacé rageusement son image. En s'y appliquant, on peut surprendre entre Charlotte et moi la forme de son visage tout en hauteur et le col de sa chemise. Comment ne pas voir dans ce geste destructeur les prémices d'une existence saccagée au départ par qui, jamais, ne s'acceptera ? A l'instant de s'annuler, élément perturbateur au sein d'un groupe soudé par l'harmonie, Branwell a-t-il eu l'intuition de ce que le destin nous réservait ? Lui qui désirait fréquenter la gloire et aspirait à la reconnaissance du grand nombre, s'est-il effacé pour n'avoir pas à se mesurer à nous, ses sœurs, que pourtant il dominait du haut de son talent ? A cette question je n'ai jamais pu répondre, ni à l'époque, ni plus tard.

★

Mais je reviens sur mes pas.

Au lendemain des obsèques de notre mère, notre tante, Elizabeth Branwell, étant retournée à Penzance pour y régler ses affaires et prendre une décision qui l'engagerait pour la vie, ce fut Maria qui eut la charge de nous donner ce que la mort venait de nous prendre : l'amour d'une mère, sa compréhension, ses soins. Nous nous accrochâmes à cette petite aussi démunie que nous comme les rescapés d'un naufrage à un radeau. Devant l'urgence de la demande, elle fit front courageusement : « Maria, je ne sais pas lacer mes bottines ! — Maria, viens vite, Anne a fait pipi dans l'escalier ! — Maria, Charlotte pleure dans son lit ! — Maria, Branwell m'a battue ! » Sa foi, sa bonté, son intelligence lui dictèrent les gestes indispensables.

Sans l'avoir jamais cherché, elle trouva le chemin de notre confiance, celui de notre cœur, répara en nous ce qu'il y avait de brisé. Puis elle entreprit d'enseigner l'alphabet à Branwell, l'indiscipliné, l'insolent, le bavard, mais aussi le plus prometteur des enfants.

« D'abord, les hommes ils sont bien plus forts que les femmes ! La preuve, moi je suis bien plus costaud que vous cinq réunies ! »

Dès qu'il sut lire, elle lui fit partager ses bonheurs de lectrice, le contenu de ses cahiers. Flatté par l'intérêt qu'on lui portait, Branwell tenta de s'emparer du pouvoir :

« Toi, Emily, tu n'as qu'à rester avec la petite ! »

Au groupe des lecteurs s'ajoutèrent bientôt Charlotte, puis Elizabeth, encore indécise dans son caractère.

« Je ne suis pas petite !
— Si, Anne, tu es petite ! »

Autour de la table de salle à manger où nous maintenaient Sarah et Nancy Garrs, les deux servantes excédées par la turbulence de toute cette marmaille, s'organisaient des jeux. Parfois l'un de nous trouvait le temps long : « Voulez-vous être sages et ne pas crier ! Que va dire papa lorsqu'il va rentrer ? Que vous ne savez pas grandir ! » Pour nous ramener au calme, Maria nous faisait la lecture. Même si nous ne comprenions pas grand-chose, nous aimions écouter sa voix charmante et appliquée : « Qui c'est Napoléon ? — Pourquoi la reine Caroline elle a des ennuis avec le roi George IV ? — Qui c'est Chateaubriand ? — Où c'est qu'elle habite la famille royale d'Angleterre ? »

« Je ne répondrai plus à vos questions. Vous en avez assez appris pour aujourd'hui !
— Qu'est-ce que c'est qu'un spectre ?
— Branwell, si tu insistes encore une fois, je te mets à la porte !
— C'est un mort qui se promène comme un vivant ! »

Notre santé morale affichant bonne mine, Maria s'inquiéta de notre père gagné par la misanthropie ; il venait d'essuyer trois refus successifs à la suite de trois demandes en mariage. Devant le désarroi d'un homme de quarante ans passés qui ne savait comment affronter seul six enfants, elle apprit à devenir adulte. Pour rompre l'isolement de ce père à l'humeur maussade, elle s'essaya à des lectures plus difficiles, notamment celle des journaux qui parvenaient au presbytère. Sur la table du bureau où nous n'avions pas le droit de pénétrer sans en demander l'autorisation, il y avait toujours le *Leeds Intelligencer* et le *Blackwood's Edinburg Magazine*.

« Où est mon journal ?
— Sur le lit de Maria.
— Maria !
— Oui, papa !
— Je t'interdis de monter les journaux dans ta chambre ! C'est moi qui décide de tes lectures ! »

A l'heure des repas, tandis que nous partagions la nourriture frugale imposée, non pas uniquement par l'ascétisme dictatorial et l'avarice de notre père comme on l'a trop souvent dit, mais par notre pauvreté, Maria demandait l'autorisation de prendre la parole. Elle posait des questions, s'enquérait avec le sérieux d'une grande personne des problèmes de l'époque. Quelle tournure prendraient les bagarres de Halifax si les patrons n'y mettaient bon ordre? Les ouvriers avaient-ils raison de protester contre leurs conditions de travail? Était-il juste que les enfants fussent employés dans des manufactures mal chauffées où ils mouraient de froid? Que pensait papa qui était dans la tradition des «évangéliques» et, bien que tolérant, plutôt conservateur, de ces dissidents qui ne recherchaient à travers Dieu que l'aventure et le désordre, bousculant les dogmes les mieux établis? Devait-on rejeter le prédéterminisme que prêchaient les calvinistes et s'écarter d'une doctrine où le salut comme la condamnation étaient décidés à l'avance? Le révérend Patrick Brontë, que tout le monde respectait à la ronde parce qu'il avait des égards pour chacun, était-il adepte du méthodisme dont il semblait accepter la doctrine touchant le salut? «Mon Dieu, mais où as-tu appris tout cela?» Maria jetait un regard éperdu de reconnaissance à notre père stupéfait par un si grand savoir: «Comment une enfant de ton âge peut-elle comprendre de tels problèmes?»

«Je vous en prie, papa, répondez-moi!
— Je tente de prêcher et de pratiquer la charité, telle que le Christ l'a enseignée.
— Vous pensez donc que nous sommes tous égaux devant Dieu?
— Oui, Maria! Non seulement je le pense, mais j'en suis certain! Je désapprouve le zèle d'une pratique d'où sont exclues la compassion et la tolérance!»

Papa se taisait souvent au milieu d'une phrase. Il regardait tristement la pomme de terre dans son assiette, l'écrasait avec sa fourchette. Son silence durait parfois quelques secondes, parfois quelques minutes. Nous, les enfants, nous attendions patiemment qu'il reprenne la parole : « C'est parce que je crois au Christ rédempteur que je cite chaque dimanche une parabole de l'Évangile. »

« *Comme ils étaient en route, quelqu'un dit à Jésus en chemin : "Je te suivrai partout où tu iras." Jésus lui dit : "Les renards ont des terriers et les oiseaux du ciel des nids ; le Fils de l'homme, lui, n'a pas où poser sa tête."* »

« Qui c'est qu'a dit ça ?
— Saint Luc !
— C'est qui saint Luc ? Un parent de Jésus ?
— Dis-moi, mon garçon, quand apprendras-tu à t'exprimer correctement ?
— Quand Maria s'occupera plus de moi ! Moi aussi je veux tout savoir ! »

Ému par cette enfant qui tentait de se hausser jusqu'à lui, notre père ne manqua jamais de répondre à Maria avec franchise, lui confiant ce qu'il pensait de la politique et des luttes au sein de l'Église. Ces discussions nous servirent d'enseignement. A l'âge où les autres lisent des contes de fées, nous, nous étions à nous poser des questions sur les vertus de la religion selon Wesley et celles, plus conformistes, de l'Église anglicane traditionnelle.

Le repas terminé, nous ne quittions jamais la salle à manger sans une prière destinée à notre mère qui nous attendait au ciel ; Dieu lui avait prouvé combien il l'aimait en la rappelant à lui.

« Si Dieu nous aimait, Il nous aurait laissé notre maman !
— Assez d'insolence, Branwell ! Il y a des choses que tu ne peux pas comprendre ! Souviens-toi d'une chose... c'est à la blessure que l'on mesure l'amour du Seigneur ! »

*Fragment*

*« Les pieds de sa sœur, de son frère*
*Essuient la rosée embaumée :*
*Elle bondit pour saluer*
*L'herbe, les fleurs et le soleil.* »

Emily Jane Brontë, août 1837.
(Traduction Pierre Leyris

*«Lorsque le révérend Patrick Brontë, désirant en apprendre davantage sur la forme d'esprit de ses six jeunes enfants, orphelins de mère, les dissimula tour à tour derrière un masque afin qu'ils lui répondent avec plus d'audace, il révéla pour la première fois, aux trois sœurs qui devaient survivre, le don béni de l'anonymat.»*

Daphné Du Maurier

Dans un coin du bureau où j'aime à situer sa haute et sévère silhouette, à gauche de la fenêtre qui donne sur le jardin, et un peu plus bas sur le cimetière dont on aperçoit le sommet des tombes, le révérend Patrick Brontë s'abandonne à la rêverie d'une fin de journée. Il songe à sa femme, aux enfants qu'elle lui a laissés en témoignage d'une belle union. Son affection est-elle ressentie aussi fortement qu'il le souhaiterait ? Une idée vient de lui traverser l'esprit ; elle lui semble bonne. Il s'approche du bureau, sort du tiroir un masque, appelle les enfants installés dans la salle d'étude du premier étage, une pièce minuscule aux murs recouverts de dessins et d'inscriptions où ils aiment s'agglutiner comme des abeilles. Un branle-bas lui annonce qu'il a été entendu. Les enfants descendent l'escalier en courant. Un visage apparaît dans l'entrebâillement de la porte ; c'est celui de Branwell. Les yeux vifs sous la masse des cheveux roux, il s'approche de son père qui tient ses mains cachées derrière son dos. Les cinq filles, plus circonspectes, suivent en file indienne. Devançant Maria qui va sur ses onze ans, Charlotte — elle n'en a que huit — donne déjà le ton. Son sérieux, la sévérité de son regard auquel rien n'échappe interrogent son père. Anne, la petite de quatre ans, clôt le cortège.

« Pourquoi nous avez-vous convoqués ?
— Tu vas bientôt le savoir, Branwell !
— Nous n'avons rien fait de mal !
— Qui vous accuse ? »

Papa montre le masque. Sans dire un mot, il le pose sur son visage, guette à travers les deux trous l'effet produit. Surpris, les enfants ne savent quelle attitude adopter. Branwell lui-même hésite ; il se demande s'il doit rire ou protester. L'inconnu qui a pris la place du père prononce des phrases que les enfants saisissent mal tant ils sont troublés. Que dit cet homme ni chair ni carton ? Il leur demande de dire la vérité, rien que la vérité, toute la vérité. En bref, il les questionne. Un père peut-il tout entendre ? C'est lui qui répond : oui. Un enfant peut-il tout dire à son père ? Certes, mais il n'ose pas. Ce masque est donc là pour métamorphoser la relation. « Qu'est-ce que ça veut dire métamorphoser ? » Le révérend gronde Branwell, le bavard. « Celui qui sera protégé par ce masque pourra dire ce qu'il pense ! » Il n'aura pas à redouter les foudres paternelles ; sa réponse, même insolente, sera reçue et considérée.

« *"Quelle est, lui demande M. Brontë, la meilleure manière de mesurer la différence d'intelligence de l'homme et de la femme ?" Rapide comme la flèche, la réponse du petit garçon jaillit: "C'est de considérer les différences de leurs corps."»*

Daphné Du Maurier.

«C'est à ton tour Emily! Prends ce masque et pose-le sur ton visage. Que dois-je faire lorsque Branwell se montre insupportable?
— Vous devez tenter de le raisonner, papa! Mais s'il n'obéit pas, comme à son habitude, vous devez lui donner une bonne et violente fessée!
— Voilà qui est bien dit, ma fille! Qu'en penses-tu, Branwell?
— Ce que j'en pense? C'est qu'Emily est une chipie et une jalouse! Elle aurait voulu être un garçon!»

Après cette scène inattendue et quelque peu théâtrale, en voici une autre. En haut du perron vient d'apparaître, bien droite dans sa robe de soie mal taillée, Miss Branwell, nouvelle venue dans ce décor. Sous le coquet bonnet, son visage adouci par une frange de faux cheveux reflète l'intelligence et un rien de malice qu'atténue le sérieux appris dès l'enfance. Patrick Brontë n'a pas eu d'effort à faire pour convaincre sa belle-sœur de demeurer quelque temps au presbytère; n'est-elle pas déjà venue deux fois aider sa sœur épuisée par les maternités? D'abord à la Woodhouse Grove Academy où demeuraient les jeunes mariés, puis à Thornton, une bourgade située à quelques milles de Haworth, où Patrick Brontë avait la charge de la paroisse?

«Je ne m'habituerai jamais à cet horrible climat!
— Il y a pire!

— Dans l'au-delà, peut-être... et encore, je ne suis pas sûre qu'il ne fasse pas meilleur en enfer ! »

A peine débarquée dans ce pays battu par le vent et les tempêtes, Miss Branwell s'est mise à regretter les douceurs et l'aménité de sa chère Cornouailles, ses arrière-saisons, son printemps, ses couchers de soleil : « Mon Dieu, que cette région est hostile à l'homme ! Je ne pensais pas qu'il y faisait si froid et si humide ! Voilà qui n'est pas bon pour les rhumatismes ! »

« Vous verrez, le corps s'y fait, de même l'esprit ! »

Hormis le froid et le vent, cette vieille fille de quarante-cinq ans ne redoute rien. Armée des principes rigoureux que le méthodisme a forgés pour les gens de sa race, elle n'a jamais connu le doute ni l'angoisse. Son beau-frère a été averti d'emblée ; elle est venue à Haworth pour l'aider à élever les enfants de sa sœur, et non pour se faire entretenir : « L'indépendance est pour moi chose si précieuse que je ne la sacrifierai qu'à l'heure où Dieu me retirera la vie ! » Bien qu'elle ne dispose que de cinquante livres de rente annuelle au regard des émoluments du pasteur qui se montent à cent soixante-dix livres, elle participera aux frais du ménage, qu'il le veuille ou non.

« Pour peu qu'on n'en mélange pas la monnaie, deux bourses valent mieux qu'une !
— Je ne vous désobligerai pas en refusant votre participation. Sachez cependant que je me sens gêné par cet excès de générosité. Me voici redevable non seulement de votre temps mais aussi de vos revenus ! »

Miss Branwell, qui n'a pas su devenir riche par le biais d'un mariage avantageux, est restée économe dans le célibat. « La liberté n'a pas de prix, mon cher ! — Ça dépend pour qui ! J'en connais qui ont plus peur d'elle que de la servitude ! » Parmi toutes ses amies pourvues d'une famille, elle est la seule à pouvoir encore affirmer ses idées sans la crainte d'un blâme. Ce sens de l'économie, de la liberté d'esprit, elle l'inculquera à ses nièces, à Charlotte notamment qui s'en souviendra au moment de refuser les propositions de mariage qu'on lui fera par convenance ou intérêt.

> « Dieu seul sait pour combien de temps je suis ici !
> — Je ne voudrais pas que vous vous sentiez prisonnière d'une situation !
> — Il est hors de question que j'abandonne à un homme seul les enfants de ma sœur ! »

Parvenue à bon port, Miss Branwell ne se démettra de ses fonctions de mère adoptive qu'à son décès, soit vingt ans plus tard. Quant à sa chère ville de Penzance, elle ne la reverra plus jamais. Le sacrifice sera de taille, même pour une âme trempée comme la sienne.

> « Puisque je suis condamnée à subir l'exil et un climat exécrable, j'aimerais avoir une chambre convenable, avec une bonne cheminée et de grands murs pour y accrocher les souvenirs qui me tiendront compagnie ! »

La demande a été entendue. Patrick Brontë lui a offert ce qu'il y avait de mieux : l'ancienne chambre de sa femme située en face de la sienne, au-dessus de la salle à manger; elle donne sur le cimetière auquel, dans cette demeure, personne ne peut échapper.

« Qu'à cela ne tienne! Je ne m'en plaindrai pas. J'ai de la sympathie pour les morts. Ils ont assez souffert pour qu'on continue à les plaindre! »

Aussitôt installée, Tante a sorti de ses malles ses travaux d'aiguille. Tandis qu'elle brode des psaumes sur un canevas, elle médite ou tend l'oreille. Que fait-on en bas? La porte d'entrée vient de claquer; on frappe à la porte du bureau. C'est certainement un paroissien qui vient chercher un remède pour son âme malade ou demander une messe pour un défunt, ou encore prier le révérend d'intervenir dans la vie dépravée d'un de ces alcooliques qui errent dans le village. A Haworth, l'ivresse court les rues. Pour défendre leur sécurité, les gens de bien ont dû fonder une Société pour la suppression du vice. Tout en tirant l'aiguille, Miss Branwell s'agace sur une pensée: si le péché poursuit ainsi son chemin, on ne pourra bientôt plus sortir dans la rue. Déjà, à peine dépassée l'église on entend venant de la taverne, le Black Bull, les insanités et les rires des ivrognes. A longueur de journée, ils sont là à échanger des insultes et des grossièretés. Dans ce coin du Yorkshire, la misère est mauvaise conseillère et personne ne semble pouvoir la museler.

« Encore ce refrain! »

Emily joue du piano. Branwell est avec elle; ses gloussements montent jusqu'au premier étage. Seul garçon au milieu d'une ribambelle de filles, il dirige la tribu. Jamais esprit n'a été aussi vif, intelligence aussi brillante, dons d'imitation aussi grands. Le dialecte du Yorkshire n'a plus rien à apprendre à qui sait si bien jouer le rustre dans la cuisine. Bien qu'elle n'apprécie guère la désinvolture et l'insolence du plaisantin, Miss Branwell croit fermement à l'avenir de ce petit rouquin qu'on ne peut qu'aimer, même si de cet amour il abuse. La fierté de la famille a basculé de son côté ; chacun sait que de lui viendront de grandes choses. Emporté par l'enthousiasme son père a décidé de lui apprendre le grec et le latin. Joli projet, mais tout cela ne dit pas à Miss Branwell qui s'occupera de l'éducation des cinq filles : « Sûrement pas moi ! » Plutôt que d'enseigner les rudiments de la grammaire, Tante préfère discuter avec son beau-frère du méthodisme ; ce sont les seuls moments où ils se rencontrent, dans l'affrontement, mais aussi dans la conciliation. Pourquoi ne chercherait-on pas une institution peu coûteuse, du moins pour les aînées, Maria et Elizabeth, qu'il serait temps d'instruire un peu sérieusement ?

> « Trop d'originalité nuit, à plus forte raison lorsqu'elle s'adresse à des fillettes comme celles-ci ! Maria tient des discours savants à Elizabeth qui l'imite ! »

Quelle heure est-il ? Le piano et les rires se sont tus. Profitant d'un moment de liberté et faussant compagnie aux adultes, les enfants se sont échappés de la maison. Qu'il fasse froid ou chaud, ils rôdent sur la lande ; pas un sentier, pas une grotte dont ils ne connaissent la géographie et les replis. Emily, encore mieux que les autres, sait où se nichent les oiseaux et où se cache le gibier : cette petite en remontrerait à un chasseur ! Curieuse enfant en vérité que la quatrième fille de Maria Branwell ! Insaisissable, mystérieuse, déjà hautaine. Il n'y a que sa sœur Anne, la plus petite, qui ait droit aux manifestations de sa tendresse. Le secret de ce cœur fermé sur lui-même est si bien gardé qu'il ne viendrait l'idée à personne de lui poser des questions: « Que fera-t-on d'elle plus tard? — Ne vous inquiétez pas, Elizabeth! Jolie comme elle est, nous trouverons toujours à la marier! » Se sentirait-elle isolée dans cette famille ou, à l'exemple des animaux pour lesquels elle a une véritable passion, défendrait-elle son territoire? Mais que signifient ces cris?

« C'est ton travail, pas le mien!
— J'le dirai à miss!
— Dis-lui c'que tu veux! Ça m'empêche pas d'penser qu't'es une foutue fainéante! »

Sarah et Nancy Garrs, les servantes, sont en train de se chamailler dans la cuisine. En voilà deux dont il faudra songer à se séparer. Justement le révérend a entendu vanter les mérites d'une veuve; encore robuste pour ses cinquante-trois ans, Tabitha Aykroyd prendra son service dès que les deux écervelées auront été renvoyées. Cette paysanne apportera au presbytère ce qui lui manque; la bonne humeur, la chaleur du peuple, le franc-parler des gens d'ici dont le patois ne craint pas les imperfections. En voilà une qui saura tenir les enfants à la maison; jamais personne n'a su aussi bien raconter les histoires macabres: « Elle donnerait froid dans le dos à un général d'Empire! » Tante se lève. Elle va mettre un morceau de tourbe dans la cheminée. Ses semelles de bois résonnent sur le plancher. « A pieds froids, gorge malade! » a-t-elle l'habitude de rétorquer à ceux qui lui font remarquer combien sa démarche est bruyante.

★

Une troisième scène s'impose à moi, menée plus rondement que les deux précédentes. Miss Branwell est en train de descendre l'escalier du presbytère refermé sur les ombres d'une fin de journée. Parvenue dans le vestibule, elle s'avance jusqu'à la porte du bureau, tend l'oreille. Le silence qui règne au rez-de-chaussée lui confirme que le pasteur est seul. Après avoir frappé deux coups secs, elle avance un nez pointu dans l'entrebâillement de la porte : « Entrez donc, Elizabeth ! Quel bon vent vous amène à cette heure ? » Avant même d'avoir pris des nouvelles de sa santé, le révérend s'enquiert des lectures de la journée : la disciple de John Wesley a-t-elle lu dans *The Methodist Magazine*, l'article consacré à la discipline du devoir ?

« Les calvinistes sont des gens dangereux, Elizabeth !
— Et pourquoi, s'il vous plaît ?
— Parce qu'ils osent prétendre que seuls les prédestinés rejoindront le Royaume ! Le Christ est venu sur terre pour racheter tous les hommes, y compris les plus mauvais !
— C'est vous qui le dites ! »

Miss Branwell semble tracassée par un problème qui ne regarde pas Dieu, mais son beau-frère. Elle sort de sa poche la précieuse tabatière, prend une pincée de tabac, la présente à ses narines. Le geste choque le révérend qui trouve la manie fâcheuse, surtout chez une femme aussi distinguée. « Je vous sens préoccupée, Elizabeth ? » Miss Branwell l'est en effet. La coqueluche qui sévit dans la maison l'a épuisée ; après avoir soigné Maria et Elizabeth, ne doit-elle pas aujourd'hui s'occuper de Charlotte et d'Emily ?

Tout en essuyant soigneusement ses verres de lunettes, Patrick Brontë joint ses plaintes à celles de sa belle-sœur. Que peut-on faire de cinq filles lorsqu'on est pauvre? « Leur donner une éducation, et éventuellement un métier ! Ne m'avez-vous pas parlé d'une institution destinée aux filles de pasteurs peu fortunés que dirige un certain Carus Wilson ? » Situé dans le Westmoreland, à Cowan Bridge, non loin de Leeds, cet établissement subventionné par de riches familles jouit d'une excellente réputation. « Vous me conseillez donc de me séparer de mes enfants ? » De son œil d'oiseau, Miss Branwell fixe son beau-frère. « C'est le sort de tous les parents, n'est-il pas vrai ? » Patrick Brontë soupire : toute vérité n'est pas agréable à entendre, mais puisque c'est dans l'intérêt de ses filles, dès ce soir il écrira pour demander la faveur d'une double admission. Miss Branwell est satisfaite ; ses nièces recevront une éducation digne de ce nom :

> « Enfin, vous vous rendez à la raison ! Je m'en réjouis autant pour elles que pour vous ! »

Ce que Tante ignore, c'est que l'institution de Cowan Bridge ne prépare pas au mariage mais à la mort.

*« Nos vêtements étaient insuffisants pour nous préserver du froid rigoureux ; nous n'avions pas de bottines, aussi la neige pénétrait-elle dans nos souliers et y fondait ; nos mains, sans gants, s'engourdissaient, se couvraient d'engelures, comme nos pieds. Je me souviens très bien de la douleur intolérable que j'éprouvais chaque soir lorsque mes pieds étaient enflammés, et de ma torture quand, chaque matin, il me fallait faire rentrer mes orteils enflés, froids et raides, dans mes chaussures. »*

Charlotte BRONTË *Jane Eyre.*
(Traduction Charlotte Maurat.)

*« Here do I wait my sisters, on our way*
*To the Hall of Arimanes — for to-night*
*Is our great festival — 'tis strange they come not. »*

G. Gordon Lord Byron,
*Manfred.*

Hélas ! ce ne fut pas le Byron des soirées de notre enfance que mes deux sœurs aînées puis, quelques mois plus tard, Charlotte et moi-même retrouvâmes derrière les hauts murs de l'institution dirigée par le révérend Carus Wilson, mais la stupeur, l'effroi que ressentent les enfants lorsqu'ils sont confrontés pour la première fois à la violence et à l'irresponsabilité des adultes.

*« J'attends ici mes sœurs, au long de ce chemin*
*Jusqu'au château d'Arimanes, car cette nuit*
*Est notre grande fête. C'est curieux, elles*
*[tardent. »*

Comme elle fut longue pour mes sœurs, la nuit de Cowan Bridge, comme elle fut douloureuse ! Si je confesse crûment cette souffrance — elle modifia à jamais nos sentiments et changea le cours de notre destinée — ce n'est pas pour faire vibrer les cordes d'une émotion facile ni pour mendier une compassion rétrospective, mais pour rendre hommage à mes aînées ; tout d'abord à Maria, la meilleure de nous toutes, brutalisée par des vieilles filles rancunières et haineuses, à Maria qui ne se révolta jamais, ni ne se plaignit d'aucune façon des traitements pourtant terribles qu'on lui fit subir jusqu'à l'instant de son agonie, puis

à Elizabeth, moins courageuse sans doute, moins grande dans l'abnégation et le sacrifice, mais aussi résignée, Elizabeth qui mourut d'épouvante quinze jours après Maria, au presbytère où papa l'avait ramenée à la hâte, enfin

à Charlotte, qui survécut avec moi et quelques autres pensionnaires au typhus qui s'abattit sur l'institution de Cowan Bridge déjà touchée par la tuberculose ; à Charlotte qui témoigna dans son œuvre maîtresse, *Jane Eyre*, de l'expérience déchirante et de la perte irréparable que nous dûmes subir à cause de la méchanceté et de l'envie d'éducateurs féroces. Dans l'homme ils ne surent voir que ce qu'il y avait de mauvais, et dans la religion que ce qu'elle enseignait de détestable.

« *L'insuffisance de nourriture était, d'autre part, désolante ; avec nos appétits dévorants d'enfants en pleine croissance, nous avions tout juste de quoi maintenir en vie un malade affaibli. Il en résulta un abus dont souffrirent durement les plus jeunes élèves : chaque fois que les grandes, affamées, en avaient l'occasion, elles contraignaient les petites, par cajoleries ou par menaces, à leur donner leur portion.* »

Ce soir, alors que le souvenir m'entraîne malgré moi vers Cowan Bridge, dans l'institution du révérend Carus Wilson, je revois ces visages de fillettes livides et affamées, enfants sacrifiées à l'imbécillité et au sadisme de misérables qui, pour se venger de l'inanité de leur existence et de la pauvreté de leur âme, tourmentèrent des êtres sans défense. Entre tous, je revois celui de Maria, exsangue, aussi entêtée dans le pardon que les autres l'étaient dans la perversité, Maria qu'une créature hargneuse et cruelle — elle avait pour fonction de nous surveiller — persécuta sans relâche.

Avant d'évoquer les derniers instants de mes deux sœurs, comment décrire nos départs successifs de Haworth? d'abord celui de Maria et d'Elizabeth, puis, un peu plus tard, celui de Charlotte, puis, plus tard encore, le mien? Comment décrire, avec quels mots assez poignants, la séparation, l'arrachement au monde de l'enfance?

« Tante, permettez-moi de rester près de vous et d'Anne. Permettez-moi de ne pas partir!
— Ma chère enfant, si ton père t'envoie dans cette pension rejoindre tes sœurs, c'est qu'il y voit ton bien!
— Pourquoi Branwell a-t-il le droit de rester ici?
— Parce que ton père se charge lui-même de son éducation!
— Pourquoi ne vous chargez-vous pas de la nôtre?
— Parce que j'en suis incapable. Nous sommes pauvres, et à l'heure de notre mort nous ne vous laisserons rien! Il faudra trouver du travail. Quels seront alors vos atouts? »

A peine suis-je capable de me souvenir de ce matin triste et froid de novembre où l'on me déposa à la diligence. Quelqu'un, je ne saurais dire qui, mon père probablement, me recommanda à un voyageur surpris de me voir monter seule dans la voiture : « C'est qu'elle n'est pas haute, cette petiote, pour partir déjà si loin ! » Il le pria de bien vouloir descendre mon maigre bagage à l'arrêt de Cowan Bridge où quelqu'un m'attendrait ; il ne savait pas qui.

« Et n'oublie pas de nous envoyer de tes nouvelles et d'embrasser tes sœurs pour nous ! »

A peine puis-je évoquer le départ brutal de la diligence, ma main tendue à la portière pour un adieu, les secousses de la voiture emportée par les chevaux, la toux insistante d'une voyageuse emmitouflée dans des châles, le paysage entr'aperçu derrière un rideau de pluie : un champ, un autre, un troupeau de moutons, des bœufs regroupés près d'une barrière, la façade d'une maison, le porche d'une église entourée de son cimetière, un bouquet d'arbres noyés dans la brume, un champ, un autre, et ainsi de suite, jusqu'au ciel de plus en plus sombre, de plus en plus bas. A peine puis-je évoquer les cahots de la diligence bousculée au sommet des côtes par les rafales de vent, les cris du cocher furieux du retard pris sur l'horaire, le bruit du fouet sur les chevaux aveuglés par la pluie, la tombée progressive de la nuit, et avec elle le glissement de l'angoisse jusqu'à la banquette où se recroqueville une enfant craintive — « Tu peux remettre ton manteau, petite ! Ça va être ton tour de descendre ! » —, le grincement des roues, la porte ouverte brutalement, la voix forte d'un homme qui crie plutôt qu'il ne demande s'il y a dans la voiture une fillette du nom de Brontë, Emily Jane Brontë, la fille du pasteur de Haworth ?

« C'est la petiote qui est dans le coin, mais elle ne vous répondra pas. Elle est muette comme une carpe. On m'a chargé de descendre son bagage. C'est vous, l'homme de l'institution de Cowan Bridge ?
— Qui voulez-vous qu'j'sois d'autre ? »

A peine puis-je évoquer la prison où nous demeurâmes plusieurs saisons, ses pièces glaciales été comme hiver, ses couloirs où l'ombre chassait la lumière dès le début de l'après-midi, ses lits humides et étroits où nous nous coulions en tremblant et où nous dormions à deux, telles des gisantes dont nous avions déjà la mine blafarde et la raideur, son réfectoire crasseux et puant, ses assiettes garnies d'une nourriture écœurante que nous ne parvenions pas à avaler, la cuvette que nous partagions à plusieurs, les poux, le silence oppressant du dortoir où nous ne pouvions même pas échanger des confidences à l'heure de nous endormir.

« Charlotte Brontë, descendez de votre lit et venez ici tout de suite !
— Oui, mademoiselle !
— Qu'étiez-vous en train de dire à votre voisine ?
— Que j'avais reçu une lettre de mon frère, mademoiselle !
— Vous savez pourtant qu'il n'est plus l'heure de bavarder ? Tendez-moi votre main afin que je lui apprenne l'obéissance et le respect des lois ! »

A peine puis-je décrire la baguette longue et flexible avec laquelle nous frappaient les maîtresses, et que n'auraient-elles pas inventé pour assouvir ce besoin de châtier et d'humilier ? A peine puis-je décrire, moi qu'il effraya tant, le révérend Carus Wilson, son air justicier tandis qu'il nous jaugeait du haut de sa redingote : « Comment ces demoiselles se sont-elles comportées cette semaine ? »

« Ont-elles laissé de la nourriture dans leurs assiettes ?
« Se sont-elles repenties publiquement de leurs mauvaises pensées ?
« Les a-t-on bien punies ? Je dois tout savoir d'elles, tout ! Ici, il n'y a pas de place pour les petits secrets !
« Qu'est-ce que c'est que cette coiffure ? Voulez-vous me faire le plaisir de couper tout ça ! »

Sa silhouette à peine esquissée, il me faut maintenant le suivre jusqu'à Tunstall, sa paroisse, où nous allions l'écouter chaque dimanche plaider pour la souffrance, la culpabilité, la contrition, le remords. Jamais homme ne se sentit plus en harmonie avec le monde que Carus Wilson lorsqu'il écrivit des livres pour les enfants, par exemple, *Les Mémoires pour la jeunesse*, ouvrage édifiant dans lequel il racontait avec une luxuriance de détails et de commentaires la damnation éternelle, les tortures de l'enfer, les supplices, l'agonie de l'âme soumise aux démons.

« Emily, viens vite !
— Que me veux-tu ?
— J'ai une sucrerie pour toi ! »

Tandis que mes six ans et mon visage qu'on se

plaisait à trouver joli m'attiraient les faveurs des autres élèves, mes sœurs affrontaient l'injustice ; Maria surtout, que son étonnante grandeur d'enfant née adulte signalait à la mesquinerie de vieilles filles amères et stériles. Certaines scènes furent si pénibles que je les ai oubliées pour n'avoir plus à en souffrir.

« Où est Maria ?
— Elle est punie !
— Encore ? »

A peine me reviennent en mémoire les visages fanés de ces femmes de trente ans, notamment celui de la répétitrice, Miss Andrews que Charlotte peignit dans son roman *Jane Eyre* sous les traits de Miss Scatcherd. Sous le moindre prétexte, elle frappait de son fouet ma sœur déjà très malade, Maria dont les seuls défauts furent la distraction et les manquements à l'horaire. A côté de cette mauvaise ombre demeure le souvenir, celui-là plus heureux, de la surintendante Miss Evans qui, en ce terrible hiver 1825, tenta de s'opposer au directeur de l'institution parce qu'il nous refusait la nourriture dont nous avions pourtant le besoin urgent.

★

Au moment d'en arriver aux adieux, à cette étreinte désespérée — elle précède l'arrachement définitif —, je ne trouve plus pour décrire Maria que des mots secs, agressifs : maigreur, toux rauque et persistante, taches de sang lavées à la hâte, sur un mouchoir, sur un col, silhouette blessée, appuyée contre un mur pour ne pas tomber, démarche hésitante.

« Où est Maria ?

— Elle a failli glisser dans l'escalier ce matin.
— Où est Maria ?
— Miss Andrews l'a punie car elle ne parvenait pas à s'habiller !
— Où est Maria ?
— Elle est mourante. Il paraît que sa famille va venir la chercher. »

Et tout de suite après ce départ, avant même qu'on ait eu le temps de comprendre ce que le cœur refuse d'accepter, le glissement d'Elizabeth en direction de la même mort, sa blessure à la tête, blessure due à une chute mystérieuse, peut-être au cours d'une crise d'épilepsie, malade elle aussi, et réfugiée auprès de Miss Evans qui tenta de la soigner avant de la confier à papa assez aveugle pour ne pas voir dans quelle institution il nous avait placées ; enfin, pour conclure, le typhus qui décima le troupeau de Carus Wilson.

Trop de chagrin nuit à l'exercice de la mémoire. Des événements eurent lieu à cette époque dont je ne me souviens pas. En revanche, quelques détails continuent à se raconter en moi. Ils sont sans importance : le soleil d'un mois de juin assez beau, le parc où nous pouvions enfin jouir de la paix — Carus Wilson et ses complices dénoncés par le typhus ayant d'autres soucis que celui de nous surveiller —, les fleurs, le gazon près de la serre où nous allions chercher refuge, les chuchotements qui nous apprenaient la mort de l'une, le départ précipité d'une autre dont l'état s'était aggravé, la venue de notre père — « Comment avez-vous pu me cacher la manière effrayante dont vous traitiez ces enfants ? Vos politesses ne visaient qu'à masquer vos violences secrètes ! Misérable que j'ai été de vous confier mes filles ! » —, son effroi devant notre aspect squelettique, ses accusations, les protestations du révérend Wilson menacé de poursuites judiciaires, notre retour à Haworth, les crises de larmes de Branwell qui venait d'assister à l'agonie d'Elizabeth et à l'enterrement de Maria, les regrets de Tante — « Nous qui pensions bien faire en vous plaçant dans cette institution ! Que Dieu nous pardonne une telle erreur ! » —, la main protectrice de Tabitha, la servante au grand cœur, sa main posée sur nos têtes :

> « Une chance, miss, qu'deux soient r'venues vivantes ! J'vas m'employer à les soigner ! »

Oui, comme elle fut longue pour mes sœurs, la nuit de Cowan Bridge, comme elle fut douloureuse !

> « *Here do I wait my sisters, on our way*
> *To the Hall of Arimanes — for to-night*
> *Is our great festival — 'tis strange they come*
> [*not.* »

*« Vent, éteins-toi dans la bruyère,*
*Ta voix folle ne me plaît pas ;*
*Je veux certes un temps sévère,*
*Mais qui soit dépourvu de toi. »*

Emily Jane BRONTË,
août 1837.
(Traduction Pierre Leyris

La Hurlevent.

N'était-ce pas le titre d'un livre que je m'étais promis d'écrire à la première personne? Balayé par le vent des Moors, mon projet en forme de rêverie s'est défait au fil du temps. Il a pris la forme que lui ont donnée des morts. Devenue le scribe d'une famille d'outre-tombe, je ne fais qu'écrire ce qu'elle me dicte, à savoir son histoire superbe et accablante. Et que lui importe mon embarras?

Alors que je souhaitais entendre la grande Emily Brontë, c'est une enfant qui demande la parole et la prend. Amaigrie, épuisée par un jeûne de huit mois, elle est assise pour l'instant à côté de son frère qui lui raconte un épisode de son roman:

> «... à ce moment de terreur, le jeune homme en tenue de soirée s'est mis à hurler! Il est sorti de sa cachette en courant, mais le monstre qui avait déjà tué sa fiancée, Elizabeth de Haworth, l'a saisi par le bas de son pantalon: "A moi, Napoléon, à moi!" a-t-il crié...
> — J'ai peur, Branwell!
> — Eh bien, ma pauvre, qu'est-ce que ça va être tout à l'heure, quand tu connaîtras la suite!»

★

Après avoir quitté Cowan Bridge en toute hâte,

elle a retrouvé, en compagnie de Charlotte et d'une mourante que l'on a enterrée quelques jours après son retour, la maison très chère, le tic-tac de l'horloge dans l'escalier, une servante qui lui tiendra lieu de mère: «Emily, vas-tu m'répondre à la fin? Où c'est-y qu't'es encore cachée?»

«Je suis dans la petite chambre avec Branwell!»

un frère, enfant talentueux, menacé par une imagination débridée...

«Et que c'est t'y qu'vous faites à pareille heure?
— Cesse de nous harceler, Taby!
— J't'as d'mandé d'tes nouvelles, à toi, Branwell?
— Non, mais je t'en donne tout de même!
— J'vas m'plaindre à n't'e révérend, p'tit insolent!»

et pour finir une jeune sœur, aussi fragile qu'une poupée de porcelaine, Anne, la nièce préférée de Tante qui dirige la maison depuis sa chambre du premier étage: «Tabitha, que se passe-t-il encore?»

«Rien d'grave, miss!
— Ne pourriez-vous faire un peu moins de bruit, et au lieu de crier, ne pourriez-vous monter voir ce qui se passe au premier étage?
— C'est qu'miss, j'ai au't'e chose à faire qu'à monter et descend'e ces fichus escaliers tout' la journée qu'Dieu a vue longue!»

lieu qu'elle ne quitte pratiquement plus que pour descendre faire la lecture à son beau-frère:

« Ce tapage est épuisant !
— Faut vous en prendre à c'gamin qu'est mal luné et p'us malin qu'l' Diable lui-même ! »

Moi qui souhaitais rencontrer Emily, et elle seule, me voilà confrontée à deux adultes — trois en comptant la robuste Tabitha — et quatre enfants. Et comment en détacher un sans faire du tort aux autres ? Qui est Emily Brontë, sinon la sœur de Charlotte, l'impulsive, la passionnée, sinon celle d'Anne, une fillette infiniment plus attachante qu'on ne l'a décrite, sinon celle de Branwell, enfant si précoce et si prometteur que son père s'inquiète déjà de son futur ? : « L'intelligence de mon fils est si vive que j'en viens à douter de savoir la rassasier ! » Ce génie en herbe ne risque-t-il pas une fièvre méningée à solliciter ainsi ses capacités cérébrales ?

« Brannii, viens vite nous raconter les exploits du capitaine Shakespeare !
— Ce soir, les filles, j'ai mieux pour vous !
— Quoi ? Dis vite !
— Les aventures de l'Empereur des Français !
— Nous n'en voulons plus, de ton méchant Napoléon ! César est bien plus sympathique que lui ! »

Brannii le magicien ; il sait écrire des deux mains en même temps, raconter avec une drôlerie ou un sérieux inimitables des histoires extraordinaires, réciter de mémoire l'article d'un journal sans oublier un seul mot, jouer du piano, dessiner, chanter mieux que personne. « Veux-tu m'fiche l'camp d'la cuisine ! — J'y suis chez moi autant que toi, Taby ! — Bon, dans c'cas t'arrêtes d'brailler ! — Brailler ? Mais tu m'insultes ! » Son vocabulaire est aussi riche que celui du pasteur dont il imite à la perfection les longs prêches.

> « ... le péché m'a donné la mort comme il est en train de vous la donner à vous, pécheurs à la mine blafarde, jeunes à la tête folle ou vieux pétrifiés par le gel des années. Vos passions se lisent sur vos visages tournés vers moi, fils de Dieu ! Vous m'avez trahi et pourtant vous me regardez ! Vous m'avez cloué sur une croix et pourtant vous continuez à chanter mes louanges ! Pourquoi tant d'hypocrisie mes frères ? En vérité, en vérité, je vous le dis ; le soleil se lèvera maintes fois sur le monde en larmes avant que je ne me donne la peine de ressusciter, et la route sera longue à remonter que celle qui mène à mon Père, car son Royaume, bande d'arriérés et d'imbéciles, n'est pas de ce monde !
>
> — Qu'es-tu encore en train de raconter à tes sœurs, mon garçon ?
> — Je joue à être ce que je serai plus tard pour de bon !
> — Que seras-tu plus tard ?
> — Un héros ! Non, c'est bête, un héros. Un prédicateur ! Non, j'aurais honte d'être inférieur à vous. Un écrivain !
> — Du calme, mon fils ! Tes talents nombreux et évidents sont encore fragiles ! »

Brannii le magnifique, enfant gâté par l'admiration, fils béni du pasteur qui ne sait plus faire un pas sans lui. Ne l'entraîne-t-il pas à la sacristie ou, lorsque le soir tombe et que le froid se fait sentir, ne l'invite-t-il pas à le rejoindre dans son bureau où le petit, fier de ses prérogatives, nettoie le fameux pistolet : « Oh, papa, s'il vous plaît, pendant que je m'occupe de votre arme, racontez-moi l'Irlande, votre pays magnifique où j'irai plus tard, quand je serai grand ! »

« Qu'aimerais-tu m'entendre te raconter ?
— L'histoire de la sorcière qu'on a trouvée pendue près du lac où vous alliez pêcher !
— Mais je te l'ai déjà racontée dix fois !
— Alors celle du fantôme qui a emporté le fils de la veuve qui attendait le retour de son mari mort à la guerre ! Vous aussi, papa, vous auriez voulu être un grand soldat, n'est-il pas vrai ?
— Sans doute. Mais Dieu a été plus prompt que ma patrie d'adoption. Avant même que j'aie eu à choisir, il m'a fait savoir que je devais me mettre à son service.
— C'est ça qu'on appelle une vocation ? »

Qui est Emily Brontë, sinon la nièce d'Elizabeth Branwell ? Celle que toute la famille et les amis surnommèrent Tante, avec un grand T, ne fut pas la vieille fille sèche et rebutante qu'on nous montre, armée de la Bible et de l'infaillibilité d'une foi saupoudrée de méthodisme à la Wesley, mais bien plutôt une femme de devoir, assez extravagante pour oser enseigner à ses nièces ce que d'autres, pourtant infiniment plus audacieuses qu'elle, ont tu à leurs filles.

« Assez de simagrées, mesdemoiselles ! Vous n'êtes plus à Cowan Bridge !
— Mais Tante...
— Il n'y a pas de mais ! Je veux voir de la clarté sur votre visage et de la franchise dans votre regard.
— Nous ne vous avons jamais menti !

— Non, mais vous me cachez l'essentiel de votre pensée !
— Qu'entendez-vous par "l'essentiel d'une pensée" ?
— Assez d'insolence, Charlotte ! Et maintenant, à genoux ! Nous allons prier Dieu pour qu'Il vous donne ces vertus qui manquent cruellement aux femmes. Au lieu de devenir ce que le Seigneur attend d'elles, ces sottes s'abaissent jusqu'à ressembler à leurs poupées ! Rien de plus navrant que ces jouets qu'on offre aux enfants sous prétexte d'occuper leurs mains ! »

★

Dans l'histoire de cette enfance à quatre, il y a un chapitre qu'aucun biographe ne passe sous silence, tant il eut d'importance. Au cours du mois de juin de l'année 1826, le révérend Patrick Brontë se rendit à Leeds. Il ramena à son fils qui allait sur ses dix ans une boîte de douze soldats. L'irruption soudaine de ces petits personnages de bois dans la vie des enfants — leur existence s'était nourrie jusque-là de contes macabres et des versets de la Bible commentée chaque soir par le pasteur — bouleversa complètement leur univers...

Le lendemain de son retour de Leeds, alors qu'il ouvre à peine les yeux — on se souvient que le fils et le père dorment dans la même chambre —, Patrick Brontë aperçoit la tête ébouriffée de Branwell debout au pied du lit : « Vous voilà enfin réveillé, papa ! — Ma parole, tu me guettais dans mon sommeil ? Veux-tu regagner ton lit ! — Je ne vous ai pas entendu rentrer cette nuit ! — Et alors, en voilà une affaire ! — C'est que... — C'est que quoi ? — Je

vais avoir dix ans ! J'espère que vous n'avez pas oublié votre promesse ! » Au lieu d'afficher un visage impassible, Patrick Brontë ne résiste pas au désir de faire plaisir à son fils. Il lui indique le paquet qui l'attend sur la table de nuit. Sans prendre le temps de remercier son père, le gamin s'empare de la boîte : « Qu'est-ce que c'est ? — Ouvre et tu verras ! — Dites-moi ! Qu'est-ce qu'il y a à l'intérieur ? Je vais mourir si je ne le sais pas tout de suite ! »
Quelques secondes plus tard, un rugissement sort de la chambre des filles réveillées en sursaut par leur frère empêtré dans une chemise de nuit trop longue pour lui : « Regardez, mesdemoiselles, regardez ce que papa m'a rapporté pour mon anniversaire ! » Charlotte, la première, émerge du sommeil. Elle éclate de rire à la vue des soldats de bois, s'empare de l'un d'eux : « Si tu acceptes de m'en offrir un, je prendrai celui-là, c'est le plus grand et le plus beau ! Je l'appellerai Wellington ! » Branwell ne proteste pas ; au contraire, dépossédé, il veut l'être davantage. Il tend les soldats à Emily qui, pour suivre l'exemple de son aînée, en choisit un qu'elle nomme aussitôt Parry. Puis vient le tour d'Anne : « Non, merci : c'est pour toi que papa a rapporté les soldats ! » Le généreux donateur insiste ; il offre à la timide un petit personnage : « Tu l'appelleras Ross ! C'est un nom qui lui ira très bien ! Et voici le mien, Naughty, ou Rogue ! Je sens, mesdemoiselles, que nous allons faire de grandes choses avec ces quatre-là ! Nous n'en avons pas fini des guerres et des batailles ! »

De cette rencontre de quatre soldats de bois

manipulés par des enfants à l'imagination flamboyante, naîtront une saga et quatre génies: Brannii, Tallii, Emmii, Annii, maîtres avant Dieu de personnages qui, en leurs noms, commettront les actions les plus odieuses: meurtres collectifs, vengeances, tortures, adultères, incestes, trahisons.

En ces années 1826-1827, comme elle semble lointaine la lecture de *L'Imitation de Jésus-Christ* que le révérend conseilla à ses filles aînées à la veille de leur départ pour Cowan Bridge! Comme ils sonnent platement les *Sermons et homélies du temps de la reine Elizabeth d'illustre mémoire*, écrits par un M. Morgan, sermons que récitait par cœur la petite Maria. A la place des paroles dictées par la foi et l'humilité, montent dans la salle d'étude du premier étage où se retrouvent les quatre enfants les plaintes des soldats morts au champ d'honneur, les cris de Rogue qui va et vient au gré des victoires, les hurlements des géants enfermés dans des palais croulant sous la richesse.

« Emmii, pourquoi boudes-tu?
— Annii et moi, nous en avons assez des guerres!
— Dans ce cas, changeons de sujet!
— Si nous partions sur une île? »

Branwell a déjà trouvé la sienne; il prendra celle de Man, Emily celle d'Aran, Anne celle de Guernesey, quant à Charlotte, elle régnera sur celle de Wight. De cette prise de pouvoir naîtra un drame intitulé *Les Insulaires* dans lequel prendront place des personnages réels, tels Christopher North, le rédacteur en chef du *Blackwood's Magazine*, l'inévitable Wellington, John Lockhart, le gendre de Walter Scott, deux ou trois hommes politiques au torysme affirmé, Michaël Sadler, Lord Bentick, tous deux choisis par Anne, et beaucoup d'autres encore, un chirurgien connu de toute l'Angleterre, expédié sur l'île de Wight par Charlotte qui, depuis qu'elle a vu mourir ses sœurs, n'ignore plus que le corps, à l'inverse de l'âme, n'est pas immortel.

«Papa, accepteriez-vous de me prêter *La Médecine moderne au foyer*?
— Ces lectures ne sont pas de ton âge!
— Je voudrais apprendre l'anatomie. Je crois que c'est plus facile de soigner le mal lorsqu'on sait où il niche.
— Soigner le mal? A ma connaissance tu ne te destines pas à la médecine?»

★

Amenée par quatre enfants dans une chambre aux murs recouverts d'inscriptions mystérieuses, j'affronte des combats, survis aux guerres napoléoniennes, traverse des salons où se pavane Walter Scott en compagnie de Wellington et autres fantômes.

*« Par la moindre brèche céleste*
*A l'expiation des nuées...*
*Par un sourire qui leur reste*
*Depuis la première journée.*

*Le jour agile nous emporte*
*Succédant au sombre matin ;*
*Les larmes de l'enfance annoncent le destin ;*
*Plus que l'homme, tristesse est forte. »*

Emily Brontë.
(Traduction Françoise d'Eaubonne.)

VOTRE présence insistante me déplaît, comme me déplaît votre guet dans la petite chambre du premier étage où vous retient, non pas quatre enfants comme vous aimeriez le faire croire, mais votre curiosité. Cet espace privilégié appartenait au souvenir ; personne n'avait le droit d'y pénétrer. Sur les murs de vagues inscriptions demeurent, mais elles ont perdu leur sens et ce n'est pas l'œil des vivants qui leur en redonnera un. Seul, en effet, vous est proposé un rôle que je vous conseille d'accepter : scribe — ce mot a été choisi par vous — d'une famille d'outre-tombe, et peut-être, qui vous plaira davantage : compagne de voyage. Me suivrez-vous ? La route est belle qui va jusqu'à Colne ou, remontant vers le nord, jusqu'à Keighley !

Si vous consentez à n'être que la main au service d'une mémoire, je vous raconterai notre vie d'alors et ce qui tint lieu d'événements dans une existence austère : la plainte du vent d'est, son impétuosité à la mauvaise saison, le jeu des nuages déchirés par des vents contraires, la tourmente des arbres à l'époque des tempêtes, l'apparition inattendue du soleil un jour de l'équinoxe d'hiver, sa disparition soudaine, le noir des orages non prémédités, la cisaille d'un éclair au loin, la chute de la foudre près du clocher, le craquement épouvantable de l'air, la promesse du crépuscule en juin, l'arrivée tant attendue de l'été.

Je vous raconterai un dimanche pris au hasard,

un dimanche où le révérend rattrapé par Dieu en plein office, et pour arracher une poignée de malheureux aux griffes de Satan, lança l'anathème au-dessus de l'assemblée saisie par la parole prophétique...

> «*Ainsi parle l'Éternel des armées; voici, j'enverrai parmi eux l'épée, la famine et la peste, et je les rendrai semblables à des figues affreuses qui ne peuvent être mangées à cause de leur mauvaise qualité.*
> «*Je les poursuivrai par l'épée, par la famine et par la peste, et je les rendrai un objet d'effroi pour tous les royaumes de la terre, un sujet de malédiction, de désolation, de moquerie et d'opprobre, parmi toutes les nations où je les chasserai...*»

Je vous raconterai notre épouvante d'enfants éduqués par Jérémie, Isaïe et quelques autres figures vengeresses toujours prêtes à cracher le feu ou à ouvrir les vannes du déluge: «Pourquoi les prendrions-nous au sérieux? Après tout, ils ont fauté comme nous!» Je vous raconterai nos terreurs d'enfants poursuivis par l'Ancien Testament: «Nous y sommes obligés! Si nous discutons leurs lois, ils nous abattront! A tour de rôle nous tomberons gravement malades! Moi je mourrai de la peste, Emily du choléra, Anne deviendra mendiante!»

> «Nous abattre? Je voudrais bien voir ça! Napoléon lui-même n'est pas parvenu à abattre l'Angleterre! A nous de leur tenir tête!
> — Tais-toi, Brannii, tu vas attirer sur nous la colère divine!
> — Celle de papa me suffit!
> — Si connaissait vos peurs, not'e révérend,

serait p'êt'e plus prudent! Si c'est pas misère d'élever d'la marmaille dans d'la tragédie! »

Je vous raconterai notre solitude, pis, notre isolement hérités de notre père qui prétendait n'avoir jamais trouvé dans ce pays de rustres et d'analphabètes un seul esprit qui s'accordât au sien. Tenu à l'écart par sa seule volonté, le vicaire perpétuel de Haworth cacha son chagrin dans un bureau où il décida, sous prétexte de soigner une maladie d'estomac — une dyspepsie chronique —, de prendre ses repas. Cette décision encouragea Tante à prendre les siens dans sa chambre, si bien que nous, les quatre enfants, nous nous retrouvâmes bientôt seuls dans la salle à manger. « Pourquoi nous abandonnent-ils ? »

« Ils ne nous abandonnent pas!
— Que font-ils alors?
— Ils préfèrent rester avec eux-mêmes!
— Je ne vois pas la différence.
— Il y en a pourtant une... Papa est malade et Tante craint le froid!
— Moi aussi, je suis malade! Hein, Taby, que je suis malade?
— D'la tête, sûrement!
— Moi aussi, je crains le froid! Ça ne m'empêche pas de prendre mes repas avec mes sœurs!
— Et qu'elles ont du mérite, pauvrettes, d'supporter un gars d'ta mesure! »

Je vous raconterai Branwell, le héros de notre enfance, toujours prêt à déclencher des batailles, à échanger un de ses personnages contre un bain de sang: « Laisse-nous tranquilles, Brannii! Tu ne vois donc pas que nous sommes en train d'écrire?
— Que m'importent vos occupations; la guerre

n'attend pas que l'ennemi soit prêt ! », des coups de pied contre une gifle de ma part, car je fus la seule à lui résister : « Sale fille ! Je le dirai à papa ! — Et moi, je lui rapporterai la manière dont tu te comportes maintenant qu'il n'y a plus personne pour te surveiller ! »

« Que se passe-t-il, les enfants ?
— Tout va bien, Tante !
— Alors, pourquoi ces cris ? »

Je vous raconterai Anne, ses retraits, ses plaintes, Anne encore trop jeune pour ne pas être terrifiée par nos exploits sanguinaires, Anne qui après être restée recroquevillée dans un coin de l'étroite et minuscule pièce, finissait par aller chercher refuge auprès de Tante, sa protectrice : « Pourquoi ces tremblements, mon enfant ? — C'est Rogue, il me fait peur ! — Rogue ? Qui est Rogue ? — C'est Naughty ! — Qui est Naughty ? — C'est Branwell ! — Ah bon, parce que maintenant pour aboutir à ton frère, il faut remonter une filière ? »

« Branwell !
— Oui, Tante.
— Lorsque je t'appelle, ce n'est pas pour m'entendre dire oui, mais pour voir ta face d'insolent ! Viens ici immédiatement ! Qu'as-tu encore fait à cette pauvre petite ?
— J'ai gagné la bataille de Waterloo devant elle ! »

Je vous raconterai la treizième année du fils Brontë, l'une des plus glorieuses de sa destinée, ses sorties discrètes par la porte de la cuisine, sa participation en tant que témoin aux bagarres de Haworth, celles-là bien réelles, qu'il allait observer au plus près afin d'en nourrir ses futurs récits. Entre John et William Brown, les fils du sacristain, deux rudes gaillards plus âgés que lui, Branwell que sa petite taille ne gênait apparemment point fit souvent une apparition remarquée et même applaudie. C'est à cette époque également qu'il se lia d'amitié avec le fils du fossoyeur, Willie Wood, un blasphémateur notoire. Dans ces deux bouches moqueuses, l'Écriture devint un sujet de plaisanterie. Aucune de nous ne fut conviée à ce partage coupable, et nous ne nous en plaignîmes point : nous n'étions que respect et crainte là où Branwell était révolte et refus.

Un soir, après nous avoir raconté les exploits scandaleux des voyous du coin, il décida brusquement d'en terminer avec l'enfance pour aborder le rivage escarpé de la littérature :

> « J'ai l'intention de fonder une revue, mesdemoiselles ! Qu'en dites-vous ?
> — Comment l'appelleras-tu ?
> — Sans fausse modestie, le *Branwell's Blackwood's Magazine* ! »

Ainsi venait de naître la chronique de Glasstown qui nous occupa pendant des mois.

Je vous raconterai aussi Charlotte, ma sœur, que la folle imagination de Branwell enflamma ; si l'un avait les idées, l'autre possédait l'outil pour les traduire. Tandis que je me rapprochais d'Anne pour laquelle j'éprouvais une tendresse presque maternelle, Charlotte, poussée par le désir de ressembler à ce frère dont elle épiait avec envie les débordements, reprit à son compte le journal de Branwell soudainement distrait par d'autres projets. Il devint sous sa plume déjà aiguisée et critique le *Blackwood's Young Men Magazine*.

Unis par une complicité singulière, et oubliant jusqu'à leur entourage, le frère et la sœur ne formèrent bientôt plus qu'un seul être. De cette union exceptionnelle naquirent des récits insolites, des textes moqueurs qui prenaient la politique pour cible, les faits divers pour modèles, les travers humains pour anecdotes. Des titres me reviennent en mémoire : *Nuits, Wellington et Parry*, l'*Histoire des jeunes hommes, Napoléon* ; des personnages aussi : Lucien Bonaparte, le duc de Wellington, Ossian, Chateaubriand et beaucoup d'autres. Puis surgirent, en décembre 1829, sous la signature du capitaine Tree (l'un des nombreux travestissements masculins de Charlotte) les *Caractères des hommes célèbres du temps présent*, celui du marquis de Duro — qui devint par la suite marquis de Douro — celui aussi de Lord C. Wellesley, l'un après l'autre appelés à faire longue carrière chez les Brontë[1].

> « Le plus âgé de ces deux jeunes messieurs, le marquis de Duro, est aujourd'hui dans sa vingt-deuxième année. En apparence, il ressemble beaucoup à sa noble mère. Il a la même taille élancée, le même nez fin de Romain (...) Son imagination est des plus débridées comme l'est le tracé de son naturel et de son esprit... »

> « Rogue a environ quarante-sept ans. Il est très grand et plutôt sec. Il est assez beau, sauf qu'il y a quelque chose d'un peu effrayant

1. Les titres des œuvres de jeunesse de Charlotte et de Branwell Brontë signalés dans ce chapitre et dans les suivants ont été relevés dans le livre de Raymond Bellour, *Charlotte Brontë/Patrick Branwell Brontë*, édité en 1972 par J.-J. Pauvert, de même les extraits des *Caractères des hommes célèbres du temps présent*, traduits par Denis Roche.

dans ses terribles yeux gris et dans son formidable front... »

« (Naughty)... Il est plein d'insolence et de brutalité. Ses meurtres sont de l'espèce la plus sauvage. Il adore torturer ses victimes avant de les tuer. En bref rien n'est jamais trop mal pour lui... »

Je vous raconterai nos lectures savantes ; tout le monde les a signalées : *Childe Harold* de Byron, la Bible, *Le Voyage du pèlerin* de Bunyan, *Le Paradis perdu* de Milton, toute l'œuvre de Shakespeare, *Les Ballades d'Ossian* de Macpherson, *The Tales of a grand father* de Walter Scott, et bien sûr *Ivanhoë*. Avec les revues hebdomadaires et les journaux que recevaient Tante et papa, ces livres furent nos lectures préférées.

« Charlotte, as-tu traduit dans une bonne langue les notes que nous avons prises hier au soir ?
— Non.
— Et pourquoi, s'il te plaît ?
— Parce que j'ai lu *Roméo et Juliette*. Crois-tu qu'un jour nous aurons le talent de Shakespeare ?
— Je l'espère bien ! »

C'est en 1830 que Charlotte, encouragée par Branwell — il attendait de sa complice des révélations qu'il n'avait pas le courage de provoquer lui-même — écrivit sous la signature de Lord Wellesley sa première histoire d'amour, *Albion et Marina*, conte moral parachevé par une mort exemplaire, car ainsi va la passion, fatalement, vers la tombe. Marina, un prénom, presque un masque ; comme les autres, il subira maintes métamorphoses, deviendra plus tard, dans ce très beau récit *The Spell an Extravaganza* (en français *Sortilège*), Marian, puis Mary, puis Maria, puis Mina ; et comment ne pas songer à notre mère mais aussi à notre sœur aînée, toutes deux allongées sous les fenêtres de ces enfants en train de reconstruire le monde ? *Albion et Marina*, nouvelle au tracé presque parfait écrite en quatre heures par une fillette de quatorze ans qui ne connaissait des turbulences du cœur que ce que *La Gazette de Leeds* voulait bien en dire ?

★

Mais j'en reviens à vous, madame. Qu'êtes-vous venue faire dans cette salle d'étude, sinon réveiller le souvenir d'une enfance qui se voulut secrète et qui le resta durant près d'un siècle, jusqu'à ce que quelqu'un se penchât sur de petits carnets recouverts d'une écriture microscopique, bien propre à lasser l'indiscrétion des adultes... des adultes d'alors, car ceux d'aujourd'hui portent des lunettes si perçantes qu'ils peuvent voir à l'intérieur des morts, là où l'âme a laissé une trace.

*« Ces horreurs, en ces mornes jours de maladie et pendant les heures agitées de la nuit, emplissaient le cœur de Mary d'une atroce angoisse qui, certes, contrebalançait toute une vie de bonheur. Puis l'adieu qui la faisait frémir, la pensée de son mari, l'accablait. Il dédaignait de cacher les douloureux tourments désormais sans espoir qui, jour après jour, lui dévoraient le cœur, au point qu'il en devenait sombre, sauvage, au bord de la folie; et elle songeait: "Que fera-t-il quand viendra la dernière heure, quand je l'aurai quitté à tout jamais?" »*

Patrick Branwell Brontë,
*La Mort de Mary Percy.*
(Traduction Marcelle Sibon.)

HIER au soir, j'ai lu *La Mort de Mary Percy* de Patrick Branwell Brontë, nouvelle écrite vraisemblablement à la fin de l'année 1833, alors qu'il avait un peu plus de seize ans, nouvelle publiée avec d'autres textes grâce à Raymond Bellour. Et puisque j'en arrive aux écrits de jeunesse de Charlotte et de Branwell, les *Juvenilia*, je voudrais ouvrir ici une parenthèse : il est très regrettable pour qui désire comprendre l'œuvre des Brontë que ce livre soit devenu introuvable, car comment ne pas reconnaître dans ces récits passionnés, ces descriptions saisissantes signées de Charlotte ou de Branwell ou des deux à la fois, et dans *La Mort de Mary Percy* en particulier, la violence, l'intensité qui sous-tendent l'œuvre des sœurs Brontë ? Violence et intensité demeurées longtemps inexplicables du fait de la méconnaissance de ces textes, et surtout de l'exclusion ultérieure de Branwell auquel ses sœurs — elles lui devaient pourtant beaucoup — ne rendirent jamais ouvertement hommage.

Dans ce récit à la concision exemplaire et d'une cruauté rare, jeté à la hâte sur le papier, on devine le halètement de l'auteur, un garçon de seize ans maintenu malgré lui en enfance par le souvenir de plusieurs morts ; notamment par celle d'une mère confrontée durant des mois à la douleur sous l'œil effrayé d'un père impuissant, à peine capable de répondre aux appels pathétiques par des bénédictions et des prières.

« *Ainsi le temps passa, et son corps décharné à l'image de la Mort, ses yeux étincelant d'un éclat anormal, sa voix étouffée jusqu'au chuchotement annoncèrent que sa mort était en vérité toute proche...* »

Comment ne pas reconnaître au long de ces pages arrachées à de petits carnets intimes, couvertes d'une écriture si serrée et si petite qu'elle ne peut être déchiffrée qu'à l'aide d'une loupe, écriture microscopique qui dénonce la présence d'une tante curieuse et d'un père mal-voyant, comment ne pas reconnaître ce sentiment du déjà vécu ou du déjà craint, cette angoisse ressentie par ceux qui se souviennent de l'instant où l'être aimé, sur le point de mourir, les a fixés de ce regard que nul ne décrira jamais vraiment, parce qu'il est de l'ordre de l'incommunicable, de l'indicible, regard révolté par l'injustice qui oblige l'homme à partir seul.

« *Alexander, si ce vœu ne semblait égoïste, ma seule prière serait que là où je vais tu puisses* maintenant *m'accompagner, à l'instant et dans la même tombe...* »

*La Mort de Mary Percy*, c'est la nôtre, cette lente, et tout à coup rapide montée des ténèbres dont nous savons — même si nous l'oublions à chaque instant de notre existence — qu'elles nous attendent quelque part ; et si ce n'est pas la mort, c'est à coup sûr l'expérience du deuil, ce refus d'être séparé *à jamais* — je souligne jamais comme Branwell a souligné maintenant — de ceux qui donnèrent un sens à notre vie.

« *Il avait la certitude que ce qu'elle disait était*

*une brillante chimère qui, dans une heure peut-être, aurait fait d'elle un cadavre sans vie, sans âme, sans au-delà. Il ne doutait pas que quoi qu'il arrivât, ils seraient séparés immédiatement et pour toujours. Ce cœur qui s'emplissait d'une noire violence à l'endroit des hommes et défiait le Ciel qu'il tenait pour imaginaire, ne pouvait faire de promesse de vie sans condamner le péché...* »

Et si *La Mort de Mary Percy* n'est pas notre expérience de la perte de l'autre, c'est en tout cas celle du propriétaire des Hauts de Hurle-Vent, le sombre et terrible Heathcliff, lequel, après avoir fomenté le mal et semé la douleur, reconnaît n'avoir d'autre désir que de rejoindre au plus vite Catherine Linton, la Cathy de son enfance, dans ce lieu qu'est l'éternité de l'amour, et peu lui importe s'il est situé aux frontières de l'enfer ou aux confins du néant. « ... *Étant seul, et sachant que deux mètres de terre meuble étaient l'unique obstacle qui nous séparât, je me dis : Il faut que je la tienne une fois encore dans mes bras ! Si elle est froide, je penserai que c'est le vent du nord qui me glace, moi ; si elle est immobile, c'est qu'elle dormira.* » Sa foi, Heathcliff la tient d'un cadavre. Ce qu'il souhaite, ce n'est point retrouver un Dieu compatissant et charitable — comme Percy, il sait que Dieu n'existe pas —, mais rejoindre là, *maintenant*, celle qu'il a poussée au suicide. « *Je pris une bêche dans ce hangar aux outils et me mis à creuser de toutes mes forces. La bêche racla le cercueil ; je continuai à travailler avec mes mains. Le bois commença de craquer près des vis. J'étais sur le point d'arriver à mon but, quand il me sembla entendre au-dessus de moi, près de l'angle de la tombe, le soupir de quelqu'un qui se penchait. "Si je puis seulement soulever le couvercle, murmurai-je, je souhaite qu'on nous recouvre de terre tous deux!"*»

Grâce à la lecture de *La Mort de Mary Percy*, récit d'autant plus violent qu'il est bref, je peux deviner ce qu'imagina, certain jour où elle se retrouva seule avec son frère, Emily, la cinquième enfant de Maria Branwell Brontë dont je viens de revivre l'agonie, corrigée il est vrai par son fils qui aurait préféré avoir pour père un Alexander Percy, être de négation et de révolte, plutôt qu'un vicaire à la foi inattaquable mais inefficace. La sœur s'approcha-t-elle du frère? Lut-elle par-dessus son épaule le texte qu'il était en train d'écrire? Il ne fait aucun doute; Emily eut connaissance de cette nouvelle. Cette scène de mort ne la renvoya pas à sa mère dont elle se souvenait à peine — elle n'avait que trois ans au moment de son décès — mais à elle-même, et à l'intérieur d'elle-même, à un amour déjà porté à son paroxysme, à un amour fou; il devint l'emblème d'une existence vouée à l'attente... de qui? de quoi? de l'Autre, d'un autre assoiffé comme elle d'Absolu, prêt à s'allier aux mêmes exigences. Mais parce qu'il n'existait pas, cet être bâti par son désir, elle s'adressa à Dieu.

«*I wish to be as God made me.*»

Sans le savoir — il en aura conscience beaucoup plus tard, quand il se vantera auprès de ses amis d'avoir écrit une partie de *Wuthering Heights*, en français *Les Hauts de Hurle-Vent*, Branwell a soulevé le voile derrière lequel se cachait Heathcliff, l'enfant abandonné par des gitans au teint basané. Tout comme Percy dont il a hérité la violence et le désespoir, Heathcliff sera cet être de misère et de solitude, peut-être parce qu'il est porteur de la malédiction, donc maudit lui-même. Ivraie mêlée à la bonne graine, il l'empoisonnera. D'un trait de plume, Branwell a esquissé pour sa sœur Emily, et non pour Charlotte, sa préférée, le héros autour duquel tournera un roman rédigé à la manière d'une confession. «*Je suis Heathcliff!*» De même que Branwell souhaitera toute sa vie devenir Alexander Percy, l'objet de sa création et de son désir, de même Emily souhaitera devenir Heathcliff; mais à la différence de son frère qui échouera, elle y parviendra.

Georges Bataille a-t-il su pourquoi, à la suite de quelle mort, Alexander Percy avait indiqué le chemin du Mal à son glorieux descendant, Heathcliff, l'usurpateur, le tyran de *Wuthering Heights*? A-t-il jamais soupçonné Branwell, l'impuissant, l'alcoolique, le raté de la famille, d'avoir indiqué à Emily la voie qui, traversant la chambre d'une mère agonisante, la mènerait vers un cercueil; au cœur d'une œuvre magistrale, il attend le lecteur innocent.

> «*L'emportement mortel de* Wuthering Heights *est si fort qu'il serait vain, selon moi, d'en parler sans épuiser, s'il est possible, la question qu'il a posée.*»

★

Mais il me faut revenir à cette année 1831 qui vit Charlotte quitter pour la seconde fois l'abri du presbytère.

Que se passa-t-il dans l'esprit du révérend Brontë pour qu'il décidât de se séparer de sa fille aînée? Pour quelles raisons refusa-t-il de l'instruire en compagnie de Branwell auquel il enseignait le latin et le grec, deux langues indispensables pour qui désirerait quelque jour accéder à la philosophie ou, suivant les traces de son père, à la théologie? Sa tête bien faite, mais traversée par les courants d'un imaginaire impétueux, son esprit trop vibrant n'auraient-ils pas eu à se féliciter de la présence de Charlotte, l'élève studieuse et appliquée d'Elizabeth Branwell? Peut-on imaginer, sans prendre le risque de se tromper, que le pasteur de Haworth, après la grave maladie qui le frappa dans le courant de l'été 1830 et l'affaiblit au point qu'il ne put circuler seul durant plusieurs semaines, s'inquiéta tout à coup du manège de ses enfants? Ils ne quittaient plus la petite salle d'étude du premier étage où chacun vaquait à ses occupations littéraires ou poétiques. De la chronique *Letters from an Englishman* à *Caractarus*, vers de facture classique inspirés des grands prêches, c'était à celui qui passionnerait l'autre: «Brannii! Lis-nous quelques vers! Ceux d'hier étaient si beaux! — Cet après-midi j'ai beaucoup mieux à faire partager, mesdemoiselles!»

«Elizabeth... je vais vous faire un aveu. Ces enfants m'inquiètent sérieusement!
— Ils sont pourtant en bonne santé.
— Ce n'est pas leur santé qui me tracasse, ce sont leurs agissements!
— Leurs agissements?
— Ne les trouvez-vous pas curieux?
— Je suis moi-même assez extravagante pour les trouver normaux!
— Alors que les autres enfants ne rêvent que de sorties et de nouvelles rencontres, eux se replient dans une chambre de six mètres carrés! La sauvagerie de mes filles est si

grande que j'en viens à me demander si demain elles ne refuseront pas de se rendre à l'office de crainte d'avoir à y croiser un regard étranger !
— Qu'elles n'aillent pas rôder avec les friponnes du coin, je trouve cela plutôt rassurant ! »

Qui étaient ces personnages que Branwell et ses sœurs ne cessaient d'évoquer ? Chassant devant eux la monotonie des jours par un meurtre ou un exploit, Sneaky, le capitaine Bud dont les idées avancées faisaient vibrer la petite assemblée, Parry, Ross, le poète Soult aux versifications redondantes, Naughty, Rogue devenu Rougue, propriétaire d'un palais baptisé *Rougue's Death and Cie*, ce monde imaginaire courait dans le presbytère du matin au soir.

« C'est simple, je ne me sens plus chez moi !
— Mais enfin, Patrick, il faut bien que ces enfants s'amusent !
— Il y a d'autres jeux. Ceux-là ne me paraissent pas innocents... Non, non, ne protestez pas ! je sais ce que je dis ! Tout comme vous, je me félicite que mes enfants n'aillent pas rôder avec n'importe qui, mais de là à les savoir enfermés des journées entières, de là à les voir lire le *Leeds Intelligencer* ou le *John Bull* comme des adultes passionnés de politique, il y a un pas !
— Moi, ce ne sont pas les filles qui m'inquiètent, c'est Branwell... Savez-vous comment il se fait appeler par ses sœurs ? Alexander Rougue !

Pirate en même temps que révolutionnaire, capturé un certain été, relâché à l'automne, repris au cours de l'hiver suivant par un dénommé Douro marquis de son état et homme si séduisant malgré sa vilenie et ses trahisons amoureuses que Charlotte s'était éprise de lui, Rougue, dont s'inquiétait Tante, vivait dans la ville de Glass Town située en Afrique, très précisément au pays des Ashantis ou encore, selon les jours, en Angria...

« Qui a encore emprunté le *Traité de géographie générale* ?
— Lequel ? Celui du révérend Goldsmith ?
— Oui, Branwell, celui du révérend Goldsmith ! Et ne prends pas cet air hypocrite ! Je t'interdis de prendre des livres dans ma bibliothèque sans me les demander ! »

Il est probable que le pasteur s'inquiéta de sa progéniture. Outre la crainte de voir ses filles réduites tôt ou tard à une situation précaire faute d'avoir reçu une éducation convenable, il s'interrogea sur leur santé ; n'allaient-elles pas s'abîmer les yeux ? « Charlotte, il est temps de songer à faire de toi une vraie jeune fille ! — Oh, papa, ne me dites pas que je vais devoir partir ! »

Personne ne sut jamais de quels arguments Patrick Brontë usa pour convaincre son aînée. Il demanda conseil à de vieux amis ; d'abord au révérend Hammond Roberson, puis à Mme Franks — celle-ci n'étant que l'ancienne Elizabeth Firth de qui, après avoir essuyé un refus de Miss Burder, il avait demandé la main au lendemain de la mort de sa femme. D'avoir écarté un parti trop chargé d'enfants ne gêna en rien Mme Franks dans l'expression de sa fidèle amitié. Elle se renseigna aussitôt, indiqua l'adresse de Miss Margaret Wooler qui dirigeait avec ses trois sœurs le pensionnat de Roe Head, situé non loin de Huddersfield.

Charlotte prépara donc ses bagages. Elle prit la route, parcourut les trente kilomètres qui séparaient Haworth de la pension Wooler. Le génie Tallii laissait derrière lui trois enfants meurtris et dépossédés ; de quel droit venait-on détruire leur monde ?

«Pourquoi avez-vous envoyé Charlotte au loin ? Est-ce juste de l'avoir arrachée à notre affection ?
— Oui, mon garçon ! Ta sœur a l'âge d'étudier. C'est de son avenir que je me préoccupe, et non de ses jeux !»

La maîtresse du marquis de Douro fit son entrée dans le monde des études un jour de janvier 1831. Frissonnante sous une robe démodée et un peu ridicule qui attira les regards moqueurs des autres élèves, elle se présenta aux sœurs Wooler. Devant tant de malaise, ces demoiselles s'interrogèrent : d'où venait cette créature minuscule et mal nourrie, effarouchée comme un oiseau tombé du nid, myope et sans grâce ? De quelle contrée perdue ? «Mademoiselle Charlotte, n'ayez pas honte de ne pas savoir ce qu'on ne vous a pas appris !» Devant son ignorance, Miss Wooler décida de mettre la fille du pasteur dans la classe des petites. Humiliée par cette décision, Charlotte écrivit à son cher ami Rougue.

Cher Alexander, cher Rougue, cher Brannii,
J'ai trouvé ici ce que je redoutais, le monde et son ironie. Ah, comme vous aviez raison lorsque vous affirmiez qu'il n'est que dérision et simulacre ! Pas un jour ne se passe sans que je verse des larmes ou rougisse d'être ce que je

suis, une élève misérable et ignorante! Je me languis de nos amis, du royaume d'Angria, de Ross, de Parry! Si vous saviez comme les journées sont longues et les soirées tristes! Comment vais-je pouvoir continuer à vivre sans vous? Deux aimables personnes m'ont offert spontanément leur amitié. Peut-être pourront-elles nous servir de modèles lorsqu'il nous faudra proposer de nouvelles victimes au marquis de Douro dont vous connaissez l'insatiabilité. L'une est blonde et l'autre brune, et toutes deux sont ravissantes. Elles ont mon âge et s'appellent Ellen Nussey et Mary Taylor. Leurs pères sont des industriels de la région. Mais je crois qu'on nous appelle pour la prière, aussi suis-je dans l'obligation de vous quitter précipitamment. A bientôt, cher Rougue. Ne m'oubliez pas dans vos pensées.

Votre Charles de Wellesley.

*« Je sais, lecteur, que tu dois espérer trouver dans ces réminiscences une description de l'Élysée, de ses mystères et de ses orgies, mais je ne le puis car, au temps où il brillait de tout son éclat, je n'étais qu'un petit enfant, et bien que je fusse certainement différent de la moyenne des enfants, je n'étais pas assez habile pour pénétrer dans l'arène de ce splendide temple de l'Enfer. Jamais je n'en franchis les portes. Je ne suis pas sûr de pouvoir en désigner l'emplacement exact ; mais, d'après ce que j'ai entendu dire plusieurs fois à mots couverts par le général Thornton, ce devait être un endroit merveilleux. »*

Charlotte Brontë,
*Quatre ans plus tôt,*
21 juillet 1837.
(Traduction Annie Villelaur.)

La croyance qui veut que les morts, parce qu'ils regrettent de n'être plus, s'accommodent des spéculations que les vivants se permettent à leur sujet repose autant sur la suffisance que sur une totale incompréhension. Ceci pour vous dire que je n'apprécie pas la façon dont vous avez mis en relief certain passage d'un roman dont personne ne connaîtra jamais la genèse, puisque moi-même je ne me souviens plus comment et quand *Wuthering Heights* germa dans mon esprit.

Voilà pour la première remarque que je me devais de faire. La seconde a trait à Charlotte dont je n'aime guère le portrait tracé avec désinvolture et brièveté. Vous la livrez au monde gauchie par la maladresse et fagotée comme une paysanne du Yorkshire. Contrairement à ce que l'on a pu croire — à ce qu'elle a cru elle-même — ma sœur ne fut pas dépourvue de charme, et il convient de rappeler que de nous trois, elle fut la seule à avoir été demandée plusieurs fois en mariage.

En cette année 1831 où vous la mettez en scène, en ce mois de janvier brumeux et froid où elle fit une apparition discrète à Roe Head, il est exact que ses compagnes ne virent au début que sa timidité maladive, sa myopie, ses imperfections ; mais elles s'attachèrent par la suite à sa personnalité qu'elles s'accordèrent à trouver remarquable. Tant il est vrai que l'on commence, à l'ordinaire, par considérer la silhouette avant de juger l'être. Ellen Nussey et Mary Taylor, signalées par vous dans une lettre de votre cru, offrirent leur amitié et leur protection à Charlotte. A peine remise d'une séparation qui l'avait ébranlée, démunie devant un monde dont elle ne connaissait ni les lois ni les règles, notre aînée se méfia. Nous reçûmes un courrier désabusé dans lequel elle nous disait combien tout lui paraissait vain et particulièrement les sentiments qu'affichaient des gens constamment en parade : puis, le temps passant, elle se laissa apprivoiser.

> « Je ne sais ce qui me retient...
> — Dites-le nous, Charlotte !
> — L'épreuve de la souffrance sans doute... J'en ai fait une si laide expérience que je crains de la retrouver partout ! »

A Ellen et à Mary, sujets privilégiés d'un destin facile, elle fit des confidences qu'elle ne se serait pas permises avec d'autres, même pas avec nous, ses sœurs. Les nouvelles venues apprirent sur notre famille des détails bouleversants que nous pensions oubliés d'elle depuis longtemps ; par exemple de quelle façon Maria avait été fouettée peu de temps avant sa mort, sa grande faiblesse l'ayant empêchée un matin de se lever ; comment Elizabeth bouleversée par ce spectacle avait eu le soir même une crise de somnambulisme, comment elle s'était blessée à la tête ; la manière aussi dont Branwell avait hurlé lorsqu'il avait vu le cadavre de Maria, puis, quelques jours plus tard, celui d'Elizabeth, les crises de convulsions qui s'en étaient suivies, ses pertes de connaissance.

> « Mais que ceci ne vous pousse pas à croire que nous avons toujours été malheureux ! L'affection qui nous lie a fini par chasser le mal. Nous ne sommes heureux que lorsque nous sommes ensemble. Branwell va bien rôder à droite et à

gauche et ma sœur Emily errer sur la lande, mais ce ne sont que de courtes séparations.

— Vos sœurs n'ont donc pas d'amies ?

— Non. Nous nous satisfaisons les uns des autres. Branwell est pour nous un bien si précieux ! Par lui nous savons tout ce qui se passe à Haworth. J'espère que vous le rencontrerez un jour. Il vous plaira, j'en suis certaine. Mon frère est un prince ; il en a le charme, l'intelligence et la séduction ! »

La singularité du comportement de ma sœur, sa perspicacité réussirent là où l'aisance aurait échoué. Après les mots d'amitié, elle reçut des cadeaux, puis des invitations : « J'espère, Charlotte, que vous accepterez de venir cet été dans le château de mes parents ! Nous serions heureux de vous y recevoir ! » Bras dessus, bras dessous, les nouvelles amies parcoururent le parc de Roe Head. Elles avaient tant de choses à se dire. L'éducation bourgeoise et raffinée de ces demoiselles — le père de Mary, Joshua Taylor, un homme dont on disait qu'il parlait couramment le français, possédait à Gomersal une manufacture — ne les avait pas préparées à une telle rencontre. Elles demeurèrent toujours reconnaissantes à ma sœur d'avoir eu assez de confiance en elles pour leur avoir livré d'aussi pénibles secrets.

Encouragée par la sympathie, Charlotte rattrapa le retard pris au cours des ans passés au presbytère : puisqu'on lui avait offert la possibilité d'accéder à la connaissance, elle devait s'en montrer digne. Son séjour dans la classe des petites prit rapidement fin ; éblouie par une si belle intelligence et un si grand courage, Miss Wooler la pria de rejoindre celle des grandes. Une fin de mois, elle prit la première place, et elle la garda jusqu'à son départ.

Ma chère Tante, mon cher papa,

Aujourd'hui les maîtresses nous ont remis nos cahiers. J'ai le plaisir de vous annoncer que les sacrifices que vous avez consentis pour moi n'auront pas été vains. Mes notes sont excellentes et j'ai reçu les compliments de Miss Wooler qui me considère comme la meilleure élève de son école.

★

Tandis que ma sœur gagnait du terrain sur le front du savoir, qu'advenait-il de nous ?

Après avoir boudé la petite salle d'étude, Branwell y refit des apparitions : « Maintenant qu'on lui a retiré ce qu'il avait de plus cher, que peut faire Alexander Percy, sinon mourir ? » Ému par ses crises de larmes ou l'état de prostration dans lequel il demeurait parfois des matinées entières, papa ne se préoccupa bientôt plus que de lui. Il refusa obstinément de suivre les conseils de Tante et du révérend William Morgan, pasteur à Bradford et parrain de Branwell, qui insistaient pour qu'il mît le pleurnicheur en pension : « Il n'a plus l'âge de vivre dans la seule compagnie de ses sœurs ! »

« C'est pourtant avec elles qu'il est le plus heureux !
— Il pourrait y exercer ses multiples talents et se faire des amis de qualité au lieu de fréquenter les fils Brown et ce garnement de Willie Wood !
— Laissons là cette discussion, Elizabeth ! Elle ne mènerait à rien ! »

Quand elle comprit que le pasteur ne changerait pas d'avis, Tante cessa de donner des conseils : « Si vous ne voulez pas vous en séparer, essayez au moins de le calmer ! » Devant le nervosisme grandissant de Branwell dont le commerce était devenu délicat, pour ne pas dire difficile, papa consulta des livres de médecine. Il y chercha le remède qui soignerait l'épilepsie dont notre frère pouvait être atteint, puis il profita de l'absence de Charlotte pour offrir à l'irascible la chambre attenante à la sienne : « Ainsi, mon garçon, tu auras plus d'aise et tu te sentiras plus libre ! — Papa, ne m'appelez plus mon garçon ! J'ai cessé d'être un enfant ! », enfin il l'invita à partager sa vie et ses préoccupations d'adulte.

« Tu as raison de me rappeler à l'ordre... tu n'es plus un enfant, et ce n'est pas moi qui m'en plaindrai ! J'ai attendu ce moment-là assez longtemps ! »

Dès cette époque, Branwell prit l'habitude de donner son opinion sur la situation économique du pays, l'importance de la religion dans les affaires, les bienfaits du torysme. Il devint le défenseur de l'Église anglicane comme l'avait été Charlotte avant lui, épousa les querelles de papa qui s'était toujours opposé à l'émancipation des catholiques. L'enseignement destiné au mâle de la famille profita aux deux filles. Nous apprîmes, entre autres informations, combien la condition des habitants de Haworth, tous employés dès l'âge de huit ans dans les manufactures de la région, était précaire, voire tragique.

« Dans ce cas, je me demande pourquoi Charlotte a pour amies des filles d'industriels ?
— Ta sœur n'a pas à entrer dans de pareilles considérations et tous les patrons ne sont pas des monstres ! Il y a parmi eux d'honnêtes gens ! »

La plupart des maisons du village, dont nous ne connaissions que les façades alors que lui, le pasteur, en connaissait les chambres misérables et sales, n'étaient pas éclairées et l'eau manquait souvent. Et s'il y avait tant de décès à Haworth — la moitié des enfants n'atteignaient pas quinze ans —, c'était à cause de la misère et du manque d'hygiène.

« Combien de fois n'ai-je pas dû me fâcher tout rouge pour qu'on nettoie les rues où pourrissent les ordures ménagères ! Ce sont les rats qui apportent la maladie ! »

C'était encore à l'extérieur, dans la campagne même, que les gens étaient le moins malheureux. Malgré la précarité de leurs revenus — la laine ne se vendant plus ou se vendant mal sur les marchés de Leeds et de Halifax — ils disposaient des produits de la terre, de maigres légumes pour se nourrir, de la tourbe pour se chauffer, et les jours de fête de la viande d'un mouton sacrifié pour la satisfaction de plusieurs familles.

« Que pouvez-vous faire pour eux dans de telles conditions ?
— Hélas, mon fils, pas grand-chose ! »

Le sentiment du devoir, la croyance en une éternité heureuse dans la mesure bien sûr où on l'avait préparée, étaient les arguments d'une religion austère. Si la prédication du dimanche insistait sur la nécessité de se préparer à une bonne mort, c'est parce que Patrick Brontë n'envisageait plus de bonheur possible sur terre : « C'est un leurre ! » Et pourtant, lui aussi, il y avait cru.

« A peine arrivé dans ce pays, j'ai compris que mes études, ma science, ma foi, mon enthousiasme ne serviraient à rien ! »

Tout ce trajet de l'esprit avait été accompli en pure

perte. Et de fait, à peine s'était-il installé dans le presbytère à la place d'un prédécesseur redouté, et même haï, qu'il avait dû faire face à la violence de ce monde rustre et sauvage. Que pouvait faire un homme seul contre les beuveries, les querelles, le viol des servantes, les combats de coqs, l'inceste, le brigandage, les hobereaux sans pitié pour le petit peuple? Que pouvait prétendre un homme sans revenus ni pouvoir face à ces petits maîtres qui se prenaient pour de grands originaux alors qu'ils n'étaient que des alcooliques! Les forces étaient trop inégales. « Tante dit qu'autrefois vous étiez un homme très gai... est-ce exact? »

« Oui, Anne... j'étais ce qu'on appelle un boute-en-train... j'aimais rire, plaisanter, surprendre, éblouir même!
— Que pourrait-on faire pour que vous redeveniez ainsi? Nous aimerions tant vous voir sourire quelquefois!
— Rien, malheureusement... C'est trop tard! »

Cette vie ressentie comme une trahison, un échec, une humiliation, ne l'empêchait pas d'affirmer la parole de l'Évangile: « Dans tout homme il y a la divinité! Dieu est partout, y compris là où on ne l'espère plus! » Cette promesse, notre père la reprenait à son compte; il nous priait, nous, ses enfants, de nous en souvenir afin de ne jamais ressembler à ce monde cruel et misérable qu'il venait de décrire; Branwell surtout devait prendre garde à ses instincts et à ses fréquentations, Branwell qui tenait de sa famille irlandaise: « Là-bas, est-ce le climat, la mer? ils sont tous fous! »

« Pourquoi ne nous parlez-vous jamais de votre famille, de votre pays?
— Avec le temps tombe l'oubli, comme le som-

meil sur l'esprit... Je vieillis, mon fils, mais ce vieillissement ne me coûte pas car je sais que je puis fonder de grands espoirs sur toi. Bientôt ce sera ton tour. Tu t'envoleras pour Londres ou pour Cambridge ! »

Ravi d'être l'élu, mon frère insistait : « Vous croyez en moi, papa, n'est-il pas vrai ? — Puisque je viens de te le dire ! » Quant à moi je me sentais... comment exprimer mon sentiment ? attristée, démunie, spoliée de ce que je croyais être mon avenir. Le portrait de cette misère indéracinable, la haine de ces hommes appelés à une mort précoce et à un combat sans merci, l'idée d'avoir un jour à quitter ce pays que j'aimais me plongeaient dans le désarroi. Malgré les récriminations de Taby qui souhaitait mon aide, je passais par la porte de la cuisine, filais en direction de la lande où m'attendait mon Dieu à moi, entre l'infini d'un ciel dont j'espérais la délivrance et une terre prête à m'engloutir. Essoufflée d'avoir couru, je tombais à genoux au milieu des bruyères, et là, assurée de ne pas être vue, j'éclatais en sanglots. Parfois je m'en prenais à Celui d'en haut : « Pourquoi les laissez-vous faire ? » A travers mes cheveux rabattus par le vent, je regardais le paysage, la sauvagerie de la nature où ne s'aventuraient que les troupeaux. Je clignais les yeux, apercevais les herbes hautes près d'un ruisseau, la rondeur d'une colline, le vol des oiseaux migrateurs et, au-delà des dernières pistes menant aux bergeries, un groupe de rochers noirs témoins d'un antique cataclysme.

Lorsque je redescendais enfin, la douleur avait disparu pour laisser place à la certitude d'être à ma place dans ce pays que n'aimait pas ma famille. Dans la lumière déclinante de l'après-midi m'apparaissait le presbytère, comme la maison de mon bonheur, de ma sécurité. La porte à peine poussée me parvenait une odeur de lessive. Assise dans un coin de la cuisine, Anne attendait mon retour en écoutant les jérémiades de Taby ; pour la punir de croire en la sorcellerie, le Christ n'en finissait pas de lui envoyer des maux : « Quand c'est p'us l'jambe qu'j'traîne comme un boulet, c'est l'œil droit qu'm'joue d'mauvais tours ! » Un élan me poussait vers ma sœur ; j'entourais sa taille, l'entraînais jusqu'au premier étage où nous réclamait l'écriture.

« Alors, Emily, tu as bien réfléchi ?
— Oui, Anne... c'est décidé ! Je me retire d'Angria pour créer mon propre État ! J'ai déjà trouvé son nom, *Gondal* !
— Et moi... que dois-je faire ?
— Ce qui te plaît ! Me suivre ou rester en Angria avec Charlotte et Branwell !
— Je préfère aller avec toi. »

★

Un jour de l'été 1831, Branwell décida d'aller rendre visite à Charlotte ; il espérait trouver à Roe Head un peu de la tendresse perdue et des idées pour sa chronique qui dépérissait faute de sang neuf. Averti par Tante, papa tenta de s'opposer à l'aventure : « Il n'est pas prudent de voyager seul en des temps où on attaque les gens sur les routes ! » A Huddersfield, des ouvriers s'étaient opposés aux patrons qui refusaient de leur accorder une augmentation de salaire sous prétexte qu'ils venaient d'acheter des machines à tisser, un gros investissement, et peu importait à ces messieurs de mettre au chômage des centaines de tisserands : seule la rentabilité comptait. « Ne vous inquiétez pas, papa... je serai prudent ! »

Notre père céda. Nous assistâmes donc au départ du voyageur. Enveloppé d'une longue cape qui cachait aux vagabonds sa musette, il nous fit signe de la main avant de disparaître à l'angle du cimetière. Nous n'eûmes pas à nous inquiéter longtemps ; deux jours plus tard il était de retour, aussi flambant qu'au départ. Délivré de son vêtement poussiéreux, il raconta à la famille avide de nouvelles comment il avait été accueilli, la surprise de Charlotte, sa présentation aux jeunes élégantes qui fréquentaient l'établissement de Miss Wooler : « J'ai évidemment été présenté à Miss Taylor et à Miss Nussey ! »

> « Ah oui, comment sont-elles ?
> — Dignes de devenir nos amies, même si ces demoiselles ont des idées un peu osées en matière de religion. On ne peut pas être parfait sur tous les fronts ! »

Son récit, après m'avoir enchantée, me mit en colère. Au cours de la nuit qui suivit son retour une question me réveilla : pourquoi n'étais-je pas née homme ? J'aurais eu les mêmes droits que Branwell. Je ne serais jamais bonne qu'à aider Taby, au mieux à suivre les traces de Charlotte qui ne songeait plus qu'à devenir la meilleure élève du pensionnat, non pas pour satisfaire une sotte ambition ou la vanité facile, mais pour répondre dès que possible à la nécessité de gagner sa vie.

Mais je me tais, car je sens monter en moi l'amertume.

*« Oh what is Man ? A wretched being*
*Tossed upon the tide of time,*
*All its rocks and whirlpools seeing,*
*Yet denied the power of fleeing*
*Waves, and gulfs of woe and crime. »*

*« O, Homme qu'es-tu ? Une créature misérable*
*Ballottée sur les flots du temps,*
*Se meurtrissant aux rocs, happée par les remous,*
*Impuissante à se soustraire*
*Aux vagues et aux abîmes du malheur et du crime. »*

Patrick Branwell Brontë
(Traduction Jane Fillion.)

On l'aura pressenti, Patrick Branwell Brontë m'est cher, autant, sinon plus que ne le serait l'être dont j'aurais entendu dire le plus grand mal, que je rencontrerais fortuitement et qui, renversant sa réputation, me séduirait d'un regard, me charmerait d'un mot, d'un trait d'esprit, d'un geste que les autres, pourtant meilleurs que lui, n'auraient pas eus à mon endroit. L'affection que je porte à cette ombre, enveloppée pour l'heure dans une longue cape de voyage, grandit au fur et à mesure de mon avancée dans l'histoire des Brontë. Depuis que je l'ai rencontré, je me sens moins seule, moins désemparée.

A l'inverse de ses sœurs défendues par l'orgueil et la timidité, Branwell est don spontané de lui-même pour le meilleur et pour le pire, et cet abandon de soi me touche plus que la réserve excessive d'une belle âme qui ne consent à se donner qu'au moment choisi par elle. Ce petit homme — comme Charlotte il oubliera de grandir — rouquin et myope avant de naître, ardent et loufoque, tendre et bavard, faible et velléitaire, m'amuse, me touche, m'enchante. Au long de cette interminable descente au royaume des morts, il prévient mes pas, tient mon bras d'aveugle, écarte sur mon passage les démons qui m'empêchent de pénétrer dans le presbytère ou m'y tiennent enfermée. Devant moi, sa meilleure spectatrice, il tente d'amadouer ses sœurs, joue le consolateur ironique en présence de Charlotte choquée par le mutisme d'Emily.

« Mais enfin... qu'a-t-elle ?
— Et tu me le demandes ?
— C'est à peine si depuis mon retour elle m'a fait la faveur de trois confidences !
— Pour elle c'est déjà beaucoup !
— Je ne vois pas de quelle manière j'aurais pu la blesser !
— Je croirais plutôt que tu la fatigues.
— Que veux-tu dire ?
— La chose me paraît claire. Ton enseignement l'épuise ! »

Après un an et demi d'internat, l'aînée vient de rentrer de Roe Head où elle a fait une brillante carrière d'étudiante. Ce succès, hélas, n'a pas étanché sa soif. Depuis qu'elle a rencontré la Culture, Charlotte se contrefait : « J'essaie de lui transmettre ce qu'on m'a enseigné... Ne ressent-elle aucun plaisir à apprendre ? »

« Si, mais son plaisir est plus discret que le tien.
— Que cherches-tu à insinuer, Branwell ?
— Face à la connaissance, tu te comportes comme une femme devant l'homme qu'elle convoite !
— Je t'interdis...
— Emily ne voit pas les choses de la même façon que toi. Son intérêt se porte ailleurs. »

Trop pudique pour assister à des effusions qui ne regardent que Charlotte et le Savoir, Branwell se détourne. Son regard se porte plus volontiers sur ses sœurs malmenées par l'aînée, volontaire et dominatrice. Sur l'ordre de leur père, Emily et

Anne se sont assises devant le bureau afin d'y recevoir un enseignement digne du pensionnat de Miss Wooler. Ces trois filles dévergondées par les études font sourire Branwell qui s'amuse de la scène: «Ne sont-elles pas touchantes, ces trois grâces attablées sagement devant la connaissance?»

«Branwell, nous n'avons que faire de tes sarcasmes!
— Que voilà un joli tableau! Vite, mes pinceaux!
— Un mot de plus, et je me plains à papa!
— Pourquoi pas à Tante, pendant que tu y es!»

A peine les cahiers fermés, chacune reprend sa personnalité et si Anne, avant de disparaître de la salle à manger, manifeste sa reconnaissance à Charlotte, Emily ne songe qu'à fuir: «Où vas-tu? — J'ai un rendez-vous! — Avec qui? — C'est un secret! — Merci de ta confiance!» Lasse de suivre le chemin des autres, Emily vient de bifurquer; sa route, même si elle est parallèle, diffère de celle de Charlotte qui s'en blesse. Dans cette démarche vers l'indépendance — elle mène au pays de Gondal — elle a accaparé Anne. La belle complicité Branwell-Charlotte, figure maîtresse de la mythologie brontéenne, vient de rencontrer sa rivale. Emily et sa jeune sœur font concurrence sur le plan de la tendresse et de la connivence avec leurs aînés dont la royauté est remise en question.

«Pourquoi ne veulent-elles plus participer à notre chronique? Elles y tenaient pourtant un rôle important!
— Parce qu'elles souhaitent être autonomes!»

Naughty, alias Rougue, alias Alexander Percy, alias Northangerland, alias Branwell sait depuis peu que la forte tête de la famille n'est pas Charlotte. S'il restait un pantalon à distribuer, ce serait à Emily qu'il faudrait l'offrir ; d'abord parce qu'elle est la plus grande, ensuite parce qu'elle est la plus déterminée, la moins influençable. Sa nature est une ; elle se raconte d'un trait et qu'importe si les autres ne la comprennent pas. « Elle est inatteignable ! »

« Pour toi, Charlotte, pas pour Anne ! As-tu vu comme elles s'entendent, se comprennent sans se parler ?
— Si Emily ne dominait pas Anne, elle n'aurait pas pour elle un tel intérêt !
— Veux-tu dire que l'autorité chez Emily prend le pas sur l'affection ? »

Parfois, c'est à Patrick Brontë de s'interroger sur la silhouette énigmatique assise à côté de lui, dans la salle à manger : « Impossible, ma fille, de ne pas retrouver en toi certains traits de mes ancêtres... Tu as leur regard, leurs attitudes... »

« Dites donc, papa, chercheriez-vous à séduire Emily ? Vous m'avez dit que c'était moi qui ressemblais à vos parents ! Or je suis aussi différent de ma sœur que John Brown l'est de moi ! »

Emily ne manque jamais de répondre à l'attention paternelle. Le visage qu'elle offre au révérend est dépouillé de tout artifice ; nu, pur et comme innocenté par l'intensité de l'émotion, il attend d'être interrogé. Le pasteur va-t-il enfin se conduire comme un père ? Va-t-il se pencher vers sa fille, lui parler? Non. L'homme n'a le droit de s'adresser directement qu'à Dieu.

« Pourquoi ne peut-on aimer ses parents et ses sœurs d'une façon toute particulière?
— D'où sors-tu cette question?
— De moi, évidemment! Encore que je ne sache pas qui est moi!
— De mieux en mieux!
— Vous ne vous rendez pas compte, papa! Vous avez beaucoup de chance! En vous, il y a un seul homme! »

L'idée de l'inceste a-t-elle jamais pénétré au presbytère? Que ce soit du côté d'Angria ou de Gondal, de l'Afrique, d'une île située dans le Pacifique ou dans le Grand Nord, l'infortune des femmes séduites par leur père, le commerce des frères incestueux ne se mesurent plus à la ligne mais à la page. « Qu'as-tu, Charlotte? Sont-ce les divagations de ton frère qui te font cet effet? Tu es aussi blanche que la nappe! » Charlotte, la guindée, la fervente tory, l'anglicane, plus encore que ses sœurs dont on ne connaîtra jamais les récits de jeunesse — ils ont été perdus ou détruits — s'en donne à cœur joie depuis des années. Devenue homme sous la plume de Lord Wellesley, qui n'est autre que le marquis de Douro, lequel n'est autre que le duc de Zamorna, figure perfide et cruelle, elle dirige une confédération, conquiert des États africains, s'adonne à des amours illicites, séduit, puis abandonne des héroïnes énamourées qui ressemblent à s'y méprendre à ses amies de pensionnat, Ellen Nussey et Mary Taylor. Ces jeunes et innocentes personnes sont également victimes des machinations d'Alexander Percy, seigneur de la somptueuse cité de Verdopolis.

« Comment as-tu osé poser une pareille question à papa ? es-tu devenu fou ?
— Aucune importance. Il n'y comprend rien !
— N'empêche que j'ai failli m'évanouir !
— On peut se demander pourquoi ?
— Imagine qu'il trouve nos carnets !
— Et alors, il serait incapable de lire un mot. Il est presque aveugle ! »

Tandis que Charlotte s'interroge sur ce flot d'indécence qui traverse ses chroniques, son complice fait tranquillement l'inventaire des jouissances imaginaires : « Et je t'invite, ma chère, à en faire autant ! Ce serait folie de ta part que de cesser d'écrire ! — Il n'est pas question de cesser d'écrire, il est question d'en terminer avec la chronique d'*Angria* ! Dieu nous jugera autant sur nos pensées que sur nos actes ! Nos écrits nous condamneront ! »

« Ce n'est pas notre faute si la vie est ainsi faite qu'elle privilégie les événements cruels et immoraux ! »

Mise en accusation, la saga d'Angria va-t-elle prendre fin ? Non. De nouveaux faits divers arrivent au presbytère, rapportés par Taby qui n'a que faire des soupçons de l'âme : à Ponden Hall — un lieu qui hantera toujours l'imagination des sœurs Brontë —, la honte a pris la forme d'un bâtard qui entraînera la mort de la mère coupable. « N'avait qu'à point pécher ! » Plus loin, à Trawden, dans une ferme isolée, un amant éconduit a été retrouvé mort dans la chambre où il s'était lui-même emmuré pour s'empêcher d'aller tuer l'infidèle. « Aurait mieux fait d'en trouver une autre ! » A Haworth, un paysan a fait monter son bœuf sur une charrette pour le jeter ensuite, lui et la carriole, dans une mare où l'animal s'est enlisé, puis noyé ; depuis cette nuit d'ivresse, le misérable erre sur les Moors à la recherche de son compagnon de travail dont le fantôme le poursuit toutes les nuits.

> « Seules la mort, la folie et la passion ont inspiré les créateurs ! Lis Shakespeare, Byron ! Sur quoi ont-ils écrit ? Sur la douleur, uniquement sur la douleur ! Le bonheur est indigne d'être raconté ! Laisse la vertu aux imbéciles, Charlotte ! »

★

On l'aura pressenti, Patrick Branwell Brontë peut dès aujourd'hui s'en remettre à moi, je ne le trahirai pas. Sa dérive — je la vois déjà se dessiner — aurait pu être la mienne si le destin m'avait fait naître dans cette Angleterre du XIX^e siècle, dressée entre l'ennui des saisons pluvieuses, la misère d'un peuple sans avenir et une religiosité coulée dans du plomb. La folie de cet être, ses menues vilenies à côté des grandes d'aujourd'hui, ses trahisons, ses tricheries demandent l'indulgence du tribunal devant lequel on le convoque depuis un siècle et demi. Mal compris de la famille dont il fut le héros avant d'en être la plaie, il se plut à jouer, et fort bien, le rôle de « *Celui par qui le scandale arrive* », et il en tira des avantages. Le silence héroïque de son père ne le sauva pas plus que la passion que lui porta sa sœur Charlotte.

Mais pour l'instant nous n'en sommes pas là, même si au presbytère les larmes coulent facilement ; elles sont dues à des lectures. *L'Anatomie de la mélancolie*, de Robert Burton, a circulé entre toutes les mains. Charlotte l'a lue en une semaine, Emily en deux jours, Branwell en une heure: «Tout ça m'est connu! Burton ne m'a rien appris!» Quant à Tante, elle a tout simplement refusé d'ouvrir le livre et a demandé qu'on ne le prête pas à Anne; cette solide femme n'a aucune appétence pour la mélancolie à laquelle elle trouve mauvaise tenue.

«Ce genre de lecture m'insupporte autant que les pleurnicheries! Rien de plus affligeant que les êtres qui se complaisent dans la douleur!»

Ellen Nussey que l'on attend d'un jour à l'autre partagera-t-elle ce sentiment? En attendant de lui poser la question, chacun est retourné à ses occupations: Anne prie et coud en compagnie de Tante, Emily taquine Tabitha tout en s'activant dans la maison, Charlotte s'exaspère: cette vie est décidément trop plate pour elle qui se sent prête à entreprendre de grandes choses. Branwell, lui, a décidé de se consacrer davantage à la musique; il s'est procuré une flûte... de là à imaginer Anne ou Emily l'accompagnant au piano! Malheureusement pour Charlotte qui sait apprécier, peut-être plus que les autres, les grandes œuvres — Mozart, Beethoven et Haendel sont ses musiciens préférés — elle ne peut jouer du piano du fait de sa trop grande myopie.

«Il me semble que tu serais plus douée que nous!
— C'est possible, mais je ne vois pas les touches! Pour changer de sujet, j'ai une bonne nouvelle à vous annoncer... Ellen s'est enfin décidée. Elle arrive après-demain!»

★

Au presbytère, l'émotion est à son comble : « Oh, Ellen, ma chère Ellen ! » A peine descendue de calèche, l'invitée glisse un mot à l'oreille de Charlotte : « Je comprends mieux votre tristesse et je vous admire de garder la santé dans un tel décor ! » La réalité de ce lieu désolé est plus terrible encore que la description qui lui en a été faite à Roe Head. Mais Ellen n'est pas fille à se complaire dans la morbidité ; elle se détourne du spectacle, pénètre d'un pas décidé dans le presbytère où l'attend le révérend Brontë, pour le coup raidi dans une tournure d'homme d'Église. Ce père que Charlotte ne pouvait évoquer sans trembler d'émotion et de respect est plus grand qu'elle ne le pensait. Affable, presque enjoué, il salue la visiteuse, se charge, en quelques phrases bien tournées, de lui faire oublier la mélancolie des lieux. L'invitée est enchantée par ce préambule à l'accent irlandais ; elle le sera encore davantage lorsque Branwell, coincé entre le buffet et son père, lui aura fait part de la joie qu'il éprouve à la revoir :

« La liberté vous va à merveille, Ellen ! »

Les salutations faites, tout le monde sort du bureau. Au passage, Charlotte présente un personnage qu'on ne saurait dédaigner sans attirer des représailles : « Ah v'la l'demoiselle dont j'entends causer d'belle date ! » Charlotte pointe un doigt en direction de Tabitha : « Taby, notre servante et notre amie ! » Miss Nussey accepte la main qu'on vient d'essuyer sur le tablier à carreaux : « Enchantée, madame ! »

« Bin en v'la une madame ! J'suis Taby pour vous aussi, Miss Ellen ! »

Ellen marque un mouvement de recul qu'elle regrette aussitôt. Elle se retourne, aperçoit par la porte entrouverte de la salle à manger deux statues au regard baissé. Devant tant de timidité, elle traverse le vestibule, s'adresse aux deux sœurs surprises par la spontanéité, le naturel, l'aisance de la visiteuse : « J'imagine que vous êtes Emily, et vous Anne ? Je vous reconnais sans vous avoir jamais vues ! » D'où vient cette aimable personne qui, d'une phrase, sait vous faire savoir qu'elle n'a que de la sympathie pour vous ? La glace est rompue. Elle le sera de la même manière au premier étage où attend Miss Branwell. Charmée par l'allure de la voyageuse, la vieille fille n'attendra pas la fin de la conversation pour lui présenter sa tabatière : « Savez-vous priser, Miss Ellen ? Ou êtes-vous comme ces sots d'ici qui ne voient là que mauvaise habitude ? Il n'y a rien de mieux que le tabac pour chasser les microbes ! »

Ce soir, le presbytère est en fête. Pour la première fois, les enfants du pasteur reçoivent une amie. Autour de la table où la famille est réunie, les questions jaillissent : Ellen a-t-elle fait bon voyage ? Comment va sa famille ? Ses frères vont-ils partir faire leurs études à l'étranger ? A-t-elle été à Londres cette année ? Où compte-t-elle passer ses vacances ? A la mer ? Comment est-ce, la mer ? L'invitée tente de répondre au mieux : « Je suis heureuse d'être parmi vous ! » Branwell coupe la parole à son père ; ce soir c'est lui le maître de maison :

« Ellen, c'est nous qui sommes honorés de vous recevoir ! »

*«L'air qui se jouait sur le front des deux jeunes filles était frais, doux et réconfortant.*
*"Notre Angleterre est une île charmante, dit Shirley, et le Yorkshire l'un de ses plus jolis endroits.*
*— Vous êtes aussi une fille du Yorkshire?*
*— Oui, par le sang et la naissance. Cinq générations de ma famille dorment sous les ailes de l'église de Briarfield; j'ai respiré mon premier souffle dans la vieille et noire demeure qui est là derriere vous."»*

Charlotte Brontë, *Shirley*.
(Traduction Guy Faroux.)

*« Elle pouvait bien, comme Charlotte l'écrivit plus tard, "n'être rien de plus qu'une jeune fille du Yorkshire, consciencieuse, intelligente, calme, bien élevée", c'est là précisément ce qu'ils admiraient. »*

Virginia MOORE.

CE portrait simplifié à l'extrême — je vois dans ce « *rien de plus* » la condescendance à laquelle ma sœur ne sut pas toujours résister — ne rend pas justice à Ellen Nussey. En revanche il montre ce que Charlotte refusa catégoriquement d'être : « *une jeune fille du Yorkshire, calme, bien élevée* ».

« Je préfère mourir tout de suite !
— Dans ce cas, suicide-toi, car je crains fort que ce ne soit là ce qu'attendent de toi papa et Tante !
— Tu en parles à ton aise, Branwell ! En ce sens, tu es bien né homme ! »

Avant d'expliquer pourquoi je ne pus, dès son retour de Roe Head, me confier à Charlotte comme je l'avais si souvent fait dans l'enfance, quand sa parole coulait en moi comme une eau bienfaisante, je voudrais ajouter quelques mots sur le séjour que Miss Nussey fit à Haworth et le plaisir que nous tirâmes de sa compagnie. A peine installée dans la maison cette jeune fille — elle ne connaissait du monde que les bienfaits d'une situation avantagée, la bienveillance d'une famille pourvue et unie, l'écho des affaires que menaient du haut de leur compétence les hommes nés Nussey —, s'attacha à nous. Sa spontanéité, sa simplicité rencontrèrent notre sympathie puis notre affection.

« Je me suis rarement autant amusée !
— Nous aussi, Ellen ! Soyez bénie d'être venue à Haworth ! »

Durant deux semaines, elle partagea nos plaisirs, nos rêvasseries, se prêta à nos jeux sans montrer de réticence. Nonobstant, nous lui cachâmes nos écrits. Pas plus que les autres, Ellen ne serait invitée à pénétrer dans le royaume de Gondal ou dans celui d'Angria.

« Comment occupez-vous votre temps en hiver, lorsqu'on ne peut pas sortir ?
— Nous lisons, ou nous cousons, ou nous jouons aux cartes.
— Vous ne vous ennuyez jamais ? »

Je me souviens que le temps, pour une fois, favorisa nos promenades. Nous fîmes de longues et belles randonnées à travers les Moors. Alors que l'invitée avançait avec prudence — elle craignait pour ses chevilles fragiles et ses pieds maladroits —, moi je filais à l'avant du cortège : « Emily, attendez-nous ! »

« Impossible de la suivre !
— Court-elle toujours ainsi ? »

Je me retournais en riant, tendais une main qu'on me refusait : « N'ayez pas peur, Ellen...

suivez-moi ! — Ah ça, jamais, j'ai bien trop peur ! — Peur de quoi ? D'un rocher ? — J'ai le vertige ! — Je n'en crois pas un mot ! Donnez-moi donc la main ! — Non, n'insistez pas, Emily ! — Tant pis pour vous... Vous ne verrez pas comme c'est joli de l'autre côté ! »

« Charlotte, rappelez-la ! Elle va tomber !
— Ne craignez rien... ma sœur est souple comme un chat ! »

Mes pieds nus pour courir plus vite et grimper sans danger, mes jupes retroussées jusqu'à la ceinture pour traverser les cours d'eau, mes cris lorsque je poursuivais un coq de bruyère, cette agitation l'étonna sans la choquer. Il y avait trop de bonté en elle. Ellen nous jugea avec son cœur : « Mon Dieu, quelle étonnante famille vous formez là ! »

« Croyez-vous ?
— Je n'ai jamais rencontré autant d'originalité. Vous êtes tous différents et pourtant vous vous ressemblez ! »

Beaucoup plus tard, quand nous eûmes tous disparu, on lui demanda un témoignage ; elle fit alors de nous un portrait incisif qui prouvait qu'en la traitant de « *rien de plus qu'une jeune fille du Yorkshire* » Charlotte lui avait fait injure. Cela dit, il est probable que pour cette jeune personne, patiente, calme et avisée, nous dûmes souvent prendre allure de fous, surtout Branwell dont l'excentricité verbale atteignit des sommets en cette saison où une oreille étrangère se tendait vers lui :

« Comment me trouvez-vous, Ellen ? Ne rou-

gissez pas! Ma question est sincère! Avez-vous une opinion sur moi?
— Si j'en ai une, elle ne peut qu'être bonne!
— La réponse est polie. J'attendais mieux!
— Quoi par exemple?
— J'aimerais plaire!
— Voyez-vous ça!
— J'aimerais séduire, subjuguer, briller comme une étoile, réchauffer autrui par mon ardeur, l'émouvoir, l'étonner par mon savoir!»

Dans ce groupe quelque peu remuant pour une personne habituée à plus de mesure, Anne apporta à l'invitée le calme dont elle avait parfois besoin: «Ma chère petite, accepteriez-vous de faire une promenade avec moi? Je me sens si bien en votre présence!»

«Soyez remerciée, Ellen, de me donner enfin la possibilité d'être utile... ici, je ne sers à personne!
— Comment pouvez-vous dire une chose pareille?
— J'en souffre beaucoup, mais à quoi cela servirait de me plaindre?... Ils n'ont pas besoin de moi!
— Je n'en crois pas un mot!
— Surtout, Ellen, que ceci reste entre nous! Charlotte ne comprendrait pas, et Emily serait fâchée!
— Je crois, ma chère petite, que vous vous faites de fausses idées sur vous-même. N'avez-vous donc aucune confiance en vous?»

Après Anne dont elle écouta avec étonnement la confession, la personne qui surprit le plus Ellen fut notre père: «Comment parvient-il encore à enseigner la bonne parole devant un tel auditoire? Je n'ai jamais vu la moindre étincelle d'intelligence briller sur le visage de ces malheureux ! »

« La foi de papa est si grande que, pour reprendre l'expression, elle soulèverait des montagnes !
— Comme vous aimez votre père, chère Anne !
— Comment ne pas l'aimer ? Il est un peu froid et distant avec nous, mais au fond il est bon. »

Ellen était presque de cet avis ; comment, en effet, ne pas aimer le pasteur de Haworth ? Sa violence, son désespoir soutenaient si bien la parole évangélique qu'elle aurait dû pourfendre l'âme la plus endurcie : « Il ne peut pas ne pas leur donner le goût de Dieu, du bon, du bien ! » Jamais Miss Nussey n'avait rencontré une telle conviction, un tel courage, une telle ardeur dans la prédication. Face à ces êtres embourbés dans une préhistoire sans fin, le révérend Brontë faisait figure de prophète et de saint.

« La compassion chez papa est si grande que rien ne le rebute. Autrefois, quand il avait encore de bons yeux, il allait porter l'espérance et la promesse de la résurrection dans les taudis et les fermes isolées. Savez-vous, Ellen, que beaucoup lui doivent de ne pas être morts mécréants ? »

Au fil des journées où elle ne cessa de s'instruire, Ellen découvrit à quelques milles de Birstall, où vivait confortablement sa famille, la misère, l'ignorance, des mœurs barbares. L'office du dimanche ne fut plus pour elle occasion de se recueillir mais d'observer, éventuellement de comprendre. « Souffrent-ils ? » Le monde n'allait pas aussi bien qu'elle l'avait cru jusque-là. La pauvreté des gens était si grande qu'ils ne possédaient même pas une paire de chaussures pour venir à l'église ; beaucoup s'y rendaient en galoches. M. Brown, le sacristain, se plaignait de son rôle : « Je sers de gendarme. Tantôt il me faut gronder le paysan qui sort une fiole de sa poche, tantôt arracher cet autre à ses ronflements, tantôt donner un coup de bâton au garnement qui fait des bêtises derrière un pilier ! » La récitation des prières ramenait un semblant de gravité. Pas pour longtemps. A peine l'Amen prononcé, le pasteur passait en revue les mauvaises actions de la semaine, car à Haworth où tout semblait se diriger vers le pire, le serviteur de Dieu était aussi le gardien du citoyen.

« *Malheur à celui qui fait boire son prochain,*
*A toi qui verses ton outre et qui l'enivres,*
*Afin de voir sa nudité !* »

Fascinée par cet homme qui montait en chaire comme on monte au combat, Ellen l'entendit plusieurs fois jeter l'anathème, invoquer le mal, demander à Dieu de punir celui que l'on avait retrouvé dans le ruisseau, cet autre accusé d'adultère, cet autre qui avait battu ses enfants à mort ; au village, le commerce des coups était plus florissant que celui des mots.

« *Tu seras rassasié de honte plus que de gloire :*
*Bois aussi toi-même, et découvre-toi !*
*La coupe de la droite de l'Éternel se tournera*
[*vers toi,*
*Et l'ignominie souillera ta gloire.* »

Au fur et à mesure que son prêche allait vers sa fin, la voix du vicaire prenait de l'ampleur ; elle montait crescendo jusqu'aux cris de la colère. Des soupirs coupables montaient des bancs où se serraient les misérables, épaule contre épaule. Le pasteur finissait toujours pas se taire, faute de souffle. Il posait ses deux mains sur le pupitre. Épuisé par l'effort, il jetait un regard de pitié à son troupeau saisi par le repentir. Son silence douloureux durait quelquefois plusieurs minutes. « Y peut toujours nous fixer avec l'œil du Justicier, on sait qu'y nous voit pas net ! L'est presque aveugle ! » Puis sonnait la cloche ; elle annonçait la fin de l'office.

> « Allez en paix, et que Dieu dans sa miséricorde ait pitié de vous ! »

Nous attendions que tout le monde eût quitté l'église pour sortir à notre tour. Parfois le papetier, M. Greenwood, venait nous saluer. Discrètement, il prenait des nouvelles de la famille, remerciait le pasteur de ses services et disparaissait sur un signe de tête. Sous la lumière de midi, nous traversions à la queue leu leu le cimetière pour regagner le presbytère. Tante ouvrait la marche, notre père la fermait. Tabitha nous ouvrait la porte : « Pourquoi n'étiez-vous pas à l'office ? » demandait Tante en pointant un menton accusateur : « J'avais trop à faire, miss ! L'repas s'prépare pas en priant et mes r'lations avec Dieu sont d'un ord'e tout particulier ! — Quelle insolence ! » Excédée, Miss Branwell se détournait de la vieille femme. Elle regardait Ellen avec bienveillance. D'une main de militaire elle montrait la place d'honneur à l'invitée qui la refusait : « A ma droite, Ellen, et ne protestez pas ! » Puis Tante prenait la parole ; elle racontait sa vie, à l'époque où elle se pavanait à Penzance. « Ne regrettez-vous pas cette existence facile ? ce climat ? »

« Le climat, certes ! L'existence sûrement pas ! La vieillesse m'aurait rattrapée là-bas comme elle m'a rattrapée ici ! »

Après le déjeuner quelqu'un décidait d'une promenade : « Où ? — Encore ! — Si tu n'es pas content, ne viens pas avec nous, Branwell ! — Vous auriez tort de prendre de grands airs... Trois filles seules, ça ne fait pas sérieux ! » Nous partions main dans la main, mais bientôt Charlotte et Ellen s'écartaient du groupe. Tout en marchant d'un pas de petites vieilles, elles évoquaient leur vie de pensionnaires à Roe Head. Leurs rires nerveux, leurs cris étouffés agaçaient Branwell qui bâillait comme un paysan mal élevé. Deux heures plus tard, vaincus par la fatigue, nous faisions demi-tour : « De ma vie, je n'aurai jamais autant marché ! Lorsque je raconterai nos randonnées à ma famille, elle n'en croira pas ses oreilles ! A Birstall, je ne quitte pratiquement pas le salon ! »

« Ceci prouve que l'air est meilleur ici que chez vous ! Il invite à plus d'hygiène ! J'espère que vos parents vous laisseront revenir ! »

En fin de journée, papa nous convoquait dans son bureau pour la prière. Aussitôt les psaumes lus, il montait l'escalier : « Ne vous couchez pas trop tard, les enfants ! » Parvenu sur le premier palier, quelque chose l'arrêtait ; un geste à accomplir dont il ne se souvenait plus : « Ah oui, l'horloge ! Je dois la remonter ! » Ce travail fait, il se retournait, guettait l'approbation des spectateurs regroupés en bas de l'escalier : « N'est-ce pas curieux ? Alors que je refais chaque soir le même geste, chaque soir se pose à moi la même question ! » Charlotte s'appliquait à montrer sa patience ; elle devait parfois garder la pose car le pasteur, peu pressé de regagner la solitude glacée de son lit, et inspiré par un souffle dont nous ne sûmes jamais de quel point cardinal il venait, se mettait à raconter des histoires effrayantes dont nous ignorâmes toujours si elles étaient destinées à la cage d'escalier ou à nous. « Quel étrange père vous avez là ! Avez-vous remarqué, pendant qu'il nous parlait, il ne nous a pas regardés une seule fois ! » Appuyée contre l'épaule de Charlotte, Ellen frissonnait :

« Pensez-vous que demain matin il nous réveillera avec son pistolet ?
— C'est probable ! »

Sur le seuil de la cuisine, Anne m'adressait un regard inquiet ; pourquoi notre père racontait-il des histoires aussi épouvantables à une étrangère ? Je songeais à notre mère ; quel geste aurait-elle eu pour cette jeune fille au corps de libellule et au regard violet ? Je lui prenais le bras. Nous montions nous coucher pendant que les trois autres continuaient à discuter dans la salle à manger.

★

Hélas, vint le jour où Ellen dut nous quitter. Nous retrouvâmes la mélancolie où nous l'avions laissée avant son arrivée. Un après-midi où le temps était passablement mauvais, Branwell eut une crise de nerfs. Au lieu de tenter de le consoler, papa lui conseilla d'aller promener son humeur à Bradford où le recevrait son parrain. De ce voyage, notre frère ramena des crayons de toutes les couleurs, des pinceaux, des aquarelles et quelques tubes de peinture à l'huile. L'odeur de l'essence de térébenthine indisposa Tante qui n'eut pas gain de cause : « Autrement dit, migraine ou pas, je n'ai plus rien à dire ? » Papa s'excusa ; son fils avait du talent, il ne lui manquait que la pratique :

« Je suis désolé, Elizabeth, mais il faut bien que ces enfants s'occupent ! De plus, je vois là un devenir possible pour Branwell. »

Cette reconnaissance nous stimula si bien que nous insistâmes pour recevoir l'enseignement d'un maître. Un dénommé Robinson vint nous donner des cours de dessin. Il nous inculqua les rudiments d'une technique que Branwell fit sienne sur-le-champ ; nous dûmes poser à tour de rôle. De cette époque date le portrait de famille que vous connaissez.

A la vue de cette œuvre pourtant bien modeste, notre père épousa les illusions de Branwell qui, alors âgé de dix-sept ans, décida de choisir la carrière artistique. Ce choix se confirma quelques mois plus tard à la suite d'une excursion à Leeds où demeurait notre maître, M. Robinson. Branwell visita une exposition au cours de laquelle il s'extasia sur une sculpture, un gigantesque buste de Satan. Cette œuvre frappa notre frère qui s'enquit de l'identité de l'artiste ; Joseph Bentley Leyland, un garçon de vingt-trois ans — il devait devenir son ami par la suite —, était le fils d'un libraire de Halifax : « Ce sculpteur, malgré sa jeunesse, a la taille d'un créateur de premier plan ! Déjà lors d'une exposition à Manchester, un

*Spartacus* lui a valu les éloges de la critique! Le Yorkshire peut être fier de lui!»

> «Voilà qui m'enthousiasme et m'encourage à poursuivre mon propre chemin! En face d'une œuvre de cette force, j'ai le sentiment d'exister enfin!»

Lorsqu'il revint de Leeds, bouleversé parce qu'il venait de découvrir, à travers un autre, ses propres dimensions, Branwell nous raconta comment, dans cette galerie, il avait été saisi par l'œuvre magistrale qui, au détour d'une salle, s'était imposée à lui. Inspiré de l'épopée de Milton, Satan, sous le ciseau de Leyland, avait la beauté démoniaque d'Alexander Percy.

> «Que ce garçon te serve d'exemple, mon fils! Mets-toi au travail!»

En attendant de prendre la route glorieuse qui le mènerait à Londres où il s'inscrirait dès que possible à la Royal Academy, Branwell s'empressa d'introduire dans sa chronique angriane un nouveau personnage. Pétri, non pas dans l'argile, mais façonné par les mots, il ressemblait au Satan de Leyland.

*« Une magnifique aube de printemps parut le lendemain de notre arrivée en ce lieu, et je me levai de bonne heure pour me promener un peu avant le petit déjeuner sur les moelleuses pelouses qui s'étendaient sous la fenêtre de ma chambre. L'image de cette splendide et vénérable suite de bâtiments qui constituent le château, des pentes de verdure ensoleillée qui l'entourent, des arbres superbes, principalement des ormes de la plus grande dimension, qui couvrent les pentes d'une ombre frémissante entrelacée de continuelles trouées de lumière, doit être imprimée dans le cœur de quiconque a lu* La Politique de Verdopolis, *et qui donc ne l'a lue ? »*

Charlotte Brontë,
*Le Grand Monde à Verdopolis.*
(Traduction Francis Ledoux.)

Hier matin, alors que le froid s'abattait brutalement sur le nord de l'Europe, j'ai songé au village de Haworth plongé au cœur de l'hiver, au clair-obscur des journées attristées par l'absence du soleil, aux pentes des Moors impraticables, aux rues glissantes, à la lande battue par le vent du nord, aux bosquets racornis, à la présence spectrale des arbres, au presbytère encerclé par le cimetière enseveli sous la neige.

Pour échapper à cette reconstitution quelque peu glaciale, j'ai ouvert le livre *The Brontë's* de Brian Wilks que j'ai acheté lors de mon séjour à Haworth dans une boutique du village. Saisie par cette sorte d'émotion que l'on ressent à regarder les photos du passé, j'ai revu le presbytère, tel qu'il est inscrit dans mon souvenir, avec ses fenêtres à petits carreaux, son fronton triangulaire au-dessus de la porte à colonnades, ce qui donne à la bâtisse par ailleurs modeste une touche de distinction et l'amorce d'un style. Puis j'ai relu les titres des ouvrages que fit éditer le révérend Patrick Brontë, prosateur et philosophe à ses heures : « *The Rural Minstrel : A Miscellany of Descriptive Poems — Cottage Poems — The Cottage in the Wood, or The Art of becoming rich and happy,* enfin *The Phenomenon or An Account in Verse of the extraordinary Disruption of a Bog* » —, une littérature probablement édifiante et pleine de bons sentiments. Enfin je suis tombée sur une photographie qui m'a frappée par sa simplicité et sa force d'évocation : composée à la manière d'une nature morte, elle met en scène trois éléments : le fameux pistolet, la montre et le bonnet de nuit du pasteur : sommeil, temps, mort, ici représentée par une arme dont il semble qu'elle ne servit qu'à réveiller les cadavres.

> « Papa, de quoi avez-vous peur, vous qui semblez si grand et si fort ?
> — De ne pas rendre grâces à Dieu comme il conviendrait que je le fasse, mon fils !
> — Et de quoi encore ?
> — Peut-être bien des insomnies... il y a des souvenirs que l'on préfère aborder en pleine lumière.
> — Et de quoi encore ?
> — Du temps.
> — Qu'est-ce qu'il vous a fait le temps ?
> — Il me mène vers la cécité. »

Mais ce qui dans cet ouvrage m'a le plus interessée, ce ne sont pas tant les photographies prises à l'intérieur du presbytère que les reproductions des dessins, des aquarelles et des peintures signés par les enfants Brontë dont le talent, ici comme dans l'écriture est incontestable.

Pour qui ignore tout de leur art, j'ai choisi une aquarelle intitulée *The Bay of Glasstown* que réalisa Charlotte, vue panoramique d'une ville — celle de la chronique angriane — flanquée au premier plan d'un château féodal aux allures de prison. Éclairée par une lumière bleutée d'un effet tout à fait surprenant, elle emprunte au fantastique et à l'Orient ses tours et ses cours intérieures refermées sur des ombres mystérieuses, ses espaces inhabités où l'être ne règne que parce qu'il est absent. Une longue esplanade, comme désœuvrée, ajoute à la singularité de cette aquarelle qui semble inspirée par une des nombreuses filatures situées non loin de Halifax — bien que désaffectées, elles sont toujours aussi imposantes, avec leurs cheminées monumentales et leurs hautes fenêtres. Je me suis laissé émouvoir aussi par les dessins d'Anne; naïfs, frais, touchants, parfois maladroits, ils évoquent la renaissance des arbres au printemps, la marche lourde d'un bœuf, l'atmosphère bucolique d'une campagne paisible et souriante, en tout cas moins rude que celle de cette partie du Yorkshire. Branwell, le caricaturiste, en dehors de quelques portraits à l'huile, nous a laissé des esquisses cruelles et cocasses; toutes dénoncent les travers humains dans ce qu'ils ont de plus ridicule. Ses dessins nous ramènent soit à la taverne du Black Bull où s'enivraient les mâles de Haworth, soit à Verdopolis ou à Glasstown, capitales imaginaires où l'on s'égorgeait tranquillement entre personnes de qualité. Rien de semblable chez Emily. Sa technique, son pinceau cernent au plus près le réel, la vie quotidienne, les compagnons de chaque instant. Plus qu'aux êtres, elle est attachée aux animaux qu'elle observe avec tant de patience qu'elle arrive à les surprendre dans le relâchement du sommeil; son chien d'abord, le dogue Keeper, à l'heure de la pause; son faucon ensuite, Hero, dont on pourrait compter les plumes.

« Cesse de bouger, Anne!
— J'ai des agacements dans la nuque!
— Tant pis!
— Tu en as de bonnes, Charlotte!
— Je te tiens enfin... ça n'est pas pour te rendre à la liberté!
— En as-tu encore pour longtemps?
— Quelques minutes... c'est cette boucle

au-dessus de ton front qui me donne le plus de travail ! »

J'aimerais terminer ce catalogue des œuvres brontéennes avec une miniature en forme de médaillon qui représente la jeune Anne peinte par sa sœur aînée. Rien de mièvre dans ce profil long et mince, mais au contraire de la distinction, de la réserve, un beau regard porté droit devant lui, une bouche charmante, un menton dessiné dans la fermeté. Le cou gracile et long rappelle celui que décrit Charlotte dans *High Life in Verdopolis*, un récit de jeunesse.

« *En dix minutes, elle fut habillée, et elle était tout à fait ravissante, dans les plis sombres et changeants de la soie qui glissaient sur sa forme svelte, sans colliers ni autres ornements autour de son rose cou de cygne...* »

Est-ce cette image enfermée dans un médaillon qu'emportera Charlotte, lorsque contrainte de gagner sa vie il lui faudra repartir pour Roe Head où Miss Wooler lui offrira une place d'institutrice ? Est-ce ce beau profil sans défense qu'elle abandonnera à Tante : « Je sais qu'avec vous, Anne ne risque rien ! — Qu'entends-tu par ne risquer rien ? Crois-tu donc que je suis la force incarnée et la clairvoyance en personne, pour protéger ta sœur contre les choses de l'esprit et de la pensée ? Si je peux guider vos consciences, je n'ai pas le pouvoir de m'immiscer dans vos songeries. La solitude d'une vieille fille comme moi lui pèsera sûrement, mais je ferai de mon mieux pour la divertir ! »

Laissant à Miss Branwell le soutien moral de sa jeune sœur, Charlotte entraînera une Emily réticente dans son sillage.

★

29 juillet 1835.

De la fenêtre du bureau, Patrick Brontë et sa belle-sœur souhaitent bonne route aux deux voyageuses. Un dernier conseil, un avis judicieux, une parole en forme de sermon, un geste de la main, et en voilà assez ! « Ne manquez pas de nous donner de vos nouvelles ! » Tous deux disparaissent de la vue des jeunes filles. Tante retourne à sa broderie et le pasteur à ses ruminations. Charlotte et Emily encadrent Anne qui, le matin même, a demandé la permission d'accompagner ses sœurs jusqu'à la diligence. Tante a bien voulu donner son assentiment : « Mais à une condition ! Que tu ne pleures pas comme une désespérée au moment de la séparation ! » Après avoir envoyé un dernier baiser de la main à Taby qui marmonne devant la maison, elles longent le cimetière, descendent les quelques marches qui donnent sur les premières maisons du village. Elles passent rapidement devant le Black Bull, descendent la rue qui mène au croisement où s'arrêtera la diligence.

Charlotte ouvre maintenant la marche. Sa petite taille accentue son allant. Son visage affiche la satisfaction de celle qui a choisi sa voie et la prend pour bonne. Derrière elle suivent ses sœurs ; elles se partagent le poids d'un sac de voyage qu'elles tiennent chacune par une anse. L'air triste d'Emily renvoie à celui d'Anne qui marche en baissant la tête pour éviter la curiosité des voisins : « Voilà les trois filles du presbytère ! Où vont-elles de ce pas ! Inutile de s'impatienter, on saura tout de l'affaire par Branwell ! » Charlotte s'inquiète de la lenteur des deux autres ; elle se retourne, fait signe à ses sœurs de hâter le pas.

« Eh bien, Emily, tu en fais une tête ! Ne dirait-on pas que tu pars pour le bagne ! »

Emily ne répond pas. Elle fixe quelque chose au loin. Charlotte détourne la tête ; ce regard de visionnaire l'exaspère. Anne a perçu l'énervement de sa sœur aînée. Elle sent l'émotion monter dans sa gorge ; pourquoi Charlotte a-t-elle fait preuve d'autant d'insistance ? Alors qu'elle ne voulait pour rien au monde aller à Roe Head, Emily, de guerre lasse, a fini par céder. Anne songe au moyen d'obéir à Tante à qui elle a promis des yeux secs. Pourquoi ne réfléchirait-elle pas à la façon d'aborder la prochaine page de son journal ?

> ... ce matin, 29 juillet 1835, date mémorable pour nous qui n'aurons même pas le plaisir de fêter l'anniversaire d'Emily — elle aura dix-sept ans demain —, j'ai accompagné mes deux sœurs jusqu'à la voiture qui les a emportées loin de mon affection et de ma tendresse. Dans la rue de Haworth que nous avons descendue précipitamment, Charlotte s'est plainte de Branwell : « Il n'a même pas daigné nous accompagner ! » Depuis quelque temps, notre frère nous néglige ; il fait bande à part. A notre compagnie, il préfère celle des mauvais garçons du pays. Emily a répondu évasivement ; mieux que nous tous, elle sait laisser à autrui l'usage de son indépendance. « Parce que tu trouves normal qu'il ait refusé de nous accompagner ? » Emily a dit à Charlotte qu'elle ne trouvait pas cela normal mais qu'elle ne voyait pas de quelle manière remédier à la chose : « Branwell est libre de ses désirs ; s'il n'est pas venu avec nous, c'est peut-être parce qu'il ne souhaitait pas nous voir partir ! » Ce qui inquiétait Emily, ce n'était pas que notre

frère fût absent : « C'est quoi alors ? » Emily a cherché les mots justes pour répondre : « Les choses ne vont pas bien en lui ! » a-t-elle fini par dire. J'ai songé que j'allais me retrouver seule avec ce « pas bien ». Cette idée m'a fait peur. De blanche, je suis devenue livide. « Mon Dieu, Anne, tu ne vas pas te trouver mal dans la rue ? » a dit Charlotte en se rapprochant de moi. Elle m'a prise par le bras avec affection : « Ma chère petite, nous ne partons que pour quelques mois ! Profite donc de notre absence pour lire et t'instruire. Demande à papa de te ramener de la bibliothèque de Ponden Hall l'*Histoire universelle* : Hume, Rollin sont des auteurs passionnants ! Et pourquoi ne t'intéresserais-tu pas aux biographies ? Lis celle qu'a écrite Moore sur le cher Byron. Et puis, n'oublie pas d'apprendre chaque jour quelques vers ; je ne l'avouerai jamais à papa, mais la poésie me paraît aussi importante que la Bible. Celle de Milton est superbe ; quant à Shakespeare, tu t'en rendras compte plus tard, malgré ses excès de langage et ses tristes vues sur l'homme, c'est tout simplement un génie ! Commence par Wordsworth, Southey, nos contemporains, et ne néglige surtout pas d'écrire pour me donner tes impressions. Même à ton âge, on a le droit d'avoir une opinion ! » Plus tard, lorsque la voiture a surgi sur la route qui va de Keighley à Halifax, j'ai cru que mon cœur allait cesser de battre. Pendant que Charlotte tendait les bagages, j'ai jeté un bras en direction d'Emily. Nous nous sommes précipitées l'une contre l'autre, bouleversées à la pensée d'avoir à nous séparer pour de longs mois. Puis l'ordre de fermer les portes a été donné par le conducteur. Emily s'est arrachée à mon étreinte. Elle est montée sans dire un mot ni se retourner. Quand la voiture a disparu, j'ai oublié la promesse que j'avais faite à Tante et j'ai éclaté en sanglots. J'espère que Dieu me pardonnera cette faiblesse.

«*Et moi, dans la bruyère et sur les monts lointains,*
*Cœur lourd, yeux pleins de larmes,*
*J'ai fui le jugement et les soucis humains;*
*Réconfort de l'azur et de son grave charme...*»

Emily Jane Brontë.
(Traduction Françoise d'Eaubonne.)

*«Emily que rien ne rebutait, rien n'effrayait, et qui nourrissait son cœur de mépris et de charité mêlés, Emily (...) pouvait aisément concevoir l'horrible, l'atroce : elle y était naturellement portée.»*

DANIEL-ROPS.

A PEINE étions-nous rendues à Roe Head que je compris, à travers ce déracinement que m'imposait ma famille, à quoi la vie m'avait condamnée. Née à Thornton, élevée à quelques milles de là sur la pente d'une de ces collines qui encerclent les Moors, j'étais devenue la plante qui meurt au cours de sa transplantation. Cet attachement forcené à une région, plus encore à un paysage, je l'éprouvais soudainement comme une dépendance.

« Que se passe-t-il ?
— Tout va bien, Charlotte !
— Pourquoi te tiens-tu constamment à l'écart ?
— Je n'ai pas envie de me mêler aux autres !
— Pourquoi ? A-t-on été désagréable avec toi ? »

A ma sœur Charlotte qui, à l'inverse de moi, se retrouvait dans un lieu dont elle connaissait déjà les habitudes, je ne pus confier le malaise que je ressentis en ces pénibles semaines. Tandis qu'elle découvrait les limites de son pouvoir et les vicissitudes d'une carrière qu'elle avait imaginée différente, je me défis silencieusement à l'écart des autres. Ce retrait, cette impuissance à participer à la vie collective ne m'empêchèrent pas de souffrir de la suffisance de certaines. J'entendis même, alors que je tentais de passer inaperçue, des conversations humiliantes pour ma sœur dont on méprisait le passé de brillante élève : « Pour qui se prend-elle, cette Brontë ? Après tout, elle n'est qu'une petite rien du tout qui tente de nous en imposer ! » Charlotte s'était trompée lourdement sur l'accueil qui lui serait réservé. Pour les autres, elle n'était qu'une institutrice qui travaillait afin de payer les études de sa sœur, laquelle sœur n'était qu'une ombre apathique et muette.

« Ne t'empresse pas de les juger.
— Ce n'est pas leur méchanceté qui me blesse, c'est leur bêtise.
— Tu verras qu'à l'usage certaines sont meilleures qu'on ne le pense.
— Je n'en doute pas, mais je n'ai pas envie d'en savoir davantage.
— Dans ce groupe, il y a certainement l'amie dont tu as besoin... puisque à moi tu ne veux rien dire, peut-être accepteras-tu de te confier à une étrangère ? »

Après les premières semaines où Charlotte dut montrer aux sœurs Wooler qu'elle était capable d'enseigner à des élèves pour lesquelles elle n'avait pas d'estime — les défaillances de l'intelligence ne rencontraient chez elle qu'irritation et impatience —, ma sœur s'inquiéta de ma santé : « Es-tu malade, Emily ? — Cesse de t'inquiéter,

Charlotte! — Comment veux-tu que je ne m'inquiète pas lorsque je te vois dépérir de la sorte?» Face à cette fille courageuse — elle tenait à vivre avec hauteur le mépris où on la tenait —, je me sentis devenir de plus en plus lâche, de plus en plus égoïste. Malheureusement, la découverte de mes défauts ne me donna pas les moyens de les soigner, et mes tentatives pour rassurer Charlotte échouèrent. Les quelques poésies destinées à nourrir l'épopée de Gondal, strophes désespérées que j'écrivis à cette époque, ne m'apportèrent ni réconfort ni plaisir. Secouée par le vent de refus qui soufflait en moi, je me crus abandonnée de Dieu; ne venait-il pas de me retirer le peu de charité dont il m'avait fait la grâce jusque-là? Refermé sur sa propre contemplation, mon esprit ne pouvait s'affranchir de lui-même ni se confier.

> «Je dispose d'une heure... veux-tu que nous allions nous promener? Je connais un très joli coin!
> — Si ça peut te faire plaisir!
> — Ce n'est pas à moi que je cherche à faire plaisir, Emily, c'est à toi!»

Au mois d'août, on put lire sur mon visage les effets de l'anorexie. La mélancolie m'inonda d'une eau crayeuse. De pâle, je devins blafarde; de mince, je devins maigre. Charlotte s'affola; elle tenta d'obtenir de moi les raisons d'un tel dépérissement. M'avait-on fait des réflexions désobligeantes? Avais-je reçu de mauvaises nouvelles du presbytère? Branwell avait-il encore fait des siennes? Affaissée sur une chaise ou recroquevillée au bord de mon lit, je la voyais aller et venir, se pencher de temps à autre pour tenter de surprendre dans mon regard une lueur d'espérance. Chagrinée de causer autant de souci, je laissais couler des larmes que je n'avais plus la force d'essuyer : « Pardonne-moi, Charlotte... pardonne-moi ! »

« Mais de quoi, Grand Dieu ?
— De toute cette peine que je te fais !
— Je n'ai rien à te pardonner ! Tout ce que je voudrais, c'est pouvoir t'aider, mais tu ne m'en donnes pas les moyens.
— La vie ne m'attendait pas. »

Ma sœur se récriait ; comment, moi, fille de pasteur, pouvais-je parler ainsi ? Comment pouvais-je douter de la générosité divine ? L'avenir me montrerait bonne figure et l'amour m'accorderait tôt ou tard ses faveurs ; mais pour que cela fût, il me fallait quitter Haworth, car de là-haut, de cette prison gardée par des tombes, rien de bon ne pouvait venir. Charlotte se taisait, attendant une approbation, un mot qui calmerait son inquiétude ; comme il ne venait pas, elle attirait une chaise, s'asseyait à côté de moi : « Eh bien, Emily, dis-moi quelque chose... Fais-moi savoir que tu m'as entendue ! » Mon silence l'effrayait tellement qu'elle me saisissait la main, la serrait de toutes ses forces, parfois elle la portait à ses lèvres :

« Je suis là, ma chère sœur, je suis là ! Tu n'es pas seule ! »

Cet acte d'amour, ce regard rempli d'attente me désolaient. Aurais-je le courage de lui dire qu'il ne pouvait y avoir d'autre futur pour moi que celui qui m'était promis à Haworth ? A défaut de rencontrer l'amour, j'avais rencontré la nature ; mariée à un paysage, je préférais mourir plutôt que d'être séparée de lui : « Ce que je veux, aucun homme ne pourra jamais me le donner ! »

> « Pourquoi dis-tu cela ? Tu ne sais pas ce que la vie te réserve !
> — Si, je le sais, Charlotte, et c'est parce que je le sais que je ne veux pas attendre ni espérer en vain ! »

A la mi-septembre, le désir de la mort m'investit. Je priai Dieu de me rappeler à lui comme il avait rappelé mes sœurs, et avant elles ma pauvre mère. J'avais suffisamment vécu pour juger l'existence. Le monde était trop ingrat pour qu'on s'y attardât, et sages ceux qui savaient le quitter à temps. Certains prêches du pasteur Brontë évoquant la douleur balbutiante de l'homme, sa révolte, son incompréhension au pied de la croix, me revinrent en mémoire. Je compris que la crucifixion n'avait pas eu lieu autrefois, dans un temps donné ; à chaque minute, Jésus souffrait à travers ceux qui acceptaient de l'accueillir ; à chaque minute, il souffrait de l'abandon des hommes ; à chaque minute, il posait la question : « Père, pourquoi m'avez-vous abandonné ? » Moi-même, j'étais devenue ce corps de déréliction où Dieu se remettait constamment en cause. Que pouvais-je faire pour combler Son attente et participer à Sa souffrance sinon lui offrir ma vie ?

C'est ainsi qu'après avoir cessé d'espérer, je cessai d'étudier ; les études ne servaient qu'à alimenter l'absurde. Éclairée par l'intuition que l'amour prête parfois, ma sœur comprit qu'à l'exemple de nos deux aînées je me dirigeais vers la mort. Elle se souvint de son impuissance de naguère et ce souvenir la secoua si fortement qu'elle décida de ma remise en liberté. Elle tenta de parler à Miss Wooler qui ne comprit pas un mot d'un discours où on voulait lui démontrer qu'une jeune fille pouvait souhaiter la mort pour la seule raison qu'on l'avait soustraite à une vie médiocre et recluse. Ce refus d'entendre ne désarma pas Charlotte. Plusieurs lettres alarmistes parvinrent au presbytère. Las d'enterrer ses filles, papa répondit très vite; il demandait à Miss Wooler de bien vouloir me faire rapratrier d'urgence, en échange de quoi il lui confierait volontiers sa troisième fille, Anne, un caractère doux, pieux, timide et conciliant, en tout cas moins original que le mien dont il disait n'avoir pas mesuré la sauvagerie. Bâtie pour l'indépendance et non pour la discipline, il m'était égal d'assumer la pauvreté qui m'attendait entre les murs où j'avais grandi.

> «... curieuse fille, en vérité, mademoiselle, et j'aurais dû tenir compte de ce caractère trempé d'une autre manière, mais un père se méprend souvent sur ce qu'il croit devoir être le bien de sa progéniture...»

Ce que Patrick Brontë avait pris pour de la force n'était qu'une faiblesse; sur elle, il me faudrait construire ma vie.

> «... pardonnez-moi, chère mademoiselle Wooler, de vous avoir mise dans l'embarras. J'en appelle à votre indulgence et à votre bonté que Charlotte m'a dit grandes...»

Au reçu de la lettre de mon père, la directrice me convoqua dans son bureau. Elle me demanda sur le ton du médecin qui s'adresse à un grand malade si je souhaitais abandonner des études à peine commencées. Au lieu de répondre, j'éclatai en sanglots : « Décidément, vous allez bien mal, mon enfant ! » La pitié l'emporta sur le dédain ; elle vint poser une main amicale sur mon épaule, me conseilla de faire mes valises au plus vite. Je vécus ce départ pourtant souhaité aussi mal que possible. Au moment d'embrasser Charlotte, la honte empourpra mon visage. Je m'excusai d'abandonner à son sort celle qui avait lutté pour mon bien. Ma sœur baissa la tête pour me cacher ses larmes : « Tu as fait ce que tu as pu, Emily ! » M'en voulait-elle de ne pas lui ressembler ? Cette question — elle ne cessa de me harceler durant tout le voyage — s'envola à la seconde où je descendis de voiture. Heureuse de retrouver Haworth, les Moors et ma famille, j'oubliai en quelques jours l'échec que je venais de lui imposer.

★

Hélas, le ciel de ce magnifique automne fut bien vite assombri par le départ d'Anne. A mon tour je l'accompagnai jusqu'à la diligence. Au moment de nous séparer, elle montra une telle fermeté, une si grande détermination que j'en demeurai confondue.

L'irréflexion me poussa vers Tabitha à laquelle je me confiais volontiers : « Je ne savais pas qu'Anne souhaitait poursuivre des études à l'extérieur ! » La brave femme eut des mots qui me réveillèrent, et sa réponse m'atteignit comme une gifle ; les qualités que je prêtais à ma sœur n'avaient pas fondu sur elle en quelques semaines. Anne m'aimait assez pour se sacrifier et partir à ma place, et moi j'étais assez égoïste pour ne pas l'avoir compris :

«Puisque t'as pas la force d'viv'e ailleurs, c'elle qui s'en ira! Elle m'a dit ça tel quel!»

Ce renoncement ne faisait qu'annoncer tous ceux qui allaient suivre. D'après les calculs que ma sœur avait faits devant Taby, il était apparu que si trois de nous gagnaient correctement leur vie, je pourrais demeurer au presbytère avec Tante et papa qui avaient besoin d'une aide et d'une présence. «Pourquoi ne pas me l'avoir dit plus tôt? Pourquoi avoir attendu son départ?»

«Y a pas pire aveugle que c'ui qui veut pas voir!
— Je ne veux pas qu'Anne se sacrifie pour moi!
— Si t'veux mon avis, c'te petiote c'est la plus courageuse et la plus entêtée d'vous quat'e!»

★

Dans ses calculs, ma sœur n'avait pas tenu compte des insuffisances de Branwell qui allait nous montrer de quel bois il était fait. Son désir de partir pour la Royal Academy de Londres ayant eu le temps de mûrir, et encouragé par la famille, il prépara ses bagages. Un matin de ce même automne il disparut à son tour. Nous n'eûmes que le temps de faire sa chambre... il était déjà de retour.

«A pas moisi sur place, ton frère! J'me demande si f'ra des racines quéque part?»

Branwell fut-il éconduit par un maître trop sévère? Eut-il en présence de témoins compromettants une crise de convulsions? Dépensa-t-il en beuveries l'argent que notre père lui avait remis?

Toujours est-il qu'il revint sept jours plus tard, sans autre excuse que le dégoût qu'il éprouvait pour une ville qui l'avait ignoré, lui et son talent. La seule information que nous obtînmes visait Leyland ; retenu à Londres pour y terminer une grande statue, il vivait chez un graveur célèbre : William Geller. « Si vous saviez papa, de quelle manière ces deux-là m'ont accueilli ! » Branwell, que cette piteuse expérience n'avait pas eu le pouvoir de modérer, abusa à nouveau notre père :

> « L'estime que me porte Leyland me dit que je dois continuer ! Il n'y a pas qu'à Londres qu'on fasse carrière ! »

Quelques mois plus tard, la lecture qu'il me fit de son dernier récit, *Les Aventures de Charles Wentworth*, me prouva que ce séjour à Londres avait été terrible. Sous la plume de son héros, Branwell décrivait l'épreuve qu'il avait dû subir, lorsque seul, misérable et angoissé, il s'était senti disparaître dans une ville prompte à engloutir ceux qui ne savaient pas l'affronter. La réalité n'avait en rien correspondu au rêve ; qui sait même si le destin, frappant un grand coup, n'avait pas foudroyé mon frère devant un public effrayé par une crise d'épilepsie dont il n'avait pas souvenance ?

Branwell s'empressa d'oublier sa malheureuse escapade londonienne au Black Bull où il prit, dès cette époque la fâcheuse habitude de se rendre chaque soir. C'est probablement là qu'on lui proposa d'entrer dans la confrérie des francs-maçons. John Brown, le sacristain, Vénérable grand maître de la loge des Trois-Grâces, invita mon frère à subir l'initiation qui ferait de lui un notable. Ses talents oratoires méritaient mieux que les oreilles des vadrouilleurs attablés dans les tavernes de la région. Branwell lui rappela qu'il n'avait que dix-neuf ans ; l'approbation de notre père était donc indispensable. Une démarche fut entreprise. Un soir de janvier, j'entendis la grosse voix de John Brown résonner dans le presbytère : « Nous serions heureux de l'accueillir parmi nous ! »

« Mais il est si jeune !
— L'âge ne fait rien à l'affaire ! Votre fils trouvera chez nous l'occasion d'améliorer son caractère ! Il ne lui manque qu'un peu de profondeur ! »

Papa entendit le conseil ; il donna son accord. Quelques jours plus tard, la confrérie des francs-maçons accepta le fils Brontë bien qu'il lui manquât deux ans pour avoir l'âge requis. La cérémonie de l'initiation l'impressionna tant qu'il mit plusieurs semaines à s'en remettre. Sous le sceau du secret qu'on lui avait demandé de garder, il nous décrivit le trajet initiatique qui l'avait amené jusqu'à l'instant décisif où, le bandeau retiré de ses yeux, il avait reconnu, rassemblés autour du Vénérable grand maître de la loge des Trois-Grâces, des hommes salués au hasard de ses promenades journalières ; ceux-là n'étaient plus les citoyens ordinaires auxquels on tendait la main, mais des frères.

Convié à des rites secrets, Branwell prit des distances avec nous. Le presbytère devint une pension où il ne séjournait plus que contraint et forcé : « Si tu faisais un effort ! Depuis que tu vas chez les francs-maçons, tu n'accordes plus une seconde à papa qui se morfond ! — J'en ai assez de jouer à l'enfant avec lui ! » A son regard, à son allure, Tabitha et moi sûmes bientôt deviner s'il revenait d'une réunion organisée par la société de Tempérance dont il était également devenu l'un des membres hypocrites, ou de Newel Hill où était située la maison dans laquelle les frères se retrouvaient à intervalles réguliers. Puis vint le 25 avril 1836, jour où mon frère se trouva catapulté jusqu'au grade de maître maçon. Armé des cinq degrés de la fraternité, il en oublia presque de nous saluer.

Tandis qu'il grimpait à l'échelle de nouvelles valeurs, le rédacteur en chef du *Blackwood's Magazine*, ignorant une gloire qui se refusait à dépasser les frontières de Haworth, prit le parti de l'humilier. Au courrier insistant, à l'envoi d'un long poème, il ne répondit pas ; la redondance des thèmes, le lyrisme de Branwell, son autosatisfaction n'eurent pas le bonheur de plaire. Mon frère souffrit-il de cette mésestime ? Je ne m'en souviens pas. Seules demeurent inscrites dans ma mémoire les soirées solitaires d'alors.

« *I am the only being whose doom*
*No tongue would ask, no eye would mourn ;*
*I never caused a thought of gloom,*
*A smile of joy, since I was born.* »

« *Je suis le seul être ici-bas dont ne s'enquiert*
*Nulle langue, pour qui nul œil n'aurait de pleurs ;*
*Jamais je n'ai fait naître une triste pensée,*
*Un sourire de joie depuis que je suis née.* »

(Traduction Pierre Leyris
© Gallimard.)

# DEUXIÈME PARTIE

« *C'est une sensation très étrange pour un être jeune et sans expérience que de se sentir tout à fait seul dans le monde, emporté à la dérive, tous liens rompus, incertain d'atteindre le port vers lequel il fait route, empêché par de nombreux obstacles de revenir vers ce qu'il a quitté.* »

Charlotte Brontë, *Jane Eyre.*
(Traduction Charlotte Maurat.)

La relecture de *Jane Eyre* m'amène au fil des pages à une Charlotte à laquelle je dois des excuses. Le mot semblera peut-être excessif; en fait, il est insuffisant. Je l'avoue, longtemps je n'ai guère eu de sympathie pour la sœur d'Emily Brontë. Quelque chose, je ne saurais dire quoi, me poussait à suspecter Charlotte de n'avoir pas été la femme admirable qu'a saluée l'Angleterre. Sous ses manières affairées, je devinais la stratégie de ces femmes sans beauté mais fort intelligentes qui, jouant de leur petite taille, finissent tôt ou tard par se propulser jusqu'au premier rang; ainsi sont relégués au fond des salles les grands gabarits. Non seulement je la voyais dominatrice en famille où son droit d'aînesse l'autorisa à prendre toutes les initiatives, mais je la devinais ambitieuse dans son commerce amical. Aussi fructueuses et sincères furent-elles, les amitiés de Charlotte l'obligèrent à modifier parfois son opinion, du moins à atténuer ses points de vue. Pour ne pas être rejetée à sa pauvreté et surtout à sa solitude, elle dut se draper dans le conservatisme. Au moment de la révolte des luddites — ces ouvriers qui luttèrent contre l'implantation des machines dévoreuses d'emplois — elle se garda de prendre trop violemment parti. Le père de Mary Taylor (on retrouvera sa silhouette avec d'autres dans son roman *Shirley*) ne fut-il pas un de ces patrons auxquels s'opposèrent les luddites? Reçue à bras ouverts par une bourgeoisie industrielle cultivée, séduisante dans ses mœurs et ses manières, Charlotte, à l'inverse d'Emily qui lui tourna le dos ou d'Anne qui en fit les frais, eut l'occasion de goûter au privilège. Nonobstant, elle ne l'épousa pas — j'use ici du verbe épouser au sens figuré mais aussi au sens propre; la fille aînée du pasteur refusa plusieurs partis avantageux. Pour elle, comme pour les autres enfants Brontë, l'appel du presbytère fut plus fort que l'appel du monde.

Je le répète, longtemps, je n'ai guère eu de sympathie pour Charlotte Brontë. Cependant, je crois que j'aurais fait le sacrifice de ma rancune si je n'avais pas eu, au cours de mes lectures, à la rencontrer si souvent. Alors que je tentais de retrouver la trace de la fuyante Emily, je ne cessais de me heurter à l'éminente Charlotte. Mon voyage à Haworth, au lieu de m'inviter à une réconciliation, n'a fait qu'aggraver le différend — l'aînée des Brontë m'exaspérait par son omniprésence, son insistance à être là où je ne souhaitais point la rencontrer. Impérieuse dans la mort comme elle le fut dans la vie, Charlotte m'invitait à me soumettre à ses exigences. Il devenait clair que je n'aurais l'autorisation de rencontrer Emily qu'après avoir rendu hommage à l'aînée qui avait su résister à la tuberculose assez longtemps pour gérer l'œuvre des trois autres, quitte à détruire des pages jugées par elle inintéressantes, trop confidentielles ou scandaleuses.

J'en étais là de mon refus, lorsqu'il m'a fallu passer à l'acte, je veux dire à l'écriture. Devant ces enfants déchirés par des drames répétés, l'idée d'injustice s'est émoussée jusqu'à disparaître derrière la tragédie familiale que je n'avais pas imaginée aussi vaste. Sans que j'y prenne garde, l'image de Charlotte s'est modifiée en moi. Elle a d'abord été cette petite fille angoissée et démunie devant la mort de ses sœurs aînées, puis, sitôt rentrée de Cowan Bridge, elle est devenue cet être affamé de tendresse qui recherchait la présence d'un frère chahuté par un imaginaire débordant: «Je veux bien partager mes idées avec toi, Charlotte, mais à une condition!»

«Laquelle? Ne me laisse pas languir! Laquelle?
— Que tu me dises tout ce qui te passe par la tête.
— Mais c'est horrible, ce que tu me demandes là!
— Peut-être... il faut de l'horrible pour vivre heureux, beaucoup d'horrible!
— Et l'enfer, qu'en fais-tu?
— Pour l'instant, rien... nous y penserons plus tard, quand nous serons grands!»

Avec les écrits de jeunesse, je suis entrée dans un monde de turbulences et de passions fondamentalement étranger à celui de l'enfance tel que le concevait alors l'éducation anglicane. Stupéfaite, et plus encore ravie, j'ai suivi le frère et la sœur sans marquer de recul jusqu'à Verdopolis, la capitale du pays d'Angria où j'ai laissé mon amertume et mes griefs aux soins de personnages imaginaires.

«Et le salut, Branwell?
— Nous partagerons celui dont papa parle à l'office du dimanche matin. Il est assez grand pour que nous en ayons une part!»

A mon insu, je me suis attachée à Charlotte comme je m'étais attachée aux autres membres de la famille. Son courage, sa volonté, ses secrètes divagations ont fini par me faire oublier son intransigeance et son goût pour les âmes astiquées comme des meubles de cuisine.

> « Crois-tu qu'il y a un seul être en nous ?
> — Ma pauvre Charlotte... quelle curieuse question ! Bien sûr que non ! »

Pour m'assurer de la solidité de ce changement d'opinion, j'ai repris la lecture de son roman *Jane Eyre* mis à l'écart quelques mois plus tôt.

> « *J'ai toujours désiré, au contraire, paraître à mon avantage et plaire autant que le permettait mon manque de beauté. Je regrettais parfois de n'être pas plus jolie ; j'aurais voulu avoir les joues roses, un nez droit, une petite bouche rouge comme une cerise, j'aurais aimé être grande, avoir un port majestueux, une taille délicatement épanouie.* »

J'y ai retrouvé l'écrivain, son style, sa lucidité, sa force, ses terribles et éblouissants autoportraits. Avant de juger les autres, Charlotte s'est jugée elle-même.

> « *C'était un malheur pour moi d'être si petite, si pâle, d'avoir des traits si irréguliers, si marqués.* »

Ce regard sans concession, dans quel miroir l'a-t-elle surpris ? A Roe Head peut-être ? Dans cette grosse maison de pierre plantée au milieu d'une prairie fleurie trois mois l'an ? A Roe Head où Charlotte s'attarde en cette longue et pénible année 1836 en compagnie d'Anne : « O Dieu, comme j'aimerais avoir pour ma jeune sœur les sentiments qui m'attachent à Emily dont j'envie, sans la comprendre, la nature singulière ! »

« Anne... Emily se confie-t-elle à toi ?
— Non... enfin, rarement.
— Pourtant, vous semblez vous comprendre.
— Oui, mais cette compréhension ne passe pas par les mots. Il y a beaucoup de silence entre nous ! »

En ces mois d'exil, à qui confier le poids de l'âme, l'embrun du cœur ? Les fidèles amies, Ellen Nussey et Mary Taylor, ne sont plus là pour tendre l'oreille aux confidences. Comment échapper à l'ennui, comment faire taire cette voix attristée qui vous dit dès le matin que rien ni personne ne vous attend, que la vie, telle qu'elle se dessine déjà, ne vous apportera que médiocrités, désillusions, chagrins ? En ces jours où l'avenir lui apparaît aussi lugubre que le présent, Charlotte admet sa faiblesse ; travailler pour le bien d'autrui, se sacrifier exige une foi qu'elle n'est plus certaine d'avoir.

« Je sais combien cet emploi te coûte, Charlotte... Si je suis ici, ce n'est pas pour prendre la place d'Emily dans ton cœur, mais pour apprendre toutes ces choses que je dois savoir afin de subvenir à mes besoins !
— Que vas-tu chercher là ? Je t'aime autant qu'Emily et je suis heureuse de pouvoir t'assister dans tes études ! Allez, va vite dormir ! »

A l'heure où les pensionnaires rejoignent leur lit, Charlotte retrouve la paix de sa chambre, ses livres, ses notes, le rêve auquel elle tient plus qu'à la vie. A côté de ce corps malhabile, incapable d'attirer les hommages, à plus forte raison de susciter le désir, rôdent des personnages dont elle connaît la secrète mécanique. Jetés sur le papier, ils vont et viennent au fil de leurs amours tumultueuses. L'idole de sa jeunesse, le duc de Wellington, a depuis longtemps été remplacée par son fils, l'irrésistible Arthur Wellesley, marquis de Douro, lequel est devenu le perfide duc de Zamorna. Métamorphosées en victimes alanguies et consentantes par l'amie à laquelle elles ont eu l'imprudence de confier leur faim et leurs désirs, Ellen Nussey et Mary Taylor ont cédé à Zamorna qui les a séduites puis abandonnées ; ce méchant homme ne sait jouir des femmes qu'à l'instant où il les bafoue, les torture et parfois les tue. « Seigneur, une idée terrible vient de me traverser l'esprit... Me pardonnerez-vous si je vous confesse qu'un instant j'ai eu le sentiment d'être vous, c'est-à-dire Dieu ; que de moi seule dépendaient des êtres, des destins ? » En ces instants où rien ne s'oppose plus aux désirs les plus extravagants, aux haines les plus subtiles, aux souffrances les plus troubles ; désirs, haines et souffrances qui cherchent, à travers l'auteur et sa plume, à se dire au mieux, qu'importe à Charlotte de n'être qu'une petite institutrice myope et disgracieuse : « Oh, comme je vous aime et je vous hais, vous qui me possédez si bien ! »

Hélas, la plume à peine posée sur le buvard, la réalité reprend ses droits. Elle frappe au cœur, là où ne guérissent jamais les blessures. La dernière a pour nom Branwell. Depuis qu'il est devenu franc-maçon, Alexander Percy se montre oublieux. Il délaisse sa complice dont il devine les tourments pour des expériences littéraires qu'il refuse de partager. Emily se charge de donner des nouvelles à sa place : « A-t-elle un mot pour moi ? »

« Évidemment, Charlotte ! D'ailleurs voici sa lettre, lis-la ! »

Que raconte la recluse ? La vie quotidienne à Haworth, les matinées froides, les nuits trop longues, la plainte d'un hibou qui est venu chercher refuge non loin du presbytère, la terre chaque semaine retournée dans un coin du cimetière où s'additionnent les tombes, les problèmes de santé de papa attristé par la désaffection de son fils, l'acharnement de Tante au bord d'une folie qui lui fait tirer l'aiguille du matin au soir ; elle vient de commencer une nouvelle tapisserie qu'elle compte mener à terme pour l'automne : « La vie a pris pour moi la forme d'un point de croix. Qu'en est-il de celle de ton père ? Que compte-t-il faire pour échapper à la neurasthénie ? » A cette question, Patrick Brontë a répondu par une démarche qui a surpris tout le monde ; il s'est inscrit à un cours de littérature ancienne : « Comment pourrez-vous suivre cet enseignement avec vos mauvais yeux ? — A défaut de le suivre avec les yeux, je le suivrai avec mes oreilles ! » Chaque semaine, il se rend à Keighley, dans un de ces *Mechanic's Institutes*, sorte de bibliothèque et lieu de conférence qui viennent d'ouvrir leurs portes aux adultes invités à parfaire leurs connaissances. Quant à Branwell, il a entrepris une correspondance qu'il n'a pu garder secrète au-delà de trois jours. Sa position de franc-maçon l'encourageant dans la recherche des honneurs, il s'est adressé aux poètes, aux critiques et autres notables de l'écriture. Surpris par son excentricité épistolaire, ces messieurs n'ont pas encore répondu : « C'est bien connu, les gens qui possèdent le pouvoir nient le talent lorsque celui-là a le défaut de loger ailleurs que chez eux!» La déception l'a rapproché d'Emily. Les veillées rassemblent le frère et la sœur autour de James Hogg, de ses contes terrifiants, de ses morts vivants, de ses incubes assoiffés de sang. «C'est bien simple, nous en sommes arrivés à échanger nos cauchemars!»

«Je me félicite de cette nouvelle entente! N'empêche que Branwell pourrait m'écrire!»

Charlotte pose la lettre sur la table. Elle soupire: «Quelle ingratitude!» Le regard attristé que lui jette Anne la ramène à ses obligations:

«Pourquoi n'es-tu jamais avec les autres? Je m'inquiète pour ta santé...
— Ne me gronde pas... je fais ce que je peux!»

Le remords jette Charlotte vers sa sœur. Elle la prend dans ses bras. Pourquoi ne puis-je me confier à cette petite qui est si bonne et si indulgente?: «Anne... me comprendrais-tu si je te disais...» Non, Anne ne comprendrait pas sa solitude, sa douleur, ce trouble du corps qui se refuse à des exigences que la morale réprouve. Anne ne comprendrait pas son dégoût: «Dieu n'aura-t-il donc jamais pitié de moi?»

«Charlotte, pourquoi te détournes-tu?»

Charlotte essuie une larme. Elle se tourne vers la fenêtre derrière laquelle se dresse un arbre, immense, solitaire: «Ce soir, j'aimerais être morte... peux-tu comprendre ça?»

*« J'ai éprouvé de brusques élancements de jalousie, j'ai passé par des moments de ténèbres inexprimables, durant lesquels mon esprit bouillonnait comme la lave. J'ai eu une impression d'étouffement et des sensations terriblement acérées qui m'ont presque rendue folle. Quand la créature que je soupçonnais d'être ma rivale se trouvait là, je devenais blême d'abomination. Et dès que je pouvais me trouver en tête-à-tête avec Zamorna, je le suppliais de me tuer tout de suite ; je m'agenouillais à ses pieds et je baignais sa main de larmes qu'il qualifiait lui-même de brûlantes. »*

Charlotte Brontë, *Le Sortilège*,
juillet 1834.
(Traduction Francis Ledoux.)

*« Charlotte d'ailleurs — en proie ce printemps-là à un accès d'hystérie religieuse qui affecta sa santé — était si occupée à déverser sur Ellen le trop-plein de ses émotions qu'il n'en restait guère pour sa propre sœur. »*

Virginia MOORE.

IL me déplaît d'avoir à parler après vous et après tant d'autres de Charlotte, mais le tort porté à sa mémoire par des indiscrétions vieilles de plus d'un siècle demande réparation. Son expérience de la douleur morale dont on s'est rassasié, la traitant parfois d'hystérie, Charlotte aurait dû la taire ; ainsi ne serait-on pas confronté aujourd'hui à ce portrait caricatural dans ce que ses vingt ans eurent de pénible, de bouleversant même. Les lettres, nombreuses il est vrai, où elle avoua à Ellen son désarroi face à une tentation difficile à surmonter, furent écrites dans des moments de fièvre et de déraison. Qui n'en a pas connu de semblables ? Destinataire indiscrète, Ellen a-t-elle été inspirée par le désir de mieux faire connaître une grande figure de l'Angleterre victorienne ? La question n'est plus à poser car le mal est fait ; avec le temps il creuse une image à laquelle mon aînée n'échappera plus.

Si j'accepte aujourd'hui d'évoquer Charlotte, ce n'est donc pas pour satisfaire une curiosité malsaine, mais uniquement pour tenter de la soustraire à un viol qui se perpétue à travers une correspondance livrée au public qui s'en délecte. Y a-t-il pires trahisons que ces lettres rédigées à la hâte et dans l'essoufflement du désespoir? «Oh, chère Ellen, comment vous décrire ce que je ressens? L'adolescence sort de moi par une déchirure, et cet abandon m'endolorit!» Plus tournée vers le monde que nous ne le fûmes, Anne et moi, Charlotte rencontra le désir, ou plus précisément, le désir du désir. Absent de sa vie comme il le fut de la nôtre, l'homme prit chez elle les allures d'un héros dont elle fit un duc, brillant et cruel. Encouragée par Branwell qui lui aussi s'identifia à ses personnages — à la différence de Charlotte, il ne put jamais s'en déprendre — ma sœur offrit sa jeunesse à une image. Ce jeu du vrai et du faux la troubla si bien qu'il lui arriva de ne plus savoir si elle était fille de pasteur, institutrice, ou Zamorna, le séducteur. Il est probable qu'elle eut pour les créatures destinées au duc — Ellen, Mary, et plus tard Martha, la jeune sœur de Mary — des regards d'homme. Cet emprunt l'encouragea-t-il à les désirer? C'est possible. Enfants d'une religion qui nous enseigna la contrition et le refus du plaisir, nous ne nous autorisâmes jamais à posséder un corps, à fortiori un sexe. Basculant du pôle féminin au pôle masculin, nous ne fûmes ni vraiment ceci, ni vraiment cela, mais ceci et cela à la fois. Mais pour en revenir à cette période difficile que vous évoquez, et plus précisément à ce dégoût dans lequel vous enfermez ma sœur pour mieux la livrer à ses démons, je crois en effet que Charlotte rencontra à Roe Head ce qu'elle n'avait cessé de fuir depuis l'adolescence: le remords, la culpabilité, l'horreur du corps.

Ses écrits, ses divagations autour d'un thème, celui de l'amour adultérin ou incestueux, lui apparurent brusquement comme autant d'aveux. Perverse, immorale, son imagination la dénonçait à la conscience ulcérée. Cette révélation fut si forte qu'elle bouleversa sa vie et mit sa santé en danger. L'idée lui vint qu'elle s'était séparée de Dieu, et cette idée l'affola. Ignorant tout de ces turpitudes imaginaires, Ellen reçut des confidences qu'elle ne comprit qu'à moitié et parfois pas du tout. Elle répondit avec maladresse et une pointe de condescendance qui insupportèrent ma sœur: « L'incompréhension de ma meilleure amie me prouve que je suis perdue! Dieu m'a abandonnée! »

> « Ma chère Emily,
> Charlotte est méconnaissable et son comportement m'inquiète. Amaigrie, fiévreuse, irascible, nul ne peut l'approcher. Pourrais-tu me donner un conseil? Cela ne fait plus de doute; notre sœur souffre d'un mal qui refuse de se confier, même à moi... »

Parce qu'elle la voyait s'enfoncer dans une dépression dont personne ne parvenait à comprendre l'origine, Anne m'adressa des lettres alarmantes. Je rédigeai plusieurs réponses que je ne me résolus pas à poster; dans son désarroi, Charlotte ne pouvait dialoguer qu'avec son mal.

★

Je crois me souvenir que c'est à cette époque que Tabitha eut un accident qui la rendit boiteuse. Il me fallut la remplacer dans des tâches qu'elle ne pouvait plus assumer. Papa envisagea de la congédier pour libérer un lit qu'on pourrait, le cas échéant, proposer à une autre servante : « Qu'en pensez-vous, Elizabeth ? »

« Demandez son avis à Emily, maintenant c'est elle qui a la charge de la maison ! »

Je m'y refusai avec violence. Cette vieille femme méritait d'être traitée comme une personne de la famille ; sa bonté, ses services passés lui donnaient des droits que je voulais voir respectés. « En voilà un ton pour me répondre ! As-tu perdu la tête pour me manquer à ce point de respect ? » Papa s'étonna bien haut de mon indignation et moi de son peu de mémoire. Nous en restâmes là jusqu'au jour où il m'invita à faire une promenade avec lui. A mi-parcours, il sortit le pistolet de sa poche : « Es-tu toujours aussi bonne tireuse ? » Nous nous essayâmes au tir ; il visa mal car il avait la vue basse ; moi j'avais son pistolet bien en main et je lui prouvai qu'il n'était pas nécessaire d'être militaire pour atteindre la cible. Mon père s'étonna : je vis dans son regard quelque chose qui ressemblait à de la méfiance : « Je me demande pourquoi tu n'es pas née homme ? »

« A dire vrai, je me pose la même question que vous. »

Durant les vacances, je revis mes sœurs. Charlotte me parut plus nerveuse qu'à l'ordinaire et Anne plus frêle qu'avant son départ. Lorsque je la serrai dans mes bras, je sentis ses os sous de faibles chairs : « Es-tu malheureuse à Roe Head ? » Anne ne me répondit pas.

Je n'eus guère le temps de me préoccuper de la santé de mes sœurs ; le soir même la bande des quatre se retrouvait dans la salle d'étude du premier étage. Traquée par ses personnages en mal de confession et par Branwell — durant son absence il avait piétiné aux portes de Verdopolis — Charlotte céda à la tentation ; elle replongea avec nous dans les délices de l'écriture. « Le temps n'existe pas pour ces enfants ! Rien ne les sortira jamais de cette maudite pièce ! » Tante et papa s'inquiétèrent de notre commerce : « A votre avis, Elizabeth, qu'y font-ils de si passionnant ? »

> « Ce qu'ils y font ? Mais de l'écriture, voyons, de l'écriture ! et de la myopie ! et des dos voûtés ! De ceci vous êtes responsable, Patrick ! Vous n'aviez pas à encourager leur vice comme vous l'avez fait ! Lorsque je vois sur vos rayonnages des Byron, des Shakespeare et autres gredins, je ne m'étonne plus de rien ! »

A l'heure de la rentrée scolaire, mes sœurs repartirent chez Miss Wooler. Le courrier reprit entre Rydings où habitait Ellen et Roe Head où se morfondait Charlotte. Après la pause d'un été trop court, réapparurent les troubles de naguère : haine de soi, mépris pour les pensées indignes, épuisement devant une tâche fastidieuse, insomnies, dégoût. De son côté, Anne passa un hiver très difficile. Sa santé déjà fragile s'altéra. Elle prit froid, souffrit d'une douleur aux poumons dont elle ne parla à personne. Sa discrétion servit la maladie, qui s'installa. Arrachée à ses tourments par une méchante toux, Charlotte se tourna vers Anne : « C'est toi qui tousses ainsi ? Depuis quand es-tu malade ? — Deux mois. — Deux mois ! » Ma sœur reconnut les symptômes d'une maladie qui la terrifiait : « Pourquoi ne m'en as-tu rien dit ? —

Parce que tu semblais préoccupée. » Anne lut dans le regard qui la fixait avec crainte un diagnostic qu'elle jugea faux : « Ce n'est pas de la tuberculose que je suis atteinte, c'est beaucoup plus grave que ça ! Les mauvaises pensées pourrissent en moi ! » Alors qu'elle semblait à l'abri des crises qui nous avaient frappées à tour de rôle, voilà qu'Anne, oubliant sa piété et le secours des prières, s'abandonnait elle aussi aux troubles de la conscience malheureuse : « Ce sont elles qui sont en train de me tuer ! » Charlotte n'écouta pas la suite du discours ; elle courut chez la directrice qui eut un geste d'agacement ; ne pouvait-on pénétrer dans son bureau plus discrètement ?

« Il faut qu'Anne voie rapidement un docteur !

— Écoutez, Charlotte, vous viendrez me parler de cela un peu plus tard. Pour l'instant j'ai des copies à corriger.

— Je vous en prie, c'est très urgent !

— Calmez-vous ! Depuis quelque temps vous perdez la tête pour un oui ou pour un non ! C'est une simple grippe ; Anne sera sur pied d'ici une semaine. »

Attaquée par un mal que seule Charlotte acceptait de reconnaître, ma sœur s'alita, convaincue qu'elle allait mourir damnée : « Dieu a cessé de m'aimer car je n'ai pas su être à la hauteur de son amour ! — Mais enfin, Anne, tu n'as jamais songé qu'à faire du bien autour de toi ! » Le médecin enfin convoqué parla d'une fièvre gastrique, mais au mal qui mûrissait dans sa tête, il ne sut donner de nom : « Donnez-lui cette potion calmante ; elle lui remettra le moral en place ! » Un soir où la malade se sentait au plus mal, elle demanda le secours d'un homme d'Église. « Je t'en supplie, Charlotte... avant que je ne meure dans le péché ! » Ma sœur alla chercher, non pas un pasteur de l'Église anglicane, mais le révérend James La Trobe, ministre d'une Église non conformiste et membre de la secte morave :

> « Je vous en prie, monsieur le ministre, ramenez cette petite à la raison ! Il n'y a pas meilleure enfant, ni plus pieuse qu'elle ! Comment peut-elle douter à ce point d'être sauvée ? »

Contrairement à nous qui avions suivi l'enseignement de papa — il n'avait jamais manqué de nous rassurer — Anne n'avait connu que la lumière avaricieuse du calvinisme dispensée par l'éducation de Tante. Parce qu'elle n'avait pas sacrifié sa personnalité, elle n'était pas digne de pénétrer dans le royaume des élus ; les pensées qu'elle avait nourries à son corps défendant la livreraient à l'enfer éternel.

> « Ma chère enfant, votre sœur m'a demandé de venir vous voir pour vous apporter la bonne parole. J'aimerais que vous l'entendiez : le Christ est mort sur la croix pour le rachat de nos péchés ! »

Le révérend James La Trobe sut trouver les mots qui atteignirent Anne en ce lieu où ne se racontaient plus que les ténèbres : « Dieu m'aime-t-il encore ? — Mais évidemment, mon enfant, plus que jamais ! » Affermie dans son désir de vivre, ma jeune sœur reprit un peu de forces au grand soulagement de Tante : « Pourquoi ne m'a-t-elle pas fait part de ses angoisses ? Décidément, cet esprit était trop bien disposé à m'entendre ! »

★

Durant l'été 1837, alors que les demoiselles Wooler déménageaient pour Dewsbury Moor où les suivraient les pensionnaires, Charlotte écrivit au poète Southey. Avec l'habileté épistolaire que nous lui enviions tous, elle lui confia son goût pour la littérature et lui adressa un poème de son cru. Une réponse lui parvint quelques mois plus tard ; le poète n'était pas insensible à l'aisance de la versification, mais il mettait en garde ma sœur contre une carrière littéraire peu faite pour les femmes qui s'y sentaient mal à l'aise. A la même époque, Branwell décida de s'adresser à William Wordsworth, le poète accablé sous le poids des honneurs. Il lui envoya un long poème et une lettre qui, sous sa plume maladroite et juvénile, devint flagorneuse. Je relus cette missive plusieurs fois, n'y vis qu'une demande bien tournée qui appelait une réponse favorable. Hélas, au lieu de s'arrêter à ce qu'avait de touchant l'appel d'un jeune homme isolé qui, somme toute, lui demandait son aide, Wordsworth ne remarqua que la grossièreté du compliment.

> « Voilà qui en dit long sur l'homme que l'Angleterre croit immense ! »

Dépité et un peu aigri, Branwell accepta de devenir secrétaire de la loge des Trois-Grâces : « Il me reviendra de rédiger les procès-verbaux ! » Ce nouveau poste ne lui apporta malheureusement pas les satisfactions qu'il en attendait. Au retour des séances auxquelles il me disait avoir assisté avec une dignité de notable, il imitait devant moi, sa seule spectatrice, le Vénérable paralysé dans le protocole. « On dirait un homme de cire ! » Les frères maçons jugés grotesques devinrent des silhouettes dessinées sur les murs de la petite salle d'étude. En fait, Branwell ne se voyait pas plus étudiant à la Royal Academy que franc-maçon ; tout cela l'assommait.

> « De fieffés hypocrites ! A peine John Brown a-t-il quitté la salle qu'il va se remplir de bière ! La dernière fois, tous les membres de la société de Tempérance étaient ivres morts, moi y compris. Il faut dire que nous abordons des sujets arides ! »

Dès cette époque, mon frère versa dans l'alcoolisme. Devant cet abandon, je tentai de l'intéresser à nos écrits : « Tu ne vas tout de même pas capituler devant un Wordsworth ! » Ma sollicitude l'aida. Il réembarqua avec Alexander Percy, comte de Northangerland, fit le tour du monde avec lui. Pendant que je rejoignais l'île de Gondal, il redessina la carte d'une Afrique imaginaire, puis celle du pays d'Angria, remania l'armée, destitua certains de leur poste, en promut d'autres : « C'est Charlotte qui va en faire une tête lorsqu'elle va apprendre tout ça ! » Notre collaboration se fit plus étroite ; je repris à mon compte certains de ses thèmes, lui prêtai les miens.

Une lettre mit fin à notre association. Anne était malade. La fièvre avait attaqué à nouveau un corps qui ne pouvait s'en défendre. Papa reçut une lettre indignée de Miss Wooler ; bravant l'autorité et les convenances, Charlotte était venue lui donner des ordres : « Si vous ne laissez pas ma sœur partir immédiatement, je l'enlève moi-même de cette maison ! » Patrick Brontë répondit sèchement ; il désirait revoir ses deux filles au plus vite.

★

« Décidément, quand les unes rentrent, les autres partent !

— Que voulez-vous, Patrick, ce ne sont plus des enfants ! Je trouve que Branwell a raison de tenter sa chance de portraitiste à Bradford ! Quant à Emily, elle fera sûrement une excellente institutrice à Law Hill ! »

*« Le soir passe d'un train rapide,*
*C'est presque l'heure du repos :*
*Quelles pensées te laisse le jour évanoui ?*
*Quelles impressions en ton sein ?*

*Le jour évanoui ? Hélas, un sentiment*
*De travail à peine accompli,*
*De faible gain acquis à frais immenses —*
*Un sentiment de chagrin seulement.* »

Emily Jane Brontë,
23 octobre 1842, 6 février 1843.
(Traduction Pierre Leyris

La petite chambre du premier étage appelée aussi salle d'étude est restée intacte. C'est là que vivait Emily. Depuis son départ pour Law Hill où elle enseigne chez Miss Patchett, personne n'y a pénétré. Près de la fenêtre où elle aimait dormir, le lit a conservé sa place. Des tiroirs empilés les uns sur les autres, des tréteaux, une boîte à couture attendent le retour de l'absente. Rendu à un calme qu'il n'avait jamais connu, le presbytère respire au rythme de trois personnes assiégées par l'âge. Tante coud dans sa chambre : « Voyons, depuis combien d'années suis-je enfermée dans cette pièce ?... Ma sœur est morte en... Seigneur, est-ce possible ! » Tabitha se lamente au rez-de-chaussée : « J'vas tout d'même pas finir comme ces vieillards qu'sont bons qu'à gémir après la vie qu'a passé au-d'ssus d'eux comme un vol d'étourneaux ? »

« Personne ici ne se plaint de votre présence !

— Vous en avez d'bonnes, miss ! M'taire avec c'te jambe qu'est même plus capab'e d'm'assister !

— D'autres connaissent des souffrances plus humiliantes. Lorsque Dieu décidera de votre heure, vous répondrez à l'appel. D'ici là, préparez-moi plutôt un bon thé ! »

Quant au révérend, depuis que son fils est parti pour Bradford où il ne désespère pas de faire une brillante carrière de portraitiste, il trouve des excuses pour fuir la maison ; tantôt c'est une visite à rendre à un malade, tantôt c'est un cours à suivre à Keighley, et du coup il est absent tout l'après-midi : « Patrick, êtes-vous là ? »

« Non, miss, l'est parti d'puis une bonne heure !

— Savez-vous où il a été ?

— Sûr qu'y m'dit pas son emploi du temps ! »

Dieu merci pour le moral de Tante — pour un peu elle se laisserait gagner par la mélancolie —, Charlotte et la petite malade ne vont pas tarder à regagner Haworth. Leur retour a été ajourné en raison de l'état de santé d'Anne. Aux dernières nouvelles, elle souffrirait d'asthme et non d'une congestion pulmonaire comme on le redoutait. « Tabitha, où en êtes-vous de mon thé ? » Tante songe qu'elle a eu grand tort de laisser partir Emily ; elle qui ne se plaît que dans cette maison, qu'avait-elle besoin de s'exiler pour aller gagner quatre sous ?

« Tabitha, m'entendez-vous ?

— J'arrive, miss ! J'étais occupée avec l'facteur qu'a pas la lettre attendue ! »

Emily, il y a un peu plus d'une semaine, a pris la diligence pour se rendre à Law Hill, situé non loin de Halifax, une ville qui fait parler d'elle en ces temps de répression brutale. La misère, il est vrai, n'a jamais fait autant de victimes. Dans certains quartiers où sévit la famine, le typhus et le froid nettoient le terrain. Le nombre des morts est si élevé que la presse, pour ne pas attrister le citoyen, préfère n'en pas parler. Les lois votées pour que soient offerts aux misérables de maigres secours ne rencontrent que la mauvaise volonté des patrons qui refusent de les appliquer. Depuis l'arrivée des machines à vapeur, ils ont trouvé le ton qu'il faut pour engager le dialogue : que ceux qui ne sont pas contents prennent la porte ! La main-d'œuvre ne manque pas, au contraire, elle pleure aux portes des usines !

« Merci, Tabitha... posez le plateau sur la table ! Eh bien, qu'attendez-vous ?

— J'dois vous dire, miss, qu'j'm'inquiète pour la petiote !

— Emily n'est plus « une petiote » et vous avez tort de vous inquiéter... les routes sont mal fréquentées, c'est vrai, mais s'il lui était arrivé quelque chose, nous le saurions depuis longtemps ! »

Pour sauver l'image de l'Angleterre, le Seigneur, qu'il soit loué, y a fait naître de belles âmes ; Oastler, le chroniqueur, par exemple. Dans les colonnes du *Leeds Mercury*, il a dénoncé avec virulence les conditions de vie des ouvriers. Malheureusement, sa flamme n'a pu réchauffer une population portée à l'apathie et à l'égoïsme. Seuls les événements qui touchent la famille princière intéressent les lecteurs. Tout le monde se souvient du 20 juin dernier, date capitale pour l'histoire de l'Angleterre, puisqu'à la mort de Guillaume IV à Windsor, une jeune fille de dix-huit ans, Victoria, a été sacrée reine. La situation économique difficile n'empêche pas la bourgeoisie de veiller à l'éducation de sa progéniture. Dans les pensionnats, on apprend aux jeunes filles des langues étrangères, l'allemand bien sûr et parfois le français, la langue de

Mme George Sand, une femme parfaitement immorale qui s'habille comme un homme, celle aussi d'un dénommé Balzac dont Tante a pu lire quelques lignes dans le *Blackwood's Magazine*, traduites de deux romans dont elle a oublié les titres. « Mes nièces ne manqueront jamais de travail. Avec leurs qualités intellectuelles et leur probité morale, elles trouveront toujours un poste d'institutrice ou de gouvernante ! » Seul Branwell pose un problème sérieux à la famille qui le chérit d'autant. Il faut avouer que *l'individu* sait divertir son monde. Comme dit Tabitha : « Posez une soupière d'vant lui, l'f'ra rire ! » Si ses sœurs se plient aux lois que le destin leur assigne, Branwell, lui, refuse toute contrainte.

« Comment se fait-il que vous vous souciiez autant d'Emily et aussi peu de Branwell ?

— C'est qu'j'sais qu'l'une joue à la forte, alors qu'est fragile, et qu'l'aut'e joue au délicat, alors qu'est un débrouillard ! »

★

Pressé d'atteindre sa majorité le 26 juin de cette année 1838, le débrouillard en question attend le succès à Fountain Street où il loge en meublé. Les notables de Bradford ne tarderont pas à venir poser pour lui ; en vérité qui ne souhaiterait avoir son portrait accroché au mur du salon ? Que diable, il trouvera bien une centaine d'amateurs dans une ville de plus de quarante mille habitants ! Voilà de quoi l'occuper un bon bout de temps ! En attendant que la corne d'abondance le couvre d'or, Tante et papa apportent leur aide matérielle à l'artiste. Chaque fin de semaine, il vient rendre visite au presbytère qui reprend vie. A peine a-t-il poussé la porte qu'il se met à raconter sa vie: « Savez-vous comment j'ai décroché ma première commande? En montrant au client le portrait que j'ai fait de mes sœurs! N'est-ce pas drôle? » Le bavard ne désespère pas de terminer celui de John Brown et celui de William, son frère: « Deux fameuses gueules que ceux-là! »

« Est-ce que tu ne te sens pas trop seul, mon fils?
— Au contraire! Je n'ai jamais vu autant de monde!
— Le monde n'a jamais peuplé la solitude. »

Tante regarde son beau-frère, trop admiratif à son goût: « Pensez-vous que Branwell soit sur la bonne voie? » Le révérend détourne les yeux avec regret; ma foi, il ne pense pas de mal de ce qu'il vient d'entendre. Il souhaiterait simplement que Branwell subvienne à ses besoins. Sa famille ne pourra pas toujours payer sa pension et son costume. Certes, le chapeau haut de forme et la redingote bien taillée pourront encore longtemps faire bonne figure devant les filateurs et les banquiers qui pourraient s'intéresser au travail de l'artiste, mais son estomac, lui, demandera à être nourri tous les jours!

« Je vous demande encore un peu de patience! Maintenant que je commence à être connu, le succès ne tardera pas! De cela, vous pouvez être certains! »

Le succès est à trois pas, aux côtés du fameux Joseph Leyland qui vient de réapparaître. Salué par la critique qui s'extasie, le sculpteur, ami des plus célèbres artistes londoniens, s'est laissé charmer par le fils Brontë. Depuis cet instant où la gloire en personne est venue s'asseoir à côté de lui au George Hotel de Bradford, Branwell surveille son idole, et que découvre-t-il? Un homme qui n'en fait qu'à sa tête, travaille quand ça lui chante, se balade quand l'envie lui en prend, paie de ses largesses le plaisir des autres, se moque de ses dettes. Et que ne donnerait pas Branwell pour avoir cette tête splendide, ces yeux noirs, cette chevelure, ce front magnifique, ce nez bien dessiné au-dessus de la bouche ironique, cette taille enfin, cette taille de héros romantique? Autour de sa majesté Leyland, combien semblent falotes les deux potiches locales: le poète Edward Collinson et le peintre Richard Weller! «Savez-vous que le grand homme m'a invité à lui rendre visite dans son atelier de Halifax?» Ce que Branwell ne dit pas à papa qui l'écoute avec fierté, c'est combien il a pris goût au verre de rhum, ou encore, lorsque après des heures de palabres on ne redoute plus rien, à la grande lampée d'un alcool français qui déverse du feu dans la gorge. Depuis qu'il fréquente les grands, la bière paraît fade à Branwell.

«Avant d'être sculpteur, Leyland s'est intéressé à la littérature! James Hogg, Kilmeny n'ont plus de secret pour lui!

— Tout cela est bien joli, mon garçon! mais lui a fait carrière; il peut aller ici et là pour son plaisir, ce qui n'est pas encore ton cas!»

★

Cette réserve a trouvé un écho chez Branwell. Depuis que Leyland a passagèrement déserté la région pour aller à Londres, le fils Brontë se demande s'il est bien fait pour portraiturer des gens insignifiants pour lesquels il n'a que mépris. Ces affairistes et ces petits-bourgeois manquent décidément de dimensions, et ce n'est pas sa sœur Charlotte, venue lui rendre visite à Fountain Street, qui dira le contraire ! On lui reproche d'abandonner ses portraits en cours de route, de faire plus acte de présence dans les tavernes de la ville que dans son atelier où il commence à s'ennuyer. On ne peut pas, hélas, être le créateur d'un Alexander Percy et le portraitiste d'un Kirby, son logeur !

Par les yeux de Branwell, c'est Percy, comte de Northangerland, qui soupèse le monde ; c'est lui qui jauge les femmes, approuve la rondeur de leur gorge, devine la forme de leur corps ; c'est lui qui sait ce qu'elles peuvent donner ou prendre. Grâce à Alexander Percy, les humiliations que l'on voudrait faire subir à Branwell se métamorphosent en hommages, les refus qu'on lui oppose en compliments, les remarques ironiques en clins d'œil complices : « Ce ne sont que des valets ! » Comblé par tant d'aventures imaginaires, de vies multiples, de conquêtes, le héros de Verdopolis ne voit même plus son double, ce pauvre petit rouquin, haut comme trois pommes, myope et maladroit à plaisir et qui, c'est un comble, est fils de pasteur !

Un détail cependant ; les cauchemars d'autrefois ont resurgi. Ils profitent de son endormissement pour venir harceler Branwell. Prisonnier de la nuit du Yorkshire, le fils Brontë est la proie d'un rêve qui le poursuit depuis des années. A peine a-t-il fermé les yeux qu'il sent le mal se glisser jusqu'à lui. « Non, papa ! » crie-t-il avec une voix d'enfant, mais ses protestations sont vaines. Dans la pièce où l'on vient de le séquestrer, des doigts s'agrippent à son bras. Il voit surgir le cadavre d'une femme, parfois celui d'une fillette; elles apparaissent lentement, comme arrachées au monde des ténèbres par une puissance effrayante. Défigurées par la mort qui a dessiné sur leurs visages un crâne, des orbites, et, dans la mâchoire entrouverte, la forme des dents, elles se tournent vers un enfant qui tente de se dégager de la main d'un homme. « Non, papa! Laissez-moi partir! » Les mortes réclament un baiser que Brannii refuse de donner. Il appelle au secours. On vient le sauver. Quelqu'un le secoue de plus en plus fort:

« Réveillez-vous! Réveillez-vous! »

Son visage à moitié caché sous le bonnet de nuit, M. Kirby est penché au-dessus de lui. Il le regarde d'un air soupçonneux: « Vous avez encore réveillé toute la maison avec votre cauchemar! » Branwell s'excuse. Il tremble, demande à son logeur de lui laisser la chandelle. Dès que l'autre a le dos tourné, il prend l'oreiller à pleins bras, y enfonce sa tête et se met à pleurer.

« *That presses on me! Raise my head...*
*I cannot breathe!...* »

★

Un jour ou l'autre Patrick Brontë, qui devine le mal dont son fils est atteint, ouvrira le *Traité moderne de médecine familiale*. Il lira avec attention le chapitre « L'alcoolisme et ses conséquences », préparera un verre d'eau sucrée dans lequel il versera quelques gouttes d'ammoniaque, le tiendra prêt au cas où Branwell, venu lui rendre visite, hurlerait dans la nuit. Au premier cri, il se lèvera, apportera la mixture à l'agité qui s'empressera de la boire, vite, très vite, avant que la mort ne l'emporte lui et ses terreurs.

*« The night is darkening round me,*
*The wild winds coldly blow;*
*But a tyrant spell has bound me*
*And I cannot, cannot go.*

*The giant trees are bending*
*Their bare boughs weighed with snow,*
*And the storm is fast descending*
*And yet I cannot go. »*

Emily Jane Brontë,
novembre 1837.

HIER au soir, alors que j'attendais de voir s'écrire des mots sans surprise, j'ai entendu l'appel au secours de Branwell à peine sorti d'un cauchemar, puis j'ai vu surgir le visage de ma mère décédée après un combat si effrayant et si inégal que Dieu lui-même dut en avoir honte, enfin j'ai vu le mien, mon visage d'institutrice, mes yeux cernés, mon front têtu, mes joues blafardes, et j'ai senti, comme autrefois à Law Hill, la douleur me saisir.

Désarçonnée par ce mal qui revenait d'un si long voyage, d'un si patient exil, ce mal dont je croyais m'être défaite à tout jamais, je me suis approchée de votre bureau ; vous étiez en train de décrire une scène, courte et violente, qui avait pour premier rôle Branwell et pour second M. Kirby furieux d'avoir été réveillé en pleine nuit. Le logeur et son bonnet de nuit à peine disparus dans les ténèbres de l'escalier, vous avez tenté de surprendre Branwell en proie au désespoir, puis vous avez convoqué mon père. Il a surgi aussitôt sous votre plume, porteur d'un livre de médecine dont j'ai immédiatement reconnu la couverture défraîchie, l'odeur de papier moisi, l'usure des pages souvent feuilletées. A ce moment, vous vous êtes souvenue d'une recette capable de dégriser un cerveau embué par l'alcool. Vous avez tendu cette mixture à Branwell qui, fou de terreur, s'est empressé de l'avaler.

Sans doute auriez-vous refermé votre manuscrit si vous n'aviez eu le sentiment d'un manque ; un élément se dérobait. Vous avez songé à moi; qu'étais-je devenue dans tout cela? Tandis que Patrick Brontë prenait conscience de la maladie de son fils, tandis que M. Kirby remontait se coucher, tandis que pleurait le portraitiste dans son oreiller, où m'étais-je cachée? Tout simplement à Law Hill, dans une bâtisse aux murs gris et tristes; à Law Hill, près de Halifax, un endroit réputé pour ses hivers glacials. Combien d'arbres aux troncs fissurés par le gel ai-je vus craquer et mourir cette année-là?

« *They are two trees in a lonely field;*
*They breathe a spell to me...* »

A l'instant me reviennent en mémoire les mots d'un poème très simple écrit à cette époque.

« *Deux arbres dans un champ désert*
*Me chuchotent un sortilège:*
*Lugubre est le secret que leur sombre ramure*
*Agite avec solennité.* »

Ces strophes traduisent bien le climat lugubre de cette année 1838 où sonna pour nous quatre l'heure des grandes séparations:

« Elizabeth, est-ce raisonnable de les envoyer à droite et à gauche? Emily est ici, Charlotte est là, Branwell ailleurs, et Anne, la pauvre petite, est seule avec nous!

— Qu'y pouvons-nous?

— Nous pourrions vivre pauvrement mais ensemble!

— C'est à eux d'en décider! »

Sans doute assumai-je la solitude plus douloureusement que Charlotte, appelée par une Miss

Wooler toute de repentir. Ma sœur venait de réintégrer son poste à Dewsbury Moor lorsqu'elle m'adressa un courrier...

> Ma chère Emily,
> J'ai trouvé ici des élèves dont le comportement et les manières n'ont hélas pas changé. La suffisance, le mépris sont de rigueur ; ils apportent à des caractères par ailleurs effacés et futiles une fausse assise que je n'ai nulle envie de voir basculer du bon côté. La maison est infiniment plus confortable que celle de Roe Head, peut-être parce qu'elle est mieux exposée et plus spacieuse. Les parquets ont une belle couleur dorée. Lorsque le soleil brille haut dans le ciel, une diagonale de lumière pénètre dans le salon qui s'illumine ; c'est alors un véritable plaisir que de demeurer là à rêvasser. Les murs des pièces principales percés de hautes fenêtres sont de belles proportions. Du bureau où je t'écris, je vois le jardin, les arbres, le ciel, et le début d'une vaste prairie. Nulle sympathie véritable de la part des autres maîtresses, mais une forme de politesse que j'apprécie. A peine ai-je terminé les cours et corrigé les devoirs, que je me replie dans ma chambre où m'attend mon écritoire. Le bonheur d'écrire ne peut être comparé à aucun autre ; il ne souffre pas de rival. A vrai dire, je n'imagine pas un homme assez talentueux et intelligent pour mériter pareil sacrifice. Si la douleur lie l'être à Dieu, l'écriture l'attache à la solitude. Je crains fort qu'il ne nous faille nous contenter de cette compagnie !

Sans doute assumai-je l'isolement plus douloureusement qu'Anne, de retour au presbytère...

Emily, sœur très chère,
J'ai cessé d'inquiéter le monde avec ma santé qui se rétablit peu à peu. Jamais je ne remercierai assez Charlotte de ce qu'elle a fait pour moi! La présence affectueuse de Tante, celle plus lointaine de papa, les visites de Branwell qui est en train de terminer à Bradford une carrière à peine commencée, sont pour beaucoup dans mon rétablissement. J'ai pris la charge des animaux et les soigne avec le plus de bonté possible. Tous s'ennuient de toi. Il suffit que je prononce ton nom devant eux: «Emily! Où est Emily?» pour qu'ils manifestent de l'impatience et de la joie, chacun à sa façon. Le temps s'est adouci et la végétation commence à croître. J'en suis heureuse car j'ai trouvé l'hiver long. Chaque jour, à l'heure de la promenade, je découvre de nouveaux bourgeons. Dans le jardin les primevères sont en fleur et la terre bouge sous les pas. Ces remuements secrets m'émeuvent. Depuis ton départ j'ai peu écrit, non pas parce que les idées me font défaut, mais parce que je ne suis pas certaine de les trouver intéressantes. J'ai tout de même rédigé une longue note où je consigne la vie de chacun, ses espoirs, ses déconvenues. Nous l'ouvrirons ensemble dans deux ans et nous verrons alors si les choses ont évolué dans le bon sens. Je t'avoue que je préférerais vivre plutôt que de mourir maintenant; il me semble que l'existence peut encore m'apporter des joies, surtout si je ne suis pas exigeante.

★

Law Hill. Un nom, presque un titre.

Il n'est point besoin pour moi de faire un effort pour me souvenir du site, de la campagne environnante, de la bâtisse plantée sans goût, du jardin mal ordonné, des lauriers, des sycomores alignés en bon ordre devant l'ancienne écurie pour les chevaux. En face de l'aile principale s'étendait une petite place pavée qui servait de cour de récréation. Lorsqu'il faisait très froid, les pensionnaires y tournaient comme des prisonnières en soufflant dans leurs mains.

Les lieux évoqués, je me revois telle que j'étais alors, déjà femme et toujours enfant, campée maladroitement sur ce que je tentais de cacher : ma singularité, mes défauts, la peur que provoquaient en moi ces quarante élèves qu'il me fallait dompter. Entre sept heures et demie du matin et neuf heures du soir, qu'avaient-elles en tête ? Le désir de m'imposer leurs lois, et plus encore que les leurs, celles de leur mère à laquelle elles avaient décidé de ressembler. Moi qui avais été élevée par un père austère, comment aurais-je pu ne pas voir dans ces mains tendues pour demander la parole, m'interroger, et parfois m'interrompre, comment aurais-je pu ne pas voir dans ces gesticulations, ces tapotements agacés, le doigt de l'épouse en puissance, de la maîtresse de maison déjà prête à donner des ordres ?

« Maman s'est plainte à Miss Patchett de l'âge de Miss Brontë. Nous méritons mieux qu'une fille de dix-neuf ans !

— Surtout qu'elle n'a aucune expérience !

— Il paraît qu'elle vient d'une famille très pauvre !

— La pauvreté n'est pas une excuse ! »

A l'heure de la récitation de texte, alors qu'on tentait dans les rangs de se moquer de ma jeunesse, combien m'étaient précieuses les lectures d'autrefois. *The Doctrine of the passions*, d'Isaac Watts, les sermons de Luther, la prose de Byron qui aurait pris figure de diable dans ce pensionnat pour jeunes filles de la bourgeoisie industrielle de Halifax.

> « Mademoiselle Johns ! Pourquoi prenez-vous ce ton stupide pour réciter un texte aussi grave ?
> — C'est vous qui le jugez stupide, Miss Brontë !
> — Ah oui...
> — Mes camarades ne sont pas de votre avis... La preuve, pas une seule n'a ri ! »

Plusieurs fois par jour les pensionnaires se regroupaient au petit bonheur des complicités et des connivences. Des chuchotements dénonçaient un groupe à moitié caché par l'ancienne écurie, un autre à l'abri du préau. Parfois une élève jetait un coup d'œil en direction du premier étage où, assise près d'une fenêtre, je corrigeais les copies : « C'est une des filles du pasteur de Haworth ! »

> « Je comprends mieux pourquoi elle est aussi sinistre !
> — Elle travaille ici pour gagner de l'argent car sa plus jeune sœur est malade et son frère est un bon à rien ! »

Aux marques d'une affection simulée, je préférais l'indifférence, voire l'agressivité, et en cela je me démarquais des autres institutrices qui, pour gagner des suffrages, se laissaient chahuter par des arrogantes à qui la position de leurs parents assurait l'impunité. Dès que je voyais pointer l'insolence, j'empruntais le regard du pasteur. Un adjectif cinglant me venait tout naturellement sur la langue que je ne retenais pas: « Sortez! Vous reviendrez lorsque vous aurez trouvé les mots d'une excuse sincère! » En somme, je ne souffrais vraiment que de la fatigue, car sur plus de dix-sept heures de travail, nous ne disposions que d'une heure et demie de liberté.

Après quelques mois de ce dur régime, la directrice de l'établissement, Miss Patchett, une belle femme d'une quarantaine d'années, coiffée à la dernière mode londonienne, et — particularité impressionnante pour les paysans de la région qui la voyaient traverser leurs terres comme une amazone de la mythologie — cavalière émérite, s'employa à me rendre la vie plus facile: « Vous me semblez particulièrement fatiguée, Miss Brontë. Qu'avez-vous? — Je dors mal. — Ce rythme vous épuise. Je vais voir s'il n'y a pas possibilité de vous remplacer une matinée ou deux par semaine! » Il est probable que si les circonstances avaient été autres, cette femme d'esprit m'aurait accordé son amitié; mais l'obligation qui lui était faite de garder ses distances avec une employée dont on ne manquait pas de lui rappeler qu'elle n'avait pas d'expérience l'obligea à la réserve. « Je vous remercie beaucoup de vos bontés, et je continuerai à faire de mon mieux, même si parfois je rencontre des difficultés avec certaines élèves! »

> « Vous devriez être plus chaleureuse. La bienveillance ne retire rien à l'autorité... au contraire, elle la renforce! J'ai remarqué qu'il y a chez vous une pointe de raideur, un refus de la gaieté... A votre âge elle est pourtant indispensable. »

Non, il n'est point besoin de faire un effort pour

me souvenir de la manière dont s'organisaient les soirées à Law Hill, lorsque Miss Patchett, après nous avoir souhaité une bonne nuit, disparaissait derrière la tenture qui cachait la porte du salon. Dans les escaliers montaient les rires et les cris des bousculées. J'attendais à l'écart la dernière demande de la journée ; un conseil pour un devoir, une indication pour la lecture du lendemain, l'orthographe d'un mot étranger dont j'étais à peine assurée. Parfois un sourire venait couronner mes efforts. Je le recevais avec gratitude et une sorte de gêne qui m'interdisait toute démonstration.

Surprise de me voir choisir, après l'enfermement avec les élèves, l'enfermement avec moi-même, mes collègues m'adressaient un bonsoir plutôt sec.

Je montais en courant jusqu'à ma chambre, une cellule sans confort, à peine de quoi dormir, se laver, écrire. Je m'asseyais à la petite table, demeurais là, les muscles tendus, comme dans l'attente d'un effort physique. La flamme de la chandelle vacillait devant mes yeux brûlants de fatigue. Je sombrais dans une sorte d'hypnose, attendais que se calment les battements de mon cœur malmené par la montée trop rapide des escaliers. Enfin, je prenais la plume, la trempais dans l'encrier, ce geste ne correspondant à rien d'autre qu'au besoin de mettre la dernière touche à un rituel que je devais respecter. Ensuite, je reposais la plume mouillée d'encre sur le buvard. Sans y prêter vraiment attention, j'écoutais Miss Patchett qui jouait du piano, une sonate dont il me semblait reconnaître les notes, mais j'étais trop absente pour aller au-delà d'une vague impression. L'attente durait parfois des heures, parfois seulement quelques minutes. Le poème venait immanquablement par la tête, je veux dire par la première strophe. Il jaillissait de moi. « *The night* » et la nuit prenait couleur, matière : « *The night is darkening round me/The wild winds coldly blow.* » Lorsque les mots se retiraient, je me levais. Le parquet craquait si fort que je m'arrêtais de marcher pour ne pas prendre le risque de réveiller quelqu'une. Ne pouvant me résigner à dormir, je restais près de l'unique fenêtre, et là, je scrutais la nuit. Prise de vertige, je fermais les yeux, tentais de retrouver à l'intérieur de ce qui en moi demeurait solide les mots d'une prière que l'on m'avait apprise autrefois. La souffrance surgissait toujours à ce moment-là. Oh, my God !

« *The night is darkening round me,*
*The wild winds coldly blow ;*
*But a tyrant spell has bound me*
*And I cannot, cannot go.* »

*«La nuit comme le jour, sans trêve, trois puissances*
*Se livrent bataille en mon être;*
*Cependant que le Ciel ne les contiendrait pas,*
*Je les enferme toutes,*
*Et je n'en serai délivrée*
*Que lorsque je serai délivrée de moi-même...*
*Qu'il vienne ce temps bienheureux*
*Où leur conflit aura pris fin!*
*Qu'il vienne, ce jour bienheureux*
*Qui me déchargera de toute ma souffrance!»*

Emily Jane Brontë,
octobre 1845.
(Traduction Mireille Best.)

*« Emily Brontë est un écrivain orienté à la fois vers l'affabulation et vers une réflexion métaphysique qu'alimentent des expériences visionnaires et une tendance plus générale au mysticisme naturel... »*

Jean-Pierre PETIT.

LA semaine dernière, j'ai senti le besoin de relire les poèmes d'Emily Brontë. Tous ou presque tous m'ont renvoyée à la solitude, au tourment de l'âme divisée, à la fatalité, à un Autre, plus masculin que féminin, à un Autre qui parle parfois à la place de l'auteur, à un Autre dépositaire d'un secret qu'il ne partagera avec personne.

Le discours de la fidélité, d'une fidélité sans faiblesse ni concession d'aucune sorte, celui de l'intransigeance du moi fragilisé, torturé par des tensions difficilement maîtrisables, du moi qui se veut créature de Dieu et créature enfantée par un pays qui importe autant que la mère disparue ; la volonté du tout ou rien ; l'ambiguïté du désir qui souhaite à son objet bien et mal en même temps... ces thèmes se répondent d'un poème à l'autre, dans une continuité qui nous échappe en raison de la destruction de la saga dans laquelle ils s'inséraient et prenaient tout leur sens.

Un fait pourtant demeure qu'Emily tient à nous rappeler : tout est impermanent sauf, peut-être, le lieu où naît l'éphémère ; lui seul existe. Dans cet univers d'intense déchirement, de douleur perpétuée à l'infini, de mort promise et souhaitée, d'angoisse récidiviste, le décor sert de pierre d'achoppement à la souffrance apprise dès l'enfance. C'est d'elle, c'est de cette mauvaise mère qu'Emily a reçu le don de voir l'invisible; il l'enserre, lui parle, la persuade...

*« Écoute, une ombre s'est dressée*
*Tout à l'heure, là où tu es;*
*Trois fleuves entouraient ses pieds,*
*Trois fleuves larges et profonds:*
*L'un était d'or, l'autre de sang,*
*Et l'autre semblait de saphir.*
*Leurs trois courants se rejoignaient,*
*Et le tumulte de leurs eaux*
*Sombrait dans une mer couleur de nuit*
*[profonde. »*

Pour avoir entendu l'appel de l'Absolu, pour avoir entendu la voix de l'Imaginaire, la fille du pasteur de Haworth, plus encore que ses sœurs, s'est vue désignée par le silence, la solitude, la nuit, par tout ce qui dans l'univers est hostile au bonheur mais favorable à l'étude et à la réflexion. Soucieuse du salut de tous autant que du sien, Emily a confié son espérance à ses cahiers. Comme ces mystiques dont on fuit la présence, tant ils nous inquiètent, nous glacent, et nous désespèrent — sans doute nous renvoient-ils à notre insignifiance? — elle a bâti son œuvre autour d'une méditation qui la menait vers une grande mort. Cet exil voulu, ce retrait entretenu jour après jour, cette fuite constante dont souffrirent ses intimes ne furent que le prélude à une fin qui est restée un mystère pour tous.

*L'Esprit perça ces flots qui n'étaient que*
*[ténèbres*
*De la flamme de son regard :*
*Une lueur soudaine embrasa l'onde immense ;*
*La mer était en feu, claire comme un soleil,*
*Plus belle, mille fois, que l'arc-en-ciel des eaux*
*Qui venaient y mourir.*

★

Mais j'avance trop vite.

En ces jours de chaleur, car l'été est enfin là, Emily est en route pour Haworth où l'on s'empresse autour de deux visiteuses : Mary Taylor et sa jeune sœur Martha décrite quelques semaines plus tôt par Charlotte conquise et enthousiaste : « Elle te séduira comme elle séduit tout le monde. Son enjouement, sa vivacité, sa conversation sont irrésistibles ! » Emily aurait préféré se retrouver seule au presbytère avec sa famille, ses animaux et ses manies : « Et surtout, que ces visites ne t'inquiètent pas ! Tu verras, il n'y a pas de personnes plus aimables que les Taylor ! » Il lui faudra songer à se montrer courtoise, chaleureuse, accueillante, à cacher sa fatigue, à distribuer ici et là un compliment.

Au sortir de la diligence, Emily lève la tête. Elle regarde le ciel comme on regarde un tableau superbe, longuement, avec reconnaissance. Dieu merci, au-dessus de Haworth, le temps est beau, paisible. Derrière les quelques maisons essaimées le long de la route, la nature invite aux randonnées : pourra-t-elle s'isoler, se promener seule, échapper aux questions ? La rue lui semble plus dure à remonter que d'habitude : « Pourquoi suis-je aussi essoufflée ! Ai-je pris tant d'années en si peu de mois ? » A peine entrée dans le cimetière, un cri l'y accueille ; il vient du presbytère.

« A-t-on idée d'avoir aussi mauvaise mine et si piètre allure ? »

Tante vient de l'apercevoir de sa fenêtre. Ce dos courbé, cette démarche déjà lasse, alourdie par le poids d'un sac de voyage font pitié à Miss Branwell ; je ne me souvenais pas qu'elle fût aussi grande et aussi mince ! Elle interroge à nouveau sa nièce : « As-tu maltraité ton corps comme tu as maltraité tes cheveux ? »

« Je porte une résille pour me vieillir.
— Allons bon !
— A Law Hill, on me reproche constamment mon âge. »

Miss Branwell, une fois n'est pas coutume, souhaiterait montrer son affection : « Dépêche-toi de venir m'embrasser avant que la tribu ne s'empare de toi ! » Emily se presse ; aura-t-elle le temps de gagner sa chambre sans se faire remarquer ? Non. C'est au tour de papa d'apparaître en haut du perron : « Ta Tante a raison, tu as mauvaise mine. Je ne t'ai jamais vue aussi blanche ! » Rappelée à la fenêtre par un adjectif qui lui paraît tout à fait insuffisant, Tante se penche en direction de son beau-frère :

« Blanche ? Vous voulez dire qu'elle est tout bonnement livide ! »

Près du muret de pierre qui sépare la lande du cimetière, Branwell bavarde avec une inconnue dont on devine le profil sous un immense chapeau de paille. Ce «livide» lancé du premier étage lui fait tourner la tête. Il se jette en avant : « Emily ! Par où es-tu passée ? Je ne t'ai pas vue arriver ! », tend le bras, désigne à l'attention de sa sœur engagée dans des présentations qu'elle aurait voulu remettre à plus tard la personne assise à côté de lui : « Voici Martha ! — Enchantée de vous connaître, Emily ! Nous étions justement en train de discuter avec Branwell d'un poème superbe, *La Vision de Don Roderick* de Walter Scott, l'un de vos auteurs préférés. J'ai trouvé ce livre dans la chambre de Charlotte et je me suis permis de le lire ! »

« C'est un cadeau de Miss Wooler qui s'est très mal conduite avec elle ! Charlotte a fait une terrible dépression. Elle ne retournera plus jamais à Dewsbury Moor !

— Crois-tu que ce soit le moment d'annoncer ce genre de nouvelle à ta sœur ? »

Branwell adresse un sourire ironique à son père exaspéré par le verbiage et l'insolence du jeune coq. Non, son empressement n'est pas déplacé ; plus vite Emily sera au courant des événements, plus vite elle s'adaptera à la bonne ambiance qui règne dans la maison :

« Tu as un air à donner froid dans le dos ! Que s'est-il passé là-haut ?

— Je te trouve bien curieux... et surtout impulsif ! »

Emily jette un regard de reproche à son frère qui joue au désinvolte devant témoin. Martha se lève. Elle repousse la chaise sur laquelle elle était installée comme une princesse ; sa jupe blanche à gros plis accompagne ses mouvements gracieux. Elle s'approche de la voyageuse, lui propose de porter son sac : « Non, merci ! » Emily n'a pas le temps d'en saisir les anses que surgit Charlotte ;

elle est accompagnée de sa chère amie Mary et d'Anne. Dans l'effervescence des retrouvailles, Emily reconnaît la pression des doigts de sa jeune sœur qui, tout en lui serrant le bras, lui glisse un mot à l'oreille: « J'espère que tu auras un peu de temps pour moi... Tu m'as tellement manqué! » Miss Branwell se rappelle au bon souvenir de sa nièce:

« Si vous la laissiez monter m'embrasser et déposer ses affaires? »

Papa s'est rapproché du groupe. Il touche l'épaule d'Emily comme s'il voulait s'assurer de sa réalité: « Bienvenue au presbytère, ma fille! » Des larmes brillent dans les yeux de la voyageuse qui se baisse pour prendre son petit bagage: « Merci, papa! » Dans sa bouche, les mots ont la dureté des cailloux. Elle s'étonne de ne pas ressentir de passion pour ces êtres qu'elle aime pourtant d'un sentiment vrai, profond.

A l'heure du dîner, Charlotte pose des questions auxquelles Emily ne sait pas répondre. Ce refus de parler de soi, de son travail, de ses idées, étonne les filles Taylor habituées à plus de loquacité et d'aisance. Bouleversée par ce regard qui l'évite, cette présence fuyante, Anne fait le tour de la table. A bout de patience, elle prend une main qu'Emily n'a pas la cruauté de lui retirer: « Pourquoi ne resterais-tu pas avec nous? Charlotte m'a dit que là-haut tu travaillais tellement que le soir tu t'endormais tout habillée sur ton lit! »

« Je dois retourner à Law Hill... je ne veux pas manquer à mes engagements! »

Branwell insiste : « Et Miss Patchett... comment est-elle ? » Emily s'interroge à haute voix : « Je ne sais qu'en dire... belle, grande, plutôt raffinée... » Elle cherche les adjectifs susceptibles de décrire la beauté d'une femme d'âge mûr, admirable cavalière, juste, bonne, et de grande moralité. Branwell s'exclame : « Tant de grâce et faire un tel métier ! » Mary se moque : « Depuis que votre frère sait que papa s'intéresse à la peinture française, il me trouve l'allure continentale... au fait, mon cher, quand vous déciderez-vous à faire mon portrait ? »

« Lorsqu'il aura les doigts usés par la paresse !
— Bigre ! Tu ne m'as pas raté, Emily. »

Pas une seule fois, durant ces courtes vacances, Emily n'a pu abandonner cette froideur protectrice ; pas même en présence de Taby qui dès le premier jour a visé la cible en plein cœur : « C'te pension d'malheur t'vaut rien ! Elle t'donne un air d'deuil et d'étrangère ! » ; pas même en présence d'Anne qui a fait des confidences à Mary : « A votre place, je me garderais d'en tirer des conséquences. Il se passe quelque chose que vous ne pouvez comprendre ! Emily vous reviendra ! » ; pas même en présence du pasteur dont les gestes maladroits, la main tendue en avant rappellent l'infirmité : « Il est en train de devenir aveugle, n'est-ce pas ? — Oui, Emily ! Nous avons vu quelqu'un de compétent à Bradford. Il faudra l'opérer dans quelque temps ; pour l'instant c'est trop tôt ! — L'opérer ! — Rassure-toi, l'opération donne en général d'excellents résultats ! » ; pas même en présence de Branwell qui depuis son retour a repris ses habitudes et sa place au Black Bull où l'on se presse pour l'entendre raconter les derniers scandales et imiter son père : dans ces moments de franche dérision, Dieu lui-même en prend pour son grade.

« Que compte-t-il faire ?
— A part se moquer de papa et amuser les ivrognes du coin, pas grand-chose. Nous avons espoir malgré tout qu'il accepte le poste qui vient de lui être proposé par M. Postlethwaite qui habite à Broughton-in-Furness dans le Cumberland ! »

Pas même en présence de ce frère que l'on devine et que l'on voudrait aider, parce que plus que tous les autres, il en a besoin : « J'ai appris par Charlotte... »

« Je sais.
— Et alors, que comptes-tu faire ?
— Pour l'instant, je termine un grand poème que j'ai commencé il y a peu de temps. Je l'ai intitulé : *Azraël.* »

★

Dans la voiture qui la reconduit à Halifax, entre Oxenhope et Hebden Bridge, Emily a une pensée pour sa famille qu'elle aime en silence et dans le secret, pour l'inquiétude frileuse d'Anne, pour la vieillesse de Tante, pour la cécité et l'hypocondrie de papa qui a fini par trouver une aide précieuse dans le verre de vin que le médecin lui a conseillé de prendre en matière de reconstituant, pour les déchirements de Charlotte harcelée par un moi trop fougueux et trop exigeant, pour l'angoisse grandissante de Branwell entraîné sur une pente dont elle ne voit pas la fin, pour Branwell qui, au cours d'une beuverie, a basculé dans le délire. N'a-t-il pas raconté devant témoins que sa petite sœur, Maria, continuait à errer sur la lande ! « Tout cela est pure folie, John ! »

« Non pas, Miss Emily !
— Vous n'allez tout de même pas croire à des choses pareilles ?
— Puisque je vous dis que Branwell nous a tout raconté ! Chaque nuit, lorsque vous dormez, Maria vient frapper à la porte du presbytère. Elle insiste, demande à entrer, dit qu'elle a froid. Branwell l'implore de partir, mais elle refuse. Sa prière est si déchirante qu'à chaque fois le pauvre garçon éclate en sanglots. Il se bouche les oreilles, se cache sous les couvertures, mais la voix est toujours là qui appelle au secours. Quelquefois votre mère apparaît elle aussi. Elle est enveloppée d'un suaire bien propre. A la place de son visage, elle a une tête de mort, avec des orbites creuses et des dents plantées dans la mâchoire. Branwell hurle. Votre père se lève. Il lui prépare une mixture ; de l'eau sucrée avec un peu d'ammoniaque dedans.
— C'est l'alcool qui le rend fou !
— L'alcool et les morts !
— Ne pourriez-vous l'empêcher de boire ? »

Dans la voiture qui la reconduit à Halifax, Emily cherche les mots d'une prière : « Oh, Seigneur Jésus, n'abandonnez pas mon frère ! »

*«Methought I saw him, but I knew him not,*
*He was so changed from what he used to be...»*

*«Je l'ai vu, mais je ne l'ai pas reconnu,*
*Il était si changé...»*

Anne Brontë.
(Traduction Mireille Hollard.)

*« A ce point de la vie d'Emily Brontë — sa vingt et unième année —, il se pose une question épineuse que nous formulerons ici sans détour : était-elle au nombre de celles que les hommes laissent insensibles et qui n'ont d'amour que pour les femmes ? »*

Virginia MOORE.

CE matin, alors que vous vous attardiez sur cette interrogation, j'ai vu se ranimer le soupçon qui plane sur ma mémoire : ai-je connu les secousses et les tumultes de l'amour ? Alors que j'étais employée à satisfaire les maigres exigences culturelles des jeunes bourgeoises de la région de Halifax, ai-je vécu une passion coupable ?

« *Et mon cœur est baigné par cette sombre [averse*
*Qui s'abat sur Gomorrhe et ses plaines en feu.*
*Mais que tes ennemis de sarcasmes te percent :*
*Mes bras noués sur toi ne serreront que [mieux !* »

La question, certes, est « épineuse », surtout si l'on songe à la position incommode qui était la mienne : fille de pasteur et nièce d'une vieille demoiselle méthodiste. Dois-je ici et maintenant en remercier le ciel ? Personne de mon vivant ne pointa sa curiosité sur une telle hypothèse qui m'eût envoyée devant le tribunal des bonnes mœurs.

«T'pourrais p'têt'e accorder plus à l'coquetterie ?

— Coquette, je le suis, mais à mes heures !

— Point nombreuses, tes heures !

— Ce ne sont pas les tiennes.

— Dans l'pays, y disent qu't'as tout d'un gars ! »

Il est vrai, ma silhouette longue et plutôt maigre, assez plate pour ne point attirer sur elle le souhait d'une maternité, mon manque d'artifice furent maintes fois dénoncés en présence de Tabitha dont on ne se méfiait pas. Parce qu'ils ne comprenaient pas le plaisir que l'on peut prendre à s'essouffler au long de randonnées solitaires où le halètement d'un chien vous tient compagnie, les gens de Haworth critiquèrent mon style et mes manières.

«Paraît qu't'as encore battu ton chien et d'belle façon ?

— Il m'y a obligée.

— Quéque c'est c'genre d'obligations ?

— Il a tenté de mordre William Brown qui voulait me parler.

— Ça fait longtemps qu'j'l'aurais renvoyé chez l'diable, l'Keeper ! N'empêche qu'à côté d'Brannii, t'as l'allure d'un fiancé au bras d'sa promise ! »

Mon frère, à qui le destin épargna l'état d'adulte, fut le seul à s'amuser de ce qui, d'une certaine manière, le déshéritait. Seul mâle de la famille, il laissa sa virilité à une sœur trop masculine : «Pourquoi n'échangerions-nous pas notre tenue ?

Je te prête mon pantalon, tu me donnes ta jupe! Imagine un peu leur tête!» Nous ne mîmes pas notre projet à exécution ; seule la crainte de blesser nous retint : « Pauvre vieux papa, il en ferait une tête ! »

Afin de ne pas étouffer dans cette enveloppe qui portait nom Emily Jane Brontë, j'entamai un dialogue avec des êtres imaginaires à qui je confiai mes frémissements, ma fierté. Ce dédoublement, ce jeu du Il et du Elle me sauva de la désespérance et de la solitude qui poussent certains au suicide. Je devins mon propre partenaire. « Emily, souhaiterais-tu être un garçon ? — Garçon, je le suis autant que Branwell ! » À l'image de Charlotte qui jusqu'à sa grande crise de conscience signa sous le nom d'un homme, puis d'un autre, et encore d'un autre, je me mis à parler par la bouche de l'amant que le destin me refusait. Cet emprunt m'épargna l'humiliation et l'amertume que m'eût apportées une vaine recherche.

> « Si nous étions homme et femme à la fois, comme tu prétends l'être, nous n'aurions pas à redouter l'avenir !
> — La mort est au bout pour tout le monde !
> — C'est possible, mais tout est permis aux hommes alors que tout est interdit aux femmes ! À peine accorde-t-on le droit de vivre à celles qui sont stériles ! »

Ce vêtement étroit et mal taillé qui nous désignait au monde, ce vêtement de future vieille fille laissée pour compte à un père infortuné, je m'en défis souvent. Sous le nom de Julius Brenzaida ou, selon les saisons, sous celui de Julius Angora, je m'adressai aux créatures de mon choix, hommes et femmes, refusant ainsi une existence soumise à un sexe et à des lois trop étroits pour me convenir. Assurée de titres masculins qui me donnaient d'autorité un passeport, je parcourus les terres de la trahison et les déserts de l'amour...

*« Noble foe, I pardon thee*
*All thy cold and scornful pride*
*For thou wast a priceless friend to me*
*When my sad heart had none beside. »*

Ces appels sans écho qui désespèrent la plupart de mes poèmes furent-ils lancés pour la première fois à Law Hill ? C'est possible. L'exil fut pour moi une épreuve très douloureuse. Afin de traverser le temps du sacrifice — je refusai de céder à l'insistance du désir qui me pressait de rentrer à Haworth plus tôt que prévu — j'appelai à mon aide l'écriture. Elle ne se fit pas prier. Nourrie de mes déceptions quotidiennes, de mes souffrances secrètes, de mes brefs enchantements, la poésie s'imposa à moi avec la même force, les mêmes exigences qu'une passion.

Plus tard, abusés par la violence de mes vers et la crudité de cette souffrance dont je fus, jusqu'à la veille de ma mort, le porte-parole, certains se posèrent une question qui court encore : avais-je quelque jour d'éblouissement prêté à une silhouette plus féminine que la mienne des attraits auxquels je n'aurais pas su résister ? Mieux. Cet élan vers un Dieu rédempteur, cette louange de l'Absolu inatteignable, cette révolte enfin, cette révolte contre la féminité dans laquelle la société m'avait enfermée, tous ces sursauts n'étaient-ils pas le langage du désir coupable, pressé de s'affranchir d'un poids trop lourd? Je n'ai aucune réponse à donner mais un remerciement à adresser à la postérité qui m'a donné tout ce que la vie m'a refusé; un amour mystérieux et inspiré, glorieux véhicule de l'écriture, la compréhension intuitive de la passion sur son versant le plus sombre, la connaissance de ce qu'on nomme le démoniaque, l'inassouvissable, cette notion du Mal dont l'histoire, par un tour de passe-passe, a déchargé Branwell et Charlotte, mes maîtres.

En me faisant ce cadeau, et en ne le faisant qu'à moi, l'histoire a commis une injustice que je me dois de dénoncer. Charlotte, Branwell, Anne sont présents dans mon œuvre comme je le suis dans la leur. On ne peut isoler nos écrits sans commettre une erreur, pire, un faux. Si certaines de nos expériences ont été divergentes, nos hantises, nos obsessions, nos espoirs, nos joies se sont entrecroisés comme les ramures du même arbre. Élevés dans la foi anglicane, l'austérité, la rigueur, nous avons poussé tous les quatre à l'angle d'un cimetière, et cette rude contrée dont nous sommes issus, nous l'avons appréhendée chacun à notre façon, mais toujours tragiquement. L'ironie de Branwell, ses saillies n'ont été que le buisson derrière lequel s'est dissimulé son désespoir.

★

« Papa, à quoi nous sert d'avoir une âme ?

— A nous sauver de l'enfer et du néant, mon fils !

— Mais n'est-elle pas un embarras avant d'être un moyen de salut ?

— Comment oses-tu parler ainsi ? Sans l'âme, tu ne serais rien de plus que le cheval des Heaton !

— Le cheval des Heaton est heureux et moi je ne le suis pas et c'est bien pourquoi...

— Silence ! J'ai assez entendu de blasphèmes pour aujourd'hui ! »

Je me souviens, Branwell n'avait pas dix ans que déjà il était toute malice et insolence. Atteint par l'intelligence comme d'autres le sont par le cancer, il s'offrit à trois filles. Ravies de nous savoir les élues de cet enfant-Dieu, mes sœurs et moi-même nous empressâmes de goûter à ce mal délicieux qu'il nous proposait de partager. Son imagination excita notre fantaisie. Devant cette coalition, la réalité recula jusqu'au fond d'un cimetière qui se métamorphosa en scène de théâtre. Au fil du temps, nous nous fîmes cadeau de nos rêves, de nos idées, de nos chimères. Ces échanges de bons et de mauvais procédés nous lièrent à jamais. A la fin de sa courte existence, Branwell parla surtout au nom des femmes et moi au nom des hommes ; Charlotte, de son côté, accusa le duc de Zamorna, son double, d'avoir fait d'elle un écrivain et une veuve. Seule Anne resta ce qu'elle était : la nièce d'Elizabeth Branwell, une jeune fille fragile et forte à la fois que le mariage et les maternités eussent épanouie.

Ces allées et venues entre deux sexes, ces va-et-vient de l'identité qui semblent dérouter certains n'affectèrent nullement nos rapports avec notre entourage qui n'y vit goutte. Le devoir nous fit monter sur les mêmes estrades, enseigner les mêmes élèves, rencontrer les mêmes hostilités. Après avoir plus ou moins tergiversé, nous finîmes par épouser la même mort tuberculeuse.

★

« Maintenant, ça suffit ! Tes sœurs t'ont assez donné l'exemple !

— Pourquoi parlez-vous au passé, Patrick ! Ses sœurs ne cessent de lui donner l'exemple ! »

J'ajouterai, pour apporter une nuance à ce qui précède, que l'un des rares moments où nos destins semblèrent diverger se situe justement vers ces années 1839-1840. Tandis que je m'éclipsais définitivement de Law Hill et regagnais le presbytère avec soulagement, Branwell, après avoir enterré sans la moindre dignité une carrière de peintre, partait pour Liverpool où l'attendait, non pas l'emploi espéré, mais la drogue. Anne, de son côté, désireuse d'accéder à l'indépendance, s'engageait comme gouvernante.

« C'est absurde ! Tu ne tiendras pas !

— C'est ce que nous verrons, Charlotte. »

A nouveau l'heure des séparations venait de sonner.

*«Father! thou hast long been dead,*
*Mother! thou art gone,*
*Brother! thou art far away,*
*And I am left alone!*

*Long before my mother died,*
*I was sad and lone,*
*And, when she departed too,*
*Every joy was flown.»*

Anne Brontë.

*« Anne avec un courage silencieux avait accepté un poste de gouvernante chez Mrs. Ingham, à Blake Hall, Mirfield. Rien ne put l'en dissuader. »*

Daphné Du Maurier.

8 avril 1839.

Depuis l'aube, il pleut sur le nord de l'Angleterre. Derrière les murets qui clôturent les pâturages, l'herbe brûlée par la neige d'un hiver interminable est recouverte d'une vase brunâtre. Après les tempêtes qui se sont abattues sur le nord de l'Écosse, le vent a brusquement changé de cap ; il pousse à l'intérieur des terres un amoncellement de nuages. Sur la route qui relie Halifax à Huddersfield, des rafales entravent la marche des chevaux qui s'éreintent à l'avant de la diligence. Entre deux coups de fouet, le conducteur assis à l'extérieur entend des bribes de conversation. Dans la voiture, des passagers discutent bruyamment ; ils s'en prennent aux derniers événements politiques : l'un trouve que la situation économiqe s'aggrave chaque jour davantage, l'autre que les menaces ouvrières détériorent un climat déjà compromis : « Les gens ont peur ! — Il y a de quoi ! Ces meneurs défient la sécurité et le confort du citoyen ! Bientôt on ne pourra même plus prendre la diligence ! — Que faire ? On ne peut plus leur proposer du travail, les machines les remplacent et à l'aise encore!»

Assise à côté d'un vieillard qui somnole, Anne s'inquiète: «Ne va-t-on pas arriver avec une heure de retard?» Le vent souffle de plus en plus fort. Il hurle aux portières, tente d'arracher la capote arrière. «Quel temps pour un mois d'avril! C'est encore pire que l'année dernière!» Un représentant en textiles tente de placer une histoire: une manifestation de tisserands à laquelle il a assisté: «Ils portaient tous des drapeaux noirs sur lesquels ils avaient inscrit "Mort!" Vous jugez de l'effet. Nous étions tous glacés!» Au lieu de mettre un point final à la scène, quelqu'un la relance: «A votre avis, qui est menacé? Les patrons ou les ouvriers qu'on laisse crever de faim?» Le représentant en textiles s'agace: «Que croyez-vous, monsieur, on voit bien que vous n'êtes pas d'ici! Ces gens-là ne se posent pas de questions! Ce sont des analphabètes! — Analphabètes? je n'en suis pas si sûr que vous, en tout cas pas assez pour ne pas savoir écrire le mot mort!»

Anne soupire. Elle se sent inconfortable entre le vieillard dont la tête vient de tomber sur son épaule et un commis voyageur qui s'étale largement à côté d'elle. «Si seulement ils pouvaient se taire!» Le silence ne dure malheureusement pas. Trop d'idées se pressent dans la tête des voyageurs. «Je ne voudrais pas être prophète de malheur, mais je prétends qu'il y a là toutes les conditions d'une guerre civile!» Une femme prend la parole: «Pas plus que vous, monsieur, je n'aime les drapeaux noirs, mais tirer sur des hommes et des femmes qui manifestent, la chose, à mon avis, n'aura pas plu à Dieu!» Le voisin d'Anne se réveille. Il s'excuse auprès de sa voisine, s'en prend au spectre de la révolution qui rôde, si on veut l'en croire, dans toutes les villes manufacturières du Yorkshire : « Il n'y a pas d'autre issue ! Il faut prendre les armes et descendre dans la rue ! » Assis près de la portière, un homme jusque-là silencieux approuve : la presse elle-même, d'ordinaire si nuancée, a pris franchement le parti des patrons, elle dénonce les agissements de furieux qui se promènent avec des barres de fer : « Pour quoi faire ? »

> « Pour briser les reins des chevaux qui pourraient les charger ! Si elle tient à rester en selle, l'armée n'a qu'à bien se tenir ! »

Le vieillard se tourne vers Anne : « Voilà ce que c'est que le socialisme ! » Effrayée par le regard qu'on lui adresse, la fille du pasteur détourne les yeux. Au-dessus d'une large collerette froissée par le châle, son visage a la pâleur d'une morte en sursis : « Et vous, mademoiselle, que pensez-vous de tout ça ? » D'un mouvement d'épaules, Anne fait savoir qu'elle n'a aucune opinion sur la question. Elle jette un coup d'œil anxieux en direction de la portière. Le cocher de Mme Ingham aura-t-il la patience d'attendre au relais de Huddersfield ?

A court de propos et peut-être de souffle, le représentant en textiles s'est tu, et avec lui tous les autres passagers. Ils observent d'un œil hébété les gouttes de pluie qui ruissellent sur la vitre embuée, écoutent la boue clapoter sous les roues. « C'est pire que l'année dernière ! — Nous n'aurons pas de printemps ! — Quel fichu temps ! » Les claquements de langue du cocher annoncent une difficulté ; l'attelage vient de s'engager dans une côte. Malgré les cris du conducteur — et l'on ne sait, à l'intérieur où règne une chaleur animale, s'il use ainsi de la voix pour se réchauffer ou faire avancer les chevaux — le rythme des sabots se fait plus lourd, plus pesant. « Pourquoi les frappe-t-il autant? Ça ne sert à rien!» Anne s'apitoie sur le sort des chevaux dont elle imagine l'effort, l'encolure ruisselante et tendue, la bave des naseaux. Pourquoi est-on impitoyable envers les animaux? Cette question posée à maintes reprises au presbytère n'a jamais reçu de réponse valable. Papa refuse de s'intéresser à un aussi mince problème; il pense que l'animal a été créé par Dieu pour les besoins de l'homme qu'il doit servir. Quant à Tante, elle accepte de cohabiter avec les animaux domestiques dans la mesure où ils se tiennent à distance respectueuse: «Emily, garde ton chien loin de ma chambre. Je ne tiens pas à attraper des puces!»

De l'autre côté de la vitre qu'une main essuie de temps à autre, défile le paysage rendu monotone par la pluie et la brume: des pâturages que l'on devine immenses, quelques arbres fantomatiques, des maisons isolées et comme enfoncées dans la terre, le sommet d'un clocher à peine visible qui signale un village planté en contrebas d'une petite colline, des moutons serrés les uns contre les autres pour lutter contre le froid, un cheval solitaire et pris de folie qui court au milieu d'une vaste prairie. «Vais-je lui ressembler et courir ainsi toute ma vie au milieu d'un espace désert, humide et froid? La solitude sera-t-elle mon lot, comme elle l'est pour ce cheval? Anne tente de sourire au lourd visage de son voisin qui s'inquiète enfin de son inconfort: «On vous laisse bien peu de place, miss... — Tout va bien, merci!»

«Vous êtes de Haworth?
— Oui.
— Il me semble vous avoir déjà vue?
— Je suis la fille du pasteur.»

La fille du pasteur et la sœur d'Emily et de

Charlotte. Que font-elles à cette heure? Assises devant un feu de tourbe, elles doivent s'inquiéter. Charlotte parle en agitant la main au-dessus de la théière. « Je n'aurais jamais dû la laisser partir... elle qui ne sait pas tenir une conversation... elle qui bégaie... elle qu'un vol de mouches effraie... sait-elle ce que représente l'état de gouvernante ? Il n'y a pas pire que ces enrichis par la banque et le charbon, et qui, de plus, possèdent des terres ! D'après mes renseignements, Joshua Ingham est un magistrat aussi entêté qu'irritable, et de ses enfants, Cunliffe et Mary, on m'a dit le plus grand mal. Tu imagines Anne face à deux petits monstres ? » Tout en écoutant Charlotte, Emily regarde par la fenêtre : « Pour quelqu'un qui s'effraie d'un vol de mouches, je la trouve plutôt courageuse d'être allée à Mirfield, surtout après le tableau que tu viens de faire ! » Blessée, Charlotte riposte : « Je n'ai pas dit cela pour me moquer d'Anne ! Je crains simplement qu'elle ne se fasse pas à certains traitements ! A son âge, on se remet mal des humiliations ! — Je sais que tu es inquiète, Charlotte, mais je crois que nous avons bien fait de la laisser partir ! Anne a besoin d'une reconnaissance qu'elle ne trouvera pas ici. » Ce discours atteint Charlotte au vif : « J'aurais dû accepter la demande en mariage du frère d' Ellen Nussey ! — J'espère que tu plaisantes ! — Non ! — Ce n'est pas une femme qu'il recherche, mais une dame de compagnie ! — Il n'y a aucune raison pour qu'Anne s'exile et que moi, l'aînée, je reste ici. J'ai décidé d'accepter la place de gouvernante que m'offrent les Sidgwick ! — Tu ne te plairas pas à Stonegrappe ! — C'est probable, mais j'irai tout de même ! »

Serrée entre deux voisins qui lui mesurent chichement la place, Anne songe à sa famille, à son père qu'elle aime d'un amour discret mais fidèle, à sa tante pour laquelle elle prie chaque jour afin que Dieu lui accorde longue vie, à ses sœurs: «Charlotte a-t-elle encore pour moi un semblant d'affection, ou ne me voit-elle qu'avec le regard du devoir?» Autant Emily lui fait confiance, autant Charlotte lui mesure son estime. «Suis-je si mince, si insignifiante pour qu'elle doute encore de moi à ce point?» Personne, à part Emily, n'a su trouver l'expression juste pour lui dire qu'elle était souhaitée, que sa place, sa vraie place, était au presbytère. Ces mots qui rassureraient sont si rarement dits dans la vie quotidienne qu'on en vient à douter de soi, de sa fonction, de son rôle, de son utilité même: «Je pourrais mourir, là, tout de suite, personne ne me regretterait vraiment!» Si seulement la bienveillance pouvait brûler la langue comme la colère ou l'aversion, le monde se porterait mieux.

«Miss! Vous dormez?

— Mon Dieu, non! Où sommes-nous?

— A Huddersfield! Le cocher de Mme Ingham vous attend dans la cour avec votre bagage!»

Depuis l'aube, il pleut sur le nord de l'Angleterre. A l'intérieur de la calèche que les Ingham ont dépêchée pour elle, Anne dialogue avec l'inquiétude. Quels mots emploiera-t-elle pour se présenter à ses futurs employeurs? Devra-t-elle prendre les enfants dans ses bras ou, au contraire, garder ses distances et leur tendre la main comme à des personnes respectables? Lui accordera-t-on un regard de sympathie? un mot aimable? M. Ingham lui souhaitera-t-il la bienvenue comme autrefois papa l'a souhaitée à Emily, alors qu'exténuée elle revenait de Law Hill pour les vacances scolaires ? « Bienvenue dans cette maison, ma fille ! »

> « *Father! thou hast long been dead,*
> *Mother! thou art gone,*
> *Brother! thou art far away,*
> *And I am left alone!* »

Dans la calèche des Ingham, la crainte a laissé place à la tristesse. Anne essuie une larme. Seigneur, songerez-vous à me donner un peu de ce dont j'ai besoin ? Je ne vous demande ni honneur, ni talent, ni richesse, juste un peu de cet amour que vous avez généreusement accordé à mes parents.

> « *Mon père connaissait trop bien la valeur de ma mère pour ne pas penser qu'elle était par elle-même une précieuse fortune, et que, si elle voulait consentir à embellir son humble foyer, il serait heureux de la prendre, à quelque condition que ce fût ; tandis que ma mère, de son côté, eût plutôt labouré la terre de ses propres mains que d'être séparée de l'homme qu'elle aimait.* »

Anne BRONTË, *Agnès Grey*.

«Papier à ouvrir
quand Anne aura vingt-cinq ans
ou à mon prochain anniversaire d'après
— si tout va bien —
Emily Jane Brontë le 30 juillet 1841

*C'est vendredi soir — il est presque neuf heures — temps pluvieux tourmenté. Je suis assise dans la salle à manger après avoir juste fini de ranger les boîtes de nos pupitres — en train d'écrire ce mémoire. Papa est au salon. Tante en haut dans sa chambre. Elle a lu le* Blackwood's Magazine *à papa. Victoria et Adelaïde sont blotties dans le hangar à tourbe. Keeper est dans la cuisine. Hero dans sa cage.»*

(Traduction Pierre Leyris.)

VOTRE manière d'aborder un chapitre en le centrant autour d'une date me rappelle les journaux que nous tenions dans le secret, ma sœur Anne et moi. Je me souviens de celui-ci :

> « *Lundi soir 26 juin 1837.*
> *Un peu après 4 heures Charlotte travaille dans la chambre de Tante Branwell lui lit Eugene Aram Anne et moi écrivons au salon — Anne un poème qui commence par "beau s'annonçait le soir, rayonnait le soleil" — moi la vie d'Agustus-Almeda Ier v. 4e page dudit belle journée assez frisquette avec de minces nuages gris mais ensoleillée...* »

Aujourd'hui, si je devais confier quelque chose de moi à un journal intime, c'est ainsi que je le ferais, sous cette forme innocente, sans prétention. Je prendrais une date au hasard, par exemple le 20 août 1839, puis j'indiquerais l'heure. Je parlerais du temps, de mon humeur...

20 août 1839.

Il est un peu moins de dix-neuf heures. Nous venons de terminer les prières et de réciter les psaumes. Ayez pitié de nous, Seigneur ! La journée a été superbe. Papa est enfermé dans son bureau. Assis près de la fenêtre, il contemple le cimetière. A quoi, à qui songe-t-il ? Au temps ? A la mort ? A Dieu auquel il rend fidèlement hommage ? A son fils peut-être? A Branwell qui lui donne des inquiétudes renforcées par la distance? Après un second voyage à Liverpool d'où il est revenu plus désordonné qu'à l'ordinaire, mais surtout fasciné par le prédicateur de Saint-jude, un orateur que l'on vient entendre de très loin: «C'était superbe! Ah, comme j'aurais voulu que vous fussiez là, papa! Devant l'assistance éblouie et incendiée par sa parole, il a sommé l'Église catholique romaine de permettre le mariage des prêtres qui pèchent par orgueil et par abstinence!» Mais où en étais-je? Ah oui, après un second voyage à Liverpool, mon frère est reparti pour Bradford où je le soupçonne de mener une vie dépravée et fiévreuse aux dépens d'amis plus riches que lui.

20 août 1839.

Il est dix-neuf heures. Enfin, à peine. J'écris ces lignes après une journée laborieuse. Ce matin, j'ai nettoyé les escaliers, j'ai astiqué les meubles du premier étage. Tante est sortie sur le palier: «En as-tu bientôt fini de ce remue-ménage ou as-tu l'intention de me faire reluire moi aussi?» Elle m'a conseillé d'arrêter là les travaux ménagers et de me reposer, mais je n'ai pas suivi ses conseils. Quand le vent souffle dans le bon sens, il faut savoir dresser la voile. Cet après-midi, j'ai donc lavé le linge de la maison car la pauvre Taby ne peut plus m'aider en rien. Il est question qu'elle aille vivre avec sa sœur dans une petite maison dont toutes deux viennent d'hériter. Cette séparation sera douloureuse pour moi; même si elle l'ignore, la brave femme occupe une grande place dans mon cœur.

20 août 1839.

Il est un peu moins de vingt heures. De mon bureau, je dirige la guerre qui se déroule dans l'île de Gondal. Les royalistes perdent du terrain et des hommes. Je ne vois pas ce que je pourrais faire pour les sauver. Les idées me manquent. Ce soir j'ai d'autres soucis en tête.

20 août 1839.

Il est près de vingt heures trente. J'ai rangé mon manuscrit dans l'écritoire et je me suis décidée à me coucher. C'est encore dans mon lit que je me sens le plus à l'abri. J'aperçois le ciel. La lune ne va pas tarder à se lever. Tante ne dort pas encore. La tête soutenue par plusieurs oreillers, elle prie pour le salut de tous, pour celui d'Anne dont elle s'inquiète. Ma jeune sœur nous adresse régulièrement de ses nouvelles ; dans l'ensemble, elles sont plutôt mauvaises. Les deux enfants Ingham lui rendent la vie impossible. J'aimerais qu'elle rentre à la maison ; de la savoir malheureuse au loin me chagrine. « Y a d'quoi t'chagriner, ma tout'belle ! J't'avais bien dit qu'elle se sacrifierait pour ta paix ! »

20 août 1839.

Il est un peu moins de vingt et une heures. Mon faucon Hero dort dans sa cage et mes oies, Adelaïde et Victoria, sont enfermées dans le hangar à tourbe. Keeper rêve dans la cuisine. Charlotte est au loin. Malgré les objections de Tante qui rechignait à la voir s'éloigner à nouveau — elle ne fait qu'aller et venir comme un capitaine de guerre — ma sœur est partie au bord de la mer, sur la côte est, avec son amie Ellen. Si seulement elle pouvait rencontrer là-bas un homme à sa convenance, intelligent et sensible ! Ces demoiselles résident dans un hôtel à Bridlington, une station balnéaire fréquentée par la bourgeoisie du Yorkshire. Même si je m'ennuie d'elle, je suis contente de savoir Charlotte en joyeuse compagnie. J'espère que la mer lui apportera l'apaisement dont elle a grandement besoin.

20 août 1839.

Il est vingt et une heures passées. De mon lit où je suis en train de rêvasser, je vois les premières étoiles. Lorsque Charlotte est là, nous essayons de les compter. Hélas, depuis son retour de chez les Sidgwick, ma sœur n'a plus de goût à rien. Elle ne veut plus être gouvernante : « Ces maîtres anglais sont des vaniteux, des gens stupides et guindés ! Lorsqu'ils s'adressent à leur personnel, ils prennent le ton d'un roi parlant à la populace ! Mme Sidgwick m'a traitée d'une façon si méprisante et pour finir si hostile, que je ne suis pas près de l'oublier ! » Je me demande ce qu'il va advenir de mon aînée. Mon inquiétude n'est pas nouvelle et je pourrais même en décrire le parcours, mais je ne vois pas de quelle manière je pourrais venir en aide à quelqu'un qui refuse tout commerce : « Je ne veux pas rester à Haworth où je dépéris ! A ce stade, ce n'est même plus une question d'argent !
— Puisque tu ne souhaites pas être institutrice, ni gouvernante, ni tout simplement fille de pasteur, pourquoi n'envisagerais-tu pas une bonne fois de te marier ? Ce n'est pas parce que les propositions qui t'ont été faites n'étaient pas valables que celles à venir ne le seront pas ! — Celles à venir ? Seigneur Dieu ! De qui puis-je attendre une demande en mariage, sinon d'un de ces vicaires ennuyeux ? Je ne vais tout de même pas épouser n'importe quel vieux garçon pour échapper à cette prison ? »

20 août 1839.

Il n'est pas encore vingt et une heures trente. J'entends les ronflements de Tante et ceux plus discrets de papa. Tout en contemplant le ciel magnifique de cette belle nuit, je songe à Charlotte et à ce qui nous sépare. Comment faire comprendre à ma sœur que j'ai besoin de solitude? Comment l'assurer de mon affection sans qu'elle en abuse aussitôt? Ma préférence pour Anne lui est intolérable et notre connivence considérée comme une trahison. Elle a oublié celle qui la liait autrefois à Branwell, à cette époque où nous, les deux petites, nous ne l'intéressions pas.

20 août 1839.

Non seulement mon aînée nie les sentiments réels et profonds que je lui porte, mais elle s'isole pour mieux souffrir d'un mal contre lequel personne ne peut rien. A quel destin ce corps tourmenté, cette âme déchirée se promettent-ils? Heureusement, Ellen l'écoute et la rassure. Plus que tout, Charlotte redoute la solitude qui la renverrait à elle-même. Malgré l'originalité de son caractère, malgré son grand talent — de nous quatre, elle est l'écrivain, en tout cas la styliste — malgré son étonnante intelligence, Charlotte ne parvient pas à sacrifier l'idée du mariage. Au lieu de la confirmer dans le célibat, la demande de Henry Nussey, celle plus récente de M. Bryce, un pasteur de l'université de Dublin, homme plutôt plaisant quoique trop familier, ont, en elle, exaspéré quelque chose.

20 août 1839.

Depuis cet instant où deux hommes lui ont fait savoir qu'ils souhaitaient la prendre pour femme, tout est devenu dérisoire: « A peine M. Bryce a-t-il eu le temps d'entrevoir qui j'étais qu'il a demandé ma main! Quelle irréflexion! Quelle irresponsabilité!» A en croire Charlotte, la vie est absurde, laide, sans espoir, et nous sommes appelées, quoi que nous fassions, à demeurer vieilles filles.

Comment la ramener à une vue plus juste des choses ? Pas plus qu'elle n'espère rencontrer le duc de Zamorna je ne compte voir apparaître Julius Angora à la porte du cimetière. Nous n'avons rien à attendre des autres, mais nous pouvons beaucoup espérer de nous-mêmes.

20 août 1839.

Pourquoi Charlotte ne garde-t-elle pas pour elle le linge douteux des confessions ? Tout n'est pas bon à dire. Entre elle et Ellen se joue une relation... je ne trouve pas le mot pour la qualifier. Il me semble qu'il y a de part et d'autre une sorte de satisfaction malsaine qui n'est bonne pour personne. Qui sait si Ellen ne finira pas par gâcher sa vie en tentant d'imiter Charlotte, et Charlotte la sienne en essayant d'être à la hauteur de ce qu'Ellen attend d'elle ? Je me demande si ma sœur, toujours prête à crouler sous le poids de péchés imaginaires, ne s'empresse pas de porter des accusations sur elle-même pour qu'Ellen les examine avec son œil de juge ?

20 août 1839.

Plongée dans mes pensées, j'en ai oublié de compter les coups de l'horloge. Il doit être très tard. De mon lit je ne vois plus qu'un rectangle noir. Il me ramène non pas à Anne, l'esseulée qui attend de mes nouvelles, mais à Charlotte. Ainsi fonctionnons-nous. Nous donnons davantage à ceux qui nous envahissent qu'à ceux qui nous aiment assez pour ne songer qu'à notre bonheur.

20 août 1839.

Que va-t-il advenir maintenant que Charlotte a décidé d'abandonner ses héros ? Au lieu de continuer à s'en faire des alliés et des amis, elle a décidé de rompre définitivement avec le duc de Zamorna et ses acolytes. L'étroite complicité qui la liait depuis l'enfance à des personnages sortis de l'enfer vient d'être rompue; la moralité n'y trouvait plus son compte. Elle a décidé de gagner à sa cause d'écrivain une société qu'elle juge pourtant sévèrement. Si Dieu lui prête plume, elle donnera aux sujets de Sa Gracieuse Majesté ce qu'ils attendent: la sagesse des sages, la méchanceté des méchants, la bonté des bons, et la victoire du bien sur le mal. En sera-t-elle capable? J'espère bien que non. Après Southey qui l'a renvoyée aux travaux d'aiguille, elle va s'adresser à Wordsworth. J'espère bien qu'il la traitera avec moins de mépris qu'il n'a traité Branwell.

20 août 1839.

J'entends les oiseaux de nuit chanter derrière le presbytère. J'aime les animaux autant que les êtres. Est-ce normal? Anne et moi nous partageons cette passion de l'humble, du discret.

20 août 1839.

J'aimerais dormir car je sens la fatigue, mais je n'y parviens pas. Trop de pensées défilent dans ma tête. Après Charlotte, c'est au tour de Branwell de me persécuter. Je connais trop peu de sa vie pour aller au-delà d'un soupçon: se droguerait-il au laudanum? Cette crainte a pris naissance en moi un matin tandis que je faisais le ménage dans la chambre de papa. J'ai vu sur la table de nuit son livre *La Médecine familiale* ouvert au chapitre «Tics». Alors qu'en général il note ses impressions dans la marge, ici, comme s'il voulait garder le secret pour lui, papa s'est contenté de souligner discrètement deux mots: laudanum, cocaïne, médicaments, ai-je lu plus loin, destinés à soigner les convulsions. Cette indication m'a donné à réfléchir. Qui sait si à Liverpool Branwell n'a pas pris un médicament dangereux pour une nature faible comme la sienne ?

20 août 1839.

De même que De Quincey qui, après s'en être servi comme remède, en est devenu la victime, qui sait si Branwell n'a pas pris goût à la cocaïne, un bon moyen pour échapper à l'empoignade de la réalité ? La drogue expliquerait son comportement bizarre, ses pleurs, ses engouements subits ; avant-hier pour la beauté de Liverpool, aujourd'hui pour les travaux de Leyland, demain pour le chemin de fer qui va transformer la région ?

20 août 1839.

Je viens d'entendre sonner minuit. Heureusement que papa ne sait pas que je veille si tard ; il se mettrait en colère. A ce sujet, j'ai quelque chose à raconter : la semaine dernière, au moment où il allait nous quitter, Branwell a posé son sac sur une chaise : « Vous ne vous intéressez donc plus à rien ? » a-t-il demandé avec violence et mépris. Papa a retiré ses lunettes : « Que cherches-tu à me faire comprendre, mon garçon, que je suis un vieil imbécile ? » Au lieu de s'expliquer tranquillement, Branwell s'est mis à crier : « Comment pouvez-vous continuer à vivre ainsi ? Vous ne savez donc pas que la vitesse est sur le point de conquérir le monde ? » Vexé de se voir traité de cette façon, papa a tourné le dos à Branwell qui l'a poursuivi : « Quand je pense à l'homme que vous étiez autrefois, j'enrage ! Allez-vous continuer à vivre dans cet immobilisme, alors qu'à quelques kilomètres d'ici, à Todmorden, des hommes posent les rails de la ligne Leeds-Manchester ? »

20 août 1839.

Mon frère s'est fait des amis parmi les ingénieurs et les bateliers qui travaillent à la construction du chemin de fer. Son goût de l'humain le porte aussi bien vers les francs-maçons que vers les gens du bas peuple. Lors de sa dernière visite, il a fait part à papa de ses nouveaux objectifs. Abandonnant une fois pour toutes l'espoir d'être reconnu en tant que peintre par une bande d'imbéciles, il veut s'engager au service de la modernité: «Grâce à mes relations, je compte trouver une place dans les chemins de fer!»

> «*C'est vendredi soir — il est presque neuf heures — temps pluvieux tourmenté. Je suis assise dans la salle à manger.*»

Si je devais raconter certaine scène vécue autrefois, c'est avec des mots comme ceux-là que je le ferais. Je choisirais un jour, un dimanche par exemple, puis je commencerais mon récit par une réplique, celle de papa: «Et tu voudrais que j'applaudisse à ce discours de fou?» Je poursuivrais avec l'intervention de Tante que je montrerais penchée au-dessus de la balustrade: «Eh bien, que se passe-t-il? Vous en faites un vacarme! — Savez-vous ce qu'il a décidé, Elizabeth? Après tous les sacrifices que nous avons consentis pour lui, savez-vous ce qu'il compte faire?» À ce moment, Branwell lèverait la tête: «Tante, demandez à papa de me lâcher! Je vais rater la diligence!»

> «Allons bon... il a déjà terminé sa carrière? Au fond, ça ne m'étonne pas! Lâchez-le! Qu'il aille porter ailleurs son incompétence et sa paresse, et vous, calmez-vous! Aucun être ne vaut qu'on offense Dieu, et vous l'offensez par votre colère!»

J'accompagnerais alors Branwell jusqu'à la diligence : « Je préfère encore crever d'un coup de couteau dans un bouge de Todmorden plutôt que de vivre avec eux ! » Je tenterais de le calmer en posant ma main sur son bras : « Prends soin de toi, Brannii... et n'hésite pas à faire appel à moi ! »

> « Ma pauvre Emily, avant de prendre soin des autres, occupe-toi de toi ! Tu ne vois pas que ces deux vieux sont en train de te détruire ? Tu ne vois donc pas qu'ils te volent ta jeunesse ? »

★

1er septembre 1839.

Papa vient de monter dans sa chambre. Au passage il m'a souhaité une bonne nuit et m'a conseillé d'aller me coucher car il me trouve mauvaise mine. J'aimerais lui obéir, mais je dois répondre à Anne qui compte sur moi pour lui donner des nouvelles de la famille. Que vais-je lui dire ? Que Keeper me tient compagnie. Que Charlotte est à la mer avec Ellen. Que Branwell rêve de devenir employé de la société des chemins de fer. Que papa est bien fatigué. Que le successeur de M. Hodgson, son ancien assistant, doit arriver ces jours-ci ; il s'appelle William Weightman et il est âgé de vingt-cinq ans. Que je m'ennuie d'elle. Que Branwell a raison ; mieux vaut mourir que de vivre ainsi. Non, cela je ne le lui dirai pas.

1er septembre 1839.

Les étoiles brillent au-dessus d'un grand rêve. En contrebas le clocher ressemble à une forteresse. A Gondal, on ferme les portes du palais. Je suis en train de relire un poème que j'ai écrit au mois de juillet dernier.

« *Compassion changed to horror then*
*And fear to meet that gaze again.*
*It was not hatred's tiger-glare,*
*Nor the wild anguish of despair;*
*It was not useless misery*
*Which mocks at friendship's sympathy.*
*No — lightning all unearthly shone*
*Deep in that dark eye's circling zone,*
*Such withering lightning as we deem*
*None but a spectre's look may beam...* »

1er septembre 1839.

De ma fenêtre, je vois les tombes briller sous la lune. Pourquoi Branwell hait-il cette maison ?

*« Alors la compassion se changeait en horreur,*
*En effroi de croiser encore ce regard.*
*Ce n'était point la férocité de la haine,*
*Ni l'angoisse frénétique du désespoir,*
*Ni la détresse en pure perte qui dédaigne*
*La sympathie que lui montrerait l'amitié,*
*Non — dans les profondeurs de cette orbite sombre*
*Flamboyait un éclair rien moins que de ce monde,*
*Un éclair si dévastateur qu'on aurait cru*
*Que nul ne le pouvait lancer qu'un œil de spectre.* »

Emily Jane Brontë,
12 juillet 1839.
(Traduction Pierre Leyris

TOUS les automnes, à un moment ou à un autre, se ressemblent. Celui de cette année déposera sur les bas-côtés de la route les mêmes feuilles que celles qui recouvrirent les sentiers des Moors en l'année 1840. Les arbres se dépouilleront de la même façon, dans l'ordre des tempêtes et avec la collaboration du vent. La pluie éteindra le violet de la bruyère qui tombera en poussière dès les premiers gels. Les oiseaux s'abattront sous les coups de fusil des Heaton et autres chasseurs de la région. Entre Stanbury et Wycoller, le paysage, après s'être enflammé, s'immobilisera au seuil de l'hiver. Cassées en pleine exaltation par les orages, les fougères se prépareront à une lente dégradation. Tout en posant pour l'amateur d'arrière-saison, la nature attendra l'instant où elle cessera de s'émouvoir. En décembre, c'en sera fini. La terre s'inquiétera une dernière fois avant de s'endormir ; aura-t-elle la force de renaître au printemps suivant ?

En cet hiver difficile pour sa santé, Taby se pose la même question : « Quéque chose m'dit qu'c'est la fin pour moi, et j'n'aurai pas l'goût d'm'plaindre d'pas voir l'printemps ! »

« Cessez de dire des sottises, Tabitha !
— J'vas pas m'déposer ici plus longtemps, et l'mieux veut qu'j'aille tenter la mort ailleurs qu'dans c'te maison qu'en a déjà trop vu ! »

Honteuse d'être à la charge d'une famille pauvre, la vieille servante a signifié son départ au révérend qui ne l'a pas retenue ; les chambres sont en nombre insuffisant au presbytère, surtout depuis l'arrivée du nouveau vicaire, William Weightman. A Emily qui se désespérait de son départ, Tabitha a répondu : « C'beau monsieur m'remplacera à l'amiable ! — Pour moi, tu es irremplaçable, Taby ! — Qu'on dit ! — Comment peux-tu mettre en doute mes sentiments ? »

« C'est pas tes sentiments qu'j'mets en doute, petite, c'est ta foi dans c'que tu crois à l'avance ! La fidélité c'est un mot, pas une pratique !
— Ma parole, mais tu me donnes une leçon ?
— D'main t'f'ra savoir que d'plus coriaces qu'toi cèdent d'vant la jeunesse, surtout quand y a d'la séduction dans l'affaire !
— Séduction ? C'est la première fois que je t'entends prononcer ce mot !
— C'est pas l'seul qu'j'aurai r'tenu d'crainte d'être reprise. C'est pas pa'ce qu'j'suis née rustre, qu'j'connais pas certaines choses du cœur ! »

Taby ne s'y est pas trompée. Ce jeune homme, vif et causant de la plus charmante manière, d'emblée a conquis son monde. Pour commencer le pasteur, enfin secondé : « De vieilles habitudes me tenaient lieu d'énergie... il était temps que vous arriviez ! — J'aimerais pouvoir vous aider davantage ! — Patientez, mon cher ! Cela viendra plus vite que vous ne le pensez ! » Depuis le mois d'août 1839, date de l'arrivée de William Weightman, le révérend remercie Dieu de l'avoir soulagé d'un surcroît d'obligations. La gentillesse du jeune homme est si grande que pour un peu son supérieur l'ajouterait à la liste de sa progéniture. Ses enfants prendraient-ils ombrage d'une telle adoption ? Non. La famille a voté à l'unanimité pour le nouveau venu. Charlotte, la critique, Anne, Emily ont fait savoir à leur père combien elles appréciaient cette présence masculine : « Il distribue trop facilement ses sourires et ses faveurs, mais sa générosité est réelle, et il vous sera d'un grand secours ! » Quant à Branwell, dès qu'il a aperçu le vicaire, il a versé dans l'enthousiasme : « Enfin, je vais pouvoir dialoguer avec un Alexander Percy en chair et en os ! Avez-vous remarqué, mesdemoiselles, combien ce beau blond est élégant ? Voilà un galant auquel les femmes ne doivent pas savoir résister ! » Cette démonstration verbale à peine terminée, Branwell est allé présenter sa sympathie au vicaire :

> « Ah çà, mon cher William... vous permettez que je vous appelle William ? Vous ne pouviez mieux tomber ! Cette maison et ses occupants vous attendaient depuis des années ! C'est bien simple, la mort elle-même a fini par admettre son inefficacité, et je n'ai jamais trouvé si bonne allure à ces tombes que depuis que je les regarde avec vous ! »

Dans le cimetière, les jeunes gens vont et viennent ; ils discutent de religion ou de philosophie sous l'œil bienveillant de Tante et de papa : « Depuis la venue de M. Weightman, ces enfants ont rajeuni ! — Ils en avaient grandement besoin, et pour ne rien vous cacher, Patrick, moi aussi ! » De sa fenêtre, Miss Branwell surveille le manège de l'assistant dont elle aime les manières raffinées, les éclats de rire superbes, le langage châtié, la douceur : « Rien n'est plus émouvant pour une femme qu'un homme qui se permet le luxe de lui emprunter un peu de sa féminité ! » Elle le voit se retourner, tendre la main à la jeune fille qui le suit : « Pour un peu, le bougre lui prendrait la taille ! » Tantôt, c'est Charlotte à la voix toujours décidée, tantôt c'est Emily la silencieuse, l'attentive, la méfiante aussi, tantôt c'est Ellen ou Mary, car les amies de Charlotte continuent à venir rendre visite à la famille Brontë. Quant à Anne, maintenue à l'écart par ce sentiment qu'elle a d'être de trop, on ne l'a guère vue aux côtés du vicaire ; et pour cause ! la pauvre enfant a presque toujours été absente : « A peine es-tu de retour que tu songes déjà à repartir ! »

> « Je ne veux pas rester sur un échec ! Ce renvoi est injuste ! »

★

Après huit mois de bons et loyaux services, Anne s'est vue remerciée sans autre forme de politesse par Mme Ingham : « Les violences que vous avez fait subir à mes enfants sont inacceptables ! — Mais, madame, il le fallait bien ! Cunliffe me griffe et me frappe, et Mary me crache dessus... Depuis que je suis ici, je n'ai pas pu prendre un seul repas en paix ! — Vous n'aviez qu'à les convaincre d'être sages ! Il y a en vous trop de minceur pour en imposer à des enfants. Dès que je vous ai vue descendre de la calèche, je l'ai su ; vous aviez l'air misérable. J'aurais dû vous remercier sur-le-champ ! Au lieu de cela j'ai perdu une année d'éducation pour mes enfants ! » Certain jour où elle est entrée sans prévenir dans la chambre de la gouvernante, Mme Ingham n'a-t-elle pas trouvé ses chers petits attachés aux pieds d'une lourde table ?

« Je ne pouvais vraiment pas faire autrement !
— Mais ne te justifie pas, Anne ! Tu as bien fait ! »

A son retour, la famille s'est inquiétée : pourquoi Anne a-t-elle accepté sans se plaindre de semblables traitements ? Parce qu'elle n'était pas certaine d'avoir raison, a-t-elle répondu sur un ton d'enfant coupable ; Mme Ingham l'a longtemps persuadée que son fils était un génie et qu'elle était une incapable. Il a fallu beaucoup de tendresse et de patience à Emily pour ramener sa sœur à la confiance. Le résultat est encore modeste ; plutôt que d'offrir sa tristesse, Anne, en attendant de repartir dans une autre famille où elle espère être mieux traitée, préfère la compagnie de Tante à celle de ses sœurs. Les prières faites en commun la rassurent à peine :

« Mais non, ma chère enfant, tu ne leur as pas fait de mal, au contraire, tu as tenté de les éduquer ! »

★

En fin de journée, l'appel pressant des autres l'invite à rejoindre la salle à manger où l'on joue aux cartes. Entre deux parties, on se jauge, on s'adresse des compliments, on s'envoie des reproches : « Pourquoi avoir joué votre dix de carreau ? » L'ironie s'exprime par la bouche d'Emily, la passion par celle de Charlotte, les regrets par celle d'Anne. William Weightman se prête aux tortures de l'inquisition. Ces demoiselles le prient d'avouer un intérêt auquel elles ne souhaitent même pas qu'il donne un nom. « Aimez-nous ! » convient mieux ici qu'« Aimez-moi ! ».

« Et voilà pour votre dame de pique ! »

Anne rougit en ramassant les cartes ; pourquoi le vicaire se tourne-t-il constamment vers elle ? Elle se refuse à croire qu'on lui trouve du charme : « Aurais-tu l'as, par hasard ? » La question qu'elle pose à Charlotte ne dit rien d'autre que : « Ne me troublez pas avec votre regard, monsieur Weightman ! Je connais trop votre goût du flirt et de la conquête pour ne pas me méfier de vous ! » Au presbytère tout le monde s'attarde sur les faiblesses du vicaire.

« Dans sa dernière lettre, Ellen me parle encore de vous !

— C'est très aimable à elle, et j'en suis fort touché ! Comment va-t-elle ?

— Bien. J'imagine que vous êtes également touché par la présence de cette fille de Stanbury qui vient chaque dimanche se recueillir à vos pieds ?

— Je ne vois pas de qui vous voulez parler !

— Pas plus que vous ne voyez qui est cette petite brunette qui fait dix milles dans l'espoir de vous croiser à la sortie de l'office ? »

Emily, qui reproche au vicaire sa versatilité, a surnommé le joli cœur « *Miss Celia Amelia* ». De son côté, William Weightman ne s'adresse plus à elle qu'en l'appelant « *Sa Seigneurie* » ou « *Mon commandant* ».

« Pourquoi es-tu si sévère avec lui ?

— Parce qu'il est dangereux pour qui aurait la naïveté de le prendre au sérieux ! Ma sévérité, comme tu dis, ne m'empêche pas de l'aimer beaucoup. »

Charlotte, pour qui il a accepté de poser en toge, lui trouve — en tant que peintre — des excuses qui s'évanouissent à l'instant où elle prend la plume. « Mon Dieu comme cet homme est ennuyeux avec ses manières de coquet ! » A peine exprimé, ce reproche se transforme en conseil, car il ne fait plus de doute qu'au château des Nussey quelqu'un a un faible pour lui. « Il a pour vous, ma chère Ellen, des sentiments si vastes qu'il ne peut que les partager avec quatre ou cinq autres, et ce serait grand dommage de souffrir d'avances égrenées aux quatre vents. Vous me rétorquerez que, malgré sa légèreté, *Celia Amelia* a des gestes inattendus et touchants ; le bouquet pour Tante, la carte d'anniversaire pour Anne, la bouteille de vin français pour papa. C'est exact, mais n'oubliez pas, ma belle, avant de tomber amoureuse de ce vaniteux, qu'il a laissé une fiancée à Westmoreland ! »

★

Dès son retour de Broughton-in-Furness où il a vécu six mois — « Déjà ! — Comment déjà ? Je n'allais pas m'attarder indéfiniment chez ce brave M. Postlethwaite ; le rôle de précepteur est trop limité pour me satisfaire ! » —, Branwell, inspiré par la présence de William, et surtout par ses nombreuses conquêtes, s'est engouffré dans un nouvel épisode de son épopée romanesque. Mais alors que jusqu'ici il ne savait se dire qu'à travers des personnages masculins, en cette saison où un jeune homme s'applique à lui montrer les mécanismes de la séduction, il ne se sent véritablement à l'aise que sous l'habit des femmes dont il imagine la fièvre et les turbulences de l'âme. Les sentiments qui l'attachent au vicaire sont si vifs que pour plaire davantage il a pris de bonnes résolutions :

« Je ne boirai plus !

— En êtes-vous certain ?

— Absolument ! Jamais présence ne m'a autant fortifié que la vôtre. J'avais besoin d'un autre homme à mes côtés ! Trop de femmes nuisaient à mon équilibre ! »

Si au presbytère on s'empresse de croire à cette promesse, au Black Bull on s'en moque : « Se fatiguera plus vite de la vertu que nous du vice ! » John Brown lui-même, le Vénérable grand maître de la loge des Trois-Grâces, ne désespère pas de voir son ami réapparaître un soir de cafard. En attendant, le repenti s'attache aux pas d'un freluquet vaguement érudit qu'il assomme de ses discours de poète incompris de tous, sauf de Hartley Coleridge qui l'a accueilli fraternellement au début de l'année, quand il était en fonction dans le Cumberland : « Il s'est intéressé à mon travail... si vous saviez, William, le bonheur que j'en ai éprouvé ! C'était la première fois que quelqu'un se penchait sur ces pages ! Au fait, accepteriez-vous de lire ma traduction des *Odes* d'Horace ? »

L'aimable vicaire ne sait pas refuser un service. Il lit d'un œil, écoute d'une oreille. Là-haut, Charlotte est en train de confier son désappointement à ses sœurs ; elle n'a reçu aucune réponse aux annonces passées dans les gazettes de la région : « Je ne puis avoir raisonnablement d'autres ambitions ! Il faut absolument que je trouve un poste de gouvernante ! » Anne tente d'intervenir : « Tu n'as pas à t'inquiéter dans l'immédiat ; c'est moi qui vais repartir ! » L'autre crie : « C'est à moi de m'engager et pas à toi ! surtout après ce qui s'est passé à Blake Hall ! » Ce petit pas rageur ne peut appartenir qu'à Charlotte. William l'entend aller et venir. Il l'imagine pâle et bien droite, avec ce profil buté et intransigeant qu'elle a parfois. Dans la vitre où monte l'ombre du soir, sa silhouette passe et repasse : « Sait-elle qu'elle est en train de se faner au fil d'une existence stérile ? » Un éclat désabusé dégringole l'escalier : « La vie nous échappe et nous sommes là à l'attendre sans bouger ! » La voix d'Anne fait écho : « Je n'ai que vingt ans, et je me sens déjà vieille. Il me semble que jamais rien d'heureux ne surviendra dans ma vie. Tout ce que je souhaite, c'est que nous restions en bonne santé pour aider Tante et papa ! »

« Vous aimez mes sœurs, n'est-ce pas, William ?
— Sans doute... je les estime. »

Le jeune curate souhaiterait apporter son aide aux trois filles du pasteur, mais leurs exigences sont si grandes, leurs critiques si aiguës, qu'il ne peut, sous peine de se remettre lui-même en question, que leur offrir son amitié : « Et moi, m'estimez-vous aussi ? » Surpris, William porte sur le frère un regard plus paternel qu'amical :

« Bien sûr... Je regrette simplement que vous ne soyez pas plus courageux, pas plus entreprenant. Il n'y a aucune raison pour que ce soit vos sœurs qui travaillent à votre place ! »

★

L'hiver est à nouveau là. L'obscurité se glisse dans le vide laissé par les jours qui raccourcissent. Emily a repris ses promenades et Charlotte continue à se morfondre entre deux crises de folle gaieté dont personne, même pas elle, ne connaît la raison. « Peut-être suis-je en train de devenir folle ? » Jamais son humeur n'a été aussi changeante. Chaque jour, elle écrit à la fidèle Ellen qui s'empresse de répondre avec la même régularité.

Dans sa lettre d'avant-hier, Charlotte a raconté comment Branwell avait trouvé un nouveau poste...

> ... le croirez-vous, chère Ellen, l'art ne l'intéresse plus ! C'est le machinisme qui l'enthousiasme ! La promesse d'un bel avenir lui a été faite par la compagnie des chemins de fer. A défaut de monnayer son talent, le voilà qui vend des billets dans une gare. Pour combien de temps ? Dieu seul le sait. Avec un caractère comme le sien, on ne sait pas s'il est parti pour deux jours ou pour deux ans. Des nouvelles arrivent de droite et de gauche que nous taisons à papa. A ce qu'on raconte, Branwell promène son éloquence de taverne en taverne. Ses connaissances littéraires, sa faconde enchantent un auditoire de choix ; débardeurs, bateliers, conducteurs de locomotives. La célébrité qui n'a pas voulu de lui à l'étage des poètes lui ouvre les bras à l'entresol des ivrognes. Le succès ne l'a pas rendu ingrat. Quand il a fini de boire avec ceux-là, il va s'enivrer à Halifax avec Leyland et sa clique. L'autre homme de la maison — j'exclus de cette liste papa — a passé brillamment ses examens de théologie. Cet hommage rendu à son travail et à ses connaissances n'a pas apaisé le séducteur ; William traîne toujours derrière lui quelques jolies figures qui ne désespèrent pas de le conquérir. Je vous embrasse, très chère, avant de fondre en larmes, tant me semble interminable l'hiver !

*« Je vois autour de moi de grises pierres tombales,*
*Chacune profile une ombre pâle.*

*Sous mon pas sans bruit le gazon se creuse*
*Et la terre cache, silencieuse,*
*Les gisants perdus dessous ce gazon ;*
*Le noir et le froid seuls sont leur maison.*
*Laissons désormais couler tous ces pleurs*
*Que le souvenir des années anciennes*
*Pouvait retenir en sa coupe en fleur... »*

Emily Jane BRONTË.
(Traduction Françoise d'Eaubonne.)

Depuis cet instant où vous avez traversé le cimetière de Haworth, vous prêtez à des morts — aujourd'hui à William Weightman, l'ancien vicaire de notre père — une mémoire, des émois, un visage, des sentiments. Les scènes que vous retracez ne sont ni justes ni fausses, mais justes et fausses à la fois. Il y a du vrai dans ces promenades à plusieurs ou à deux, dans ces flirts à peine ébauchés, dans ces jeux de cartes. Il y a également du vrai dans vos portraits : Charlotte, pointue et violente à ses heures, Anne, blessée par un monde injuste et sans pitié, Branwell, ravi d'avoir trouvé un ami sincère. Où se situe donc le faux ? Dans le manque de subtilité. Il faudrait une encre de meilleure qualité pour recréer l'ambiance des journées noyées sous la pluie ou immobilisées par le brouillard, un autre pinceau pour évoquer la couleur d'un automne trop vite incendié et trop vite éteint, la blancheur d'un hiver paralysé par le gel.

Plus de rigueur et moins d'emportement conviendraient mieux à un paysage grandiose mais austère, à une nature sauvage mais dépourvue d'angles et de précipices, à un chemin maintes fois parcouru. C'est là, sur cette lande, au cœur de ces Moors que j'appris à me taire pour entendre bien, à ne plus condamner pour comprendre et pardonner. C'est encore là, à l'heure des grandioses couchers de soleil, que j'ai reçu la promesse d'une éternité heureuse.

« Ta patience est exaspérante !
— Tu voudrais me voir me révolter ?
— Oui !
— Contre quoi, Charlotte ?
— Contre tout ce qui nous oppresse... contre ce pays, cet enfermement, ces gens incultes ! N'attends-tu donc rien de la vie ?
— Elle me donne ce qu'elle peut ! »

Ces états extrêmes, ces tensions, ces bondissements intérieurs aidèrent Charlotte à rompre avec l'adolescence et ses chimères ; ils brisèrent Branwell qui n'en eut jamais la maîtrise.

« C'est-à-dire rien !
— Pour toi peut-être, pas pour moi ! »

Au lieu d'accompagner mes aînés sur le chemin de la révolte, la sagesse me conseilla de m'en remettre pour toujours à un pays. De lui, d'une maison, d'un cimetière reconnu chaque matin derrière une fenêtre, d'une tour, d'un clocher, d'une perspective, je reçus le droit de vivre sans nourrir de vaines espérances. Alors qu'enfant je désespérais de voir s'évanouir l'été, j'accueillis jeune fille toutes les saisons avec une égalité d'humeur qui étonna mon entourage. Les orages et les tempêtes, après m'avoir effrayée, me devinrent aussi nécessaires que le calme des belles journées ; leur violence apaisait la mienne.

Un jour de promenade, alors que j'observais la nature autour de moi, le jeu de l'ombre et de la lumière me renvoya à celui du bien et du mal. Où se disait l'un, où se déclarait l'autre ? Qui connaissait les règles de ce jeu-là ? Dès lors, je me méfiai des gens vertueux, de leurs bontés, de leurs services. Comme la mère qui protège l'enfant disgracié, je me rapprochai du mal auquel je trouvai des excuses et une utilité ; celle de mettre en valeur le bien. Il m'arriva même de le préférer au bien ou à ce qu'on me présentait comme tel. Le sentier qui menait à ma vérité n'était pas droit, et ce n'était pas dans les livres de théologie de mon père que je trouverais la réponse aux questions qui se posaient en moi. Je ne pouvais me fier qu'à ma bonne volonté et à mes réflexions.

« A quoi songez-vous, Elizabeth ?
— A Emily !
— Heureusement qu'elle se plaît ici ! Sans elle, que deviendrions-nous ?
— Des vieillards grincheux et mal entretenus !
— Cette petite ne sait que faire pour m'être agréable, et pourtant je ne l'ai jamais sentie aussi lointaine, aussi distante !
— Elle l'a toujours été.
— J'ai le sentiment de ne plus exister pour elle ! »

Durant ces années où je me retrouvai — maintenant que mon frère et mes sœurs n'étaient plus là — seule fille au presbytère entre Tante, papa et William Weightman gêné par ma personne qu'il jugeait probablement trop austère, je fis l'inventaire de ce qui me séparait des autres et de leurs convictions. Je profitai du peu d'empressement du charmant vicaire pour m'adonner à nouveau à la poésie. Ces aveux plus ou moins déguisés n'étaient destinés qu'à moi, et s'il voulait bien les entendre, à un Dieu plus compatissant que celui dont l'Église anglicane m'avait montré les traits courroucés. Je crois que c'est à cette époque que commença à se dérouler en moi une sorte de rêverie peuplée d'images fulgurantes, d'interrogations ouvertes sur l'infini, de visions d'effroi. Je ne la confiai à personne, ni à Charlotte employée comme gouvernante chez les White, des nouveaux riches tapageurs qui l'exhibaient comme un objet de luxe exposé à l'envie des voisins, ni à Anne exilée à Thorp Green chez M. et Mme Robinson où elle devait demeurer jusqu'en 1845...

> Emily, sœur très chère,
> J'ai retrouvé ici la solitude, notre lot à tous, mais aussi une plus grande compréhension que chez les Ingham dont je mesure après coup la méchanceté à mon endroit. Les lieux ne sont beaux que parce qu'ils sont peuplés d'arbres ; immenses, à l'égal du temps qui ne se lasse de rien, même pas de nous voir nous débattre, ils entourent la propriété qui est vaste. Les maîtres ressemblent aux hectares qui s'étendent devant le château ; un peu plats et d'humeur égale. M. Robinson est un homme très riche, mais sans forfanterie. Il m'ignore avec courtoisie et ne s'adresse à moi qu'en cas de nécessité. Son épouse est plus loquace que lui. Elle est belle et s'intéresse surtout aux frivolités vestimentaires. Le couple s'ennuie dans l'intimité, aussi y a-t-il souvent des invités. Quant aux petites demoiselles, elles sont ravissantes et irritables. J'ai un peu de temps. Je l'emploie à écrire mon roman, *Solala Vernon's Life*, dont j'aimerais te lire quelques pages ; malheureusement, il y a fort à parier que cette joie ne me sera pas donnée avant longtemps.

J'aurais probablement vécu ainsi jusqu'à la fin de mon existence, me satisfaisant d'une lettre, d'une pensée chaleureuse, si Charlotte, pour fuir les humiliations auxquelles elle était à nouveau exposée, n'avait pas eu l'idée de créer un pensionnat. Le projet me sembla peu raisonnable ; de plus il mettait un terme à ma tranquillité. Pourtant, je l'approuvai ; mes sœurs ne pouvaient continuer à se sacrifier pour mon confort.

★

« Emily ! Où es-tu ?

— Je suis dans la cuisine, Tante !

— Veux-tu monter un instant ? Je viens de recevoir une lettre de Branwell qui me préoccupe. »

Nous en étions là de ce projet, lorsque Branwell fut nommé chef de gare, non pas comme il l'avait espéré dans une de ces grandes villes remuantes, toile de fond pour des exploits scandaleux et des rêves de grandeur, mais à Luddenden Foot, une bourgade perdue et triste, sans autre horizon que le flanc assombri des montagnes et une rivière paresseuse, la Calder. Cette nomination qui n'avait rien de flatteur fut mal accueillie. Non seulement elle ne rehaussait pas son prestige, mais elle l'éloignait d'un commerce amical dont il avait besoin autant que de sa famille. Perdu dans cette gare où ne passaient que de pauvres ouvriers irlandais, quelques représentants de commerce essoufflés et une poignée de voyageurs sans coloration précise, Branwell perdit la foi en lui-même.

Ma chère Tante,

L'aurais-je cherché, je n'aurais pas trouvé mieux ; voici enfin le lieu idéal pour y creuser ma tombe. Moi qui croyais avoir vécu dans

> l'endroit le plus triste du monde, je m'aperçois qu'il y a pire. Luddenden Foot, où je viens d'être nommé chef de gare, ressemble à ces villages de montagne isolés et pauvres où l'on ne rencontre que des êtres apathiques et terreux, des familles misérables qui comptent chacune plusieurs suicidés, par pendaison, en général. Je me suis laissé dire qu'il tombait deux fois plus d'eau ici, dans la vallée, que sur les plateaux, ce qui m'amène à compter trois cents jours de pluie par an. Comment résister à un tel déluge? Seul Noé pourrait me répondre.

Je reçus à mon tour une lettre dans laquelle Branwell m'avouait sa défaite. Pris de panique à la perspective de se retrouver seul dans un endroit aussi sinistre, il s'était mis à la recherche de nouveaux amis. Un bringueur dénommé Francis Grundy, ingénieur des chemins de fer, d'autres bâtis sur le même modèle, devinrent ses partenaires.

> ... pour l'instant je n'ai trouvé de sortie de secours que du côté des tavernes. La boisson me donne des joies de courte durée suivies de longs maux de tête. Mais ceci importe peu. Je suis prêt à tout pour quelques minutes d'oubli!

Mon frère trouva chez ces êtres une amitié sincère mais nuisible à sa santé. La gare étant trop exiguë pour qu'il y passât plus de quelques heures par jour, il confia ses scrupules et ses devoirs de chef de gare à un employé qui vendait les billets.

> ... que veux-tu, ma chère, le temps n'est plus où je pouvais contempler mon image et lui

décerner des médailles. Je préfère me moquer de mes espoirs plutôt que de remuer leurs cendres !

Tôt dans l'après-midi, le chef de gare filait discrètement par la porte de derrière. A peine avait-il fait quelques pas qu'il rencontrait le long du canal une âme en peine. Il l'invitait à venir étancher sa soif dans la taverne la plus proche. « Pourquoi un gars aussi brillant que toi croupit-il dans un trou pareil ? » demandait l'invité ébloui par la verve de son hôte.

« Si j'accepte de vivre ici, c'est parce que j'y vois mon intérêt. En réalité, je ne suis pas chef de gare, mais écrivain. Je suis en train de terminer un roman !

— Ton chef-d'œuvre, tu pourrais l'écrire ailleurs !

— Pourquoi changer de décor ? Celui-là en vaut un autre ! Mais ceci serait trop long à t'expliquer ! En un mot, je méprise la réalité, et non seulement je la méprise, mais je ne la vois pas !

— Méfie-toi, mon gars... c'est comme ça qu'on devient aveugle ! »

Mon frère crut-il jamais à ses vantardises ? Si j'en crois le portrait qu'il fit de lui-même, sûrement pas.

*... son maigre visage au long nez, constellé de taches de rousseur, et surmonté d'une épaisse toison rousse, était sans cesse agité de tics et de mouvements nerveux. Au lieu de regarder son interlocuteur en face, il détournait les yeux, des yeux encore agrandis par d'épaisses lunettes et lorsqu'il parvenait enfin à balbu-*

*tier quelques mots, il les noyait aussitôt dans un torrent de paroles incohérentes.*

En fin de semaine, le bavard venait rendre visite à papa et à Tante ; il nous arrachait à la mollesse du dimanche. Nous écoutions ses récits, buvions ses paroles. « Et alors, que se passe-t-il là-bas, mon fils ? Es-tu toujours aussi enthousiaste ? »

> « La machine à vapeur va changer le monde ! Personne ne s'y reconnaîtra plus ! Il n'y a qu'ici que les choses refusent de bouger ! »

Ce que nous ignorâmes toujours, c'est qu'au moment de monter dans la diligence qui le ramenait sur les lieux de son exil, Branwell s'effondrait : « Comment puis-je tromper de la sorte des êtres qui m'aiment et me font confiance ? » se demandait-il honteux de sa performance hypocrite. Des larmes coulaient sous ses lunettes ; elles lavaient sa mauvaise conscience : « Je ne vais tout de même pas me culpabiliser pour si peu ? Si mes mensonges font leur bonheur, pourquoi les en priverais-je ? » Aussitôt rendu à destination, il allait noyer ses regrets dans un de ces lieux où l'on savait le recevoir. Dès qu'ils le voyaient apparaître sur la route, échevelé, nerveux, ses admirateurs poussaient des cris : « Alors... comment va le pasteur ? Est-il toujours parent du Christ ? » Branwell racontait sa journée ; il se moquait de nous, les crédules. Entre deux verres, le remords le rattrapait. Il sortait sa fiole de laudanum, en avalait une gorgée. Parfois une crise de convulsions le jetait à terre. A peine calmé, il se remettait à boire pour montrer qu'il était plus fort que le mal. Le petit matin déposait une peau livide sur son visage d'ivrogne. Douloureux, titubant, il finissait par rentrer chez lui. A peine avait-il pénétré dans sa chambre qu'il s'affalait sur son lit. Quelques heures plus tard, la migraine ou un cauchemar le réveillait. Il gémissait pendant des heures tout en écoutant tomber la pluie, calme et régulière. Sur le coup de midi, la voix du facteur montait jusqu'à lui. « M. Brontë est-il là ? J'ai une lettre pour lui ! » Sa joie était si grande qu'il en oubliait la nausée. Il descendait en courant les escaliers : « De qui ? » criait-il en traversant la salle d'attente : « De qui ? » Hélas ! elle n'était ni de Coleridge qui n'avait jamais accusé réception de sa version des *Odes* d'Horace, ni du rédacteur en chef du *Blackwood's Magazine*. Postée à Upperwood House où demeuraient les White, elle venait de Charlotte.

> Cher Branwell,
> J'ai une grande nouvelle à t'apprendre qui va sûrement t'étonner...

Ma sœur lui annonçait que Tante venait d'accepter de financer ses études et les miennes, car je l'accompagnerais en Belgique. Pour Charlotte qui ambitionnait d'ouvrir une école, la connaissance de l'allemand et du français était indispensable. Quant à Anne, la famille la dédommagerait plus tard de ce qu'elle ne pouvait lui donner aujourd'hui. « Ça, pour une nouvelle, c'est une nouvelle ! » C'en était donc fini de la complicité des enfants Brontë ; nous n'avions plus besoin de lui.

« Moi aussi, j'aurais aimé aller faire des études à l'étranger ! »

« *Derrière elle étaient deux rangées de Flamandes vulgaires, parmi lesquelles se faisaient remarquer deux ou trois exemples de cette difformité physique et morale que l'on rencontre si fréquemment en Belgique et en Hollande, et qui semble prouver que le climat y est assez insalubre pour amener la dégénérescence de l'esprit et du corps.* »

Charlotte Brontë, *Le Professeur.*
(Traduction Henriette Loreau.)

AVANT de me rendre à Bruxelles, rue d'Isabelle où Mme Héger dirigeait un pensionnat pour jeunes filles, j'ai lu le premier roman de Charlotte Brontë, *The Professor*, une œuvre glaciale comme un courant d'air, cruelle et étonnamment rancunière. Accompagnée de personnages pour la plupart entêtés et méchants — le talent de Charlotte n'est jamais aussi percutant que lorsqu'elle assassine —, j'ai traversé des lieux qui n'existent plus depuis longtemps, à savoir la maison et le jardin où vécurent les deux sœurs Brontë. Il y avait là une famille composée d'un couple et de plusieurs enfants en bas âge, trois ou quatre professeurs et un groupe de pensionnaires... «... *assemblage de créatures vulgaires, insignifiantes, mal tournées et stupides, vicieuses et répulsives...*» Rien de moins ! Heureusement que Charlotte était myope ! Qu'aurait-elle écrit si elle avait eu bonne vue ?

«Maintenant que nous nous connaissons mieux, mesdemoiselles, j'aimerais vous poser une question. Qu'êtes-vous venues chercher à Bruxelles ?
— Des connaissances.
— Bigre ! En quoi ?
— En français plus particulièrement ! Ma sœur Emily et moi, nous souhaitons ouvrir un pensionnat !»

Ce que Charlotte ne dit pas à Mme Héger assise

en face d'elle sur un sofa, c'est que ce goût pour la culture française, elle le doit à la famille Taylor. Joshua, le père de Mary et de Martha, n'a jamais cessé de lorgner du côté de la France qu'il qualifie d'attrayante. Le filateur est fasciné par la superficialité et l'immoralité des Français. « Je suis certain, Charlotte, que les Parisiens vous séduiraient ! — J'en doute, monsieur ! — Tiens donc, et pourquoi ? — Ce que j'en connais me suffit ; ce sont des gens indiscrets et vaniteux, et les préceptes de l'Église romaine ne les ramèneront certainement pas à plus de tenue ! — Seriez-vous intolérante, jeune personne ? — Si c'est être intolérante que de voir dans l'impudicité un odieux défaut, alors je suis intolérante ! — Comment savez-vous que les Français sont impudiques ? En avez-vous déjà rencontré ? — Non, mais mon père m'a toujours recommandé de me méfier des papistes ! »

Dès qu'il a su que Charlotte s'intéressait aux belles-lettres, Joshua Taylor lui a fait envoyer un colis de romans français. Ils ont été reçus au presbytère avec circonspection. Papa, qui ne connaît pas la langue, s'est contenté de jeter un coup d'œil critique sur la typographie. Tante les a soupesés avec inquiétude : « L'immoralité pèse lourd dans ce pays ! » Emily les a feuilletés. Seule Charlotte a tenté de les lire : « Mes connaissances sont vraiment insuffisantes ! » Malgré tout, ce survol lui a permis d'y sentir les relents d'une sensibilité dépravée.

★

« Mesdemoiselles, qui parmi vous a déjà lu les œuvres de George Sand, d'Eugène Sue, de Paul de Kock ? Personne ? Tant pis. Nous laisserons de côté ces auteurs populaires au profit d'autres plus difficiles. Ce semestre, nous étudierons Victor Hugo, Chateaubriand, Bossuet. »

Sous la férule de M. Héger, le mari de la directrice, Charlotte et Emily étudient les grands auteurs français. L'enthousiasme, l'irritabilité, l'impatience du professeur de lettres choquent les deux Anglaises habituées à plus de retenue. Emily, qui a eu la faiblesse de céder aux instances de sa sœur en venant à Bruxelles, se voit contrainte d'obéir à un maître dont elle n'apprécie pas les façons ; et c'est faire bien peu de cas de la personnalité de l'élève que de lui demander de parodier l'auteur étudié : « Il me semble, monsieur, que chacun devrait écrire les choses à sa façon ! »

« Voyez-vous ça !

— Victor Hugo ne m'inspire pas ! Je ne me reconnais pas plus en lui que je ne me reconnais en d'autres !

— La langue, pour être bien maniée, demande une discipline que vous devez vous imposer ! »

Emily, bien qu'elle ait la parole difficile, a décidé de ne pas s'en laisser remontrer ; jamais elle n'empruntera rien à personne, et c'est déjà bien assez d'avoir délaissé sa propre langue !

« J'ai bien aimé votre devoir de français, "Le palais de la mort". Vos thèmes ne sont pas faciles, mais vous ne l'êtes pas plus qu'eux. Ce que vous refusez de comprendre, c'est que l'autre a peut-être quelque chose à vous donner, et d'abord sa langue. La pensée n'existe que parce qu'il y a des mots pour l'énoncer. Plus votre vocabulaire sera riche, plus votre pensée s'épanouira. Plus tard, lorsque vous voudrez la formuler mieux, vous irez emprunter à l'allemand ou au français des mots que vous ne trouverez pas dans votre langue ! »

M. Héger qui n'aime rien tant que mater qui lui résiste, apprécie infiniment plus Emily que sa sœur. Il estime son courage et cette sorte de détermination qu'ont parfois les femmes qui refusent aux hommes le droit de les influencer.

« Votre sœur, mademoiselle Charlotte, aurait intérêt à se servir davantage de son esprit d'analyse. C'est sa plus grande qualité. »

Tandis que Charlotte plie devant un homme qui la fascine, la trouble et l'interroge jusque dans ses rêves, tandis qu'elle erre à la frontière du désir, Emily ne songe qu'à rentrer au pays. Indifférente à l'opinion que l'on a d'elle, elle étudie sans passion, récite sans voix, écoute sans plaisir. Autant l'aînée recherche l'approbation, autant la plus jeune refuse les compliments qui l'agacent.

« Pourquoi es-tu si dure avec M. Héger ? Il n'a pour toi que des bontés et des attentions ! Beaucoup d'élèves t'envient !

— J'espère que tu ne fais pas partie du nombre ! M. Héger est un homme intelligent, brillant, mais versatile. Je n'aime pas ces êtres qui passent de la violence à la douceur sans raison. Ce sont des amuseurs ; ils jouent avec la sensibilité des autres ! »

Malgré ces différences de point de vue, jamais les deux sœurs ne se sont senties aussi proches que dans ce milieu étranger. D'emblée, elles l'ont jugé hostile, vindicatif, alors qu'il n'était qu'ironique.

La tenue démodée des filles Brontë, leur maintien trop strict, leurs manières guindées ont attiré la moquerie des coquettes qui se préparent à un mariage honorable. « Dieu, que ces Anglaises sont ridicules et pédantes ! Elles ont la raideur des oies et la méchanceté des corbeaux ! » Mais là où Charlotte s'indigne de se voir rejetée, Emily, elle, ne semble nullement affectée.

« Fais comme moi, ignore-les ! »

Heureusement, la ville où naquit Charles Quint offre aux deux exilées la splendeur de ses maisons bourgeoises et le mystère de ses cours intérieures. Lorsqu'elles sont par trop excédées par les cloches de Sainte-Gudule qui sonnent les offices catholiques, Charlotte et Emily quittent la pension. Elles se promènent le long des avenues, admirent les façades entretenues comme des jolies femmes, longent les jardins qui protègent de l'indiscrétion les villas des notables, s'enfoncent dans les rues de plus en plus sombres, de plus en plus étroites, jusqu'à la vieille place gardée par les anciens palais.

Tout en se plaignant de la répétitrice de français ou des difficultés de la langue, elles s'arrêtent devant les vitrines où sont exposés des chapeaux ridicules copiés sur des modèles parisiens, évitent celles où s'étalent les victuailles destinées à ce qu'elles appellent, dans leur ascétisme anglican, la voracité flamande, tombent en arrêt devant des brassées de fleurs, jettent un coup d'œil fureteur à l'intérieur d'une taverne dont la porte est restée ouverte, y devinent une silhouette affalée qui leur rappelle Branwell.

Ramenées malgré elles à Luddenden Foot que leur frère, d'après ce qu'a écrit Tante, a dû quitter en catastrophe, elles songent à la tristesse que doit ressentir leur père devant les indélicatesses de Branwell. A la suite de la visite du vérificateur des comptes, la compagnie des chemins de fer a congédié le chef de gare qui oubliait de tenir ses comptes à jour.

> ... vous décrire la réaction de votre père me demanderait un talent que je n'ai pas. La scène a viré au drame. J'ai cru, un moment, qu'il allait frapper Branwell !

Les larmes du fils, son repentir, n'ont pas eu le pouvoir de faire oublier au père l'affront fait à son nom : « Sors de mon bureau, voleur ! »

> ... si je vous disais, mes chères petites, que les deux hommes ne se saluent même plus. Lorsque l'un s'avance dans une pièce, l'autre se retire. Ce manège est puéril. J'ai tenté de les réconcilier, peine perdue. L'ambiance est à la rancune de part et d'autre. Heureusement que William Weightman revient après-demain. Sa présence souriante, sa cordialité détendront l'atmosphère. Je compte sur lui pour remettre un peu de plomb dans la tête mal accrochée de Branwell. Votre chère Taby est venue aux nouvelles : elle s'inquiète de vous savoir au loin et se plaint de ne plus vivre parmi nous. Je me demande s'il ne faudra pas la reprendre un jour ou l'autre ; enfin, nous aviserons ! Ah oui, j'oubliais le principal ! Keeper est insupportable ! Je dis bien, insupportable ! Jamais je n'ai vu un chien se tenir aussi mal. Même Martha Brown n'en arrive plus à bout ! Quel besoin Emily avait-elle de ramener cet animal impossible à la maison ?

★

En ce dimanche après-midi, alors que Tante doit suivre d'une oreille inquiète le pas lourd et entêté du révérend enfermé dans son bureau, à Bruxelles où le soleil brille enfin, ses nièces remontent une avenue fréquentée par les familles qui ont décidé de faire prendre l'air à leurs enfants et à leurs garde-robes. Quelques ombrelles distinguées et parfaitement inutiles valsent au-dessus des têtes des élégantes accompagnées, comme il se doit, d'un mari en redingote. L'air est à la douceur et aux chuchotements. Quelque chose comme de la joie circule sous un groupe d'arbres où se sont donné rendez-vous des bonnes d'enfants. Emily regarde ce monde dont elle devine les mœurs : « Comment peut-on vivre dans une ville ? » Elle a pris de l'avance sur sa sœur qui rouspète derrière elle : « Quand cesseras-tu de marcher aussi vite ? Nous ne sommes pas sur les Moors ! »

« Quand tu cesseras, toi, de marcher aussi lentement !

— Je n'ai pas tes longues jambes ! »

Le nez baissé, Charlotte est en train de réfléchir : malgré la lettre vexante de Wordsworth — il a finalement répondu à l'envoi d'une de ses nouvelles — ne devrait-elle pas se mettre sans plus tarder à... Non, ce ne serait pas raisonnable. Ces messieurs ont probablement raison ; les femmes n'ont pas les qualités requises pour devenir de bonnes romancières ! Il raconterait quoi, ce roman ? L'aventure d'un professeur et de son élève, leur amour. L'élève serait sage et studieuse, d'humeur mélancolique, et sans prétention. Le professeur serait un homme remarquable, brillant, vif, cultivé, mais dominé par une épouse surnommée «Madame».

« Charlotte, si tu te dépêchais un peu... nous allons être en retard, et Madame ne sera pas contente ! »

Au lieu de protester, Charlotte adresse un regard interrogateur à sa sœur qui vient de s'arrêter au milieu de la rue : « Emily... si tu devais faire le portrait de Madame, quels termes emploierais-tu ? »

« Je la ferais mourir en début de chapitre pour n'avoir pas à faire son portrait. »

Pour la première fois depuis longtemps, Charlotte éclate de rire : « Merci, Seigneur, pour ce délicieux instant ! » Emily hausse les sourcils : « Pourquoi cet éclat ? Ai-je assez d'humour pour avoir oublié que j'en avais ? »

« Tu ne peux pas comprendre... tu sais qu'elle m'a proposé de nous garder six mois de plus ?

— Il n'est pas question pour moi de rester une journée de plus que prévu !

— Nous pourrions payer notre pension et nos études en donnant, toi des cours de musique, et moi des cours d'anglais. Qu'en penses-tu ?

— Je viens de te répondre clairement.

— Un peu trop vite, Emily. J'aimerais que tu y réfléchisses ! »

*«... tandis que les circonstances passent devant mon fauteuil, j'épie la marche qu'elles suivent; je garde le silence, tant qu'elles vont comme je le désire; je ne bats pas des mains et je ne crie pas bravo! Je n'attire pas l'attention des voisins; Je n'excite pas leur envie en disant que je suis heureuse; je me tais, je reste passive. L'événement au contraire vient-il à mal tourner, ma vigilance redouble sans que je parle davantage; mon tricot va toujours, ma bouche est close, mais j'arrive à mon but sans que personne ait deviné mon expédient.»*

Charlotte Brontë, *Le Professeur.*
(Traduction Henriette Loreau.)

VOTRE manière d'aborder le chapitre précédent est parfaitement déplaisante, injuste et malhonnête. En effet, au lieu d'évoquer notre séjour à Londres où nous nous rendîmes en compagnie de notre père affolé à la perspective de nous voir partir au loin, ou notre traversée, longue et pénible, de la Manche qui garde l'Angleterre du continent, vous avez préféré commencer par la critique de Charlotte Brontë, l'écrivain. Toutefois, à la différence de ses nombreux admirateurs qui font d'abord la louange de *Jane Eyre*, son œuvre maîtresse, vous avez choisi d'aiguiser votre méchante humeur sur son premier roman, *The Professor*.

Mise dans l'obligation de défendre un livre pour lequel je n'ai ni sympathie particulière, ni aversion, je ferai deux remarques. La première c'est que la réalité fut infiniment plus douloureuse que vous ne vous plaisez à la décrire. Déchirée par un amour sans réciprocité, Charlotte, alors qu'elle rédigeait cette œuvre en forme de confession, n'évita pas les mots fâcheux de la rancune. Elle sombra ici et là, au hasard de la méchanceté et de l'aigreur ; mais l'âme la plus claire ne traverse-t-elle pas des zones d'ombre ? S'il y a dans ce roman un ressentiment qui raccourcit les silhouettes, déforme les profils, caricature les âmes, il y a également des phrases éblouissantes, une virtuosité de la langue, des descriptions superbes de la Belgique et de Bruxelles en particulier que vous vous gardez d'évoquer.

Voilà pour l'œuvre que vous tentez de discréditer ; maintenant, en ce qui concerne la culture française dont vous semblez douter qu'elle ait jamais intéressé ma sœur, je vous renvoie à la lettre qu'elle m'écrivit lors de son second séjour à Bruxelles,

> « *Dear Emily : I send you this nice little book of* Psaumes de David *as it will enable you to polish up your French. I shall never be satisfied until you are to read Racine, Corneille, and Molière sufficiently well to thoroughly appreciate all their thousand beauties.* »

lettre qui prouve à quel point cette langue et les grands auteurs français comptèrent pour elle qui désirait me faire partager ses découvertes.

Mais j'en reviens à notre séjour en Belgique et à ses conséquences. A peine remises de notre voyage, nous reçûmes à Bruxelles, de la part des autres pensionnaires, un accueil plutôt pénible. L'incompréhension précéda tout autre sentiment. Personne, dans cette capitale ouverte sur les affaires du monde, n'imagina un seul instant ce qu'avait été notre existence avant notre débarquement. Moquées dès le soir de notre arrivée dans une langue étrangère, humiliées par une bande de filles habituées à un luxe déroutant pour nous, nous ne soutînmes pas la comparaison. Isolées, démunies, nous demeurâmes dans le coin du dortoir qu'on nous avait réservé. Par la suite nous n'eûmes ni le courage ni le désir de revenir sur des gestes, sur des mots, vers une amitié possible. Plus malheureuses qu'hostiles, nous continuâmes à renvoyer à certaines qui aimaient qu'on plie devant elles leur mépris et leur sottise, ce qu'elles ne nous pardonnèrent pas. Le dédain nous coûta cher. « Vous pourriez vous excuser, mademoiselle Brontë ! — De quoi ? répondait ma sœur au lieu de se taire. — De m'avoir bousculée ! Le fait de venir d'une île ne vous donne pas tous les droits ! — Si j'avais manqué de politesse, ce n'est pas ici que je l'eusse apprise ! »

« Votre prétention ne trouvera pas à se satisfaire ici ! Nous vous connaissons trop bien et vous jugeons pour ce que vous êtes, des anglicanes ! »

Au lieu de laisser s'éteindre la colère accumulée au cours des mois, Charlotte vida la querelle dans un roman qui ne lui renvoya rien de bon. De filles lourdes et sans esprit, marquées surtout par l'entêtement, elle fit des personnages monstrueux et malfaisants.

Mais j'arrête là l'évocation, car voici que vient d'apparaître celle qui fut au centre du drame, «Madame», la maîtresse de céans. A l'instant me reviennent en mémoire certaines scènes aux accents doucereux. Point n'est besoin pour moi de faire un effort pour revoir des rondeurs, une coquetterie, du charme, le pincement d'une bouche qui retient des mots trop vifs, une façon de dodeliner de la tête comme une petite fille ou une vieille dame — l'une et l'autre se ressemblent souvent — des manières flatteuses et grimacières destinées non pas à séduire mais à mettre autrui à son service. Omniprésente dans deux romans de Charlotte, d'abord dans *The Professor* puis, plus tard, dans *Villette*, Mme Héger gagna l'immortalité grâce au talent de sa rivale qui alimenta le souvenir jusqu'à l'écœurement. La revanche de Charlotte fut totale; «Madame», qui se cacha derrière le paravent de la stratégie, figure aujourd'hui sur le catalogue de la nudité complète. Radiographié par l'œil de la vengeance, analysé sous tous ses angles, ce caractère porté vers la dissimulation se raconte au lecteur par le menu détail. Nul doute, Mme Héger subit une torture depuis un siècle et demi. Elle est là, présente dans chaque phrase, dans chaque virgule, dans chaque point. La passion refoulée devint l'encre d'une histoire décidée à ne pas s'asphyxier dans une fin trop brutale. Souffrance et dépit se glissèrent sous une plume qui croyait décrire des événements réels, une situation assumée, des faits indiscutables, cependant qu'elle mettait en scène la rivalité de deux femmes; l'échec de l'une, la victoire silencieuse de l'autre, mieux armée et infiniment plus habile.

Au moment de la saluer de loin, comme une vieille connaissance qu'on se garde d'approcher, je revois Madame telle qu'elle fut: forte, insidieuse, secrète, infranchissable. Aussi suis-je tentée de rendre hommage au savoir-faire de Charlotte qui, même si elle en força les traits, parvint à décrire — il y fallait de la virtuosité — l'hypocrisie dans ce qu'elle a de plus subtil. Jamais femme n'emprunta autant de masques que Mme Héger. Faussement chaleureuse à l'heure des contrats où l'employée félicitée de mille manières voyait se réduire son salaire, douce et silencieuse à la seconde où elle sentait sa sécurité menacée, Madame ne se laissa jamais gagner par l'impatience et la nervosité. Sa bouche sut toujours retenir les mots qui l'auraient livrée à autrui.

★

« Mesdemoiselles, je vous présente M. Héger ; il sera pour vous plus qu'un maître, un ami, et qui sait ? un élève ; l'anglais est une si belle langue, pourquoi ne la lui apprendriez-vous pas ? »

La directrice nous présenta son époux d'une phrase tirée au cordeau, comme l'homme d'affaires présente à des clients son principal collaborateur : « Quelle curieuse femme, Emily... ne trouves-tu pas ? »

« Je ne l'aime guère.
— Pourquoi... elle est plutôt aimable !
— Il me semble que quelque chose se cache derrière son amabilité... pourquoi se donne-t-elle tant de mal ? Après tout, elle ne nous connaît pas ! »

Bien vite, Madame intrigua Charlotte ; comment une femme engagée depuis plusieurs années dans la maturité, de toute évidence plus vieille que son mari, pouvait-elle diriger au présent une pension réputée et conjuguer au futur une vie familiale en mettant régulièrement des enfants au monde ? « Où va-t-elle puiser son énergie ? » A quel élixir faisait-elle appel pour retenir un époux aussi bouillant ? Quel était le secret qui faisait d'elle une maîtresse femme, une épouse, une amante, une mère ? L'envie qui jusque-là avait épargné Charlotte l'attaqua le jour où, devant un miroir, elle se souvint de son âge. « Pourquoi ne m'a-t-on jamais aimée ? » Elle jeta un œil nouveau sur les bras, la gorge, la taille, les mouvements de jupe qui avaient arraché un homme de la trempe et de la dimension de M. Héger au célibat. « Suis-je moins désirable que cette future matrone ? » L'envie, en gagnant du terrain, entraîna Charlotte sur des terres où son élégance morale cessa d'être à l'aise. Elle lui fit guetter les rides d'un visage constamment souriant, et à défaut des rides, les marques de l'usure, et à défaut les traces de l'embonpoint, bref, tout ce qui l'eût autorisée à se regarder, elle, Charlotte, avec moins d'animosité : « Je suis de plus en plus laide, ne trouves-tu pas, Emily ? »

> « Non, mais sans doute n'est-ce pas la réponse que tu souhaites ? A force de te torturer, laide tu le deviendras vraiment ! Pourquoi cherches-tu à te comparer à d'autres ? »

Le visage de Madame ne prit point ombrage de l'observation de la jalouse. Il resta lisse comme celui d'une jeune fille, lisse, frais et reposé, et son corps, malgré une grossesse avancée, garda une belle prestance. « Je ne sais pourquoi, mais le temps passant, je ne puis plus regarder Madame sans ressentir une profonde antipathie. J'imagine que ce sentiment vient de l'hypocrisie que je devine en elle. »

> « J'ai le sentiment inverse... alors qu'au départ j'étais mal à l'aise, je le suis moins maintenant. Il me semble que dans ce couple elle est l'élément courageux. Certes, son ambition est grande et son habileté parfaite, mais la gestion de cette maison ne doit pas être facile. Quant à M. Héger, c'est un homme qu'il faut savoir surveiller ! »

Sur le cahier des charges où elle notait scrupuleusement ses réflexions, Charlotte consigna sa déception. Madame promettait son amitié afin de mieux assujettir. Sa stratégie était parfaite.

« Même Emily se laisse séduire par elle ! » C'était à qui lui donnerait satisfaction ! Son mari, choisi par ce regard et séduit par cette voix, les professeurs, les pensionnaires, tous succombaient à son charme et personne ne songeait à se révolter. Charlotte qui s'était crue privilégiée n'était qu'un objet entre les mains de Madame qui la manipulait avec sa sournoiserie habituelle : « J'ai beau me débattre, je vais et je viens à sa guise ! » A force d'observation, ma sœur acquit un peu de ce que la plantureuse Belge possédait en abondance : du sang-froid et assez de cran pour s'imposer comme professeur.

> « J'ai une proposition à vous faire, mademoiselle Charlotte. Seriez-vous prête à remplacer le professeur d'anglais ? Il ne me donne plus satisfaction et plutôt que d'aller chercher à l'extérieur quelqu'un pour le remplacer, je me demande si vous ne seriez pas heureuse d'occuper ce poste ? Cela dit, vous avez constaté combien les enfants sont difficiles ! Il vous faudra les mater dès le premier cours ! »

Charlotte remplaça au pied levé et pour un salaire dérisoire le professeur renvoyé par Madame parce qu'il pesait trop lourd sur la comptabilité. Du même coup, elle obtint la considération de M. Héger, surpris de découvrir en son élève autant de compétence et de courage : « Votre timidité cache votre personnalité ! Je ne vous aurais pas crue capable de dompter un pareil troupeau ! » Hélas ! les sentiments du maître ne dépassèrent jamais l'estime ; le temps de saluer au passage le nouveau professeur d'anglais, et Constantin Héger avait déjà regagné l'ombre de sa femme où il se plaisait plus qu'ailleurs.

Je me suis souvent posé la question ; ma sœur, si

elle avait eu plus de malice, aurait-elle pu mettre en péril le couple Héger? Je ne le crois pas. Madame veillait trop bien sur le sommeil de son mari. Par la suite, sûre de son pouvoir, elle provoqua une situation qu'une autre, moins audacieuse, aurait évitée: «Mademoiselle Charlotte, j'aimerais que vous donniez des cours privés à M. Héger!»

«Mais Madame...
— L'anglais tôt ou tard lui sera nécessaire!»

*La petite créature laide et noire* si souvent décrite à Ellen et qui portait nom Héger devint, l'espace d'une saison l'élève de Miss Brontë. L'attirance que ma sœur ressentait pour le maître devint amour. M. Héger joua à l'étudiant. Aveugle et sourd à ce qui n'était pas sa famille et son enseignement, il ne devina rien de l'adoration qu'on lui portait. Cet homme bien intentionné traversa la vie de Charlotte avec l'inconscience d'un jeune chien. Il s'amusa de ses peurs, s'indigna de ses manques, s'enthousiasma de ses trouvailles: «Bravo! Jamais vous ne m'avez remis un si bon devoir! Il y a en vous une veine peu commune, Charlotte! Travaillez!»

«Vous croyez vraiment que...
— La voilà qui bafouille... oui, je crois que... ah non, vous n'allez pas pleurer parce que je vous fais un compliment!»

Ma sœur ne m'autorisa jamais à l'aider. Au contraire, elle continua à nier: «Pour qui me prends-tu, Emily? Je trouve que M. Héger est un professeur exceptionnel, ça ne va pas au-delà!» Tout en continuant à condamner les autres au nom d'une morale que je ne partageai jamais avec elle, Charlotte laissa dériver ses pensées en direction d'un amour impossible et coupable qu'elle refusa de reconnaître. Sa pudeur éteignit des images trop brûlantes. Jalouse d'une femme mariée, de surcroît mère de famille, elle me supplia d'accepter l'offre de Madame qui nous proposait de rester quelques mois de plus à Bruxelles, non pas en tant qu'élèves mais comme professeurs.

★

L'automne était déjà là lorsque la mort, après une longue éclipse, refit brutalement son apparition. Elle épargna à l'assistant de papa les ennuis de la vieillesse ; nous apprîmes par Branwell que William Weightman était mort le 6 septembre des suites du choléra ou d'une mauvaise dysenterie. Bouleversé par la perte d'un garçon qu'il aimait comme un fils, notre père lui avait rendu hommage en l'église de Haworth : « Comme à son habitude, quand il est personnellement touché, il a prêché sublimement. Nous étions tous en larmes ! »

A peine avions-nous eu le temps de nous remettre de cette secousse que nous reçûmes une lettre du château de Koekelberg situé dans la banlieue de Bruxelles. Mary Taylor nous apprenait dans une lettre à peine compréhensible que sa sœur Martha avait rendu l'âme. Enterrée en toute hâte, comme une voleuse ou une avortée, elle reposait enfin : « Dieu sera assez compatissant pour tenir compte des souffrances de son agonie et lui pardonner ses péchés. Il ne faut pas regretter ce départ précipité ; Martha est mieux là où elle est ! » Cette lettre nous choqua ; le cadavre d'une jeune fille de vingt-trois ans ne valait-il pas quelques larmes et des regrets ? Qu'avait donc fait Martha pour mériter une si brève épitaphe ? Nous en étions là de nos interrogations lorsque nous parvint une troisième lettre, celle-là encore plus pénible que les deux précédentes. Branwell, encore lui, l'avait postée à Haworth :

> Mes chères,
> J'ai une mauvaise nouvelle à vous annoncer. Tante est au plus mal. Elle est alitée depuis une quinzaine de jours. Elle souffre d'une douleur au ventre intolérable. Papa et moi ne savons comment lui porter secours et nous craignons pour sa vie. Ce matin, elle m'a demandé de vous écrire : elle ne voudrait pas partir avant de vous avoir revues toutes les trois. J'adresse par le même courrier une lettre à Anne.

Cette lettre nous fut remise au moment où nous nous apprêtions à descendre pour donner le cours de neuf heures. L'émotion nous cloua sur place. Ne nous voyant pas, Madame monta dans notre chambre : « Eh bien, que se passe-t-il ? La cloche a sonné depuis cinq minutes ! Êtes-vous paralysées l'une et l'autre ? » Sans un mot, Charlotte tendit la lettre à Mme Héger qui s'empressa de la lire. Son visage changea aussitôt d'expression. Sur un ton maternel que nous ne lui connaissions pas, elle nous invita à faire nos bagages :

> « Les épreuves passées, vous pourrez revenir. Vous serez toujours les bienvenues dans cette maison ! »

Lorsque nous arrivâmes à Haworth, Tante était déjà enterrée.

*« Leur bonheur cessa donc quand les circonstances leur firent sentir à chacun que l'intérêt de l'un n'était pas l'objet principal des pensées de l'autre... »*

Emily BRONTË,
*Les Hauts de Hurle-Vent.*
(Traduction Frédéric Delebecque.)

Au premier étage, la chambre de Miss Branwell est restée telle qu'elle était de son vivant. Les objets, les bibelots ramenés de Penzance, sa ville natale, la tapisserie qu'elle n'a pas eu le temps de terminer semblent attendre son retour. Aucun des enfants Brontë n'a encore osé les toucher ; l'inventaire se fera plus tard. Sur la table de nuit, la bible que Tante ne manquait jamais de feuilleter avant de remettre son sommeil à Dieu rappelle la piété de la défunte. A côté, les œuvres spirituelles de Mme Elizabeth Rowe — lettres amicales adressées à la mort rédemptrice — affirment que le bonheur terrestre est une illusion qu'il faut savoir chasser de l'esprit ; de même qu'il faut savoir juguler, avant qu'ils ne prennent trop de place, les élans dirigés vers l'art en général et la littérature en particulier, un exercice dangereux pour l'âme insidieusement détournée de sa vraie voie. En regard de l'immortalité qui attend l'homme de l'autre côté de la fosse, tout est vain.

« Je crois que papa nous a appelés.
— En es-tu certaine ?
— Non, mais nous ferions mieux de descendre pour nous en assurer. »

Au rez-de-chaussée, le révérend attend ses enfants avec lesquels il veut s'entretenir. Saisi tout à coup par ce silence qu'il ne parvient plus à rompre depuis que sa belle-sœur est décédée — n'a-t-elle pas été sa fidèle alliée durant vingt ans ? —, il sort de son bureau. La main posée sur le bouton de la porte, il tourne son regard agrandi par le verre épais des lunettes vers les jeunes gens qui descendent l'escalier en file indienne.

« Père, vous nous avez demandés ?
— En effet. »

Réunis après des mois de séparation, Branwell et ses sœurs observent le pasteur dont le visage amaigri ne parvient pas à cacher l'anxiété. Il attend que quelqu'un prenne la parole, l'interpelle, l'accuse même : « Vous n'avez pas su être un père pour nous ! » ou : « Qu'avez-vous fait pour Tante durant ces longues années ? L'avez-vous seulement aidée à mourir dignement ? » Hélas ! la péritonite, comme autrefois le cancer de sa femme et la tuberculose de ses filles, s'est moquée de ses prêches et de ses prières. A l'heure des grandes échéances, l'homme ne peut rien pour l'homme ; la naissance est solitaire et la mort l'est aussi.

Branwell, pour une fois, soutient le regard paternel. Il devine la question que le pasteur doit se poser : à quand le prochain enterrement ? Ce matin, la fatigue est si grande, le poids des ans si lourd qu'il accepterait volontiers de mourir, ne fût-ce que pour échapper à la demande silencieuse de ces jeunes gens tendus dans une même espérance : Père, pouvons-nous compter sur vous, maintenant que Tante n'est plus ? Bien sûr que non. Personne ne peut compter sur lui. En enterrant William Weightman, plus encore qu'un fils, un véritable ami, le révérend a senti la fraternité mourir en lui. Aujourd'hui où la mort a décidé de faire place nette, une question se pose : où en est-il du désarroi ? Père de ces quatre enfants qu'il ne comprend pas, qu'il n'a jamais compris, pas plus qu'eux ne le comprennent — ne leur a-t-il pas tout caché de sa vie intérieure, de ses tentations suicidaires, de ses élans charnels, de ses faiblesses devant la bouteille de vin cachée dans son bureau ? —, il avance dans la solitude, et sa foi, bousculée par les derniers événements, lui demande des comptes.

> « Entrez et fermez la porte ! Il fait froid comme en hiver ! »

Pourtant ce matin, alors qu'il voudrait ne plus être, ne plus sentir, ne plus penser, ne plus juger ses semblables, alors qu'il voudrait rejoindre Maria, l'épouse parfaite et trop tôt perdue, va-t-il, poussé par la faiblesse, répondre à des interrogations qu'il a toujours fuies et dire à ses enfants qui attendent de lui l'autorisation de devenir adultes ce qu'il pense en ce moment de complet découragement ? Ceci par exemple : Vivez pendant qu'il en est temps ! fuyez ce pays, ces gens obtus et violents, cette Église étriquée ! allez là où vos désirs vous appellent... Ou encore ceci : Si Dieu nous a créés à son image, ce que je crois, alors c'est nous qui avons la charge de Dieu et pas Lui de nous, et personne ne nous donnera le père protecteur dont nous avons besoin ! En créant le monde, Dieu a oublié la souffrance qui se venge de cet affront ; le Seigneur a besoin de nos prières... Ou encore ceci : Comme votre mère, Elizabeth était une chrétienne fervente ; pourtant, comme votre mère, elle est morte dans l'épouvante et le déchirement des entrailles.

> « Qu'avez-vous papa ?... Vous sentez-vous mal ? Vous êtes tout pâle ! »

Non, Patrick Brontë ne parlera pas de son désespoir ni de sa détresse ; il n'en a pas le droit. Les bras du crucifié se sont refermés sur lui dès le jour où il a décidé de lui consacrer sa vie. Enlacé à Dieu et à son Église glorieuse, il sait, même si ce soir il se défend de l'espérance, que la rébellion ne peut qu'enténébrer l'esprit.

« Que se passe-t-il ? Vous nous convoquez dans votre bureau, et vous vous taisez ! »

Branwell s'énerve. Il prononce un mot qui a souvent retenti dans la maison : « Papa ! » Patrick Brontë a été condamné par la fatalité à porter ce nom que le veuvage a alourdi et auquel il ne sait pas répondre : papa sans passion, sans tendresse, papa lointain, tragiquement démuni en face de la demande de quatre personnalités menacées et pourtant fortes. « Ils attendent de moi un mot de réconfort ! » Il fait un pas en direction du groupe : « J'aurais voulu faire mieux ! »

« Faire mieux... que voulez-vous dire ?
— J'aurais voulu vous écouter davantage, vous comprendre, me conduire comme un bon père ! »

Des larmes apparaissent dans les yeux de ses filles troublées par un si terrible aveu. Il pose la main sur l'épaule d'Anne dont il connaît le chagrin, car plus que les autres, elle a été aimée de la morte qui n'a pas manqué d'ensemencer une âme gagnée d'avance. Mais que pouvait-on opposer à une telle foi ? Élevée sur les terres arides du calvinisme, la pauvre enfant devra lutter pour s'accorder quelques miettes de bonheur.

« Pense à toi, ma petite fille... Ne t'impose pas des charges trop lourdes... je sais que Tante pensait différemment de moi, mais sur ce point elle avait tort ! »

Le révérend s'écarte du groupe. Il va jusqu'à son bureau, prend une lettre cachetée: «Je vous ai demandé de descendre car nous allons ouvrir le testament de Tante. Elle me l'a remis il y a quelque temps en me priant de m'y conformer en tous points.» L'inquiétude se glisse dans les rangs. Pourquoi papa est-il si pressé ? La défunte est encore présente dans le presbytère, et l'on parle de partager ses biens !

«Nous pouvons peut-être remettre à plus tard l'ouverture de cette lettre... rien ne presse!»

Patrick Brontë lève la tête. Il fixe Emily debout près du bureau : « Charlotte insiste pour retourner à Bruxelles le plus vite possible et je n'ai pas les moyens de payer son voyage ! » Emily se tourne vers Charlotte qui regarde ostensiblement par la fenêtre : « Tu es donc si pressée de retourner chez les Héger ? » L'aînée est surprise par le ton ; elle sursaute, accepte de croiser le regard d'Emily: « Oui, assez ! Vu mon âge, je n'ai plus de temps à perdre ! » Branwell prend Anne à témoin : « Tu vois, lorsqu'on a eu la chance d'aller vivre sur le continent, on ne peut plus supporter l'île ! » Papa pousse un soupir ; lassitude ou agacement ?

« Asseyez-vous... ne restez pas debout ! »

Le pasteur vient de décacheter l'enveloppe. A l'aide d'une loupe, il déchiffre silencieusement les dernières volontés de sa belle-sœur, puis il lève la tête, regarde longuement Branwell. Le fils de la maison s'interroge: pourquoi ce regard insistant? Tante lui aurait-elle tout donné? Il a un geste en direction de ses sœurs qui ne bougent ni ne disent mot. Pâles, retirées en elles-mêmes, elles attendent de savoir si Miss Branwell, par affection pour son neveu, les a déshéritées. Le révérend commence la lecture d'un texte écrit par une personne qui, sans aucun doute, avait bonne tête. Après avoir effleuré Branwell, la fortune vient de couronner les trois filles. Le neveu chéri de Tante hérite du coffret auquel la morte attachait grand prix, mais les nièces, elles, reçoivent chacune une rente de trois cents livres, soit la totalité de l'argent épargné par la belle-sœur de Patrick Brontë.

« Ah çà, par exemple ! »

Branwell — il a déjà oublié les sacrifices consentis par Tante pour lui permettre de devenir peintre — cherche sur le visage de ses sœurs la raison d'une pareille injustice, et parce qu'il ne la trouve consignée nulle part, il se lève, tousse plusieurs fois de suite, se rassoit : « Ah çà... je suis stupéfait ! » Les mains posées à plat sur les cuisses, il attend la promesse qui le rassurera ; on ne peut l'abandonner à la gêne ! Hélas ! son mauvais sort ne semble intéresser personne. Va-t-il protester ? Dire combien ce partage est déloyal ? Après tout, n'est-ce pas lui qui, malgré sa peur horrible de la mort, a aidé Tante à partir ? Non. Quelque chose en lui s'apaise. Il pousse un long soupir. Maintenant qu'il a perdu son dernier soutien, il ne lui reste plus qu'à attendre le secours de la Providence : il n'avait pas à nourrir les illusions de Tante : « La pauvre vieille a toujours cru à mon futur ! »

« Ne faites pas cette tête, papa ! Je suis surpris mais content que Tante ait songé à mes sœurs plutôt qu'à moi ! Puisqu'elles désirent ouvrir une école, elles auront besoin de cet argent ! »

Patrick Brontë adresse un regard de gratitude à son fils : « Voilà ce que j'appelle une belle réaction !

Je n'en attendais pas moins de toi, mon fils!» Le déshérité aurait préféré un silence embarrassé à un compliment trop vite fait: «Cela dit, je trouve injuste qu'Emily et Charlotte aient pu partir à l'étranger et pas moi! Moi aussi j'aurais aimé me frotter à d'autres esprits! Moi aussi j'aurais aimé trouver un maître!» Emily s'insurge: «M. Héger est peut-être un maître pour Charlotte, il ne l'est pas pour moi!» Le pasteur s'inquiète; d'où vient cette passion? Que cache ce remue-ménage? Il n'a pas le temps de s'interroger longtemps.

«N'empêche qu'il t'a appris des choses que sans lui tu n'aurais jamais découvertes! Ton orgueil te jouera des tours, Emily!»

Cet avertissement jette un froid que Charlotte a décidé d'ignorer. Elle sort de sa poche la lettre que M. Héger lui a remise au moment du départ, la tend à son père. Le révérend la prend avec précaution, comme si elle était trempée dans du poison. Il la pose sur son bureau: «A quoi bon me la donner? Tu sais bien que je ne lis pas le français!», la saisit à nouveau, la soupèse; que dit ce Belge? «Si tu me la traduisais?» Charlotte s'empresse d'obéir malgré les protestations d'Emily qui connaît le contenu de la lettre.

«“Cher révérend Brontë: c'est avec peine que je vois partir Charlotte et Emily rappelées à Haworth par de cruels devoirs. J'ose espérer que c'est un au revoir et non un adieu que j'aurai à leur dire au moment du départ. Ce regret exprime mieux que mille phrases l'estime que je porte à vos deux filles dont la sensibilité et l'intelligence...”

— Assez!»

Le pasteur paraît satisfait de la traduction : « Si tu te calmais, Emily ? » Ainsi ses filles ont laissé rue d'Isabelle un souvenir si excellent que M. et Mme Héger seraient heureux de les accueillir à nouveau dans leur établissement où une place leur est offerte. « ... car il serait regrettable, cher révérend Brontë, de laisser s'épuiser des talents aussi exceptionnels sans leur donner leur chance ! »

« Comme vous le constatez, papa, malgré les objections d'Emily, nous sommes attendues et souhaitées.

— J'en suis heureux... et fier ! »

Maintenant qu'elle a obtenu le consentement de son père, Charlotte s'adresse à Emily qui l'interrompt dès la première phrase : « Je ne retournerai pas à Bruxelles ! » Le visage fermé, elle tourne le dos à Charlotte qui insiste : « Mais enfin, Emily... ne fais pas ta mauvaise tête... Réfléchis à ce que tu perds ! »

« C'est tout réfléchi ! Je ne retournerai pas à Bruxelles !

— Tu pourrais recevoir des leçons de musique des meilleurs professeurs, améliorer ton français, perfectionner ton style, perdre ta timidité... N'oublie pas que tu vas avoir bientôt vingt-cinq ans ! »

Entraînée par un désir si impérieux qu'elle en oublie la prudence, Charlotte s'acharne sur une cause perdue d'avance ; il lui faudra se présenter seule rue d'Isabelle : « Nous avons tant à apprendre avant d'être capables d'enseigner nous-mêmes, que refuser une telle proposition me paraît pure folie ! » Excédé par une discussion d'où il est exclu, Branwell s'interroge à haute voix : « Je croyais avoir lu sous ta plume que les Belges et les catholiques détestaient les Anglais ? — Est-ce si grave ? On peut parfaitement vivre à Bruxelles en ignorant les Flamands ! »

« Et la famille Héger, tu l'ignoreras aussi ? »

Emily est si furieuse qu'elle en bégaie : « Et Mme Héger, tu passeras à côté d'elle sans la voir ? » Charlotte se lève ; elle tremble de tous ses membres. « Sans doute te crois-tu assez forte pour vivre à côté d'elle sans en souffrir ? » Charlotte a un geste en direction de son père : « Papa, dites-lui de se taire ! A-t-elle bientôt fini de me violenter ? » Patrick Brontë est sur le point de se fâcher à son tour. Il va exiger le silence lorsque la plus jeune de ses filles demande la parole :

« Puis-je dire un mot après cet échange auquel je ne comprends rien ? Après tout, nous avons à choisir notre voie, Branwell et moi ! »

La surprise est totale ; depuis quand Anne a-t-elle cette autorité, cette pointe d'aigreur ? Le pasteur est confus : « Évidemment, ma petite fille... tu as droit à la parole comme tes sœurs qui viennent d'ailleurs d'en abuser... Personne ici ne te l'a jamais interdite, c'est toi qui refusais de la prendre ! »

« Juste avant de quitter Thorp Green, je me suis préoccupée de l'avenir de Branwell.
— Tiens donc ! C'est une délicate pensée.
— Tante ne lui ayant rien laissé, j'imagine qu'il va devoir gagner sa vie ?
— Mais certainement, et le plus vite possible ! »

Que signifie ce dialogue entre le père et la fille ?

Branwell fixe sa sœur ; contre toute attente, le salut viendrait-il de la plus faible ? « Je t'écoute. Qu'as-tu à me proposer ? — M. et Mme Robinson, auxquels j'ai parlé de toi, seraient prêts à t'offrir un poste de précepteur. M. Robinson est peut-être étroit d'idées, mais sa femme est charmante, et tout me dit que tu t'attacheras à Edmund, leur fils unique. De nous quatre, tu es le seul à aimer les enfants, n'est-il pas vrai ? »

Au rez-de-chaussée, dans le bureau du révérend Brontë, les jeunes gens rangent leur chaise. Une fois de plus, ils vont devoir se séparer. Ils partiront à tour de rôle, demain, après-demain, dans une semaine ou deux. Seule Emily restera au presbytère avec son père et son chien. Le silence reprendra sa vraie place...

*« Je ne pleurerai pas de te voir me quitter.*
*Il n'est rien d'aimable ici-bas,*
*Et doublement m'affligera, ce sombre monde*
*Tant que ton cœur y pâtira.*

*Je ne pleurerai pas : la splendeur de l'été*
*Nécessairement s'enténèbre ;*
*L'histoire la plus heureuse, quand on la suit,*
*Se termine avec le tombeau !* »

(Traduction Pierre Leyris
© Gallimard.)

alors reviendront les mots, car la poésie ne se donne que dans la solitude.

*«Je regardai de nouveau derrière moi. Je vis le clocher du village et, derrière, la vieille maison du presbytère éclairée par un rayon de soleil; ce rayon était le seul, car tout le village et les collines environnantes étaient dans l'ombre formée par les nuages. Je saluai ce rayon de soleil comme un heureux présage pour ma maison. J'implorai avec ferveur la bénédiction du ciel pour ses habitants et me détournai vivement, car je voyais les rayons du soleil disparaître.»*

Anne Brontë, *Agnès Grey.*
(Traduction Ch. Romey et A. Rolet.)

CETTE scène — vous auriez pu l'intituler « L'ouverture du testament » — a ranimé en moi le souvenir de la période qui suivit la mort de Tante emportée brutalement par une occlusion intestinale, période où Anne repartit avec Branwell chez les Robinson.

« Que penses-tu de la proposition de ta sœur, mon garçon ?

— Elle me paraît excellente, et je l'en remercie. Ce qui m'étonne, c'est qu'Anne ait pensé à moi. Je croyais qu'elle ne se souciait que d'Emily !

— La preuve en est que non ! »

Alors que je ne songeais qu'à me soustraire à l'influence et à l'emprise de Charlotte, la tenace : « Parce que moi, je ne me soucie pas d'elle en l'encourageant à repartir pour Bruxelles avec moi ? — Ce n'est pas ce que j'ai dit, Charlotte ! — Non, mais c'est ce que vous pensez tous ! » Anne n'avait calculé que mon bonheur. Grâce à elle, à son sacrifice maquillé en choix, je restai à Haworth comme je l'avais souhaité, entre mes animaux et un père atteint de mélancolie.

« Tu t'es toujours mépris sur mes sentiments, Branwell. Ce n'est pas parce que je me soucie d'Emily que je suis indifférente au reste du monde !

— Anne, mon incompréhension est excusable. Je ne t'ai jamais entendue parler de toi. Je crois que c'est la première fois que tu t'exprimes en ma présence aussi longtemps ! »

Oui, je me souviens de l'intervention inattendue de ma jeune sœur, de l'étonnement qu'elle suscita en ce jour où nous nous retrouvâmes réunis autour d'un testament aux dispositions déconcertantes, de la proposition qu'elle fit à Branwell stupéfait d'être tour à tour déshérité par Tante dont il avait pourtant été le neveu préféré, et sauvé par une sœur dont il n'avait jamais rien attendu.

Beaucoup de mots ne furent pas dits que je regrette encore aujourd'hui ; ils nous auraient permis de nous retrouver, Anne et moi. Le miracle de l'échange, nous le vécûmes que dans la première jeunesse, à cette époque où l'innocence et la spontanéité nous liaient comme les épis de blé sur la couronne des moissons. Mon passage à Law Hill, puis mon séjour à Bruxelles où Charlotte m'accapara totalement, enfin son long exil à Thorp Green où elle demeura jusqu'en 1845 ne nous séparèrent pas, mais ils rendirent difficiles les échanges et les rencontres. Jusqu'à la fin ou presque, il est vrai, la saga de Gondal, notre œuvre commune, ne cessa de nous mobiliser ; à travers l'incongruité des situations et l'inconvenance des aveux faits à des êtres imaginaires, elle nous rappelait combien nous nous aimions. Cette complicité, cette interminable conversation écrite nous valurent la jalousie de Charlotte que son divorce littéraire d'avec Branwell, puis sa passion contrariée pour M. Héger avaient rendue susceptible et vulnérable à l'extrême.

★

Pauvre Charlotte !

Je l'avoue ; ce n'est pas sans embarras que j'en arrive à ce second séjour à Bruxelles. Il fut pour ma sœur l'épreuve la plus douloureuse de sa vie, celle qui devient blessure incicatrisable dans le corps de désir et d'amour.

> Chère Emily,
> Par suite du retard de mon train, je n'ai vu de Londres que les ténèbres des rues et l'eau noire de la Tamise remuée par les rats. J'ai eu si peur de me perdre ou de me faire voler mes bagages que j'ai embarqué le soir même sur le bateau. J'ai passé la nuit seule à bord avec un marin et le capitaine qui a eu pitié de moi et m'a hébergée. Je préfère ne pas voir dans cette aventure un présage funeste pour la suite, mais j'en garde néanmoins un souvenir qui m'obsède... je t'entends d'ici me dire : « Encore tes hantises, Charlotte ! » Oh, comme tu me manques, chère sœur !

Après un voyage angoissant qui augurait mal de l'avenir, Charlotte arriva à Bruxelles un matin du mois de janvier 1843. M. et Mme Héger l'accueillirent avec chaleur, comme une amie de longue date. Ils la reçurent dans leur appartement personnel avant de la mener jusqu'à l'estrade du professeur. Ma sœur gagna à sa cause une classe de jeunes filles au gouvernement pourtant difficile. Les premiers mois de cet exil souhaité furent presque heureux. Charlotte n'était-elle pas parvenue à ses fins ? Elle avait réussi à quitter Haworth où elle refusait de vivre maintenant qu'elle avait gagné compétence et savoir, et elle avait découvert, en même temps que Mme Héger qui l'espionnait derrière les judas de la rue d'Isabelle, qu'elle était capable d'être un excellent professeur mais aussi une élève appliquée : « Parce que vous apprenez également l'allemand ?

Le français ne vous suffit pas ! — Ce sera un atout supplémentaire lorsque que le moment sera venu d'ouvrir ma propre école ! — Et quand comptez-vous mettre ce projet à exécution ? — Mon Dieu, mais dès que j'en serai capable ! »

L'existence aurait pu se dérouler de cette manière si entre l'anglais, le français et l'allemand, ne s'était glissé le discours de la passion d'un maniement infiniment plus redoutable que celui des langues étrangères. Ma sœur, qui prenait chaque compliment pour un aveu, se mit à espérer plus.

> Ma chère Emily,
> Tu ne reconnaîtrais pas M. Héger. Il est infiniment plus doux et plus aimable que lors de notre premier séjour. Autrefois, jamais il ne se serait adressé à moi de cette façon attentive et courtoise...

La sympathie qu'on lui portait, au lieu de satisfaire une espérance raisonnable, alimenta un désir secret et coupable.

> ... sais-tu qu'il me demande des nouvelles de ma santé et s'intéresse à mes projets ?

La main amicale posée sur son épaule, le salut un peu appuyé, le mouvement du petit doigt pour lui montrer qu'on l'avait remarquée, la moindre réflexion sur sa bonne mine : « Vous avez bien dormi, Charlotte ? Ne répondez pas ! Je le vois à votre teint splendide ! » devinrent des signes qu'il n'y avait pas à discuter. Égarée par des attentions sans conséquence, Charlotte fit fausse route. Elle s'écarta d'une amitié possible pour nourrir un sentiment qui n'avait de réalité que dans son esprit.

... je n'ai plus le goût de sortir tant je me plais rue d'Isabelle !

Pour se consacrer tout entière à ses chimères, elle rompit avec le monde. Les sorties du dimanche après-midi devinrent si ennuyeuses qu'elle y mit un terme. Sous des prétextes divers, elle déclina les offres de divertissement. La famille Héger, qui s'était félicitée de la voir s'épanouir dans le petit milieu non catholique de Bruxelles, la vit revenir à sa solitude d'antan. Après avoir cherché les raisons de ce repli et épié les symptômes dénonciateurs d'un état subodoré de longue date, Madame commença à s'inquiéter du comportement du professeur d'anglais : Charlotte ne risquait-elle pas de rencontrer M. Héger ailleurs que dans une salle d'étude ?

« Depuis un certain temps, je m'alarme pour vous, Charlotte.
— Et pourquoi donc, Madame ?
— Il me semble que vous vous attristez. Avez-vous des ennuis de santé ? de cœur ? Non... vous savez que vous pouvez tout me dire, je suis votre amie ! »

Mais je crois avoir déjà raconté tout cela, l'efficacité, la sournoiserie de Madame qui s'ingénia à découvrir ce qu'elle soupçonnait depuis l'année précédente. Parla-t-elle à son innocent mari de la découverte qu'elle venait de faire ou, sans rien dire, le sépara-t-elle habilement de son élève ? Dans les semaines qui suivirent, l'humeur de Constantin Héger vira à la maussaderie. Arraché par quelques manigances subtiles de son épouse à la bienheureuse somnolence des consciences fortes de leur ignorance, il porta les yeux sur une Charlotte qui venait de découvrir quel fléau était l'amour non partagé. « Quelle tristesse se dégage de cette pauvre fille ! » M. Héger se détourna avec précipitation d'un commerce amical dont sa femme, subtilement, venait de lui faire voir les embûches. Son travail l'absorba tellement que du jour au lendemain il cessa de donner des leçons de littérature à sa brillante élève.

Alors qu'elle avait pris l'habitude, lorsque le temps le permettait, d'aller bavarder avec lui dans le jardin où il soignait ses rosiers, elle ne l'y trouva plus. Charlotte chercha vainement les raisons d'un aussi soudain refroidissement : pourquoi la fuyait-on et qu'avait-elle fait qui l'eût rendue à ce point indésirable ? S'était-elle montrée arrogante ? Au lieu de discuter l'admiration qu'elle portait à son maître, objet ingrat d'un attachement dont il n'était pas digne, elle tourna sa réflexion du côté de ses compétences. « Quelle bêtise ai-je encore faite sans m'en rendre compte ? »

Pour renouer un lien auquel elle tenait plus que tout, ma sœur fit comprendre à Madame combien elle avait d'estime pour l'établissement qui lui faisait l'honneur de l'employer. Mais cette manœuvre indigne ne lui apporta qu'humiliation, car Madame, atteinte d'une crise de surdité, ignora ses compliments. Il était clair qu'on ne souhaitait plus rien d'elle.

> Ma chère Emily,
> Faut-il que je sois ingrate pour oser trouver le temps long à Bruxelles où il n'a jamais fait aussi beau. Vue du jardin que je ne quitte guère avant la tombée de la nuit, car je ne désespère pas d'y rencontrer un soir M. Héger à qui je parlerai en toute simplicité — veut-on ma démission oui ou non ? —, la tour de Sainte-Gudule est superbe. L'approche des grandes vacances me pousse vers une sorte d'angoisse chaque jour plus

intense. Que se passe-t-il ? Seraient-ce les effets de l'exil ?

Au mois d'août, les portes du pensionnat s'ouvrirent toutes grandes, comme sous l'action d'un coup de vent purificateur. Après s'y être étiolées une partie de l'année, les pensionnaires quittèrent ces lieux d'incarcération ; des familles, des affections les attendaient ailleurs. L'établissement se vida peu à peu. Les enseignantes suivirent les enseignées. Seule Charlotte qui n'avait pas les moyens du voyage Bruxelles-Haworth aller-retour resta rue d'Isabelle en compagnie de la cuisinière, une femme passablement sourde avec laquelle il lui était impossible d'échanger plus de dix mots.

Avant de partir pour sa maison de campagne, M. Héger se souvint à temps de l'élève injustement traitée ; mû par la compassion ou peut-être par le remords, il se précipita dans la salle d'étude, fit cadeau à Charlotte de plusieurs livres qu'il lui conseilla de lire pendant son absence afin de parfaire sa connaissance du romantisme français. « Oh, monsieur, vous ne pouviez pas me faire plus plaisir ! Moi qui croyais que... — Vous n'allez pas encore pleurer ? Allez, allez, un peu de nerf, que diable ! » Sa joie ne dura que le temps de feuilleter les ouvrages offerts entre deux portes. Charlotte comprit bien vite qu'elle n'aurait pas le courage de vivre sereinement une solitude aussi pesante durant un mois et demi ; depuis qu'elle ne pouvait plus s'en remettre à Dieu, l'obsession qui avait pris le visage de M. Héger l'étreignait du matin au soir : « O, Seigneur, délivrez-moi de cet amour ! »

Le soir même Charlotte, qui se sentait vraiment trop seule dans l'immense salle à manger, décida de prendre ses repas à la cuisine. Après le repas qu'elle avala rapidement et pour fuir la loquacité de la cuisinière qui voulait l'entretenir dans un hurlement de sourde de ses réflexions, elle monta au premier étage, se heurta à elle-même et fondit en larmes.

Cher papa,
En ces jours de grande chaleur, ma pensée va vers vous que j'imagine assis dans votre bureau, lieu de fraîcheur, ou marchant sur la lande entre Emily et Keeper. De la chambre où je vous écris, j'entends le chant des oiseaux et je sens l'odeur des roses. Hélas ! je ne puis partager ce bonheur car tout le monde a fui la rue d'Isabelle.

Tout en observant l'avancée de l'ombre entre la double rangée des lits, Charlotte pensa que si M. et Mme Héger avaient eu la moindre sympathie pour elle, ils l'auraient invitée à les accompagner, ne fût-ce qu'une semaine. D'après la cuisinière, la maison dans laquelle les Héger passaient l'été était si spacieuse que l'Anglaise aurait pu vivre sous le même toit sans les importuner : « Un rien de bonté, un minimum de prévenances, rien de tel pour rendre les gens heureux, pas vrai, mademoiselle Charlotte ! »

« J'aurais même pu garder les enfants !
— Mais Madame ne sait rien de ces choses du cœur ! »

Chère Ellen,
Je vis seule depuis quinze jours, ou plus exactement, je vis avec une sourde qui dort à l'autre bout de la maison, si bien que je peux aller et venir au gré de mes insomnies, pleurer, sangloter, me plaindre à haute voix, hurler, personne ne m'entend. Un choix s'offre à moi : demeurer ici où je désespère, ou retourner à Haworth où je dépéris. A votre avis, quelle est l'agonie la moins pénible ?

Au seuil de la seconde quinzaine, Charlotte commença à maigrir. La cuisinière s'en aperçut ; elle conseilla à ma sœur d'aller consulter un médecin : « Vous n'allez tout de même pas tomber malade alors qu'il n'y a plus personne ici pour vous soigner ? » Ma sœur s'y refusa ; elle seule pouvait se sauver du désespoir. Les promenades en ville, l'étude de l'allemand, la lecture lui apporteraient tôt ou tard la paix dont elle avait besoin. Malheureusement, toutes ses tentatives échouèrent ; il suffisait d'une pensée mal maîtrisée, d'un regard porté sur un objet appartenant à M. Héger pour faire basculer le bel échafaudage de la volonté ; le mal qu'elle croyait avoir vaincu resurgissait plus virulent. Ces récidives journalières accrurent son désespoir. Ma sœur, un temps, se crut la proie des démons. Un prêtre de l'Église romaine eut droit à sa visite et à son désarroi. Que lui confessa-t-elle ? Son amour coupable, des élans charnels, un désir de mort, des idées de meurtre, sa jalousie pour une femme qui, à côté d'elle, comptabilisait tranquillement son bonheur ? Tout cela sans doute.

Cette existence torturante, rythmée par les cloches de Sainte-Gudule, le chant des oiseaux et l'appel lancé deux fois par jour par la cuisinière, Charlotte ne l'oublia jamais. Encore aujourd'hui, son œuvre témoigne d'une douleur si poignante qu'on ne peut pas ne pas être bouleversé par elle.

*Ne me laissez pas penser à eux trop souvent, trop et trop tendrement, implorai-je ; laissez-moi me contenter de puiser un breuvage tempéré, dans cette vivante rivière ; ne me laissez pas courir assoiffée ni m'adresser passionnément à ses eaux accueillantes ; ne me laissez pas imaginer en elles un goût plus suave que n'en connaissent les fontaines de la terre. Oh ! Dieu veuille que je puisse me sentir suffisamment soutenue par des rapports occasionnels, amicaux, rares, brefs, qui ne demandent point un don total...*

*« Aucun astre n'éclairera ma nuit prochaine ;*
*Aucun croissant d'espoir ne brillera pour moi ;*
*Je ne m'afflige point que le Ciel m'enténèbre,*
*Je n'ai jamais langui après des voies divines,*

*Ni demandé dans la dure tâche de vivre*
*Que le Ciel m'encourage ou que le Ciel m'assiste ;*
*Mon destin, je l'ai vu sans masque,*
*Je l'ai subi sans une larme. »*

Emily Jane Brontë,
10 février 1844.
(Traduction Pierre Leyris,

CERTAINS lieux, à fortiori certains êtres, indisposent, oppressent, accablent même. Ainsi s'expliquent les difficultés rencontrées au cours de la rédaction de ces biographies où l'auteur doit suivre les fantômes auxquels il a décidé de redonner vie. Alors qu'il pensait les diriger à sa guise, ce sont les morts qui décident ; ils l'obligent à voyager quand il souhaiterait s'attarder sur place, l'immobilisent dans un lieu qu'il se serait contenté de traverser, l'introduisent auprès de personnages antipathiques, bref, l'amènent à fréquenter des êtres qu'il aurait volontiers contournés. C'est dire combien ce séjour forcé à Bruxelles m'a coûté de gêne et de lassitude. Pourquoi le cacherais-je ? Les Héger m'ennuient, M. Constantin notamment. Parce que je ne porte pas en moi un duc de Zamorna en mal d'incarnation, je ne peux projeter sur ce petit homme à moustache, *laid et noir*, une passion digne de celle que vécut Charlotte.

Attachée à Emily, comme elle je me plais à Haworth où je me trouve à nouveau. L'hiver y est rude et violent. À peine peut-on sortir du presbytère sans être aveuglé par des tourbillons de neige. Vu des fenêtres, le cimetière ressemble à un immense linceul troué ici et là par les angles d'une croix plus haute que les autres. À l'intérieur de la maison, chacun vaque à ses occupations, réduites, il est vrai, du fait de la saison. Keeper lui-même en a fini de ses incessantes allées et venues ; il ne quitte plus la cuisine. Son caractère s'est amélioré avec l'âge ; il fait alliance depuis peu avec le chat qui a fini par lui laisser une place près de l'âtre où rougeoient jour et nuit des morceaux de tourbe.

Après des drames qu'elle a préféré taire à sa famille, Charlotte a quitté la rue d'Isabelle. Elle est rentrée définitivement de Bruxelles, laissant à sa rivale victorieuse et ravie un homme assez lâche pour ne pas l'avoir secourue. Emily a appris que Madame, jusqu'au bout, a joué la carte de l'hypocrisie. Une fois voté le départ de l'indésirable Anglaise, elle a attendu patiemment le moment qui lui permettrait de mettre son plan à exécution. Sa voix n'a jamais été altérée par la colère : au contraire, elle l'a baissée d'un ton, surtout les derniers mois : « Mademoiselle Charlotte, je ne critique pas votre travail, mais l'importance excessive que vous vous accordez. Certes, vos intentions sont louables, mais votre excès de zèle importune ! »

« Je ne sais plus à qui m'adresser dans cette maison.

— Que dites-vous là ?

— Tout le monde me fuit !

— Sottise !

— Si je suis réservée on m'accuse de froideur, et si je suis chaleureuse on me trouve trop familière !

— Votre irritabilité est maladive ! Vous devriez songer à la faire soigner ! »

Doucereuse, insistante, Madame a obtenu gain de cause sans avoir à user des armes de la légitimité ou de la menace. Sa froideur de stratège, son sang-froid, ses manigances secrètes ont gagné une bataille que l'ardeur de Charlotte a perdue : « Oh, Emily, si tu savais... j'ai subi sa présence et son espionnage de tous les instants comme une torture. Les murs, les plafonds, les placards... j'avais l'impression que tout me surveillait ! »

« Pourquoi n'es-tu pas rentrée plus tôt ?
— À la fin, je n'en pouvais plus. Il m'arrivait de me réveiller la nuit parce que j'étais convaincue qu'elle me guettait dans mon sommeil.
— Je comprends mieux la lettre alarmante de Mary Taylor... Elle croyait que tu étais en train de devenir folle !
— Si j'étais restée quinze jours de plus, je le serais devenue. Ma seule satisfaction, c'est d'avoir évité la faute professionnelle qui lui aurait permis de me mettre à la porte comme une incapable ! »

De guerre lasse, Charlotte a donc donné sa démission à celle qui, silencieusement, l'attendait depuis des mois. Nonobstant ce sacrifice, elle garde sur le cœur le poids d'un amour incompris. « Emily, peux-tu me dire ce qu'a ta sœur ? Elle a toujours la larme à l'œil ! — À mon avis, pas grand-chose, papa. Une dépression due à la fatigue et au brusque changement de climat. Elle ira beaucoup mieux d'ici quelques semaines ! — Je l'espère, car ce spectacle est navrant ! » De Belgique, l'aînée des Brontë a rapporté une humeur chagrine et une santé chancelante. Que ce soit à Haworth ou à Thorp Green où vivent Anne et Branwell, on s'interroge, on s'inquiète : que s'est-il passé à Bruxelles pour qu'une fille aussi énergique soit à ce point affectée et déprimée ? Alors qu'elle devrait se féliciter d'avoir retrouvé sa place au presbytère et l'affection confiante des siens qui ne demandent qu'à la réconforter, elle évite tout dialogue et s'isole dans un mutisme qui ne lui ressemble pas. Tous les prétextes lui sont bons pour fuir la compagnie, si aimable soit-elle. La migraine sert d'excuse : « Je vais m'étendre, je ne me sens pas bien ! » Elle s'enferme dans la chambre de Tante, ne la quitte qu'à la nuit tombée, les yeux rougis et le visage lavé par les larmes.

« Charlotte ! Charlotte, m'entends-tu ?
— Oui... que me veux-tu ?
— J'ai préparé du thé... si tu descendais en prendre une tasse avec moi ? »

★

Un matin de printemps, la douceur du temps, l'odeur des jeunes pousses, la délicatesse du ciel ont invité Charlotte à l'espérance. Elle a songé avec sympathie aux projets abandonnés deux ans plus tôt : « Pourquoi n'ouvririons-nous pas une pension pour jeunes filles ? » Cette idée a pris la route. Quelques jours plus tard, Charlotte a soumis à Emily une lettre formulaire qui a été adressée à toutes les familles susceptibles d'être intéressées. Un volumineux courrier est parti : accompagné de recommandations chaleureuses, il proposait un enseignement de qualité pour un prix modeste : « Où logeras-tu les élèves ? » a demandé le révérend, surpris qu'on puisse envisager semblable hébergement dans une maison de petites dimensions. « Mais dans le presbytère ! »

« Tu n'y comptes tout de même pas !
— Eh bien, nous verrons d'ici là ! »

Hélas ! pour Charlotte, le problème d'hébergement ne se posera pas ; ses projets tourneront vite court, car d'élèves, elle n'en trouvera pas une seule. Les familles démarchées répondront que la situation géographique de Haworth, son rude climat ne conviendraient pas à leurs filles. Après les autres, ce projet mourra de sa belle mort.

« Notre séjour à Bruxelles n'aura servi à rien !
— Je ne suis pas de cet avis. Il aura servi à nous prouver qu'il n'y a de salut qu'en nous. La paix, l'espérance et la joie sont en toi, Charlotte, nulle part ailleurs ! »

Les paroles d'Emily ne trouveront pas d'écho. À nouveau, Charlotte sentira l'angoisse frapper à une porte qu'elle ne saura pas tenir fermée. Les frayeurs, les désirs monteront en elle comme par le passé. Elle se précipitera dans la cuisine, donnera des ordres à Martha qui ne comprendra pas ce halètement, puis elle reviendra sur ses pas, passera la tête dans l'entrebâillement de la porte de la salle à manger : « Emily, je monte me coucher... j'ai une migraine si terrible que j'en suis aveugle ! — Veux-tu que je te prépare une tisane ? — Non, c'est inutile ! » Charlotte ira cacher son désespoir au premier étage, dans la chambre hantée par le souvenir de la vieille méthodiste. À peine la porte tirée sur elle, une longue, une terrible plainte s'échappera de sa poitrine oppressée. « Je voudrais mourir ! » Elle ira s'asseoir près de la fenêtre comme une femme épuisée par les turbulences de la vie, et elle restera ainsi, des heures et des heures. « Je voudrais mourir ! » Plus tard, elle retirera ses lunettes, portera un doigt à ses yeux ; elle les pressera, comme pour repousser la douleur à l'intérieur du crâne. Les larmes jailliront. « Je voudrais mourir ! » Elle songera alors à Bruxelles, aux rares moments de bonheur qu'elle y a vécus. Constantin Héger apparaîtra devant elle ; elle l'entendra rire, se moquer, gronder. Elle soupirera : « Oh, mon Dieu, si seulement je pouvais mourir, là, tout de suite ! » L'apparition de John Brown traversant le cimetière interrompra sa mélancolique divagation. Elle ira chercher un livre pour se distraire, toujours le même, un recueil de poèmes français que lui a donné M. Héger le matin de son départ. Elle l'ouvrira au hasard, lira quelques strophes et refermera le livre. « Pourquoi m'interdit-il de lui écrire ? » Elle se souviendra de la réponse du maître, se blessera contre les mots, durs, secs, méchants, imaginera la main qui les a tracés...

> Mademoiselle Charlotte, je vous ordonne de maîtriser vos émotions et de m'écrire moins souvent. Parlez-moi davantage de vos projets, et moins de vos états d'âme. Tout est excessif en vous, même votre déférence à mon endroit !

Elle ira s'asseoir devant son bureau, et là, elle cédera à la tentation. Sa lettre commencera par une excuse : « Pardonnez-moi de ne pas vous obéir, je sais que je ne devrais pas vous écrire, mais voilà bientôt six mois que je suis sans nouvelles de vous ! » Elle s'inquiétera de la santé de Mme Héger, ainsi, lorsque Madame fouillera dans les tiroirs de son mari et lira la lettre, elle y trouvera immédiatement son nom. Ensuite, et toujours en français, elle lui confiera les soucis que lui donne son père qui survit péniblement à une désespérance que seules ses filles peuvent comprendre, parce qu'il faut avoir contemplé ce visage de vieillard aux yeux fermés pour savoir ce qu'est l'enfermement. Puis elle parlera d'Emily, la besogneuse qui s'occupe avec le même soin des bêtes et des gens, pétrit le pain ou épluche les légumes tout en apprenant l'allemand dans un livre ouvert sur la table de cuisine. Elle décrira la vie de Branwell et d'Anne, tous deux employés dans une riche famille de la région d'York ; son frère et sa sœur, dont les nouvelles sont plutôt rassurantes malgré l'accent nostalgique de certaines remarques. Elle terminera en parlant d'elle, de sa solitude — « immense, monsieur, surtout depuis que je n'ai plus le bonheur d'échanger des idées avec vous ! » — de son regret de ne pouvoir devenir écrivain, mais elle a retenu la leçon de Southey et de Wordsworth, celle de son maître également : « Je sais qu'une femme ne peut nourrir un projet aussi ambitieux ! » En fin de lettre, elle se plaindra de ne pouvoir continuer à enseigner, trouvera l'excuse de la cécité de son père qu'elle ne peut décemment laisser aux seuls soins d'Emily. Ce récapitulatif terminé, elle taira la lenteur des journées désertées par l'enthousiasme, l'anxiété des soirées sans but, l'arrivée angoissante de la nuit, la lente agonie de sa jeunesse tendue vers un amour qu'on lui refuse et que Dieu condamne. Un peu plus tard, Emily la verra quitter le presbytère comme une voleuse.

« Où cours-tu ainsi ?
— Je vais chez le papetier ! »

Emily devinera la lettre cachée dans la poche du manteau. « Pauvre Charlotte ! » Elle s'apitoiera, imaginera l'accueil réservé à semblable message ; le mouvement agacé de la main, les commentaires irrités d'un homme qui n'a que faire de la passion d'une Anglaise, même si elle lit Pascal dans le texte. Les abandons épistolaires de Charlotte ne rencontreront que mépris et incompréhension. « La famille Héger l'a condamnée, et elle s'entête à refuser cette condamnation ! » Pour échapper à ces images négatives et humiliantes, Emily se précipitera dans le bureau du pasteur qui l'accueillera avec un sursaut : « Eh bien, que t'arrive-t-il ? »

« Voulez-vous que je vous lise le journal ? »

Si papa refuse son aide, elle ira se dégourdir les

jambes sur la lande, ou bien elle se jettera dans son journal.

> ... aujourd'hui, il fait un temps frais et pluvieux. À Gondal, les royalistes ont livré une bataille aux révolutionnaires. Charlotte est allée poster une lettre qu'elle aurait mieux fait de garder pour elle. J'écris dans la cuisine ; c'est encore là que je me sens le mieux, entre Keeper et mon faucon...

À peine clos le procès-verbal d'une journée aussi insignifiante que les autres, la force d'une image l'avertira qu'un poème commence à s'écrire. Capturée par l'œuvre en cours, elle se laissera entraîner vers cette sorte de ravissement inquiet, toujours prêt à glisser vers l'insatisfaction, parce que le désir de dire, de raconter, renaît au bout de chaque phrase, en bas de chaque paragraphe. Puis elle songera à ses sœurs et à son frère, livrés comme elle à l'inassouvissement ; si l'écriture n'a rassasié aucun d'eux, elle les a tous sauvés du néant.

> « Encore quelqu'un qui vient nous déranger ! Tais-toi, Keeper ! »

Un bruit de sabots lui signalera la visite d'un paroissien venu demander conseil au révérend. Elle fera taire Keeper qui, de dépit, mordillera le pied de sa chaise. L'écho de la discussion la distraira de son travail.

> ... aujourd'hui, jeudi, papa est malade. Il a une forte grippe mais il refuse de garder le lit. Un paroissien est venu lui rendre visite. Charlotte est rentrée de la poste. Elle se morfond dans la chambre de Tante où elle a élu domicile ; elle

pense que je suis assez égoïste pour ignorer sa souffrance. J'ai enfin reçu des nouvelles d'Anne qui a écrit un beau poème à mon intention. Le projet d'ouvrir un pensionnat a dû être abandonné. Serons-nous encore en vie dans cinq ans ?

# TROISIÈME PARTIE

*February 2, 1844*

*«No sighs for me, no sympathy,*
*No wish to keep my soul below;*
*The heart is dead since infancy,*
*Unwept-for let the body go.»*

*«Pour moi ni sympathie, ni soupirs, ni regret*
*Que mon âme soit en partance;*
*Puisque le cœur est mort dès sa première enfance,*
*Que le corps s'en aille impleuré.»*

(Traduction Pierre Leyris.)

DANS cet espace clos où se replie l'écrivain, vous attendez que viennent vers vous une silhouette, un visage, éventuellement un profil. Qui vous remettra sur la piste ? Anne ? Branwell ? Prisonnier d'un emploi qui le retient au loin, il n'est plus là pour vous soutenir ou vous tendre la main. Charlotte, peut-être ? Je la vois. Emportée par un mouvement de tout le corps, elle est en train de descendre précipitamment la grand-rue de Haworth. La voici qui entre chez le papetier. On s'empresse autour d'elle, on l'interroge. Comment se portent les habitants du presbytère ? L'isolement d'un printemps gâché par le mauvais temps n'est-il pas difficile à vaincre ? « Le cimetière doit être peu visité ces jours-ci ? » En effet, à part les membres de la famille Brontë, nul ne le traverse.

« Il paraît que mademoiselle Emily a été mordue par un chien enragé ?

— C'est exact. Elle n'a rien trouvé de mieux que de brûler la plaie elle-même avec un tisonnier !

— Courageuse personne... Et comment va le révérend ?

— Comme un aveugle. »

Charlotte s'est rendue au village pour y effectuer des achats. Ce matin encore, son panier sera lourd à porter.

« Il me faut également de l'encre et quelques feuilles de papier de belle qualité. »

Les gestes nerveux du commerçant lui rappellent ceux du maître bruxellois, alors qu'il rangeait précipitamment les copies sur son bureau. Ce souvenir la renvoie au pire de ce que contient sa mémoire : la séparation, l'abandon de l'être qu'on aime sans espoir. Elle grimace un remerciement, arrache le paquet des mains du papetier surpris par une précipitation jugée grossière dans un pays où le temps ne presse qu'à l'instant de mourir, disparaît sur un au revoir mal articulé et à peine perceptible : « Celle-là n'a décidément plus sa raison. Depuis qu'elle a séjourné sur le continent, elle se prend pour une autre ! » Dans la rue, Charlotte essuie discrètement une larme. Le coup d'œil jeté à la bouteille d'encre la réconforte. Elle songe à la longue lettre circonstanciée qu'elle va écrire à Ellen, au soulagement qu'elle en tirera.

Ma chère Ellen,
Le printemps tarde comme à son habitude. Il fait encore plus froid que la semaine dernière où une sérieuse chute de neige a brûlé les premiers bourgeons. Le vent souffle du matin au soir. Il est si violent et si glacial que nous ne pouvons même pas aller nous promener. Je comprends les parents qui ont refusé de nous confier leurs filles. Qui choisirait de vivre dans un tel pays ? L'échec que nous venons d'essuyer a profondément affecté mon moral et celui d'Anne. S'il est pour l'une et pour l'autre symbole d'une fin — celle de nos dernières espérances —, il libère Emily d'un énorme souci. Ma sœur redoutait de voir arriver des étrangères. Elle ne m'en a jamais rien dit, mais je la connais. Il y a quelques jours, nous avons eu une discussion

qui a failli virer à la dispute. Je ne peux tout de même pas lui en vouloir de se satisfaire d'une vie médiocre ?

Depuis quelque temps, Charlotte n'écoute plus que sa détresse et moi les pulsations d'une maison où j'aime aller et venir. Chacune à notre façon, nous remontons le chemin de l'égoïsme. Le sien tourne autour d'une pension étrangère, le mien autour d'un presbytère. L'anodin a cessé d'exister entre nous et les conflits abondent. Encore hier matin, alors que je sortais brusquement de ma chambre, je l'ai bousculée : « Tu pourrais t'excuser, Emily ! »

« Tu ne m'as pas laissé le temps de le faire ! »

Elle a caché son visage. Au lieu d'ignorer son chagrin, j'ai eu la maladresse de le lui renvoyer : « Pourquoi pleures-tu ? — Laisse-moi tranquille ! » a-t-elle crié avec haine. J'ai voulu la prendre par les épaules, mais elle m'a repoussée : « Tu ne peux pas me comprendre ! Là où tu es, tu ne peux comprendre personne ! » Dire que je me suis sentie blessée, non ; impuissante, oui. Elle s'est enfermée dans sa chambre où elle a dû écrire une lettre à sa seconde confidente, Mary Taylor, à qui elle a pris l'habitude de confier son dénuement, la déchirure ressentie chaque matin quand le facteur disparaît sans avoir déposé une lettre de Bruxelles. Peut-être s'est-elle plainte de moi ?

> ... Emily n'aime personne. Son dogue, un arbre comptent autant que moi. Oh, Mary, je ne sais où me conduit la vie, vers quel désert ? Il n'y a pas un soir où je ne demande à Dieu de me rappeler à lui tant l'idée d'avoir à me réveiller le lendemain me remplit d'effroi ! Où vais-je trouver le courage de vivre encore ?

★

Sur le point de quitter définitivement le château de son père pour partir pour la Nouvelle-Zélande, Mary a invité Charlotte à Huntsworth. Le jour de la séparation, l'audacieuse voyageuse a conseillé à ma sœur de suivre son exemple: « Regardez-vous en face... Le temps passe, et vous n'avez plus vingt ans ! Vous serez bientôt ce qu'on appelle ici une vieille fille sans devenir ! »

« Oh, Mary, comment pouvez-vous me dire des choses aussi brutales ?

— Arrachez-vous à ce cimetière.... Quittez votre père qui n'est qu'un égoïste !

— Vous savez bien qu'il est quasiment aveugle et qu'il a besoin d'aide !

— Qu'à cela ne tienne... Emily s'occupera de lui ! Vous êtes trop intelligente pour sacrifier votre avenir. Le désœuvrement est en train de vous tuer ! Faites comme moi, faites comme ces milliers de femmes libres, indépendantes, courageuses, quittez l'Angleterre et sa poussière ! »

Lorsque Charlotte, émue, bouleversée, m'a rapporté cette conversation, j'ai dû convenir que Mary avait raison ; le destin l'attendait ailleurs. Elle avait trop d'envergure pour une contrée aussi étriquée que la nôtre : « Comment peux-tu me dire cela, toi qui te plais ici ? — Je me plais ici car je n'attends plus rien, ce qui n'est pas ton cas. — Je ne vais tout de même pas te laisser seule avec un aveugle ? — Et pourquoi pas ? — Jamais je n'en aurai le courage ! »

L'intervention de Mary Taylor m'a rappelée à l'ordre. Comment pouvais-je goûter à la paix alors qu'à côté de moi un être dépérissait ? Le moment était venu de prouver que non seulement je pouvais rester seule au presbytère avec papa mais que j'étais capable également de tenir un rôle de gestionnaire. J'ai donc proposé ce qu'on n'aurait probablement jamais songé à me demander : Charlotte accepterait-elle de me confier l'héritage que Tante nous avait laissé ? « Avec ton assentiment et celui d'Anne, je veillerai à sa gestion. La lecture de journaux spécialisés m'aidera à faire des placements avantageux. Ces gains te permettront de voyager un peu. »

« Banquière ? Voilà un talent que je ne m'attendais pas à trouver chez toi !
— Il faut bien que quelqu'un se préoccupe de cet argent !

À peine avais-je fait cette proposition qu'Anne et Branwell sont venus nous rendre visite. Au cours d'un repas pris en commun, papa s'est interrogé sur ma véritable nature : « Décidément, tu m'étonneras toujours ! »

« Qu'est-ce qui vous étonne si fort ?
— Tu te conduis comme un homme !
— Que voulez-vous dire par là ? Que je manque de modestie ?
— Tu tires au pistolet mieux que quiconque, dresses ton chien comme un dompteur, et voilà que tu t'occupes de placements ! Si seulement ton frère avait tes qualités ! »

Piqué au vif, Branwell a dressé la tête ; qu'était-on en train de lui reprocher ? son manque de virilité ? son refus de prendre des initiatives ? Il s'est lancé dans un discours véhément qui a coupé l'appétit à la communauté stupéfaite par tant d'aigreur. Non seulement Branwell rejetait les vertus dont notre père aurait voulu le voir paré, mais son ambition était placée ailleurs, derrière d'autres guichets. Le sérieux, l'attachement aux choses vaines, la gestion d'un patrimoine misérable n'étaient pas de nature à mobiliser un caractère comme le sien qui n'appréciait que l'extraordinaire, le singulier, le jamais vu. Perdu dans des spéculations égoïstes, papa ignorait tout de ses enfants. « Si vous avez des reproches à me faire, adressez-vous directement à moi et pas à Emily ! — À quoi ça servirait ? Tu ne me réponds jamais ! — Que voulez-vous que je réponde ? — Ce que tu penses, si toutefois tu parviens à penser juste ! »

> « Je n'ai pas plus de goût pour le tir au pistolet que pour le dressage des chiens ou les placements d'argent ! Tout cela m'insupporte !
>
> — Je serais curieux de savoir s'il y a quelque chose dans le monde qui ne t'insupporte pas ?
>
> — Au lieu de vous plaindre de trouver ces qualités chez une de vos filles, ce qui, entre parenthèses, est offensant pour elle, félicitez-vous-en !
>
> — Je t'interdis de t'adresser à moi sur ce ton !
>
> — Dans ce cas, ne vous étonnez pas que je me taise en votre présence ! »

Mon frère a gardé le silence toute la journée et personne n'a pu le convaincre de mettre un terme à cette sotte bouderie. « Je n'y suis pour rien, Branwell ! Les compliments de papa ne me causent ni plaisir ni déplaisir, mais ton mutisme me chagrine ! — Emily, laisse-moi tranquille, veux-tu ? »

De son séjour à Luddenden Foot, Branwell a gardé le regret des soirées passées en compagnie des mariniers et des Irlandais brûlés par l'alcool. Combien courtes étaient alors les nuits ! Combien beau le ciel qu'on regardait couché dans les prairies de l'été, excitantes les soirées où on se faisait des serments avinés et sans suite, folles les histoires qu'on se racontait à tour de rôle ! Et ce n'est pas le salaire de précepteur que lui remet solennellement le stupide et austère M. Robinson qui lui fera oublier les plaisirs d'autrefois. « Sache que si je reste à Thorp Green, c'est contre mon gré ! J'ai accepté ce poste pour être agréable à papa qui n'est qu'un vieux radoteur ! »

Au fur et à mesure qu'il avance dans la vie, les démons se réveillent en Branwell. Pourquoi n'est-il pas resté l'enfant aimé d'un héros, d'un Alexander Percy, comte de Northangerland, génie arraché par le pouvoir de l'imagination aux insignifiances de la vie provinciale ? Pourquoi n'a-t-il pas su convaincre le rédacteur en chef du *Blackwood's Magazine* de son talent ? Le destin ne donne-t-il donc bonne place qu'aux médiocres ?

★

> Emily, sœur très chère,
> Il semblerait que depuis notre retour, les choses se soient gâtées en Branwell. La tristesse, l'amertume lui font suite. Pour ma part, je ne sais plus comment l'aborder. Son humeur est telle que prendre de ses nouvelles, c'est l'offenser. J'imagine que les réflexions pessimistes de papa ont fait mauvaise route en lui. Le goût qu'il a toujours eu pour sa personne le rend sensible à des compliments dont il devrait s'écarter ; ils ne sont sincères qu'à la surface. À diverses reprises, Branwell s'est mis en frais auprès des jeunes filles de la maison ; après avoir fait la cour à l'aînée qui s'est moquée de lui, il a tenté de se rendre intéressant auprès de la

seconde, trop rustre pour le comprendre. Cet insuccès, au lieu de l'inviter à un recul, l'a poussé sur le versant où logent les maîtres. M. et Mme Robinson l'invitent chaque soir à la conversation. De se sentir écouté l'aide à supporter un état qu'il juge par ailleurs intolérable.
Je te tairais tout ceci si depuis une semaine ou deux je n'avais une inquiétude. À qui, en vérité, s'adressent les discours de Branwell ? Qui tente-t-il de convaincre de son malheureux sort ? Mon regard se porte sur quelqu'un, mais j'espère me tromper, car l'affaire serait grave...

A Thorp Green, sous les arbres du parc qu'il traverse deux fois par jour, Branwell soliloque. Lorqu'il n'en peut plus de ce grondement intérieur, il va cacher sa colère derrière les murs d'un pavillon que ses employeurs ont mis à sa disposition. C'est là qu'il reçoit Anne lorsqu'elle a besoin d'un mot de réconfort. « Pourquoi te laisses-tu tracasser de la sorte par ces gamines ! Tu n'es pas leur bonne ! » Plus portée vers autrui que vers elle-même, Anne oublie ses propres ennuis pour s'intéresser à ceux de Branwell : « Mon Dieu, mais quelle mauvaise mine tu as ! Tu n'as pas bu, j'espère ? » Un grognement lui répond ; il l'envoie en enfer.

« Je n'en peux plus ! »

De quoi ? Après tant d'échecs professionnels, de tribulations, Branwell n'est-il pas satisfait d'être enfin posé dans une famille, certes capricieuse, mais qui sait apprécier le brio de sa conversation ? Au lieu de l'apaiser, cette interrogation le met hors de lui : « Si c'est pour me faire un prêche à la manière de Tante, tu peux regagner ta chambre ! Je ne suis pas d'humeur à l'entendre ! »

« Je t'en supplie, Branwell... cesse de boire... Un jour ou l'autre, les Robinson le remarqueront ! Ressaisis-toi !
— Ressaisir qui ? Il n'y a plus de Branwell ! »

«*Madame... écoutez-moi bien. Ne trouvez-vous pas étrange qu'une personne en ayant invité une autre à dîner dispose devant ce convive un service d'assiettes mais oublie la nourriture ? De même, n'est-il pas étrange que vous m'accueilliez ici en me refusant le seul plaisir qui puisse me plaire ? Je vois que vous vous préparez à partir, mais si mon séjour dans cette maison doit être bref, pourquoi me le rendre désagréable ? Pourquoi tenter d'infliger une gelée nocturne aux feuilles naissantes qui ne demandent pour atteindre leur plein développement qu'une heure ou deux de rosée matinale et de soleil tiède ?*»

Patrick Branwell Brontë,
*Et ceux qui sont las se reposent.*
(Traduction Marcelle Sibon.)

ALORS que je croyais l'avoir perdu, j'ai retrouvé Branwell. Il se promenait dans le parc du château des Robinson que pour des raisons que j'ignore encore il ne semble plus pressé de quitter. À son regard, à ses gestes, à son allure, j'ai compris qu'en lui quelque chose avait changé; le fils du pasteur n'est plus décidé à recevoir des leçons de morale: son père n'est qu'un vieux radoteur et ses sœurs des dévotes! Son vocabulaire s'est endurci, mais son cœur, au fond, est toujours aussi compatissant, et ce jeu de méchant ne convainc personne. Si Branwell fait souffrir, c'est par inadvertance; rien en lui ne se réjouit de voir couler des larmes. Quant à son physique il a subi peu de modifications. Sa silhouette est toujours aussi courte, ses cheveux en brosse toujours aussi durs, son grand front toujours aussi bombé. Seuls ses yeux, sous les lunettes, se sont creusés; mais peut-être n'est-ce qu'une impression due à un léger amaigrissement? Au-dessus de la bouche moqueuse, son nez tout en finesse fait ressortir la faiblesse du menton.

«Anne, comment me trouves-tu?
— Qu'est-ce qui t'inquiète?
— Mme Robinson m'a dit que j'avais l'air tendu et crispé!»

Peut-on l'en condamner? Branwell passe à côté du réel sans le voir: «Tout en moi est vrai... même et surtout ce que les autres disent faux!» Hier soir encore, il a donné un aperçu de son caractère à sa sœur, scandalisée qu'on puisse traiter la vérité avec pareille désinvolture :

> « Pourquoi as-tu menti ? Tu n'as jamais refusé un poste au *Blackwood's Magazine* !
> — J'ai vécu cet instant tant de fois par la pensée que cela revient au même ! »

Pour le moment, il est le précepteur d'Edmund, un jeune gaillard avec lequel il s'entend fort bien — les enfants ont pour le fils Brontë des élans et une confiance que n'ont jamais eus les adultes. L'adaptation à ce poste a été lente, difficile, mais le résultat — provisoire — est satisfaisant : « Je vais finir par me plaire dans cette maison ! — Je croyais que tu n'en pouvais plus ? — Mon humeur a changé depuis qu'on est bon pour moi ! » À qui Branwell doit-il cette soudaine bonté ? À M. Robinson animé par le repentir ? Certes pas : « Je n'ai jamais croisé homme aussi ennuyeux, aussi austère, un véritable pisse-froid ! » Aux invités qui hantent le château et circulent dans le salon de Thorp Green ? « Ces propriétaires terriens sont assommants et leur prétention n'a d'égale que leur idiotie ! » À Mme Robinson, alors ?

> ... une femme, cher ami Leyland, d'une distinction exceptionnelle et d'une qualité de cœur rare. Non pas indifférente et froide comme je l'ai cru durant des mois passés dans l'ignorance de ce qui se préparait pour moi, mais chaleureuse et ouverte !

Juste retour des choses ; après avoir rêvé de conquérir sous des noms d'emprunt, Branwell souhaite être aimé sous le sien. L'objet de ses pensées n'est autre que la maîtresse de céans, une femme aux charmes indéniables qui, avec le concours du hasard, aurait pu être sa mère. Mais n'est-ce pas une mère que recherche ce garçon mal grandi ? N'est-ce pas la protection féminine qui a si cruellement fait défaut à sa jeunesse ? N'est-ce pas le regard de tendresse, la main posée sur la tête de l'enfant que recherche le précepteur d'Edmund ?

> « Que pourrais-je faire pour vous être agréable, madame ?
> — Rester près de moi.
> — Je vous sens si triste.
> — Je le suis... cette pluie pénètre jusqu'au cœur. Que lisez-vous en ce moment ?
> — *Manfred* de Byron.
> — Si vous m'en lisiez un passage ? »

À Thorp Green, j'ai retrouvé Branwell installé aux pieds d'une Lydia Robinson alanguie dans une robe de soie. Assis près d'une fenêtre où venait mourir la lumière grisâtre d'une journée pluvieuse, il lui faisait la lecture. La tête renversée sur le dossier du sofa, la maîtresse de maison écoutait avec ravissement la voix chaleureuse et parfaitement modulée du précepteur de son fils ; dans la bouche du jeune homme, l'amour n'était plus un mot vague, une idée confuse, mais un état bouleversant, indiscutable.

> « Voilà des phrases qu'on aimerait avoir écrites soi-même, tant elles sont belles et sonnent juste ! Continuez, je vous prie... continuez ! »

Cette femme d'âge mûr, gracieuse autant qu'attentive, n'est pas la sage épouse qu'a cru Branwell. Tenue à la fidélité par un serment de pure convenance, mariée depuis des années à un homme pour lequel elle n'éprouve que de la sympathie, elle a choisi des moyens détournés pour faire savoir au précepteur combien elle était sensible à sa présence : « Continuez, je vous prie... continuez ! »

> ... au respect que je lui porte vient de s'ajouter une passion que je ne mesure plus. Mais chut ! La chose doit demeurer secrète. Je ne peux la livrer qu'à un ami comme vous. Cette révélation, si elle était connue, ne nous apporterait que des tracas. Le scandale serait si grand qu'il me faudrait partir d'ici et je ne peux imaginer cette éventualité sans frémir ! Lydia est mariée à un homme étroit d'idées et terre à terre qui ne respecte que la fortune et le conformisme. Imaginez la scène qu'il nous ferait !

Amenée par Branwell à une réflexion à laquelle elle s'est longtemps refusée, Lydia Robinson s'apitoie sur elle-même. Qu'a-t-elle connu de l'amour, de ses frémissements ? La sagesse apprise dès le berceau demandait à être bousculée, eh bien, voilà qui est fait ! Ce soupir, cette main qui s'abandonne sont pour Branwell autant d'aveux.

> « *Écoute-moi, écoute-moi, ô Astarté !*
> *Ma bien-aimée, oh, parle-moi ! J'ai tant souffert,*
> *Oh ! j'ai tant enduré... Regarde-moi ! La tombe*
> *Ne t'a changée pas plus que je n'ai fait pour toi.* »

Tout en continuant sa lecture, Branwell lève la tête au-dessus des pages, le temps de constater que Lydia Robinson a les yeux fermés : « Continuez, je vous en prie... continuez ! »

> « *Tu m'as aimé trop fort, comme moi je t'aimais ;*
> *Nous ne fûmes pas faits pour torturer l'un*
> *[l'autre,*
> *Si le plus mortel péché fut de nous aimer*

*Comme nous avons fait. Dis que tu ne me hais...*
*Car j'ai porté le châtiment pour tous les deux...* »

... la lecture nous rapproche et nous unit ; c'est à elle que nous devons nos seuls moments de bonheur. Elle nous permet des confidences d'une audace incroyable. Lydia, enfin Mme Robinson, aime m'entendre. J'ai l'impression que ma voix lui plaît. Elle me regarde rarement : craint-elle de découvrir un aveu dans mes yeux ? C'est probable ; la pudeur de ma bien-aimée est si grande ! Oh, cher Leyland, si vous saviez combien délicieux sont ces moments où nous communions dans la beauté du style et la perfection des sentiments !

Cette perfection confiée à l'ami Leyland est-elle durable ? Non, car voici que s'avancent des trouble-fête. « Que fait ce petit rien du tout ? Ne devrait-il pas être auprès d'Edmund ? » Les trois filles de Mme Robinson, Lydia, Elizabeth et Mary, viennent d'entrer à pas de loup dans le salon. Elles observent le tableau d'un œil stupéfait en même temps que furieux. Que signifie tout cela ? Ce freluquet et cette femme indolente sont-ils en train de jouer une scène de séduction, et depuis quand la représentation dure-t-elle ? « Ce rouquin est ridicule à souhait ! Lui si petit, s'asseoir sur un tabouret ! On dirait un enfant aux pieds de sa mère ! » Requis par sa lecture, Branwell n'a pas conscience du geste de sa main qui trace dans l'espace des mots que sa bouche articule à la manière d'un comédien.

« Lui n'est pas brillant, mais maman est encore plus ridicule. Elle ressemble à une sainte en prière ! »

Les demoiselles Robinson ont décidé de quitter la pièce sans être vues. Elles abandonnent Byron à une mère alanguie sous la charge d'un plaisir coupable et un précepteur trop prévenant pour être honnête. Toutes trois vont déverser leur hargne et leur antipathie dans le petit salon qui sert de salle d'étude. « Comment un jeune homme peut-il courtiser une femme aussi vieille que maman ? Branwell n'est qu'un coquin ! » Offensées au nom du père parti pour surveiller ses terres, Elizabeth s'interroge :

> « Que dirait papa s'il savait que maman profite de son absence pour se faire lire des choses dégoûtantes !
>
> — Nous allons bientôt le savoir car nous allons tout lui raconter ! »

L'aînée des filles à qui l'âge a déjà beaucoup appris ne partage pas l'ardeur des deux justicières : « Nous n'avons rien à gagner d'un scandale ! Nous serions les premières à en pâtir. Miss Brontë serait renvoyée en même temps que son frère. N'oubliez pas que c'est elle qui l'a fait engager ! Elle a la responsabilité de cette vilaine affaire ! » L'argument a du poids ; plusieurs années de vie commune ont créé des liens solides et personne ne souhaite le départ d'Anne : « N'empêche que son frère n'a pas à faire le malin en la présence de maman ! » L'idée d'un marchandage germe dans l'esprit de l'une d'elles :

> « Je propose que nous gardions le secret quitte à le monnayer par la suite, quand maman nous refusera quelque chose ! »

À Thorp Green, en ce printemps 1845, trois chipies guettent Branwell qui ne se doute de rien. « Qu'ont-elles à me regarder de cette façon insistante ? J'avais l'impression de ne pas leur plaire, et voilà qu'elles ne me quittent plus d'un pas ! »

« Que puis-je pour vous, mesdemoiselles ?
— Pour nous, pas grand-chose !
— Pourquoi riez-vous ? Ma question est-elle si comique ? »

Pris au piège d'une passion qui envahit son esprit et lui dicte un but, le précepteur des Robinson poursuit la conquête d'une femme pour laquelle il ne devrait avoir que de l'estime, du respect et de l'admiration. « Le malheur est peut-être au bout, mais qu'importe ! Je n'ai jamais vécu aussi intensément ! » Après avoir suivi un enseignement qui aurait dû ne s'adresser qu'à son fils, Mme Robinson réfléchit à l'insignifiance de son existence oisive, c'est du moins ce qu'affirme Branwell dans les lettres très enflammées et confidentielles qu'il adresse régulièrement à son meilleur ami. Épouse d'un homme sans dimension ni perspective, si scrupuleux dans la gestion de son patrimoine qu'il en est devenu insupportable et ennuyeux, l'ancienne Miss Gisborne, fille du révérend du même nom, attend le veuvage et les retombées d'une fortune qui fera d'elle l'une des femmes les plus riches de la région. Ses silences, ressentis par tous comme autant de marques d'indifférence ou de mépris, sont pris par Branwell pour des appels pressants auxquels il lui faut répondre : « Vous m'avez demandé ? »

« Non.
— Puis-je vous faire la lecture ? Je viens de terminer *Othello*. Il y a un passage admirable sur la jalousie.
— Je n'ai pas le désir d'en savoir plus sur un sentiment que j'ignore. Mais si vous souhaitez faire la lecture à mes filles, elles en seront ravies ! »

Sous ce coup de vent, Branwell s'éteint. Il jette un coup d'œil autour de lui, s'alarme; que signifie ce recul? Pourquoi Lydia Robinson a-t-elle refusé au précepteur le plaisir d'une lecture dans l'intimité? L'a-t-il contrariée sans le vouloir?

> ... il y a des moments où l'envie de mourir me saisit à nouveau, comme ce soir, par exemple, où je me retrouve seul comme au pire d'un passé qui n'est pas si lointain. Pourquoi m'a-t-elle répondu sur ce ton hautain? Quel souhait n'ai-je pas entendu? Heureusement, j'ai toujours ma petite fiole de laudanum à portée de main. Qu'en pensez-vous, homme sensible? Vaut-il mieux souffrir sainement, je veux dire à jeun, ou être heureux grâce à la drogue?

★

Alors que tombe le crépuscule, Branwell s'adonne sans retenue à la mélancolie et à l'amertume. Il marche pour marcher, au hasard, sans plaisir. Sous les arbres du parc dont il a appris à connaître tous les détours, le crépuscule glisse en direction des fourrés. « Qu'attend le bonhomme pour mourir? À plus de quarante ans, il a l'âge! Je me vois d'ici, époux d'une femme admirable et riche. Oh, comme je saurais l'aimer et lui donner ce qu'elle n'a jamais reçu! »

> « Branwell, peux-tu monter un instant? J'ai à te parler! »

Penchée à la fenêtre de sa chambre, Anne a l'expression des mauvais jours. « Aurai-je encore droit à une leçon de morale? » Il traverse l'allée gravillonnée, dépose sa bouteille de laudanum dans la pénombre d'un massif, jette un coup d'œil en direction des fenêtres du rez-de-chaussée, aperçoit le profil de Madame et le dos de Monsieur qui se pavane dans le salon. Il monte l'escalier.

« Que me veux-tu ?
— Donne-toi la peine d'entrer pour le savoir ! »

La porte à peine poussée, il s'affale sur le lit. Sa sœur le regarde d'un air sévère et désapprobateur : « Je te préviens tout de suite... je ne suis pas d'humeur à entendre tes reproches ! » Anne s'assoit à l'écart ; cet homme avachi l'irrite et la met mal à l'aise : « Autant que tu le saches avant les autres... je ne reviendrai pas à Thorp Green après les congés scolaires. »

« Tu plaisantes ?
— En ai-je l'air ?
— Mais que dira Mme Robinson ?
— Ce qu'elle voudra. »

Branwell pousse un juron. La position assise lui convient soudain mieux que la position couchée. Il pousse un doigt en direction de sa sœur : « Tu ne peux pas faire ça à des gens qui ont été si bons pour toi ! » Ses paroles tombent dans le vide ; Anne ne demeurera pas davantage dans une maison où, dès le départ, elle s'est déplu : « J'ai assez souffert de la solitude ici. Il est temps pour moi de rentrer à la maison ! — Es-tu si pressée d'aller t'y cloîtrer ? » Branwell cherche à sauver la situation. Il insiste, va de la menace à la prière avec une facilité qui désarçonne sa sœur : « Crois-tu donc que je n'aie pas remarqué ton manège ? — Quel manège ? — Personne dans cette maison, à part M. Robinson, n'est aveugle ! Pas plus tard que cet après-midi, Elizabeth et Edmund ont menacé leur mère de tout

révéler à leur père si elle ne passait pas leur caprice !
— Je ne comprends rien à tout cela ! Qu'ai-je donc fait ? »

« La cour à Mme Robinson, qui a eu l'impudeur d'y répondre ! »

Quelques jours plus tard, Anne a signifié à ses employeurs qu'elle ne reviendrait pas après les vacances. Vexée qu'une salariée ait pu prendre une initiative réservée aux maîtres, Mme Robinson a donné son accord sur un ton qui n'a trompé personne. « Si vous en avez décidé ainsi ! » Menacé par ce départ, Branwell a repris goût à l'alcool. Au château, où l'on ressent le départ d'Anne comme une insulte et une trahison, chacun se pose la question : pourquoi le précepteur qui suivait de trop près la maîtresse des lieux se tient-il à l'écart maintenant que l'on souhaiterait le divertissement de sa conversation ?

« J'imagine qu'il est dans sa chambre, madame.
— Quel curieux personnage ! Depuis que vous avez décidé de nous quitter, c'est à peine s'il daigne encore nous saluer, nous ses maîtres ! »

Anne s'excuse pour les manquements de son frère ; si Branwell continue à refuser l'aide de Dieu, que va-t-il advenir de lui ? « Vos sœurs ou vous-même songerez à lui préparer un trousseau léger ! » Dès la fin juillet, il partira avec la famille Robinson qui passera l'été au bord de la mer : « Il risque de faire très chaud à Scarborough ! »

« Mais certainement, madame ! »

*« "... je veux tenir ta main, en preuve que je ne t'ai pas fâchée ou, du moins, en signe qu'à la réprimande de l'offense tu mêles l'absolution de l'offenseur. Allons, en tant qu'hôtesse, tu dois mettre ta main dans la mienne... ou je n'aurai d'autre choix que de partir sur-le-champ ou d'ouvrir tout un sac de querelles. Dieu bénisse les doigts qui de leur seul contact me redonnent de longs jours de vie."*

*« Ainsi parla M. Percy, avec un peu de hâte et beaucoup d'ardeur en lui saisissant la main au passage, et la dominant de sa haute taille avec une expression où l'amour le disputait à la tristesse ; son regard implorait le pardon de son front, la sympathie de ses yeux... »*

Patrick Branwell Brontë,
*Et ceux qui sont las se reposent.*
(Traduction Marcelle Sibon.)

*« Il ne subsiste aucune lettre relatant ce qui se passa exactement au mois de juillet 1845, époque où Branwell fut renvoyé de son poste. Dans cette histoire, tout n'est que on-dit, potins et conjectures... »*

Daphné Du Maurier.

Ainsi mon frère a été renvoyé par M. Robinson trop heureux de montrer son mépris à plus intelligent et plus pauvre que lui. Si je n'apprécie pas la brutalité du procédé, je me garde de juger le motif. Que s'est-il passé ? Nous ne le saurons probablement jamais. Quelle que soit la vérité, M. Robinson, dans une lettre adressée à notre père, a sommé Branwell de cesser toutes relations avec sa famille.

> ... s'il ne se le tient pas pour dit, je n'hésiterai pas à déclencher un scandale qui éclaboussera le nom des Brontë !

Dans cette triste affaire, c'est encore notre père qui a été le plus touché. Dès l'instant où il a pris connaissance de cette lettre humiliante, il s'est replié sur lui-même, refusant tout dialogue. Depuis le départ du coupable pour Liverpool où il est allé consoler une dépression qui menace de s'installer, papa a cessé de nous voir et de nous entendre. Il n'a même pas demandé à Anne comment, après cinq années d'absence, elle trouvait la maison et ses coutumes. En somme, nous n'existons plus pour lui.

« Papa, voulez-vous que l'une de nous vous fasse la lecture du *Blackwood's* ?

— Non, merci.

— Ça fait plus d'une semaine que vous ne suivez plus l'actualité ! Vous qui autrefois vouliez être au courant de tout !

— Plus rien ne m'importe ! »

Au long des journées interminables, pour lui et pour nous, nous ne l'apercevons que quelques minutes, le temps de lui servir ses repas. Il continue à aller et venir dans son bureau. Parfois un grognement nous parvient ; il vient de se cogner contre un meuble. À la cécité, et comme pour se punir d'avoir fait de son fils un être indésirable, il a ajouté le mutisme. La prière du soir qui, hier encore, nous donnait l'occasion d'échanger quelques mots avec lui, n'est plus qu'un bref remuement des lèvres : « Maintenant, laissez-moi seul ! »

« Seul ? mais papa, ne l'êtes-vous pas toute la journée ? »

Jamais Patrick Brontë n'aura été aussi proche du refus. Après tant d'années passées dans l'obéissance, pour un peu, il se révolterait contre le destin. Il y a quelques jours, à l'église où il continue malgré tout à prêcher la bonne parole, sa voix est descendue si bas dans la douleur que nous avons craint qu'il n'éclate en sanglots devant ses paroissiens. Charlotte était si bouleversée qu'à la fin de l'office elle nous a demandé de la laisser seule avec lui ; peut-être accepterait-il enfin de se confier ? « Qu'a-t-il donc fait de si terrible pour qu'on puisse menacer ainsi notre nom ? » a-t-il fini par murmurer. Rien ne semble devoir changer ; le fils continue à torturer le père, et personne ne peut mettre un terme au mal qui lie deux êtres décidés à ne pas se comprendre.

Cette situation nous est devenue insupportable, à nous, les filles. Pourquoi le cacher ? Branwell remue tant d'émotions et de sensations violentes que nous évitons de prononcer son nom. Qu'adviendra-t-il à son retour, car il ne saurait tarder à rentrer ? « Nous le mettrons au pas ! — N'y compte surtout pas, Charlotte ! Ce n'est pas de cette façon que tu parviendras à le calmer ! » Sommes-nous responsables de son état, de ses crises ? Et si c'est le cas, qu'avons-nous fait ou que lui avons-nous refusé pour qu'il soit devenu ce misérable que l'on doit accompagner comme un malade ? Là où se débat Branwell, les reproches ne servent à rien : « Charlotte, promets-moi que tu ne le harcèleras pas ! Tes remarques, tes conseils ne feraient que l'enfoncer plus avant dans ce désir qu'il a de se perdre ! — Doit-on le laisser tout piétiner sur son passage ? — Je n'ai pas dit cela ! »

> « Non, mais tu le penses ! Sais-tu qu'avant de partir il a encore volé de l'argent pour acheter de la cocaïne ? »

Dieu merci, Anne apporte à cette maison hantée par les passions la note de bonheur dont, personnellement, j'ai besoin. La joie que j'éprouve auprès d'elle, retrouvée après cinq ans d'absence, est si intense, le sentiment que je lui porte si profond qu'il m'arrive de me réveiller la nuit afin de savourer cette certitude ; Anne est de retour à Haworth et elle ne retournera pas chez les Robinson ! Dans ces moments où je parviens jusqu'au cœur de l'autre, je découvre combien je m'étais méprise ; rien ne vaut la présence d'un être cher auprès duquel on peut se taire. Mais je dois me garder de l'excès de mes sentiments ; seul Dieu sait combien il me faut lutter contre moi-même pour atteindre, au-delà de l'ardeur qui m'anime en toutes choses, le détachement qui, le moment venu, me permettra de regarder la mort en face.

Quant à Charlotte, avec laquelle j'apprécie de partager la vie quotidienne, elle est toujours mécontente de son sort. Anne et moi ne savons que faire pour porter remède à l'état de désenchantement chronique qui est le sien. Son voyage à Hatergate, dans le Derbyshire où elle est allée rejoindre Ellen afin de tenir avec elle le presbytère de Henry, son frère, absent pour quelques jours, n'a pas amélioré son humeur. À peine ai-je eu le temps de la serrer dans mes bras qu'elle m'a mise en garde :

« Je te préviens, Emily, à partir de maintenant, Branwell n'aura plus affaire à papa, mais à moi !

— Tu veux donc la guerre ?

— Il n'a pas le droit de briser nos vies ! »

★

Comme c'était à prévoir, Branwell est rentré de Liverpool encore plus déprimé que le jour de son départ. John Brown qui était chargé de le surveiller nous a signalé que notre malheureux frère n'avait fait que se lamenter durant tout le voyage. Ce qu'il nous a caché, c'est que, plutôt que de le garder contre la tentation, il s'est empressé de partager un péché qu'ils cultivent en commun. Les arrière-salles enfumées où on purifie l'eau avec du whisky ont dû avoir souvent leurs visites.

« Mais, mademoiselle Charlotte...

— Il n'y a pas de mais, John ! Branwell a un visage de malade. De quelle manière avez-vous passé votre temps à Liverpool ? »

Même si elle est excessive, l'irritation de Charlotte est excusable. À peine débarqué, l'ex-secrétaire de la société de Tempérance s'est empressé de filer au Black Bull où le réclamait la bande d'ivrognes prompte à s'extasier devant son éloquence facile. D'irritable, Branwell est devenu odieux, insultant, brutal : « Je n'ai pas d'ordre à recevoir de toi, Charlotte, et je te prie de sortir de ma chambre ! Tu me donnes encore plus mal à la tête qu'un mauvais alcool ! »

« J'en ai assez de tes agissements indignes ! »

Au cours d'une scène plus pénible que les autres, Charlotte a crié si fort que l'écho de sa voix nous est parvenu dans le cimetière où Anne et moi étions en train de nous promener. « Tu ferais bien d'oublier tes amours scandaleuses et de chercher un nouvel emploi ! Haworth ne te vaut rien ; tu n'y fais que des bêtises ! » Affolées, Anne et moi sommes revenues sur nos pas. Du seuil de la chambre où se disputaient le frère et la sœur, nous avons aperçu Branwell ; la tête dans l'oreiller il pleurait à chaudes larmes : « Calme-toi, Charlotte... tu ne vois donc pas dans quel état il est ! »

« Ce n'est pas du chagrin qu'il devrait ressentir, mais du remords ! Séduire une femme qui pourrait être sa mère ! »

Branwell s'est assis sur son lit : « Tais-toi ! Tu n'as pas le droit de juger Lydia Robinson ! » Il s'est emparé de la fiole de laudanum cachée sous son oreiller, en a bu une longue rasade : « Es-tu devenu fou ? » Horrifiée par ce geste qu'elle n'avait pas eu le temps de prévenir, Charlotte a poussé un cri : « Si tu veux te suicider, va le faire ailleurs ! » Branwell a protesté : « Il n'y a que papa qui ait le droit de me chasser de cette maison ! » Charlotte a perdu son sang-froid ; elle s'est précipitée sur lui, l'a saisi par le col de sa chemise : « Si tu continues, tu seras comme ces ouvriers sans travail qui traînent leur misère dans les ruisseaux ! »

« Charlotte, lâche-le ! »

Branwell a fini par se dégager. Le visage défiguré par les larmes, il a regardé Charlotte avec haine : « Il n'y a que Lydia Robinson qui ait su me comprendre et m'aimer ! Ma pauvre Charlotte, tu es incapable de comprendre la passion ! »

« Petit imbécile ! Crois-tu être le seul à être tourmenté par l'amour ? Cette Lydia Robinson n'est qu'une vaniteuse sans morale ! »

Alerté par le tapage, papa est sorti de son bureau. Il a monté quelques marches, a jeté un regard d'aveugle en direction du palier : « Que signifie ce vacarme ? » Charlotte est sortie de la chambre. Elle s'est penchée au-dessus de la balustrade : « Excusez-moi ! Je n'aurais pas dû me mettre dans un tel état, mais il est vraiment insupportable ! »

« À quoi sert de t'excuser si tu dois recommencer à crier demain ?

— Vous êtes beaucoup trop faible envers lui.

— Je le suis également envers toi pour accepter de t'entendre hurler de la sorte. Heureusement que nous n'avons pas de voisins ! Tout le monde serait au courant de nos histoires ! »

Depuis cette scène, Branwell s'acharne sur lui-même. Le dégoût, le remords, la honte, tout cet attirail de la conscience maladive, lui font rechercher l'oubli dans les plaisirs douteux. Lorsqu'il n'est pas attablé au Black Bull, il est vautré sur son lit. Des lettres non terminées sont éparpillées sur le sol ; elles sont adressées à ses anciens complices, le sculpteur Leyland et l'ingénieur Grundy. Toutes racontent la même histoire.

> ... oh, ami, comment vous décrire l'ambiance qui règne dans cette maison dirigée par des femmes hostiles ? Charlotte me refuse jusqu'au droit de souffrir et d'aimer. Son mépris est si grand que j'évite de me montrer pour n'avoir pas à croiser son regard. Il n'y a pas un jour où je ne désire retourner à Thorp Green. Seule l'idée d'y provoquer un drame dont aurait à souffrir ma bien-aimée me retient !

★

Après avoir combattu en vain, mes sœurs et moi en sommes arrivées à l'acceptation silencieuse. Notre frère souffre-t-il de cet abandon ? Son esprit semble si embourbé, si démis de sa puissance que je me demande si quelqu'un, en dehors de cette femme qu'il idéalise à distance, peut encore l'atteindre ? Lorsqu'il se décide, au soir de journées passées à boire et à discuter, à rentrer au presbytère, il profère des paroles si étranges que nous nous enfermons pour n'avoir pas à l'affronter.

Pour échapper à la folie de l'être cher persécuté par ses démons, nous sommes retournées à l'écriture. Chaque soir, quand tout est rendu au calme, nous nous lisons quelques pages. J'ai gardé pour moi le secret de mes poèmes — ils me confessent trop intimement pour que je les lise à mes sœurs — et j'ai commencé un roman dont j'ai trouvé le titre au cours d'une promenade solitaire sur les Moors : *Wuthering Heights*. Nelly Dean, la narratrice, ressemble par certains côtés à Taby qui est de retour au presbytère où elle compte finir ses jours. Quant à Catherine Earnshaw, mon héroïne, elle doit beaucoup à la chère Martha Taylor dont l'enthousiasme, l'ardeur et la mort mystérieuse ont laissé une trace profonde en moi.

Au lieu de suivre la voie de l'imagination, mes sœurs se sont engouffrées dans leur passé. Toutes deux ont choisi de parler de leur profession à la première personne, mais si Anne, dans *Agnes Grey*, reste femme et jeune fille, Charlotte, dans *The Professor,* a choisi d'être un homme. Malgré une préférence pour le livre d'Anne, j'aime la confession de William Crimsworth, le professeur de Charlotte, et j'attends de savoir qui gagnera la partie ; de la sournoise et silencieuse Zoraïde Reuter ou de la pure et innocente Frances, Evans, Henri ?

Nous n'écrivons plus ensemble comme autrefois, mais chacune de notre côté ; Charlotte dans l'ancienne chambre de Tante, Anne dans la salle à manger où elle se plaît plus qu'ailleurs, et moi dans la salle d'étude. J'ai repoussé mon lit contre le mur du fond et ai installé mon bureau contre la fenêtre. En ces courtes nuits d'été, le spectacle que m'offrent les étoiles me tient éveillée jusqu'à minuit. Tout en rêvant de choses et d'autres, j'ai une pensée pour papa dont j'imagine le visage nu, sans lunettes, la bouche entrouverte et les cheveux blancs ; parviendrons-nous à le convaincre de se faire opérer de la cataracte ? Je pense aussi à Anne, couchée sur le côté, avec cet air d'ange meurtri et craintif, à Branwell étendu tout habillé en travers du lit.

Lorsqu'il est rentré tout à l'heure, mon frère est tombé deux fois dans l'escalier. Réveillée par ses jurons et les aboiements de Keeper, Charlotte, derrière la cloison qui nous sépare, a demandé à Dieu de nous délivrer de sa présence et de ses agissements. Cette prière m'a arraché des larmes. Cette peur que sème Branwell autour de lui, ce dégoût, cet effroi vont-ils le séparer des êtres qui lui étaient attachés ? Va-t-il connaître la solitude des maudits ?

*Parmi tous les cœurs qui jamais t'aimèrent,*
*Comme il en est peu qui te pleurent !*
*Et pourquoi le mien doit-il donc, ce soir,*
*Être ému de pareille peine ?*

*How few, of all the hearts that loved,*
*Are grieving for thee now !*
*And why should mine, to-night, be moved*
*With such a sense of woe ?*

*Too often, thus, when left alone*
*Where none my thoughts can see,*
*Comes back a worth, a passing tone*
*From thy strange history.*

Emily Jane BRONTË, 11 mars 1844.
(Traduction Pierre Leyris,

*« Miss Eyre, avez-vous jamais habité une ville ?*
*— Non, monsieur.*
*— Avez-vous beaucoup fréquenté le monde ?*
*— Je n'ai fréquenté personne, à part les élèves et les maîtresses de Lowood, et maintenant, les hôtes de Thornfield.*
*— Avez-vous beaucoup lu ?*
*— Je n'ai lu que les livres qui se sont trouvés à ma disposition ; ils n'ont été ni nombreux ni très remarquables.*
*— Vous avez vécu une vie de nonne... »*

Charlotte Brontë, *Jane Eyre*.
(Traduction Charlotte Maurat.)

En ce mois d'août 1846, tandis que le soleil brille au-dessus des Moors glorifiés par la bruyère, me voici à Manchester, dans une chambre aux volets clos. Un malade y repose. Encore trop faible pour signaler sa présence autrement que par le mouvement d'une main à peine levée au-dessus du drap, il tente d'attirer l'attention de sa garde-malade : « Quelle heure est-il ? — Dix minutes de plus que tout à l'heure, papa ! »

« Moi qui ai vécu enfermé dans un bureau, je ne savais pas que le temps pouvait être si long ! »

Patrick Brontë, que le célèbre Dr Wilson vient d'opérer de la cataracte, repose immobile au long des journées interminables, fastidieuses, remplies de nuit. Sous le bandeau, ses paupières baissées pèsent sur les yeux douloureux : « Vais-je devoir rester ainsi encore longtemps ? — Quelques jours ! Vous avez entendu ce que vous a dit le chirurgien ce matin ? Si vous ne restez pas tranquille, il ne répond de rien ! »

Pendant que le vieillard se laisse gagner par une songerie morose, accaparée principalement par les derniers exploits de son malheureux fils, le bruit d'une plume lui confirme que sa fille n'est pas loin : « Charlotte, à quoi es-tu occupée ? » Un mensonge est déjà prêt : « J'écris une lettre à Emily ! »

« Grand Dieu, mais combien a-t-elle de pages ?

— Pas plus que d'habitude !

— Je ne connais personne qui passe autant de temps à écrire des lettres !

— Ne pas avoir trouvé d'emblée les mots justes m'a obligé à la recommencer trois fois ! »

Charlotte, qui a dû accompagner son père à Manchester, écrit dans la pièce voisine. Elle profite de ce séjour forcé dans une ville de suie et de misère pour mettre en œuvre un second roman. Il aura pour titre le nom de son héroïne, *Jane Eyre*, et parce qu'elle a décidé de confesser sans vanité ni détours l'essentiel d'une existence vouée au départ à la solitude, il ne cachera rien de la détresse d'une orpheline et des horreurs de certains pensionnats où l'on maltraite les enfants. Alors que dans *The Professor* elle s'indignait à tort et à travers, ici elle ne fera pas appel à la morale ni aux préjugés, mais aux sentiments. Malgré une enfance tragique, *Jane Eyre* l'orpheline, la gouvernante, ne se laissera pas abattre. L'injustice du sort, la malignité de son entourage seront les ressorts d'un caractère qui finira par vaincre le mal. Elle luttera contre l'hypocrisie d'une société sans pitié et finira par gagner ce que Charlotte n'a pu conquérir à Bruxelles ; l'amour d'un maître.

« Charlotte, où en es-tu de ta lettre ?

— Je l'ai presque terminée.

— N'oublie pas de rassurer tout le monde.

— Soyez tranquille.

— Et demande à Branwell de se comporter un peu plus dignement que d'habitude ! Prie-le d'avoir pour ses sœurs quelques bontés ! »

Tout comme les poèmes des trois sœurs qui viennent d'être publiés aux frais de leurs auteurs, ce roman sera soustrait au jugement de papa qui n'en aura pas connaissance. Pourquoi cette cachotterie indigne d'une fille aussi prévenante et attachée à son père ? Pour lui éviter une contrariété de plus : le pasteur n'apprécierait pas de savoir que ses filles ont dépensé une partie de l'héritage de Tante pour faire éditer ce qu'il qualifierait de niaiseries. Comme tous les hommes, y compris les plus grands : Southey, Wordsworth, Constantin Héger et autres, Patrick Brontë méprise la production féminine : « Qu'ont-elles besoin de raconter publiquement leurs histoires intimes ? Je trouve ces amusettes sans aucun intérêt ! » Ces dames font dans la confidence indiscrète et l'évanouissement impudique. Il suffit de lire les revues pour constater l'indigence des feuilletons féminins : « Heureusement que la plupart n'ont pas de mari... elles leur feraient honte ! Les femmes ne savent pas s'exprimer sans abuser du lyrisme. Je les trouve plus à l'aise dans les contes pour la jeunesse où il n'est point nécessaire à la pensée d'avoir de la profondeur, et à l'esprit du jugement ! » Et ce ne sont pas les demoiselles Brontë éduquées en compagnie des Shakespeare, Byron, Walter Scott et autres athlètes qui diront le contraire. Convaincues comme leur père de la fragilité et de la triste condition de leur sexe, elles se sont gardées de la critique en prenant soin de venir au monde littéraire sous des noms d'emprunt à consonance masculine. Toutefois, pour ne point s'abandonner tout à fait à l'anonymat, elles ont conservé leurs initiales. Charlotte, Emily et Anne sont devenues Currer, Ellis et Acton Bell.

« Charlotte, pourrais-tu me lire une page de la Bible ? Cet après-midi, je n'ai aucune patience !

— Volontiers, papa... Mais donnez-moi encore quelques minutes ! »

Charlotte vient de poser sa plume sur le buvard. Elle soupire, regarde par la fenêtre le va-et-vient de la rue, a une pensée déplaisante pour l'homme étendu dans la pièce d'à côté : « Pourquoi n'a-t-il jamais été capable de respecter mes activités ? Mary Taylor avait raison, papa est un tyran ! » Va-t-elle retourner auprès du malade, obtempérer comme il le lui demande ? Quelque chose la retient devant sa table de travail, un souvenir dont elle ne peut dire s'il est bon ou mauvais, un souvenir qui s'inscrit dans une matinée pluvieuse de l'automne 1845. Il commence par un regard, et ce regard, le sien, voit ce qu'il ne devrait pas voir : les poèmes d'Emily empilés comme des notes sans importance au fond d'un tiroir.

★

Alors qu'elle cherchait des papiers, Charlotte a découvert les poèmes de sa sœur cachés derrière le rempart de journaux anciens. Certains, vieux de plusieurs années, n'étaient pas terminés. Écrits à la hâte, ils ne semblaient pas avoir grande importance pour leur auteur qui les avait probablement oubliés. Au lieu de respecter le secret, la curieuse a lu quelques vers, puis d'autres, puis d'autres encore...

« *Il aurait moins pesé, le monde entier, qu'un [cœur*
*Qui de la sorte enferme une douleur si dense ;*
*L'approche de la mort ne peut pas faire peur*
*Lorsqu'on a tout connu de l'humaine [souffrance.* »

L'expérience qui se racontait là, sur ces pages couvertes d'une écriture fine, serrée, pressée d'aller au but, l'aveu de la douleur, le désir éperdu d'un

Ailleurs, la grandeur des visions, la force des images ont bouleversé Charlotte. Stupéfaite de découvrir en elle tant d'ignorance, elle a reconnu son égoïsme et son orgueil ; n'avait-elle pas toujours été convaincue de sa supériorité, y compris dans la souffrance ?

« *L'ombre du désespoir eût lassé*
*Quiconque autre que moi, qui de tout temps*
*[l'assume ;*
*Aux côtés du malheur j'ai toujours avancé :*
*Je suis enfant de l'Amertume.* »

Ainsi, Emily, que rien ne distinguait des autres membres de la famille, était un être de passions refoulées et de déchirements. Ce regard clair et honnête, ce sourire, ce dévouement silencieux cachaient une peine si grande, une solitude si impitoyable qu'elles ne pouvaient s'exprimer que dans le secret de l'écriture destinée à soi-même. Depuis toujours, Emily savait combien était vaine la révolte de Branwell, inutiles les espoirs de ses sœurs, dérisoires leurs projets. Assombrie par la présence de la mort qui faisait route à ses côtés, elle avait acquis cette force qui consiste à croire en soi, y compris dans la souffrance la plus totale. Son attachement à elle-même et aux êtres était d'autant plus fort qu'elle le savait menacé. Ainsi marchait-elle désespérée, et pourtant parfaitement paisible, portée par une connaissance que les autres n'avaient pas, vers ce lieu qu'elle appelait du beau nom d'Immortalité.

« *Arrière donc, soupirs ! Arrière donc, pitié !*
*Auprès de tous je suis à charge ;*
*Dès l'enfance mon cœur mourut à l'amitié :*
*Laissez mon corps prendre le large !* »

Charlotte a repoussé le tiroir de la commode.

Allait-elle avouer sa curiosité et prendre le risque de fâcher Emily qui ne lui pardonnerait pas d'avoir pénétré dans son monde intérieur par effraction ? Un appel lancé de la salle à manger l'a invitée à rejoindre ses sœurs : « Eh bien, mais que t'arrive-t-il ? La soupe va être froide ! »

« Je viens de commettre une indiscrétion qui m'en a plus appris que trente ans de vie ! »

Anne s'est étonnée avec beaucoup de gentillesse et de naïveté ; Charlotte indiscrète ? « Je n'en crois pas un mot ! » Emily qui était en train de donner une leçon de politesse à Keeper le mendiant a jeté un regard malicieux à sa sœur : « La confiance d'Anne est si grande que devant elle on se sent parfaite ! Je suis plus réservée qu'elle ; je te crois capable de commettre une indiscrétion. » Une seconde, Charlotte a espéré qu'elle irait au-delà de cette taquinerie, mais sa sœur s'en est tenue là. L'aînée s'est assise avec gêne : « Je n'ai pas très faim ! » Elle a attendu une question qui n'est pas venue ; ce geste coupable à demi avoué ne semblait intéresser personne. « Si j'avais du poil et m'appelais Keeper, elle essaierait d'en savoir davantage, malheureusement je ne suis que sa sœur ! » Plus tard, alors qu'elles déjeunaient en silence, Charlotte a regardé le beau front d'Emily plongée dans une rêverie : « Elle n'attend même pas la fin du repas. La voilà déjà partie ! Qui pourrait croire que sous ce visage pâle et transparent courent des eaux si noires ? Qui pourrait songer que cette douceur cache une violence si terrible qu'elle ne peut s'adresser qu'à la mort ? »

« Emily ?

— Oui, Charlotte ! Tu m'as parlé ? Excuse-moi, je n'ai pas entendu ce que tu me disais.

— J'ai découvert des papiers qui ne m'étaient pas destinés, et je les ai lus. »

Emily a laissé tomber sa fourchette sur la table. « Tu ne vas pas me dire que... » Foudroyée par ce regard, Charlotte n'a même pas songé à mentir ; d'avoir découvert le talent de sa sœur lui donnait tous les droits, y compris celui de la blesser : « Eh bien, justement... si ! Pourquoi m'as-tu caché que tu écrivais de si beaux poèmes ? C'est impardonnable de les avoir laissés dans un tiroir depuis des années ! » Emily a failli s'étouffer de colère : « Qui t'a autorisée à fouiller dans ce tiroir qui m'est réservé ! Qui ? » La dure voix de sa maîtresse a réveillé Keeper qui s'est mis à aboyer.

« Je cherchais des papiers. Ne les trouvant pas, j'ai ouvert ce tiroir sans songer à mal... les poèmes étaient là... oh, ce chien ! ne pourrais-tu pas le faire taire ou lui dire de sortir !

— Les poèmes étaient là... Et alors, étais-tu obligée de les lire ?

— Non... mais aussi, pourquoi faut-il que tu fasses mystère de tout ? Si je ne t'ai jamais fait lire les miens, ce n'est pas parce que je veux les garder secrets, mais parce que je pense qu'ils ne t'intéresseraient pas. J'avoue qu'ils sont loin d'avoir la valeur des tiens ! »

Une larme a coulé sur la joue d'Emily, une larme qu'elle n'a pas songé à essuyer : « Comment as-tu pu faire une chose pareille ? C'est comme si tu m'avais salie ! » Cette scène qui semblait l'exclure a tellement troublé Anne qu'elle, si patiente et si paisible, a frappé la table de son poing : « Cessez de vous disputer ! Et toi, Emily, fais taire ton chien ! Il va réveiller papa qui est en train de se reposer ! » Tandis que Charlotte lançait une main en direction de sa sœur qui la refusait, Anne a quitté la table. « Dehors, sale bête ! Dehors ! » Elle a ouvert la porte de la salle à manger, a poussé le chien à l'extérieur. « Il est vrai que Charlotte aurait pu te demander ton autorisation, mais tu la lui aurais refusée ! » Surprise de ne pas trouver chez sa complice le secours dont elle avait besoin en un pareil moment, Emily a crié :

« Je ne supporte pas cette idée !
— Quelle idée ?
— D'avoir été souillée !
— Ton orgueil est sans limites, Emily ! Charlotte n'est pas une violeuse ! Moi aussi, j'écris des poèmes.
— C'est ton droit !
— Parfaitement, c'est mon droit ! Et je serais très heureuse si l'une de vous et même toutes les deux acceptiez de les lire ! »

Charlotte a saisi l'aide que sa jeune sœur venait de lui proposer : « Il faut les publier, et les nôtres avec les tiens ! Il suffit de faire une sélection ! » Emily s'est levée : « Où voulez-vous en venir ? Vos poèmes vous appartiennent, libre à vous de les faire publier, mais ne comptez pas sur les miens ! Et maintenant, laisse-moi passer, je veux sortir ! » Charlotte est restée clouée contre la porte :

« Au lieu de fuir ainsi, écoute-moi cinq minutes... la beauté appartient à tout le monde ! Tu ne peux pas refuser de comprendre cela ! Que ce soit toi ou quelqu'un d'autre qui l'ait traduite, peu importe, ton devoir est de la rendre à l'humanité qui en a besoin !
— Jamais ! »

Il a fallu beaucoup de temps et de patience à Charlotte pour obtenir gain de cause. De guerre lasse, Emily a enfin cédé. À ses poèmes, ses sœurs ont joint les leurs, revus et corrigés. Charlotte, qui n'a jamais rechigné devant la tâche, a envoyé un courrier à plusieurs éditeurs londoniens pour leur demander s'ils accepteraient de publier un recueil de poèmes signés par trois frères. L'un d'eux a répondu par l'affirmative en précisant toutefois que ce serait à compte d'auteur. Charlotte a donc prélevé sur l'héritage de Tante la somme de trente et une livres et dix shillings qu'elle a adressés à MM. Aylott et Jones.

Les poèmes de Currer, Ellis et Acton Bell ont été lus par deux ou trois critiques qui se sont montrés plutôt satisfaits. Des coupures de presse sont arrivées au presbytère ; on les a lues en cachette ; elles faisaient l'éloge du talent des frères Bell. Quelques mois plus tard, ne recevant aucune nouvelle de Londres, Charlotte a demandé des comptes à l'éditeur qui a répondu avec une sobriété de circonstance que deux exemplaires avaient été vendus.

« Voilà qui me confirme dans mon attitude ! »

Si Emily a vécu cet échec comme un affront, Charlotte et Anne, décidées plus que jamais à imposer leurs noms, ont trouvé que le destin venait de leur donner une sage leçon ; dorénavant elles ne publieraient plus à compte d'auteur.

★

« Charlotte, mais enfin, que fais-tu ? »

Arrachée à ses pensées, Charlotte sursaute. Tout en rangeant les pages noircies, elle songe au jour qui la consacrera, elle et ses sœurs. « J'arrive, papa ! »

« Je te croyais endormie... »

Dans la chambre où l'attend un long corps immobile et un visage aux yeux bandés, le révérend semble prier. Il lui fait un petit signe de la main comme pour s'excuser : « Pardonnez-moi ! Je n'aurais pas dû vous faire attendre aussi longtemps ! » Patrick Brontë émet un vœu ; il est sincère : « J'espère que cette opération sera une réussite : ainsi, je pèserai moins sur ta vie ! »

« Vous ne pesez pas sur ma vie, vous lui donnez un sens, c'est très différent... Quel passage aimeriez-vous que je vous lise ? »

*« Hatred and vengeance, my eternal portion,*
*Scarce can endure delay of execution,*
*Wait, with impatient readiness, to seize my*
*Soul in a moment... »*

*« Haine et vengeance, mon lot éternel,*
*Supportant mal tout délai,*
*Attendent, avec une frémissante impatience,*
*De se saisir de mon âme... »*

Patrick Branwell Brontë.
(Traduction Jane Fillion.)

Depuis le retour de Charlotte et de notre père — il a recouvré partiellement la vue et peut aller et venir sans l'aide de personne — l'anxiété s'est installée dans le presbytère. Branwell, vous vous en doutez, est à l'origine de ces nouveaux tracas. Sa santé qui semblait s'être améliorée durant le séjour de papa à Manchester, s'est derechef dégradée, et gravement. Derrière le supplice qu'il s'impose et impose à autrui, je devine l'activité d'un Alexander Percy. Le mois dernier, j'ai tenté de lui parler, d'attirer son attention sur ce qui se jouait si dangereusement en lui. Hélas ! le ciel au-dessus de notre rencontre n'était pas aussi serein que je l'eusse souhaité ; mon frère a refusé de m'entendre. La démence poursuit son chemin ; elle mine un être qui ne peut plus s'en défendre. À peine lui parle-t-on de lui, de ce qu'il représente pour nous qu'il ricane, désigne d'un doigt dégoûté les tableaux qui ornent les murs de sa chambre :

« Voilà tout ce qui reste du fils Brontë, quatre misérables croûtes ! Si je te disais que je me hais ? Que ces cris, ces hurlements qui sortent de moi me font horreur ? Que votre condamnation me pétrifie en même temps qu'elle m'invite à vous renvoyer votre jugement !

— Si tu songeais un peu moins à toi et un peu plus aux autres, tu te haïrais moins !

— Si je te disais que je vous accuse de ce que je suis devenu ! Votre religion, vos propos de dévotes offusquées, vos manières d'être, vos yeux baissés m'exaspèrent ! Vous êtes restées les nièces de Tante, sages, économes, de petites gratte-papier ! Si j'avais à faire votre portrait aujourd'hui, je le ferais avec des teintes si plombées que rien qu'à le regarder vous vous mettriez toutes les trois à pleurer ! La seule qui échappera au triste sort que je prévois pour vous, c'est Charlotte ; sa méchanceté la gardera ! »

À l'exception de notre aînée qui a pris le parti discutable du mépris, nous ne lui marchandons pas nos soins ; et s'il ne tenait qu'à moi, mon frère serait le malade le plus choyé d'Angleterre. Malheureusement, il refuse toute aide. La violence souffle si fort en lui qu'il ne sait bien qu'insulter, maudire. Le souvenir de Lydia Robinson le ronge comme un mal incurable auquel il tient plus qu'à tout. Chaque matin il ravive la blessure de crainte qu'elle ne se cicatrise dans la journée. Combien d'années la souffrance prendra-t-elle ses quartiers chez lui avant de le détruire ?

La semaine dernière, après une beuverie, Branwell a mis le feu à son lit. Je suis arrivée à temps pour éteindre le début d'incendie. Les gifles, les appels, les coups ne le ramenant pas à la conscience, Anne est allée chercher de toute urgence le médecin. Devant l'épave qui gisait dans le lit noirci par les flammes, le docteur s'est montré pessimiste : « Je ne lui donne pas six mois de vie ! » Devant un verdict aussi rédhibitoire, notre père s'est écrié : « Comment peut-on livrer un homme soûl à l'irrémédiable ? » Le docteur a insisté ; il tenait à sa vérité : « Votre fils se drogue depuis des années. La cocaïne mélangée à l'alcool détruit le système nerveux. Il est probable qu'avant de tomber dans le coma, il a eu une crise de delirium. La prochaine peut lui être fatale ! » Ces dernières paroles ont été entendues par Branwell que nous pensions sans connaissance. Il s'est dressé sur son lit comme un spectre: «Guérissez-moi!» a-t-il crié en jetant deux bras suppliants. Papa s'est approché du malade. Lorsqu'il a reconnu qui venait à son secours, Branwell s'est mis à hurler:

«Je vous en supplie, ne me laissez pas mourir! Aidez-moi à guérir, et je vous prouverai que je puis être autre chose qu'un misérable!»

Remué au plus profond de lui-même, notre pauvre père a pris son fils dans ses bras: «Calme-toi, mon petit! Bien sûr que tu vas guérir! D'ailleurs, nous allons tout faire pour cela!» L'enfant d'autrefois s'est accroché aux épaules du vieillard et il a crié sa terreur: «Par pitié, papa! Par pitié!» Ses mains se sont enfoncées dans le tissu noir de la veste. Toute sa force était là, au bout de ses doigts: «La mort me fait si peur!»

Offensé par un spectacle qui mettait sa tranquillité en danger, le médecin s'est esquivé sur la pointe des pieds. Charlotte et moi l'avons suivi jusqu'à la porte du jardin. La parole de réconfort que nous quémandions en silence n'est pas venue. Avant de nous quitter, l'homme nous a conseillé de surveiller le malade jour et nuit: «Il n'a plus sa tête à lui. Dans une crise, le pire peut lui traverser l'esprit!»

«Vous croyez qu'il pourrait se tuer?

— Oui... mais il peut aussi mettre le feu au presbytère, tout casser, vous frapper... que sais-je?

— Vous êtes en train de décrire la folie, docteur!

— C'est hélas ce dont il s'agit... Le delirium rend les gens fous!»

Le visage de Charlotte s'est vidé de son sang. Je lui ai tendu un bras auquel elle s'est accrochée : « Je ne parviens pas à y croire ! Un homme aussi doué, aussi intelligent que lui ! Je vous en prie, faites quelque chose pour l'arracher à cet horrible état ! Au fond, la nature est bonne, elle ne peut laisser un être se détruire en quelques mois ! »

« Il ne s'agit pas de mois, mademoiselle Charlotte, mais d'années... j'arrive trop tard !

— Si Dieu le veut...

— Je suis désolé, mais je ne peux rien faire pour lui, ni avec Dieu, ni sans Dieu. Son cerveau a trop souffert ; les lésions cérébrales sont irréversibles. Quant à son foie, il a la grosseur de celui d'un homme de soixante-dix ans qui aurait abusé de la vie. »

Depuis ce drame, l'angoisse règne au premier étage. Pour éviter « ce pire » dont la science nous menace, nous avons retiré sa lampe à Branwell, puis nous lui avons demandé de réintégrer la chambre de papa. « Jamais ! Pour qui me prenez-vous ? Pour un enfant malade ? » Ses protestations ont été inutiles ; pour une fois nous avons tenu bon. Ce retour à l'enfance vécu comme une humiliation le tourmente si fort qu'il nous provoque et nous injurie du matin au soir.

Et ce n'est pas tout. Alors qu'il avait décidé de relire ses notes et de suivre notre exemple en se remettant à l'écriture — il caresse le projet d'un roman depuis longtemps — il est retombé au plus bas de la dépression. À nouveau, plus rien ne l'intéresse. Les allées et venues du facteur, nos chuchotements l'indiffèrent. Sait-il seulement que les paquets que nous retournent les éditeurs contiennent des manuscrits refusés ? Et s'il le savait, se réjouirait-il de notre insuccès ? Je ne le pense pas. Branwell est violent, mais il n'est pas mauvais bougre.

Vautré sur son lit, il s'adonne à la neurasthénie : « Laisse-moi tranquille ! — Mais enfin, il faut bien que je change tes draps ! — Ils sont bien bons pour moi ! » Invariablement, ses journées se terminent au Black Bull. Les pronostics médicaux tiennent leurs promesses ; pas une nuit ne se passe sans qu'il réveille la maison : « Qu'avais-tu encore à hurler de la sorte ? Ne pourrais-tu pas te maîtriser un peu ? À cause de toi, papa ne peut plus dormir ! »

« Si tu sais comment interdire la porte aux cauchemars, donne-moi ta recette !

— Je n'ai pas envie de plaisanter ! Il en va de la santé de papa ! »

Martyrisé par ce fils unique, notre père finit peu à peu par ne plus se ressembler. Il suit avec une attention désespérée les symptômes d'un mal qu'il ne peut combattre qu'en priant. Les efforts d'Anne, les miens, ne servent plus à rien. Ou Branwell est trop ivre pour prêter attention à ce que nous lui disons, ou il vocifère contre ce qu'il appelle nos prêches, ou il pleure comme un enfant abandonné par le sort. À ses larmes pitoyables, je préfère encore ses hurlements ou ses accusations, la plupart dirigées contre Charlotte qu'il traite d'hypocrite, d'ambitieuse et de puritaine. L'ascendant que notre aînée a sur papa exaspère Branwell qui voit dans cette complicité récente la coalition de deux êtres forts face à sa faiblesse : « Mieux vaut être détesté qu'ignoré ! »

« Crois-tu donc que nous te détestions ?

— Toi, je ne sais pas, mais Charlotte sûrement ! Réponds-moi franchement, Emily, suis-je à ce point repoussant qu'il faille s'écarter de moi dans l'escalier, sortir de la pièce où je pénètre, détourner son regard du mien ? »

Cette question a fait son chemin. J'ai profité de ce que Branwell était en visite chez les Brown pour aller frapper à la porte de Charlotte. Elle était en train d'écrire à Ellen qui, mieux que quiconque, peut comprendre ce que nous vivons puisque deux des fils Nussey sont atteints de maladie mentale. Le but de ma visite a été deviné dès la première seconde : « Je n'ai d'autre souhait que de le voir quitter cette maison ! » Cette entrée en matière n'a pas servi mon éloquence. J'ai bafouillé : « Charlotte... — Je t'en prie, Emily, nous n'allons tout de même pas recommencer à nous disputer pour lui ? — Pourquoi refuses-tu de lui parler ? Branwell souffre de ton mépris et de ton abandon ! » Ma sœur a lancé son menton en avant : « Sa maladie est une excuse ! Il s'en sert pour nous émouvoir. Sais-tu que la semaine passée il a profité de mon absence pour extorquer un souverain à papa ? Le pauvre homme ne saura jamais rien lui refuser ! »

« Pourquoi tant d'aigreur ? Il est évident qu'il est malade ! »

Au regard qu'elle m'a lancé, j'ai compris que mon intervention ne servirait qu'à envenimer la relation déjà difficile du frère et de la sœur. J'ai voulu quitter la pièce, mais elle m'a saisie par le bras : « Je ne peux même plus descendre en ville ! »

« À peine ai-je fait trois pas qu'une bonne âme vient me raconter ses exploits ! Le dernier te concerne. Il a été jusqu'à se vanter d'avoir écrit

*Wuthering Heights*. J'imagine qu'il a trouvé ton manuscrit. Toujours est-il qu'il en a lu un passage à ses complices. "Que pensez-vous, messieurs, de mon œuvre ? — Elle est aussi impayable que toi ! Ton Heathcliff, personne n'y croira. Il est trop sombre et méchant pour être vrai !" »

Charlotte m'a fixée en silence ; elle a attendu un mot de réprobation que je n'ai pas prononcé : « Alors, tu ne dis rien ? — Tout cela n'est pas bien grave ! — Parce que pour toi, s'approprier le travail d'autrui ne porte pas à conséquence ? — Dans ce cas précis, non. Branwell est encore plus malade que je ne le croyais. À mon avis, il en sait beaucoup plus long que nous sur nos transactions avec les éditeurs de Londres. — Et le fait de colporter cette pénible histoire d'amour avec Lydia Robinson ne te choque pas non plus ? » J'ai dû montrer de l'abattement car Charlotte m'a offert sa chaise :

« De Keighley à Halifax, tout le monde sait que Mme Robinson est amoureuse de son ancien précepteur ! Ce qui m'étonne, c'est que nous n'ayons pas eu d'histoires avec la famille, surtout maintenant que M. Robinson est mort ! »

J'ai tenté de faire comprendre à ma sœur que les amours tumultueuses de Branwell lui étaient intolérables parce qu'elles ressemblaient aux siennes, mais elle a refusé de m'entendre. Seul lui importait de me raconter comment Edmund Robinson était mort à l'âge de quarante-six ans d'une phtisie qui l'avait emporté en quelques jours. Bafoué jusque dans la mort par son ancien précepteur, il s'était apparemment refusé à la vengeance. Sa femme et ses enfants — à l'exception de la fille aînée enlevée par un homme de théâtre — avaient hérité de la totalité de ses biens. Ce témoignage de confiance posthume révélait néanmoins une faiblesse qui sauvait la réputation de Branwell, le séducteur. Si Lydia Robinson n'était pas accourue à Haworth, c'était parce que le défunt stipulait dans son testament que le remariage de sa femme ou sa mauvaise conduite la priveraient de son héritage. Acculée à la richesse, la malheureuse souffrait l'enfer de la séparation du fait d'un mari assez jaloux pour continuer à la persécuter jusque dans la tombe. Elle se devait au souvenir de son mari et à un veuvage sans éclaircie.

> « Est-ce possible qu'il ait songé un seul instant qu'une femme de cet âge l'épouserait ? William m'a raconté qu'on l'a retrouvé étendu et sans connaissance dans l'arrière-salle du Black Bull où un messager serait venu lui apporter la nouvelle !
>
> — Pourquoi n'aurait-il pas droit lui aussi à la souffrance ? Il s'est peut-être évanoui lorsqu'il a su qu'il ne reverrait jamais Lydia Robinson ?
>
> — Ne s'est-il pas tout simplement trouvé mal à la suite d'une forte prise de laudanum ? »

Depuis cet entretien, Charlotte m'évite. Elle m'en veut d'avoir pour Branwell une compréhension, une indulgence que je n'ai jamais eues pour elle. J'ai songé plusieurs fois à lui dire toute mon affection — le mot amour serait trop fort et il me semble plus juste de le réserver à Anne infiniment plus démunie. Pourquoi me suis-je tue ? J'ai craint d'aller au-delà des mots aimables. Une phrase en appelant une autre, je lui aurais peut-être avoué que je n'apprécie pas sa complaisance envers elle-même et son intransigeance envers les autres. Elle m'aurait répondu qu'elle est la première à se critiquer. J'aurais dû l'admettre en signalant toutefois que son autocritique ne vise qu'une partie de la cible ; Charlotte s'imagine que son ambition, ses désirs, sa passion pour M. Héger, bref, que toutes ces tribulations me sont inconnues. Elle m'idéalise tout en m'estimant incapable de percevoir les remous du cœur. Mes poèmes ne lui ont rien appris. En la rappelant à l'ordre de la tolérance et de la compassion, je pourrais troubler l'écrivain en elle ; celui-là a besoin d'être traité avec égard et délicatesse. *Jane Eyre*, le roman qu'elle est en train d'écrire, est une œuvre forte, superbe, à l'égal des plus grandes, et il ne saurait être question pour moi d'en perturber le cours.

« Emily, que s'est-il passé entre Charlotte et toi ?

— Absolument rien, Anne !

— Est-ce à cause de Branwell ?

— Même pas.

— Que te reproche-t-elle ?

— Mes silences... Ils n'ont pas le sens qu'elle veut leur donner.

— Pourquoi ne le lui dis-tu pas ?

— Parce que ça ne servirait à rien. »

Dorénavant, plus rien ne pourra me contraindre aux aveux. On ne mène bien que les combats secrets.

*«Ni Emily ni Anne n'étaient savantes; elles ne songeaient point à emplir leur cruche à la fontaine d'autres esprits; elles écrivaient toujours sous l'impulsion de la nature, sous la dictée de l'intuition, et d'après les réserves d'observations que leur expérience limitée leur avait permis d'amasser. Je puis tout résumer en disant que pour des étrangers elles n'étaient rien, pour des observateurs superficiels moins que rien, mais que, pour ceux qui les avaient connues toute leur vie dans l'intimité d'une étroite parenté, elles étaient véritablement bonnes et grandes.»*

Currer BELL,
19 septembre 1850.
(Traduction Pierre Leyris.)

On ne saurait taire la joie — elle est rare en ces jours où le père et le fils s'affrontent constamment — qu'a provoquée l'acceptation par l'éditeur T.C. Newby des deux manuscrits d'Anne et d'Emily, et quelques mois plus tard, après ce premier succès tempéré par les atermoiements de l'éditeur en question, la joie plus grande encore qu'a suscitée l'agrément par MM. Smith and Elder du second manuscrit de Charlotte, *Jane Eyre*. Si ces messieurs ont refusé *The Professor* auquel ils trouvaient maintes qualités, mais aussi trop de défauts, ils ont littéralement été transportés par la dernière œuvre de Currer Bell. Devançant la parution de *Wuthering Heights* et d'*Agnès Grey* que T.C. Newby ne semble plus pressé de publier, *Jane Eyre* vient de conquérir l'Angleterre victorienne.

Currer Bell dont on ignore la véritable identité — certains prétendent avoir décelé sous la vigueur de l'écriture une tournure féminine — raconte au long d'un roman au style droit et nerveux, tourné vers un mystère qui ne s'éclaircira qu'à la fin, la vie éprouvante d'une femme, gouvernante de son état, ses débuts d'orpheline, son adolescence malheureuse, sa solitude de jeune fille, son combat au nom d'un amour qui ne la décevra pas. Touchée par les accents pathétiques de ce nouveau talent, la critique ne s'est pas trompée ; après l'éditeur, M. Smith et son collaborateur, M. Williams, un homme d'importance dans le Londres littéraire où sa parole tient lieu de garantie, elle a versé dans l'enthousiasme. Quant à l'intelligentsia qui donne le ton dans les salons, elle qui jusque-là se moquait des bons sentiments, elle a brusquement changé de cap et vogue vers la vertu affichée à la devanture des libraires sous le nom d'un inconnu... ou d'une inconnue.

Jamais auteur n'a autant intrigué le monde : « Qui est donc Currer Bell ? » Seules quelques ladies abusées par l'âge et le conformisme osent critiquer un ouvrage qui, même s'il est à la mode et alimente les conversations, insulte la femme anglaise dans ce qu'elle a de plus noble et de plus représentatif.

> « *Mrs. Sarah Ellis, auteur de ces manuels typiques sur la conduite de la femme victorienne :* Filles d'Angleterre, Épouses d'Angleterre *et* Femmes d'Angleterre, *subodora également qu'il s'agissait de deux auteurs "car l'œuvre contient des passages dont le lecteur est tenté de dire qu'aucun homme n'aurait pu les écrire s'il l'avait voulu ; et d'autres dont le lecteur est encore plus tenté de dire qu'aucune femme n'aurait* voulu *les écrire si elle l'avait pu".* »

En cet automne 1847, tandis qu'Anne et Emily attendent avec impatience la parution de leurs romans oubliés par M. Newby — le peu scrupuleux éditeur songe à la meilleure façon d'utiliser le succès de *Jane Eyre* — Charlotte se laisse émouvoir par la rumeur flatteuse qui lui arrive de Londres. Hissée jusqu'à cette gloire qu'elle a toujours convoitée, elle jouit de son triomphe sous le nom d'emprunt qui continue à la cacher au monde.

> « Depuis quelque temps, mademoiselle Charlotte n'est plus la même ! Je l'ai rencontrée pas plus tard qu'hier ! Elle semblait si préoccupée

qu'elle ne m'a même pas vue ! Deviendrait-elle prétentieuse ? »

En vérité, cette célibataire de trente ans, au physique sans grâce et à la réserve trop grande, à laquelle pour un peu on souhaiterait un bon mari et des enfants, vit dans la crainte de sombrer corps et âme dans l'orgueil. Mais aussi, comment s'en garder lorsqu'on vous renvoie dès la première ligne d'un livre un profil agrandi par la consécration ? Déjà, au groupe des enthousiastes de la première heure, viennent se joindre quelques grands noms dont celui de Sa Gracieuse Majesté, la reine Victoria, touchée par la noblesse du ton et le sentiment hautement religieux de *Jane Eyre* qui, on ne sait comment, s'est frayé une voie jusqu'à la bibliothèque de Buckingham Palace ; celle aussi de Thackeray, le tranchant, l'impitoyable, soudainement bouleversé par l'histoire très morale d'une gouvernante en mal d'amour et de légalité, Thackeray à qui Currer Bell dédiera la seconde édition de son livre. Quant aux imprudents qui oseront par la suite émettre un semblant de réserve sur la vraisemblance du récit, qu'ils prennent garde ! Charlotte en a fini avec l'humilité ; elle n'est plus femme à s'en laisser imposer et sait trouver les mots pour défendre son œuvre.

Ce beau succès va-t-il en entraîner d'autres derrière lui ? Non, car à l'inverse des malheurs qui se présentent en série, un bienfait arrive souvent seul. Sur le presbytère où l'on jouit d'un heureux secret partagé à trois, le ciel va s'assombrir. Alors qu'ils auraient dû bénéficier de l'accueil réservé à *Jane Eyre*, les romans d'Ellis et d'Acton Bell publiés par Newby avec un retard savamment calculé font les frais d'une critique portée sur la comparaison : « *Une chose est certaine : poésie ou roman, les meilleures œuvres (et de loin) sont signées Currer Bell* », d'une critique décidée, cette fois, à rappeler à l'ordre les frères Bell qui en prennent décidément trop à leur aise. Trois ? Rien n'est moins évident ! Ne s'agirait-il pas d'une seule personne assez astucieuse pour signer ses ouvrages sous des prénoms différents ?

« C'est odieux !
— Charlotte, ta colère n'arrangera rien !
— Mais enfin, c'est un mensonge !
— Et alors ? Il ne porte atteinte qu'à Emily et à moi ! Le succès de *Jane Eyre* étant maintenant assuré, tu n'as plus à te faire d'inquiétude !
— Vous avez un sang-froid que je n'ai pas. Quand je relis ce qu'on a osé écrire sur vos romans, j'en suis tout simplement malade ! »

Ellis Bell, plus encore qu'Acton, attire sur elle les foudres de la critique offensée par le choix d'un sujet jugé « *malencontreux, pénible à l'extrême, déplaisant* ». Dans *Wuthering Heights*, un roman « *informe et interminable* » où s'affrontent plusieurs générations de démons, l'auteur, à n'en pas douter un homme malsain, décrit avec une « *désolante minutie* » des intrigues effrayantes, le tourment des âmes ruinées dès la naissance, la traîtrise des uns, la lâcheté des autres, la malhonnêteté de tous, en bref, l'univers dégradant que recherchent inlassablement les êtres qui ont du goût pour la souffrance. De l'alcoolisme meurtrier de Hindley, le frère de l'héroïne prêt à tuer son fils Hareton, à la haine de Heathcliff qui s'acharne à gérer le mal comme on gère un capital, en passant par la cruauté et le sadisme d'un vieux bigot, la veulerie de Linton, l'enfant corrompu et avili par un père à côté duquel il mourra —réellement — de frayeur, ce ne sont d'un bout à l'autre du roman que turpitudes, bassesses, désordres rassemblés sur quelques milles d'une contrée dont on se demande à Londres si elle n'est pas située dans une cervelle malade plutôt que sur l'île de Sa Gracieuse Majesté. « Peut-être penseriez-vous, chers amis lecteurs, qu'à côté de ces misères humaines, l'auteur nous ferait partager les joies que procure à l'œil un beau décor ? Eh bien, pas du tout ! » Aux descriptions « *d'intérieurs sinistres* » répondent celles d'un paysage désolé et menaçant, gardé à vue par un ciel prêt à choir, des arbres rabougris et tordus « *déformés par la rudesse du climat* », un paysage bousculé par les fureurs imprévisibles d'une nature hostile à l'homme.

En résumé, si la lecture de *Jane Eyre* — son auteur a su aller puiser son inspiration au confluent des belles émotions — touche le lecteur « *jusqu'aux larmes* », celle de *Wuthering Heights* le livre bel et bien au supplice. On sort de ce roman anéanti, brisé. Un sentiment d'horreur saisit le lecteur et lui fait douter de l'humanité. En son esprit révulsé demeure le souvenir terrifiant de Heathcliff, le héros satanique d'Ellis Bell, celui aussi de Cathy, l'enfant capricieuse, volontaire et acharnée, sur laquelle s'est fixé l'amour d'un monstre, celui enfin des amants réunis dans la boue d'une fosse qu'ils ne partageront avec personne, pas même avec Dieu. « *Nous rencontrons assez de mesquinerie, assez de turpitudes, assez d'afflictions dans cette vallée de larmes pour que l'Artiste ne se croie pas obligé de choisir son intrigue et ses personnages dans un aussi morne catalogue...* »

★

En ce début d'année 1848, alors qu'Emily et Anne rencontrent incompréhension et refus, Charlotte se plaît à revivre, dans l'intimité de sa chambre, la scène où, poussée par l'orgueil et ses deux sœurs, elle a fait savoir à Patrick Brontë qu'il était le père d'un écrivain reconnu par ses pairs.

Après une hésitation qui a mis ses nerfs à l'épreuve et sa patience à bout, elle est allée frapper à la porte du bureau. « Oui, entrez ! » Debout devant la fenêtre, le vieillard guettait le retour de Branwell disparu à la suite d'une altercation : « Ah, c'est toi ! » Dès qu'il a vu sa fille porteuse d'un livre qui semblait lui brûler les doigts, papa s'est enquis du but de sa visite : « Pourquoi prends-tu un air aussi embarrassé ? »

« Je vous ai apporté un roman à lire.

— Tu sais bien que je lis le moins possible !

— J'aimerais que vous me disiez ce que vous en pensez.

— *Jane Eyre* : le titre a le mérite d'être simple et il est facile à retenir. Qui est ce Currer Bell ? Tu le connais ? »

Quand il a su qu'il s'agissait d'un roman écrit à la maison, un roman de femme, ou plutôt une amusette de vieille fille, Patrick Brontë s'est inquiété : « Mon Dieu, mais combien cette épaisse publication a-t-elle pu coûter ! » Comme pour s'excuser d'avoir commis une œuvre dont on ne semblait guère pressé de connaître le contenu, Charlotte a sorti de sa poche quelques coupures de presse : « Ce sont les articles que j'ai découpés dans différents journaux ; ils vantent les mérites de mon livre. » Étonné qu'on ait pu consacrer du temps à l'œuvre d'une inconnue, le pasteur en a demandé la lecture : « Lis-moi cette prose. Je doute qu'elle m'intéresse, mais on ne sait jamais ! » Charlotte a lu les critiques qui faisaient l'éloge de son talent. « Me voilà proprement stupéfait ! » a lancé le pasteur au bout d'un moment.

« Ce n'est pas la stupéfaction que je guette en vous, mais la fierté ! Si mon livre pouvait vous plaire, j'en serais heureuse, car votre opinion m'importe plus que toute autre ! »

Durant cet après-midi consacré à la lecture, le pasteur s'est découvert un titre sur lequel il ne comptait plus : géniteur d'une enfant de la gloire. Au détour de pages émouvantes, il a fait connaissance avec le talent de sa fille aînée, avec son style brillant, sa verve, sa causticité, son audace. Au long d'une confession menée de main de maître, *Jane Eyre* lui a dévoilé les secrets de Charlotte. « Et moi qui croyais la connaître ! » Patrick Brontë n'avait donc pas prêché ni prié en vain ; sa foi, son ardeur, ses convictions qui n'avaient pas su émouvoir Branwell avaient germé ailleurs ; la récolte était de qualité. « Et quel humour ! Je m'y reconnais tout à fait ! Celle-là est bien ma fille ! » Prenant le livre sous le bras, il a traversé le vestibule, s'est engouffré dans la salle à manger où ses trois filles attendaient son verdict : « Savez-vous que votre sœur a écrit un roman sous un faux nom ? » Emily et Anne ont posé leurs travaux d'aiguille sur la table.

« Je ne m'attendais pas à lire un si beau livre ! Le style est excellent, la forme sans défaillance et le contenu émouvant ! »

Il a jeté un coup d'œil admiratif et respectueux à son aînée : « Où as-tu été chercher toutes ces trouvailles ? », puis il a demandé sur un ton mal assuré : « As-tu donc tant souffert ? » Charlotte a bafouillé : « Heu... oui... enfin, que croyez-vous donc ? Souffert ? Pas plus que mes sœurs ! » Patrick Brontë a eu un haut-le-corps :

« Qu'entends-tu par pas plus que tes sœurs ? N'êtes-vous pas heureuses ? Qu'avez-vous à reprocher à la vie ? »

Anne et Emily ont détourné les yeux. Quant à Charlotte, elle a eu ce mouvement de la main qui accompagne une phrase interrogative : « M. Lewes, dans le *Frazer's Magazine*, m'a reproché de mieux entendre l'imaginaire que le réel ! Croyez-vous qu'il ait raison ? »

« Oui... plutôt.
— Si je laissais à ma seule expérience le soin de s'exprimer, je n'aurais guère à raconter ! »

Anne a saisi la main de Charlotte : « Mon Dieu, mais c'est qu'elle va le contrarier ! Tout cela va trop vite pour lui ! » Elle l'a posée sur la table, l'a maintenue fermement sous la sienne.

« L'expérience ne te manque pourtant pas ! Peu de femmes de ton âge et de ta condition ont eu l'occasion de voyager comme tu l'as fait ! »

Avant de quitter la salle à manger, Patrick Brontë a demandé un conseil à celle en qui il avait toujours eu confiance : Emily. Simple et sans ambition, et comme ces êtres qui s'effacent en donnant toujours davantage, sa cadette savait tout des choses bonnes et mauvaises ; minutieuse au point de verser dans la maniaquerie, scrupuleuse, elle ne répondrait qu'après avoir réfléchi :

« Penses-tu qu'il soit souhaitable, toi qui le connais mieux que nous, de parler à ton frère de cette publication ?
— Il faut au contraire la lui cacher.
— Pourquoi ?
— Il verrait là une injustice du sort. Branwell a tout tenté pour être publié. »

Ces mots ont touché un cœur qui n'avait pas su s'endurcir. Le pasteur a montré un visage pitoyable : « Pourquoi me persécute-t-il ? » Tout en fixant ses filles, il a songé aux raisons qui l'avaient poussé à s'entêter sur le seul de ses enfants qui ne pouvait répondre à son amour : « Je suis pourtant prêt à l'impossible pour l'aider ! » Sa douleur a atteint Emily qui s'est tournée vers Charlotte : « Qu'en penses-tu ? Ne crois-tu pas qu'il faille laisser Branwell dans l'ignorance ? » Charlotte a fini par répondre par l'affirmative, mais plus tard, alors que ses deux sœurs se réjouissaient du succès remporté par *Jane Eyre* auprès de leur père pourtant si difficile à attendrir, elle a laissé poindre un regret ; il lui était pénible d'accueillir sa gloire sous un faux nom : « Maintenant que papa est au courant, pourquoi cacher notre identité au monde ? » Cette remarque a rencontré une telle opposition de la part d'Emily que Charlotte a dû se fâcher :

« Je ne t'autorise pas à me parler sur ce ton ! Ce que j'ai fait, je l'ai fait pour le bien de nous trois !

— Surtout pour le tien !

— Comment peux-tu dire une chose pareille ?

— Je ne voulais pas voir publier mon roman ! La critique m'a donné raison en m'insultant. Je te préviens que si quelqu'un apprend qui je suis, je ne t'adresserai plus la parole, car je considérerai que tu m'as trahie ! »

Stupéfaite, Charlotte a observé ce visage ennemi ; était-il vraiment celui d'Emily ? Me croit-elle capable de renier une promesse, même s'il m'en coûte ? Pour lui plaire, je suis prête aux concessions les plus discutables, les plus stupides ! « Tu me parles comme à une ennemie ! Je ne troublerai pas ta paix ! »

> «Je n'en suis plus aussi sûre, Charlotte. Le succès est en train de te gagner à sa cause. Il n'y a pas pire amant que celui-là!»

Charlotte s'est sentie dépossédée. Le cadeau que lui avait donné son père venait de lui être retiré brutalement par l'être qu'elle aimait le plus au monde: «Pourquoi me repousses-tu sans cesse?» Emily brodait près de la fenêtre. Elle a posé son travail sur ses genoux, a regardé longuement sa sœur, sans hargne, sans colère, avec une sorte de bonté attristée: «Je ne te repousse pas, Charlotte! J'essaie de me préserver de toi, c'est tout.» Anne a profité du silence pour annoncer à ses sœurs qu'elle ne ferait rien pour les contrarier, ni l'une ni l'autre. Ce qui lui importait, c'était de terminer son second roman, *The Tenant of Wildfell Hall* et éventuellement de le voir publié: «Emily, l'admiration que je te porte ne va pas jusqu'à partager ton renoncement. Comme Charlotte, je regrette un peu l'anonymat que tu nous imposes, mais je respecterai moi aussi ton désir.» Emily a caressé Keeper qui venait de pénétrer dans la pièce:

> «Comprenez-moi bien... La critique serait élogieuse, ma position serait la même. Je ne veux pas avoir affaire avec ce monde-là! Si j'avais su que vous ne partagiez pas mon désir, j'aurais repris mon manuscrit et je vous aurais laissées publier les vôtres!»

Sur le soir, Anne a été prise d'une violente quinte de toux. Rien ne semblant pouvoir la calmer, elle a fini par monter se coucher. Un souvenir s'est rappelé à Charlotte: la toux insistante de Maria dans la nuit de Cowan Bridge. «Emily, j'ai peur!» a-t-elle mur-

muré. Sa sœur a continué à ranger sa boîte à couture : « Moi aussi. C'est cette discussion qui l'a contrariée ! Le corps est sensible aux choses de la tête ! Anne pense probablement comme moi, même si ses discours tendent à dire le contraire. Personne n'a plus peur du monde qu'elle ! »

*« Mes grandes souffrances en ce monde ont été les souffrances de Heathcliff, je les ai toutes observées et ressenties dès le début : ma grande pensée dans la vie c'est lui-même. Si tout le reste périssait et qu'il demeurât, lui, je continuerais d'être, moi aussi, et si tout le reste demeurait et que lui fût anéanti, l'univers me deviendrait formidablement étranger : je ne semblerais plus en faire partie. Mon amour pour Linton est comme le feuillage des bois : le temps le changera, je m'en rends bien compte, comme l'hiver change les arbres. Mon amour pour Heathcliff ressemble aux rocs éternels du sous-sol... »*

Emily Brontë, *Wuthering Heights*.
(Traduction Pierre Leyris.)

De même que la ruse n'est d'aucun secours pour le corps frappé par une maladie incurable, de même la méditation sur les vanités terrestres n'apprend pas à enterrer ceux que l'on aime. Depuis les funérailles de notre malheureux frère emporté par une mort qu'il aura défiée jusqu'à l'ultime instant, je m'évite. Il m'arrive pourtant de jeter au miroir un regard creux et brillant de fièvre ; il m'indique que l'œuvre de mort est en train de s'accomplir en moi comme elle s'est accomplie en Branwell. Je ne suis différente d'un cadavre que par la faculté que j'ai conservée d'accomplir mon travail, d'aller et venir comme un automate ou une aveugle.

« Emily, pourquoi n'écris-tu plus ?
— Emily, pourquoi ne nous parles-tu plus ?
— Emily, pourquoi refuses-tu de jouer avec Keeper ?
— Emily, pourquoi ne souris-tu plus à personne ? »

J'ai cessé de donner et de recevoir. Comme l'arbre déjà mort, j'attends la foudre qui m'abattra. Ô Branwell, comment avons-nous pu te laisser partir ainsi ? Depuis ton enterrement, la souffrance m'étreint avec une telle force qu'elle m'étouffe. Je déambule dans la maison à la manière d'une asthmatique qui sait qu'elle ne retrouvera plus jamais le souffle. Je m'étais pourtant employée à devancer ta mort ; ne pensais-je pas sottement que de m'y préparer en réduirait les effets le moment venu ? Au lieu de me porter secours, ce lâche calcul a fortifié en moi le dégoût. L'écriture a cessé d'être un secours ; les mots, les phrases me font horreur comme me font horreur les potions que Charlotte voudrait me faire prendre sous prétexte que je tousse. Je n'aspire plus qu'au silence, à l'oubli, au sommeil éternel, à la délivrance :

*Divitiae si affluant, nolite cor opponere.*

« Si les richesses abondent, veuillez ne pas y attacher votre cœur. » Le mien est attaché à la douleur qui, si je n'y prends pas garde, finira par devenir mon unique bien. Pourtant, au lendemain des obsèques, j'ai fait ce que la foi recommande en pareil cas ; je m'en suis remise à Dieu, pas à celui de mon père, ce Dieu de puissance et de gloire, mais à celui auquel je crois plus que jamais ; au Dieu de la compassion. Je l'ai imploré de sauver l'âme de Branwell, d'oublier sa révolte et son avilissement. Les prières n'allégeant pas mon chagrin, je suis retournée à la vie et à ses simulacres. Je me suis imposé des tâches ménagères, ai voulu mettre de l'ordre dans les affaires de mon frère. Parce que Martha refusait de pénétrer dans la chambre du mort, j'ai nettoyé moi-même la pièce. Après avoir encaustiqué les meubles, j'ai mis des draps propres dans son lit, puis j'ai brossé ses vêtements :

« Emily, pour qui prépares-tu cette chambre ? Pour un fantôme ? »

Tout est prêt pour sa prochaine visite. À peine aura-t-il poussé la porte que Branwell apercevra sa deuxième paire de chaussures, la première étant descendue avec lui dans la tombe. Disposées avec soin sous la redingote rafraîchie par la brosse, elles lui rappelleront ses visites au Black Bull et les traversées du cimetière où j'allais le relever en pleine nuit avant qu'il n'attrape une pneumonie.

« *Still, still that tomb's eternal shade*
*Oppressed my heart with sickening fear...* »

« *Depuis toujours, les ténèbres de la tombe*
*Ont empli mon cœur de terreur...* »

Depuis les funérailles de Branwell, un souvenir m'obsède. Il a trait à une scène maintes fois vécue. Je revois mon frère; chassé de la taverne où il accumule des dettes et fait scandale, il remonte péniblement la rue, longe l'église, apparaît à l'entrée du cimetière. Il va de droite et de gauche comme s'il était perdu, tourne sur lui-même, appelle quelqu'un d'une voix pâteuse, probablement Mme Robinson, la femme de son rêve, remariée au mieux de ses intérêts à un certain Scott. Il tente quelques pas, essaie d'assurer son équilibre mis en péril par un coup de vent plus fort que les autres, disparaît de ma vue. Je quitte mon poste, descends silencieusement les escaliers, me glisse à l'extérieur. Je l'appelle doucement : « Branwell... Branwell, où es-tu ? » Agenouillé entre deux tombes, en contrebas du sentier, il tente de se relever tout en fixant d'un œil mauvais Keeper qui m'a devancée : « Tu ne pourrais pas tenir ce chien enfermé ? Il va finir par me mordre ! » Je siffle Keeper, lui ordonne de rebrousser chemin, mais l'animal renifle le malheur à trois pas. Il hésite à laisser sa maîtresse avec un ivrogne accroupi dans la boue. « Et d'abord, que viens-tu faire ici ? J'en ai assez de ta surveillance ! Fais comme les autres, laisse-moi crever en paix ! » Ma pitié l'exaspère. Il cherche le moyen de me blesser; des insultes viennent tout naturellement sur ses lèvres. Il hurle : « Ne te défendras-tu donc jamais ? » Nous nous observons en silence. Va-t-il tenter de se relever? Non, il connaît son corps et ses limites : « Je ne veux pas que tu me regardes ! » crie-t-il en plongeant son visage dans son chapeau. Je lui tends deux mains qu'il repousse avec violence : « Ne me touche pas ! Ne me touche surtout pas ! » Au-dessus de nous le vent pousse la nuit vers des cieux moins austères. « Des ingrates, voilà ce que vous êtes ! Vous vous êtes servies de moi, puis vous m'avez mis à l'écart de vos projets... parce que vous vous figurez peut-être que je ne suis au courant de rien ? » Il tombe à la renverse. J'entends le bruit de sa tête qui vient de heurter la dalle. Je me précipite, le prends par les épaules, le secoue : « Redresse-toi, Branwell, nous allons rentrer à la maison avant que tu ne prennes froid ! » Il a l'air d'un cadavre abandonné. Un ronflement sort de sa bouche entrouverte au-dessus du menton mal rasé : « Branwell, redresse-toi ou je vais chercher Charlotte ! » Cette menace le réveille. Il s'assoit : « C'est ça, va chercher cette garce pour qu'elle vienne me juger du haut de sa grandeur ! » Il arrache à un vase une poignée de fleurs artificielles qu'il me tend en criant : « Qu'en penses-tu, ne suis-je pas un joli cadavre ? Vous allez bientôt pouvoir me pleurer ! » Il a perdu ses lunettes : « Oh, je vous vois d'ici, Charlotte, comme d'habitude, en début de cortège, toi au milieu et Anne, la sacrifiée, à la fin ! » Il éclate d'un mauvais rire : « À vous trois, vous m'avez dépossédé du meilleur de moi-même ! » Il cherche ses lunettes à tâtons, ne les trouve pas : « Je ne veux plus voir toutes ces choses affreuses, ces serpents, ces rats ! Qu'ai-je fait pour que Dieu me punisse de cette façon ? — Tu bois trop, Branwell ! Tu bois beaucoup trop ! Mais à quoi sert de te le dire ? Tu ne veux entendre personne ! » Il me fixe avec un regard désespéré : « Ne comprends-tu donc pas ? Je ne peux plus m'arrêter de boire ! Dès que je suis à jeun, je souffre dans tout le corps ! Oh, comme je voudrais être mort ! » Sa douleur me traverse. Je m'agenouille près de lui, attire son visage contre ma poitrine. Ses cheveux mouillés collent à mon corsage et la pluie se mêle à nos larmes. Il sanglote : « Comment fais-tu pour être aussi bonne ? » Nous nous étreignons comme deux amants que la vie va bientôt séparer. Jusqu'à ma mort je sentirai le poids de sa tête sur mon épaule, son haleine d'ivrogne, l'abandon de son corps épuisé. Je l'aide à se relever, le pousse vers une croix contre laquelle il prend appui. La verticalité l'effraie ; il lâche un juron qui meurt dans une sorte de halètement animal. Je prends son bras, le passe autour de mon cou. Le sentier est difficile à remonter. Il traîne ses jambes comme un hémiplégique. La mort est là ; je la vois dans ses membres engourdis et enflés, dans son profil de plus en plus creusé ; je la sens dans ses suffocations, son déséquilibre, toutes ces trahisons du corps qui dénoncent un mal qui ne disparaîtra qu'avec le malade. Tandis qu'il gémit dans mon cou, se plaint et s'accuse, je le vois sur son lit mortuaire. Sa peau sera plus grise, ses yeux plus enfoncés, sa bouche plus molle, mais l'expression ultime est déjà là. « Pauvre vieux papa, pourquoi me suis-je acharné sur lui qui ne me voulait que du bien ? » Des mots me reviennent en mémoire, des bribes du discours de Bildad à Job : « *... Ses pas assurés seront à l'étroit : malgré ses efforts, il tombera. Car il met les pieds sur un filet. Il marche dans les mailles. Il est saisi au piège par le talon. Et le filet s'empare de lui. Le cordeau est caché dans la terre. Et la trappe est sur son sentier. Des terreurs l'assiègent, l'entourent...* » Nous finissons par pénétrer dans le presbytère. Sur le seuil de la cuisine où brûle une lampe, Keeper observe silencieusement ces deux corps qui tentent d'atteindre l'escalier.

Ô Branwell, comment t'oublier, toi, l'âme de cette maison ? Sur la table de nuit de ta chambre où je viens prier chaque jour, la dernière lettre de ton ami, l'ingénieur Grundy, te signale en des termes embarrassés que la compagnie des chemins de fer Manchester Hebden Bridge refuse ta candidature ; ton passé joue contre toi ; malgré ton bon vouloir d'aujourd'hui, tu ne réintégreras pas un poste où tu t'es autrefois illustré. Francis Grundy ajoute qu'il a bien reçu ton dernier poème, mais qu'il n'a pas encore eu le loisir de lui accorder toute l'attention que ce texte mérite. Quelques lignes au ton désabusé font mention de tes amours malheureuses avec Lydia Robinson ; elles ne cherchent pas à t'écarter de cette illusion qui t'aide à vivre. Plus loin, il fait état de tes dettes et d'une demande d'argent que tu aurais faite au sculpteur Leyland.

Cette lettre découverte après ta mort a réveillé en moi la culpabilité. J'ai compris qu'au moment où Anne publiait avec un certain succès son second roman, *The Tenant of Wildfell Hall* — roman dans lequel tu fais figure de mauvais héros —, toi tu ne récoltais que des refus : le nôtre, celui de la compagnie des chemins de fer, celui de Lydia Robinson devenue entre-temps Lady Scott, celui des magazines qui n'ont même pas pris la peine de te retourner tes poèmes. L'activité de mes sœurs emportées par le désir de réussir là où les autres échouent, la mienne, nos cachotteries vis-à-vis de toi que nous ne voulions en aucun cas voir mêlé à nos travaux et à nos démarches, me sont apparues comme autant de trahisons.

Des détails me sont revenus qui ont ajouté à ma honte : regards détournés, chuchotements imbéciles, murmures, et cette honte a ravivé le souvenir en moi. Je t'ai revu dans maintes situations humiliantes ; à peine franchissais-tu le seuil de la pièce où nous cultivions une complicité reconstruite à trois que cessaient les conciliabules. Comme un nuage dans un ciel limpide, tu assombrissais notre existence et nous t'en voulions presque de vivre encore. Ta mine rembrunie, tes manières tourmentées nous encourageaient à garder le silence. Dans la salle à manger où tu descendais de plus en plus rarement, nos phrases de politesse, nos remarques sur le temps allaient vers ton assiette, jamais vers ton visage que nous cherchions à éviter : « Tu as vu son regard... il a encore bu du laudanum cette nuit ! — Pauvre papa, il ne sait plus ce que c'est que de passer une nuit tranquille ! » La rougeur fautive d'Anne, mon empressement à te servir, le silence de Charlotte violentée par ta seule présence, ces attitudes auraient dû te pousser au soupçon. As-tu jamais eu vent de nos déboires et de nos succès littéraires ?

Ô Branwell, pourquoi es-tu mort dans le silence ? Pourquoi ne nous as-tu pas rappelées à l'ordre de la fraternité ? Pourquoi nous as-tu laissées jusqu'à la fin à nos indignes cachotteries ? Enfant père de trois sœurs qui sans toi n'auraient jamais osé s'aventurer dans l'écriture, tu t'es laissé distancer. Au lieu de nous lancer un appel que nous n'aurions pas manqué d'entendre : « Ne m'abandonnez pas ! », tu t'es refermé sur un mal que par commodité nous avons appelé « vice ». Cette maladie nous a servi d'alibi ; nous sommes sorties de ta vie comme tu étais sorti de la nôtre. Peu à peu, nous avons fini par oublier tout ce que nous te devions : idées folles, désirs, passion...

Ô mon frère, sans doute l'as-tu su avant moi ? Il n'y a pas d'amour sans haine.

*« O Percy ! Percy ! where art thou ?...*
*I've sacrified my God for thee,*
*And yet thou wilt not come to me !...*
*Methought I saw a sudden beam*
*Of passing brightness through the room*
*Like lightning vanish... Percy, come !*
*Leave me not in the dark ; t'is cold.*
*And something stands beside my bed...*
*Oh, loose me from its icy hold*
*That presses on me ! Raise my head...*
*I cannot breathe !»*

*« O Percy ! Percy ! où es-tu ?...*
*Pour toi j'ai sacrifié mon Dieu,*
*Mais près de moi tu te refuses à revenir !...*
*Il m'a semblé apercevoir un brusque rai*
*D'une vive lumière illuminant la chambre.*
*Plus brève que l'éclair... Percy, reviens !*
*Ne me laisse pas dans les ténèbres ; j'ai froid.*
*Et à mon chevet se dresse une ombre...*
*Oh, arrache-moi à son étreinte glacée*
*Qui m'oppresse ! Soulève ma tête...*
*Je ne puis respirer !... »*

Patrick Branwell Brontë.
(Traduction Jane Fillion.)

EN cet automne 1848, comment aborder le décès des trois enfants Brontë sans paraphraser la mort? Rien de plus odieux que les beaux mots qui se pavanent autour des cadavres. Et pourtant... Avant d'assister à la mort de mon héroïne, Emily Brontë, à celle de sa sœur Anne, je vais devoir vivre celle de Branwell, en ce dimanche de septembre, au terme de sa courte existence.

Peu avant d'aller à l'église où, ce matin encore, va officier leur père, les trois sœurs se sont rendues auprès du malade dont l'état s'est aggravé depuis la veille. C'est un spectacle terrifiant que ce visage défait, ces cheveux collés par la fièvre, ces yeux de supplicié, cette boursouflure de la chair, ce mouvement des doigts qui se crispent sur la peur. Étendu sur son lit, Branwell fixe ses sœurs en silence. Il attend le sourire qui le réconforterait — on ne sourit pas à un cadavre — mais aucun signe ne lui parvient.

« Priez pour moi... »

Anne répond par un brusque mouvement de tête; l'émotion lui a volé la voix. Elle sort la première. Charlotte et Emily la suivent en silence. Toutes trois étouffent un sanglot dans leur mouchoir: « Est-ce possible de mourir ainsi ? » demande l'une d'elles. À l'extérieur les attendent un ciel bas, les poussées terribles du vent d'est, le froid d'un automne pourri par les pluies, le cri des oiseaux rassemblés sur le clocher : « Nous n'aurions pas dû le laisser seul ! »

« Il n'est pas seul... John Brown a décidé de rester avec lui. »

Assis sur une chaise, le sacristain a pris la main de l'agonisant. Il la serre affectueusement : « Dieu est infiniment bon et sa clémence est infinie ! » murmure-t-il à l'oreille de Branwell. Celui-ci tourne péniblement la tête. Il lance à son ami un regard de gratitude : « Crois-tu que Dieu me pardonnera mes péchés ? » À peine la question posée, il entrevoit une réponse ; ce n'est pas celle qu'il attendait. Son corps se crispe : « Vite ! Vite !... John, je vais mourir ! » Le sacristain s'affole. Il court jusqu'à la fenêtre, lance un appel en direction du pasteur et de ses filles qui sont en train de traverser le cimetière :

« Branwell... revenez... Branwell ! »

Lorsque le mourant aperçoit le pasteur dans l'encadrement de la porte, il tente de lui dire quelque chose. Une atroce plainte monte de sa poitrine. Il glisse une jambe à l'extérieur du lit, veut se lever, courir vers ce père si longtemps bafoué, lui demander sa protection, son pardon peut-être.

« Ne t'agite pas, mon petit ! »

Les forces lui manquent. Branwell se renverse sur l'oreiller. Un dernier hoquet sort de sa bouche. Quand Patrick Brontë comprend que son fils est mort, il pousse un cri. Ses jambes plient sous lui ; il tombe à genoux. Tandis qu'il pleure dans la nuit de ses mains collées sur son visage, la douleur tâtonne en lui ; elle cherche une voie, le lieu où elle pourra se déverser librement. Ses membres s'engourdissent, se paralysent. Seul son cerveau continue à fonctionner ; il ramène des mots, les enfonce dans le cœur. « Seigneur, sauvez-moi de l'épouvante ! Je ne suis qu'un enfant sans défense ! » Il récite un psaume : « *Voici, tu as donné à mes jours la largeur de la main ! Et ma vie est comme un rien devant toi/ Oui, tout homme debout n'est qu'un souffle.* » La souffrance le laboure entre les omoplates : « Mon fils est mort et je suis vivant ! » Il demande à Dieu de lui retirer la vie comme il vient de la retirer à Branwell : « Tuez-moi, Seigneur ! Tuez-moi vite ! » Des idées folles le traversent. La pensée du suicide le frôle. Il songe que maintenant, il va devoir dormir seul, dans cette chambre où tout lui rappellera l'enfant égaré, perdu à jamais. Son ministère, sa foi en Dieu ne lui épargneront pas les tourments de l'absence, le poids de l'obsession. Il devra vivre avec un fantôme. Nuit après nuit, les cauchemars, les hallucinations, les terreurs de Branwell lui reviendront en mémoire, et lorsqu'il se réveillera en sueur, avec ce sentiment horrible bloqué dans sa poitrine : « Branwell, où es-tu, mon garçon ? » il n'aura plus à accuser son fils de ses insomnies. Peu à peu, il en arrivera à penser qu'il ne l'a pas compris, qu'à le vouloir trop parfait, digne des éloges qu'il aurait souhaité pouvoir lui décerner, il l'a détruit. Parce qu'il y a de l'honnête homme en lui, il demandera pardon au défunt.

« Papa, puis-je vous aider ? »

Quelqu'un vient de poser une main sur son épaule ; Charlotte peut-être, ou Anne qui a tant de douceur et si peu d'exigence. Pourquoi n'aime-t-il pas davantage ses filles ? Parce qu'il ne les comprend pas ; elles sont trop pudiques, trop secrètes. Ainsi, en ce moment où il voudrait pouvoir serrer le cadavre contre lui, leur présence le lui interdit. Il voudrait protester: « Laissez-moi seul ! Vous ne comprenez donc pas que vous me gênez ? » mais la pensée du mal qu'il provoquerait injustement le retient.

« Papa... m'entendez-vous ? »

Emily s'écarte à regret du vieillard agenouillé. Dans le lit défait, Branwell la fixe. Elle regarde ses membres inertes, son visage figé, deux gouttes de sang coagulées au coin des lèvres entrouvertes sur un cri que seules les ténèbres ont entendu. Elle se retourne, cherche à qui porter secours : « Je suis là ! » dit l'être en elle. « Je suis là ! » mais personne ne peut recevoir son amour, même pas Charlotte qui la repousse : « Laisse-moi ! » La tête penchée en avant pour ne pas voir le cadavre, l'aînée vient de reculer jusqu'à la porte. Alors qu'elle se voudrait calme et digne, elle tremble comme une malade sur le point de céder à une crise de convulsions. D'où vient cette faiblesse qui l'humilie devant les siens, devant ce frère dont elle ne peut affronter la dépouille ? Elle serre son mouchoir sur sa bouche, lutte contre les sanglots : « Laisse-moi, te dis-je ! » La présence insistante d'Emily l'oblige à lever les yeux. Malgré sa myopie, le cadavre lui apparaît avec précision. L'horreur lui saute au visage ; ce n'est pas une répétition comme il y en a eu tant ; Branwell est mort.

« Charlotte ! »

Elle se précipite sur le palier, tire la porte et tombe à genoux comme son père quelques minutes plus tôt. La migraine frappe à ses tempes, serre sa tête comme un étau. « Seigneur, ayez pitié de nous ! » La souffrance fraie la voie au passé. Des images resurgissent qu'elle croyait avoir classées une fois pour toutes : la salle d'étude de la pension bruxelloise, les reflets de la lumière sur les feuilles du rhododendron de Madame, une craie, le tableau noir, le sécateur de M. Héger dont elle entend de plus en plus nettement le pas, la voix, le rire, une phrase en français : « Comment va la petite Anglaise, ce matin ? » Charlotte se débat : « Je ne veux pas m'évanouir ! » Elle se sent emportée par un sentiment qu'elle a connu autrefois, alors qu'elle errait misérablement dans les rues de Bruxelles ; la solitude, l'épouvante, l'effroyable solitude. Mon Dieu, vais-je devoir perdre tous ceux que j'aime avant de disparaître moi-même ? Une envie de vomir la prend. Elle pose sa main contre le mur.

Derrière la porte qui cache son évanouissement, Anne et Emily aident leur père à se relever. Tous trois s'approchent du cadavre ; ils le fixent avec une sorte d'étonnement. Avec ce sang-froid qui étonnera toujours son entourage, Emily ferme les yeux de son frère. Elle dispose ses mains en croix sur sa poitrine, écarte une mèche de son front et ajuste le drap autour de son corps. Ces gestes accomplis, elle s'adresse à Anne qui la fixe d'un œil épouvanté : « Oh, ma petite ! » Comme si elle avait attendu cette autorisation pour avouer son chagrin, Anne éclate en sanglots : « Emily, j'ai si peur pour lui, pour nous tous ! Qu'avons-nous fait pour que Dieu nous rende aussi malheureux ! »

★

Jeudi 24 septembre 1848.

Au sommet de la colline de Haworth, on enterre le fils du pasteur, Patrick Branwell Brontë, mort à trente et un ans des conséquences de l'alcoolisme et de la tuberculose. Sous le porche de l'église, John Brown, l'ingénieur Grundy et le sculpteur Leyland évoquent la triste fin de vie de l'amuseur de la région, son humeur vacillante, ses amours, son talent mal employé, sa déchéance physique. S'il a laissé des dettes, Branwell a également laissé de bons souvenirs : « Voilà quelqu'un qu'on n'oubliera pas de si tôt ! » À Leyland qui s'enquiert de la manière dont il est mort, John Brown répond que Dieu s'est souvenu à temps de la belle âme que cachait le rouquin sous ses airs de m'as-tu-vu. Deux jours avant son décès, Branwell s'est réconcilié avec son père et il a pardonné à Dieu de n'avoir jamais exaucé ses souhaits : « Toute la famille était autour de lui, y compris la vieille Taby qui ne tient pourtant plus debout ! Seule Charlotte n'a pas cédé à la charité ; elle a laissé partir son frère sans lui adresser un mot de compassion ! » Le mépris habite cette tête bien faite, assez naïve toutefois pour croire encore que le village ignore sa double identité et son commerce littéraire.

« Currer Bell, c'est bien elle, n'est-ce pas ?
— Évidemment que c'est elle !
— Pourquoi le cache-t-elle ?
— Allez savoir ! »

Aussi grand soit-il, le talent de Charlotte ne lui donnera pas les centimètres qui lui manquent et la bonté qu'elle a perdue. La gloire est mauvaise conseillère. La preuve ! Face au cadavre de son frère, elle n'a trouvé d'autre échappatoire que la maladie. Elle a laissé à ses sœurs et à son père le soin de veiller le mort jusqu'à sa mise en bière. La migraine, toutefois, n'a pas ankylosé sa main ; prompte à décrire ses états d'âme, Charlotte a rédigé plusieurs lettres que John Brown est allé poster : « Jamais famille n'aura utilisé autant d'encre ni noirci autant de pages ! La plume, chez les Brontë, est le véhicule des nerfs ! »

« Je croyais qu'il n'y avait que Branwell qui écrivait !

— Les trois sœurs ont suivi son exemple pour mieux le dépasser ! Anne elle-même, la timide, l'effacée, écrit des romans outranciers. Dans le dernier, il paraît qu'elle met en scène un Branwell au pire de lui-même. Porté par le vice et le mensonge, son héros ressemble de si près au modèle que Charlotte s'est presque fâchée !

— Comment savez-vous tout cela ?

— Martha, ma sœur, est servante au presbytère ! »

Seule Emily s'est détachée de l'écriture. Tournée vers un secret qu'elle refuse de partager, elle ne quitte plus la maison : « Même Keeper n'y comprend plus rien ! » Le dogue tourne inlassablement autour de sa maîtresse comme s'il cherchait à la protéger d'un mal que les autres ne voient pas encore. La mélancolie n'a pas affecté son courage ; elle s'affaire dans la maison comme par le passé, pétrit le pain, cuisine, coud, rend service à chacun. Cette activité de tous les instants ne rassure pas Charlotte qui s'inquiète : « Anne... me diras-tu ce qu'elle a ? » La petite n'en sait pas plus que l'aînée : « Est-elle malade... je veux dire, est-elle malade de la tête comme Branwell ? — Je n'en sais rien ! Ce que je sais c'est qu'Emily a décidé d'échapper à la prison du corps et au mauvais gouvernement de l'esprit. Elle accepte ce que nous refusons : l'inéluctable. La mort ne lui cause aucune frayeur ; au contraire, elle l'attend comme une délivrance. »

« Et nous ? Ne comptons-nous donc plus ?

— De moins en moins !

— C'est la mort de Branwell qui est la cause de son état !

— Non, Charlotte, c'est nous ! Nous n'aurions jamais dû aller à Londres ! »

De fait, dans le courant du mois de juillet dernier, et pour mettre un terme à certains bruits malveillants qu'a propagés Newby, Anne et Charlotte se sont rendues à Londres où elles ont rencontré les éditeurs de *Jane Eyre* pour une mise au point. « Je suis Currer Bell ! » a dit Charlotte à M. Smith stupéfait de découvrir en cette créature minuscule et démodée un grand écrivain. « Je me suis déplacée pour vous dire que M. Newby mentait. Ce n'est pas moi qui ai écrit *The Tenant of Wildfell Hall*, mais Acton Bell que voici. Nous sommes trois sœurs ! » Lorsqu'elle a su que Charlotte avait eu l'imprudence d'avouer qu'Ellis Bell était une femme, Emily s'est fâchée : « Moi qui t'avais demandé de garder le secret de mon identité ! Quand cesseras-tu de disposer des autres comme de toi-même ? »

« Depuis ce moment le dialogue est rompu.
— D'où vient qu'Emily soit si secrète ?
— Personne ne le saura jamais ! »

★

Au sommet de la colline, on enterre le fils du pasteur, un brave garçon qui n'a pas su éviter le pire pour lui-même. Derrière le cercueil s'avancent les parents du défunt, ses amis, les gens du village. Le révérend porte le deuil avec la raideur d'un officier. À sa droite Charlotte et Anne, à sa gauche Emily.

« N'empêche que c'était Branwell, le génie de la famille ! »

John Brown vient de disparaître dans l'église où le requiert le service religieux.

« *Frappe et le jette au sol, pour que d'autres*
*[fleurissent*
*Là où poussait ce rejeton exténué,*
*Et que, du moins, son corps en pourrissant*
*[nourrisse*
*Ce dont il a jailli : L'Éternité.* »

(10 avril 1845.)
(Traduction Pierre Leyris

*« My darling, thou wilt never know*
*The grinding agony of woe*
*That we have borne for thee...*

*Since thou art spared such pain*
*We will not wish thee here again. »*

*« Chère, jamais tu ne sauras*
*combien pour toi la douleur*
*nous a broyés...*

*Puisque cette douleur t'a été épargnée,*
*nous ne souhaiterons pas que tu reviennes ici-bas. »*

Charlotte BRONTË,
24 décembre 1848.
(Traduction Jacques Blondel.)

MADAME,

Votre poursuite aura été inutile. Ma sœur Emily est décédée. Le secret que vous avez tenté de lui arracher est descendu avec elle dans la tombe. Jusqu'au dernier instant, elle aura refusé le secours de notre affection et l'aide du médecin. Elle est entrée dans la mort les yeux grands ouverts. À peine a-t-elle laissé échapper un appel en forme d'excuse. Je n'ai pas su s'il s'adressait à nous, ou à l'enfant qui s'est réveillée en elle à l'instant de mourir. Sa mise en terre a eu lieu le vendredi 22 décembre de l'année 1848, c'est-à-dire, à huit jours près, trois mois après celle de notre malheureux frère. Son agonie a été terrible. Peut-être devrais-je la tenir au secret, mais la douleur en moi est si intense que je ne résiste pas au désir de la confier à une étrangère.

Au lendemain de l'enterrement de Branwell, ma sœur a commencé par montrer des signes de faiblesse. Sur l'instant, je n'ai voulu voir qu'un accès de mélancolie. Au-delà d'un deuil déchirant, Emily ne souffrait-elle pas de se voir refuser la reconnaissance à laquelle son œuvre avait droit? Cette question n'est pas insignifiante; vous en conviendrez lorsque vous saurez que j'ai découvert après sa mort des coupures de presse serrées dans son écritoire. Parmi elles figurait en bonne place l'article paru dans le journal *L'Atlas* où un critique faisait l'éloge de mon talent poétique comparé à celui de mes deux sœurs qu'il jugeait nettement inférieur.

Malheureusement, les jours passant, j'ai dû me rendre à l'évidence ; il ne s'agissait pas d'une crise de découragement. L'état d'Emily était plus grave que je ne l'avais cru. Amaigrie, pâle et fiévreuse, elle s'est bientôt mise à tousser comme au pire d'une crise pulmonaire : « As-tu de la fièvre ? — Non, Charlotte ! Ne te soucie pas de moi ! » Son essoufflement quand elle montait les escaliers, des douleurs du côté du cœur, les secousses soudaines de la poitrine déchirée m'ont mise sur la piste ; à travers ces symptômes, il me semblait reconnaître la tuberculose. L'idée m'est venue que Branwell, avant de partir, avait ensemencé un terrain préparé de longue date. Était-il possible que ce fût la grande et solide Emily qui eût récolté les germes de l'abominable maladie ? Cette découverte, au soir d'une mauvaise journée, m'a terrifiée. J'ai réfléchi au moyen d'y faire face. Le lendemain matin, alors qu'elle était en train de pétrir de la pâte à pain dans la cuisine, j'ai tenté d'attirer ma sœur sur un terrain où je savais que je rencontrerais de sérieuses difficultés. Je l'ai suppliée de se laisser ausculter par un médecin, « de ton choix, bien entendu ! ». Elle a refusé ma demande avec une véhémence qui m'a laissée sans voix ; jamais elle ne s'offrirait au diagnostic de qui était incapable de la soigner.

Comme toujours, la pensée de notre malheureux père est venue ajouter à mon désarroi. Après la mort de son fils, comment lui annoncer la maladie d'Emily et son refus catégorique de se soigner ? Comment épargner sa vieillesse, du moins dans l'immédiat ? Le silence m'a semblé être la seule réponse possible. Je lui ai donc tu mes craintes ; mieux, je lui ai menti : « Charlotte, je m'inquiète pour Emily. Je la trouve fatiguée et encore plus silencieuse que d'habitude. C'est elle qui tousse toute la journée? — Non, papa. Nous toussons toutes les trois!» La santé de ma sœur s'aggravant de jour en jour, j'ai fini par m'en remettre à Anne dont j'ai découvert à cette occasion le courage silencieux. Au lieu d'accroître mon tourment en m'offrant le sien, ma jeune sœur a tenté de me rassurer avec les arguments qui avaient été les miens; affectée par la disparition de celui qui avait illuminé, mais aussi ruiné notre vie, elle reprendrait bien vite le dessus. Un fortifiant lui redonnerait l'appétit perdu ces derniers mois, car il était urgent qu'elle reprît du poids en même temps que des couleurs. Hélas, pas plus que la mienne, cette intervention pourtant habilement menée n'a porté ses fruits. Quelque chose en Emily se désespérait de vivre encore: «Si maladie il y a, je vous demande de ne plus en faire état devant moi!»

Tandis qu'autour du presbytère se dépouillaient les arbres, tandis que tournoyaient les dernières feuilles sous un vent glacial, nous avons vu Emily s'affaiblir. Sapée par une force souterraine infiniment plus puissante que le misérable secours que nous tentions de lui apporter, elle a commencé à s'éteindre sous nos yeux. Le rythme de sa respiration s'est modifié; il nous a semblé que son souffle ne s'exhalait plus de ses poumons que par saccades, comme si elle allait puiser son inspiration très bas, dans les profondeurs dévorées par la tuberculose. La fièvre s'est installée; elle a fardé ses joues, creusé son regard, s'est glissée dans la paume de ses mains. Sa toux est devenue de plus en plus insistante, de plus en plus rauque. Au cours de ces nuits où personne ne pouvait dormir ni aller lui porter la potion qui l'aurait soulagée, combien de fois me suis-je bouché les oreilles pour ne plus l'entendre? Pourquoi ma sœur s'infligeait-elle une pareille torture? Quel péché en elle réclamait punition?

À la mi-novembre, je suis allée chercher dans les livres de médecine un soutien que je savais illusoire. Tous m'ont renvoyée à une mort rapide. Au chapitre Phtisie, j'ai lu le mot « saignements ». Le soir même, j'ai découvert un mouchoir taché de sang. Lorsque je l'ai interrogée, Emily m'a répondu qu'elle s'était coupé le doigt en épluchant des pommes de terre. Plus perspicace, plus fine, plus intelligente que jamais, elle a eu pour nous des regards qui disaient qu'elle savait tout de notre inquiétude, de notre désespoir, de notre attente. L'angoisse se faisant de plus en plus grande, j'ai demandé à l'amical Williams de Londres des conseils que ma sœur a refusé d'entendre ; elle ne se soignerait pas, c'était inutile. Devant ce refus, j'ai demandé l'adresse d'un éminent spécialiste que j'ai consulté par correspondance. Je lui ai adressé une longue lettre circonstanciée dans laquelle je décrivais avec minutie les symptômes de ce que nous nous acharnions à appeler une fluxion de poitrine. Ne recevant pas de réponse, je me suis adressée à la chère Ellen qui a reçu mes plaintes avec sa tendresse habituelle. Autorisée à me confier, je lui ai parlé de cette angoisse qui grandissait en moi comme une plante carnivore. Je lui ai également raconté comment j'essayais maladroitement d'éloigner la malade des contraintes de la vie quotidienne, de quelle façon elle m'avait repoussée lorsque j'avais voulu la décharger d'un poids : « Lâche cette soupière, Charlotte ! Nous allons finir par la laisser tomber ! Pour qui me prends-tu ? Pour une mourante ? » L'appellation avait sonné si fort, si cruellement que j'en avais perdu contenance. Depuis cet incident je la laissais nous servir comme par le passé.

Derrière son dos, Anne et moi avons commencé à échanger des regards horrifiés ; pas plus que moi, la pauvre petite ne savait comment mettre un terme à cette atroce danse macabre. Tandis qu'Emily vaquait dans la maison, l'image de Catherine Earnshaw criant à Nelly Dean, la servante, sa décision de mourir pour fuir la souffrance, s'est imposée à nous. Dans son unique roman, ma sœur avait-elle eu l'intuition de sa fin prochaine ? S'était-elle laissé guider par ses héros dans sa manière d'accueillir la mort, ou était-ce la mort qui, après avoir joué avec son imagination, s'était incarnée en elle ?... Ne meurs pas, Emily ! Ne meurs pas, sœur très chère, de toi, de ta présence, de ton dévouement, de ton amour nous avons besoin ! Reste parmi nous ! Ne meurs pas !... Durant ces trois mois, pas une seule fois Emily n'a entendu notre prière. Sans pitié pour son corps squelettique, pitoyable jusque dans les gestes les plus simples, comme celui de tendre son assiette à Anne, de remplir la carafe d'eau, de donner à manger à ses animaux, de coudre près de la fenêtre, elle a marché d'un pas égal jusqu'au tombeau. Son courage a été si grand que la maladie, l'espace de quelques jours, a reculé devant lui. Le temps d'une folle espérance, de croire en une guérison miraculeuse, son point de côté avait disparu et sa respiration était devenue plus ample, plus apaisée. La vie s'était remise à couler en elle avec une vigueur qui l'étonnait autant que nous : « Mon Dieu, comme c'est bon de ne plus souffrir ! de pouvoir oublier son corps ! Je ne savais plus ce que c'était de respirer ! »

Hélas, à peine avions-nous eu le temps de remercier le ciel que le mal a resurgi en une autre place. Une diarrhée s'est déclarée qui ne l'a plus quittée. Nous avons cru qu'elle accepterait enfin de s'aliter. Mais non ! Garder le lit, c'eût été reconnaître une maladie à laquelle elle refusait droit de cité ; c'eût été aussi affoler notre père : « Rassure papa, Charlotte ! Dis-lui que tout va bien ! Je ne veux pas qu'il se tourmente pour moi ! » Ce jeu qui consistait à nier la mort devant un vieillard déjà déchiré par la perte d'un être aimé, ce jeu a pris fin un soir. Convoquée dans son bureau, je n'ai pu émettre un son. Entre nous le silence a duré plusieurs minutes, le temps que s'évanouissent les mots : agonie, derniers devoirs, sacrements. « Comment va Anne ? » a-t-il fini par me demander. « Beaucoup mieux, papa ! » Il a dodeliné de la tête : « Enfin, l'écho d'une bonne nouvelle ! » puis il a pris cet air résigné et pitoyable de l'homme sans indulgence pour lui-même ; moi qui ai pour mission d'accompagner l'être en détresse, je me cache dans mon bureau pendant que ma fille cadette est en train de mourir !

Le 19 décembre 1848, vaincue par une maladie qu'elle aura refusée jusqu'au bout, Emily a rendu les armes. Si j'emploie une expression guerrière, c'est parce qu'elle correspond à la façon dont est morte ma sœur, en héroïne et en combattante. Cette funeste journée a commencé un peu avant l'aube. Anne est venue me trouver dans ma chambre. Elle m'a demandé si, comme elle, j'avais entendu Emily gémir dans son sommeil. Cette interrogation a ranimé un pressentiment qui m'avait torturée une partie de la nuit. J'ai offert à Anne un peu d'espace dans mon lit. Ensemble, nous avons attendu un appel qui n'est pas venu. Lorsque, sur le coup de huit heures, nous avons perçu du bruit dans la chambre d'à côté, nous nous sommes empressées auprès de la malade et nous l'avons suppliée de regagner son lit ; la journée était très froide et aucune urgence ne l'attendait au rez-de-chaussée. Devant ce regard déjà mort, ce visage cadavérique, j'ai dû faire un effort pour cacher mon désespoir. Deux heures plus tard, j'ai laissé l'agonisante aux soins d'Anne. Je me suis habillée, puis j'ai fui le presbytère en passant par la porte de derrière.

Depuis la nouvelle lune, le temps était à la neige. Un fort vent d'est soufflait par rafales. Engouffré dans ma cape, je l'ai senti, pénétrant, hostile. Une sorte de haine pour ce pays m'a saisie. J'ai dû éteindre en moi les mots de la malédiction, contenir une coulée de violence qui m'inondait comme un poison. Tournant le dos à ce presbytère où s'étaient étiolées nos vies, à ce père prêcheur, à cette agonisante entêtée, je me suis mise à courir en direction des Moors sans trop savoir ce que j'allais y chercher : la délivrance, l'oubli, la mort peut-être ? L'essoufflement a mis un terme à ma course ; cependant j'ai continué à marcher. Le sentier creusé par les dernières pluies est devenu de plus en plus difficile, presque impraticable, mais quelque chose me poussait en avant. Lorsque je me suis retrouvée à bonne distance de la dernière ferme, lorsque j'ai su que personne ne pouvait m'entendre, je me suis mise à crier : « Assez ! Assez ! » J'ai insulté mon sort, non pas avec les mots savants de l'écrivain — que m'importait la gloire alors que l'amour était en train de m'abandonner ? — mais avec ceux, malhabiles et grossiers, de l'être vaincu par la fatalité. Puis j'ai pleuré, puis j'ai demandé à Dieu de me rappeler à lui ; pas plus que Currer Bell, Charlotte Brontë ne voulait vivre !

Parvenue au sommet de la colline qui donne sur le village, je me suis retournée, affaiblie par cette course sans but, et j'ai vu le paysage tel qu'il n'avait jamais cessé d'apparaître à ma sœur, avec ce ciel immense, extraordinaire, indescriptible, et la vastitude des terres sans obstacle, habitées ici et là par le squelette d'un arbre à moitié mort, prêt à s'offrir à la foudre ou à plier sous la tempête, et le mouvement des collines semblables et pourtant différentes, et le spectacle de ce qui nous poussait à mourir avant terme ; celui de la mélancolie, de la solitude, du grandiose renoncement de l'hiver. Devant cette lande métamorphosée par un regard qui, à travers un roman, l'avait rendue immortelle, devant l'infini de cette nature indifférente à la détresse humaine, j'ai enfin compris combien ma sœur avait dû souffrir ; combien, aussi, elle avait lutté pour échapper à l'isolement définitif de celui qui sait que l'objet égaré dans la première enfance est irrémédiablement perdu. Devant cette perte sans guérison, Emily avait choisi de mourir afin de n'avoir plus à se trahir. L'enfer n'était pas dans un Ailleurs dont la pensée avait terrorisé Branwell, mais ici où l'on ne pouvait que dépérir de n'être pas.

Submergée, anéantie, j'ai épousé le désir de la malade et je me suis mise à hurler : « Emily, ne combats plus, *mon bel amour* ! N'écoute plus nos prières ! Pars ! Va-t'en ! Le bonheur est ailleurs ! » Le vent a emporté mon cri, comme il emporte tout. Il l'a poussé droit devant lui, en direction de la grange des Grimshaw, et ce bâtiment de pierre noire m'a renvoyée à la ferme des *Hauts de Hurle-Vent* où va mourir Heathcliff, le sombre héros du roman d'Emily. « *Je n'ai qu'un désir, à quoi tendent tout mon être et toutes mes facultés. Ils y ont tendu si longtemps et avec tant de constance que je suis convaincu qu'il sera satisfait — et bientôt — parce qu'il a dévoré mon existence : je suis englouti dans l'avant-goût de sa réalisation. Ma confession ne m'a pas soulagé ; mais elle pourra expliquer des phases de mon humeur, qui, autrement seraient inexplicables. O Dieu ! c'est une longue lutte, et je voudrais qu'elle fût finie !* » À quelle préhistoire, à quel être maudit ma sœur avait-elle emprunté cette voix ? Comment avait-elle pu nous taire la présence de cet étranger qui, en elle, exigeait l'absolu d'un amour vécu dans la mort? Branwell l'avait-il jamais aidée à survivre à la puissance destructrice de ses personnages? Et Heathcliff, était-il le porte-parole d'Emily ou celui du fère et de la sœur réunis dans une création commune? À ce moment j'ai songé que la folie à laquelle j'avais toujours refusé sympathie était une façon de s'extraire de l'intolérable, de l'inadmissible.

J'allais faire demi-tour, lorsque j'ai aperçu une touffe de bruyère que le gel n'avait pas encore complètement grillée. C'était cela que j'étais venue chercher sur les Moors, le mauve fané d'une fleur que ma sœur avait aimée. J'en ai cueilli un brin, puis je me suis hâtée de regagner le presbytère. Sans prendre la peine de retirer ma cape et mes chaussures boueuses, je suis montée à l'étage. Mon geste, hélas, n'a pas su ramener dans les yeux d'Emily la moindre étincelle de vie; elle a regardé la bruyère posée sur l'oreiller sans manifester d'intérêt; elle n'était déjà plus là.

En fin de matinée, elle a demandé à se lever. Anne et moi n'avons rien fait pour l'en dissuader car nous savions que ce serait inutile. Nous lui avons tendu ses vêtements comme deux figurantes muettes et terrorisées. Elle s'est habillée avec lenteur et maladresse. Ensuite, elle a descendu l'escalier, mais au lieu d'aller directement à la cuisine, elle s'est dirigée vers la salle à manger, et là elle s'est assise dans le fauteuil à bascule. Tandis qu'Anne et moi faisions semblant d'écrire, nous l'avons entendue demander son peigne à Martha. Nous ignorerait-elle jusqu'au bout? À l'instant de le passer dans sa chevelure, ses doigts ont cédé au relâchement des muscles et le peigne est tombé dans l'âtre. Elle l'a regardé brûler; elle n'avait même plus la force de se pencher pour l'écarter des braises. À midi, le vague de son regard a cédé brusquement devant la peur qui venait d'inonder le cerveau. Dans un appel désespéré, Emily a avoué son effroi devant la mort: «*Je veux bien voir un docteur maintenant!*» Quand nous avons voulu l'aider à regagner son lit, elle s'est débattue: «Je veux rester ici!» Ce combat perdu à l'avance nous a rappelé celui de Branwell. Anne et moi l'avons étendue sur le canapé où elle a rendu le dernier soupir quelques minutes plus tard.

Madame,

Votre poursuite aura été vaine. Ma sœur Emily est morte. Son âme captive a abandonné la prison du corps et les replis de la conscience. Elle n'a plus à lutter contre les imperfections du monde et les rigueurs d'une religion qu'elle a toujours contestée. Nous qui souhaitions la garder près de nous comme on garde un objet précieux et irremplaçable, nous avons dû l'accompagner jusqu'à sa dernière demeure. Nous étions peu nombreux à son enterrement. Papa ouvrait le cortège avec Keeper qui a assisté au service funèbre avec une dignité tout humaine. Malgré plusieurs accès de sanglots du côté des femmes, la cérémonie s'est déroulée dans le calme. Un moment, j'ai cru que de là où elle était, Emily nous adressait un message de paix, mais cette impression n'a pas duré. Au retour, elle nous attendait; à peine avions-nous fait trois pas dans le presbytère à jamais déserté par celle qui lui avait donné une âme, que le désespoir s'abattait sur nous. Taillé dans l'épaisseur de l'air, le souvenir d'Emily était partout.

Alors que je m'abandonnais à une crise de larmes, Anne est allée voir papa. Sa visite a été de courte durée: «Il ne veut de personne... que pouvons-nous faire pour lui porter secours?» Il faut croire que dans ces moments d'extrême souffrance, l'imagination montre peu d'audace; nous sommes restées à court de procédés devant ce vieillard accablé. Au lieu de répondre à la douleur avec les gestes de l'habitude, il est monté au premier étage. Nous l'avons entendu aller et venir durant plusieurs heures. Sur le soir, il s'est assis devant la chambre d'Emily ; sa douleur est descendue jusqu'à nous : « Ma chère fille, pourquoi nous as-tu abandonnés, toi aussi ? » Rien ne semblant pouvoir l'écarter de cette porte entrebâillée, j'ai dû aller chercher le médecin. Il a su convaincre le pauvre homme de regagner la pénombre du rez-de-chaussée.

Madame,

Dois-je l'avouer ? En ce début d'automne 1849, je connus une douleur si poignante que je souhaitai maintes fois mon trépas. Heureusement, la présence de la fidèle Ellen venue nous rendre visite me fut d'un grand réconfort. Un jour de bruine, alors que nous nous promenions bras dessus bras dessous sur la lande, je lui posai la question qui me harcelait depuis des mois : pourquoi Emily avait-elle refusé toute assistance ? la tuberculose avait-elle servi la cause du suicide ? Mon amie refusa de répondre ; plus encore que pour nous, ses intimes, Emily demeurerait une énigme pour les étrangers : « Votre sœur était unique. Conservez son souvenir comme on conserve un joyau : ne le ternissez pas avec des spéculations négatives ! »

Durant la quinzaine qui suivit le départ d'Ellen, je me remis à l'écriture. Malheureusement cet exercice ne me fut d'aucun secours. *Shirley*, le personnage féminin de mon nouveau roman, héritière aussi lointaine que séduisante, ne serait jamais Emily Jane Brontë que je désirais venger des critiques humiliantes et sottes. Ellen avait eu raison de me mettre en garde ; ma sœur avait été un être exceptionnel et ma plume ne la ressusciterait pas. Je refermai mon écritoire ; celle qui avait hurlé son désespoir sur les Moors avant de se répandre en lamentations auprès d'une morte continuerait encore longtemps à gémir en moi. Currer Bell dont on attendait avec impatience le second roman ne pouvait qu'avouer son impuissance ; la littérature refusait de se mesurer à la mort.

Un matin, alors que j'errais de pièce en pièce à la recherche d'un travail qui m'occuperait les mains et l'esprit, je reconnus ma jeune sœur dans l'entrebâillement de la porte de la salle à manger. L'avais-je à ce point perdue de vue ? Assise dans le fauteuil, elle regardait fixement le feu avec cet air qu'ont les gens hantés par une image obsédante. La tristesse de son profil amaigri et sans défense m'émut au point de m'arracher des larmes. Alors que la discrétion me soufflait de signaler ma présence, je restai là, à moitié cachée par le battant de la porte. Dieu, dans sa compassion infinie, aimait-il mieux que je ne l'aimais moi-même, cet être démuni dont j'avais pourtant envié le pouvoir ? Malgré sa bienveillance envers moi qu'elle aimait à sa manière, Anne m'avait volé l'amour d'Emily, et cela j'étais incapable de le lui pardonner. Sans elle, sans son regard violet, sans sa fragilité captieuse, Emily aurait probablement eu pour moi un sentiment plus profond que cette affection distante et presque paresseuse. Avant de mourir, elle aurait pris le temps de reconnaître mon amour. Mais ce geste, elle n'avait jamais pu le faire car jusqu'à la fin elle était restée à l'écoute d'Anne qui n'avait cessé de la réclamer avec insistance et douceur. J'en étais là de mes réflexions, lorsque ma sœur détourna la tête. Elle m'aperçut sur le seuil de la pièce. Je m'avançai vers elle : « Comme tu sembles triste, ma chère petite ! — Charlotte, crois-tu que je vais mourir moi aussi ? »

Quelques semaines plus tard, la toux, le manque d'appétit, une fièvre persistante me rappelèrent des symptômes que je ne connaissais que trop bien. Convoqué à nouveau dans une maison où il avait fini par prendre des habitudes, le médecin dut répondre à Anne qui le priait de lui dire la vérité : « C'est malheureusement la phtisie ! — Je vais donc devoir mourir ? » Comme s'il avait l'intuition de ce qui se passait à quelques mètres de lui, papa sortit de son bureau. Il salua le docteur : « Comment la trouvez-vous ? » puis il s'avança vers la malade, et dans un geste inattendu chez un homme aussi froid, il lui prit les deux mains : « Tu vas te soigner, n'est-ce pas, ma petite fille ? » Anne reçut son inquiétude comme un cadeau : « Sur ce point, papa, vous pouvez me faire confiance ! » A l'inverse d'Emily qui avait refusé le secours de la médecine, Anne souhaitait guérir. J'étais en train de regarder le dos du père penché sur sa fille malade, et le profil du médecin dressé à l'écart, quand je compris avec horreur qu'il me faudrait assister à un troisième enterrement. Je reculai jusqu'à la table contre laquelle je pris appui. Ainsi, le rêve fait dans ma jeunesse où je m'entendais appeler désespérément mon frère et mes sœurs qui venaient de disparaître était prémonitoire. Je voulus vaincre ce pressentiment abominable, en vain. Je dus m'asseoir. Lorsque papa se retourna pour me prendre à témoin de la promesse que venait de lui faire la malade, il eut un geste de frayeur : « Qu'as-tu, Charlotte ? Est-ce donc si grave ? »

Dès le mois de mars, je sus que ma sœur n'atteindrait pas l'été. Bouleversée au-delà de ce qu'au pire moment j'avais pu imaginer, je compris que je n'économiserais pas ma souffrance ; à l'heure de l'agonie, Anne m'était devenue aussi chère qu'Emily. Alors que le temps était venu de s'en remettre à Dieu, Anne prêta l'oreille à une bouche ignorante et légère qui tentait de lui redonner espoir alors qu'il n'y avait plus lieu d'en avoir : « Pourquoi n'iriez-vous pas à Scarborough où l'air est si bon ? — Charlotte, as-tu entendu ce que Mme Franks est en train de me conseiller ? » J'essayai de détourner ma sœur d'un projet qui me paraissait dangereux : « Anne, as-tu songé aux fatigues du voyage ? — Oui, bien sûr ! mais une fois sur place, j'aurai tout le temps de me reposer ! L'air est si doux au bord de la mer... Peut-être puis-je encore guérir ? » Abusée par l'espérance, la malheureuse ignorait que seul un miracle pouvait la sauver ; mais comment aurions-nous pu en espérer un ? Pas plus qu'elle n'avait cédé devant les supplications de Branwell et le courage d'Emily, la mort ne se laisserait déjouer par la confiance d'Anne.

Ma sœur a-t-elle jamais compris pourquoi je marquai tant de réticence à l'accompagner dans un voyage dont je savais qu'elle ne reviendrait pas ? J'en doute. « Pourquoi me refuses-tu ce dernier cadeau ? Crois-tu donc que je suis perdue ? » Son insistance me renvoya à la culpabilité de ne pas l'avoir aimée autant qu'Emily. Je finis par céder. Une lettre partit pour le château de Nussey ; elle demandait à Ellen si elle voulait bien nous accompagner jusqu'à la station balnéaire de Scarborough. Mon amie me fit savoir sur-le-champ que nous pouvions compter sur sa présence et son affection. J'annonçai la bonne nouvelle à Anne et je fis nos valises. Le jour du départ, ma sœur ne put se rendre à la diligence ; la tuberculose avait creusé tant de cavernes dans ses poumons qu'elle ne pouvait plus faire trois pas sans manquer de s'évanouir. Inquiète de ne pas nous trouver à Leeds, où nous devions prendre le train toutes les trois, Ellen vint le jour même à Haworth. Sa nature confiante redonna de l'énergie à la malade. Nous partîmes finalement le jeudi 24 mai et le voyage s'effectua mieux que je ne le pensais. Parvenues à York, Anne nous demanda de l'emmener jusqu'à la cathédrale. Ce détour lui coûta quelques heures de vie et lui valut une grande émotion : « Si les hommes sont capables de construire une si belle œuvre, c'est parce qu'ils sont fils de Dieu ! »

Nous pensions avoir pris de l'avance sur la mort. Il n'en était rien. Elle nous attendait à Scarborough où nous arrivâmes le 26 mai dans la journée. Aussitôt descendues du train, j'appelai un fiacre qui nous mena à la pension de famille où j'avais réservé un petit appartement. Assise près de la fenêtre, Anne put enfin contempler les dunes au loin. Elle se souvint de ses dernières vacances avec les Robinson : « Je vous dois tant de bonheur à toutes les deux ! Je n'aurais pas voulu mourir sans avoir revu la mer ! » Ce changement d'air fut trop brutal ; dès le lendemain de notre arrivée, ses forces déclinèrent. Elle demanda à rentrer car elle ne voulait pas mourir sans avoir revu papa. Appelé en toute hâte, le médecin ne put que confirmer ce que nous savions déjà : il était trop tard pour envisager ce voyage. Anne mourut peu après cette visite. Au moment de nous quitter, elle me fit signe d'approcher mon oreille de sa bouche : « Je vous ai tous beaucoup aimés mais je n'ai pas su vous le dire. Ne pleure pas, Charlotte. Là où je vais, il n'y a pas de souffrance ! »

Madame,

Anne est décédée le lundi 27 mai 1849, c'est-à-dire cinq mois après Emily et huit mois après Branwell. Même si sa mort a été moins déchirante que ne l'a été celle d'Emily, elle a déposé en moi un lit d'amertume. Afin d'épargner un troisième enterrement à papa, je l'ai fait inhumer à Scarborough, dans le cimetière de l'église St. Mary. Étonné de ne voir derrière cette jeune morte que deux femmes en pleurs, le pasteur nous a offert son aide. Nous l'avons refusée car Ellen et moi désirions fuir la ville au plus vite. Quelques heures plus tard, nous nous sommes quittées sur le quai de la gare.

À Haworth, Keeper m'attendait sur le pas de la porte. Lorsqu'elle a compris que je rentrais seule, la pauvre bête est retournée dormir dans la chambre d'Emily. D'un accord tacite, papa et moi avons refusé d'associer nos désespoirs. Après une accolade, chacun a regagné son poste. Je me suis attelée à mille tâches, mais aucune n'a eu le pouvoir de chasser la douleur. Quoi que j'entreprenne, je sais que là-haut les chambres sont inhabitées, que dans la penderie attendent des vêtements qui ne seront plus jamais portés, que ce soir encore le silence tombera en même temps que la lumière. Avec la nuit s'avancera la monstrueuse, l'horrible solitude. A peine couchée, je ressentirai cette impression d'étouffement qui m'oblige à m'asseoir. J'allumerai la lampe, essaierai de lire, mais les mots traverseront mon esprit sans y laisser la moindre trace. Alors je prierai Dieu, je lui demanderai de m'envoyer la résignation. Le visage de Branwell surgira comme au plus beau jour de l'adolescence, puis celui d'Emily, rieur ou sévère, puis le regard violet d'Anne. Devant ces images rassemblées autour de trois pierres tombales, je pleurerai jusqu'à l'aube. L'heure venue de me lever, et avant de me rendre à la cuisine, je me laverai le visage pour y effacer la trace des larmes. La tête plongée dans la cuvette, j'entendrai papa descendre les escaliers. Il ira s'installer derrière son bureau, attendra que je vienne lui apporter son plateau. Lorsque j'entrerai dans la pièce, je lui ferai remarquer qu'il fait trop sombre pour lire déjà ; il me jettera un regard de gratitude, me fera comprendre combien ma présence et mes attentions lui sont chères, indispensables. Je m'exercerai devant lui au simulacre qui consiste à faire croire à l'autre qu'on a du courage ; je lui parlerai du temps, de la ponctualité de

Martha, de la visite de son vicaire, M. Bell Nicholls. Nous nous quitterons sans avoir évoqué le moindre souvenir. Dans l'après-midi, je monterai à l'étage pour aller chercher refuge dans les manuscrits qu'ont laissés mes sœurs. Je relirai certaines pages que je connais par cœur, en déchirerai d'autres trop personnelles pour être lues par des étrangers. Les reproches qu'on pourrait me faire n'arrêteront pas ma main ; au contraire, mon désir de purification n'en sera que plus fort. Le monde ne connaîtra de l'intimité des Brontë que ce qu'il doit connaître.

Plus tard, beaucoup plus tard, lorsque je me sentirai à nouveau en possession de mes moyens, je rédigerai des préfaces pour présenter mes sœurs, exalter l'œuvre poétique d'Emily, rendre hommage à celle d'Anne. La gestion du destin posthume de ces deux êtres me redonnera un peu de ce que j'ai perdu en les enterrant. Lorsque j'en aurai terminé avec ce travail, je m'enhardirai jusqu'à retourner auprès de Branwell. Je jetterai un coup d'œil à ses textes éparpillés, les rangerai dans un tiroir où le destin a voulu qu'ils restent.

Un jour viendra qui sera date d'anniversaire. J'irai déposer un bouquet sur une tombe, une brassée de bruyère sur une autre. Plusieurs saisons s'écouleront avant que je ne me décide à me rendre là-bas, dans ce pays où Anne attend ma visite : « Papa, je vais devoir vous quitter pour quelques jours. Je vais faire un pèlerinage à Scarborough ! » Au moment de nous séparer, le pauvre homme m'embrassera avec des larmes dans les yeux : « J'aurais tellement voulu la serrer une dernière fois dans mes bras. Elle était la plus fragile de vous trois, mais d'une certaine manière la plus humaine aussi, et si pieuse ! C'est peut-être pour cela que je l'aimais tout particulièrement. J'aurais dû le lui dire avant qu'elle nous quitte ! »

Puis viendra l'été suivi d'un automne enflammé.

Avec les pluies torrentielles de l'arrière-saison renaîtront les vieilles peurs. Je songerai aux moyens de rompre la solitude. L'idée du mariage me rendra visite. Au lieu de la chasser, j'accepterai qu'elle fasse route en moi. Je rêverai de deux bras, d'un regard, d'une présence. La tendresse ne me fera plus peur comme autrefois. Je remarquerai que le vicaire de papa, M. Arthur Bell Nicholls, a des attentions à mon endroit : « Tu ne vas tout de même pas te marier à ton âge ? À quoi cela ressemblerait-il ? » Après s'être indigné, papa invitera sa fidèle gouvernante à prendre le thé avec lui. Il tentera de se confesser, n'y parviendra pas : « Te sens-tu bien, Charlotte ? — Mais oui, pourquoi me posez-vous cette question ? — Parce que je te trouve de plus en plus nerveuse ! Est-ce la présence de ce malheureux Bell Nicholls qui te met dans cet état ? » Tout en jouant avec la cuillère, j'observerai ce profil de vieillard, la forme du grand nez, la blancheur éclatante de la chevelure, la tristesse des yeux tombants, l'ossature volontaire du menton. Je songerai à ce que diront plus tard ceux qui ne l'ont pas connu. J'imaginerai les adjectifs auxquels ils feront appel pour cerner la complexité d'une nature aussi austère. Qui comprendra jamais ce qu'a vécu cet homme malheureux, les raisons qui l'ont poussé à se cacher, y compris de ses enfants ? Rendra-t-on jamais à Patrick Brontë, égoïste et misanthrope certes, avare presque, sa véritable dimension ? Au lieu d'attaquer l'époque en la dévoilant dans toute sa tragédie, le calomniera-t-on ?

Madame,

Je vous ai dit, je crois, tout ce que j'avais à vous dire. Le reste appartient au secret.

*« Quand Charlotte Brontë meurt, le 31 mars 1855, moins d'un an après son mariage avec Arthur Bell Nicholls, vicaire de son père, ses livres comptent déjà parmi les classiques de la littérature anglaise. »*

Raymond BELLOUR.

Phtisique comme ses sœurs, Charlotte est morte dans les bras de son mari. Elle avait trente-neuf ans et était enceinte de plusieurs mois.

Patrick Brontë, qui avait lutté contre un mariage ajourné de son fait durant plusieurs années, a reçu la nouvelle de sa mort comme une délivrance : « Cette fois, ça y est... le pire vient de m'arriver... plus rien ne peut m'atteindre car j'ai tout perdu ! Oh, Martha, pourquoi Charlotte ne m'a-t-elle pas écouté ? Je savais qu'elle n'était pas faite pour la vie conjugale et les grossesses ! Elle n'en avait pas la force ! Son destin était d'être écrivain ! »

Bien qu'on ne possède aucune preuve, on est en droit de supposer qu'avant de disparaître, Charlotte-Currer Bell a été le censeur des Brontë. Certains poèmes d'Emily, la presque totalité de ceux d'Anne, la saga de *Gondal* composée par les deux sœurs pendant une quinzaine d'années n'ont jamais été retrouvés. Quant au manuscrit du second roman d'Emily, nul ne saura jamais s'il a été détruit par l'auteur lui-même ou par Charlotte. A-t-il seulement existé ? Seule pourrait nous répondre une morte ; la main posée sur les lèvres, elle ressemble à l'une de ces statues qui recommandent le silence dans les cimetières où continuent à s'égarer les vivants.

« *Ce n'est pas une lâche que mon âme,*
*Elle ne tremble pas en ce monde tourmenté d'orages :*
*Je vois briller les gloires du Ciel*
*Et la Foi brille à leur égal, me cuirassant contre la*
[*Crainte.* »

Emily Jane Brontë, 2 janvier 1846.
(Traduction Pierre Leyris,

## PRINCIPAUX OUVRAGES CONSULTÉS

*Les œuvres des sœurs Brontë*

Anne Brontë :
*Agnès Grey*, trad. Ch. Romey et A. Rolet, Gallimard, 1978.
*La Recluse de Haworth* (The Tenant of Wildfell Hall), trad. Georges Charbonnier et André Frédérique, L'Élan, Paris, 1947.

Charlotte Brontë :
*Jane Eyre*, trad., préface et notes de Charlotte Maurat, Le Livre de Poche, 1984.
*Villette*, trad. Albine Loisy et Brian Telford, Gallimard, 1979.
*Le Professeur* (The Professor), trad. Henriette Loreau, Gallimard, 1949.
*Shirley*, trad. Guy Faroux, Nouvelles Éditions latines, 1951.

Emily Brontë :
*Les Hauts de Hurle-Vent* (Wuthering Heights), trad. Frédéric Delebecque, Payot, Paris, 1984.
*Wuthering Heights*, trad. Pierre Leyris, J.-J. Pauvert, 1972.
*Poèmes*, choisis et traduits d'après la leçon des

manuscrits par Pierre Leyris, *Poésie*/Gallimard, 1983.
*Emily Brontë/Poèmes*, trad. Françoise d'Eaubonne, Seghers, 1964.
*The Complete Poems of Emily Jane Brontë*, edited from the manuscripts by C. W. Hatfield, Columbia University Press, New York, 1941.

*Autres ouvrages*

BATAILLE Georges, *La Littérature et le Mal*, Gallimard, 1957.
BAY André, *Lettres à quelques-unes*, Mercure de France, 1964.
BELLOUR Raymond, *Emily Brontë - Wuthering Heights*, trad. Pierre Leyris, choix établi et présenté par R. Bellour, J.-J. Pauvert, 1972. — *Charlotte Brontë - Patrick Branwell Brontë*, choix établi et présenté par R. Bellour, J.-J. Pauvert, 1972.
BLONDEL Jacques, *Emily Brontë - Expériences spirituelles et création poétique*, Presses Universitaires de France, 1956.
CREVEL René, *Les Sœurs Brontë, Filles du Vent*, Illustrations de Marie Laurencin, Les Quatre Chemins, 1930.
DANIEL-ROPS, *Où passent les anges*, Les Écrits, Bruxelles, 1943; réédité par Plon, 1947.
D'EAUBONNE Françoise, *Emily Brontë/Essai suivi d'un choix de poèmes*, Seghers, 1964 (coll. Poètes d'aujourd'hui).
DU MAURIER Daphné, *Le Monde infernal de Branwell Brontë*, Albin Michel, 1962.
LE GUERN Joseph, *Anne Brontë (1820-1849) - La vie et l'œuvre*, tomes I et II, Atelier de reproduction des

thèses, université de Lille-III, diffusion Librairie Honoré Champion, 1977.

MAURAT Charlotte, *Le Secret des Brontë ou Charlotte Brontë d'après les « Juvenilia », ses lettres et ceux qui l'ont connue*, Buchet-Chastel, 1967.

MOORE Virginia, *Emily Brontë*, trad. Mireille Hollard, Gallimard, 1939.

PETERS Margaret, *Charlotte Brontë : une âme tourmentée*, trad. Guy Le Clech, Stock, 1979 (coll. Femmes de leur temps).

PETIT Jean-Pierre, *L'Œuvre d'Emily Brontë : la vision et les thèmes*, L'Hermès, 1972.

Également cité dans cet ouvrage : *Manfred*, de G. Gordon lord Byron, trad. Florence Guilhot et Jean-Louis Paul, Ressouvenances, 1985.

# RÉFÉRENCES DES TEXTES CITÉS

Pages 9, 22, 49, 59, 83, 177, 203, 218, 273, 330, 343, 357, 391, 451, 474 : Emily Brontë, *Poèmes*, traduction de Pierre Leyris, coll. Poésie, Gallimard.

Pages 14-15, 16, 17, 46, 47, 109-110, 319, 462 : extraits des *Hauts de Hurle-Vent*, traduction de Frédéric Delebecque, Payot.

Page 20 : *Les Sœurs Brontë, Filles du vent*, illustrations de Marie Laurencin, éd. Les Quatre Chemins.

Pages 21, 111 : Georges Bataille, *La Littérature et le Mal*, Gallimard.

Pages 27, 39, 141 : Charlotte Brontë, *Shirley*, traduction de Guy Faroux, Nouvelles Éditions latines.

Page 29 : Jacques Blondel, *Emily Brontë, expériences spirituelles et création poétique*, PUF ; pages 310, 453 : textes traduits par J. Blondel, *ibid.*

Pages 51, 143, 193, 241 : Virginia Moore, *Emily Brontë*, traduction de Mireille Hollard, Gallimard ; page 239 : texte cité par V. Moore, *ibid.*

Pages 61, 62-63, 129, 212, 251, 383 : Daphné Du Maurier, *Le Monde infernal de Branwell Brontë*, traduction de Jane Fillion, Albin Michel ; pages 383, 405, 435, 441 : textes reproduits par D. Du Maurier, *ibid.*

Pages 71, 74, 181, 186, 393 : Charlotte Brontë, *Jane Eyre*, traduction de Charlotte Maurat, Le Livre de Poche.

Pages 73, 374-375 : Byron, *Manfred*, traduction de Florence Guilhot et Jean-Louis Paul, éd. Ressouvenances.

Pages 95, 165, 227, 241, 285, 398, 399 : *Emily Brontë*, Essai suivi d'un choix de poèmes, par Françoise d'Eaubonne, coll. Poètes d'aujourd'hui, Seghers ; pages 230-231 : texte traduit par Mireille Best, *ibid.*

Pages 105, 108, 109, 369, 381 : textes traduits par Marcelle Sibon dans *Juvenilia*, éd. par Raymond Bellour, J.-J. Pauvert.

Page 117 : texte traduit par Anne Villelaur, dans *Charlotte Brontë/Branwell Brontë*, éd. par Raymond Bellour, J.-J. Pauvert ; pages 155, 191 : textes traduits par Francis Ledoux, *ibid.*

Pages 259, 261 : *Emily Brontë, Wuthering Heights*, éd. par Raymond Bellour, J.-J. Pauvert ; page 53 : « Sur Emily Brontë par Ellen Nussey », traduction de Ginette Billard et Jeanne Villardebo, *ibid.* ; pages 417, 431 : textes traduits par Pierre Leyris, *ibid.* ; page 423 : texte traduit par Didier Coupayre, *ibid.*

Page 167 : Daniel-Rops, *Où passent les anges*, Plon.

Pages 177, 215, 244, 271, 357, 391 : *The Complete Poems of Emily Jane Brontë*, Hatfield, Columbia University Press, New York.

Page 239 : Jean-Pierre Petit, *L'Œuvre d'Emily Brontë : la vision et les thèmes*, L'Hermès.

Page 249 : poème relevé dans *Anne Brontë (1820-1849), la vie et l'œuvre,* tome I, par Joseph Le Guern, Honoré Champion.

Pages 257, 331 : Anne Brontë, *Agnès Grey*, traduction de Ch. Romey et A. Rolet, Gallimard.

Pages 297, 299, 307 : Charlotte Brontë, *Le Professeur*, traduction d'Henriette Loreau, Gallimard.

Page 341-342 : Charlotte Brontë, *Villette*, traduction d'Albine Loisy et Brian Telford, Gallimard.

Page 420 : Margaret Peters, *Charlotte Brontë, une âme tourmentée*, traduction de Guy Le Clech, Stock.

Composition réalisée par COMPOFAC - PARIS

---

IMPRIMÉ EN FRANCE PAR BRODARD ET TAUPIN
Usine de La Flèche (Sarthe).
LIBRAIRIE GÉNÉRALE FRANÇAISE - 6, rue Pierre-Sarrazin - 75006 Paris.

ISBN : 2 - 253 - 04705 - 8

30/6509/1